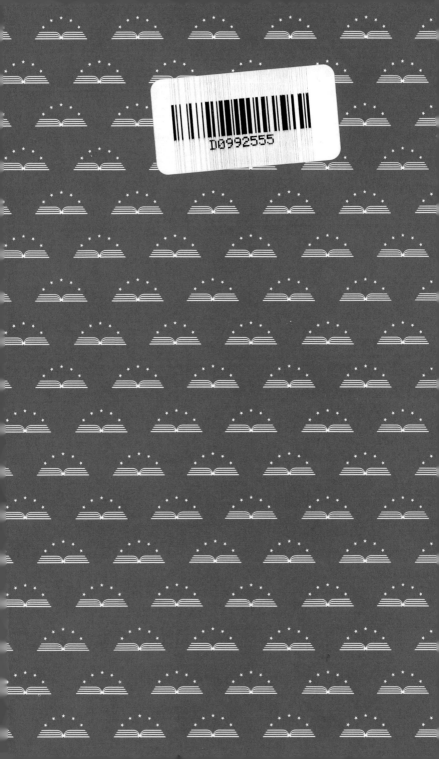

ISAAC BASHEVIS SINGER

ISAAC BASHEVIS SINGER

COLLECTED STORIES:
GIMPEL THE FOOL
to
THE LETTER WRITER

Gimpel the Fool & Other Stories
The Spinoza of Market Street
Short Friday & Other Stories
The Séance & Other Stories

THE LIBRARY OF AMERICA

Distributed to the trade
in the United States by Penguin Putnam Inc.
and in Canada by Penguin Books Canada Ltd.

Library of Congress Catalog Number: 2003066055
For cataloging information, see end of Notes.
ISBN 1–931082–61–8

———

First Printing
The Library of America—149

Manufactured in the United States of America

The publishers wish to thank H. Axel Schupf
for his support toward publication of this volume.

ILAN STAVANS

IS THE EDITOR OF THIS VOLUME

Contents

GIMPEL THE FOOL

AND OTHER STORIES

Contents

Gimpel the Fool

I AM Gimpel the Fool. I don't think myself a fool. On the contrary. But that's what folks call me. They gave me the name while I was still in school. I had seven names in all: imbecile, donkey, flax-head, dope, glump, ninny, and fool. The last name stuck. What did my foolishness consist of? I was easy to take in. They said, "Gimpel, you know the rabbi's wife has been brought to childbed?" So I skipped school. Well, it turned out to be a lie. How was I supposed to know? She hadn't had a big belly. But I never looked at her belly. Was that really so foolish? The gang laughed and hee-hawed, stomped and danced and chanted a good-night prayer. And instead of the raisins they give when a woman's lying in, they stuffed my hand full of goat turds. I was no weakling. If I slapped someone he'd see all the way to Cracow. But I'm really not a slugger by nature. I think of myself: Let it pass. So they take advantage of me.

I was coming home from school and heard a dog barking. I'm not afraid of dogs, but of course I never want to start up with them. One of them may be mad, and if he bites there's not a Tartar in the world who can help you. So I made tracks. Then I looked around and saw the whole market place wild with laughter. It was no dog at all but Wolf-Leib the Thief. How was I supposed to know it was he? It sounded like a howling bitch.

When the pranksters and leg-pullers found that I was easy to fool, every one of them tried his luck with me. "Gimpel, the Czar is coming to Frampol; Gimpel, the moon fell down in Turbeen; Gimpel, little Hodel Furpiece found a treasure behind the bathhouse." And I like a golem believed everyone. In the first place, everything is possible, as it is written in the Wisdom of the Fathers, I've forgotten just how. Second, I had to believe when the whole town came down on me! If I ever dared to say, "Ah, you're kidding!" there was trouble. People got angry. "What do you mean! You want to call everyone a liar?" What was I to do? I believed them, and I hope at least that did them some good.

I was an orphan. My grandfather who brought me up was already bent toward the grave. So they turned me over to a baker, and what a time they gave me there! Every woman or girl who came to bake a batch of noodles had to fool me at least once. "Gimpel, there's a fair in heaven; Gimpel, the rabbi gave birth to a calf in the seventh month; Gimpel, a cow flew over the roof and laid brass eggs." A student from the yeshiva came once to buy a roll, and he said, "You, Gimpel, while you stand here scraping with your baker's shovel the Messiah has come. The dead have arisen." "What do you mean?" I said. "I heard no one blowing the ram's horn!" He said, "Are you deaf?" And all began to cry, "We heard it, we heard!" Then in came Rietze the Candle-dipper and called out in her hoarse voice, "Gimpel, your father and mother have stood up from the grave. They're looking for you."

To tell the truth, I knew very well that nothing of the sort had happened, but all the same, as folks were talking, I threw on my wool vest and went out. Maybe something had happened. What did I stand to lose by looking? Well, what a cat music went up! And then I took a vow to believe nothing more. But that was no go either. They confused me so that I didn't know the big end from the small.

I went to the rabbi to get some advice. He said, "It is written, better to be a fool all your days than for one hour to be evil. You are not a fool. They are the fools. For he who causes his neighbor to feel shame loses Paradise himself." Nevertheless the rabbi's daughter took me in. As I left the rabbinical court she said, "Have you kissed the wall yet?" I said, "No; what for?" She answered, "It's the law; you've got to do it after every visit." Well, there didn't seem to be any harm in it. And she burst out laughing. It was a fine trick. She put one over on me, all right.

I wanted to go off to another town, but then everyone got busy matchmaking, and they were after me so they nearly tore my coat tails off. They talked at me and talked until I got water on the ear. She was no chaste maiden, but they told me she was virgin pure. She had a limp, and they said it was deliberate, from coyness. She had a bastard, and they told me the child was her little brother. I cried, "You're wasting your time. I'll never marry that whore." But they said indignantly, "What a way to talk! Aren't you ashamed of yourself? We can take you to the rabbi and have you fined for giving her a bad name." I saw then that I wouldn't escape them so easily and I thought: They're set on making me their butt. But when you're married the husband's the master, and if that's all right with her it's agreeable to me too. Besides, you can't pass through life unscathed, nor expect to.

I went to her clay house, which was built on the sand, and the whole gang, hollering and chorusing, came after me. They acted like bear-baiters. When we came to the well they stopped all the same. They were afraid to start anything with Elka. Her mouth would open as if it were on a hinge, and she had a fierce tongue. I entered the house. Lines were strung from wall to wall and clothes were drying. Barefoot she stood by the tub, doing the wash. She was dressed in a worn hand-me-down gown of plush. She had her hair put up in braids and pinned across her head. It took my breath away, almost, the reek of it all.

Evidently she knew who I was. She took a look at me and said, "Look who's here! He's come, the drip. Grab a seat."

I told her all; I denied nothing. "Tell me the truth," I said, "are you really a virgin, and is that mischievous Yechiel actually your little brother? Don't be deceitful with me, for I'm an orphan."

"I'm an orphan myself," she answered, "and whoever tries to twist you up, may the end of his nose take a twist. But don't let them think they can take advantage of me. I want a dowry of fifty guilders, and let them take up a collection besides. Otherwise they can kiss my you-know-what." She was very plain-spoken. I said, "It's the bride and not the groom who gives a dowry." Then she said, "Don't bargain with me. Either a flat 'yes' or a flat 'no'—Go back where you came from."

I thought: No bread will ever be baked from *this* dough. But ours is not a poor town. They consented to everything and proceeded with the wedding. It so happened that there was a dysentery epidemic at the time. The ceremony was held at the cemetery gates, near the little corpse-washing hut. The fellows got drunk. While the marriage contract was being drawn up I heard the most pious high rabbi ask, "Is the bride a widow or a divorced woman?" And the sexton's wife answered for her, "Both a widow and divorced." It was a black moment for me. But what was I to do, run away from under the marriage canopy?

There was singing and dancing. An old granny danced opposite me, hugging a braided white *chalah*. The master of revels made a "God 'a mercy" in memory of the bride's parents. The schoolboys threw burrs, as on Tishe b'Av fast day. There were a lot of gifts after the sermon: a noodle board, a kneading trough, a bucket, brooms, ladles, household articles galore. Then I took a look and saw two strapping young men carrying a crib. "What do we need this for?" I asked. So they said, "Don't rack your brains about it. It's all right, it'll come in handy." I realized I was going to be rooked. Take it another way though, what did I stand to lose? I reflected: I'll see what comes of it. A whole town can't go altogether crazy.

II

At night I came where my wife lay, but she wouldn't let me in. "Say, look here, is this what they married us for?" I said. And she said, "My monthly has come." "But yesterday they took you to the ritual bath, and that's afterward, isn't it supposed to be?" "Today isn't yesterday," said she, "and yesterday's not today. You can beat it if you don't like it." In short, I waited.

Not four months later she was in childbed. The townsfolk hid their laughter with their knuckles. But what could I do? She suffered intolerable pains and clawed at the walls. "Gimpel," she cried, "I'm going. Forgive me!" The house filled with women. They were boiling pans of water. The screams rose to the welkin.

The thing to do was to go to the House of Prayer to repeat Psalms, and that was what I did.

The townsfolk liked that, all right. I stood in a corner saying Psalms and prayers, and they shook their heads at me. "Pray, pray!" they told me. "Prayer never made any woman pregnant." One of the congregation put a straw to my mouth and said, "Hay for the cows." There was something to that too, by God!

She gave birth to a boy. Friday at the synagogue the sexton stood up before the Ark, pounded on the reading table, and announced, "The wealthy Reb Gimpel invites the congregation to a feast in honor of the birth of a son." The whole House of Prayer rang with laughter. My face was flaming. But there was nothing I could do. After all, I *was* the one responsible for the circumcision honors and rituals.

Half the town came running. You couldn't wedge another soul in. Women brought peppered chick-peas, and there was a keg of beer from the tavern. I ate and drank as much as anyone, and they all congratulated me. Then there was a circumcision, and I named the boy after my father, may he rest in peace. When all were gone and I was left with my wife alone, she thrust her head through the bed-curtain and called me to her.

"Gimpel," said she, "why are you silent? Has your ship gone and sunk?"

"What shall I say?" I answered. "A fine thing you've done to me! If my mother had known of it she'd have died a second time."

She said, "Are you crazy, or what?"

"How can you make such a fool," I said, "of one who should be the lord and master?"

"What's the matter with you?" she said. "What have you taken it into your head to imagine?"

I saw that I must speak bluntly and openly. "Do you think this is the way to use an orphan?" I said. "You have borne a bastard."

She answered, "Drive this foolishness out of your head. The child is yours."

"How can he be mine?" I argued. "He was born seventeen weeks after the wedding."

She told me then that he was premature. I said, "Isn't he a little too premature?" She said, she had had a grandmother who carried just as short a time and she resembled this grandmother of hers as one drop of water does another. She swore to it with such oaths that you would have believed a peasant at the fair if he had used them. To tell the plain truth, I didn't believe her; but when I talked it over next day with the schoolmaster he told me that the very same thing had happened to Adam and Eve. Two they went up to bed, and four they descended.

"There isn't a woman in the world who is not the granddaughter of Eve," he said.

That was how it was; they argued me dumb. But then, who really knows how such things are?

I began to forget my sorrow. I loved the child madly, and he loved me too. As soon as he saw me he'd wave his little hands and want me to pick him up, and when he was colicky I was the only one who could pacify him. I bought him a little bone teething ring and a little gilded cap. He was forever catching the evil eye from someone, and then I had to run to get one of those abracadabras for him that would get him out of it. I worked like an ox. You know how expenses go up when there's an infant in the house. I don't want to lie about it; I didn't dislike Elka either, for that matter. She swore at me and cursed, and I couldn't get enough of her. What strength she had! One of her looks could rob you of the power of speech. And her orations! Pitch and sulphur, that's what they were full of, and yet somehow also full of charm. I adored her every word. She gave me bloody wounds though.

In the evening I brought her a white loaf as well as a dark one, and also poppyseed rolls I baked myself. I thieved because of her and swiped everything I could lay hands on: macaroons, raisins, almonds, cakes. I hope I may be forgiven for stealing from the Saturday pots the women left to warm in the baker's oven. I would take out scraps of meat, a chunk of pudding, a chicken leg or head, a piece of tripe, whatever I could nip quickly. She ate and became fat and handsome.

I had to sleep away from home all during the week, at the bakery. On Friday nights when I got home she always made an excuse of some sort. Either she had heartburn, or a stitch in the side, or hiccups, or headaches. You know what women's excuses are. I had a bitter time of it. It was rough. To add to it, this little brother of hers, the bastard, was growing bigger. He'd put lumps on me, and when I wanted to hit back she'd open her mouth and curse so powerfully I saw a green haze floating before my eyes. Ten times a day she threatened to

divorce me. Another man in my place would have taken
French leave and disappeared. But I'm the type that bears it
and says nothing. What's one to do? Shoulders are from God,
and burdens too.

One night there was a calamity in the bakery; the oven
burst, and we almost had a fire. There was nothing to do but
go home, so I went home. Let me, I thought, also taste the
joy of sleeping in bed in mid-week. I didn't want to wake the
sleeping mite and tiptoed into the house. Coming in, it
seemed to me that I heard not the snoring of one but, as it
were, a double snore, one a thin enough snore and the other
like the snoring of a slaughtered ox. Oh, I didn't like that! I
didn't like it at all. I went up to the bed, and things suddenly
turned black. Next to Elka lay a man's form. Another in my
place would have made an uproar, and enough noise to rouse
the whole town, but the thought occurred to me that I might
wake the child. A little thing like that—why frighten a little
swallow, I thought. All right then, I went back to the bakery
and stretched out on a sack of flour and till morning I never
shut an eye. I shivered as if I had had malaria. "Enough of
being a donkey," I said to myself. "Gimpel isn't going to be a
sucker all his life. There's a limit even to the foolishness of a
fool like Gimpel."

In the morning I went to the rabbi to get advice, and it
made a great commotion in the town. They sent the beadle for
Elka right away. She came, carrying the child. And what do
you think she did? She denied it, denied everything, bone and
stone! "He's out of his head," she said. "I know nothing of
dreams or divinations." They yelled at her, warned her, hammered on the table, but she stuck to her guns: it was a false accusation, she said.

The butchers and the horse-traders took her part. One of
the lads from the slaughterhouse came by and said to me,
"We've got our eye on you, you're a marked man." Meanwhile
the child started to bear down and soiled itself. In the rabbinical court there was an Ark of the Covenant, and they couldn't
allow that, so they sent Elka away.

I said to the rabbi, "What shall I do?"

"You must divorce her at once," said he.

"And what if she refuses?" I asked.

He said, "You must serve the divorce. That's all you'll have to do."

I said, "Well, all right, Rabbi. Let me think about it."

"There's nothing to think about," said he. "You mustn't remain under the same roof with her."

"And if I want to see the child?" I asked.

"Let her go, the harlot," said he, "and her brood of bastards with her."

The verdict he gave was that I mustn't even cross her threshold—never again, as long as I should live.

During the day it didn't bother me so much. I thought: It was bound to happen, the abscess had to burst. But at night when I stretched out upon the sacks I felt it all very bitterly. A longing took me, for her and for the child. I wanted to be angry, but that's my misfortune exactly, I don't have it in me to be really angry. In the first place—this was how my thoughts went—there's bound to be a slip sometimes. You can't live without errors. Probably that lad who was with her led her on and gave her presents and what not, and women are often long on hair and short on sense, and so he got around her. And then since she denies it so, maybe I was only seeing things? Hallucinations do happen. You see a figure or a mannikin or something, but when you come up closer it's nothing, there's not a thing there. And if that's so, I'm doing her an injustice. And when I got so far in my thoughts I started to weep. I sobbed so that I wet the flour where I lay. In the morning I went to the rabbi and told him that I had made a mistake. The rabbi wrote on with his quill, and he said that if that were so he would have to reconsider the whole case. Until he had finished I wasn't to go near my wife, but I might send her bread and money by messenger.

III

Nine months passed before all the rabbis could come to an agreement. Letters went back and forth. I hadn't realized that there could be so much erudition about a matter like this.

Meanwhile Elka gave birth to still another child, a girl this time. On the Sabbath I went to the synagogue and invoked a blessing on her. They called me up to the Torah, and I named the child for my mother-in-law—may she rest in peace. The louts and loudmouths of the town who came into the bakery gave me a going over. All Frampol refreshed its spirits because of my trouble and grief. However, I resolved that I would always believe what I was told. What's the good of *not* believing? Today it's your wife you don't believe; tomorrow it's God Himself you won't take stock in.

By an apprentice who was her neighbor I sent her daily a corn or a wheat loaf, or a piece of pastry, rolls or bagels, or, when I got the chance, a slab of pudding, a slice of honeycake, or wedding strudel—whatever came my way. The apprentice was a goodhearted lad, and more than once he added something on his own. He had formerly annoyed me a lot, plucking my nose and digging me in the ribs, but when he started to be a visitor to my house he became kind and friendly. "Hey, you, Gimpel," he said to me, "you have a very decent little wife and two fine kids. You don't deserve them."

"But the things people say about her," I said.

"Well, they have long tongues," he said, "and nothing to do with them but babble. Ignore it as you ignore the cold of last winter."

One day the rabbi sent for me and said, "Are you certain, Gimpel, that you were wrong about your wife?"

I said, "I'm certain."

"Why, but look here! You yourself saw it."

"It must have been a shadow," I said.

"The shadow of what?"

"Just of one of the beams, I think."

"You can go home then. You owe thanks to the Yanover rabbi. He found an obscure reference in Maimonides that favored you."

I seized the rabbi's hand and kissed it.

I wanted to run home immediately. It's no small thing to be separated for so long a time from wife and child. Then I reflected: I'd better go back to work now, and go home in the evening. I said nothing to anyone, although as far as my heart was concerned it was like one of the Holy Days. The women teased and twitted me as they did every day, but my thought was: Go on, with your loose talk. The truth is out, like the oil upon the water. Maimonides says it's right, and therefore it is right!

At night, when I had covered the dough to let it rise, I took my share of bread and a little sack of flour and started homeward. The moon was full and the stars were glistening, something to terrify the soul. I hurried onward, and before me darted a long shadow. It was winter, and a fresh snow had fallen. I had a mind to sing, but it was growing late and I didn't want to wake the householders. Then I felt like whistling, but I remembered that you don't whistle at night because it brings the demons out. So I was silent and walked as fast as I could.

Dogs in the Christian yards barked at me when I passed, but I thought: Bark your teeth out! What are you but mere dogs? Whereas I am a man, the husband of a fine wife, the father of promising children.

As I approached the house my heart started to pound as though it were the heart of a criminal. I felt no fear, but my heart went thump! thump! Well, no drawing back. I quietly lifted the latch and went in. Elka was asleep. I looked at the infant's cradle. The shutter was closed, but the moon forced its way through the cracks. I saw the newborn child's face and loved it as soon as I saw it—immediately—each tiny bone.

Then I came nearer to the bed. And what did I see but the apprentice lying there beside Elka. The moon went out all at once. It was utterly black, and I trembled. My teeth chattered. The bread fell from my hands, and my wife waked and said, "Who is that, ah?"

I muttered, "It's me."

"Gimpel?" she asked. "How come you're here? I thought it was forbidden."

"The rabbi said," I answered and shook as with a fever.

"Listen to me, Gimpel," she said, "go out to the shed and see if the goat's all right. It seems she's been sick." I have forgotten to say that we had a goat. When I heard she was unwell I went into the yard. The nannygoat was a good little creature. I had a nearly human feeling for her.

With hesitant steps I went up to the shed and opened the door. The goat stood there on her four feet. I felt her every-where, drew her by the horns, examined her udders, and found nothing wrong. She had probably eaten too much bark. "Good night, little goat," I said. "Keep well." And the little beast answered with a "Maa" as though to thank me for the good will.

I went back. The apprentice had vanished.

"Where," I asked, "is the lad?"

"What lad?" my wife answered.

"What do you mean?" I said. "The apprentice. You were sleeping with him."

"The things I have dreamed this night and the night before," she said, "may they come true and lay you low, body and soul! An evil spirit has taken root in you and dazzles your sight." She screamed out, "You hateful creature! You moon calf! You spook! You uncouth man! Get out, or I'll scream all Frampol out of bed!"

Before I could move, her brother sprang out from behind the oven and struck me a blow on the back of the head. I thought he had broken my neck. I felt that something about me was deeply wrong, and I said, "Don't make a scandal. All that's needed now is that people should accuse me of raising spooks and *dybbuks*." For that was what she had meant. "No one will touch bread of my baking."

In short, I somehow calmed her.

"Well," she said, "that's enough. Lie down, and be shattered by wheels."

Next morning I called the apprentice aside. "Listen here, brother!" I said. And so on and so forth. "What do you say?" He stared at me as though I had dropped from the roof or something.

"I swear," he said, "you'd better go to an herb doctor or some healer. I'm afraid you have a screw loose, but I'll hush it up for you." And that's how the thing stood.

To make a long story short, I lived twenty years with my wife. She bore me six children, four daughters and two sons. All kinds of things happened, but I neither saw nor heard. I believed, and that's all. The rabbi recently said to me, "Belief in itself is beneficial. It is written that a good man lives by his faith."

Suddenly my wife took sick. It began with a trifle, a little growth upon the breast. But she evidently was not destined to

live long; she had no years. I spent a fortune on her. I have forgotten to say that by this time I had a bakery of my own and in
Frampol was considered to be something of a rich man. Daily
the healer came, and every witch doctor in the neighborhood
was brought. They decided to use leeches, and after that to try
cupping. They even called a doctor from Lublin, but it was too
late. Before she died she called me to her bed and said, "Forgive me, Gimpel."

I said, "What is there to forgive? You have been a good and
faithful wife."

"Woe, Gimpel!" she said. "It was ugly how I deceived you
all these years. I want to go clean to my Maker, and so I have
to tell you that the children are not yours."

If I had been clouted on the head with a piece of wood it
couldn't have bewildered me more.

"Whose are they?" I asked.

"I don't know," she said. "There are a lot . . . but they're
not yours." And as she spoke she tossed her head to the side,
her eyes turned glassy, and it was all up with Elka. On her
whitened lips there remained a smile.

I imagined that, dead as she was, she was saying, "I deceived
Gimpel. That was the meaning of my brief life."

IV

One night, when the period of mourning was done, as I lay
dreaming on the flour sacks, there came the Spirit of Evil himself and said to me, "Gimpel, why do you sleep?"

I said, "What should I be doing? Eating *kreplach*?"

"The whole world deceives you," he said, "and you ought
to deceive the world in your turn."

"How can I deceive all the world?" I asked him.

He answered, "You might accumulate a bucket of urine
every day and at night pour it into the dough. Let the sages of
Frampol eat filth."

"What about the judgment in the world to come?" I said.

"There is no world to come," he said. "They've sold you a
bill of goods and talked you into believing you carried a cat in
your belly. What nonsense!"

"Well then," I said, "and is there a God?"

He answered, "There is no God either."

"What," I said, "*is* there, then?"

"A thick mire."

He stood before my eyes with a goatish beard and horn, long-toothed, and with a tail. Hearing such words, I wanted to snatch him by the tail, but I tumbled from the flour sacks and nearly broke a rib. Then it happened that I had to answer the call of nature, and, passing, I saw the risen dough, which seemed to say to me, "Do it!" In brief, I let myself be persuaded.

At dawn the apprentice came. We kneaded the bread, scattered caraway seeds on it, and set it to bake. Then the apprentice went away, and I was left sitting in the little trench by the oven, on a pile of rags. Well, Gimpel, I thought, you've revenged yourself on them for all the shame they've put on you. Outside the frost glittered, but it was warm beside the oven. The flames heated my face. I bent my head and fell into a doze.

I saw in a dream, at once, Elka in her shroud. She called to me, "What have you done, Gimpel?"

I said to her, "It's all your fault," and started to cry.

"You fool!" she said. "You fool! Because I was false is everything false too? I never deceived anyone but myself. I'm paying for it all, Gimpel. They spare you nothing here."

I looked at her face. It was black; I was startled and waked, and remained sitting dumb. I sensed that everything hung in the balance. A false step now and I'd lose Eternal Life. But God gave me His help. I seized the long shovel and took out the loaves, carried them into the yard, and started to dig a hole in the frozen earth.

My apprentice came back as I was doing it. "What are you doing boss?" he said, and grew pale as a corpse.

"I know what I'm doing," I said, and I buried it all before his very eyes.

Then I went home, took my hoard from its hiding place, and divided it among the children. "I saw your mother tonight," I said. "She's turning black, poor thing."

They were so astounded they couldn't speak a word.

"Be well," I said, "and forget that such a one as Gimpel ever existed." I put on my short coat, a pair of boots, took the bag that held my prayer shawl in one hand, my stick in the other, and kissed the *mezzuzah*. When people saw me in the street they were greatly surprised.

"Where are you going?" they said.

I answered, "Into the world." And so I departed from Frampol.

I wandered over the land, and good people did not neglect me. After many years I became old and white; I heard a great deal, many lies and falsehoods, but the longer I lived the more I understood that there were really no lies. Whatever doesn't really happen is dreamed at night. It happens to one if it doesn't happen to another, tomorrow if not today, or a century hence if not next year. What difference can it make? Often I heard tales of which I said, "Now this is a thing that cannot happen." But before a year had elapsed I heard that it actually had come to pass somewhere.

Going from place to place, eating at strange tables, it often happens that I spin yarns—improbable things that could never have happened—about devils, magicians, windmills, and the like. The children run after me, calling, "Grandfather, tell us a story." Sometimes they ask for particular stories, and I try to please them. A fat young boy once said to me, "Grandfather, it's the same story you told us before." The little rogue, he was right.

So it is with dreams too. It is many years since I left Frampol, but as soon as I shut my eyes I am there again. And whom do you think I see? Elka. She is standing by the washtub, as at our first encounter, but her face is shining and her eyes are as radiant as the eyes of a saint, and she speaks outlandish words to me, strange things. When I wake I have forgotten it all. But while the dream lasts I am comforted. She answers all my queries, and what comes out is that all is right. I weep and implore, "Let me be with you." And she consoles me and tells me to be patient. The time is nearer than it is far. Sometimes she strokes and kisses me and weeps upon my face. When I awaken I feel her lips and taste the salt of her tears.

No doubt the world is entirely an imaginary world, but it is only once removed from the true world. At the door of the hovel where I lie, there stands the plank on which the dead are taken away. The gravedigger Jew has his spade ready. The grave waits and the worms are hungry; the shrouds are prepared—I carry them in my beggar's sack. Another *shnorrer* is waiting to inherit my bed of straw. When the time comes I will go joyfully. Whatever may be there, it will be real, without complication, without ridicule, without deception. God be praised: there even Gimpel cannot be deceived.

Translated by Saul Bellow

The Gentleman from Cracow

AMID thick forests and deep swamps, on the slope of a hill, level at the summit, lay the village of Frampol. Nobody knew who had founded it, or why just there. Goats grazed among the tombstones which were already sunk in the ground of the cemetery. In the community house there was a parchment with a chronicle on it, but the first page was missing and the writing had faded. Legends were current among the people, tales of wicked intrigue concerning a mad nobleman, a lascivious lady, a Jewish scholar, and a wild dog. But their true origin was lost in the past.

Peasants who tilled the surrounding countryside were poor; the land was stubborn. In the village, the Jews were impoverished; their roofs were straw, their floors dirt. In summer many of them wore no shoes, and in cold weather they wrapped their feet in rags or wore sandals made of straw.

Rabbi Ozer, although renowned for his erudition, received a salary of only eighteen *groszy* a week. The assistant rabbi, besides being ritual slaughterer, was teacher, matchmaker, bath attendant, and poorhouse nurse as well. Even those villagers who were considered wealthy knew little of luxury. They wore cotton gabardines, tied about their waists with string, and tasted meat only on the Sabbath. Gold coin was rarely seen in Frampol.

But the inhabitants of Frampol had been blessed with fine children. The boys grew tall and strong, the girls handsome. It was a mixed blessing, however, for the young men left to marry girls from other towns, while their sisters, who had no dowries, remained unwed. Yet despite everything, inexplicably, though the food was scarce and the water foul, the children continued to thrive.

Then, one summer, there was a drought. Even the oldest peasants could not recall a calamity such as this one. No rain fell. The corn was parched and stunted. There was scarcely anything worth harvesting. Not until the few sheaves of wheat had been cut and gathered did the rain come, and with it hail which destroyed whatever grain the drought had spared.

Locusts huge as birds came in the wake of the storm; human voices were said to issue from their throats. They flew at the eyes of the peasants who tried to drive them away. That year there was no fair, for everything had been lost. Neither the peasants nor the Jews of Frampol had food. Although there was grain in the large towns, no one could buy it.

Just when all hope had been abandoned and the entire town was about to go begging, a miracle occurred. A carriage drawn by eight spirited horses, came into Frampol. The villagers expected its occupant to be a Christian gentleman, but it was a Jew, a young man between the ages of twenty and thirty, who alighted. Tall and pale, with a round black beard and fiery dark eyes, he wore a sable hat, silver-buckled shoes, and a beaver-trimmed caftan. Around his waist was a green silk sash. Aroused, the entire town rushed to get a glimpse of the stranger. This is the story he told: He was a doctor, a widower from Cracow. His wife, the daughter of a wealthy merchant, had died with their baby in childbirth.

Overwhelmed, the villagers asked why he had come to Frampol. It was on the advice of a Wonder Rabbi, he told them. The melancholy he had known after his wife's death, would, the rabbi assured him, disappear in Frampol. From the poorhouse the beggars came, crowding about him as he distributed alms—three groszy, six groszy, half-gulden pieces. The stranger was clearly a gift from Heaven, and Frampol was not destined to vanish. The beggars hurried to the baker for bread, and the baker sent to Zamosc for a sack of flour.

"One sack?" the young doctor asked. "Why that won't last a single day. I will order a wagonload, and not only flour, but cornmeal also."

"But we have no money," the village elders explained.

"God willing, you will repay me when times are good," and saying this, the stranger produced a purse crammed with golden ducats. Frampol rejoiced as he counted out the coins.

The next day, wagons filled with flour, buckwheat, barley, millet, and beans, drove into Frampol. News of the village's good fortune reached the ears of the peasants, and they came to the Jews, to buy goods, as the Egyptians had once come to Joseph. Being without money, they paid in kind; as a result, there was meat in town. Now the ovens burned once more;

the pots were full. Smoke rose from the chimneys, sending the odors of roast chicken and goose, onion and garlic, fresh bread and pastry, into the evening air. The villagers returned to their occupations; shoemakers mended shoes; tailors picked up their rusted shears and irons.

The evenings were warm and the sky clear, though the Feast of the Tabernacles had already passed. The stars seemed unusually large. Even the birds were awake, and they chirped and warbled as though in midsummer. The stranger from Cracow had taken the best room at the inn, and his dinner consisted of broiled duck, marchpane, and twisted bread. Apricots and Hungarian wine were his dessert. Six candles adorned the table. One evening after dinner, the doctor from Cracow entered the large public room where some of the more inquisitive townspeople had gathered and asked,

"Would anyone care for a game of cards?"

"But it isn't Chanukah yet," they answered in surprise.

"Why wait for Chanukah? I'll put up a gulden for every groszy."

A few of the more frivolous men were willing to try their luck, and it turned out to be good. A groszy meant a gulden, and one gulden became thirty. Anyone played who wished to do so. Everybody won. But the stranger did not seem distressed. Banknotes and coins of silver and gold covered the table. Women and girls crowded into the room, and it seemed as though the gleam of the gold before them was reflected in their eyes. They gasped in wonderment. Never before in Frampol had such things happened. Mothers cautioned their daughters to take pains with their hair, and allowed them to dress in holiday clothes. The girl who found favor in the eyes of the young doctor would be fortunate; he was not one to require a dowry.

II

The next morning, matchmakers called on him, each extolling the virtues of the girl he represented. The doctor invited them to be seated, served them honey cake, macaroons, nuts, and mead, and announced:

"From each of you I get exactly the same story: Your client is beautiful and clever and possesses every possible distinction. But how can I know which of you is telling the truth? I want the finest of them all as my wife. Here is what I suggest: Let there be a ball to which all the eligible young women are invited. By observing their appearance and behavior, I shall be able to choose among them. Then the marriage contract will be drawn and the wedding arranged."

The matchmakers were astounded. Old Mendel was the first to find words. "A ball? That sort of thing is all right for rich Gentiles, but we Jews have not indulged in such festivities since the destruction of the Temple—except when the Law prescribes it for certain holidays."

"Isn't every Jew obliged to marry off his daughters?" asked the doctor.

"But the girls have no appropriate clothes," another matchmaker protested. "Because of the drought they would have to go in rags."

"I will see that they all have clothes. I'll order enough silk, wool, velvet, and linen from Zamosc to outfit every girl. Let the ball take place. Let it be one that Frampol will never forget."

"But where can we hold it?" another matchmaker interjected. "The hall where we used to hold weddings has burned down, and our cottages are too small."

"There's the market place," the gentleman from Cracow suggested.

"But it is already the month of Heshvan. Any day now, it will turn cold."

"We'll choose a warm night when the moon is out. Don't worry about it."

To all the numerous objections of the matchmakers, the stranger had an answer ready. Finally they agreed to consult the elders. The doctor said he was in no hurry, he would await their decision. During the entire discussion, he had been carrying on a game of chess with one of the town's cleverest young men, while munching raisins.

The elders were incredulous when they heard what had been proposed. But the young girls were excited. The young men approved also. The mothers pretended to hesitate, but finally gave their consent. When a delegation of the older men sought out Rabbi Ozer for his approval, he was outraged.

"What kind of charlatan is this?" he shouted. "Frampol is not Cracow. All we need is a ball! Heaven forbid that we bring down a plague, and innocent infants be made to pay for our frivolity!"

But the more practical of the men reasoned with the rabbi, saying, "Our daughters walk around barefoot and in tatters now. He will provide them with shoes and clothing. If one of them should please him he would marry her and settle here. Certainly that is to our advantage. The synagogue needs a new roof. The windowpanes of the house of study are broken, the bathhouse is badly in need of repairs. In the poorhouse the sick lie on bundles of rotting straw."

"All this is true. But suppose we sin?"

"Everything will be done according to the Law, Rabbi. You can trust us."

Taking down the book of the Law, Rabbi Ozer leafed through it. Occasionally he stopped to study a page, and then, finally, after sighing and hesitating, he consented. Was there any choice? He himself had received no salary for six months.

As soon as the rabbi had given his consent there was a great display of activity. The dry goods merchants traveled immediately to Zamosc and Yanev, returning with cloth and leather paid for by the gentleman from Cracow. The tailors and seamstresses worked day and night; the cobblers left their benches only to pray. The young women, all anticipation, were in a feverish state. Vaguely remembered dance steps were tried out. They baked cakes and other pastries, and used up their stores of jams and preserves which they had been keeping in readiness for illness. The Frampol musicians were equally active. Cymbals, fiddles, and bagpipes, long forgotten and neglected, had to be dusted off and tuned. Gaiety infected even the very old, for it was rumored that the elegant doctor planned a banquet for the poor where alms would be distributed.

The eligible girls were wholly concerned with self-improvement. They scrubbed their skin and arranged their hair; a few even visited the ritual bath to bathe among the married women. In the evenings, faces flushed, eyes sparkling, they met at each other's houses, to tell stories and ask riddles. It was difficult for them, and for their mothers as well, to sleep at night. Fathers sighed as they slept. And suddenly the young girls of Frampol seemed so attractive that the young men who had contemplated marrying outside of town fell in love with them. Although the young men still sat in the study-house poring over the Talmud, its wisdom no longer penetrated to them. It was the ball alone that they spoke of now, only the ball that occupied their thoughts.

The doctor from Cracow also enjoyed himself. He changed his clothes several times daily. First it was a silk coat worn with pom-pommed slippers, then a woolen caftan with high boots. At one meal he wore a pelerine trimmed with beaver tails, and at the next a cape embroidered with flowers and leaves. He breakfasted on roast pigeon which he washed down with dry wine. For lunch he ordered egg noodles and blintzes, and he was audacious enough to eat Sabbath pudding on weekdays. He never attended prayer, but instead played all sorts of games: cards, goats and wolves, coin-pitching. Having finished lunch, he would drive through the neighborhood with his coachman. The peasants would lift their hats as he passed, and bow almost to the ground. One day he strolled through Frampol with a gold-headed cane. Women crowded to the windows to observe him, and boys, following after him, picked up the rock candy he tossed them. In the evenings he and his companions, gay young men, drank wine until all hours. Rabbi Ozer constantly warned his flock that they walked a downhill path led by the Evil One, but they paid no attention to him. Their minds and hearts were completely possessed by the ball, which would be held at the market place in the middle of that month, at the time of the full moon.

III

At the edge of town, in a small valley close to a swamp, stood a hut no larger than a chicken coop. Its floor was dirt, its window was boarded; and the roof, because it was covered with green and yellow moss, made one think of a bird's nest that had been forsaken. Heaps of garbage were strewn before the hut, and lime ditches furrowed the soggy earth. Amidst the refuse there was an occasional chair without a seat, a jug missing an ear, a table without legs. Every type of broom, bone, and rag seemed to be rotting there. This was where Lipa the Ragpicker lived with his daughter, Hodle. While his first wife was alive, Lipa had been a respected merchant in Frampol where he occupied a pew at the east wall of the synagogue. But after his wife had drowned herself in the river, his condition declined rapidly. He took to drink, associated with the town's worst element, and soon ended up bankrupt.

His second wife, a beggar woman from Yanev, bore him a daughter whom she left behind when she deserted him for non-support. Unconcerned about his wife's departure, Lipa allowed the child to shift for herself. Each week he spent a few days collecting rags from the garbage. The rest of the time he was in the tavern. Although the innkeeper's wife scolded him, she received only abusive answers in reply. Lipa had his success among the men as a tale-spinner. He attracted business to the place with his fantastic yarns about witches and windmills and devils and goblins. He could also recite Polish and Ukrainian rhymes and had a knack for telling jokes. The innkeeper allowed him to occupy a place near the stove, and from time to time he was given a bowl of soup and a piece of bread. Old friends, remembering Lipa's former affluence, occasionally presented him with a pair of pants, a threadbare coat, or a shirt. He accepted everything ungraciously. He even stuck out his tongue at his benefactors as they turned away from him.

As in the saying, "Like father, like son," Hodle inherited the vices of both parents—her drunken father, her begging mother. By the time she was six, she had won a reputation as a glutton and thief. Barefoot and half naked, she roamed the town, entering houses and raiding the larders of those who were not home. She preyed on chickens and ducks, cut their throats with glass, and ate them. Although the inhabitants of Frampol had often warned her father that he was rearing a wanton, the information did not seem to bother him. He seldom spoke to her and she did not even call him father. When she was twelve, her lasciviousness became a matter for discussion among the women. Gypsies visited her shack, and it was rumored that she devoured the meat of cats and dogs, in fact, every kind of carcass. Tall and lean, with red hair and green eyes, she went barefoot summer and winter, and her skirts were made of colored scraps discarded by the seamstresses. She was feared by mothers who said she wove spells that blighted the young. The village elders who admonished her received brazen answers. She had the shrewdness of a bastard, the quick tongue of an adder, and when attacked by street urchins, did not hesitate to strike back. Particularly skilled in swearing, she had an unlimited repertoire. It was like her to call out, "Pox on your tongue and gangrene in your eyes," or, possibly, "May you rot till the skunks run from your smell."

Occasionally her curses were effective, and the town grew wary of incurring her anger. But as she matured she tended to avoid the town proper, and the time came when she was almost forgotten. But on the day that the Frampol merchants, in preparation for the ball, distributed cloth and leather among the town's young women, Hodle reappeared. She was now about seventeen, fully grown, though still in short skirts; her face was freckled, and her hair disheveled. Beads, such as those worn by gypsies, encircled her throat, and on her wrists were bracelets made from wolves' teeth. Pushing her way through the crowd, she demanded her share. There was nothing left but a few odds and ends, which were given to her. Furious with her allotment, she hastened home with it. Those who had seen what had happened laughed, "Look who's going to the ball! What a pretty picture she'll make!"

At last the shoemakers and tailors were done; every dress fit, every shoe was right. The days were miraculously warm, and the nights as luminous as the evenings of Pentecost. It was the morning star that, on the day of the ball, woke the entire town. Tables and benches lined one side of the market. The cooks had already roasted calves, sheep, goats, geese, ducks, and chicken, and had baked sponge and raisin cakes, braided bread and rolls, onion biscuits and ginger bread. There were mead and beer and a barrel of Hungarian wine that had been brought by the wine dealer. When the children arrived they brought the bows and arrows with which they were accustomed to play at the Omer feast, as well as their Purim rattles and Torah flags. Even the doctor's horses were decorated with willow branches and autumn flowers, and the coachman paraded them through the town. Apprentices left their work, and

yeshiva students their volumes of the Talmud. And despite
Rabbi Ozer's injunction against the young matrons' attending the ball, they dressed in their wedding gowns and went,
arriving with the young girls, who also came in white, each
bearing a candle in her hand as though she were a bridesmaid.
The band had already begun to play, and the music was lively.
Rabbi Ozer alone was not present, having locked himself in
his study. His maidservant had gone to the ball, leaving him
to himself. He knew no good could come of such behavior,
but there was nothing he could do to prevent it.

By late afternoon all the girls had gathered in the market
place, surrounded by the townspeople. Drums were beaten.
Jesters performed. The girls danced; first a quadrille, then a
scissor dance. Next it was Kozack, and finally the Dance of
Anger. Now the moon appeared, although the sun had not yet
set. It was time for the gentleman from Cracow. He entered on
a white mare, flanked by bodyguards and his best man. He
wore a large-plumed hat, and sliver buttons flashed on his
green coat. A sword hung at his side, and his shiny boots
rested in the stirrups. He resembled a gentleman off to war
with his entourage. Silently he sat in his saddle, watching the
girls as they danced. How graceful they were, how charmingly
they moved! But one who did not dance was the daughter of
Lipa the Ragpicker. She stood to one side, ignored by them all.

IV

The setting sun, remarkably large, stared down angrily like a
heavenly eye upon the Frampol market place. Never before
had Frampol seen such a sunset. Like rivers of burning sulphur, fiery clouds streamed across the heavens, assuming the
shapes of elephants, lions, snakes, and monsters. They seemed
to be waging a battle in the sky, devouring one another, spitting, breathing fire. It almost seemed to be the River of Fire
they watched, where demons tortured the evil-doers amidst
glowing coals and heaps of ashes. The moon swelled, became
vast, blood-red, spotted, scarred, and gave off little light. The
evening grew very dark, dissolving even the stars. The young
men fetched torches, and a barrel of burning pitch was prepared. Shadows danced back and forth as though attending a

ball of their own. Around the market place the houses seemed to vibrate; roofs quivered, chimneys shook. Such gaiety and intoxication had never before been known in Frampol. Everyone, for the first time in months, had eaten and drunk sufficiently. Even the animals participated in the merrymaking. Horses neighed, cows mooed, and the few roosters that had survived the slaughter of the fowl crowed. Flocks of crows and strange birds flew in to pick at the leavings. Fireflies illumined the darkness, and lightning flashed on the horizon. But there was no thunder. A weird circular light glowed in the sky for a few moments and then suddenly plummeted toward the horizon, a crimson tail behind it, resembling a burning rod. Then, as everyone stared in wonder at the sky, the gentleman from Cracow spoke:

"Listen to me. I have wonderful things to tell you, but let no one be overcome by joy. Men, take hold of your wives. Young men, look to your girls. You see in me the wealthiest man in the entire world. Money is sand to me, and diamonds are pebbles. I come from the land of Ophir, where King Solomon found the gold for his temple. I dwell in the palace of the Queen of Sheba. My coach is solid gold, its wheels inlaid with sapphires, with axles of ivory, its lamps studded with rubies and emeralds, opals and amethysts. The Ruler of the Ten Lost Tribes of Israel knows of your miseries, and he has sent me to be your benefactor. But there is one condition. Tonight, every virgin must marry. I will provide a dowry of ten thousand ducats for each maiden, as well as a string of pearls that will hang to her knees. But make haste. Every girl must have a husband before the clocks strike twelve."

The crowd was hushed. It was as quiet as New Year's Day before the blowing of the ram's horn. One could hear the buzzing of a fly.

Then one old man called out, "But that's impossible. The girls are not even engaged!"

"Let them become engaged."

"To whom?"

"We can draw lots," the gentleman from Cracow replied. "Whoever is to be married will have his or her name written on a card. Mine also. And then we shall draw to see who is meant for whom."

"But a girl must wait seven days. She must have the prescribed ablutions."

"Let the sin be on me. She needn't wait."

Despite the protestations of the old men and their wives, a sheet of paper was torn into pieces, and on each piece the name of a young man or young woman was written by a scribe. The town's beadle, now in the service of the gentleman from Cracow, drew from one skullcap the names of the young men, and from another those of the young women, chanting their names to the same tune with which he called up members of the congregation for the reading of the Torah.

"Nahum, son of Katriel, betrothed to Yentel, daughter of Nathan. Solomon, son of Cov Baer, betrothed to Tryna, daughter of Jonah Lieb." The assortment was a strange one, but since in the night all sheep are black, the matches seemed reasonable enough. After each drawing, the newly engaged couple, hand in hand, approached the doctor to collect the dowry and wedding gift. As he had promised, the gentleman from Cracow gave each the stipulated sum of ducats, and on the neck of each bride he hung a strand of pearls. Now the mothers, unable to restrain their joy, began to dance and shout. The fathers stood by, bewildered. When the girls lifted their dresses to catch the gold coins given by the doctor, their legs and underclothing were exposed, which sent the men into paroxysms of lust. Fiddles screeched, drums pounded, trumpets blared. The uproar was deafening. Twelve-year-old boys were mated with "spinsters" of nineteen. The sons of substantial citizens took the daughters of paupers as brides; midgets were coupled with giants, beauties with cripples. On the last two slips appeared the names of the gentleman from Cracow and Hodle, the daughter of Lipa the Ragpicker.

The same old man who had called out previously said, "Woe unto us, the girl is a harlot."

"Come to me, Hodle, come to your bridegroom," the doctor bade.

Hodle, her hair in two long braids, dressed in a calico skirt, and with sandals on her feet, did not wait to be asked twice. As soon as she had been called she walked to where the gentleman from Cracow sat on his mare, and fell to her knees. She prostrated herself seven times before him.

"Is it true, what that old fool says?" her prospective husband asked her.

"Yes, my lord, it is so."

"Have you sinned only with Jews or with Gentiles as well?"

"With both."

"Was it for bread?"

"No. For the sheer pleasure."

"How old were you when you started?"

"Not quite ten."

"Are you sorry for what you have done?"

"No."

"Why not?"

"Why should I be?" she answered shamelessly.

"You don't fear the tortures of hell?"

"I fear nothing—not even God. There is no God."

Once more the old man began to scream, "Woe to us, woe to us, Jews! A fire is upon us, burning, Jews, Satan's fire. Save your souls, Jews. Flee, before it is too late!"

"Gag him," the gentleman from Cracow commanded.

The guards seized the old man and gagged him. The doctor, leading Hodle by the hand, began to dance. Now, as though the powers of darkness had been summoned, the rain and hail began to fall; flashes of lightning were accompanied by mighty thunderclaps. But, heedless of the storm, pious men and women embraced without shame, dancing and shouting as though possessed. Even the old were affected. In the furor, dresses were ripped, shoes shaken off, hats, wigs and skullcaps trampled in the mud. Sashes, slipping to the ground, twisted there like snakes. Suddenly there was a terrific crash. A huge bolt of lightning had simultaneously struck the synagogue, the study house, and the ritual bath. The whole town was on fire.

Now at last the deluded people realized that there was no natural origin to these occurrences. Although the rain continued to fall and even increased in intensity, the fire was not extinguished. An eerie light glowed in the market place. Those few prudent individuals who tried to disengage themselves from the demented crowd were crushed to earth and trampled.

And then the gentleman from Cracow revealed his true identity. He was no longer the young man the villagers had welcomed, but a creature covered with scales, with an eye in his chest, and on his forehead a horn that rotated at great speed. His arms were covered with hair, thorns, and elflocks, and his tail was a mass of live serpents, for he was none other than Ketev Mriri, Chief of the Devils.

Witches, werewolves, imps, demons, and hobgoblins plummeted from the sky, some on brooms, others on hoops, still others on spiders. Osnath, the daughter of Machlath, her fiery hair loosened in the wind, her breasts bare and thighs exposed, leaped from chimney to chimney, and skated along the eaves. Namah, Hurmizah the daughter of Aff, and many other she-devils did all sorts of somersaults. Satan himself gave away the bridgroom, while four evil spirits held the poles of the canopy, which had turned into writhing pythons. Four dogs escorted the groom. Hodle's dress fell from her and she stood naked. Her breasts hung down to her navel and her feet were webbed. Her hair was a wilderness of worms and caterpillars. The groom held out a triangular ring and, instead of saying, "With this ring be thou consecrated to me according to the laws of Moses and Israel," he said, "With this ring, be thou desecrated to me according to the blasphemy of Korah and Ishmael." And instead of wishing the pair good luck, the evil spirits called out, "Bad luck," and they began to chant:

> *"The curse of Eve, the Mark of Cain,*
> *The cunning of the snake, unite the twain."*

Screaming for the last time, the old man clutched at his head and died. Ketev Mriri began his eulogy:

> *"Devil's dung and Satan's spell*
> *Bring his ghost to roast in hell."*

V

In the middle of the night, old Rabbi Ozer awoke. Since he was a holy man, the fire which was consuming the town had no power over his house. Sitting up in bed he looked about, wondering if dawn were already breaking. But it was neither day nor night without. The sky was a fiery red, and from the distance came a clamor of shouts and songs that resembled the howling of wild beasts. At first, recalling nothing, the old man wondered what was going on. "Has the world come to an end? Or have I failed to hear the ram's horn heralding the Messiah? Has He arrived?" Washing his hands, he put on his slippers and overcoat and went out.

The town was unrecognizable. Where houses had been, only chimneys stood. Mounds of coal smoldered here and there. He called the beadle, but there was no answer. With his cane, the rabbi went searching for his flock.

"Where are you, Jews, where are you?" he called piteously.

The earth scorched his feet, but he did not slacken his pace. Mad dogs and strange beings attacked him, but he wielded his cane against them. His sorrow was so great that he felt no fear. Where the market place used to be, a terrible sight met him. There was nothing but one great swamp, full of mud, slime, and ashes. Floundering in mud up to their waists, a crowd of naked people went through the movements of dance. At first, the rabbi mistook the weirdly moving figures for devils, and was about to recite the chapter, "Let there be contentment," and other passages dealing with exorcism, when he recognized the men of his town. Only then did he remember the doctor from Cracow, and the rabbi cried out bitterly, "Jews, for the sake of God, save your souls! You are in the hands of Satan!"

But the townspeople, too entranced to heed his cries, continued their frenzied movements for a long time, jumping like frogs, shaking as though with fever. With hair uncovered and breasts bare, the women laughed, cried, and swayed. Catching a yeshiva boy by his sidelocks, a girl pulled him to her lap. A woman tugged at the beard of a strange man. Old men and women were immersed in slime up to their loins. They scarcely looked alive.

Relentlessly, the rabbi urged the people to resist evil. Reciting the Torah and other holy books, as well as incantations and the several names of God, he succeeded in rousing some of them. Soon others responded. The rabbi had helped the first man from the mire, then that one assisted the next, and so on. Most of them had recovered by the time the morning star appeared. Perhaps the spirits of their forbears had interceded, for although many had sinned, only one man had died this night in the market place square.

Now the men were appalled, realizing that the devil had be-witched them, had dragged them through muck; and they wept.

"Where is our money?" the girls wailed, "And our gold and our jewelry? Where is our clothing? What happened to the wine, the mead, the wedding gifts?"

But everything had turned to mud; the town of Frampol, stripped and ruined, had become a swamp. Its inhabitants were mud-splashed, denuded, monstrous. For a moment, for-getting their grief, they laughed at each other. The hair of the girls had turned into elflocks, and bats were entangled there. The young men had grown gray and wrinkled; the old were yellow as corpses. In their midst lay the old man who had died. Crimson with shame, the sun rose.

"Let us rend our clothes in mourning," one man called, but his words evoked laughter, for all were naked.

"We are doomed, my sisters," lamented a woman.

"Let us drown ourselves in the river," a girl shrieked. "Why go on living?"

One of the yeshiva boys said, "Let us strangle ourselves with our sashes."

"Brothers, we are lost. Let us blaspheme God," said a horse dealer.

"Have you lost your minds, Jews?" cried Rabbi Ozer, "Re-pent, before it is too late. You have fallen into Satan's snare, but it is my fault, I take the sin upon myself. I am the guilty one. I will be your scapegoat, and you shall remain clean."

"This is madness!" one of the scholars protested, "God for-bid that there be so many sins on your holy head!"

"Do not worry about that. My shoulders are broad. I should have had more foresight. I was blind not to realize that the Cracow doctor was the Evil One. And when the shepherd is blind, the flock goes astray. It is I who deserve the punish-ment, the curses."

"Rabbi, what shall we do? We have no homes, no bed clothes, nothing. Woe to us, to our bodies and to our souls."

"Our babies!" cried the young matrons, "Let us hurry to them!"

But it was the infants who had been the real victims of the passion for gold that had caused the inhabitants of Frampol to transgress. The infants' cribs were burned, their little bones were charred. The mothers stooped to pick up little hands, feet, skulls. The wailing and crying lasted long, but how long can a whole town weep? The gravedigger gathered the bones and carried them to the cemetery. Half the town began the prescribed seven days of mourning. But all fasted, for there was no food anywhere.

But the compassion of the Jews is well known, and when the neighboring town of Yanev learned what had happened, clothing, bed linen, bread, cheese, and dishes were collected and sent to Frampol. Timber merchants brought logs for building. A rich man offered credit. The next day the reconstruction of the town was begun. Although work is forbidden to those in mourning, Rabbi Ozer issued a verdict that this was an exceptional case: the lives of the people were in danger. Miraculously, the weather remained mild; no snow fell. Never before had there been such diligence in Frampol. The inhabitants built and prayed, mixed lime with sand, and recited psalms. The women worked with the men, while girls, forgetting their fastidiousness, helped also. Scholars and men of high position assisted. Peasants from the surrounding villages, hearing of the catastrophe, took the old and infirm into their homes. They also brought wood, potatoes, cabbages, onions and other food. Priests and bishops from Lublin, hearing of events that suggested witchcraft, came to examine witnesses. As the scribe recorded the names of those living in Frampol, Hodle, the daughter of Lipa the Ragpicker, was suddenly remembered. But when the townspeople went to where her hut had been, they found the hill covered with weeds and bramble, silent save for the cries of crows and cats; there was no indication that human beings had ever dwelt there.

Then it was understood that Hodle was in truth Lilith, and that the host of the netherworld had come to Frampol because of her. After their investigations, the clergymen from Lubin, greatly astonished at what they had seen and heard, returned home. A few days later, the day before the Sabbath, Rabbi Ozer died. The entire town attended his funeral, and the town preacher said a eulogy for him.

In time, a new rabbi came to the community, and a new town arose. The old people died, the mounds in the cemetery sifted down, and the monuments slowly sank. But the story, signed by trustworthy witnesses, can still be read in the parchment chronicle.

And the events in the story brought their epilogue: the lust for gold had been stifled in Frampol; it was never rekindled. From generation to generation the people remained paupers. A gold coin became an abomination in Frampol, and even silver was looked at askance. Whenever a shoemaker or tailor asked too high a price for his work he was told, "Go to the gentleman from Cracow and he will give you buckets of gold."

And on the grave of Rabbi Ozer, in the memorial chapel, there burns an eternal light. A white pigeon is often seen on the roof: the sainted spirit of Rabbi Ozer.

Translated by Martha Glicklich and Elaine Gottlieb

The Wife Killer

A Folk Tale

I AM from Turbin, and there we had a wife killer. Pelte was his name, Pelte the Wife Killer. He had four wives and, may it not be held against him, he sent them all off to the other side. What women saw in him, I don't know. He was a little man, thickset, gray, with a scraggly beard and bulging blood-shot eyes. Merely to look at him was frightful. And as for his stinginess—you never saw anything like it. Summer and winter he went about in the same padded caftan and rawhide boots. Yet he was rich. He had a sizeable brick house, a storeroom full of grain, and property in town. He had an oak chest which I remember to this day. It was covered with leather and bound with copper hoops, for protection in case of fire. To keep it safe from thieves, he had it nailed to the floor. It was said that he kept a fortune in it. All the same, I cannot understand how a woman could go to the bridal canopy with such a man. The first two wives at least had the excuse that they came from poor homes. The first one—poor soul may you live long—was an orphan, and he took her just as she was, without any dowry. The second one, on the other hand—may she rest in peace—was a widow without a cent to her name. She didn't have even an undershirt, if you'll pardon the expression. Today people talk of love. They think that once upon a time men were angels. Nonsense. Clumsy creature that he was, he fell head over heels in love with her, so that all Turbin snickered. He was already a man in his forties and she was a mere child, eighteen years or even less. In short, kind souls intervened, relatives took a hand in the matter, and things came to a head.

Right after the wedding the young wife began to complain that he wasn't acting right. Strange tales were told—may God not punish me for my words. He was spiteful all the time. Before he went to pray in the morning, she would ask him, "What do you want for lunch? Soup or borscht?" "Soup," he might say. So she'd make him soup. He'd return later and complain, "Didn't I tell you to make borscht?" She'd argue,

37

"You said yourself that you wanted soup." And he would say, "So now I am a liar!" And before you could turn around he was already in a rage, and would grab a slice of bread and a head of garlic, and run back to the synagogue to eat there. She would run after him and shout, "I'll cook you a borscht! Don't shame me before people!" But he wouldn't even look back. In the synagogue young men sat studying. "What happened that you eat here?" they would ask him. "My wife chased me out," he would say. To make a long story short, he drove her to the grave with his tantrums. When people advised her to divorce him, he threatened to run off and abandon her. Once he did run away and was caught on the Yanov road, near the turnpike. The woman saw that she was lost, so she simply lay down in bed and died. "I am dying because of him," she said. "May it not be held against him." The entire town was aroused. Some butchers and young bloods wanted to teach him a lesson, because she was of their class, but the community would not allow it—after all, he was a well-to-do man. The dead are buried, as people say, and what the earth swallows is soon forgotten.

Some years passed and he didn't remarry. Perhaps he didn't want to, perhaps there was no suitable opportunity; anyway, he remained a widower. Women gloated over this. He became even stingier than before, and so unkempt that it was positively disgusting. He ate a bit of meat only on Saturday: scraps or derma. All week he ate dry food. He baked his own bread of corn and bran. He didn't buy wood. Instead, he went out at night with a sack, to pick up the chips near the bakery. He had two deep pockets and whatever he saw, he put into them: bones, bark, string, shards. He hid all these in his attic. He piled heaps of stuff as high as the roof. "Every little thing comes in handy," he used to say. He was a scholar in the bargain, and could quote Scripture on every occasion, though as a rule he talked little.

Everybody thought he would remain alone the rest of his life. Suddenly the terrible news spread that he was engaged to Reb Falik's Finkl. How should I describe Finkl to you! She was the most beautiful woman in town, and of the very best family. Her father, Reb Falik, was a magnate. It was said that he bound his books in silk. Whenever a bride was led to the *mikveh,* the musicians would stop before his windows and play a tune. Finkl was his only child. There had been seven and she alone survived. Reb Falik married her off to a rich young man from Brod, one in a million, learned and wise, a real aristocrat. I saw him only once as he went by, with curly *peios* and a flowered caftan and fine shoes and white socks. Blood and milk. But it was fated otherwise. Right after the Seven Blessings he collapsed. Zishe the Healer was called, and he put leeches on him and bled him, but what can you do against fate? Reb Falik rushed a carriage to Lublin to bring a doctor, but Lublin is far, and before you knew it, it was all over with him. The entire town wept, as on Yom Kippur at Kol Nidre. The old rabbi— may he rest in peace—delivered the eulogy. I am only a sinful woman and I don't know much of learned matters, but I remember to this day what the rabbi said. Everybody memorized the eulogy. "He ordered black and got white . . ." the rabbi began. In the Gemorra this is about a man ordering pigeons, but the rabbi—peace be on him—made it mean wedding garments and burial shrouds. Even enemies mourned. We girls soaked our pillows at night. Finkl, delicate pampered Finkl, lost her speech in her great grief. Her mother was no longer living and Reb Falik, too, didn't survive long. Finkl inherited all his wealth, but what use was money? She refused to hear of anyone.

Suddenly we heard that Finkl was going to marry Pelte. The news came on a wintry Thursday evening, and a chill went through everyone. "The man is of the devil!" my mother cried out. "Such a one should be ridden out of town." We youngsters were petrified. I used to sleep by myself but that night I crawled into bed with my sister. I was in a fever. Later we learned that the match had been arranged by a man who was a bit of this and a bit of that and a general nuisance. It was said that he had borrowed a Gemorra from Pelte and found a hundred-ruble note among its pages. Pelte had a habit of hiding paper money in books. What one thing had to do with the other I didn't know—I was still a child then. But what difference does it make? Finkl consented. When God wants to punish someone, He deprives him of reason. People ran to her, they tore their hair trying to dissuade her, but she wouldn't change her mind. The wedding was on the Sabbath after

Shevuoth. The canopy was set up before the synagogue, as is the custom when a virgin gets married, but it seemed to all of us that we were attending a funeral. I was in one of the two rows of girls who stand holding candles in their hands. It was a summer evening and the air was still, but when the groom was led past, the flames began to flicker. I shook with fear. The fiddles started to play a wedding tune, but it was a wail, not music that they made. The bass viol mourned. I wouldn't wish anyone ever to hear the like. To tell you the truth, I'd rather not go on with the story It might give you nightmares, and I myself don't feel up to it. What? You do want to hear more. Very well. You will have to take me home. Tonight I won't walk home alone.

II

Where was I? Yes, Finkl got married. She looked more like a corpse than a bride. The bridesmaids had to support her. Who knows? Maybe she had changed her mind. But was it her fault? It was all from Above. I once heard of a bride who ran away from under the canopy. But not Finkl. She would rather be burned alive than humiliate anyone.

Need I tell you how it all ended? Can't you guess yourselves? May all the enemies of Israel come to such an end. I must say that this time he didn't pull his usual tricks. On the contrary, he tried to comfort her. But he gave off a black melancholy. She tried to lose herself in household duties. And young women came to visit her. There was a constant going back and forth, as with a woman in confinement. They told stories, they knitted, they sewed and asked riddles, anything to distract Finkl. Some even began to hint that perhaps it wasn't such an impossible match. He was rich, and a scholar too. Mightn't he become human living with her? It was reckoned that Finkl would become pregnant and have a baby and get used to her lot. Aren't there many unsuitable marriages in the world! But it wasn't fated that way. Finkl miscarried and had a hemorrhage. They had to bring a doctor from Zamoscz. He advised her to keep herself occupied. She did not become pregnant again, and then her troubles began. He tormented her, everybody knew that. But when she was asked: "What is he doing to you?" she would only say, "Nothing." "If he does nothing to you, why do you have such brown and blue rings around your eyes? And why do you go about like a lost soul?" But she would only say: "I don't know why myself."

How long did this go on? Longer than anyone expected. We all thought she wouldn't last more than a year, but she suffered for three and a half years. She faded like a light. Relatives tried to send her to the hot baths, but she refused to go. Things reached such a pass that people began to pray for her end. One mustn't say it, but death is preferable to such a life. She, too, cursed herself. Before she died, she sent for the rabbi to have him write her will. She probably wanted to leave her wealth for charitable purposes. What else? Leave it to her murderer? But again fate intervened. Some girl suddenly cried "Fire!" and everyone ran to look after his own things. It turned out that there had been no fire. "Why did you cry 'fire'?" the girl was asked. And she explained that it wasn't she who had shouted, but that something inside her had cried out. Meanwhile Finkl died, and Pelte inherited her property. Now he was the richest man in town, but he haggled over the cost of the grave till he got it for half-price.

Until then he hadn't been called Wife Killer. A man is twice widowed—such things happen. But after this he was always called Pelte the Wife Killer. *Cheder* boys pointed at him: "Here comes the Wife Killer." After the Seven Days of Mourning, the rabbi sent for him. "Reb Pelte," he said, "you are now the richest man in Turbin. Half the stores in the market place belong to you. With God's help you have become great. It is time you changed your ways. How long will you live apart from everyone else?" But no words impressed him. Talk of one thing to him, and he answers something entirely different; or he bites his lips and says nothing—you might as well talk to the wall. When the rabbi saw that it was a waste of time, he let him go.

For a time he was silent. He began to bake his own bread again, and to collect chips and cones and dung for fuel. He was shunned like the plague. He seldom came to the synagogue. Everybody was glad not to see him. On Thursdays he went around with his book to collect debts or interest. He had everything written down and never forgot a thing. If a storekeeper said that he hadn't the money to pay him and asked him to come some other time, he wouldn't go but stayed right there, staring with his bulging eyes, till the storekeeper got tired of it and gave him his last cent. The rest of the week he hid away somewhere in his kitchen. At least ten years passed this way, perhaps eleven; I don't remember any more. He must have been in his late fifties, or perhaps in his sixties. Nobody tried to arrange a match for him.

And then something happened, and this is what I want to tell you about. As I live, one could write a book about it; but I will make it short. In Turbin there lived a woman who was called Zlateh the Bitch. Some called her Zlateh the Cossack. From her nicknames you can guess for yourselves what sort of a person she was. It is not right to gossip about the dead, but the truth must be told—she was the lowest and meanest sort. She was a fishwife and her husband had been a fisherman. It's shameful to tell what she did in her youth. She was a slut—everyone knew that. She had a bastard somewhere. Her husband used to work in the poorhouse. There he beat and robbed the sick. How he suddenly got to be a fisherman I don't know, but that makes no difference. Fridays they used to stand in the market place with a basket of fish and curse everyone, whether they bought or not. Curses tumbled from her mouth as from a torn sack. If someone complained that she cheated on the weight, she would grab a fish by the tail and strike out. She tore the wig from the head of more than one woman. Once she was accused of stealing, so she went to the rabbi and falsely swore before black candles and the board on which the dead are washed that she was innocent. Her husband was named Eber, a strange name; he came from far off in Poland. He died and she became a widow. She was so wicked that all through the funeral she howled, "Eber, don't forget to take along all troubles." After the Seven Days of Mourning, she again sold fish in the market place. Since she was a shrew and abused everyone, people taunted her. One woman said to her, "Aren't you going to remarry, Zlateh?" And she answered, "Why not? I'm still a tasty dish." Yet she was already an old hag. "Whom will you marry, Zlateh?" people asked her, and she thought a moment and said, "Pelte."

The women thought she was joking and they laughed. But it was no joke, as you will soon hear.

III

One woman said to her, "But he is a Wife Killer!" And Zlateh answered, "If he is a Wife Killer, I am a worse Husband Killer. Eber wasn't my first husband." Who could tell how many she had before him? She wasn't a native of Turbin—the devil brought her from somewhere on the other side of the Vistula. Nobody paid any attention to what she said, but hardly a week passed before everybody heard that Zlateh hadn't been talking at random. Nobody knew whether she sent a matchmaker or arranged the match herself, but the marriage was going through. The whole town laughed—a fitting pair, falsehood and wickedness. Everybody said the same, "If Finkl were alive and saw who was inheriting her place, she would die of grief." Tailors' apprentices and seamstresses at once began to wager who would outlast whom. The apprentices said that nobody was a match for Pelte the Wife Killer, and the seamstresses argued that Zlateh was younger by some years and that not even Pelte had a chance once she opened her mouth. Anyway, the wedding took place. I wasn't there. You know that when a widower takes a widow, there's little fuss. But others who were there had lots of fun. The bride was all decked out. On Saturday she came to the women's gallery in the synagogue wearing a hat with a feather. She couldn't read. That Saturday I happened to take a new bride to the synagogue, and Zlateh stood right near me. She took Finkl's seat. She talked and jabbered all the time so that I didn't know what to do with myself for shame. And do you know what she said? She abused her husband. "He won't last long with me around," she said; just like that. A bitch—no doubt about it.

For some time nobody talked about them. After all, a whole town can't always bother with such scum. Then suddenly there was an outcry again. Zlateh had hired a maid, a little woman who had been abandoned by her husband. The maid started telling horrible stories. Pelte and Zlateh were at war—not just they, that is, but their stars. All sorts of things happened. Once Zlateh stood in the middle of the room and the chandelier fell down; it missed her by an inch. "The Wife Killer is at his tricks again," she said. "I'll show him something." The next day Pelte was walking in the market place; he slipped and fell into a ditch and nearly broke his neck. Every day something new happened. One time the soot in the chimney caught fire, and the entire house almost burned down; another time the cornice of the wardrobe fell and barely missed Pelte's skull. Everybody could see plainly that one or the other would have to go. It is written somewhere that every man is followed by devils—a thousand on the left and ten thousand on the right. We had a *malamed* in town, a certain Reb Itche the Slaughtered—that's what he was called—a very fine man who knew all about "those" matters. He said that this was a case of war between "them." At first things were fairly quiet; that is, people talked, but the unfortunate couple didn't say a thing. But in the end, Zlateh came running to the rabbi all atremble. "Rabbi," she shouted, "I can't stand it any more. Just think of it: I prepared dough in a trough and covered it with a pillow. I wanted to get up early to bake bread. In the middle of the night I see—the dough is on my bed. It's his work, Rabbi. He's made up his mind to finish me." At that time Reb Eisele Teumim, a true saint, was rabbi in the town. He couldn't believe his own ears. "Why should a man play such tricks?" he asked. "Why? You tell me why!" she answered. "Rabbi, send for him, let him tell it himself." The *shames* was sent and he brought Pelte. Naturally, he denied everything. "She is giving me a bad name," he cried. "She wants to get rid of me and get my money. She cast a spell to make water collect in the cellar. I went down there to get a piece of rope and was nearly drowned. Besides, she brought on a plague of mice." Pelte declared on oath that at night Zlateh whistled in bed, and that as soon as she started whistling there was a squeaking and a rushing of mice from all the holes. He pointed to a scar over his eyebrow and said that a mouse had bitten him there. When the rabbi realized whom he had to deal with, he said, "Take my advice and get divorced. It will be better for both of you." "The rabbi is right," Zlateh said. "I am willing, this very minute, but let him give me a settlement of half the property." "I won't give you the price of a pinch of snuff!" Pelte shouted.

"What's more, you will pay me a fine." He grabbed his cane and wanted to strike her. He was held back with difficulty. When the rabbi saw that he would get nowhere in this case, he said, "Go your ways and leave me to my studies." So they went away.

From that time on the town had no rest. It was frightening to pass by their house. The shutters were always closed, even in the day time. Zlateh stopped selling fish, and all they did was fight. Zlateh was a giant of a woman. She used to go to the landowners' ponds and help spread the nets. She would get up in the middle of the night in winter, and in the worst frosts she never used a fire-pot. "The devil won't take me," she'd say. "I'm never cold." And now she suddenly aged. Her face blackened and was wrinkled like that of a woman of seventy. She started coming to strangers' houses to ask for advice. Once she came to my mother—peace be on her—and begged to be allowed to stay overnight. My mother looked at her as one demented. "What happened?" she asked. "I'm afraid of him," Zlateh said. "He wants to get rid of me. He makes winds in the house." She said that though the windows were sealed outside with clay and inside with straw, strong winds blew in her bedroom. She also swore that her bed would rise beneath her, and that Pelte spent half the nights in the outhouse—if you'll pardon the expression. "What does he do there so long?" my mother asked. "He has a mistress there," Zlateh said. I happened to be in the alcove and heard all this. Pelte must have had dealings with the Unclean Ones. My mother shuddered. "Listen to me, Zlateh," she said, "give him the 'dozen lines' and run for your life. If they were to give me my weight in gold, I wouldn't live under the same roof with anyone like that." But a Cossack never changes. "He won't get rid of me just like that," Zlateh said. "Let him give me a settlement." In the end, my mother made up a bed for her on the bench. We didn't shut an eye that night. Before dawn she got up and left. Mother couldn't fall asleep again and lit a taper in the kitchen. "You know," she said to me, "I have a feeling that she won't get out of his hands alive. Well, it won't be a big loss." But Zlateh wasn't Finkl. She didn't give up so easily, as you will soon hear.

IV

What did she do? I don't know. People told all sorts of stories, but you can't believe everything. We had an old peasant woman in town, Cunegunde. She must have been a hundred years old, maybe older. Everybody knew that she was a witch. Her whole face was covered with warts, and she walked almost on all fours. Her hut was at the end of town, on the sand, and it was full of all kinds of animals: rabbits and guinea pigs, cats and dogs, and all kinds of vermin. Birds flew in and out of the windows. The place stank. But Zlateh became a frequent visitor and spent whole days there. The woman knew how to pour wax. If a peasant was sick, he would come to her, and she'd pour molten wax which formed all sorts of strange figures and showed what the sickness came from—though it did little good.

As I was saying, people in town said this Cunegunde taught Zlateh a charm. Anyway, Pelte became a changed man, soft as butter. She wanted him to transfer the house to her name, so he hired a team of horses and went to town to register the transfer. Then she started meddling in his stores. Now it was she who went about on Thursdays with the interest and rent book. She asked for increases right away. The storekeepers cried that they were losing their shirts, so she said, "In that case you can go begging." A meeting was held, and Pelte was called. He was so weak that he could barely walk. He was completely deaf. "There is nothing I can do," he said. "Everything belongs to her. If she wants to, she can drive me out of the house." She would have, too, but he hadn't transferred everything to her yet. He was still bargaining with her. Neighbors said that she was starving him. He used to go into houses and beg for a piece of bread. His hands shook. Everybody saw that Zlateh was having her way. Some were glad—he was being punished for Finkl. Others argued that Zlateh would ruin the town. It's not a small matter when so much property gets into the hands of such a beast. She began to build and to dig. She brought craftsmen from Yanov and they started measuring the streets. She put on a wig, with silver combs, and she carried a purse and a parasol, like a real aristocrat. She burst into homes early in the morning, before the beds were made, and she pounded on tables and shouted, "I'll throw you out with your junk. I'll have you locked up in the Yanov jail! I'll make beggars out of you!" Poor people tried to fawn on her, but she wouldn't even listen. Then people realized that it isn't wise to wish for a new king.

One afternoon the door of the poorhouse opened, and Pelte came in, dressed like a beggar. The man in charge of the poorhouse turned pale as a ghost. "Reb Pelte," he exclaimed, "what are you doing here?" "I came to stay here," Pelte answered. "My wife has thrown me out." To make a long story short, Pelte had transferred all his possessions to Zlateh, everything, down to the last thread, and then she chased him out. "But how does one do a thing like that?" he was asked. "Don't even ask," he answered. "She fixed me! I barely came out alive." The poorhouse was in an uproar. Some cursed Pelte. "As if the rich don't have enough as it is—now they come to eat the food of the poor," they cried. Others pretended sympathy. In short, Pelte was given a bundle of straw to spread in the corner, and he lay down. The whole town came running to see the sight. I, too, was curious and ran to see. He sat on the floor like a mourner and stared at everybody with his bulging eyes. People asked him, "Why do you sit here, Reb Pelte, what happened to all your power?" At first he didn't answer at all, as if they weren't talking to him, and later he said, "She isn't finished with me yet." "What will you do to her?" the beggars jeered. They made a laughing-stock of him. But don't jump at conclusions. You know the old saying: He laughs best who laughs last.

For several weeks Zlateh was a regular demon. She turned the whole town upside down. Right in the middle of the market place, near the stores, she had a pit dug and hired men to mix lime. Logs were brought and heaps of brick were piled up so that no one could pass. Roofs were torn down and a notary came from Yanov to make a list of all her tenants' belongings. Zlateh bought a carriage and a team of fiery horses, and she went riding every afternoon. She started wearing shoes with pointed tips and let her hair grow. She also began to pal around with the *goyim* of the Christian streets. She bought two vicious dogs, regular killers, so that it was dangerous to pass by her house. She stopped selling fish. What did she need it for? But out of habit, she had to have fish around, so she filled bathtubs in her house and stocked them with carp and pike. She even kept a big tub full of *treif* fish, and lobsters and frogs and eels. It was rumored in town that she would become an apostate any day. Some said that on Pesach the priest had come to her house to sprinkle it with holy water. People feared that she might inform on the community—someone like that is capable of anything.

Suddenly, she came running to the rabbi. "Rabbi," she said, "send for Pelte. I want a divorce." "What do you want a divorce for?" the rabbi asked her. "Do you want to remarry?" "I don't know," she said. "Maybe yes and maybe no. But I don't want to be the wife of a Wife Killer. I'm willing to compensate him with something." The rabbi sent for Pelte and he came crawling. Everybody in town stood outside the rabbi's house. Poor Pelte, he consented to everything. His hands shook as in a fever. Reb Moishe the Scribe sat down to write out the divorce. I remember him as if this happened yesterday. He was a small man and had a tic. He ruled the paper with his penknife, and then he wiped the goose quill on his skull cap. The witnesses were instructed how to sign divorce. My husband, peace be on him, was one of the witnesses because he wrote a good hand. Zlateh sat comfortably on a chair and sucked candy. And, yes, I forgot to mention it, she put down two hundred rubles. Pelte recognized them—he had had a habit of marking his money. The rabbi ordered silence, but Zlateh boasted to the women that she was considering marrying a "possessor," but that "as long as the Wife Killer is my husband, I am not sure of staying alive." When she said this she laughed so that everybody outside heard her.

When everything was ready, the rabbi began questioning the couple. I still remember his words. "Hear me, Paltiel, son of Schneour Zalman"—that was the name by which Pelte was called up to the reading of the Torah—"do you want to divorce your wife?" He said something more, from the *Gemorra*, but I can't say it as he did. "Say 'yes,'" he ordered Pelte. "Say 'yes' once, not twice." Pelte said "yes." We could hardly hear him. "Hear me, Zlateh Golde, daughter of Yehuda Treitel, do you want to divorce your husband, Paltiel?" "Yes!" Zlateh shouted, and as she said this she swayed and fell to the floor in a faint. I saw this myself, and I tell you the truth; I felt my brain bursting in my head. I thought I'd collapse too. There was a great outcry and commotion. Everybody rushed to revive her. They poured water on her and stuck pins into her and rubbed her with vinegar and pulled her hair. Azriel the Healer came running and cupped her then and there. She still breathed, but it wasn't the same Zlateh. May God preserve us. Her mouth was twisted to one side and the spittle ran out of it; her eyes were rolled up and her nose was white, like that of a corpse. The women who stood near, heard her mumble, "The Wife Killer! He overcame me!" These were her last words.

At the funeral there was almost a riot. Now Pelte was again on his high horse. Beside his own property he now also had her wealth. Her jewelry alone was worth a fortune. The burial society wanted a big sum, but Pelte wouldn't budge. They shouted, they warned, they abused him. They threatened him with excommunication. Might as well talk to the wall! "I won't give a penny, let her rot," he said. They would have left her lying around, too, but it was summertime and there was a heat wave just then, and people feared an epidemic. In short, some women performed the rites—what other choice was there? The pall-bearers refused to carry her, so a wagon was hired. She was buried right near the fence, among the stillbirths. All the same, Pelte said *kaddish* after her—this he did.

From then on the Wife Killer remained alone. People were so afraid of him, they avoided passing by his house. Mothers of pregnant young women did not allow his name to be mentioned, unless they first put on two aprons. *Cheder* boys fingered their fringes before pronouncing his name. And nothing came of all the construction and remodelling. The bricks were carried off, the lime was stolen. The carriage and its team of horses disappeared—he must have sold them. The water in the bathtubs dried up, and the fish died. There was a cage with a parrot in the house. It squawked, "I'm hungry"—it could talk Yiddish—until at last it starved to death. Pelte had the shutters nailed tight and never opened them again. He didn't even go out to collect the pennies from the storekeepers. All day he lay on his bench and snored, or simply dozed. At night he'd go out to collect chips. Once each week, they sent him two loaves of bread from the bakery, and the baker's wife would buy him some onions, garlic, radishes and, on occasion, a piece of dry cheese. He never ate meat. He never came to the synagogue on Saturdays. There was no broom in his house and the dirt gathered in heaps. Mice ran about even during the day and spider webs hung from the rafters. The roof leaked and wasn't repaired. The walls rotted and caved in. Every few weeks it was rumored that things were not well with the Wife Killer, that he was sick, or dying. The burial society rubbed its hands in anticipation. But nothing happened. He outlived everyone. He lived so long that people in Turbin began to hint that he might live forever. Why not? Maybe he had some special kind of blessing, or the Angel of Death forgot him. Anything can happen.

Rest assured that he was not forgotten by the Angel of Death. But when that happened I was no longer in Turbin. He must have been a hundred years old, maybe older. After the funeral his entire house was turned upside down, but nothing of value was found. The chests had rotted away. The gold and silver were gone. The money and notes turned to dust the minute a breeze touched them. All the digging in the heaps of rubbish was wasted. The Wife Killer had outlived everything: his wives, his enemies, his money, his property, his generation. All that was left after him—may God forgive me for saying so—was a heap of dust.

Translated by Shlomo Katz

By the Light of Memorial Candles

A s the darkness grew more intense, so did the frost. In the study house, though the clay oven had been heated, frost patterned the windows, and icicles hung from the frames. The beadle had extinguished the oil lamps, but two memorial candles, one tall, the other short, remained burning in the *menorah* at the east wall. The short one, burning since the day before, had grown thick with melted tallow. From the memorial candles, it is said, one can surmise the fate of those in whose memory they were kindled; the flames flicker and sputter when the soul of the departed has not found peace. And as the flames quiver, everything else appears to do so, the posts of the reading table, the rafters supporting the ceiling, the chandeliers on their chains, and even the Holy Ark, carved with lions and tablets. In summer, a fly or moth, falling into the wick, will cause the flickering; but there are no flies or moths in winter.

Benches, on three sides of the clay oven, supported wandering beggars who slept there at night. But tonight, although it was past midnight, they could not fall asleep. One of them, a short, freckled man, with straw-colored hair, a round red beard, and angry eyes, cut his toenails with a pocket knife. Another, fleshy-faced, calf-eyed, with white hair curling like wood shavings over his huge head, dried his foot rags. A tall man, sooty as a stoker's shovel, roasted potatoes, the red hot coals reflecting their glow on his face. A man, husky and pockmarked, a tumor on his forehead, and a beard like dirty cotton, lay, immobile, as if paralyzed, his eyes fixed somewhere on the wall.

The man with the huge head spoke, spitting out his words as though his tongue too were oversized. He said, "How can you tell when a man has already been married? If I say I'm still a bachelor, who can say I'm not?"

"So, if you're a bachelor, what of it?" the red-haired man answered. "Do you think the most important man in town will marry his daughter to you? You're a tramp and you'll remain one; there's no escape. You'll keep on wandering across the land with your beggar's pack; like me, for example. Once I was a craftsman, a saddle-maker; I made saddles for the nobility. But after my wife died I couldn't work any longer. I was restless and had to wander off. I became a beggar."

With fingers that no longer reacted to fire, the tall man rolled a potato out of the bed of coals. "Does anyone want a bite? I'd work, if I could find a job. But no one wants carvers any more. Long ago everything came from the carver, jewelry boxes, containers for holiday citrus, cases for the Book of Esther. I would carve cornices on wardrobes, headboards for beds, door panels. Once I was invited by a town to carve a Holy Ark for the synagogue. People from all over the country came to look at it. I stayed there for two years. But today you buy things readymade, with a few decorations thrown in. It wasn't I, but my father, may he rest in peace, who wanted to be a carver. For five generations back our family were carvers. But what's the use? It's a dying craft. Well, there was nothing to do but beg."

For a while no one spoke. The red-bearded beggar, having cut his last toenail, wrapped his nail shavings and two splinters from the bench in a piece of paper, and threw them into the fire. On the day of reckoning, the two splinters would be witnesses to the fact that he had not desecrated any parts of his body by casting them into the rubbish. Then he stared at the beggar with the tumor.

"Hey you, whatever-your-name-is, over there! How did you get that way?"

The man with the tumor made no response.

"What's the matter—are you mute?"

"I am not mute."

"Then why don't you speak? Does it cost anything?"

"If one is silent, one is silent."

"A word," the carver remarked, "is like a gold coin to him."

The red-bearded beggar began to whet his pocket knife on an edge of the oven.

"Will you be here for the Sabbath?"

"Of course."

"Then we can talk later. Pretty cold, eh? The roofs are cracking. I've heard that the entire winter sowing has frozen under the snow. This means famine."

"Oh, what won't people say! It's never cold under the snow. Even before the grain has split in the earth, the landowners have sold it. It's the grain merchants who lose out."

"What do they lose? When the harvest is bad, prices go wild, and that makes profits even bigger. The poor man is the one who always suffers most."

"Well, what do you expect? Everyone can't be rich; some must be poor too," the red-beard argued. "But surely the man doomed to be poor must be pitied. Not that I mind being hungry on weekdays—but if a miser boards you on the Sabbath, you're out of luck! When the Sabbath is scanty, you're hungry all week. Where I come from, the Sabbath overnight roasts are fat ones. But here everything is lean, even the pudding."

The man with the tumor suddenly grew talkative. "All the same one keeps from starving. You eat a lot, or you eat a little. As they say, the stomach stretches. If I get a piece of bread and an onion, I'm happy."

"One can't walk very far on bread and onion."

The man with the tumor sat up.

"You just start your feet walking and they do the rest. When you're home, you do as you please; but as soon as you've left home, you have to keep moving. In one town today, in another tomorrow. A day here, a night there. Who watches over you? I used to make a pretty good living. I had a trade for which there is always a demand. I come from Tsivkev and I was the gravedigger there. It may be a small place, but people die everywhere. I was a gravedigger for the old, the young— the hell-beadle. There was a burial society in our town, but its members were busy in the villages all week long, buying pig bristles from the peasants to make brushes. The burden was entirely mine. I had to cleanse the bodies and sew the shrouds. I lived in a hut opposite the cemetery. My wife became sick. One day I realized she would soon die. She took a little soup and then it was all over. For forty years, like a pair of pigeons, we had lived together. Suddenly she lay down and died. With my own hands I buried her. People hate a gravedigger. Is he to blame? I had no wish to harm anyone. For my part, people can live forever. But that's how it is. Well, when my own wife died, I even had to bury her.

"Corpses, they would say, roam the graveyard at night. One heard of the ghost of this person, that person, little fires, phantoms. But for thirty years I was a gravedigger and saw nothing. I walked into the synagogue in the middle of the night, but no voice ever called me to the reading table. When you die, everything's over. Even if there is a hereafter, a corpse in this world is nothing but a pile of flesh and bones.

"Once in a while, when a stranger died in our town, the body was left in the cleansing room overnight. Since I was the watchman, I would light two candles at its head and chant psalms. But how long can you chant psalms? My lids would begin to droop; I'd lie down on the bench and doze. The wind would blow out the candles and I'd be alone in the dark with the corpse. Once I forgot to take along my pillow stuffed with hay. I couldn't go home because it was raining and I didn't want to wake my wife, so, forgive me for saying so, I took the body, and placed it beneath my head. As sure as I'm here in the synagogue, it's no lie."

"It isn't everyone who could do that," the red-bearded man said.

"I'd go mad with fear," said the calf-eyed beggar with the huge head.

"You don't go mad so easily. Are you afraid of a slaughtered goose? A human corpse is like a dead goose. Why do you think the corpse needs to be watched? To keep the mice away.

"As I said, I made a good living. But when my wife died, I grew lonely. We had no children. The matchmakers had some suggestions, but how can you let a stranger take the place of a woman you've lived with for so many years? Others might do it; I couldn't. All day long I stared at her grave. Once the matchmaker sent a woman to the hut. She began to sweep the floor. She was supposed to size me up, but the moment I saw her take the broom, I felt nauseated and had to send her away. Since becoming a widower, I have learned to boil a pot of potatoes in their skins. I even started to bake bread in the oven on Friday mornings. But without a wife, there's no one to talk to. Yes, I was lonely, but I had funds. I could even give alms to the poor. Charity, my brothers, is the best deed."

II

"Then why did you become a vagabond?" the red-bearded man asked.

"Shh. Don't rush. Haste makes waste. I've said already that one has nothing to fear from a corpse. But here's the story. About five years ago there was an epidemic in our county. Every year, especially in the fall, there are epidemics that kill infants. They die like flies from smallpox, measles, scarlet fever, and the croup. Once I buried eight children in a day. It's not a hard job. Shrouds aren't needed, a cotton cloth will do; you open a shallow ditch—and that's it. The cleansing doesn't amount to much either. Yes, the mothers cry, but that's how they are. But this time, it was the grown-ups who were hit by the epidemic—cholera. They had cramps in their legs; rubbing them with alcohol didn't help. They'd vomit, get diarrhea—the usual symptoms. Even the barber-healer caught it and died. The man who tried to fetch the doctor from Zamosc was overcome on the way by cramps, and died as he reached the inn. Yes, the angel of death reaped his harvest.

"I became a one-man burial society because the other members of the society were afraid to return to town. With a mute, I traveled from house to house in search of corpses, and took them away immediately, because most of our families live in one room and you can't mix the dead with the sick. It was a bad time. Since the bodies had to be cleansed and shrouds made for them, they couldn't be buried the same day. The cleansing room was filled with corpses. At night I'd light the candles and sit down to recite psalms. One night there were nine corpses, five men and four women. They were scarcely covered by the sheets. In an epidemic, everything is upside down.

"And do you know that those who die of cholera make strange faces? I had to tie the chin of one young man who seemed to be laughing. But he went on laughing. One woman looked as though she were screaming. It just happened that she screamed a good deal when she was alive.

"Corpses are cold, but those who die of cholera remain warm. The forehead is hot when you touch it. On other nights I used to drop off for a bit, but I didn't sleep a wink that night.

"They say a gravedigger has no pity. Nonsense. My heart bled for the young people. Why should their years be cut short? It was raining hard outside. Although it was the month of Cheshvan, there was thunder and lightning, as in the summer. Heaven was weeping. The few graves I had dug were flooded.

"There was a seventeen-year-old girl, a shoemaker's daughter, among the corpses, a girl already engaged. Her father, Zellig the Shoemaker, used to mend my boots. He had three sons but he adored her, for she was his only daughter. But the whole family had become ill and I couldn't leave the corpse among them. Before taking her away, I tested her nostrils with a feather, but it didn't move. I covered her with a sack in the cleansing room. Her cheeks remained red, but in cholera, as I told you, the face of the corpse has the color of life. 'Father in heaven,' I argued, 'why do they deserve this? For years parents must wait to enjoy their children, and then before you know it the dance is over.'

"As I sang psalms, the cover on the girl seemed to stir. I thought I had imagined it; corpses don't move. Again I sang psalms, and again the cover stirred. It must be clear to you men by now that I don't scare easily; nevertheless a chill ran down my spine. I reasoned with myself: a mouse or skunk must be pulling the sack. But just then the sack fell off. The corpse raised its head. I heard her gasp, 'Water, water!' That's exactly what she said.

"Now I know what a fool I was; she was still alive. The dead aren't thirsty. She must have been in what they call a cataleptic trance. But at the time I was so terrified that I ran out of the cleansing room, shouting for help. I ran so fast, I almost broke my legs. I kept shouting, but no one heard me. The cemetery was far from town and the rain was pouring. I called, 'Hear, O Israel,' and anything else that came into my head. I just made it to the edge of town, but everyone was afraid to open up when I knocked on the shutters. They thought I was mad, I guess. Finally a few butchers and some coachmen woke up and came with me, lanterns in hand. On the way back to the cemetery they kept teasing. 'Getz,' they said—my name is Getz—, 'you should be ashamed of yourself. It's only fright that makes you see things. Others will laugh at you.' Although they played tough, they themselves were shaken.

"In our town, the gutters are flooded when it rains. We waded in water up to our knees. It's not too clever to catch a cold during an epidemic. We were soaked.

"When we entered the cleansing room we found the girl lying there with arms outspread and no cover. They rubbed her, shook her, blew at her, but she was really dead now. They began to make fun of me and to scold. Butchers will always be butchers. I swore that she had been covered with a sack and had thrown it off when she tried to sit up, but they told me it had only seemed that way. One called it a mirage, another a vision, a dream, God knows what. They made me look foolish. But there wasn't much time to argue, for everyone had to return home. I drew the girl's arms and legs together, covered her with a sack and once more started singing psalms. But now I was jumpy. My heart was like a drum. I swallowed a little whisky from a bottle I had handy, but it didn't help. I kept one eye on the psalms, the other on the corpses. If something like this could happen, how could one be sure of anything? The wind tried to blow out the candles. I had a match box with me, and I didn't mean to be left in the dark, not for a moment. I was happy when morning came.

"I forgot to mention that we didn't tell the girl's parents, for they would have been horrified. And, who knows, maybe she could have been saved. But it was too late. The next day I was ready to leave town, but you can't leave in the midst of an epidemic. I no longer wanted to watch corpses by myself, so I hired the mute to keep me company. True, he slept all the time, but he was a human being.

"Now each grave I dug, each corpse I cleansed, worried me. I kept thinking of that girl, of her sitting up and whispering, 'Water, water!' When I slept, she was in my dreams. Now I had all sorts of ideas. Who knows? Maybe she wasn't the only one. Maybe other corpses had wakened in their graves. I was sorry I had buried my wife the day she died. Never, until then, had I been afraid to look a corpse in the face. They say you forget all you know when you look at the face of a corpse; but what did I know? Nothing! But now, when a corpse was brought in, I didn't look at it. It always seemed that the corpse was winking, trying to say something and not being able to. Winter, meanwhile, was howling and whistling outside, like seven witches that had hanged themselves. And I was alone, because the mute had been unwilling to stay. But one doesn't leave a job easily. At night, on my bed, I kept turning and twisting, unable to sleep.

"One night I felt a scratching in my ear, not from without, but within. I awoke and heard my wife. She whispered: 'Getz!' I must have dreamt it; the dead don't talk. But the ear is delicate. I can stand all kinds of pain, but not a tickle in my ear. The ear, you know, is near the brain. The wind had grown quiet. Now, men, I will tell you something. I lit a candle and dressed. I stuffed a sack with linen, a coat, and a loaf of bread, and left, in the middle of the night, with no good-bys. The town owed me a month's pay, but it didn't matter. I didn't even take leave of my wife's grave, which I was supposed to do. I left everything, and I went off."

"Without money?"

"I had a few rubles in a little bag."

"Scared?" the red-bearded beggar asked.

"Not scared, but upset. I meant to become a merchant, but somehow I couldn't keep my mind on business. What does a man need by himself? A slice of bread and a glass of water. People are good to one."

"And your ear? Does your wife still call?"

"No one calls. My ear has cotton in it."

"Why cotton?"

"To keep it from catching cold. No other reason."

The beggars were silent. In the stillness, one heard the coals rustling in the oven. The first to speak was the beggar with the huge head.

"If it had happened to me, I'd have dropped dead."

"If you're destined to live, you live."

"Maybe, after all, it was your wife," said the carver.

"And maybe you're the Rabbi of Lublin," answered the gravedigger.

"She might have wanted to tell you something," the red-bearded man said.

"What could she want to tell me? I never took another in her place."

The short memorial candle flickered and went out. In the study house, the light grew dimmer. An odor of tallow and burnt wick drifted across from the *menorah* on the east wall. Slowly and silently, the beggars lay down on their benches.

Translated by Martha Glicklich and Elaine Gottlieb

The Mirror

THERE is a kind of net that is as old as Methuselah, as soft as a cobweb and as full of holes, yet it has retained its strength to this day. When a demon wearies of chasing after yesterdays or of going round in circles on a windmill, he can install himself inside a mirror. There he waits like a spider in its web, and the fly is certain to be caught. God has bestowed vanity on the female, particularly on the rich, the pretty, the barren, the young, who have much time and little company.

I discovered such a woman in the village of Krashnik. Her father dealt in timber; her husband floated the logs to Danzig; grass was growing on her mother's grave. The daughter lived in an old house, among oaken cupboards, leather-lined coffers, and books bound in silk. She had two servants, an old one that was deaf and a young one who carried on with a fiddler. The other Krashnik housewives wore men's boots, ground buckwheat on millstones, plucked feathers, cooked broths, bore children, and attended funerals. Needless to say, Zirel, beautiful and well-educated—she had been brought up in Cracow—had nothing to talk about with her small-town neighbors. And so she preferred to read her German song book and embroider Moses and Ziporah, David and Bathsheba, Ahasuereus and Queen Esther on canvas. The pretty dresses her husband brought her hung in the closet. Her pearls and diamonds lay in her jewel box. No one ever saw her silk slips, her lace petticoats, nor her red hair which was hidden under her wig, not even her husband. For when could they be seen? Certainly not during the day, and at night it is dark.

But Zirel had an attic which she called her boudoir, and where hung a mirror as blue as water on the point of freezing. The mirror had a crack in the middle, and it was set in a golden frame which was decorated with snakes, knobs, roses, and adders. In front of the mirror lay a bearskin and close beside it was a chair with armrests of ivory and a cushioned seat. What could be more pleasant than to sit naked in this chair, and rest one's feet on the bearskin, and contemplate oneself? Zirel had much to gaze at. Her skin was white as satin, her breasts as full as wineskins, her hair fell across her shoulders, and her legs were as slender as a hind's. She would sit for hours on end delighting in her beauty. The door fastened and bolted, she would imagine that it opened to admit either a prince or a hunter or a knight or a poet. For everything hidden must be revealed, each secret longs to be disclosed, each love yearns to be betrayed, everything sacred must be desecrated. Heaven and earth conspire that all good beginnings should come to a bad end.

Well, once I learned of the existence of this luscious little tidbit, I determined that she would be mine. All that was required was a little patience. One summer day, as she sat staring at the nipple on her left breast, she caught sight of me in the mirror—there I was, black as tar, long as a shovel, with donkey's ears, a ram's horns, a frog's mouth, and a goat's beard. My eyes were all pupil. She was so surprised that she forgot to be frightened. Instead of crying, "Hear, O Israel," she burst out laughing.

"My, how ugly you are," she said.

"My, how beautiful you are," I replied.

She was pleased with my compliment. "Who are you?" she asked.

"Fear not," I said. "I am an imp, not a demon. My fingers have no nails, my mouth has no teeth, my arms stretch like licorice, my horns are as pliable as wax. My power lies in my tongue; I am a fool by trade, and I have come to cheer you up because you are alone."

"Where were you before?"

"In the bedroom behind the stove where the cricket chirps and the mouse rustles, between a dried wreath and a faded willow branch."

"What did you do there?"

"I looked at you."

"Since when?"

"Since your wedding night."

"What did you eat?"

"The fragrance of your body, the glow of your hair, the light of your eyes, the sadness of your face."

"Oh, you flatterer!" she cried. "Who are you? What are you doing here? Where do you come from? What is your errand?"

I made up a story. My father, I said, was a goldsmith and my mother a succubus; they copulated on a bundle of rotting rope in a cellar and I was their bastard. For some time I lived in a settlement of devils on Mount Seir where I inhabited a mole's hole. But when it was learned that my father was human I was driven out. From then on I had been homeless. She-devils avoided me because I reminded them of the sons of Adam; the daughters of Eve saw in me Satan. Dogs barked at me, children wept when they saw me. Why were they afraid? I harmed no one. My only desire was to gaze at beautiful women—to gaze and converse with them.

"Why converse? The beautiful aren't always wise."

"In Paradise the wise are the footstools of the beautiful."

"My teacher taught me otherwise."

"What did your teacher know? The writers of books have the brains of a flea; they merely parrot each other. Ask me when you want to know something. Wisdom extends no further than the first heaven. From there on everything is lust. Don't you know that angels are headless? The Seraphim play in the sand like children; the Cherubim can't count; the Aralim chew their cud before the throne of Glory. God himself is jovial. He spends his time pulling Leviathan by the tail and being licked by the Wild Ox; or else he tickles the Shekhinah, causing her to lay myriads of eggs each day, and each egg is a star."

"Now I know you're making fun of me."

"If that's not the truth may a funny bone grow on my nose. It's a long time since I squandered my quota of lies. I have no alternative but to tell the truth."

"Can you beget children?"

"No, my dear. Like the mule I am the last of a line. But this does not blunt my desire. I lie only with married women, for good actions are my sins; my prayers are blasphemies; spite is my bread; arrogance, my wine; pride, the marrow of my bones. There is only one other thing I can do besides chatter."

This made her laugh. Then she said: "My mother didn't bring me up to be a devil's whore. Away with you, or I'll have you exorcised."

"Why bother," I said. "I'll go. I don't force myself on anyone. *Auf wiedersehen.*"

I faded away like mist.

II

For seven days Zirel absented herself from her boudoir. I
dozed inside the mirror. The net had been spread; the victim
was ready. I knew she was curious. Yawning, I considered my
next step. Should I seduce a rabbi's daughter? deprive a bridegroom of his manhood? plug up the synagogue chimney? turn
the Sabbath wine into vinegar? give an elflock to a virgin? enter a ram's horn on Rosh Hashana? make a cantor hoarse? An
imp never lacks for things to do, particularly during the Days
of Awe when even the fish in the water tremble. And then as I
sat dreaming of moon juice and turkey seeds, she entered. She
looked for me, but could not see me. She stood in front of the
mirror but I didn't show myself.

"I must have been imagining," she murmured. "It must
have been a daydream."

She took off her nightgown and stood there naked. I knew
that her husband was in town and that he had been with her
the night before although she had not gone to the ritual
bath—but as the Talmud puts it, "a woman would rather have
one measure of debauchery than ten of modesty." Zirel,
daughter of Roize Glike, missed me, and her eyes were sad.
She is mine, mine, I thought. The Angel of Death stood ready
with his rod; a zealous little devil busied himself preparing the
cauldron for her in hell; a sinner, promoted to stoker, collected
the kindling wood. Everything was prepared—the snow drift
and the live coals, the hook for her tongue and the pliers for
her breasts, the mouse that would eat her liver and the worm
that would gnaw her bladder. But my little charmer suspected
nothing. She stroked her left breast, and then her right. She
looked at her belly, examined her thighs, scrutinized her toes.
Would she read her book? trim her nails? comb her hair? Her
husband had brought her perfumes from Lenczyc, and she
smelled of rosewater and carnations. He had presented her
with a coral necklace which hung around her neck. But what is
Eve without a serpent? And what is God without Lucifer? Zirel

was full of desire. Like a harlot she summoned me with her eyes. With quivering lips she uttered a spell:

Swift is the wind,
Deep the ditch,
Sleek black cat,
Come within reach.
Strong is the lion,
Dumb the fish,
Reach from the silence,
And take your dish.

As she uttered the last word, I appeared. Her face lit up.

"So you're here."

"I was away," I said, "but I have returned."

"Where have you been?"

"To never-never land. I was in Rahab the Harlot's palace in the garden of the golden birds near the castle of Asmodeus."

"As far as that?"

"If you don't believe me, my jewel, come with me. Sit on my back, and hold on to my horns, and I'll spread my wings, and we'll fly together beyond the mountain peaks."

"But I don't have a thing on."

"No one dresses there."

"My husband won't have any idea where I am."

"He'll learn soon enough."

"How long a trip is it?"

"It takes less than a second."

"When will I return?"

"Those who go there don't want to return."

"What will I do there?"

"You'll sit on Asmodeus' lap and plait tresses in his beard. You'll eat almonds and drink porter; evenings you'll dance for him. Bells will be attached to your ankles, and devils will whirl with you."

"And after that?"

"If my master is pleased with you, you will be his. If not, one of his minions will take care of you."

"And in the morning?"

"There are no mornings there."

"Will you stay with me?"

"Because of you I might be given a small bone to lick."

"Poor little devil, I feel sorry for you, but I can't go. I have a husband and a father. I have gold and silver and dresses and furs. My heels are the highest in Krashnik."

"Well, then, good-by."

"Don't hurry off like that. What do I have to do?"

"Now you are being reasonable. Make some dough with the whitest of flour. Add honey, menstrual blood, and an egg with a bloodspot, a measure of pork fat, a thimbleful of suet, a goblet of libatory wine. Light a fire on the Sabbath and bake the mixture on the coals. Now call your husband to your bed and make him eat the cake you have baked. Awaken him with lies and put him to sleep with profanity. Then when he begins to snore, cut off one half of his beard and one earlock, steal his gold, burn his promissory notes, and tear up the marriage contract. After that throw your jewels under the pig butcher's window—this will be my engagement gift. Before leaving your house, throw the prayer book into the rubbish and spit on the *mezuzah*, at the precise spot where the word *Shadai* is written. Then come straight to me. I'll bear you on my wings from Krashnik to the desert. We'll fly over fields filled with toadstools, over woods inhabited by werewolves, over the ruins of Sodom where serpents are scholars, hyenas are singers, crows are preachers, and thieves are entrusted with the money for charity. There ugliness is beauty, and crooked is straight; tortures are amusement, and mockery, the height of exaltation. But hurry, for our eternity is brief."

"I'm afraid, little devil, I'm afraid."

"Everyone who goes with us is."

She wished to ask questions, to catch me in contradictions, but I made off. She pressed her lips against the mirror and met the end of my tail.

III

Her father wept; her husband tore his hair; her servants searched for her in the woodshed and in the cellar; her mother-in-law poked with a shovel in the chimney; carters and butchers hunted for her in the woods. At night, torches were lit and the voices of the searchers echoed and re-echoed:

"Zirel, where are you? Zirel! Zirel!" It was suspected that she had run off to a convent, but the priest swore on the crucifix that this was not so. A wonder worker was sent for, and then a sorceress, an old Gentile woman who made wax effigies, and finally a man who located the dead or missing by means of a black mirror; a farmer lent them his blood hounds. But when I get my prey, it is reprieved by no one. I spread my wings and we were off. Zirel spoke to me, but I did not answer. When we came to Sodom, I hovered a moment over Lot's wife. Three oxen were busy licking her nose. Lot lay in a cave with his daughters, drunk as always.

In the vale of shadow which is known as the world everything is subject to change. But for us time stands still! Adam remains naked, Eve lustful, still in the act of being seduced by the serpent. Cain kills Abel, the flea lies with the elephant, the flood falls from heaven, the Jews knead clay in Egypt, Job scratches at his sore-covered body. He will keep scratching until the end of time, but he will find no comfort.

She wished to speak to me, but with a flutter of wings I disappeared. I had done my errand. I lay like a bat blinking sightless eyes on a steep cliff. The earth was brown, the heavens yellow. Devils stood in a circle wiggling their tails. Two turtles were locked in an embrace, and a male stone mounted a female stone. Shabriri and Bariri appeared. Shabriri had assumed the shape of a squire. He wore a pointed cap, a curved sword; he had the legs of a goose and a goat's beard. On his snout were glasses, and he spoke in a German dialect. Bariri was ape, parrot, rat, bat, all at once. Shabriri bowed low and began to chant like a jester at a wedding:

> *Argin, margin,*
> *Here's a bargain.*
> *A pretty squirrel,*
> *Name of Zirel.*
> *Open the door,*
> *To love impure.*

He was about to take her in his arms when Bariri screamed, "Don't let him touch you. He has scabs on his head, sores on his legs, and what a woman needs he doesn't have. He acts the great lover, but a capon is more amorous. His father was like that also, and so was his grandfather. Let me be your lover. I am the grandson of the Chief Liar. In addition I am a man of wealth and good family. My grandmother was lady-in-waiting to Machlath, daughter of Naama. My mother had the honor to wash Asmodeus' feet. My father, may he stay in hell forever, carried Satan's snuffbox."

Shabriri and Bariri had grasped Zirel by the hair, and each time they pulled they tore out a tuft. Now Zirel saw how things were and she cried out, "Pity, pity!"

"What's this we have here?" asked Ketev Mariri.

"A Krashnik coquette."

"Don't they have better than that?"

"No, it's the best they've got."

"Who dragged her in?"

"A little imp."

"Let's begin."

"Help, help," Zirel moaned.

"Hang her," Wrath, the Son of Anger, screamed. "It won't help to cry out here. Time and change have been left behind. Do what you are told; you're neither young nor old."

Zirel broke into lamentations. The sound roused Lilith from her sleep. She thrust aside Asmodeus' beard and put her head out of the cave, each of her hairs, a curling snake.

"What's wrong with the bitch?" she asked. "Why all the screaming?"

"They're working on her."

"Is that all? Add some salt."

"And skim the fat."

This fun has been going on for a thousand years, but the black gang does not weary of it. Each devil does his bit; each imp makes his pun. They pull and tear and bite and pinch. For all that, the masculine devils aren't so bad; it's the females who really enjoy themselves, commanding: Skim boiling broth with bare hands! Plait braids without using the fingers! Wash the laundry without water! Catch fish in hot sand! Stay at home and walk the streets! Take a bath without getting wet! Make butter from stones! Break the cask without spilling the wine! And all the while the virtuous women in Paradise gossip; and the pious men sit on golden chairs, stuffing themselves with the meat of Leviathan, as they boast of their good deeds.

Is there a God? Is He all merciful? Will Zirel ever find salvation? Or is creation a snake primeval crawling with evil? How can I tell? I'm still only a minor devil. Imps seldom get promoted. Meanwhile generations come and go, Zirel follows Zirel, in a myriad of reflections—a myriad of mirrors.

Translated by Norbert Guterman

The Little Shoemakers

The Shoemakers and Their Family Tree

THE family of the little shoemakers was famous not only in Frampol but in the outlying district—in Yonev, Kreshev, Bilgoray, and even in Zamoshoh. Abba Shuster, the founder of the line, appeared in Frampol some time after Chmielnitzki's pogroms. He brought himself a plot of ground on the stubby hill behind the butcher stalls, and there he built a house that remained standing until just the other day. Not that it was in such fine condition—the stone foundation settled, the small windows warped, and the shingled roof turned a moldy green and was hung with swallows' nests. The door, moreover, sank into the ground; the banisters became bowlegged; and instead of stepping up onto the threshold, one was obliged to step down. All the same, it did survive the innumerable fires that devastated Frampol in the early days. But the rafters were so rotten that mushrooms grew on them, and when wood dust was needed to staunch the blood of a circumcision, one had only to break off a piece of the outer wall and rub it between one's fingers. The roof, pitched so steeply that the chimneysweep was unable to climb onto it to look after the chimney, was always catching fire from the sparks. It was only by the grace of God that the house was not overtaken by disaster.

The name of Abba Shuster is recorded, on parchment, in the annals of the Frampol Jewish community. It was his custom to make six pairs of shoes every year for distribution among widows and orphans; in recognition of his philanthropy the synagogue called him to the reading of the Torah under the honorific title, *Murenu*, meaning "our teacher."

His stone in the old cemetery had vanished, but the shoemakers knew a sign for the grave—nearby grew a hazelnut tree. According to the old wives, the tree sprang from Reb Abba's beard.

Reb Abba had five sons; they settled, all but one, in the neighboring towns; only Getzel remained in Frampol. He continued his father's charitable practice of making shoes for the poor, and he too was active in the gravediggers' brother-hood.

The annals go on to say that Getzel had a son, Godel, and that to Godel was born Treitel, and to Treitel, Gimpel. The shoemaker's art was handed down from one generation to the next. A principle was fast established in the family, requiring the eldest son to remain at home and succeed his father at the workbench.

The shoemakers resembled one another. They were all short, sandy-haired, and sound, honest workmen. The peo-ple of Frampol believed that Reb Abba, the head of the line, had learned shoemaking from a master of the craft in Brod, who divulged to him the secret of strengthening leather and making it durable. In the cellar of their house the little shoe-makers kept a vat for soaking hides. God knows what strange chemicals they added to the tanning fluid. They did not dis-close the formula to outsiders, and it was handed on from fa-ther to son.

As it is not our business to deal with all the generations of the little shoemakers, we will confine ourselves to the last three. Reb Lippe remained without heir till his old age, and it was taken for a certainty that the line would end with him. But when he was in his late sixties his wife died and he married an overripe virgin, a milkmaid, who bore him six children. The eldest son, Feivel, was quite well to do. He was prominent in community affairs, attended all the important meetings, and for years served as sexton of the tailors' synagogue. It was the custom in this synagogue to select a new sexton every Sim-chath Torah. The man so selected was honored by having a pumpkin placed on his head; the pumpkin was set with lighted candles, and the lucky fellow was led about from house to house and refreshed at each stop with wine and strudel or honey-cakes. However, Reb Feivel happened to die on Sim-chath Torah, the day of rejoicing over the Law, while dutifully making these rounds; he fell flat in the market place, and there was no reviving him. Because Feivel had been a notable philan-thropist, the rabbi who conducted his services declared that the candles he had borne on his head would light his way to Paradise. The will found in his strongbox requested that when he was carried to the cemetery, a hammer, an awl, and a last should be laid on the black cloth over his coffin, in sign of the fact that he was a man of peaceful industry who never cheated his customers. His will was done.

Feivel's eldest son was called Abba, after the founder. Like the rest of his stock, he was short and thickset, with a broad yellow beard, and a high forehead lined with wrinkles, such as only rabbis and shoemakers have. His eyes were also yellow, and the over-all impression he created was that of a sulky hen. Nevertheless he was a clever workman, charitable like his forebears, and unequaled in Frampol as a man of his word. He would never make a promise unless he was sure he could fulfill it; when he was not sure he said: who knows, God willing, or maybe. Furthermore he was a man of some learning. Every day he read a chapter of the Torah in Yiddish translation and occupied his free time with chapbooks. Abba never missed a single sermon of the traveling preachers who came to town, and he was especially fond of the Biblical passages which were read in the synagogue during the winter months. When his wife, Pesha, read to him, of a Sabbath, from the Yiddish translation of the stories in the Book of Genesis, he would imagine that he was Noah, and that his sons were Shem, Ham, and Japheth. Or else he would see himself in the image of Abraham, Isaac, or Jacob. He often thought that if the Almighty were to call on him to sacrifice his eldest son, Gimpel, he would rise early in the morning and carry out his commands without delay. Certainly he would have left Poland and the house of his birth and gone wandering over the earth where God sent him. He knew the story of Joseph and his brothers by heart, but he never tired of reading it over again. He envied the ancients because the King of the Universe revealed Himself to them and performed miracles for their sake, but consoled himself by thinking that from him, Abba, to the Patriarchs, there stretched an unbroken chain of generations— as if he too were part of the Bible. He sprang from Jacob's loins; he and his sons were of the seed whose number had become like the sand and the stars. He was living in exile because the Jews of the Holy Land had sinned, but he awaited the Redemption, and he would be ready when the time came.

Abba was by far the best shoemaker in Frampol. His boots were always a perfect fit, never too tight or too roomy. People who suffered from chilblains, corns, or varicose veins were especially pleased with his work, claiming that his shoes relieved them. He despised the new styles, the gimcrack boots and slippers with fancy heels and poorly stitched soles that fell apart with the first rain. His customers were respectable burghers of Frampol or peasants from the surrounding villages, and they deserved the best. He took their measurements with a knotted string, as in the old days. Most of the Frampol women wore wigs, but his wife, Pesha, covered her head with a bonnet as well. She bore him seven sons, and he named them after his forefathers—Gimpel, Getzel, Treitel, Godel, Feivel, Lippe, and Chananiah. They were all short and sandy-haired like their father. Abba predicted that he would turn them into shoemakers, and as a man of his word he let them look on at the workbench while they were still quite young, and at times taught them the old maxim—good work is never wasted.

He spent sixteen hours a day at the bench, a sack spread on his knees, gouging holes with the awl, sewing with a wire needle, tinting and polishing the leather or scraping it with a piece of glass; and while he worked he hummed snatches from the canticles of the Days of Awe. Usually the cat huddled nearby and watched the proceedings as though she were looking after him. Her mother and grandmother had caught mice, in their time, for the little shoemakers. Abba could look down the hill through the window and see the whole town and a considerable distance beyond, as far as the road to Bilgoray and the pine woods. He observed the groups of matrons who gathered every morning at the butcher stalls and the young men and idlers who went in and out of the courtyard of the synagogue; the girls going to the pump to draw water for tea, and the women hurrying at dusk to the ritual bath.

Evenings, when the sun was setting, the house would be pervaded by a dusky glow. Rays of light danced in the corners, flicked across the ceiling, and set Abba's beard gleaming with the color of spun gold. Pesha, Abba's wife, would be cooking *kasha* and soup in the kitchen, the children would be playing, neighboring women and girls would go in and out of the house. Abba would rise from his work, wash his hands, put on his long coat, and go off to the tailors' synagogue for evening prayers. He knew that the wide world was full of strange cities and distant lands, that Frampol was actually no bigger than a dot in a small prayer book; but it seemed to him that his little town was the navel of the universe and that his own house stood at the very center. He often thought that when the Messiah came to lead the Jews to the Land of Israel, he, Abba, would stay behind in Frampol, in his own house, on his own hill. Only on the Sabbath and on Holy Days would he step into a cloud and let himself be flown to Jerusalem.

II
Abba and His Seven Sons

Since Gimpel was the eldest, and therefore destined to succeed his father, he came foremost in Abba's concern. He sent him to the best Hebrew teachers and even hired a tutor who taught him the elements of Yiddish, Polish, Russian, and arithmetic. Abba himself led the boy down into the cellar and showed him the formula for adding chemicals and various kinds of bark to the tanning fluid. He revealed to him that in most cases the right foot is larger than the left, and that the source of all trouble in the fitting of shoes is usually to be found in the big toes. Then he taught Gimpel the principles for cutting soles and inner soles, snub-toed and pointed shoes, high heels and low; and for fitting customers with flat feet, bunions, hammer toes, and calluses.

On Fridays, when there was always a rush of work to get out, the older boys would leave *cheder* at ten in the morning and help their father in the shop. Pesha baked *chalah* and prepared their lunch. She would grasp the first loaf and carry it, hot from the oven, blowing on it all the while and tossing it from hand to hand, to show it to Abba, holding it up, front and back, till he nodded approval. Then she would return with a ladle and let him sample the fish soup, or ask him to taste a crumb of freshly baked cake. Pesha valued his judgment. When she went to buy cloth for herself or the children she brought home swatches for him to choose. Even before going to the butcher she asked his opinion—what should she get, breast or roast, flank or ribs? She consulted him not out of fear or because she had no mind of her own, but simply because she had learned that he always knew what he was talking about. Even when she was sure he was wrong, he would turn out to be right, after all. He never browbeat her, but merely cast a glance to let her know when she was being a fool. This was also the way he handled the children. A strap hung on the wall, but he seldom made use of it; he had his way by kindness. Even strangers respected him. The merchants sold him hides at a fair price and presented no objections when he asked for credit. His own customers trusted him and paid his prices without a murmur. He was always called sixth to the reading of the Torah in the tailors' synagogue—a considerable honor —and when he pledged or was assessed for money, it was never necessary to remind him. He paid up, without fail, right after the Sabbath. The town soon learned of his virtues, and though he was nothing but a plain shoemaker and, if the truth be told, something of an ignoramus, they treated him as they would a distinguished man.

When Gimpel turned thirteen, Abba girded the boy's loins in sackcloth and put him to work at the bench. After Gimpel, Getzel, Treitel, Godel, and Feivel became apprentices. Though they were his own sons and he supported them out of his earnings, he nevertheless paid them a wage. The two youngest boys, Lippe and Chananiah, were still attending the elementary *cheder*, but they too lent a hand at hammering pegs. Abba and Pesha were proud of them. In the morning the six workers trooped into the kitchen for breakfast, washed their six pairs of hands with the appropriate benediction, and their six mouths chewed the roasted groats and corn bread.

Abba loved to place his two youngest boys one on each knee, and sing an old Frampol song to them:

> *A mother had*
> *Ten little boys,*
> *Oh, Lord, ten little boys!*
>
> *The first one was Avremele,*
> *The second one was Berele,*
> *The third one was called Gimpele,*
> *The fourth one was called Dovid'l*
> *The fifth one was called Hershele. . . .*

And all the boys came in on the chorus:

Oh, Lord, Hershele!

Now that he had apprentices, Abba turned out more work, and his income grew. Living was cheap in Frampol, and since the peasants often made him a present of a measure of corn or a roll of butter, a sack of potatoes or a pot of honey, a hen or a goose, he was able to save some money on food. As their prosperity increased, Pesha began to talk of rebuilding the house. The rooms were too narrow, the ceiling was too low. The floor shook underfoot. Plaster was peeling off the walls, and all sorts of maggots and worms crawled through the woodwork. They lived in constant fear that the ceiling would fall on their heads. Even though they kept a cat, the place was infested with mice. Pesha insisted that they tear down this ruin and build a larger house.

Abba did not immediately say no. He told his wife he would think it over. But after doing so, he expressed the opinion that he would rather keep things as they were. First of all, he was afraid to tear down the house, because this might bring bad luck. Second, he feared the evil eye—people were grudging and envious enough. Third, he found it hard to part with the home in which his parents and grandparents, and the whole family, stretching back for generations, had lived and died. He knew every corner of the house, each crack and wrinkle. When one layer of paint peeled off the wall, another, of a different color, was exposed; and behind this layer, still another. The walls were like an album in which the fortunes of the family had been recorded. The attic was stuffed with heirlooms—tables and chairs, cobbler's benches and lasts, whetstones and knives, old clothes, pots, pans, bedding, salting boards, cradles. Sacks full of torn prayer books lay spilled on the floor.

Abba loved to climb up to the attic on a hot summer's day. Spiders spun great webs, and the sunlight, filtering in through cracks, fell upon the threads in rainbows. Everything lay under a thick coat of dust. When he listened attentively he would hear a whispering, a murmuring and soft scratching, as of some unseen creature engaged in endless activity, conversing in an unearthly tongue. He was sure that the souls of his forefathers kept watch over the house. In much the same way he loved the ground in which it stood. The weeds were as high as a man's head. There was a dense growth of hairy and brambly vegetation all about the place—the very leaves and twigs would catch hold of one's clothing as though with teeth and claws. Flies and midges swarmed in the air and the ground crawled with worms and snakes of all descriptions. Ants had raised their hills in this thicket; field mice had dug their holes. A pear tree grew in the midst of this wilderness; every year, at the time of the Feast of the Tabernacle, it yielded small fruit with the taste and hardness of wood. Birds and bees flew over this jungle, great big golden-bellied flies. Toadstools sprang up after each rain. The ground was unkept, but an unseen hand guarded its fertility.

When Abba stood here looking up at the summer sky, losing himself in contemplation of the clouds, shaped like sailboats, flocks of sheep, brooms, and elephant herds, he felt the presence of God, His providence and His mercy. He could virtually see the Almighty seated on His throne of glory, the earth serving Him as a footstool. Satan was vanquished; the angels sang hymns. The Book of Memory in which were recorded all the deeds of men lay open. From time to time, at sunset, it even seemed to Abba that he saw the river of fire in the nether world. Flames leaped up from the burning coals; a wave of fire rose, flooding the shores. When he listened closely he was sure he heard the muffled cries of sinners and the derisive laughter of the evil host.

No, this was good enough for Abba Shuster. There was nothing to change. Let everything stand as it had stood for ages, until he lived out his allotted time and was buried in the cemetery among his ancestors, who had shod the sacred community and whose good name was preserved not only in Frampol but in the surrounding district.

III
Gimpel Emigrates to America

Therefore the proverb says: Man proposes, God disposes.

One day while Abba was working on a boot, his eldest son, Gimpel, came into the shop. His freckled face was heated, his sandy hair disheveled under the skullcap. Instead of taking his place at the bench, he stopped at his father's side, regarded him hesitantly, and at last said, "Father, I must tell you something."

"Well, I'm not stopping you," replied Abba.

"Father," he cried, "I'm going to America."

Abba dropped his work. This was the last thing he expected to hear, and up went his eyebrows.

"What happened? Did you rob someone? Did you get into a fight?"

"No, Father."

"Then why are you running away?"

"There's no future for me in Frampol."

"Why not? You know a trade. God willing, you'll marry some day. You have everything to look forward to."

"I'm sick of small towns; I'm sick of the people. This is nothing but a stinking swamp."

"When they get around to draining it," said Abba, "there won't be any more swamp."

"No, Father, that's not what I mean."

"Then what do you mean?" cried Abba angrily. "Speak up!"

The boy spoke up, but Abba couldn't understand a word of it. He laid into synagogue and state with such venom, Abba could only imagine that the poor soul was possessed: the Hebrew teachers beat the children; the women empty their slop pails right outside the door; the shopkeepers loiter in the streets; there are no toilets anywhere, and the public relieves itself as it pleases, behind the bathhouse or out in the open, encouraging epidemics and plagues. He made fun of Ezreal the Healer and of Mecheles the Marriage Broker, nor did he spare the rabbinical court and the bath attendant, the washerwoman and the overseer of the poorhouse, the professions and the benevolent societies.

At first Abba was afraid that the boy had lost his mind, but the longer he continued his harangue, the clearer it became that he had strayed from the path of righteousness. Jacob Reifman, the atheist, used to hold forth in Shebreshin, not far from Frampol. A pupil of his, a detractor of Israel, was in the habit of visiting an aunt in Frampol and had gathered quite a following among the good-for-nothings. It had never occurred to Abba that his Gimpel might fall in with this gang.

"What do you say, Father?" asked Gimpel.

Abba thought it over. He knew that there was no use arguing with Gimpel, and he remembered the proverb: A rotten apple spoils the barrel. "Well," he replied, "what can I do? If you want to go, go. I won't stop you."

And he resumed his work.

But Pesha did not give in so easily. She begged Gimpel not to go so far away; she wept and implored him not to bring shame on the family. She even ran to the cemetery, to the graves of her forefathers, to seek the intercession of the dead. But she was finally convinced that Abba was right: it was no use arguing. Gimpel's face had turned hard as leather, and a mean light showed in his yellow eyes. He had become a stranger in his own home. He spent that night out with friends, and returned in the morning to pack his prayer shawl and phylacteries, a few shirts, a blanket, and some hard-boiled eggs—and he was all set to go. He had saved enough money for passage. When his mother saw that it was settled, she urged him to take at least a jar of preserves, a bottle of cherry juice, bedding, pillows. But Gimpel refused. He was going to steal over the border into Germany, and he stood a better chance if he traveled light. In short, he kissed his mother, said good-by to his brothers and friends, and off he went. Abba, not wanting to part with his son in anger, took him in the wagon to the station at Reivetz. The train arrived in the middle of the night with a hissing and whistling, a racket and din. Abba took the headlights of the locomotive for the eyes of a hideous devil, and shied away from the funnels with their columns of sparks and smoke and their clouds of steam. The blinding lights only intensified the darkness. Gimpel ran around with his baggage like a madman, and his father ran after him. At the last moment the boy kissed his father's hand, and Abba called after him, into the darkness, "Good luck! Don't forsake your religion!"

The train pulled out, leaving a smell of smoke in Abba's nostrils and a ringing in his ears. The earth trembled under his feet. As though the boy had been dragged off by demons! When he returned home and Pesha fell on him, weeping, he said to her, "The Lord gave and the Lord has taken away. . . ."

Months passed without word from Gimpel. Abba knew that this was the way with young men when they leave home—they forget their dearest ones. As the proverb says: Out of sight, out of mind. He doubted that he would ever hear from him, but one day a letter came from America. Abba recognized his son's handwriting. Gimpel wrote that he crossed the border safely, that he saw many strange cities and spent four weeks on board ship, living on potatoes and herring because he did not want to touch improper food. The ocean was very deep and the waves as high as the sky. He saw flying fish but no mermaids or mermen, and he did not hear them singing. New York is a big city, the houses reach into the clouds. The trains go over the roofs. The gentiles speak English. No one walks with his eyes on the ground, everybody holds his head high. He met a lot of his countrymen in New York; they all wear short coats. He too. The trade he learned at home has come in very handy. He is *all right*; he is earning a living. He will write again, a long letter. He kisses his father and mother and his brothers, and sends regards to his friends.

A friendly letter after all.

In his second letter Gimpel announced that he had fallen in love with a girl and bought her a diamond ring. Her name is Bessie; she comes from Rumania; and she works *at dresses.* Abba put on his spectacles with the brass frames and spent a long time puzzling this out. Where did the boy learn so many English words? The third letter stated that he was married and that *a reverend* had performed the service. He inclosed a snapshot of himself and wife.

Abba could not believe it. His son was wearing a gentleman's coat and a high hat. The bride was dressed like a countess in a white dress, with train and veil; she held a bouquet of flowers in her hand. Pesha took one look at the snapshot and began to cry. Gimpel's brothers gaped. Neighbors came running, and friends from all over town: they could have sworn that Gimpel had been spirited away by magic to a land of gold, where he had taken a princess to wife—just as in the storybooks the pack merchants brought to town.

To make a long story short, Gimpel induced Getzel to come to America, and Getzel brought over Treitel; Godel followed Treitel, and Feivel, Godel; and then all five brothers brought the young Lippe and Chananiah across. Pesha lived only for the mail. She fastened a charity box to the doorpost, and whenever a letter came she dropped a coin through the slot. Abba worked all alone. He no longer needed apprentices because he now had few expenses and could afford to earn less; in fact, he could have given up work altogether, as his sons sent him money from abroad. Nevertheless he rose at his usual early hour and remained at the bench until late in the evening. His hammer sounded away, joined by the cricket on the hearth, the mouse in its hole, the shingles crackling on the roof. But his mind reeled. For generations the little shoemakers had lived in Frampol. Suddenly the birds had flown the coop. Was this a punishment, a judgment, on him? Did it make sense?

Abba bored a hole, stuck in a peg, and murmured, "So—you, Abba know what you're doing and God does not? Shame on you, fool! He will be done. Amen!"

IV

The Sack of Frampol

Almost forty years went by. Pesha had long since died of cholera, during the Austrian occupation. And Abba's sons had grown rich in America. They wrote every week, begging him to come and join them, but he remained in Frampol, in the same old house on the stubby hill. His own grave lay ready, next to Pesha's, among the little shoemakers; the stone had already been raised; only the date was missing. Abba put up a bench by the side of her grave, and on the eve of Rosh Hashonoh or during fasts, he went there to pray and read Lamentations. He loved it in the cemetery. The sky was so much clearer and loftier than in town, and a great, meaningful silence rose from the consecrated ground and the old gravestone overgrown with moss. He loved to sit and look at the tall white birches, which trembled even when no breeze blew, and at the crows balancing in the branches, like black fruit. Before she died Pesha made him promise that he would not remarry and that he would come regularly to her grave with news of the children. He kept his promise. He would stretch out alongside the mound and whisper into her ear, as if she were still alive, "Gimpel has another grandchild. Getzel's youngest daughter is engaged, thank God. . . ."

The house on the hill was nearly in ruins. The beams had rotted away, and the roof had to be supported by stone posts. Two of the three windows were boarded over because it was no longer possible to fit glass to the frames. The floor was all but gone, and the bare ground lay exposed to the feet. The pear tree in the garden had withered; the trunk and branches were covered with scales. The garden itself was now overgrown with poisonous berries and grapes, and there was a profusion of the burrs that children throw about on Tishe b'Av. People swore they saw strange fires burning there at night, and claimed that the attic was full of bats which fly into girls' hair. Be that as it may, an owl certainly did hoot somewhere near the house. The neighbors repeatedly warned Abba to move out of this ruin before it was too late—the least wind might knock it over. They pleaded with him to give up working—his sons were showering him with money. But Abba stubbornly rose at dawn and continued at the shoemaker's bench. Although yellow hair does not readily change color, Abba's beard had turned completely white, and the white, staining, had turned yellow again. His brows had sprouted like brushes and hid his eyes, and his high forehead was like a piece of yellow parchment. But he had not lost his touch. He could still turn out a stout shoe with a broad heel, even if it did take a little longer. He bored holes with awl, stitched with the needle, hammered his pegs, and in a hoarse voice sang the old shoemaker's song:

> "A mother bought a billygoat,
> The shocket killed the billygoat,
> Oh, Lord, the billygoat!
> Avremele took its ears,
> Berele took its lung,
> Gimpele took the gullet,
> And Dovid'l took the tongue,
> Hershele took the neck. . . ."

As there was no one to join him, he now sang the chorus alone:

"Oh, Lord, the billygoat!"

His friends urged him to hire a servant, but he would not take a strange woman into the house. Occasionally one of the neighbor women came in to sweep and dust, but even this was too much for him. He got used to being alone. He learned to cook for himself and would prepare soup on the tripod, and on Fridays even put up the pudding for the Sabbath. Best of all, he liked to sit alone at the bench and follow the course of his thoughts, which had become more and more tangled with the years. Day and night he carried on conversations with himself. One voice asked questions, the other answered. Clever words came to his mind, sharp, timely expressions full of the wisdom of age, as though his grandfathers had come to life again and were conducting their endless disputations inside his head on matters pertaining to this world and the next. All his thoughts ran on one theme: What is life and what is death, what is time that goes on without stopping, and how far away is America? His eyes would close; the hammer would fall out of his hand; but he would still hear the cobbler's characteristic rapping—a soft tap, a louder one, and a third, louder still—as if a ghost sat at his side, mending unseen shoes. When one of the neighbors asked him why he did not go to join his sons, he would point to the heap on the bench and say, "*Nu*, and the shoes? Who will mend them?"

Years passed, and he had no idea how or where they vanished. Traveling preachers passed through Frampol with disturbing news of the outside world. In the tailors' synagogue, which Abba still attended, the young men spoke of war and anti-Semitic decrees, of Jews flocking to Palestine. Peasants who had been Abba's customers for years suddenly deserted him and took their trade to Polish shoemakers. And one day the old man heard that a new world war was imminent. Hilter—may his name vanish!—had raised his legions of barbarians and was threatening to grab up Poland. This scourge of Israel had expelled the Jews from Germany, as in the days of Spain. The old man thought of the Messiah and became terribly excited. Who knows? Perhaps this was the battle of

Gog and Magog? Maybe the Messiah really was coming and the dead would rise again! He saw the graves opening and the little shoemakers stepping forth—Abba, Getzel, Treitel, Gimpel, his grandfather, his own father. He called them all into his house and set out brandy and cakes. His wife, Pesha, was ashamed to find the house in such condition, but "Never mind," he assured her, "we'll get someone to sweep up. As long as we're all together!" Suddenly a cloud appears, envelops the town of Frampol—synagogue, House of Study, ritual bath, all the Jewish homes, his own among them—and carries the whole settlement off to the Holy Land. Imagine his amazement when he encounters his sons from America. They fall at his feet, crying, "Forgive us, Father!"

When Abba pictured this event his hammer quickened in tempo. He saw the little shoemakers dress for the Sabbath in silks and satins, in flowing robes with broad sashes, and go forth rejoicing in Jerusalem. They pray in the Temple of Solomon, drink the wine of Paradise, and eat of the mighty steer and Leviathan. The ancient Jochanan the Shoemaker, renowned for his piety and wisdom, greets the family and engages them in a discussion of Torah and shoemaking. Sabbath over, the whole clan returns to Frampol, which has become part of the Land of Israel, and re-enters the old home. Even though the house is as small as ever, it has miraculously grown roomy enough, like the hide of a deer, as it is written in the Book. They all work at one bench, Abbas, Gimpels, Getzels, Godels, the Treitels and the Lippes, sewing golden sandals for the daughters of Zion and lordly boots for the sons. The Messiah himself calls on the little shoemakers and has them take his measure for a pair of silken slippers.

One morning, while Abba was wandering among his thoughts, he heard a tremendous crash. The old man shook in his bones: the blast of the Messiah's trumpet! He dropped the boot he had been working on and ran out in ecstasy. But it was not Elijah the Prophet proclaiming the Messiah. Nazi planes were bombing Frampol. Panic spread through the town. A bomb fell near the synagogue, so loud that Abba felt his brain shudder in his skull. Hell opened before him. There was a blaze of lightning, followed by a blast that illuminated all of Frampol. A black cloud rose over the courtyard of the synagogue. Flocks of birds flapped about in the sky. The forest was burning. Looking down from his hill, Abba saw the orchards under great columns of smoke. The apple trees were blossoming and burning. Several men who stood near him threw themselves down on the ground and shouted to him to do the same. He did not hear them; they were moving their lips in dumbshow. Shaking with fright, his knees knocking together, he re-entered the house and packed a sack with his prayer shawl and phylacteries, a shirt, his shoemaker's tools, and the paper money he had put away in the straw mattress. Then he took up a stick, kissed the *mezzuzah*, and walked out the door. It was a miracle that he was not killed; the house caught fire the moment he left. The roof swung out like a lid, uncovering the attic with its treasures. The walls collapsed. Abba turned about and saw the shelf of sacred books go up in flames. The blackened pages turned in the air, glowing with fiery letters like the Torah given to the Jews on Mount Sinai.

V
Across the Ocean

From that day on, Abba's life was transformed beyond recognition—it was like a story he had read in the Bible, a fantastic tale heard from the lips of a visiting preacher. He had abandoned the house of his forefathers and the place of his birth and, staff in hand, gone wandering into the world like the Patriarch Abraham. The havoc in Frampol and the surrounding villages brought Sodom and Gomorrah to mind, burning like a fiery furnace. He spent his nights in the cemetery together with the other Jews, lying with his head on a gravestone—he too, as Jacob did at Beth-El, on the way from Beer Sheba to Haran.

On Rosh Hashonoh the Frampol Jews held services in the forest, with Abba leading the most solemn prayer of the Eighteen Benedictions because he was the only one with a prayer shawl. He stood under a pine tree, which served as an altar, and in a hoarse voice intoned the litany of the Days of Awe. A cuckoo and a woodpecker accompanied him, and all the birds roundabout twittered, whistled, and screeched. Late summer gossamers wafted through the air and trailed onto Abba's beard. From time to time a lowing sounded through the forest, like a blast on the ram's horn. As the Day of Atonement drew near, the Jews of Frampol rose at midnight to say the prayer for forgiveness, reciting it in fragments, whatever they could remember. The horses in the surrounding pastures whinnied and neighed, frogs croaked in the cool night. Distant gunfire sounded intermittently; the clouds shone red. Meteors fell; flashes of lightning played across the sky. Half-starved little children, exhausted from crying, took sick and died in their mothers' arms. There were many burials in the open fields. A woman gave birth.

Abba felt he had become his own great-great-grandfather, who had fled Chmielnitzki's pogroms, and whose name is recorded in the annals of Frampol. He was ready to offer himself in Sanctification of the Name. He dreamed of priests and Inquisitions, and when the wind blew among the branches he heard martyred Jews crying out, "Hear, O Israel, the Lord our God, the Lord is One!"

Fortunately Abba was able to help a good many Jews with his money and shoemaker's tools. With the money they hired wagons and fled south, toward Rumania; but often they had to walk long distances, and their shoes gave out. Abba would stop under a tree and take up his tools. With God's help, they surmounted danger and crossed the Rumanian frontier at night. The next morning, the day before Yom Kippur, an old widow took Abba into her house. A telegram was sent to Abba's sons in America, informing them that their father was safe.

You may be sure that Abba's sons moved heaven and earth to rescue the old man. When they learned of his whereabouts they ran to Washington and with great difficulty obtained a visa for him; then they wired a sum of money to the consul in Bucharest, begging him to help their father. The consul sent a courier to Abba, and he was put on the train to Bucharest. There he was held a week, then transferred to an Italian seaport, where he was shorn and deloused and had his clothes steamed. He was put on board the last ship for the United States.

It was a long and severe journey. The train from Rumania to Italy dragged on, uphill and down, for thirty-six hours. He was given food, but for fear of touching anything ritually unclean he ate nothing at all. His phylacteries and prayer shawl got lost, and with them he lost all track of time and could no longer distinguish between Sabbath and weekdays. Apparently he was the only Jewish passenger on board. There was a man on the ship who spoke German, but Abba could not understand him.

It was a stormy crossing. Abba spent almost the whole time lying down, and frequently vomited gall, though he took nothing but dry crusts and water. He would doze off and wake to the sound of the engines throbbing day and night, to the long, threatening signal blasts, which reeked of fire and brimstone. The door of his cabin was constantly slamming to and fro, as though an imp were swinging on it. The glassware in the cupboard trembled and danced; the walls shook; the deck rocked like a cradle.

During the day Abba kept watch at the porthole over his bunk. The ship would leap up as if mounting the sky, and the torn sky would fall as though the world were returning to original chaos. Then the ship would plunge back into the ocean, and once again the firmament would be divided from the waters, as in the Book of Genesis. The waves were a sulphurous yellow and black. Now they would saw-tooth out to the horizon like a mountain range, reminding Abba of the Psalmist's words: "The mountains skipped like rams, the little hills like lambs." Then they would come heaving back, as in the miraculous Parting of the Waters. Abba had little learning, but Biblical references ran through his mind, and he saw himself as the prophet Jonah, who fled before God. He too lay in the belly of a whale and, like Jonah, prayed to God for deliverance. Then it would seem to him that this was not ocean but limitless desert, crawling with serpents, monsters, and dragons, as it is written in Deuteronomy. He hardly slept a wink at night. When he got up to relieve himself, he would feel faint and lose his balance. With great difficulty he would regain his feet and, his knees buckling under, go wandering, lost, down the narrow, winding corridor, groaning and calling for help until a sailor led him back to the cabin. Whenever this happened he was sure that he was dying. He would not even receive decent Jewish burial, but be dumped in the ocean. And he made his confession, beating his knotty fist on his chest and exclaiming, "Forgive me, Father!"

Just as he was unable to remember when he began his voyage, so he was unaware when it came to an end. The ship had already been made fast to the dock in New York harbor, but Abba hadn't the vaguest notion of this. He saw huge buildings and towers, but mistook them for the pyramids of Egypt. A tall man in a white hat came into the cabin and shouted something at him, but he remained motionless. At last they helped him dress and led him out on deck, where his sons and daughters-in-law and grandchildren were waiting. Abba was bewildered; a crowd of Polish landowners, counts and countesses, gentile boys and girls, leaped at him, hugged him, and kissed him, crying out in a strange language, which was both Yiddish and not Yiddish. They half led, half carried him away, and placed him in a car. Other cars arrived, packed with Abba's kinfolk, and they set out, speeding like shot arrows over bridges, rivers, and roofs. Buildings rose up and receded, as if by magic, some of the buildings touching the sky. Whole cities lay spread out before him; Abba thought of Pithom and Rameses. The car sped so fast, it seemed to him the people in the streets were moving backward. The air was full of thunder and lightning; a banging and trumpeting, it was a wedding and a conflagration at once. The nations had gone wild, a heathen festival . . .

His sons were crowding around him. He saw them as in a fog and did not know them. Short men with white hair. They shouted, as if he were deaf.

"I'm Gimpel!"

"Getzel!"

"Feivel!"

The old man closed his eyes and made no answer. Their voices ran together; everything was turning pell-mell, topsy-turvy. Suddenly he thought of Jacob arriving in Egypt, where he was met by Pharaoh's chariots. He felt, he had lived through the same experience in a previous incarnation. His beard began to tremble; a hoarse sob rose from his chest. A forgotten passage from the Bible stuck in his gullet.

Blindly he embraced one of his sons and sobbed out, "Is this you? Alive?"

He had meant to say: "Now let me die, since I have seen thy face, because thou art yet alive."

VI
The American Heritage

Abba's sons lived on the outskirts of a town in New Jersey. Their seven homes, surrounded by gardens, stood on the shore of a lake. Every day they drove to the shoe factory, owned by Gimpel, but on the day of Abba's arrival they took a holiday and prepared a feast in his honor. It was to be held in Gimpel's house, in full compliance with the dietary laws. Gimpel's wife, Bessie, whose father had been a Hebrew teacher in the old country, remembered all the rituals and observed them carefully, going so far as to cover her head with a kerchief. Her sisters-in-law did the same, and Abba's sons put on the skullcaps they had once worn during Holy Days. The grandchildren and great-grandchildren, who did not know a word of Yiddish, actually learned a few phrases. They had heard the legends of Frampol and the little shoemakers and the first Abba of the family line. Even the gentiles in the neighborhood were fairly well acquainted with this history. In the ads Gimpel published in the papers, he had proudly disclosed that his family belonged to the shoemaking aristocracy:

Our experience dates back three hundred years to the Polish city of Brod, where our ancestor, Abba, learned the craft from a local master. The community of Frampol, in which our family worked at its trade for fifteen generations, bestowed on him the title of Master in recognition of his charitable services. This sense of public responsibility has always gone hand in hand with our devotion to the highest principles of the craft and our strict policy of honest dealing with our customers.

The day Abba arrived, the papers in Elizabeth carried a notice to the effect that the seven brothers of the famous shoe company were welcoming their father from Poland. Gimpel received a mass of congratulatory telegrams from rival manufacturers, relatives, and friends.

It was an extraordinary feast. Three tables were spread in Gimpel's dining-room; one for the old man, his sons, and daughters-in-law, another for the grandchildren, and the third for the great-grandchildren. Although it was broad daylight, the tables were set with candles—red, blue, yellow, green— and their flames were reflected from the dishes and silverware, the crystal glasses and the wine cups, the decanters reminiscent of the Passover Seder. There was an abundance of flowers in every available corner. To be sure, the daughters-in-law would have preferred to see Abba properly dressed for the occasion, but Gimpel put his foot down, and Abba was allowed to spend his first day in the familiar long coat, Frampol style. Even so, Gimpel hired a photographer to take pictures of the banquet—for publication in the newspapers—and invited a rabbi and a cantor to the feast to honor the old man with traditional song.

Abba sat in an armchair at the head of the table. Gimpel and Getzel brought in a bowl and poured water over his hands for the benediction before eating. The food was served on silver trays, carried by colored women. All sorts of fruit juices and salads were set before the old man, sweet brandies, cognac, caviar. But Pharaoh, Joseph, Potiphar's wife, the Land of Goshen, the chief baker, and the chief butler spun round and round in his head. His hands trembled so that he was unable to feed himself, and Gimpel had to help him. No matter how often his sons spoke to him, he still could not tell them apart. Whenever the phone rang he jumped—the Nazis were bombing Frampol. The entire house was whirling round and round like a carousel; the tables were standing on the ceiling and everyone sat upside down. His face was sickly pale in the light of the candles and the electric bulbs. He fell asleep soon after the soup course, while the chicken was being served. Quickly they led him to the bedroom, undressed, him, and called a doctor.

He spent several weeks in bed, in and out of consciousness, fitfully dozing as in a fever. He even lacked the strength to say his prayers. There was a nurse at his bedside day and night. Eventually he recovered enough to take a few steps outdoors, in front of the house, but his senses remained disordered. He would walk into clothes closets, lock himself into the bathroom and forget how to come out; the doorbell and the radio frightened him; and he suffered constant anxiety because of the cars that raced past the house. One day Gimpel brought

him to a synagogue ten miles away, but even here he was bewildered. The sexton was clean-shaven; the candelabra held
electric lights; there was no courtyard, no faucet for washing
one's hands, no stove to stand around. The cantor, instead of
singing like a cantor should, babbled and croaked. The congregation wore tiny little prayer shawls, like scarves around
their necks. Abba was sure he had been hauled into church to
be converted. . . .

When spring came and he was no better, the daughters-in-
law began to hint that it wouldn't be such a bad idea to put
him in a home. But something unforeseen took place. One
day, as he happened to open a closet, he noticed a sack lying
on the floor which seemed somehow familiar. He looked again
and recognized his shoemaker's equipment from Frampol:
last, hammer and nails, his knife and pliers, the file and the awl,
even a broken-down shoe. Abba felt a tremor of excitement;
he could hardly believe his eyes. He sat down on a footstool
and began to poke about with fingers grown clumsy and stale.
When Bessie came in and found him playing with a dirty old
shoe, she burst out laughing.

"What are you doing, Father? Be careful, you'll cut yourself,
God forbid!"

That day Abba did not lie in bed dozing. He worked busily
till evening and even ate his usual piece of chicken with greater
appetite. He smiled at the grandchildren when they came in to
see what he was doing. The next morning, when Gimpel told
his brothers how their father had returned to his old habits,
they laughed and thought nothing more of it—but the activity
soon proved to be the old man's salvation. He kept at it day
after day without tiring, hunting up old shoes in the clothes
closets and begging his sons to supply him with leather and
tools. When they gave in, he mended every last pair of shoes in
the house—man, woman, and child's. After the Passover holidays the brothers got together and decided to build a little hut
in the yard. They furnished it with a cobbler's bench, a stock
of leather soles and hides, nails, dyes, brushes—everything
even remotely useful in the craft.

Abba took on new life. His daughters-in-law cried, he
looked fifteen years younger. As in the Frampol days, he now
rose at dawn, said his prayers, and got right to work. Once

again he used a knotted string as a measuring tape. The first pair of shoes, which he made for Bessie, became the talk of the neighborhood. She had always complained of her feet, but this pair, she insisted, were the most comfortable shoes she had ever worn. The other girls soon followed her example and also had themselves fitted. Then came the grandchildren. Even some of the gentile neighbors came to Abba when they heard that in sheer joy of the work he was turning out custom-made shoes. He had to communicate with them, for the most part, in gestures, but they got along very well. As for the younger grandchildren and the great-grandchildren, they had long been in the habit of standing at the door to watch him work. Now he was earning money, and he plied them with candies and toys. He even whittled a stylus and began to instruct them in the elements of Hebrew and piety.

One Sunday, Gimpel came into the workshop and, no more than half in earnest, rolled up his sleeves and joined Abba at the bench. The other brothers were not to be outdone, and on the following Sunday eight work stools were set up in the hut. Abba's sons spread sackcloth aprons on their knees and went to work, cutting soles and shaping heels, boring holes and hammering pegs, as in the good old days. The women stood outside, laughing, but they took pride in their men, and the children were fascinated. The sun streamed in through the windows, and motes of dust danced in the light. In the high spring sky, lofting over the grass and the water, floated clouds in the form of brooms, sailboats, flocks of sheep, herds of elephants. Birds sang; flies buzzed; butterflies fluttered about.

Abba raised his dense eyebrows, and his sad eyes looked around at his heirs, the seven shoemakers: Gimpel, Getzel, Treitel, Godel, Feivel, Lippe, and Chananiah. Their hair was white, though yellow streaks remained. No, praise God, they had not become idolaters in Egypt. They had not forgotten their heritage, nor had they lost themselves among the unworthy. The old man rattled and bumbled deep in his chest, and suddenly began to sing in the stifled, hoarse voice:

"A mother had
Ten little boys,
Oh, Lord, ten little boys!

The sixth one was called Velvele,
The seventh one was Zeinvele,
The eighth one was called Chenele,
The ninth one was called Tevele,
The tenth one was called Judele . . ."

And Abba's sons came in on the chorus:

"Oh, Lord, Judele!"

Translated by Isaac Rosenfeld

Joy

RABBI BAINISH of Komarov, having buried Bunem, his third son, stopped praying for his ailing children. Only one son and two daughters remained, and all of them spat blood. His wife, frequently breaking into the solitude of his study would scream, "Why are you so silent? Why don't you move heaven and earth?" With clenched fists raised, she would wail, "What good are your knowledge, your prayers, the merits of your ancestors, your prolonged fasts? What does He have against you—our Father in Heaven? Why must all His anger be directed against you?" In her despair she once snatched a sacred book and threw it on the floor. Silently, Rabbi Bainish picked it up. His invariable answer was, "Leave me alone!"

Though he was not yet fifty, the rabbi's beard, so thin that the hairs could be numbered, had turned white as the beard of an old man. His tall body stooped. His stern black eyes looked past everyone. No longer did he comment on the Torah nor preside over meals. For weeks now he had not appeared at the House of Study. Though his followers came from other towns to visit him, they had to return without being allowed even a greeting. Behind his bolted door he sat, silent; it was a pregnant silence. The crowd, his "bread and butter" Hassidim, gradually dispersed among other rabbis. Only his intimate circle, the old Hassidim, the wise ones, stayed. When Rebecca, his youngest daughter, died, the rabbi did not even follow her hearse. He gave orders to his sexton, Avigdor, to close the shutters, and they remained closed. Through a heart-shaped aperture in the shutters, came the meager light whereby the rabbi looked through books. He no longer recited the texts out loud; he merely thumbed the pages, opening a book at one place and then at another, and with one eye closed, stared vacantly beyond the pages and the walls. Dipping his pen in the inkwell, he would move a sheet of paper close to him, but he could not write. He would fill a pipe, but it remained unlit. There was no indication that he had touched the breakfast and supper that had been brought to his study. Weeks, months, went by like this.

One summer day the rabbi appeared at the House of Study. Several boys and young men were studying there, while a couple of old men, hangers-on, were meditating. Since their rabbi had been absent for so long, all of them were frightened at the sight of him. Taking a step in one direction, and then a step back, the rabbi asked, "Where is Abraham Moshe of Borisov?"

"At the inn," said a young man who had not yet been struck dumb.

"Would you ask him to come to me, please?"

"I will, Rabbi."

The young man left immediately for the inn. Walking to the bookshelves, the rabbi drew out a book at random, glanced at a page, and then replaced the book. In his unbuttoned robe, his long fringed garment, his short trousers, white stockings, with hat pushed back on his head, his earlocks unkempt, his eyebrows contracted, he stood there. The House of Study was so still that water could be heard dripping in the basin, and flies humming around the candlesticks. The grandfather clock, with its long chains and pomegranates on the dial, creaked and struck three. Through the open windows peeped the fruit trees in the orchard; one heard the chirping of birds. In the slanting pillars of dust, tiny particles vibrated, no longer matter, and not yet spirit, reflecting rainbow hues. The rabbi beckoned to a boy who had only recently left the Hebrew school and had begun to read the Talmud on his own.

"What's your name, eh?"

"Moshe."

"What are you studying?"

"The first treatise."

"What chapter?"

"Shur Shenagah ath haparah."

"How do you translate that?"

"A bull gored a cow."

The rabbi stamped his slippered foot. "Why did the bull gore the cow? What had the cow done to him?"

"A bull does not reason."

"But He who created the bull can reason."

The boy did not know the answer to that one. The rabbi pinched his cheek.

"Well, go study," he said, returning to his room.

Reb Abraham Moshe came to him shortly afterwards. He was a small, youthful-faced man, with white beard and ear-locks, wearing a floor length robe, a thick, moss-green sash, and carrying a long pipe that reached to his knees. Over his skull cap he wore a high cap. His eccentricities were well known. He would recite the morning prayer in the afternoon, and the afternoon prayer long after others had returned from the evening service. He chanted psalms at Purim, and during the Kol Nidre prayer, he slept. On Passover eve when everyone celebrated at the Passover feast, he would study a Commentary of the Talmudic Treatises on Damages and Compensations. It was rumored that once, at the tavern, he had won a game of chess from a general, and that the general had rewarded him with a license to sell brandy. His wife ran the business; he himself, spent more time at Komarov than at home. He would say that living at Komarov was like standing at the foot of Mount Sinai; the air itself purified one. In a more jocular mood, he would comment that there was no need to study at Komarov; it was sufficient to loiter on a bench in the House of Study and inhale the Torah as one breathed. The Hassidim knew that the rabbi held Reb Abraham Moshe in the highest esteem, discussed esoteric doctrine with him, and asked his advice. Reb Abraham Moshe was always seated at the head of the table. Nevertheless, each time he visited the rabbi, he spruced up like a young man. He would wash his hands, button his caftan, curl his earlocks, and comb his beard. He would enter with reverence, as one enters the house of a saint.

The rabbi had not sent for him since Rebecca's death; this in itself was an indication of the depth of the rabbi's grief. Reb Abraham Moshe did not shuffle now, as customarily, but walked briskly, almost running. When he had reached the rabbi's door he halted for a moment, touched his cap, his chest, wiped his brow with his handkerchief, and then walked in mincingly. The rabbi, having opened one of the shutters, sat smoking his pipe in the grandfather's chair with the ivory armrests. A half-full glass of tea stood on the table, a roll beside it. Apparently, the rabbi had recovered.

"Rabbi, I'm here," said Reb Abraham Moshe.

"So I see. Be seated."

"Thank you."

The rabbi remained silent a while. Placing his narrow hand on the table edge, he stared at the white nails of his long fingers. Then he said, "Abraham Moshe, it's bad."

"What's bad?"

"Abraham Moshe, it's worse than you think."

"What could be worse?" asked Abraham Moshe, ironically.

"Abraham Moshe, the atheists are right. There is no justice, no Judge."

Reb Abraham Moshe was accustomed to the rabbi's harsh words. At Komarov, even the Lord of the Universe would not be spared. But to be rebellious is one thing; to deny God, another. Reb Abraham Moshe turned pale. His knees shook.

"Then who rules the world, Rabbi?"

"It's not ruled."

"Who then?"

"A total lie!"

"Come, come . . ."

"A heap of dung . . ."

"Where did the dung come from?"

"In the beginning was the dung."

Reb Abraham Moshe froze. He wanted to speak, but his arguments caught in his throat. Well, it's his grief that talks, he thought. Nevertheless, he marvelled. If Job could endure it, so should the rabbi.

"What should we do, then, Rabbi?" Reb Abraham Moshe asked hoarsely.

"We should worship idols."

To keep from falling, Reb Abraham Moshe gripped the table edge.

"What idols?" he asked. Everything inside him seemed to tighten.

The rabbi laughed briefly. "Don't be frightened; I won't send you to the priest. If the atheists are right, what's the difference between Terah and Abraham? Each served a different idol. Terah, who was simpleminded, invented a clay god. Abraham invented a Creator. It is what one invents that matters. Even a lie must have some truth in it."

"You are merely being facetious," Reb Abraham Moshe stammered. His palate felt dry, his throat contracted.

"Well, stop trembling! Sit down!"

Reb Abraham Moshe sat down. The rabbi rose from his seat, walked to the window, and stood there a long time, staring into space. Then he walked to the book cabinet. The cabinet, which smelled of wine and snuffed-out valedictory candles, contained a spice-box, and citron box, and a Chanukah candelabra. The rabbi, taking out a Zohar, opened it at random, stared at the page, nodded, and then, smacking his lips, exclaimed, "A nice invention, very nice!"

II

More and more Hassidim departed. In the House of Study, on Saturdays, scarcely a quorum remained. The sextons, all but Avigdor, had left. Finding her solitude unbearable, the rabbi's wife went for a long visit to her brother, the rabbi of Biala. Reb Abraham Moshe stayed at Komarov. He spent one Sabbath each month with his family in his native town. If a man were not to be deserted when his body was sick, he reasoned, then he certainly should not be left alone during the sickness of his soul. If their rabbi were committing sins, God forbid, then one would be interdicted from associating with him, but actually, his piety was now greater than before. He prayed, studied, visited the ritual bathhouse. And he was so ardent in his charity, that he sold his dearest possessions—the silver candlesticks, the large Chanukah candelabra, his gold watch, the Passover tray—and gave the proceeds to the poor. Reb Abraham Moshe told him reproachfully he was squandering his inheritance, but the rabbi replied, "Poor men *do* exist. That's one thing of which we can be certain."

The summer went by and the month of Elul came. On week days, Avigdor, the sexton, blew the ram's horn at the House of Study. Komarov used to be crowded to capacity during the month of Elul; there were not enough beds at the inns, and young people would sleep in storerooms, barns, attics. But this year, it was quiet at Komarov. The shutters remained closed at the inns. Grass grew wild in the rabbi's courtyard; there was no one to trample it. Gossamer threads floated through the air. The apples, pears, and plums ripened on the trees in the orchard, because the boys who used to pick them were gone. The chirping of birds sounded louder than ever. Moles dug up numerous mounds of earth. Certain bushes sprouted berries of a poisonous sort. One day, the rabbi, on his way to the bathhouse, plucked one such berry. "If a thing like this can turn one into a corpse," he thought, "what is a corpse?" He sniffed it and threw it away. "If everything hinges on a berry, then all our affairs are berries." The rabbi entered the bathhouse. "Well, demons, where are you?" he said aloud, and his words were thrown back at him by the echo, "At least let there be devils." He sat on the bench, undressed, removed his fringed garment, and examined it. "Threads and knots and nothing else. . . ."

The water was cold, but it made no difference to him. "Who is cold? And if one is cold, what of it?" The coldness cut his breath, and he clung to the railing. Then he plunged and stayed for a long while under the water. Something within him was laughing. "As long as you breathe, you must breathe." The rabbi dried himself and dressed. Returning to his study, he opened a Cabbala book, The Two Tablets of the Covenant. Here it was written that "the rigor of the law should be sweetened to deprive Satan of his nourishment." "Well, and what if it's a fairy tale?" The rabbi squinted one eye while the other kept staring. "The sun? Close your eyes and there is no sun. The birds? Stuff your ears and there are no birds. Pain? Swallow a wild berry, and the pain is gone. What is left, then? Nothing at all. The past no longer exists and the future has yet to come. The conclusion is that nothing exists beyond the moment. Well, if so, we really have nothing to worry about."

No more than thirty Hassidim gathered at Komarov for Rosh Hashona. Although the rabbi appeared at the service in his cloak and shawl, one could not tell if he prayed, for he was silent. After the service the Hassidim sat at the table, but their rabbi's seat was vacant. An old man chanted a little song and the others gave him a rattling accompaniment. Reb Abraham Moshe repeated a comment the rabbi had made on the Torah twenty years ago. Thank God, the rabbi was alive, though for all practical purposes, he was dead.

Avigdor brought to the rabbi's room, a decanter of wine, apples with honey, the head of a carp, two challahs, a quarter of a chicken with stewed carrots, and a slice of pineapple for the blessing of the first fruit. But although it was already evening, the rabbi had touched nothing.

During the month of Elul he had fasted. His body felt as though it had been hollowed. Hunger still gnawed somewhere in his stomach, but it was a hunger unrelated to him. What had he, Bainish of Komarov, to do with food? Must one yield to the body's lusts? If one resists, what does it do—die? "Let it die, if that's what it wants. I am satisfied." A golden-green fly flew in through the open window from the other side of the curtain, and settled on the glazed eye of the carp. The rabbi murmured, "Well, what are you waiting for? Eat. . . ."

As the rabbi sat half-awake, half-slumbering in his old chair, his arms on the arm rests, engrossed in thoughts he did not know he was thinking, divested of all external things, he suddenly caught sight of his youngest daughter, Rebecca. Through the closed door she had entered and stood there, erect, pale, her hair plaited in two tresses, wearing her best gold-embroidered dress, a prayer book in one hand, a handkerchief in the other. Forgetting that she had died, the rabbi looked at her, half-surprised. "See, she's a grown girl, how come she's not a bride?" An extraordinary nobility spread over her features; she looked as though she had just recovered from an illness; the pearls of her necklace shone with an unearthly light, with the aura of the Days of Awe. With an expression of modesty and love she gazed at the rabbi.

"Happy holiday, Father."

"Happy holiday, happy new year," the rabbi said.

"Father, say grace."

"What? Of course, of course."

"Father, join the guests at table," she said, half-commanding, half-imploring.

An icy shudder ran through the rabbi's spine. "But she's dead!" At once his eyes were drenched with tears, and he jumped to his feet as though to rush toward her. Through the mist of tears Rebecca's form became distorted, grew longer and partly blurred, but she still loomed before him. The rabbi noticed the silver clasp of her prayer book and the lace of her handkerchief. Her left pigtail was tied with a white ribbon. But her face, as though veiled, dissolved into a blotch. The rabbi's voice broke.

"My daughter, are you here?"

"Yes, Father."

"Why have you come?"

"For you."

"When?"

"After the holidays."

She seemed to withdraw. In the whirling mist her form lost its substance, but her dress continued to drag on the floor in folds and waves like a golden train, and a glow arose from it. Soon this too dissolved, and nothing remained but a sense of wonder, a supernatural tang, a touch of heavenly joy. The rabbi did not weep, but luminous drops fell on his white silken robe embroidered with flowers and leaves. There was a fragrance of myrtle, cloves and saffron. He had a cloying sensation in his mouth, as if he had eaten marzipans.

The rabbi remembered what Rebecca had told him. He put on his fur hat, stood up, and opened the door leading to the House of Study. It was time for the evening prayer, but the old men had not yet left the table.

"Happy holiday, my friends," the rabbi said in a cheerful voice.

"Happy holiday, Rabbi."

"Avigdor, I want to say grace."

"I'm ready, Rabbi."

Avigdor brought the wine, and the rabbi, chanting a holiday tune, recited the prayer. He washed his hands with the appropriate blessing and said the prayer for bread. After taking some broth, the rabbi commented on the Torah, a thing he had not done in years. His voice was low, though audible. The rabbi took up the question of why the moon is obscured on Rosh Hashona. The answer is that on Rosh Hashona one prays for life, and life means free choice, and freedom is Mystery. If one knew the truth how could there be freedom? If hell and paradise were in the middle of the market place, everyone would be a saint. Of all the blessings bestowed on man, the greatest lies in the fact that God's face is forever hidden from him. Men are the children of the Highest, and the Almighty plays hide and seek with them. He hides His face, and the children seek Him while they have faith that He exists. But what if, God forbid, one loses faith? The wicked live on denials; denials in themselves are also a faith, faith in evil-doing, and from it one can draw strength for the body. But if the pious man loses his faith, the truth is shown to him, and he is recalled. This is the symbolic meaning of the words, "When a man dies in a tent": when the pious man falls from his rank, and becomes, like the wicked, without permanent shelter, then a light shines from above, and all doubts cease. . . .

The rabbi's voice gradually grew weaker. The old men leaned toward him, intently listening. The House of Study was so still that one could hear the candles flicker. Reb Abraham Moshe paled. He realized the meaning hidden behind all this. The moment Rosh Hashona was over, he mailed some letters, having sat until daybreak writing them. The rabbi's wife returned from Biala, and for Yom Kippur the Hassidim arrived in great number. The rabbi had returned to his former self. During the Sukkoth holidays he commented on the Torah in his arbor. On Hashanah Raba he prayed all through the night, until dawn, with his Hassidim. On Simchas Torah, he never wearied of dancing around the reading stand. His Hassidim said later that Komarov had not, even under the old rabbi, blessed be his memory, celebrated that holiday with such gusto. To each of his Hassidim the rabbi spoke personally, asking about his family, and carefully reading each petition. He helped the children decorate the arbor with lanterns, ribbons, bunches of grapes. With his own hands, he wove baskets of lulab leaves for the myrtles. He pinched the cheeks of boys who had come with their fathers, and gave them cookies. As a rule, the rabbi prayed late and alone, but on the day following Succoth, he prayed in the House of Study with the first quorum. After the service he asked for a glass of coffee. Reb Abraham Moshe and a circle of young men stood watching the rabbi drink coffee. Between swallows, he puffed his pipe. He said, "I want you to know that the material world has no substance."

After breakfast, the rabbi said grace. Then he ordered his bed made ready and murmured something about his old prayer shawl. The moment he lay down he became moribund. His face grew as yellow as his fringed garment. His eyelids closed. Covered with wrinkles, his forehead assumed a strange aspect. Life could literally be seen departing from him; his body shrank and altered. The rabbi's wife wanted to call the doctor, but the rabbi signalled her not to do so. Opening his eyes, he looked toward the door. Between the door jambs, beside the *mezuseh*, all of them were standing—his four sons and two daughters, his father, blessed be his memory, and his grandfather. Reverently, they all looked in his direction, expectantly, with arms outstretched. Each of them emitted a different light. They bent forward as though restrained by an invisible fence. "So that's the way it is," the rabbi thought. "Well, now everything is clear." He heard his wife sob, and wanted to comfort her, but no strength remained in his throat and lips. Suddenly, Reb Abraham Moshe leaned over him, as though realizing that the rabbi wished to speak, and the rabbi murmured, "One should always be joyous."

Those were his final words.

Translated by Norbert Guterman and Elaine Gottlieb

From the Diary of One Not Born

WHERE man does not walk, where cattle do not tread, Friday the thirteenth of the thirteenth month, between day and night, behind the Black Mountains, in the wasted woodland, at the castle of Asmodeus, by the light of a charmed moon.

I, the author of these line, was blessed by a good fortune that comes to only one in ten thousand: I was not born. My father, a yeshivah student, sinned as did Onan, and from his seed I was created—half spirit, half demon, half air, half shade, horned like a buck and winged like a bat, with the mind of a scholar and the heart of a highwayman. I am and I am not. I whistle down chimneys and dance in the public bath; I overturn the pot of Sabbath food in a poor man's kitchen; I make a woman unclean when her husband returns from a trip. I like to play all kinds of pranks. Once, when a young rabbi was preaching his first sermon in the synagogue on the Great Sabbath before the Passover, I turned myself into a fly and bit the learned man on the tip of his nose. He flicked me off, but I flew to the lobe of his ear. He stretched out his hand to drive me away, but I danced off onto his high forehead, and paraded around between the deep rabbinical furrows. He preached and I sang, and I had the pleasure of hearing this newly hatched scholar, still wet behind the ears, scramble the text and forget the profundities which he had expected to pour from his sleeve. Oh yes, his enemies had a gay Sabbath! And oh, how his wife berated him that evening! Indeed, the quarrel between man and wife went so far that, I blush to tell you, she would not let him into her bed Passover night, when every Jewish husband should be a king and every Jewish wife, a queen. And if it had been destined for her to conceive Messiah then, I nipped that in the bud!

Since my life span is eternal, and since I don't have to worry about making a living, bringing up children, or accounting for my deeds, I do just as I please. Evenings, I watch the women at the ritual baths, or make my way into the bedrooms of pious folk and listen to the forbidden talk between man and wife. I enjoy reading other people's letters and counting up the amounts in women's nest-eggs. So sharp are my ears that I can hear thoughts behind the skull, and although I have no mouth and am dumb as a fish, I can, when the occasion arises, make a cutting remark. I have no need of money, but I like to commit petty thieveries. I steal pins from women's dresses and loosen their bows and knots. I hide important papers and wills—what malicious deeds do I not do! For instance——

A Jewish landowner, Reb Paltiel, a learned man of a distinguished family and a charitable nature, became impoverished. His cows stopped giving milk, his land became barren, his bees made no more honey. Things went from bad to worse. Reb Paltiel could see that his luck was turning, and he said to himself, "Well—I'll die a poor man." He had a few volumes of the Talmud and a Psalter, so he sat down to study and pray, thinking, "The Lord giveth and the Lord taketh away. As long as I have bread I will eat, and when that, too, is gone, the time will have come to take a sack and a stick and go begging."

The man had a wife, Grene Peshe, and she had a wealthy brother, Reb Getz, in Warsaw. So she began to nag her husband, "What's the sense of sitting here and waiting until the last loaf is eaten? Go to Warsaw and tell my brother what has happened." Her husband was a proud man, however, and he replied, "I don't want any favors from anyone. If it is God's will that I be provided for, he will give me from his full hand, and if it is my fate to be a pauper, this trip will be a needless self-abasement."

But, as women have been given nine measures of garrulousness and only half a measure of faith, she pleaded and insisted until he capitulated. He put on his shabby fur coat with the moth-eaten foxtails, took a covered wagon to Reivitz, from thence to Lublin, and then he was bounced and jounced for days between Lublin and Warsaw.

The trip was long and arduous, the covered wagon jogging along for nearly a week. Nights, Reb Paltiel slept at wayside inns. It was right after the Feast of Tabernacles, when the skies are heavy with rain. The wagon wheels sank deep into the mire; their spokes were covered with mud. To make a long story short: the Warsaw Croesus, Reb Getz, grimaced, complained, bit his beard and muttered that new-found relatives, both on his side and on his wife's, were crawling out of the cracks in the walls. And finally he took out a five hundred gulden note, gave it to his needy brother-in-law, and bade him farewell, half warmly, half coldly, smiling and sighing, and asking to be remembered to his sister. A sister is, after all, a sister, one's own flesh and blood.

Reb Paltiel took the bank note, put it into his breast pocket, and started home. Truly, the humiliation he had suffered was worth more than five times five hundred gulden. But what's a man to do? Obviously, there's a time for honors and a time for indignities. And anyway, the indignities were in the past and the five hundred gulden were in his pocket. And with such a sum one could buy cows and horses and goats, and repair the roof and pay taxes, and take care of heaven knows how many other necessaries! I was right there (I happened, at the time, to be a flea in Reb Paltiel's beard), and I whispered to him, "Well, what do you say? The fact is that Grene Peshe isn't so crazy!" He answered me, "Evidently it was decreed. Who knows? Maybe heaven wanted me to atone for some sin, and from now on my luck will be better."

On the last night of the return trip, a heavy snow fell, and then there was a severe frost. The wagon couldn't move over the icy road, and Reb Paltiel had to take a sleigh. He arrived home frozen, exhausted from the long journey, hoarse and worn. He went into the house immediately. His wife, Grene Peshe, was sitting by the hearth warming herself. When she saw him she let out a shriek, "Woe is me—what you look like! I've seen them bury healthier looking specimens!" When he heard these lamentations, Reb Paltiel stuck his hand into his breast pocket, drew out the banknote, laid it down and announced, "Take it, it's yours." And he gave her the gift of charity which had cost him so much. Grene Peshe's face went from joy to gloom and back to joy. "So, well, I had expected a thousand," she said. "But five hundred isn't to be sneezed at, either."

And as she was saying these words, I sprang out of Reb Paltiel's beard and sat myself on Grene Peshe's nose. I jumped with such force that the poor woman dropped the paper, and it fell into the fire. And before either of them could cry out, a green and blue flame shot up, and of the five hundred gulden only an ash remained.

Well, what purpose will be served by telling you what he said and what she answered? You can imagine it yourself. I leaped back into Reb Paltiel's beard, and stayed there until—and I hate to have to tell you this—he was forced to take a sack and a stick and go begging. Try to hang a flea! Try to run away from bad luck? Try to figure out where the evil spirit is! . . .

When I returned to the Black Mountains and told Asmodeus what I had done, he pinched my ear and repeated the story to his wife, Lilith, and she laughed with such abandon that the desert rang with the echoes of her glee, and she, herself, the Queen of Satan's Court, tweaked my nose:

"You're really a first rate little devil!" she said to me. "Some day you'll do big things!"

II

Where the heavens are copper and the earth iron, on a field of toadstools, in a ruined outhouse, on a dung heap, in a pot without a bottom, on a Sabbath night during the winter solstice, not to be thought of now, nor later, nor at night, Amen Selah!

The false prophecies of my mistress, Lilith, have been fulfilled. I am no longer an imp, but a full-grown devil—and a male, at that. I can disguise myself as a human, play my malicious pranks, and make men's eyes deceive them. True, I can be driven off by a holy spell, but these days who knows Cabala? The little rabbis can pour salt on my tail. Their amulets are nothing but waste paper to me; their charms make me laugh. More than once I've left a souvenir of devil-dung in one of their skullcaps, or tied knots in their beards.

Yes, I do frightful things. I'm a demon among demons, an evil one among evil ones. One moonlit night I turned myself into a sack of salt and lay down by the roadside. Soon a wagon came along. Seeing the full sack, the driver stopped his horse, jumped out and hoisted me onto the cart. Who wouldn't take something for nothing? I was heavy as lead, and the ignoramus could hardly lift me. As soon as I was in the wagon, he opened the mouth of the sack and took a lick—evidently he wanted to find out whether I was salt or sugar. In a second I had become a calf, and I'll give you three guesses where he was licking me. When he saw what he was doing, the poor wretch nearly went crazy. His hands and feet began to tremble. "What's going on here?" he cried. "Where the devil am I?" Suddenly I flapped my wings and flew away like an eagle. The drayman arrived home a sick man. And now he goes around with an amulet and a piece of charmed amber, but they'll do him as much good as cupping a corpse.

One winter I came to the village of Turbin, in the form of a solicitor collecting for the needy in the Holy Land. I went from house to house, opening the metal alms-boxes which hung on the doors and taking out the small change, mostly worn half-pennies. From one of the houses came the smell of an overheated oven. The owner was a maiden in her thirties, both of whose parents were dead. She supported herself by baking cookies for the yeshiva students. She was short and stout, with a large bosom and an even larger what-do-you-call-it. The house was warm, the air redolent of cinnamon and poppy seeds, and it occurred to me that there would be nothing to be lost by marrying this old maid for a while. I smoothed my red sidelocks, combed my beard with my fingers, blew my frostbitten nose, and had a chat with the girl. One word led to another—I told her I was a childless widower. "I'm not a big earner, but I have a few hundred gulden in a purse beneath my fringed garment."

"Is your wife dead long?" she asked, and I answer, "It'll be three years the Fast of Esther."

She asks, "What was the matter with her?" and I reply, "She died in childbirth," and groan.

She can see that I'm an honest fellow—why else would a man mourn three years after his wife? In short, it's a match. The women of the town take the orphan under their wings. They collect a dowry for her. They supply her with tablecloths, napkins, sheets, shirts, petticoats, drawers. And since she is a virgin, they erect the wedding canopy in the synagogue court. The wedding presents are given, everyone dances with the newlyweds, and the bride is carried off to her bedroom.

"Good luck!" the best man says to me. "I hope next year there'll be a circumcision feast!"

The guests leave. The night is long and dark. The bedroom is warm as an oven and black as Egypt. My bride is already in bed, under a down quilt—she had plucked the down herself—waiting for her husband. I grope around in the darkness; for the sake of appearances I undress, cough softly, and whisper to myself. "Are you tired?" I ask.

"Not so tired," she answers.

"You know," I say, "the other one, peace to her soul, was always tired. Poor thing, she was weak."

"Don't talk about her now," my wife admonishes. "May she put in a word for us in heaven."

"I want to tell you something," I say, "but don't get upset. On her deathbed she asked me to give her my holy word that I wouldn't marry again."

"You didn't promise?"

"Did I have any choice? You know it's forbidden to grieve the dying."

"You should have asked the rabbi what to do," the cookie baker says to me. "Why didn't you tell me earlier?"

"What's the matter, are you afraid she'll come back to choke you?"

"God forbid!" she answers. "How am I to blame? I knew nothing about it."

I get into bed, my body icy. "Why are you so cold?" my wife asks.

"Do you really want to know?" I say. "Come closer and I'll whisper it into your ear."

"Nobody can hear you," she says, astonished.

"There's a saying that the walls have ears," I reply.

She cocks her ear, and I spit right into it. She shudders and sits up. The bed boards squeak. The straw mattress begins to sag and crack.

"What are you doing?" she shrieks. "Is that supposed to be clever?"

Instead of answering, I begin to titter.

She says, "What kind of game is this? It may be all right for a child, but not for a grown man."

"And how do you know I'm not a child?" I answer. "I'm a child with a beard. Billy goats have beards, too."

"Well then," she says, "if you want to babble, babble. Good night."

And she turns her face to the wall. For a while we both lie quietly. And then I give her a pinch where she's fattest. My wife shoots up into the air. The bed shakes. She lets out a scream. "Are you crazy, or what? What are you pinching me for? Heaven help me—what kind of hands have I fallen into?"

And she begins to weep hoarsely—as can only a friendless orphan who has waited over thirty years for her lucky day and then finds herself espoused to a monster. A robber's heart would have melted. I'm sure that God himself shed a tear that night. But a devil is a devil.

At daybreak, I creep out of the house and go over to the rabbi's. The rabbi, a saintly man, is already at his studies, and is shocked to see me. "God bless a Jew," he says, "why so early?"

"It's true that I'm a stranger here, and only a poor man, but the town didn't have to wish a whore on me!"

"A whore!"

"What else is a bride who isn't a virgin?" I ask.

The rabbi tells me to wait for him in the study house and goes to wake up his wife. She gets dressed (even forgetting to wash her hands) and rouses some of her cronies. A little knot of women, including the rabbi's wife, goes over to my bride's to investigate and to look at the bed sheets. Turbin is no Sodom. If there's a sin, the town has to know about it!

My wife weeps bitterly. She swears that I hadn't come near her all night. She insists that I'm crazy, that I pinched her and spat in her ear, but the women shake their heads. They bring the defendant to the rabbi. They parade her through the market place, the townsfolk peering from every window. The study house is crowded. My wife moans and wails. She vows that no man has ever touched her, including me.

"He's a madman," she says, and turns on me. But I insist that she's lying.

"As a matter of fact," I announce, "let a doctor examine her."

"Where will we find a doctor in Turbin?" they ask.

"All right," I say, "then take her to Lublin. There's still some decency in the world," I screech. "I'll see to it that all of Poland hears about this! I'll tell the Rabbinical Council the whole story!"

"Be sensible. How are we to blame?" asked one of the elders.

"It's the responsibility of all of Israel," I answer piously. "Whoever heard of a town letting a girl stay unmarried until she's over thirty and having her bake cookies for the yeshiva students?"

My wife realizes that I'm trying to ruin her business, too, and she rushes up to me with clenched fists. She's ready to hit me, and she would have, if she hadn't been restrained.

"Now, people," I scream. "See how shameless she is?"

By now it's apparent to everyone that I'm the honorable one, not she. In short, the rabbi says, "We still have a God in heaven. Divorce her and get rid of her."

"I beg your pardon," I say, "but I had expenses. The wedding cost me a good hundred gulden."

And so the bargaining begins. From her cookie baking my wife has managed to save, penny by penny, some seventy-odd gulden. They urge me to settle for that, but I'm adamant.

"Let her sell the wedding presents," I say.

And the girl shrieks, "Take everything! Tear out my insides!" And she claws at her face and cries out, "Oh, mother, I wish I were lying in the grave with you!" She beats her fists on the table, overturning the ink bottle, and sobs, "If this could happen to me, there's no God."

The beadle dashes over and slaps her, and she falls to the floor, her dress pulled up, her kerchief off her head. They try to lift her up, but she kicks, flails her arms and laments, "You're not Jews, but beasts!"

Nevertheless, that evening I collect my hundred gulden. The scribe sits down to write out the divorce papers. Suddenly I announce that I have to go out for a moment—and I never return. They search for me half the night. They call me, halloo after me; they hunt high and low. My wife becomes a permanent grass widow. And so, to spite God, the town and her own bad luck, she throws herself into the well.

Asmodeus himself praised my little job.

"Not bad," he said. "You're on the way." And he sent me to Machlath, the daughter of Namah, the she-devil who teaches young demons the paths of corruption.

Translated by Nancy Gross

The Old Man

A T the beginning of the Great War, Chaim Sachar of Krochmalna Street in Warsaw was a rich man. Having put aside dowries of a thousand rubles each for his daughters, he was about to rent a new apartment, large enough to include a Torah-studying son-in-law. There would also have to be additional room for his ninety-year-old father, Reb Moshe Ber, a Turisk Hassid, who had recently come to live with him in Warsaw.

But two years later, Chaim Sachar's apartment was almost empty. No one knew where his two sons, young giants, who had been sent to the front, had been buried. His wife and two daughters had died of typhus. He had accompanied their bodies to the cemetery, reciting the memorial prayer for the three of them, pre-empting the most desirable place at the prayer stand in the synagogue, and inviting the enmity of other mourners, who accused him of taking unfair advantage of his multiple bereavement.

After the German occupation of Warsaw, Chaim Sachar, a tall, broad man of sixty who traded in live geese, locked his store. He sold his furniture by the piece, in order to buy frozen potatoes and moldy diced peas, and prepared gritty blackish noodles for himself and his father, who had survived the grandchildren.

Although Chaim Sachar had not for many months been near a live fowl, his large caftan was still covered with goose down, his great broad-brimmed hat glistened with fat, and his heavy, snub-toed boots were stained with slaughterhouse blood. Two small eyes, starved and frightened, peered from beneath his disheveled eyebrows; the red rims about his eyes were reminiscent of the time when he could wash down a dish of fried liver and hard-boiled eggs with a pint of vodka every morning after prayer. Now, all day long, he wandered through the market place, inhaling butchershop odors and those from restaurants, sniffing like a dog, and occasionally napping on porters' carts. With the refuse he had collected in a basket, he fed his kitchen stove at night; then, rolling the sleeves over his hairy arms, he would grate turnips on a grater. His father, meanwhile, sat warming himself at the open kitchen door, even though it was midsummer. An open Mishna treatise lay across his knees, and he complained constantly of hunger.

As though it were all his son's fault, the old man would mutter angrily, "I can't stand it much longer . . . this gnawing. . . ."

Without looking up from his book, a treatise on impurity, he would indicate the pit of his stomach and resume his mumbling in which the word "impure" recurred like a refrain. Although his eyes were a murky blue, like the eyes of a blind man, he needed no glasses, still retained some of his teeth, yellow and crooked as rusty nails, and awoke each day on the side on which he had fallen asleep. He was disturbed only by his rupture, which nevertheless, did not keep him from plodding through the streets of Warsaw with the help of his pointed stick, his "horse," as he called it. At every synagogue he would tell stories about wars, about evil spirits, and of the old days of cheap and abundant living when people dried sheepskins in cellars and drank spirits directly from the barrel through a straw. In return, Reb Moshe Ber was treated to raw carrots, slices of radish, and turnips. Finishing them in no time, he would then, with a trembling hand, pluck each crumb from his thinning beard—still not white—and speak of Hungary, where more than seventy years before, he had lived in his father-in-law's house. "Right after prayer, we were served a large decanter of wine and a side of veal. And with the soup there were hard-boiled eggs and crunchy noodles."

Hollow-cheeked men in rags, with ropes about their loins, stood about him, bent forward, mouths watering, digesting each of his words, the whites of their eyes greedily showing, as if the old man actually sat there eating. Young yeshiva students, faces emaciated from fasts, eyes shifty and restless as those of madmen, nervously twisted their long earlocks around their fingers, grimacing, as though to suppress stomach-aches, repeating ecstatically, "That was the time. A man had his share of heaven and earth. But now we have nothing."

For many months Reb Moshe Ber shuffled about searching for a bit of food; then, one night in late summer, on returning home, he found Chaim Sachar, his first-born, lying in bed, sick, barefoot, and without his caftan. Chaim Sachar's face was as red as though he had been to a steam bath, and his beard was crumpled in a knot. A neighbor woman came in, touched his forehead, and chanted, "Woe is me, it's that sickness. He must go to the hospital."

Next morning the black ambulance reappeared in the court-yard. Chaim Sachar was taken to the hospital; his apartment was sprayed with carbolic acid; and his father was led to the disinfection center, where they gave him a long white robe and shoes with wooden soles. The guards, who knew him well, gave him double portions of bread under the table and treated him to cigarettes. The Sukkoth holiday had passed by the time the old man, his shaven chin concealed beneath a kerchief, was allowed to leave the disinfection center. His son had died long before, and Reb Moshe Ber said the memorial prayer, *kaddish*, for him. Now alone in the apartment, he had to feed his stove with paper and wood shavings from garbage cans. In the ashes he baked rotten potatoes, which he carried in his scarf, and in an iron pot, he brewed chicory. He kept house, made his own candles by kneading bits of wax and suet around wicks, laun-dered his shirt beneath the kitchen faucet, and hung it to dry on a piece of string. He set the mousetraps each night and drowned the mice each morning. When he went out he never forgot to fasten the heavy padlock on the door. No one had to pay rent in Warsaw at that time. Moreover, he wore his son's boots and trousers. His old acquaintances in the Houses of Study, envied him. "He lives like a king!" they said, "He has inherited his son's fortune!"

The winter was difficult. There was no coal, and since sev-eral tiles were missing from the stove, the apartment was filled with thick black smoke each time the old man made a fire. A crust of blue ice and snow covered the window panes by November, making the rooms constantly dark or dusky. Overnight, the water on his night table froze in the pot. No matter how many clothes he piled over him in bed, he never felt warm; his feet remained stiff, and as soon as he began to doze, the entire pile of clothes would fall off, and he would have to climb out naked to make his bed once more. There was no kerosene; even matches were at a premium. Although he recited chapter upon chapter of the Psalms, he could not fall asleep. The wind, freely roaming about the rooms, banged the doors; even the mice left. When he hung up his shirt to dry, it would grow brittle and break, like glass. He stopped washing himself; his face became coal black. All day long he would sit in the House of Study, near the red-hot iron stove. On the shelves, the old books lay like piles of rags; tramps stood around the tin-topped tables, nondescript fellows with long matted hair and rags over their swollen feet—men who, having lost all they had in the war, were half-naked or covered only with torn clothes, bags slung over their shoulders. All day long, while orphans recited *kaddish*, women stood in throngs around the Holy Ark, loudly praying for the sick, and filling his ears with their moans and lamentations. The room, dim and stuffy, smelled like a mortuary chamber from the numerous anniversary candles that were burning. Every time Reb Moshe Ber, his head hanging down, fell asleep, he would burn himself on the stove. He had to be escorted home at night, for his shoes were hobnailed, and he was afraid he might slip on the ice. The other tenants in his house had given him up for dead. "Poor thing—he's gone to pieces."

One December day, Reb Moshe Ber actually did slip, receiving a hard blow on his right arm. The young man escorting him, hoisted Reb Moshe Ber on his back, and carried him home. Placing the old man on his bed without undressing him, the young man ran away as though he had committed a burglary. For two days the old man groaned, called for help, wept, but no one appeared. Several times each day he said his Confession of Sins, praying for death to come quickly, pounding his chest with his left hand. It was quiet outside in the daytime, as though everyone had died; a hazy green twilight came through the windows. At night he heard scratching noises as though a cat were trying to climb the walls; a hollow roar seemed to come repeatedly from underground. In the darkness the old man fancied that his bed stood in the middle of the room and all the windows were open. After sunset on the second day he thought he saw the door open suddenly, admitting a horse with a black sheet on its back. It had a head as long as a donkey's and innumerable eyes. The old man knew at once that this was the Angel of Death. Terrified, he fell from his bed, making such a racket that two neighbors heard it. There was a commotion in the courtyard; a crowd gathered, and an ambulance was summoned. When he came to his senses, Reb Moshe Ber found himself in a dark box, bandaged and covered up. He was sure this was his hearse, and it worried him that he had no heirs to say *kaddish*, and that therefore the peace of his grave would be disturbed. Suddenly he recalled the verses he would have to say to Duma, the Prosecuting Angel, and his bruised, swollen face twisted into a corpselike smile:

> *What man is he that liveth and shall not see death?*
> *Shall he deliver his soul from the grave?*

II

After Passover, Reb Moshe Ber was discharged from the hospital. Completely recovered, he once more had a great appetite but nothing to eat. All his possessions had been stolen; in the apartment only the peeling walls remained. He remembered Jozefow, a little village near the border of Galicia, where for fifty years he had lived and enjoyed great authority in the Turisk hassidic circle, because he had personally known the old rabbi. He inquired about the possibilities of getting there, but those he questioned merely shrugged their shoulders, and each said something different. Some assured him Jozefow had been burned to the ground, wiped out. A wandering beggar, on the other hand, who had visited the region, said that Jozefow was more prosperous than ever, that its inhabitants ate the Sabbath white bread even on week days. But Jozefow was on the Austrian side of the border, and whenever Reb Moshe Ber broached the subject of his trip, men smiled mockingly in their beards and waved their hands. "Don't be foolish, Reb Moshe Ber. Even a young man couldn't do it."

But Reb Moshe Ber was hungry. All the turnips, carrots, and watery soups he had eaten in public kitchens had left him with a hollow sensation in his abdomen. All night he would dream of Jozefow knishes stuffed with ground meat and onions, of tasty concoctions of tripe and calf's feet, chicken fat and lean beef. The moment he closed his eyes he would find himself at some wedding or circumcision feast. Large brown rolls were

piled up on the long table, and Turisk hassidim in silken caftans with high velvet hats over their skull caps, danced, glasses
of brandy in their hands, singing:

> *What's a poor man*
> *Cooking for his dinner?*
> *Borscht and potatoes!*
> *Borscht and potatoes!*
> *Faster, faster, hop-hop-hop!*

He was the chief organizer of all those parties; he quarreled
with the caterers, scolded the musicians, supervised every detail, and having no time to eat anything, had to postpone it all
for later. His mouth watering, he awoke each morning, bitter
that not even in his dream had he tasted those wonderful
dishes. His heart pounded; his body was covered with a cold
perspiration. The light outside seemed brighter every day, and
in the morning, rectangular patterns of sunlight would waver
on the peeling wall, swirling, as though they mirrored the
rushing waves of a river close by. Around the bare hook for a
chandelier on the crumbling ceiling, flies hummed. The cool
golden glow of dawn illuminated the window panes, and the
distorted image of a bird in flight was always reflected in
them. Beggars and cripples sang their songs in the courtyard
below, playing their fiddles and blowing little brass trumpets.
In his shirt, Reb Moshe Ber would crawl down from the one
remaining bed, to warm his feet and stomach and to gaze at
the barefoot girls in short petticoats who were beating red
comforters. In all directions feathers flew, like white blossoms,
and there were familiar scents of rotten straw and tar. The old
man, straightening his crooked fingers, pricking up his long
hairy ears as though to hear distant noises, thought for the
thousandth time that if he didn't get out of here this very summer, he never would.

"God will help me," he would tell himself. "If he wills it, I'll
be eating in a holiday arbor at Jozefow."

He wasted a lot of time at first by listening to people who
told him to get a passport and apply for a visa. After being
photographed, he was given a yellow card, and then he had
to stand with hordes of others for weeks outside the Austrian consulate on a crooked little street somewhere near the

Vistula. They were constantly being cursed in German and punched with the butts of guns by bearded, pipe-smoking soldiers. Women with infants in their arms wept and fainted. It was rumored that visas were granted only to prostitutes and to men who paid in gold. Reb Moshe Ber, going there every day at sunrise, sat on the ground and nodded over his Beni Issachar treatise, nourishing himself with grated turnips and moldy red radishes. But since the crowd continued to increase, he decided one day to give it all up. Selling his cotton-padded caftan to a peddler, he bought a loaf of bread, and a bag in which he placed his prayer shawl and phylacteries, as well as a few books for good luck; and planning to cross the border illegally, he set out on foot.

It took him five weeks to get to Ivangorod. During the day, while it was warm, he walked barefoot across the fields, his boots slung over his shoulders, peasant fashion. He fed on unripened grain and slept in barns. German military police often stopped him, scrutinized his Russian passport for a long time, searched him to see that he was not carrying contraband, and then let him go. At various times, as he walked, his intestines popped out of place; he lay on the ground and pushed them back with his hands. In a village near Ivangorod he found a group of Turisk hassidim, most of them young. When they heard where he was going and that he intended to enter Galicia, they gaped at him, blinking, then, after whispering among themselves, they warned him, "You're taking a chance in times like these. They'll send you to the gallows on the slightest pretext."

Afraid to converse with him, lest the authorities grow suspicious, they gave him a few marks and got rid of him. A few days later, in that village, people spoke in hushed voices of an old Jew who had been arrested somewhere on the road and shot by a firing squad. But not only was Reb Moshe alive by then; he was already on the Austrian side of the border. For a few marks, a peasant had taken him across, hidden in a cart under a load of straw. The old man started immediately for Rajowiec. He fell ill with dysentery there and lay in the poorhouse for several days. Everyone thought he was dying, but he recovered gradually.

Now there was no shortage of food. Housewives treated Reb Moshe Ber to brown buckwheat with milk, and on Saturdays he even ate cold calf's foot jelly and drank a glass of brandy. The moment his strength returned, he was off again. The roads were familiar here. In this region, the peasants still wore the white linen coats and quadrangular caps with tassels that they had worn fifty years ago; they had beards and spoke Ukrainian. In Zamosc the old man was arrested and thrown into jail with two young peasants. The police confiscated his bag. He refused gentile food and accepted only bread and water. Every other day he was summoned by the commandant who, as though Reb Moshe Ber were deaf, screamed directly into his ear in a throaty language. Comprehending nothing, Reb Moshe Ber simply nodded his head and tried to throw himself at the commandant's feet. This went on until after Rosh Hashonah; only then did the Zamosc Jews learn that an old man from abroad was being held in jail. The rabbi and the head of the community obtained his release by paying the commandant a ransom.

Reb Moshe Ber was invited to stay in Zamosc until after Yom Kippur, but he would not consider it. He spent the night there, took some bread, and set out on foot for Bilgorai at daybreak. Trudging across harvested fields, digging turnips for food, he refreshed himself in the thick pinewoods with whitish berries, large, sour and watery, which grow in damp places and are called Valakhi in the local dialect. A cart gave him a lift for a mile or so. A few miles from Bilgorai, he was thrown to the ground by some shepherds who pulled off his boots and ran away with them.

Reb Moshe Ber continued barefoot, and for this reason did not reach Bilgorai until late at night. A few tramps, spending the night in the House of Study, refused to let him in, and he had to sit on the steps, his weary head on his knees. The autumnal night was clear and cold; against the dark yellow, dull glow of the starry sky, a flock of goats, silently absorbed, peeled bark from the wood that had been piled in the synagogue courtyard for winter. As though complaining of an unforgettable sorrow, an owl lamented in a womanish voice, falling silent and then beginning again, over and over. People with wooden lanterns in their hands came at daybreak to say the *Selichoth* prayers. Bringing the old man inside, they placed him near the stove and covered him with discarded prayer shawls from the chest. Later in the morning they brought him a heavy pair of hobnailed, coarse-leathered military boots. The boots pinched the old man's feet badly, but Reb Moshe Ber was determined to observe the Yom Kippur fast at Jozefow, and Yom Kippur was only one day off.

He left early. There were no more than about four miles to travel, but he wanted to arrive at dawn, in time for the *Selichoth* prayers. The moment he had left town, however, his stiff boots began to cause him such pain, that he couldn't take a step. He had to pull them off and go barefoot. Then there was a downpour with thunder and lightning. He sank knee deep in puddles, kept stumbling, and became smeared with clay and mud. His feet swelled and bled. He spent the night on a haystack under the open sky, and it was so cold that he couldn't sleep. In the neighboring villages, dogs kept barking, and the rain went on forever. Reb Moshe Ber was sure his end had come. He prayed God to spare him until the *Nilah* prayer, so that he might reach heaven purified of all sin. Later, when on the eastern horizon, the edges of clouds began to glow, while the fog grew milky white, Reb Moshe Ber was infused with new strength and once again set off for Jozefow.

He reached the Turisk circle at the very moment when the hassidim had assembled in the customary way, to take brandy and cake. A few recognized the new arrival at once, and there was great rejoicing for he had long been thought dead. They brought him hot tea. He said his prayers quickly, ate a slice of white bread with honey, gefilte fish made of fresh carp, and kreplach, and took a few glasses of brandy. Then he was led to the steam bath. Two respectable citizens accompanied him to the seventh shelf and personally whipped him with two bundles of new twigs, while the old man wept for joy.

Several times during Yom Kippur, he was at the point of fainting, but he observed the fast until it ended. Next morning the Turisk hassidim gave him new clothes and told him to study the Torah. All of them had plenty of money, since they traded with Bosnian and Hungarian soldiers, and sent flour to what had been Galicia in exchange for smuggled tobacco. It was no hardship for them to support Reb Moshe Ber. The Turisk hassidim knew who he was—a hassid who had sat at the table of no less a man than Reb Motele of Chernobel! He had actually been a guest at the famous wonder-rabbi's home!

A few weeks later, the Turisk hassidim, timber merchants, just to shame their sworn enemies, the Sandzer hassidim, collected wood and built a house for Reb Moshe Ber and married him to a spinster, a deaf and dumb village girl of about forty.

Exactly nine months later she gave birth to a son—now he had someone to say *kaddish* for him. As though it were a wedding, musicians played at the circumcision ceremony. Well-to-do housewives baked cakes and looked after the mother. The place where the banquet was held, the assembly room of the Turisk circle, smelled of cinnamon, saffron, and the women's best Sabbath dresses. Reb Moshe Ber wore a new satin caftan and a high velvet hat. He danced on the table, and for the first time, mentioned his age:

"And Abraham was a hundred years old," he recited, "when his son Isaac was born unto him. And Sarah said: God hath made me laugh so that all who hear will laugh with me."

He named the boy Isaac.

Translated by Norbert Guterman and Elaine Gottlieb

Fire

I WANT to tell you a story. It isn't from a book—it happened to me personally. I've kept it secret all these years, but I know now I'll never leave this poorhouse alive. I'll be carried straight from here to the morgue. So I want the truth known. I'd have had the rabbi and the town elders here, and got them to record it in the community book, but why embarrass my brother's children and grandchildren? Here is my story.

I come from Janow near Zomosc. The place is called Poorman's Kingdom, for obvious reasons. My father, God bless his memory, had seven children, but lost five of them. They grew up strong as oaks and then down they fell. Three boys and two girls! No one knew what was wrong. The fever got them one after the other. When Chaim Jonah, the youngest, died, my mother—may she intercede for me in heaven—went out like a candle. She wasn't ill, she just stopped eating and stayed in bed. Neighbors dropped in and asked, "Beile Rivke, what's wrong?" and she answered, "Nothing. I'm just going to die." The doctor came and she was bled; they applied cups and leeches, exorcised the evil eye, washed her with urine, but nothing worked. She shriveled up until she was nothing but a bag of bones. When she had said her Confession of Sins she called me to her side. "Your brother Lippe will make his way in the world," she said, "but you, Leibus, I pity."

Father never liked me. I don't know why. Lippe was taller than me, he took after Mother's family. He was smart in school though he didn't study. I studied, but it didn't help. What I heard went in one ear and out the other. Even so I can find my way around in the Bible. I was soon taken out of *cheder*.

My brother Lippe was, as the saying goes, the apple of Father's eye. When my brother did something wrong, Father looked the other way, but God forbid that I should make a mistake. He had a weighty hand; every time he smacked me I saw my dead grandmother. As far back as I can remember it was like that. The slightest thing and off came his belt. He beat me black and blue. It was always, "Don't go here, don't go there." In the synagogue, for example, all the other boys fooled around during the services, but if I left out a single "Amen," I got my "reward." At home I did all the work. We had a handmill, and all day long I ground buckwheat; I was also water-carrier and wood-chopper; I made the fire and cleaned the outhouse. Mother protected me while she was alive, but after she was gone, I was a stepchild. Don't think it didn't eat into me, but what could I do? My brother Lippe shoved me around too.—"Leibus, do this. Leibus, do that."— Lippe had his friends; he liked to drink; he hung around the tavern.

There was a pretty girl in our town, Havele. Her father owned a drygoods store. He was well fixed, and he had his ideas about a son-in-law. My brother had other ideas. He set his trap carefully. He paid the matchmakers not to bring her proposals. He spread a rumor that someone in her family had hanged himself. His friends helped out, and in return they got their share of brandy and poppy seed cake. Money was no problem for him. He just opened Father's drawer and took what he pleased. In the end Havele's father was beaten down, and gave consent to the marriage to Lippe.

The whole town celebrated the engagement. The bride-groom does not usually bring a dowry, but Lippe persuaded Father to give him two hundred gulden. He also got a wardrobe fit for a landlord. At the wedding there were two bands, one from Janow and one from Bilgorai. That is how he started on his way up. But it was different for the younger brother; he didn't even get a new pair of pants. Father had promised me clothes, but he put off ordering from day to day, and by the time he had bought the material it was too late to have it made up. I went to the wedding in rags. The girls laughed at me. Such was my luck.

I thought I would go the way of my other brothers and sisters. But I was not fated to die. Lippe got married; as the saying goes, he started off on the right foot. He became a successful dealer in grain. Near Janow there was a watermill belonging to Reb Israel David, son of Malka, a fine man. Is-rael David took a liking to my brother and sold him the mill for a song. I don't know why he sold it; some said that he wanted to go to the Holy Land, others that he had relatives in Hungary. Whatever the reason, shortly after selling the mill, he died.

Havele had one child after another, each prettier than the last; they were such marvels, people came just to look at them. The dowry Father had given Lippe undermined his own business; he was left without a cent. The business collapsed, as well as his strength, but if you think that my brother Lippe gave him a helping hand, you're very much mistaken. Lippe neither saw nor heard anything, and Father took his bitterness out on me. What he had against me I don't know; sometimes a man conceives such a hatred for his child. No matter what I said, it was wrong, and no matter how much I did, it was not enough.

Then Father fell ill, and everyone could see he would not last long. My brother Lippe was busy making money. I took care of Father. It was I who carried the bedpan; it was I who washed, bathed, combed him. He couldn't digest anything; he kept spitting up whatever he ate. The disease spread to his legs too, so he couldn't walk. I had to bring him everything, and whenever he saw me he looked at me as though I were dirt. Sometimes he wore me out so that I wanted to run from him to the end of the world, but how can you leave your own father? And so I suffered in silence. The final weeks were just hell: Father swearing and groaning. I have never heard more horrible curses. My brother Lippe would drop in twice a week and ask with a smile, "Well, how are you, Father? No better?" and the moment Father saw him, his eyes brightened. I have forgiven him, and may God forgive him too: does a man know what he is doing?

It took him two weeks to die and I can't begin to describe his agony. Every time he opened his eyes he stared at me in rage. After the funeral, his will was found under a pillow; I was dispossessed. Everything was left to Lippe—the house, the handmill, the cupboard, the chest of drawers, even the dishes. The town was shocked; such a will, people said, was illegal. There was even a precedent to this effect in the Talmud. It was suggested that Lippe give me the house, but he merely laughed. Instead he sold it immediately, and moved the handmill and the furniture to his own place. I was left the pillow.

This is the truth pure and simple. May I be no less pure when I come before God!

I began to work for a carpenter and I could scarcely earn a living. I slept in a shed; Lippe forgot that he had a brother. But who do you suppose said *kaddish* for Father? There was always some reason why it couldn't be Lippe: I lived in town, there weren't enough men at the mill for the service, it was too far away for him the get to *shul* on Saturday. At first they gossiped about his treatment of me, but then people began to say he must have his reasons. When a man is down, everyone likes to walk on him.

I was now no longer young and still unmarried. I had grown a beard but no one thought of a match for me. If a match-maker did come, what he offered was the dregs of the dregs. But why should I deny it, I did fall in love. The girl was the cobbler's daughter and I used to watch her emptying slops. But she became engaged to a cooper. Who wants an orphan? I was no fool; it hurt. Sometimes I couldn't sleep at night. I would toss about in my bed as if I had a fever. Why? What had I done to my father? I decided that I would stop saying *kaddish*, but a year had almost gone by. Besides how can you take revenge on the dead?

And now let me tell you what happened.

One Friday night I lay in my shed on a pile of shavings. I had worked hard; in those days one began at dawn, and the price of the candle was deducted from one's wages. I hadn't even had time to go to the bathhouse. On Fridays we got no lunch, so we should have a keener appetite for the Sabbath dinner, but at dinner the carpenter's wife always dished out less to me than to the others. Everyone else got a nice piece of fish, I got the tail. I would choke on the first mouthful of bone. The soup was watery, and my portion of meat was the chicken legs, along with some strings of muscle. It was not only that you couldn't chew it, but if you swallowed it, according to the Talmud, it weakened your memory. I didn't even get enough *challah*, and as for any of the sweets, I never got a taste. So I had gone to sleep hungry.

It was winter, and bitter cold in my shed. There was an aw-ful racket—the mice. I lay on my pile of shavings, with rags for covers, burning with rage. What I wanted was to get my hands on my brother Lippe. Havele also came into my mind; you might expect a sister-in-law to be kinder than a brother, but she had time only for herself and her little dolls. The way she dressed you would have thought she was a great lady; the few times she came to *shul* to attend a wedding, she wore a plumed hat. Wherever I went I would hear told how Lippe had bought this, Havele had bought that; their main business, it seemed, was adorning themselves. She treated herself to a skunk coat, and then to a fox fur; she paraded herself in flounces while I lay like a dog, my belly growling with hunger. I cursed them both. I prayed that God would send them plagues, and everything else I could think of. Gradually I fell asleep.

But then I awoke; it was the middle of the night and I felt that I must take revenge. It was as if some devil had seized me by the hair and shouted. "Leibus, it is time for revenge!" I got up; in the darkness I found a bag which I filled with shavings. Such things are forbidden on the Sabbath, but I had forgotten my religion: surely there was a *dybbuk* in me. I dressed quietly, took the bag with the shavings, two flints and a wick, and sneaked out. I would set fire to my brother's house, the mill, the granary, everything.

It was pitch dark out and I had a long way to go. I kept away from the town. I cut across swampy pastures, over fields and meadows. I knew that I would lose everything—this world and the next. I even thought of my mother lying in her grave: what would she say? But when you're mad you can't stop. You bite off your tongue to spite your face, as the saying goes. I wasn't even worried about running into someone I knew. I just wasn't myself.

I walked and walked, and the wind blew; the cold cut into me. I sank into snow over my knees, and climbed out of one ditch only to fall into another. As I passed by the hamlet known as "The Pines," dogs attacked me. You know how it is: when one dog barks, all the rest join in. I was pursued by a pack, and I thought I would be torn to pieces. It was a miracle that the peasants didn't wake and take me for a horse thief; they would have done away with me on the spot. I was on the verge of giving up the whole thing; I wanted to drop the bag and hurry back to bed. Or I thought of simply wandering away, but my *dybbuk* kept inciting me: "Now or never!" I trudged on and on. Wood shavings aren't heavy, but if you carry a bagful long enough you feel it. I began to sweat, but I kept on going at the risk of my life.

And now listen to this coincidence.

As I walked I suddenly saw a red glow in the sky. Could it be dawn? No, that didn't seem possible. It was early winter; the nights were long. I was very close to the mill and I walked faster. I almost ran. Well, to make a long story short, I arrived at the mill to find it on fire. Can you imagine that? I had come to set a building on fire and it was already burning. I stood as though paralyzed, with my head spinning; it seemed to me that I was losing my mind. Maybe I was: for the very next moment I threw down my bag of shavings and began to scream for help. I was about to run to the mill when I remembered Lippe and his family, and so I rushed to the house; it was a blazing inferno. It seemed they had all been overcome by smoke. Beams were burning; it was as bright as on Simchas Torah. Inside it felt like an oven, but I ran to the bedroom, smashed open a window, seized my brother, and threw him into the snow. I did the same with his wife and children. I almost choked to death but I rescued them all. No sooner had I finished, than the roof collapsed. My screams had awakened the peasants and now they came running. They revived my brother and his family. The chimney and a pile of ashes were all that was left of the house but the peasants managed to put out the fire in the mill. I caught sight of the bag of shavings and threw it into the fire. My brother and his family found shelter with some neighbors. By this time it was daylight.

My brother's first question was, "How did it happen? How come you're here?" My sister-in-law rushed at me to scratch my eyes out. "He did it! He set the fire!" The peasants also questioned me. "What devil brought you here?" I didn't know what to say. They began to club me. Just before I was battered to a pulp, my brother held up his hand. "No more, neighbors. There is a God and He'll punish him," and with that he spat in my face.

Somehow or other I managed to get home; I didn't walk, I dragged myself. Like a crippled animal I pulled myself along on all fours. A few times I paused to cool my wounds in the snow. But when I got home my real troubles began. Everyone asked, "Where were you? How come you knew your brother's house was on fire?" Then they learned that I was suspected. The man I worked for came to my shed and raised the roof when he found that one of his bags was missing. All Janow said that I had set my brother's house on fire, and on the Sabbath no less.

Things couldn't have been worse. I was in danger of being jailed, or pilloried in the synagogue yard. I didn't wait, I made myself scarce. A carter took pity on me and drove me to Zamosc that Saturday night. He carried no passengers, only freight, and he squeezed me in among the barrels. When the story of the fire reached Zamosc, I left for Lublin. There I became a carpenter and married. My wife bore me no children; I worked hard but I had no luck. My brother Lippe became a millionaire—he owned half of Janow—but I never had a line from him. His children married rabbis and wealthy businessmen. He is no longer alive—he died weighted down with riches and honors.

Until now I have told this story to no one. Who would have believed it? I even kept it a secret that I was from Janow. I always said that I was from Shebreshin. But now that I'm on my deathbed, why should I lie? What I've told is the truth, the whole whole truth. There's only one thing I don't understand and won't understand it until I'm in my grave: why did a fire have to break out in my brother's house on just that night? Some time ago it occurred to me that it was my anger that started that fire. What do you think?

"Anger won't make a house burn."

"I know. . . . Still there's that expression, 'burning anger!'"

"Oh, that's just a way of talking."

Well, when I saw that fire I forgot everything and rushed to save them. Without me they would have all been ashes. Now that I'm about to die, I want the truth known.

Translated by Norbert Guterman

The Unseen

Nathan and Temerl

THEY say that I, the evil spirit, after descending to earth in order to induce people to sin, will then ascend to heaven to accuse them. As a matter of fact, I am also the one to give the sinner the first push, but I do this so cleverly that the sin appears to be an act of virtue; thus, other infidels, unable to learn from the example, continue to sink into the abyss.

But let me tell you a story. There once lived a man in the town of Frampol who was known for his wealth and lavish ways. Named Nathan Jozefover, for he was born in Little Joze-fov, he had married a Frampol girl and settled there. Reb Nathan, at the time of this story, was sixty, perhaps a bit more. Short and broad-boned, he had, like most rich people, a large paunch. Cheeks red as wine showed between the clumps of short black beard. Over small twinkling eyes his eyebrows were thick and shaggy. All his life, he had eaten, drunk, and made merry. For breakfast, his wife served him cold chicken and raisin bread, which, like a great landowner, he washed down with a glass of mead. He had a preference for dainties such as roast squab, necks stuffed with chopped milt, pancakes with liver, egg noodles with broth, etc. The townspeople whispered that his wife, Roise-Temerl, prepared a noodle-pudding for him every day, and if he so desired made a Sabbath dinner in the middle of the week. Actually, she too liked to indulge.

Having plenty of money and no children, husband and wife apparently believed that good cheer was in order. Both of them, therefore, became fat and lazy. After their lunch, they would close the bedroom shutters and snore in their feather-beds as though it were midnight. During the winter nights, long as Jewish exile, they would get out of bed to treat them-selves to gizzard, chicken livers, and jam, washed down with beet soup or apple juice. Then, back to their canopied beds they went to resume their dreams of the next day's porridge.

Reb Nathan gave little time to his grain business, which ran itself. A large granary with two oaken doors stood behind the house he had inherited from his father-in-law. In the yard there were also a number of barns, sheds, and other buildings. Many of the old peasants in the surrounding villages would sell their grain and flax to Nathan alone, for, even though others might offer them more, they trusted Nathan's honesty. He never sent anyone away empty-handed, and sometimes even advanced money for the following year's crop. The simple peasants, in gratitude, brought him wood from the forest, while their wives picked mushrooms and berries for him. An elderly servant, widowed in her youth, looked after the house and even assisted in the business. For the entire week, with the exception of market day, Nathan did not have to lift a finger.

He enjoyed wearing fine clothes and telling yarns. In the summer, he would nap on a bed among the trees of his orchard, or read either the Bible in Yiddish, or simply a story book. He liked, on the Sabbath, to listen to the preaching of a *magid*, and occasionally to invite a poor man to his house. He had many amusements: for example, he loved to have his wife, Roise Temerl, tickle his feet, and she did this whenever he wished. It was rumored that he and his wife would bathe together in his own bathhouse, which stood in his yard. In a silk dressing gown embroidered with flowers and leaves, and wearing pompommed slippers, he would step out on his porch in the afternoon, smoking a pipe with an amber bowl. Those who passed by greeted him, and he responded in a friendly fashion. Sometimes he would stop a passing girl, ask her this and that, and then send her off with a joke. After the reading of the *Perek* on Saturday, he would sit with the women on the bench, eating nuts or pumpkin seeds, listening to gossip, and telling of his own encounters with landowners, priests, and rabbis. He had traveled widely in his youth, visiting Cracow, Brody, and Danzig.

Roise Temerl was almost the image of her husband. As the saying goes: when a husband and wife sleep on one pillow finally they have the same head. Small and plump, she had cheeks still full and red despite her age, and a tiny talkative mouth. The smattering of Hebrew, with which she just found her way through the prayer books, gave her the right to a leading role in the women's section of the Prayer House. She often led a bride to the synagogue, was sponsor at a circumcision, and occasionally collected money for a poor girl's trousseau. Although a wealthy woman, she could apply cups to the sick, and would adroitly cut out the pip of a chicken. Her skills included embroidery and knitting. She possessed numerous jewels, dresses, coats, and furs, all of which she kept in oaken chests as protection against moths and thieves.

Because of her gracious manner, she was welcomed at the butcher's, at the ritual bath, and wherever else she went. Her only regret was that she had no children. To make up for this, she gave charitable contributions and engaged a pious scholar to pray in her memory after her death. She took pleasure in a nest-egg she had managed to save over the years, kept it hidden somewhere in a bag, and now and then enjoyed counting the gold pieces. However, since Nathan gave her everything she needed, she had no idea of how to spend the money. Although he knew of her hoard, he pretended ignorance, realizing that "stolen water is sweet to drink," and did not begrudge her this harmless diversion.

II
Shifra Zirel the Servant

One day their old servant became ill and soon died. Nathan and his wife were deeply grieved, not only because they had grown so accustomed to her that she was almost a blood relative, but she had also been honest, industrious, and loyal, and it would not be easy to replace her. Nathan and Roise Temerl wept over her grave, and Nathan said the first *kaddish*. He promised that after the thirty day mourning period, he would drive to Janow to order the tombstone she deserved. Nathan, actually, did not come out a loser through her death. Having rarely spent any of her earnings, and being without a family, she had left everything to her employers.

Immediately after the funeral, Roise Temerl began to look for a new servant, but could not find any that compared to the first. The Frampol girls were not only lazy, but they could not bake and fry to Roise Temerl's satisfaction. Various widows, divorced women, and deserted wives were offered her, but none had the qualifications that Roise Temerl desired. Of

every candidate presented at her house, she would make in-
quiries on how to prepare fish, marinate borscht, bake pastry,
struddle, egg cookies, etc.; what to do when milk and borscht
sour, when a chicken is too tough, a broth too fat, a Sabbath
pudding overdone, a porridge too thick or too thin, and other
tricky questions. The bewildered girl would lose her tongue
and leave in embarrassment. Several weeks went by like this,
and the pampered Roise Temerl, who had to do all the chores,
would clearly see that it was easier to eat a meal than prepare
one.

Well, I, the Seducer, could not stand by and watch
Nathan and his wife starve; I sent them a servant, a wonder
of wonders.

A native of Zamosc, she had even worked for wealthy families in Lublin. Although at first she had refused—even if she
were paid her weight in gold—to go to an insignificant spot
like Frampol, various people had intervened, Roise Temerl had
agreed to pay a few gulden more than she had paid previously,
and the girl, Shifra Zirel, decided to take the job.

In the carriage that had to be sent to Zamosc for her and her
extensive luggage, she arrived with suitcases, baskets, and
knapsacks, like a rich bride. Well along in her twenties, she
seemed no more than eighteen or nineteen. Her hair was
plaited in two braids coiled at the sides of her head; she wore a
checkered shawl with tassels, a cretonne dress, and narrow
heeled shoes. Her chin had a wolf-like sharpness, her lips were
thin, her eyes shrewd and impudent. She wore rings in her ears
and around her throat a coral necklace. Immediately, she found
fault with the Frampol mud, the clay taste of the well water,
and the lumpy home-made bread. Served over-cooked soup by
Roise Temerl on the first day, she took a drop of it with her
spoon, made a face, and complained, "It's sour and rancid!"

She demanded a Jewish or Gentile girl as an assistant, and
Roise Temerl, after a strenuous search, found a Gentile one,
the sturdy daughter of the bath attendant. Shifra Zirel began
to give orders. She told the girl to scrub the floors, clean the
stove, sweep the cobwebs in corners, and advised Roise Temerl
to get rid of the superfluous pieces of furniture, various rickety
chairs, stools, tables, and chests. The windows were cleaned,
the dusty curtains removed, and the rooms became lighter and

more spacious. Roise Temerl and Nathan were amazed by her first meal. Even the emperor could ask for no better cook. An appetizer of calves' liver and lungs, partly fried and partly boiled, was served before the broth, and its aroma titillated their nostrils. The soup was seasoned with herbs unobtainable at Frampol, such as paprika and capers, which the new servant had apparently brought from Zamosc. Dessert was a mixture of applesauce, raisins, and apricots, flavored with cinnamon, saffron, and cloves, whose fragrance filled the house. Then, as in the wealthy homes of Lublin, she served black coffee with chicory. After lunch, Nathan and his wife wanted to nap as usual, but Shifra Zirel warned them that it was unhealthful to sleep immediately after eating, because the vapors mount from the stomach to the brain. She advised her employers to walk back and forth in the garden a few times. Nathan was brimful of good food, and the coffee had gone to his head. He reeled and kept repeating, "Well, my dear wife, isn't she a treasure of a servant?"

"I hope no one will take her away," Roise Temerl said. Knowing how envious people were, she feared the Evil Eye, or those who might offer the girl better terms.

There is no sense going into detail about the excellent dishes Shifra Zirel prepared, the babkas and macaroons she baked, the appetizers she introduced. The neighbors found Nathan's rooms and his yard unrecognizable. Shifra Zirel had whitewashed the walls, cleaned the sheds and closets, and hired a laborer to weed the garden and repair the fence and railing of the porch. Like the mistress of the house rather than its servant, she supervised everything. When Shifra Zirel, in a woolen dress and pointed shoes, went for a stroll on Saturdays, after the pre-cooked *cholent* dinner, she was stared at not only by common laborers and poor girls, but by young men and women of good families as well. Daintily holding up her skirt, she walked, her head high. Her assistant, the bathhouse attendant's daughter, followed, carrying a bag of fruit and cookies, for Jews could not carry parcels on the Sabbath. From the benches in front of their houses women observed her and shook their heads. "She's as proud as a landowner's wife!" they would comment, predicting that her stay in Frampol would be brief.

III
Temptation

One Tuesday, when Roise Temerl was in Janow visiting her sister, who was ill, Nathan ordered the Gentile girl to prepare a steam bath for him. His limbs and bones had been aching since morning, and he knew that the only remedy for this was to perspire abundantly. After putting a great deal of wood in the stove around the bricks, the girl lighted the fire, filled the vat with water, and returned to the kitchen.

When the fire had burnt itself out, Nathan undressed and then poured a bucket of water on the red hot bricks. The bathhouse filled with steam. Nathan, climbing the stairs to the high shelf where the steam was hot and dense, whipped himself with a twig broom that he had prepared previously. Usually Roise Temerl helped him with this. When he perspired she poured the buckets of water, and when she perspired he poured. After they had flogged each other with twig brooms, Roise Temerl would bathe him in a wooden tub and comb him. But this time Roise Temerl had had to go to Janow to her sick sister, and Nathan did not think it wise to wait for her return, since his sister-in-law was very old and might die and then Roise Temerl would have to stay there seven days. Never before had he taken his bath alone. The steam, as usual, soon settled. Nathan wanted to go down and pour more water on the bricks, but his legs felt heavy and he was lazy. With his belly protruding upward, he lay on his back, flogging himself with the broom, rubbing his knees and ankles, and staring at the bent beam on the smoke-blackened ceiling. Through the crack, a patch of clear sky stared in. This was the month of Elul, and Nathan was assailed by melancholy. He remembered his sister-in-law as a young woman full of life, and now she was on her deathbed. He too would not eat marchpanes nor sleep on eiderdown forever, it occurred to him, for some day he would be placed in a dark grave, his eyes covered with shards, and worms would consume the body that Roise Temerl had pampered for the nearly fifty years that she had been his wife.

Probing his soul, Nathan lay there, belly upward, when he suddenly heard the chain clank, the door creak. Looking about, he saw to his amazement, that Shifra Zirel had entered. Barefoot, with a white kerchief around her head, she was dressed only in a slip. In a choking voice, he cried out, "No!" and hastened to cover himself. Upset, and shaking his head, he beckoned her to leave, but Shifra Zirel said, "Don't be afraid, master, I won't bite you."

She poured a bucket of water over the hot bricks. A hissing noise filled the room, and white clouds of steam quickly rose, scalding Nathan's limbs. Then Shifra Zirel climbed the steps to Nathan, grabbed the twig broom, and began to flog him. He was so stunned, he became speechless. Choking, he almost rolled off the slippery shelf. Shifra Zirel, meanwhile, continued diligently to whip him and to rub him with a cake of soap she had brought. Finally, having regained his composure, he said, hoarsely, "What's the matter with you? Shame on you!"

"What's there to be ashamed about?" the servant asked airily, "I won't harm the master . . ."

For a long time she occupied herself combing and massaging him, rubbing him with soap, and drenching him with water, and Nathan was compelled to acknowledge that this devilish woman was more accomplished than Roise Temerl. Her hands, too, were smoother; they tickled his body and aroused his desire. He soon forgot that this was the month of Elul, before the Days of Awe, and told the servant to lock the wooden latch of the door. Then, in a wavering voice, he made a proposition.

"Never, uncle!" she said resolutely, pouring a bucket of water on him.

"Why not?" he asked, his neck, belly, head, all his limbs dripping.

"Because I belong to my husband."

"What husband?"

"The one I'll have some day, God willing."

"Come on, Shifra Zirel," he said, "I'll give you something— a coral necklace, or a brooch."

"You're wasting your breath," she said.

"A kiss at least!" he begged.

"A kiss will cost twenty-five coins," Shifra Zirel said.

"Groszy and threepence pieces?" Nathan asked, efficiently, and Shifra Zirel answered, "Gulden."

Nathan reflected. Twenty-five gulden was no trifle. But I, the Old Nick, reminded him that one does not live forever, and that there was no harm in leaving a few gulden less behind. Therefore, he agreed.

Bending over him, placing her arms about his neck, Shifra Zirel kissed him on the mouth. Half kiss and half bite, it cut his breath. Lust arose in him. He could not climb down, for his arms and legs were trembling, and Shifra Zirel had to help him down and even put on his dressing gown. "So that's the kind you are . . ." he murmured.

"Don't insult me, Reb Nathan," she admonished, "I'm pure."

"Pure as a pig's knuckle," Nathan thought. He opened the door for her. After a moment, glancing anxiously about to make sure he was not seen, he left also. "Imagine such a thing happening!" he murmured. "What impudence! A real whore!" He resolved never again to have anything to do with her.

IV
Troubled Nights

Nathan lay at night on his eiderdown mattress, wrapped in a silken blanket, his head propped up by three pillows, but he was robbed of sleep by my wife Lilith and her companions. He had droused off, but was awake; he began to dream something, but the vision frightened him, and he rose with a start. Someone invisible whispered something into his ear. He fancied, for a moment, that he was thirsty. Then his head felt feverish. Leaving his bed, he slipped into his slippers and dressing gown, and went to the kitchen to scoop up a mug of water. Leaning over the barrel, he slipped and almost fell in. Suddenly he realized that he craved Shifra Zirel with the craving of a young man. "What's the matter with me?" he murmured, "This can only be a trick of the devil." He started to walk to his own room, but found himself going to the little room where the servant slept. Halting at the doorway, he listened. A rustling came from behind the stove, and in the dry wood something creaked. The pale glow of a lantern flashed outside; there was a sigh. Nathan recalled that this was Elul, that God-fearing Jews rise at dawn for the *Selichot* prayers. Just as he was about to turn back, the servant opened the door and asked in an alert tone, "Who's there?"

"I am," Nathan whispered.

"What does the master wish?"

"Don't you know?"

She groaned and was silent, as though wondering what to do. Then she said, "Go back to bed, master. It's no use talking."

"But I can't sleep," Nathan complained in a tone he sometimes used with Roise Temerl, "Don't send me away!"

"Leave, master," Shifra Zirel said in an angry voice, "or I'll scream!"

"Hush. I won't force you, God forbid. I'm fond of you. I love you."

"If the master loves me then let him marry me."

"How can I? I have a wife!" Nathan said, surprised.

"Well, what of it? What do you think divorce is for?" she said and sat up.

"She's not a woman," Nathan thought, "but a demon." Frightened by her and her talk he remained in the doorway, heavy, bewildered, leaning against the jamb. The Good Spirit, who is at the height of his power during the month of Elul, reminded him of *The Measure of Righteousness*—which he had read in Yiddish—stories of pious men, tempted by landowners' wives, she-demons, whores, but who had refused to succumb to the temptation. "I'll send her away at once, tomorrow, even if I must pay her wages for a year," Nathan decided. But he said, "What's wrong with you? I've lived with my wife for almost fifty years! Why should I divorce her now?"

"Fifty years is sufficient," the brazen servant answered.

Her insolence, rather than repelling him, attracted him the more. Walking to her bed, he sat on the edge. A vile warmth arose from her. Seized by a powerful desire, he said, "How can I divorce her? She won't consent."

"You can get one without her consent," said the servant, apparently well-informed.

Blandishments and promises would not change her mind. To all Nathan's arguments, she turned a deaf ear. Day was already breaking when he returned to his bed. His bedroom walls were gray as canvas. Like a coal glowing on a heap of ashes, the sun arose in the east, casting a light, scarlet as the fire of hell. A crow, alighting on the windowsill, began to caw with its curved black beak, as though trying to announce a piece of bad news. A shudder went through Nathan's bones. He felt that he was his own master no longer, that the Evil Spirit, having seized the reins, drove him along an iniquitous path, perilous and full of obstacles.

From then on Nathan did not have a moment's respite.

While his wife, Roise Temerl, observed the mourning period for her sister in Janow, he was roused each night, and driven to Shifra Zirel, who, each time, rejected him.

Begging and imploring, he promised valuable gifts, offered a rich dowry and inclusion in his will, but nothing availed him. He vowed not to return to her, but his vow was broken each time. He spoke foolishly, in a manner unbecoming to a respectable man, and disgraced himself. When he woke her, she not only chased him away, but scolded him. In passing from his room to hers in the darkness, he would stumble against doors, cupboards, stoves, and he was covered with bruises. He ran into a slop basin and spilled it. He shattered glassware. He tried to recite a chapter of the Psalms that he knew by heart and implored God to rescue him from the net I had spread, but the holy words were distorted on his lips and his mind was confused with impure thoughts. In his bedroom there was a constant buzz and hum from the glowworms, flies, moths, and mosquitoes with which I, the Evil One, had filled it. With eyes open and ears intent, Nathan lay wide awake, listening to each rustle. Roosters crowed, frogs croaked in the swamps, crickets chirped, flashes of lightning glowed strangely. A little imp kept reminding him: Don't be a fool, Reb Nathan, she's waiting for you; she wants to see if you're a man or a mouse. And the imp hummed: Elul or no Elul, a woman's a woman, and if you don't enjoy her in this world it's too late in the next. Nathan would call Shifra Zirel and wait for her to answer. It seemed to him that he heard the patter of bare feet, that he saw the whiteness of her body or of her slip in the darkness. Finally, trembling, afire, he would rise from his bed to go to her room. But she remained stubborn. "Either I or the mistress," she would declare. "Go, master!"

And grabbing a broom from the pile of refuse, she would smack him across the back. Then Reb Nathan Jozefover, the richest man in Frampol, respected by young and old, would return defeated and whipped to his canopied bed, to toss feverishly until sunrise.

V

Forest Road

Roise Temerl, when she returned from Janow and saw her husband, was badly frightened. His face was ashen; there were bags under his eyes; his beard, which until recently had been black, was now threaded with white; his stomach had become loose, and hung like a sack. Like one dangerously ill, he could barely drag his feet along. "Woe is me, even finer things than this are put in the grave!" she exclaimed. She began to question him, but since he could not tell her the truth, he said he was suffering from headaches, heartburn, stitches, and similar ailments. Roise Temerl, though she had looked forward to seeing her husband and had hoped to enjoy herself with him, ordered a carriage and horses and told him to see a doctor in Lublin. Filling a suitcase with cookies, jams, juices, and various other refreshments, she urged him not to spare money, but to find the best of doctors and to take all the medication he prescribed. Shifra Zirel too, saw her master depart, escorting the carriage on foot as far as the bridge, and wishing him a speedy recovery.

Late at night, by the light of the full moon, while the carriage drove along a forest road and shadows ran ahead, I, the Evil Spirit, came to Reb Nathan and asked, "Where are you going?"

"Can't you see? To a doctor."

"Your ailment can't be cured by a doctor," I said.

"What shall I do then? Divorce my old wife?"

"Why not?" I said to him, "Did not Abraham drive his bondwoman, Hagar, into the wilderness, with nothing but a bottle of water, because he preferred Sarah? And later, did he not take Keturah and have six sons with her? Did not Moses, the teacher of all Jews, take, in addition to Zipporah, another wife from the land of Kush; and when Miriam, his sister, spoke against him, did she not become leprous? Know ye, Nathan, you are fated to have sons and daughters, and according to the law, you should have divorced Roise Temerl ten years after marrying her? Well, you may not leave the world without begetting children, and Heaven, therefore, has sent you Shifra Zirel to lie in your lap and become pregnant and bear healthy children, who after your death, will say *kadish* for you and will inherit your possessions. Therefore do not try to resist, Nathan, for such is the decree of Heaven, and if you do not execute it, you will be punished, you will die soon, and Roise Temerl will be a widow anyway and you will inherit hell."

Hearing these words, Nathan became frightened. Shuddering from head to foot, he said, "If so, why do I go to Lublin? I should, rather, order the driver to return to Frampol."

And I replied, "No, Nathan. Why tell your wife what you're about to do? When she learns you plan to divorce her and take the servant in her place, she will be greatly grieved, and may revenge herself on you or the servant. Rather follow the advice Shifra Zirel gave you. Get divorce papers in Lublin and place them secretly in your wife's dresses; this will make the divorce valid. Then tell her that doctors had advised you to go to Vienna for an operation since you have an internal growth. And before leaving, collect all the money and take it along with you, leaving your wife only the house and the furniture and her personal belongings. Only when you are far from home, and Shifra Zirel with you, you may inform Roise Temerl that she is a divorcee. In this way you will avoid scandal. But do not delay, Nathan, for Shifra Zirel won't tarry, and if she leaves you, you might be punished and perish and lose this world as well as the next."

I made more speeches, pious and impious, and at daybreak, when he fell asleep, I brought him Shifra Zirel, naked, and showed him the images of the children she would bear, male and female, with side whiskers and curls, and I made him eat imaginary dishes she had prepared for him: they tasted of Paradise. He awoke from these visions, famished, and consumed with desire. Approaching the city, the carriage stopped at an inn, where Nathan was served breakfast and a soft bed prepared for him. But on his palate there remained the savor of the pancake he had tasted in his dream. And on his lips he could almost feel Shifra Zirel's kisses. Overcome with longing, he put on his coat again, and told his hosts he must hurry to meet merchants.

In a back alley where I led him, he discovered a miserly scribe, who for five gulden, wrote the divorce papers and had them signed by witnesses, as required by law. Then Nathan, after purchasing numerous bottles and pills from an apothecary, returned to Frampol. He told his wife he had been examined by three doctors, that they had all found he had a tumor in his stomach, and that he must go at once to Vienna to be treated by great specialists or he would not last the year. Shaken by the story, Roise Temerl said, "What's money? Your health means far more to me." She wanted to accompany him, but Nathan reasoned with her and argued, "The trip will cost double; moreover, our business here must be looked after. No, stay here, and God willing, if everything goes well, I'll be back, we'll be happy together." To make a long story short, Roise Temerl agreed with him and stayed.

The same night, after Roise Temerl had fallen asleep, Nathan rose from bed and quietly placed the divorce papers in her trunk. He also visited Shifra Zirel in her room to inform her of what he had done. Kissing and embracing him, she promised to be a good wife and faithful mother to his children. But in her heart, jeering, she thought: You old fool, you'll pay dearly for falling in love with a whore.

And now starts the story of how I and my companions forced the old sinner, Nathan Jozefover, to become a man who sees without being seen, so that his bones would never be properly buried, which is the penalty for lechery.

VI
Nathan Returns

A year passed, Roise Temerl now had a second husband, having married a Frampol grain dealer, Moshe Mecheles, who had lost his wife at the same time as she had been divorced. Moshe Mecheles was a small red-bearded man, with heavy red eyebrows and piercing yellow eyes. He often disputed with the Frampol rabbi, put on two pairs of phylacteries while praying, and owned a water mill. He was always covered with white flour dust. He had been rich before, and after his marriage to Roise Temerl, he took over her granaries and customers and became a magnate.

Why had Roise Temerl married him? For one thing, other people intervened. Secondly, she was lonely, and thought that another husband might at least partially replace Nathan. Third, I, the Seducer, had my own reasons for wanting her married. Well, after marrying, she realized she had made a mistake. Moshe Mecheles had odd ways. He was thin, and she tried to fatten him, but he would not touch her dumplings, pancakes, and chickens. He preferred bread with garlic, potatoes in their skins, onions and radishes, and once a day, a piece of lean boiled beef. His stained caftan was never buttoned; he wore a string to hold up his trousers, refused to go to the bath Roise Temerl would heat for him, and had to be forced to change a shirt or a pair of underpants. Moreover he was rarely at home; he either traveled for business or attended community meetings. He went to sleep late, and groaned and snored in his bed. When the sun rose, so did Moshe Mecheles, humming like a bee. Although close to sixty, Roise Temerl still did not disdain what others like, but Moshe Mecheles came to her rarely, and then it was only a question of duty. The woman finally conceded that she had blundered, but what could be done? She swallowed her pride and suffered silently.

One afternoon around Elul time, when Roise Temerl went to the yard to pour out the slops, she saw a strange figure. She cried out; the basin fell from her hands, the slops spilled at her feet. Ten paces away stood Nathan, her former husband. He was dressed like a beggar, his caftan torn, a piece of rope around his loins, his shoes in shreds, and on his head only the lining of a cap. His once pink face was now yellow, and the clumps of his beard were gray; pouches hung from his eyes. From his disheveled eyebrows he stared at Roise Temerl. For a moment it occurred to her that he must have died, and this was his ghost before her. She almost called out: Pure Soul, return to your place of rest! But since this was happening in broad daylight, she soon recovered from her shock and asked in a trembling voice:

"Do my eyes deceive me?"

"No," said Nathan, "It is I."

For a long time husband and wife stood silently gazing at each other. Roise Temerl was so stunned that she could not speak. Her legs began to shake, and she had to hold on to a tree to keep from falling.

"Woe is me, what has become of you?" she cried.

"Is your husband at home?" Nathan asked.

"My husband?" she was bewildered, "No . . ."

About to ask him in, Roise Temerl remembered that according to law, she was not permitted to stay under the same roof with him. Also, she feared that the servant might recognize him. Bending, she picked up the slop basin.

"What happened?" she asked.

Haltingly, Nathan told her how he had met Shifra Zirel in Lublin, married her, and been persuaded by her to go to her relatives in Hungary. At an inn near the border, she deserted him, stealing everything, even his clothes. Since then, he had wandered all over the country, slept in poorhouses, and like a beggar, made the rounds of private homes. At first he had thought he would obtain a writ signed by one hundred rabbis, enabling him to remarry, and he had set out for Frampol. Then he had learned that Roise Temerl had married again, and he had come to beg her forgiveness.

Unable to believe her eyes, Roise Temerl kept staring at him. Leaning on his crooked stick, as a beggar might, he never lifted his eyes. From his ears and nostrils, thatches of hair protruded. Through his torn coat, she saw the sackcloth, and through a slit in it, his flesh. He seemed to have grown smaller.

"Have any of the townspeople seen you?" she asked.

"No. I came through the fields."

"Woe is me. What can I do with you now?" she exclaimed, "I am married."

"I don't want anything from you," Nathan said, "Farewell."

"Don't go!" Roise Temerl said, "Oh, how unlucky I am!"

Covering her face with her hands, she began to sob. Nathan moved aside.

"Don't mourn for me," he said, "I haven't died yet."

"I wish you had," she replied, "I'd be happier."

Well, I, the Destroyer, had not yet tried all my insidious tricks. The scale of sins and punishment was not yet balanced. Therefore, in a vigorous move, I spoke to the woman in the language of compassion, for it is known that compassion, like any other sentiment, can serve evil as well as good purposes. Roise Temerl, I said, he is your husband; you lived with him for fifty years, and you cannot repudiate him, now that he has fallen. And when she asked, "What shall I do? After all, I cannot stand here and expose myself to derision," I made a suggestion. She trembled, raised her eyes, and beckoned Nathan to follow her. Submissively, he walked behind her, like any poor visitor who does everything that the lady of the house tells him to do.

VII
The Secret of the Ruin

In the yard, behind the granary, near the bathhouse, stood a ruin in which many years before, Roise Temerl's parents had lived. Unoccupied now, its ground floor windows were boarded, but on the second floor there were still a few well preserved rooms. Pigeons perched on the roof, and swallows had nested under the gutter. A worn broom had been stuck in the chimney. Nathan had often said the building should be razed, but Roise Temerl had insisted that while she was alive her parents' home would not be demolished. The attic was littered with old rubbish and rags. Schoolboys said that a light emanated from the ruin at midnight, and that demons lived in the cellar. Roise Temerl led Nathan there now. It was not easy to enter the ruin. Weeds that pricked and burned obstructed the path. Roise Temerl's skirt caught on thorns sharp as nails. Little mole-hills were everywhere. A heavy curtain of cobwebs barred the open doorway. Roise Temerl swept them away with a rotten branch. The stairs were rickety. Her legs were heavy and she had to lean on Nathan's arm. A thick cloud of dust arose, and Nathan began to sneeze and cough.

"Where are you taking me?" he asked, bewildered.

"Don't be afraid," Roise Temerl said, "It's all right."

Leaving him in the ruin, she returned to the house. She told the servant to take the rest of the day off, and the servant did not have to be told twice. When she had gone, Roise Temerl opened the cabinets that were still filled with Nathan's clothes, took his linen from the chest, and brought everything to the ruin. Once more she left, and when she returned it was with a basket containing a meal of rice and pot roast, tripe with calves' feet, white bread, and stewed prunes. After he had gobbled his supper and licked off the prune plate, Roise Temerl drew a bucket of water from the well and told him to go to another room to wash. Night was falling, but the twilight lingered a long time. Nathan did as Roise Temerl instructed, and she could hear him splash and sigh in the next room. Then he changed his clothes. When Roise Temerl saw him, tears streamed from her eyes. The full moon that shone through the window made the room bright as daylight, and Nathan, in a clean shirt, his dressing gown embroidered with leaves and flowers, in his silken cap and velvet slippers, once again seemed his former self.

Moshe Mecheles happened to be out of town, and Roise Temerl was in no hurry. She went again to the house and returned with bedding. The bed only needed to be fitted with boards. Not wanting to light a candle, lest someone notice the glow, Roise Temerl went about in the dark, climbed to the attic with Nathan, and groped until she found some old slats for the bed. Then she placed a mattress, sheets, and pillow on it. She had even remembered to bring some jam and a box of cookies so that Nathan could refresh himself before going to sleep. Only then did she sit down on the unsteady stool to rest. Nathan sat on the edge of the bed.

After a long silence, he said, "What's the use? Tomorrow I must leave."

"Why tomorrow?" said Roise Temerl, "Rest up. There's always time to rot in the poorhouse."

Late into the night they sat, talking, murmuring. Roise Temerl cried and stopped crying, began again and was calm again. She insisted that Nathan confess everything to her, without omitting details, and he told her again how he had met Shifra Zirel, how they had married, how she had persuaded him to go with her to Pressburg, and how she had spent the night full of sweet talk and love play with him at an inn. And at daybreak, when he fell asleep, she had arisen and untied the bag from his neck. He also told Roise Temerl how he had been forced to discard all shame, to sleep in beggars' dormitories, and eat at strangers' tables. Although his story angered her, and she called him blockhead, stupid fool, ass, idiot, her heart almost dissolved with pity.

"What is there to do now?" she kept murmuring to herself, over and over again. And I, the Evil Spirit, answered: Don't let him go. The beggar's life is not for him. He might die of grief or shame. And when Roise Temerl argued that because she was a married woman she had no right to stay with him, I said: Can the twelve lines of a bill of divorcement separate two souls who have been fused by fifty years of common life? Can a brother and sister be transformed by law into strangers? Hasn't Nathan become part of you? Don't you see him every night in your dreams? Isn't all your fortune the result of his industry and effort? And what is Moshe Mecheles? A stranger, a lout. Wouldn't it be better to fry with Nathan in hell, rather than serve as Moshe Mecheles' footstool in Heaven? I also recalled to her an incident in a story book, where a landowner, whose wife had eloped with a bear tamer, later forgave her and took her back to his manor.

When the clock in the Frampol church chimed eleven, Roise Temerl returned home. In her luxurious, canopied bed, she tossed, like one in a fever. For a long time, Nathan stood beside his window, looking out. The Elul sky was full of stars. The owl on the roof of the synagogue screeched with a human voice. The caterwauling of cats reminded him of women in labor. Crickets chirped, and unseen saws seemed to be buzzing through tree trunks. The neighing of horses that had grazed all night came through the fields with the calls of shepherds. Nathan, because he stood on an upper floor, could see the whole little town at a glance, the synagogue, the church, the slaughterhouse, the public bathhouse, the market, and the side streets where Gentiles lived. He recognized each shed, shack, and board in his own yard. A goat stripped some bark from a tree. A field mouse left the granary to return to its nest. Nathan watched for a long time. Everything about him was familiar and yet strange, real and ghostly, as though he were no longer among the living—only his spirit floated there. He recalled that there was a Hebrew phrase which applied to him, but he could not remember it exactly. Finally, after trying for a long time, he remembered: *one who sees without being seen.*

VIII

One Who Sees Without Being Seen

In Frampol the rumor spread that Roise Temerl, having quarreled with her maid, had dismissed her in the middle of her term. This surprised the housewives, because the girl was reputedly industrious and honest. Actually, Roise Temerl had dismissed the girl to keep her from discovering that Nathan lived in the ruin. As always, when I seduce sinners, I persuaded the couple that all this was provisional, that Nathan would stay only until he had recovered from his wandering. But I made certain that Roise Temerl welcomed the presence of her hidden guest and that Nathan enjoyed being where he was. Even though they discussed their future separation each time they were together, Roise Temerl gave Nathan's quarters an air of permanency. She resumed her cooking and frying for him, and once more brought him her tasty dishes. After a few days, Nathan's appearance changed remarkably. From pastries and puddings, his face became pink again, and once more, like that of a man of wealth, his paunch protruded. Once more he wore embroidered shirts, velvet slippers, silken dressing gowns, and carried batiste handkerchiefs. To keep him from being bored by his idleness, Roise Temerl brought him a Bible in Yiddish, a copy of the *Inheritance of the Deer*, and numerous story books. She even managed to procure some tobacco for his pipe, for he enjoyed smoking one, and she brought from the cellar bottles of wine and mead that Nathan had stored for years. The divorced couple had banquets in the ruin.

I made certain that Moshe Mecheles was seldom at home; I sent him to all kinds of fairs, and even recommended him as arbiter in disputes. It did not take long for the ruin behind the granary to become Roise Temerl's only comfort. Just as a miser's thoughts constantly dwell on the treasure he has buried far from sight, so Roise Temerl thought only of the ruin and the secret in her heart. Sometimes she thought that Nathan had died and she had magically resurrected him for a while; at other times, she imagined the whole thing a dream. Whenever she looked out of her window at the moss-covered roof of the ruin, she thought: No! It's inconceivable for Nathan to be there; I must be deluded. And immediately, she had to fly there, up the rickety stairs, to be met half-way by Nathan in person, with his familiar smile and his pleasant odor. "Nathan, you're here?" she would ask, and he would respond, "Yes, Roise Temerl, I'm here and waiting for you."

"Have you missed me?" she would ask, and he would answer:

"Of course. When I hear your step, it's a holiday for me."

"Nathan, Nathan," she would continue, "Would you have believed a year ago that it would end like this?"

And he would murmur, "No, Roise Temerl, it is like a bad dream."

"Oh Nathan, we have already lost this world, and I'm afraid we'll lose the other also," Roise Temerl said.

And he replied, "Well, that's too bad, but hell too is for people, not for dogs."

Since Moshe Mecheles belonged to the Hassidim, I, Old Rebel, sent him to spend the Days of Awe with his rabbi. Alone, Roise Temerl bought Nathan a prayer shawl, a white robe, a prayer book, and prepared a holiday meal for him. Since on Rosh Hashona, there is no moon, he ate the evening meal in darkness, blindly dunked a slice of bread in honey, and tasted an apple, a carrot, the head of a carp, and offered a blessing for the first fruit, over a pomegranate. He stood praying during the day in his robe and prayer shawl. The sound of the ram's horn came faintly to his ears from the synagogue. At the intermission between the prayers, Roise Temerl visited him in her golden dress, her white, satin-lined coat, and the shawl embroidered with silver threads, to wish him a happy new year. The golden chain he had given her for their betrothal hung around her neck. A brooch he had brought to her from Danzig quivered on her breast, and from her wrist dangled a bracelet he had bought her a Brody. She exuded an aroma of honey cake and the women's section of the synagogue. On the evening before the Day of Atonement, Roise Temerl brought him a white rooster as a sacrificial victim and prepared for him the meal to be eaten before commencing the fast. Also, she gave the synagogue a wax candle for his soul. Before leaving for the *Minchah* prayer at the synagogue, she came to bid him good-by, and she began to lament so loudly that Nathan feared she would be heard. Falling into his arms, she clung to him and would not be torn away. She drenched his face with tears and howled as though possessed. "Nathan, Nathan," she wailed, "may we have no more unhappiness," and other things that are said when a member of a family dies, repeating them many times. Fearing she might faint and fall, Nathan had to escort her downstairs. Then, standing at the window, he watched the people of Frampol on their way to the synagogue. The women walked quickly and vigorously, as though hurrying to pray for someone on his deathbed; they held up their skirts, and when two of them met, they fell into each other's arms and swayed back and forth as if in some mysterious struggle. Wives of prominent citizens knocked at doors of poor people and begged to be forgiven. Mothers, whose children were ill, ran with arms outstretched, as though chasing someone, crying like madwomen. Elderly men, before leaving home, removed their shoes, put on white robes, prayer shawls, and white skull caps. In the synagogue yard, the poor sat with alms' boxes on benches. A reddish glow spread over the roofs, reflecting in the window panes, and illuminating pale faces. In the west, the sun grew enormous; clouds around it caught fire, until half the sky was suffused with flames. Nathan recalled the River of Fire, in which all souls must cleanse themselves. The sun sank soon below the horizon. Girls, dressed in white, came outside and carefully closed shutters. Little flames played on the high windows of the synagogue, and inside, the entire building seemed to be one great flicker. A muted hum arose from it, and bursts of sobbing. Removing his shoes, Nathan wrapped himself in his shawl and robe. Half reading and half remembering, he chanted the words of Kol Nidre, the song that is recited not only by the living but by the dead in their graves. What was he, Nathan Jozefover, but a dead man, who instead of resting in his grave, wandered about in a world that did not exist?

IX

Footprints in the Snow

The High Holidays were over. Winter had come. But Nathan was still in the ruin. It could not be heated, not only because the stove had been dismantled, but because smoke, coming from the chimney, would make people suspicious. To keep Nathan from freezing, Roise Temerl provided him with warm clothes and a coal pot. At night he covered himself with two feather quilts. During the day he wore his fox fur and had felt boots on his feet. Roise Temerl also brought him a little barrel of spirits with a straw in it, which he sipped each time he felt cold, while eating a piece of dried mutton. From the rich food with which Roise Temerl plied him, he grew fat and heavy. In the evenings he stood at the window watching with curiosity the women who went to the ritual bath. On market days he never left the window. Carts drove into the yard and peasants unloaded sacks of grain. Moshe Mecheles, in a cotton padded jacket, ran back and forth, crying out hoarsely. Although it pained Nathan to think that this ridiculous fellow disposed of his possessions and lay with his wife, Moshe Mecheles' appearance made him laugh, as though the whole thing were a kind of prank that he, Nathan, had played on his competitor. Sometime he felt like calling to him: Hey, there, Moshe Mecheles! while throwing him a bit of plaster or a bone.

As long as there was no snow, Nathan had everything he needed. Roise Temerl visited him often. At night Nathan would go out for a walk on a path that led to the river. But one night a great deal of snow fell, and the next day Roise Temerl did not visit him, for she was afraid someone might notice her tracks in the snow. Nor could Nathan go out to satisfy his natural needs. For two days he had nothing warm to eat, and the water in the pail turned to ice. On the third day Roise Temerl hired a peasant to clear the snow between the house and the granary and she also told him to clear the snow between the granary and the ruin. Moshe Mecheles, when he came home was surprised and asked, "Why?", but she changed the subject, and since he suspected nothing, he soon forgot about it.

Nathan's life, from then on, became increasingly difficult. After each new snowfall, Roise Temerl cleared the path with a shovel. To keep her neighbors from seeing what went on in the yard, she had the fence repaired. And as a pretext for going to the ruin, she had a ditch for refuse dug close to it. Whenever she saw Nathan, he said it was time for him to take his bundle and leave, but Roise Temerl prevailed on him to wait. "Where will you go?" she asked. "You might, God forbid, drop from exhaustion." According to the almanac, she argued, the winter would be a mild one, and summer would begin early, weeks before Purim, and he only had to get through half the month of Kislev, besides Teveth and Shevat. She told him other things. At times, they did not even speak, but sat silently, holding hands and weeping. Both of them were actually losing strength each day. Nathan grew fatter, more blown up; his belly was full of wind; his legs seemed leaden; and his sight was dimming. He could no longer read his story books. Roise Temerl grew thin, like a consumptive, lost her appetite, and could not sleep. Some nights she lay awake, sobbing. And when Moshe Mecheles asked her why, she said it was because she had no children to pray for her after she was gone.

One day a downpour washed away the snow. Since Roise Temerl had not visited the ruin for two days, Nathan expected her to arrive at any moment. He had no food left; only a bit of brandy remained at the bottom of the barrel. For hours on end he stood waiting for her at the window, which was misted over with frost, but she did not come. The night was pitch black and icy. Dogs barked, a wind blew. The walls of the ruin shook; a whistling sound ran through the chimney, and the eaves rattled on the roof. In Nathan's house, now the house of Moshe Mecheles, several lamps seemed to have been lighted; it seemed extraordinarily bright, and the light made the surrounding darkness thicker. Nathan thought he heard the rolling of wheels, as though a carriage had driven to the house. In the darkness, someone drew water from the well, and someone poured out the slops. The night wore on, but despite the late hour, the shutters remained open. Seeing shadows run back and forth, Nathan thought important visitors might have come and were being treated to a banquet. He remained staring into the night until his knees grew weak, and with his last bit of strength, he dragged himself to his bed and fell into a deep sleep.

The cold awoke him early next morning. With stiff limbs he arose and barely propelled himself to the window. More snow had fallen during the night, and a heavy frost had set in. To his amazement, Nathan saw a group of men and women standing around his house. He wondered, anxiously, what was going on. But he did not have to wonder long, for suddenly the door swung open, and four men carried out a coffin hearse covered with a black cloth. "Moshe Mecheles is dead!" Nathan thought. But then he saw Moshe Mecheles following the coffin. It was not he, but Roise Temerl who had died.

Nathan could not weep. It was as though the cold had frozen his tears. Trembling and shaking, he watched the men carrying the coffin, watched the beadle rattling his alms box and the mourners wading through deep snowdrifts. The sky, pale as linen, hung low, meeting the blanketed earth. As though drifting on a flood, the trees in the fields seemed to be afloat in whiteness. From his window, Nathan could see all the way to the cemetery. The coffin moved up and down; the crowd, following it, thinned out and at times vanished entirely, seemed to sink into the ground and then emerge again. Nathan fancied for a moment that the cortege had stopped and no longer advanced, and then, that the people, as well as the corpse, were moving backward. The cortege grew gradually smaller, until it became a black dot. Because the dot ceased to move, Nathan realized that the pall bearers had reached the cemetery, and that he was watching his faithful wife being buried. With the remaining brandy, he washed his hands, for the water in his pail had turned to ice, and he began to murmur the prayer for the dead.

X
Two Faces

Nathan had intended to pack his things and leave during the night, but I, the Chief of the devils, prevented him from carrying out his plan. Before sunrise he was seized with powerful stomach cramps; his head grew hot and his knees so weak that he could not walk. His shoes had grown brittle; he could not put them on; and his legs had become fat. The Good Spirit counseled him to call for help, to shout until people heard and came to rescue him, because no man may cause his own death, but I said to him: Do you remember the words of King David: "Let me rather fall into God's hands, than into the hands of people?" You don't want Moshe Mecheles and his henchmen to have the satisfaction of revenging themselves on you and jeering. Rather die like a dog. In short, he listened to me, first, because he was proud, and second, because he was not fated to be buried according to law.

Gathering together his last remnants of strength, he pushed his bed to the window, to lie there and watch. He fell asleep early and awoke. There was day, and then night. Sometimes he heard cries in the yard. At other times he thought someone called him by name. His head, he fancied, had grown monstrously large and burdensome, like a millstone carried on his neck. His fingers were wooden, his tongue hard; it seemed bigger than the space it occupied. My helpers, goblins, appeared to him in dreams. They screamed, whistled, kindled fires, walked on stilts, and carried on like Purim players. He dreamed of floods, then of fires, imagined the world had been destroyed, and then that he hovered in the void with bats' wings. In his dreams he also saw pancakes, dumplings, broad noodles with cheese, and when he awoke his stomach was as full as though he had actually eaten; he belched and sighed, and touched his belly that was empty and aching all over.

Once, sitting up, he looked out of the window, and saw to his surprise that people were walking backward, and marveled at this. Soon he saw other extraordinary things. Among those who passed, he recognized men who had long been dead. "Do my eyes deceive me?" he wondered, "Or has Messiah come, and has he resurrected the dead?" The more he looked the more astonished he became. Entire generations passed through the town, men and women with packs on their shoulders and staffs in their hands. He recognized, among them, his father and grandfather, his grandmothers and great-aunts. He watched workers build the Frampol synagogue. They carried bricks, sawed wood, mixed plaster, nailed on eaves. School-boys stood about, staring upward and calling a strange word he could not understand, like something in a foreign tongue. As in a dance around the Torah, two storks circled the building. Then the building and builders vanished, and he saw a group of people, barefooted, bearded, wild-eyed, with crosses in their hands, lead a Jew to the gallows. Though the black-bearded young man cried heart-rendingly, they dragged him on, tied in ropes. Bells were ringing; the people in the streets ran away and hid. It was midday, but it grew dark as the day of an eclipse of the sun. Finally, the young man cried out: "Shema Yisroel, the Lord our God, the Lord is One," and was left hanging, his tongue lolling out. His legs swayed for a long time, and hosts of crows flew overhead, cawing hoarsely.

On his last night, Nathan dreamed that Roise Temerl and Shifra Zirel were one woman with two faces. He was overjoyed at her appearance. "Why have I not noticed this before?" he wondered. "Why did I have to go through this trouble and anxiety?" He kissed the two-faced female, and she returned his kisses with her doubled lips, pressing against him her two pairs of breasts. He spoke words of love to her, and she responded in two voices. In her four arms and two bosoms, all his questions were answered. There was no longer life and death, here nor there, beginning nor end. "The truth is twofold," Nathan exclaimed, "This is the mystery of all mysteries!"

Without a last confession of his sins, Nathan died that night. I at once transported his soul to the nether abyss. He still wanders to this day in desolate spaces, and has not yet been granted admittance to hell. Moshe Mecheles married again, a young woman this time. She made him pay dearly, soon inherited his fortune, and squandered it. Shifra Zirel became a harlot in Pressburg and died in the poorhouse. The ruin still stands as before, and Nathan's bones still lie there. And, who can tell, perhaps another man, who sees without being seen, is hiding in it.

Translated by Norbert Guterman and Elaine Gottlieb

THE SPINOZA
OF MARKET STREET

Contents

The Spinoza of Market Street

D R. NAHUM FISCHELSON paced back and forth in his garret room in Market Street, Warsaw. Dr. Fischelson was a short, hunched man with a grayish beard, and was quite bald except for a few wisps of hair remaining at the nape of the neck. His nose was as crooked as a beak and his eyes were large, dark, and fluttering like those of some huge bird. It was a hot summer evening, but Dr. Fischelson wore a black coat which reached to his knees, and he had on a stiff collar and a bow tie. From the door he paced slowly to the dormer window set high in the slanting room and back again. One had to mount several steps to look out. A candle in a brass holder was burning on the table and a variety of insects buzzed around the flame. Now and again one of the creatures would fly too close to the fire and sear its wings, or one would ignite and glow on the wick for an instant. At such moments Dr. Fischelson grimaced. His wrinkled face would twitch and beneath his disheveled moustache he would bite his lips. Finally he took a handkerchief from his pocket and waved it at the insects.

"Away from there, fools and imbeciles," he scolded. "You won't get warm here; you'll only burn yourself."

The insects scattered but a second later returned and once more circled the trembling flame. Dr. Fischelson wiped the sweat from his wrinkled forehead and sighed, "Like men they desire nothing but the pleasure of the moment." On the table lay an open book written in Latin, and on its broad-margined pages were notes and comments printed in small letters by Dr. Fischelson. The book was Spinoza's *Ethics* and Dr. Fischelson had been studying it for the last thirty years. He knew every proposition, every proof, every corollary, every note by heart. When he wanted to find a particular passage, he generally opened to the place immediately without having to search for it. But, nevertheless, he continued to study the *Ethics* for hours every day with a magnifying glass in his bony hand, murmuring and nodding his head in agreement. The truth was that the more Dr. Fischelson studied, the more puzzling sentences, unclear passages, and cryptic remarks he found. Each sentence contained hints unfathomed by any of the students of Spinoza. Actually the philosopher had anticipated all of the criticisms of pure reason made by Kant and his followers. Dr. Fischelson was writing a commentary on the *Ethics*. He had drawers full of notes and drafts, but it didn't seem that he would ever be able to complete his work. The stomach ailment which had plagued him for years was growing worse from day to day. Now he would get pains in his stomach after only a few mouthfuls of oatmeal. "God in Heaven, it's difficult, very difficult," he would say to himself using the same intonation as had his father, the late Rabbi of Tishevitz. "It's very, very hard."

Dr. Fischelson was not afraid of dying. To begin with, he was no longer a young man. Secondly, it is stated in the fourth part of the *Ethics* that "a free man thinks of nothing less than of death and his wisdom is a meditation not of death, but of life." Thirdly, it is also said that "the human mind cannot be absolutely destroyed with the human body but there is some part of it that remains eternal." And yet Dr. Fischelson's ulcer (or perhaps it was a cancer) continued to bother him. His tongue was always coated. He belched frequently and emitted a different foul-smelling gas each time. He suffered from heartburn and cramps. At times he felt like vomiting and at other times he was hungry for garlic, onions, and fried foods. He had long ago discarded the medicines prescribed for him by the doctors and had sought his own remedies. He found it beneficial to take grated radish after meals and lie on his bed, belly down, with his head hanging over the side. But these home remedies offered only temporary relief. Some of the doctors he consulted insisted there was nothing the matter with him. "It's just nerves," they told him. "You could live to be a hundred."

But on this particular hot summer night, Dr. Fischelson felt his strength ebbing. His knees were shaky, his pulse weak. He sat down to read and his vision blurred. The letters on the page turned from green to gold. The lines became waved and jumped over each other, leaving white gaps as if the text had disappeared in some mysterious way. The heat was unbearable, flowing down directly from the tin roof; Dr. Fischelson felt he was inside of an oven. Several times he climbed the four steps to the window and thrust his head out into the cool of the evening breeze. He would remain in that position for so long his knees would become wobbly. "Oh it's a fine breeze," he would murmur, "really delightful," and he would recall that according to Spinoza, morality and happiness were identical, and that the most moral deed a man could perform was to indulge in some pleasure which was not contrary to reason.

II

Dr. Fischelson, standing on the top step at the window and looking out, could see into two worlds. Above him were the heavens, thickly strewn with stars. Dr. Fischelson had never seriously studied astronomy but he could differentiate between the planets, those bodies which like the earth, revolve around the sun, and the fixed stars, themselves distant suns, whose light reaches us a hundred or even a thousand years later. He recognized the constellations which mark the path of the earth in space and that nebulous sash, the Milky Way. Dr. Fischelson owned a small telescope he had bought in Switzerland where he had studied and he particularly enjoyed looking at the moon through it. He could clearly make out on the moon's surface the volcanoes bathed in sunlight and the dark, shadowy craters. He never wearied of gazing at these cracks and crevasses. To him they seemed both near and distant, both substantial and insubstantial. Now and then he would see a shooting star trace a wide arc across the sky and disappear, leaving a fiery trail behind it. Dr. Fischelson would know then that a meteorite had reached our atmosphere, and perhaps some unburned fragment of it had fallen into the ocean or had landed in the desert or perhaps even in some inhabited region. Slowly the stars which had appeared from behind Dr. Fischelson's roof rose until they were shining above the house across the street. Yes, when Dr. Fischelson looked up into the heavens, he became aware of that infinite extension which is, according to Spinoza, one of God's attributes. It comforted Dr. Fischelson to think that although he was only a weak, puny man, a changing mode of the absolutely infinite Substance, he was nevertheless a part of the cosmos, made of the same matter as the celestial bodies; to the extent that he was a part of the Godhead, he knew he could not be destroyed. In such moments, Dr. Fischelson experienced the *Amor Dei Intellectualis* which is, according to the philosopher of Amsterdam, the highest perfection of the mind. Dr. Fischelson breathed deeply, lifted his head as high as his stiff collar permitted and actually felt he was whirling in company with the earth, the sun, the stars of the Milky Way, and the infinite host of galaxies known only to infinite thought. His legs became light and weightless and he grasped the window frame with both hands as if afraid he would lose his footing and fly out into eternity.

When Dr. Fischelson tired of observing the sky, his glance dropped to Market Street below. He could see a long strip extending from Yanash's market to Iron Street with the gas lamps lining it merged into a string of fiery dots. Smoke was issuing from the chimneys on the black, tin roofs; the bakers were heating their ovens, and here and there sparks mingled with the black smoke. The street never looked so noisy and crowded as on a summer evening. Thieves, prostitutes, gamblers, and fences loafed in the square which looked from above like a pretzel covered with poppy seeds. The young men laughed coarsely and the girls shrieked. A peddler with a keg of lemonade on his back pierced the general din with his intermittent cries. A watermelon vendor shouted in a savage voice, and the long knife which he used for cutting the fruit dripped with the blood-like juice. Now and again the street became even more agitated. Fire engines, their heavy wheels clanging, sped by; they were drawn by sturdy black horses which had to be tightly curbed to prevent them from running wild. Next came an ambulance, its siren screaming. Then some thugs had a fight among themselves and the police had to be called. A passerby was robbed and ran about shouting for help. Some wagons loaded with firewood sought to get through into the courtyards where the bakeries were located but the horses could not lift the wheels over the steep curbs and the drivers berated the animals and lashed them with their whips. Sparks rose from the clanging hoofs. It was now long after seven, which was the prescribed closing time for stores, but actually business had only begun. Customers were led in stealthily through back doors. The Russian policemen on the street, having been paid off, noticed nothing of this. Merchants continued to hawk their wares, each seeking to out-shout the others.

"Gold, gold, gold," a woman who dealt in rotten oranges shrieked.

"Sugar, sugar, sugar," croaked a dealer of overripe plums.

"Heads, heads, heads," a boy who sold fishheads roared.

Through the window of a *Chassidic* study house across the way, Dr. Fischelson could see boys with long sidelocks swaying over holy volumes, grimacing and studying aloud in sing-song voices. Butchers, porters, and fruit dealers were drinking beer in the tavern below. Vapor drifted from the tavern's open door like steam from a bathhouse, and there was the sound of loud music. Outside of the tavern, streetwalkers snatched at drunken soldiers and at workers on their way home from the factories. Some of the men carried bundles of wood on their shoulders, reminding Dr. Fischelson of the wicked who are condemned to kindle their own fires in Hell. Husky record players poured out their raspings through open windows. The liturgy of the high holidays alternated with vulgar vaudeville songs.

Dr. Fischelson peered into the half-lit bedlam and cocked his ears. He knew that the behavior of this rabble was the very antithesis of reason. These people were immersed in the vainest of passions, were drunk with emotions, and, according to Spinoza, emotion was never good. Instead of the pleasure they ran after, all they succeeded in obtaining was disease and prison, shame and the suffering that resulted from ignorance. Even the cats which loitered on the roofs here seemed more savage and passionate than those in other parts of the town. They caterwauled with the voices of women in labor, and like demons scampered up walls and leaped onto eaves and bal-conies. One of the toms paused at Dr. Fischelson's window and let out a howl which made Dr. Fischelson shudder. The doctor stepped from the window and, picking up a broom, brandished it in front of the black beast's glowing, green eyes. "Scat, begone, you ignorant savage!"—and he rapped the broom handle against the roof until the tom ran off.

When Dr. Fischelson had returned to Warsaw from Zurich where he had studied philosophy, a great future had been predicted for him. His friends had known that he was writing an important book on Spinoza. A Jewish Polish journal had invited him to be a contributor; he had been a frequent guest at several wealthy households and he had been made head librarian at the Warsaw synagogue. Although even then he had been considered an old bachelor, the matchmakers had proposed several rich girls for him. But Dr. Fischelson had not taken advantage of these opportunities. He had wanted to be as independent as Spinoza himself. And he had been. But because of his heretical ideas he had come into conflict with the rabbi and had had to resign his post as librarian. For years after that, he had supported himself by giving private lessons in Hebrew and German. Then, when he had become sick, the Berlin Jewish community had voted him a subsidy of five hundred marks a year. This had been made possible through the intervention of the famous Dr. Hildesheimer with whom he corresponded about philosophy. In order to get by on so small a pension, Dr. Fischelson had moved into the attic room and had begun cooking his own meals on a kerosene stove. He had a cupboard which had many drawers, and each drawer was labelled with the food it contained—buckwheat, rice, barley, onions, carrots, potatoes, mushrooms. Once a week Dr. Fischelson put on his widebrimmed black hat, took a basket in one hand and Spinoza's *Ethics* in the other, and went off to the market for his provisions. While he was waiting to be served, he would open the *Ethics*. The merchants knew him and would motion him to their stalls.

"A fine piece of cheese, Doctor—just melts in your mouth."

"Fresh mushrooms, Doctor, straight from the woods."

"Make way for the Doctor, ladies," the butcher would shout. "Please don't block the entrance."

During the early years of his sickness, Dr. Fischelson had still gone in the evening to a café which was frequented by Hebrew teachers and other intellectuals. It had been his habit to sit there and play chess while drinking a half a glass of black coffee. Sometimes he would stop at the bookstores on Holy

Cross Street where all sorts of old books and magazines could be purchased cheap. On one occasion a former pupil of his had arranged to meet him at a restaurant one evening. When Dr. Fischelson arrived, he had been surprised to find a group of friends and admirers who forced him to sit at the head of the table while they made speeches about him. But these were things that had happened long ago. Now people were no longer interested in him. He had isolated himself completely and had become a forgotten man. The events of 1905 when the boys of Market Street had begun to organize strikes, throw bombs at police stations, and shoot strike breakers so that the stores were closed even on weekdays had greatly increased his isolation. He began to despise everything associated with the modern Jew—Zionism, socialism, anarchism. The young men in question seemed to him nothing but an ignorant rabble intent on destroying society, society without which no reasonable existence was possible. He still read a Hebrew magazine occasionally, but he felt contempt for modern Hebrew which had no roots in the Bible or the Mishnah. The spelling of Polish words had changed also. Dr. Fischelson concluded that even the so-called spiritual men had abandoned reason and were doing their utmost to pander to the mob. Now and again he still visited a library and browsed through some of the modern histories of philosophy, but he found that the professors did not understand Spinoza, quoted him incorrectly, attributed their own muddled ideas to the philosopher. Although Dr. Fischelson was well aware that anger was an emotion unworthy of those who walk the path of reason, he would become furious, and would quickly close the book and push it from him. "Idiots," he would mutter, "asses, upstarts." And he would vow never again to look at modern philosophy.

IV

Every three months a special mailman who only delivered money orders brought Dr. Fischelson eighty rubles. He expected his quarterly allotment at the beginning of July but as day after day passed and the tall man with the blond moustache and the shiny buttons did not appear, the Doctor grew anxious. He had scarcely a groshen left. Who knows—possibly the Berlin Community had rescinded his subsidy; perhaps Dr. Hildesheimer had died, God forbid; the post office might have made a mistake. Every event has its cause, Dr. Fischelson knew. All was determined, all necessary, and a man of reason had no right to worry. Nevertheless, worry invaded his brain, and buzzed about like the flies. If the worst came to the worst, it occurred to him, he could commit suicide, but then he remembered that Spinoza did not approve of suicide and compared those who took their own lives to the insane.

One day when Dr. Fischelson went out to the store to purchase a composition book, he heard people talking about war. In Serbia somewhere, an Austrian Prince had been shot and the Austrians had delivered an ultimatum to the Serbs. The owner of the store, a young man with a yellow beard and shifty yellow eyes, announced, "We are about to have a small war," and he advised Dr. Fischelson to store up food because in the near future there was likely to be a shortage.

Everything happened so quickly. Dr. Fischelson had not even decided whether it was worthwhile to spend four groschen on a newspaper, and already posters had been hung up announcing mobilization. Men were to be seen walking on the street with round, metal tags on their lapels, a sign that they were being drafted. They were followed by their crying wives. One Monday when Dr. Fischelson descended to the street to buy some food with his last kopecks, he found the stores closed. The owners and their wives stood outside and explained that merchandise was unobtainable. But certain special customers were pulled to one side and let in through back doors. On the street all was confusion. Policemen with swords unsheathed could be seen riding on horseback. A large crowd had gathered around the tavern where, at the command of the Tsar, the tavern's stock of whiskey was being poured into the gutter.

Dr. Fischelson went to his old café. Perhaps he would find some acquaintances there who would advise him. But he did not come across a single person he knew. He decided, then, to visit the rabbi of the synagogue where he had once been librarian, but the sexton with the six-sided skull cap informed him that the rabbi and his family had gone off to the spas. Dr. Fischelson had other old friends in town but he found no one at home. His feet ached from so much walking; black and green spots appeared before his eyes and he felt faint. He stopped and waited for the giddiness to pass. The passers-by jostled him. A dark-eyed high school girl tried to give him a coin. Although the war had just started, soldiers eight abreast were marching in full battle dress—the men were covered with dust and were sunburnt. Canteens were strapped to their sides and they wore rows of bullets across their chests. The bayonets on their rifles gleamed with a cold, green light. They sang with mournful voices. Along with the men came cannons, each pulled by eight horses; their blind muzzles breathed gloomy terror. Dr. Fischelson felt nauseous. His stomach ached; his intestines seemed about to turn themselves inside out. Cold sweat appeared on his face.

"I'm dying," he thought. "This is the end." Nevertheless, he did manage to drag himself home where he lay down on the iron cot and remained, panting and gasping. He must have dozed off because he imagined that he was in his home town, Tishevitz. He had a sore throat and his mother was busy wrapping a stocking stuffed with hot salt around his neck. He could hear talk going on in the house; something about a candle and about how a frog had bitten him. He wanted to go out into the street but they wouldn't let him because a Catholic procession was passing by. Men in long robes, holding double edged axes in their hands, were intoning in Latin as they sprinkled holy water. Crosses gleamed; sacred pictures waved in the air. There was an odor of incense and corpses. Suddenly the sky turned a burning red and the whole world started to burn. Bells were ringing; people rushed madly about. Flocks of birds flew overhead, screeching. Dr. Fischelson awoke with a start. His body was covered with sweat and his throat was now actually sore. He tried to meditate about his extraordinary dream, to find its rational connection with what was happening to him and to comprehend it *sub specie eternitatis*, but none of it made sense. "Alas, the brain is a receptacle for nonsense," Dr. Fischelson thought. "This earth belongs to the mad."

And he once more closed his eyes; once more he dozed; once more he dreamed.

V

The eternal laws, apparently, had not yet ordained Dr. Fischelson's end.

There was a door to the left of Dr. Fischelson's attic room which opened off a dark corridor, cluttered with boxes and baskets, in which the odor of fried onions and laundry soap was always present. Behind this door lived a spinster whom the neighbors called Black Dobbe. Dobbe was tall and lean, and as black as a baker's shovel. She had a broken nose and there was a mustache on her upper lip. She spoke with the hoarse voice of a man and she wore men's shoes. For years Black Dobbe had sold breads, rolls, and bagels which she had bought from the baker at the gate of the house. But one day she and the baker had quarreled and she had moved her business to the market place and now she dealt in what were called "wrinklers" which was a synonym for cracked eggs. Black Dobbe had no luck with men. Twice she had been engaged to baker's apprentices but in both instances they had returned the engagement contract to her. Some time afterwards she had received an engagement contract from an old man, a glazier who claimed that he was divorced, but it had later come to light that he still had a wife. Black Dobbe had a cousin in America, a shoemaker, and repeatedly she boasted that this cousin was sending her passage, but she remained in Warsaw. She was constantly being teased by the women who would say, "There's no hope for you, Dobbe. You're fated to die an old maid." Dobbe always answered, "I don't intend to be a slave for any man. Let them all rot."

That afternoon Dobbe received a letter from America. Generally she would go to Leizer the Tailor and have him read it to her. However, that day Leizer was out and so Dobbe thought of Dr. Fischelson whom the other tenants considered a convert since he never went to prayer. She knocked on the door of the doctor's room but there was no answer. "The heretic is probably out," Dobbe thought but, nevertheless, she knocked once more, and this time the door moved slightly. She pushed her way in and stood there frightened. Dr. Fischelson lay fully clothed on his bed; his face was as yellow as wax; his Adam's apple stuck out prominently; his beard pointed upward.

Dobbe screamed; she was certain that he was dead, but—no—his body moved. Dobbe picked up a glass which stood on the table, ran into the corridor, filled the glass with water from the faucet, hurried back, and threw the water into the face of the unconscious man. Dr. Fischelson shook his head and opened his eyes.

"What's wrong with you?" Dobbe asked. "Are you sick?"

"Thank you very much. No."

"Have you a family? I'll call them."

"No family," Dr. Fischelson said.

Dobbe wanted to fetch the barber from across the street but Dr. Fischelson signified that he didn't wish the barber's assistance. Since Dobbe was not going to the market that day, no "wrinklers" being available, she decided to do a good deed. She assisted the sick man to get off the bed and smoothed down the blanket. Then she undressed Dr. Fischelson and prepared some soup for him on the kerosene stove. The sun never entered Dobbe's room, but here squares of sunlight shimmered on the faded walls. The floor was painted red. Over the bed hung a picture of a man who was wearing a broad frill around his neck and had long hair. "Such an old fellow and yet he keeps his place so nice and clean," Dobbe thought approvingly. Dr. Fischelson asked for the *Ethics*, and she gave it to him disapprovingly. She was certain it was a gentile prayer book. Then she began bustling about, brought in a pail of water, swept the floor. Dr. Fischelson ate; after he had finished, he was much stronger and Dobbe asked him to read her the letter.

He read it slowly, the paper trembling in his hands. It came from New York, from Dobbe's cousin. Once more he wrote that he was about to send her a "really important letter" and a ticket to America. By now, Dobbe knew the story by heart and she helped the old man decipher her cousin's scrawl. "He's lying," Dobbe said. "He forgot about me a long time ago." In the evening, Dobbe came again. A candle in a brass holder was burning on the chair next to the bed. Reddish shadows trembled on the walls and ceiling. Dr. Fischelson sat propped up in bed, reading a book. The candle threw a golden light on his forehead which seemed as if cleft in two. A bird had flown in through the window and was perched on the table. For a moment Dobbe was frightened. This man made her think of witches, of black mirrors and corpses wandering around at night and terrifying women. Nevertheless, she took a few steps toward him and inquired, "How are you? Any better?"

"A little, thank you."

"Are you really a convert?" she asked although she wasn't quite sure what the word meant.

"Me, a convert? No, I'm a Jew like any other Jew," Dr. Fischelson answered.

The doctor's assurances made Dobbe feel more at home. She found the bottle of kerosene and lit the stove, and after that she fetched a glass of milk from her room and began cooking kasha. Dr. Fischelson continued to study the *Ethics*, but that evening he could make no sense of the theorems and proofs with their many references to axioms and definitions and other theorems. With trembling hand he raised the book to his eyes and read, "The idea of each modification of the human body does not involve adequate knowledge of the human body itself. . . . The idea of the idea of each modification of the human mind does not involve adequate knowledge of the human mind."

VI

Dr. Fischelson was certain he would die any day now. He made out his will, leaving all of his books and manuscripts to the synagogue library. His clothing and furniture would go to Dobbe since she had taken care of him. But death did not come. Rather his health improved. Dobbe returned to her business in the market, but she visited the old man several times a day, prepared soup for him, left him a glass of tea, and told him news of the war. The Germans had occupied Kalish, Bendin, and Cestechow, and they were marching on Warsaw. People said that on a quiet morning one could hear the rumblings of the cannon. Dobbe reported that the casualties were heavy. "They're falling like flies," she said. "What a terrible misfortune for the women."

She couldn't explain why, but the old man's attic room attracted her. She liked to remove the gold-rimmed books from the bookcase, dust them, and then air them on the window sill. She would climb the few steps to the window and look out through the telescope. She also enjoyed talking to Dr. Fischelson. He told her about Switzerland where he had studied, of the great cities he had passed through, of the high mountains that were covered with snow even in the summer. His father had been a rabbi, he said, and before he, Dr. Fischelson, had become a student, he had attended a yeshiva. She asked him how many languages he knew and it turned out that he could speak and write Hebrew, Russian, German, and French, in addition to Yiddish. He also knew Latin. Dobbe was astonished that such an educated man should live in an attic room on Market Street. But what amazed her most of all was that although he had the title "Doctor," he couldn't write prescriptions. "Why don't you become a real doctor?" she would ask him. "I am a doctor," he would answer. "I'm just not a physician." "What kind of a doctor?" "A doctor of philosophy." Although she had no idea of what this meant, she felt it must be very important. "Oh my blessed mother," she would say, "where did you get such a brain?"

Then one evening after Dobbe had given him his crackers and his glass of tea with milk, he began questioning her about where she came from, who her parents were, and why she had not married. Dobbe was surprised. No one had ever asked her such questions. She told him her story in a quiet voice and stayed until eleven o'clock. Her father had been a porter at the kosher butcher shops. Her mother had plucked chickens in the slaughterhouse. The family had lived in a celler at No. 19 Market Street. When she had been ten, she had become a maid. The man she had worked for had been a fence who bought stolen goods from thieves on the square. Dobbe had had a brother who had gone into the Russian army and had never returned. Her sister had married a coachman in Praga and had died in childbirth. Dobbe told of the battles between the underworld and the revolutionaries in 1905, of blind Itche and his gang and how they collected protection money from the stores, of the thugs who attacked young boys and girls out on Saturday afternoon strolls if they were not paid money for security. She also spoke of the pimps who drove about in carriages and abducted women to be sold in Buenos Aires.

Dobbe swore that some men had even sought to inveigle her into a brothel, but that she had run away. She complained of a thousand evils done to her. She had been robbed; her boy friend had been stolen; a competitor had once poured a pint of kerosene into her basket of bagels; her own cousin, the shoe-maker, had cheated her out of a hundred rubles before he had left for America. Dr. Fischelson listened to her attentively. He asked her questions, shook his head, and grunted.

"Well, do you believe in God?" he finally asked her.

"I don't know," she answered. "Do you?"

"Yes, I believe."

"Then why don't you go to synagogue?" she asked.

"God is everywhere," he replied. "In the synagogue. In the marketplace. In this very room. We ourselves are parts of God."

"Don't say such things," Dobbe said. "You frighten me."

She left the room and Dr. Fischelson was certain she had gone to bed. But he wondered why she had not said "good night." "I probably drove her away with my philosophy," he thought. The very next moment he heard her footsteps. She came in carrying a pile of clothing like a peddler.

"I wanted to show you these," she said. "They're my trousseau." And she began to spread out, on the chair, dresses —woolen, silk, velvet. Taking each dress up in turn, she held it to her body. She gave him an account of every item in her trousseau—underwear, shoes, stockings.

"I'm not wasteful," she said. "I'm a saver. I have enough money to go to America."

Then she was silent and her face turned brick-red. She looked at Dr. Fischelson out of the corner of her eyes, timidly, inquisitively. Dr. Fischelson's body suddenly began to shake as if he had the chills. He said, "Very nice, beautiful things." His brow furrowed and he pulled at his beard with two fingers. A sad smile appeared on his toothless mouth and his large flut-tering eyes, gazing into the distance through the attic window, also smiled sadly.

VII

The day that Black Dobbe came to the rabbi's chambers and announced that she was to marry Dr. Fischelson, the rabbi's wife thought she had gone mad. But the news had already reached Leizer the Tailor, and had spread to the bakery, as well as to other shops. There were those who thought that the "old maid" was very lucky; the doctor, they said, had a vast hoard of money. But there were others who took the view that he was a run-down degenerate who would give her syphilis. Although Dr. Fischelson had insisted that the wedding be a small, quiet one, a host of guests assembled in the rabbi's rooms. The baker's apprentices who generally went about barefoot, and in their underwear, with paper bags on the tops of their heads, now put on light-colored suits, straw hats, yellow shoes, gaudy ties, and they brought with them huge cakes and pans filled with cookies. They had even managed to find a bottle of vodka although liquor was forbidden in wartime. When the bride and groom entered the rabbi's chamber, a murmur arose from the crowd. The women could not believe their eyes. The woman that they saw was not the one they had known. Dobbe wore a wide-brimmed hat which was amply adorned with cherries, grapes, and plumes, and the dress that she had on was of white silk and was equipped with a train; on her feet were high-heeled shoes, gold in color, and from her thin neck hung a string of imitation pearls. Nor was this all: her fingers sparkled with rings and glittering stones. Her face was veiled. She looked almost like one of those rich brides who were married in the Vienna Hall. The baker's apprentices whistled mockingly. As for Dr. Fischelson, he was wearing his black coat and broad-toed shoes. He was scarcely able to walk; he was leaning on Dobbe. When he saw the crowd from the doorway, he became frightened and began to retreat, but Dobbe's former employer approached him saying, "Come in, come in, bridegroom. Don't be bashful. We are all brethren now."

The ceremony proceeded according to the law. The rabbi, in a worn satin gabardine, wrote the marriage contract and then had the bride and groom touch his handkerchief as a token of agreement; the rabbi wiped the point of the pen on his skullcap. Several porters who had been called from the street to make up the quorum supported the canopy. Dr. Fischelson put on a white robe as a reminder of the day of his death and Dobbe walked around him seven times as custom required. The light from the braided candles flickered on the walls. The shadows wavered. Having poured wine into a goblet, the rabbi chanted the benedictions in a sad melody. Dobbe uttered only a single cry. As for the other women, they took out their lace handkerchiefs and stood with them in their hands, grimacing. When the baker's boys began to whisper wisecracks to each other, the rabbi put a finger to his lips and murmured, "*Eh nu oh,*" as a sign that talking was forbidden. The moment came to slip the wedding ring on the bride's finger, but the bridegroom's hand started to tremble and he had trouble locating Dobbe's index finger. The next thing, according to custom, was the smashing of the glass, but though Dr. Fischelson kicked the goblet several times, it remained unbroken. The girls lowered their heads, pinched each other gleefully, and giggled. Finally one of the apprentices struck the goblet with his heel and it shattered. Even the rabbi could not restrain a smile. After the ceremony the guests drank vodka and ate cookies. Dobbe's former employer came up to Dr. Fischelson and said, "*Mazel tov,* bridegroom. Your luck should be as good as your wife." "Thank you, thank you," Dr. Fischelson murmured, "but I don't look forward to any luck." He was anxious to return as quickly as possible to his attic room. He felt a pressure in his stomach and his chest ached. His face had become greenish. Dobbe had suddenly become angry. She pulled back her veil and called out to the crowd, "What are you laughing at? This isn't a show." And without picking up the cushion-cover in which the gifts were wrapped, she returned with her husband to their rooms on the fifth floor.

Dr. Fischelson lay down on the freshly made bed in his room and began reading the *Ethics.* Dobbe had gone back to her own room. The doctor had explained to her that he was an old man, that he was sick and without strength. He had promised her nothing. Nevertheless she returned wearing a silk nightgown, slippers with pompoms, and with her hair hanging down over her shoulders. There was a smile on her face, and she was bashful and hesitant. Dr. Fischelson trembled and the *Ethics* dropped from his hands. The candle went out. Dobbe

groped for Dr. Fischelson in the dark and kissed his mouth.
"My dear husband," she whispered to him, "*Mazel tov.*"

What happened that night could be called a miracle. If Dr.
Fischelson hadn't been convinced that every occurrence is in
accordance with the laws of nature, he would have thought
that Black Dobbe had bewitched him. Powers long dormant
awakened in him. Although he had had only a sip of the
benediction wine, he was as if intoxicated. He kissed Dobbe
and spoke to her of love. Long forgotten quotations from
Klopstock, Lessing, Goethe, rose to his lips. The pressures
and aches stopped. He embraced Dobbe, pressed her to himself, was again a man as in his youth. Dobbe was faint with
delight; crying, she murmured things to him in a Warsaw
slang which he did not understand. Later, Dr. Fischelson
slipped off into the deep sleep young men know. He dreamed
that he was in Switzerland and that he was climbing mountains—running, falling, flying. At dawn he opened his eyes; it
seemed to him that someone had blown into his ears. Dobbe
was snoring. Dr. Fischelson quietly got out of bed. In his long
nightshirt he approached the window, walked up the steps
and looked out in wonder. Market Street was asleep, breathing with a deep stillness. The gas lamps were flickering. The
black shutters on the stores were fastened with iron bars. A
cool breeze was blowing. Dr. Fischelson looked up at the sky.
The black arch was thickly sown with stars—there were green,
red, yellow, blue stars; there were large ones and small ones,
winking and steady ones. There were those that were clustered in dense groups and those that were alone. In the
higher sphere, apparently, little notice was taken of the fact
that a certain Dr. Fischelson had in his declining days married
someone called Black Dobbe. Seen from above even the
Great War was nothing but a temporary play of the modes.
The myriads of fixed stars continued to travel their destined
courses in unbounded space. The comets, planets, satellites,
asteroids kept circling these shining centers. Worlds were
born and died in cosmic upheavals. In the chaos of nebulae,
primeval matter was being formed. Now and again a star tore
loose, and swept across the sky, leaving behind it a fiery
streak. It was the month of August when there are showers
of meteors. Yes, the divine substance was extended and had

neither beginning nor end; it was absolute, indivisible, eternal, without duration, infinite in its attributes. Its waves and bubbles danced in the universal cauldron, seething with change, following the unbroken chain of causes and effects, and he, Dr. Fischelson, with his unavoidable fate, was part of this. The doctor closed his eyelids and allowed the breeze to cool the sweat on his forehead and stir the hair of his beard. He breathed deeply of the midnight air, supported his shaky hands on the window sill and murmured, "Divine Spinoza, forgive me. I have become a fool."

Translated by Martha Glicklich and Cecil Hemley

The Black Wedding

AARON NAPHTALI, Rabbi of Tzivkev, had lost three-fourths of his followers. There was talk in the rabbinical courts that Rabbi Aaron Naphtali alone had been responsible for driving away his Chassidim. A rabbinical court must be vigilant, more adherents must be acquired. One has to find devices so that the following will not diminish. But Rabbi Aaron Naphtali was apathetic. The study house was old and toadstools grew unmolested on the walls. The ritual bath fell to ruin. The beadles were tottering old men, deaf and half-blind. The rabbi passed his time practicing miracle-working cabala. It was said that Rabbi Aaron Naphtali wanted to imitate the feats of the ancient ones, to tap wine from the wall and create pigeons through combinations of holy names. It was even said that he molded a golem secretly in his attic. Moreover, Rabbi Naphtali had no son to succeed him, only one daughter named Hindele. Who would be eager to follow a rabbi under these circumstances? His enemies contended that Rabbi Aaron Naphtali was sunk in melancholy, as were his wife and Hindele. The latter, at fifteen, was already reading esoteric books and periodically went into seclusion like the holy men. It was rumored that Hindele wore a fringed garment underneath her dress like that worn by her saintly grandmother after whom she had been named.

Rabbi Aaron Naphtali had strange habits. He shut himself in his chamber for days and would not come out to welcome visitors. When he prayed, he put on two pairs of phylacteries at once. On Friday afternoons, he read the prescribed section of the Pentateuch—not from a book but from the parchment scroll itself. The rabbi had learned to form letters with the penmanship of the ancient scribes, and he used this script for writing amulets. A little bag containing one of these amulets hung from the neck of each of his followers. It was known that the rabbi warred constantly with the evil ones. His grandfather, the old Rabbi of Tzivkev, had exorcised a dybbuk from a young girl and the evil spirits had revenged themselves upon the grandson. They had not been able to bring harm to the old man because he had been blessed by the Saint of Kozhenitz. His son, Rabbi Hirsch, Rabbi Aaron Naphtali's father, died young. The grandson, Rabbi Aaron Naphtali, had to contend with the vengeful devils all his life. He lit a candle, they extinguished it. He placed a volume on the bookshelf, they knocked it off. When he undressed in the ritual bath, they hid his silk coat and his fringed garment. Often, sounds of laughter and wailing seemed to come from the rabbi's chimney. There was a rustling behind the stove. Steps were heard on the roof. Doors opened by themselves. The stairs would screech although nobody had stepped on them. Once the rabbi laid his pen on the table and it sailed out through the open window as if carried by an unseen hand. The rabbi's hair turned white at forty. His back was bent, his hands and feet trembled like those of an ancient man. Hindele often suffered attacks of yawning; red flushes spread over her face, her throat ached, there was a buzzing in her ears. At such times incantations had to be made to drive away the evil eye.

The rabbi used to say, "They will not leave me in peace, not even for a moment." And he stamped his foot and asked the beadle to give him his grandfather's cane. He rapped it against each corner of the room and cried out, "You will not work your evil tricks on me!"

But the black hosts gained ascendency just the same. One autumn day the rabbi became ill with erysipelas and it was soon apparent that he would not recover from his sickness. A doctor was sent for from a nearby town, but on the way the axle of his coach broke and he could not complete the journey. A second physician was called for, but a wheel of his carriage came loose and rolled into a ditch, and the horse sprained his leg. The rabbi's wife went to the memorial chapel of her husband's deceased grandfather to pray, but the vindictive demons tore her bonnet from her head. The rabbi lay in bed with a swollen face and a shrunken beard, and for two days he did not speak a word. Quite suddenly he opened an eye and cried out, "They have won!"

Hindele, who would not leave her father's bed, wrung her hands and began to wail in despair, "Father, what's to become of me?"

The rabbi's beard trembled. "You must keep silent if you are to be spared."

There was a great funeral. Rabbis had come from half of Poland. The women predicted that the rabbi's widow would not last much longer. She was white as a corpse. She hadn't enough strength in her feet to follow the hearse and two women had to support her. At the burial she tried to throw herself into the grave and they could barely restrain her. All through the Seven Days of Mourning, she ate nothing. They tried to force a spoon of chicken broth into her mouth, but she was unable to swallow it. When the Thirty Days of Mourning has passed, the rabbi's wife still had not left her bed. Physicians were brought to her but to no avail. She herself foresaw the day of her death and she foretold it to the minute. After her funeral, the rabbi's disciples began to look around for a young man for Hindele. They had tried to find a match for her even before her father's death, but her father had been difficult to please. The son-in-law would eventually have to take the rabbi's place and who was worthy to sit in the Tzivkev rabbinical chair? Whenever the rabbi finally gave his approval, his wife found fault with the young man. Besides, Hindele was known to be sick, to keep too many fast days and to fall into a swoon when things did not go her way. Nor was she attractive. She was short, frail, had a large head, a skinny neck, and flat breasts. Her hair was bushy. There was an insane look in her black eyes. However, since Hindele's dowry was a following of thousands of Chassidim, a candidate was found, Reb Simon, son of the Yampol Rabbi. His older brother having died, Reb Simon would become Rabbi of Yampol after his father's death. Yampol and Tzivkev had much in common. If they were to unite, the glory of former times would return. True, Reb Simon was a divorced man with five children. But as Hindele was an orphan, who would protest? The Tzivkev Chassidim had one stipulation—that after his father's death, Reb Simon should reside in Tzivkev.

Both Tzivkev and Yampol were anxious to bring the union about. Immediately after the marriage contract was written, wedding preparations were begun, because the Tzivkev rabbinical chair had to be filled. Hindele had not yet seen her husband-to-be. She was told that he was a widower, and nothing was said about the five children. The wedding was a noisy one. Chassidim came from all parts of Poland. The followers of the Yampol court and those of the Tzivkev court began to address one another by the familiar "thou." The inns were full. The innkeeper brought straw mattresses down from the attic and put them out in corridors, granaries, and tool sheds, to accommodate the large crowd. Those who opposed the match foretold that Yampol would engulf Tzivkev. The Chassidim of Yampol were known for their crudeness. When they played, they became boisterous. They drank long draughts of brandy from tin mugs and became drunk. When they danced, the floors heaved under them. When an adversary of Yampol spoke harshly of their rabbi, he was beaten. There was a custom in Yampol that when the wife of a young man gave birth to a girl, the father was placed on a table and lashed thirty-nine times with a strap.

Old women came to Hindele to warn her that it would not be easy to be a daughter-in-law in the Yambol court. Her future mother-in-law, an old woman, was known for her wickedness. Reb Simon and his younger brothers had wild ways. The mother had chosen large women for her sons and the frail Hindele would not please her. Reb Simon's mother had consented to the match only because of Yampol's ambitions regarding Tzivkev.

From the time that the marriage negotiations started until the wedding, Hindele did not stop crying. She cried at the celebration of the writing of the marriage contract, she cried when the tailors fitted her trousseau, she cried when she was led to the ritual bath. There she was ashamed to undress for the immersion before the attendants and the other women, and they had to tear off her stays and her underpants. She would not let them remove from her neck the little bag which contained an amber charm and the tooth of a wolf. She was afraid to immerse herself in the water. The two attendants who led her into the bath, held her tightly by her wrists and she trembled like the sacrificial chicken the day before Yom Kippur. When Reb Simon lifted the veil from Hindele's face after the wedding, she saw him for the first time. He was a tall man with a broad fur hat, a pitch-black disheveled beard, wild eyes, a broad nose, thick lips, and a long moustache. He gazed at her like an animal. He breathed noisily and smelled of perspiration. Clusters of hair grew out of his nostrils and ears. His hands, too, had a growth of hair as thick as fur. The moment Hindele saw him she knew what she had suspected long before—that her bridegroom was a demon and that the wedding was nothing but black magic, a satanic hoax. She wanted to call out "Hear, O Israel" but she remembered her father's death-bed admonition to keep silent. How strange that the moment Hindele understood that her husband was an evil spirit, she could immediately discern what was true and what was false. Although she saw herself sitting in her mother's living room, she knew she was really in a forest. It appeared to be light, but she knew it was dark. She was surrounded by Chassidim with fur hats and satin gabardines, as well as by women who wore silk bonnets and velvet capes, but she knew it was all imaginary and that the fancy garments hid heads grown with elf-locks, goose-feet, unhuman navels, long snouts. The sashes of the young men were snakes in reality, their sable hats were actually hedgehogs, their beards clusters of worms. The men spoke Yiddish and sang familiar songs, but the noise they made was really the bellowing of oxen, the hissing of vipers, the howling of wolves. The musicians had tails, and horns grew from their heads. The maids who attended Hindele had canine paws, hoofs of calves, snouts of pigs. The wedding jester was all beard and tongue. The so-called relatives on the groom's side were lions, bears, boars. It was raining in the forest and a wind was blowing. It thundered and flashed lightning. Alas, this was not a human wedding, but a Black Wedding. Hindele knew, from reading holy books, that demons sometimes married human virgins whom they later carried away behind the black mountains to cohabit with them and sire their children. There was only one thing to do in such a case—not to comply with them, never willingly submit to them, to let them get everything by force as one kind word spoken to Satan is equivalent to sacrificing to the idols. Hindele remembered the story of Joseph De La Rinah and the misfortune that befell him when he felt sorry for the evil one and gave him a pinch of tobacco.

II

Hindele did not want to march to the wedding canopy, and she planted her feet stubbornly on the floor, but the bridesmaids dragged her. They half-pulled her, half-carried her. Imps in the images of girls held the candles and formed an aisle for her. The canopy was a braid of reptiles. The rabbi who performed the ceremony was under contract to Samael. Hindele submitted to nothing. She refused to hold out her finger for the ring and had to be forced to do so. She would not drink from the goblet and they poured some wine into her mouth. Hobgoblins performed all the wedding rites. The evil spirit who appeared in the likeness of Reb Simon was wearing a white robe. He stepped on the bride's foot with his hoof so that he might rule over her. Then he smashed the wine glass. After the ceremony, a witch danced toward the bride carrying a braided bread. Presently the bride and groom were served the so-called soup, but Hindele spat everything into her handkerchief. The musicians played a Kossack, an Angry Dance, a Scissors Dance and a Water Dance. But their webbed roosters' feet peeped out from under their robes. The wedding hall was nothing but a forest swamp, full of frogs, mooncalves, monsters, each with his ticks and grimaces. The Chassidim presented the couple with assorted gifts, but these were devices to ensnare Hindele in the net of evil. The wedding jester recited sad poems and funny poems, but his voice was that of a parrot.

They called Hindele to dance the Good-Luck dance, but she did not want to get up, knowing it was actually a Bad-Luck dance. They urged her, pushed her, pinched her. Little imps stuck pins into her thighs. In the middle of the dance, two she-demons grabbed her by the arms and carried her away into a bedroom which was actually a dark cave full of thistles, scavengers, and rubbish. While these females whispered to her the duties of a bride, they spat in her ear. Then she was thrown upon a heap of mud which was supposed to be linen. For a long while, Hindele lay in that cave, surrounded by darkness, poison weeds and lice. So great was her anxiety that she couldn't even pray. Then the devil to whom she was espoused entered. He assailed her with cruelty, tore off her clothes, martyred her, abused her, shamed her. She wanted to scream for help but she restrained herself knowing that if she uttered a sound she would be lost forever.

All night long Hindele felt herself lying in blood and pus. The one who had raped her snored, coughed, hissed like an adder. Before dawn a group of hags ran into the room, pulled the sheet from under her, inspected it, sniffed it, began to dance. That night never ended. True, the sun rose. It was not really the sun, though, but a bloody sphere which somebody hung in the sky. Women came to coax the bride with smooth talk and cunning but Hindele did not pay any attention to their babble. They spat at her, flattered her, said incantations, but she did not answer them. Later a doctor was brought to her, but Hindele saw that he was a horned buck. No, the black powers could not rule her, and Hindele kept on spiting them. Whatever they bade her do, she did the opposite. She threw the soup and marchpane into the slop can. She dumped the chickens and squab which they baked for her into the outhouse. She found a page of a psalter in the mossy forest and she recited psalms furtively. She also remembered a few passages of the Torah and of the prophets. She acquired more and more courage to pray to God-Almighty to save her. She mentioned the names of holy angels as well those of her illustrious ancestors like the Baal Shem, Rabbi Leib Sarah's, Rabbi Pinchos Korzer and the like.

Strange, that although she was only one and the others were multitudes, they could not overcome her. The one who was disguised as her husband tried to bribe her with sweet-talk and gifts, but she did not satisfy him. He came to her but she turned away from him. He kissed her with his wet lips and petted her with clammy fingers, but she did not let him have her. He forced himself on her, but she tore at his beard, pulled at his sidelocks, scratched his forehead. He ran away from her bloody. It became clear to Hindele that her power was not of this world. Her father was interceding for her. He came to her in his shroud and comforted her. Her mother revealed herself to her and gave her advice. True, the earth was full of evil spirits, but up above angels were hovering. Sometimes Hindele heard the angel Gabriel fighting and fencing with Satan. Bevies of black dogs and crows came to help him, but the saints drove them away with their palm leaves and hosannahs.

The barking and the crowing were drowned out by the song which Hindele's grandfather used to sing Saturday evenings and which was called "The Sons of the Mansion."

But horror of horrors, Hindele became pregnant. A devil grew inside her. She could see him through her own belly as through a cobweb: half-frog, half-ape, with eyes of a calf and scales of a fish. He ate her flesh, sucked her blood, scratched her with his claws, bit her with his pointed teeth. He was already chattering, calling her mother, cursing with vile language. She had to get rid of him, stop his gnawing at her liver. Nor was she able to bear his blasphemy and mockery. Besides, he urinated in her and defiled her with his excrement. Miscarriage was the only way out, but how bring it on? Hindele struck her stomach with her fist. She jumped, threw herself down, crawled, all to get rid of that devil's bastard, but to no avail. He grew quickly and showed inhuman strength, pushed and tore at her insides. His skull was of copper, his mouth of iron. He had capricious urges. He told her to eat lime from the wall, the shell of an egg, all kinds of garbage. And if she refused, he squeezed her gall bladder. He stank like a skunk and Hindele fainted from the stench. In her swoon, a giant appeared to her with one eye in his forehead. He talked to her from a hollowed tree saying, "Give yourself up, Hindele, you are one of us."

"No, never."

"We will take revenge."

He flogged her with a fiery rod and yelled abuses. Her head became as heavy as a millstone from fear. The fingers of her hands became big and hard like rolling pins. Her mouth puckered as from eating unripe fruit. Her ears felt as if they were full of water. Hindele was not free any more. The hosts rolled her in muck, mire, slime. They immersed her in baths of pitch. They flayed her skin. They pulled the nipples of her breasts with pliers. They tortured her ceaselessly but she remained mute. Since the males could not persuade her, the female devils attacked her. They laughed with abandon, they braided their hair around her, choked her, tickled her, and pinched her. One giggled, another cried, another wiggled like a whore. Hindele's belly was big and hard as a drum and Belial sat in her womb. He pushed with elbows and pressed with his skull.

Hindele lay in labor. One she-devil was a mid-wife and the other an aide. They had hung all kinds of charms over her canopied bed and they put a knife and a Book of Creation under her pillow, the way the evil ones imitate the humans in all manners. Hindele was in her birth throes, but she remembered that she was not allowed to groan. One sigh and she would be lost. She must restrain herself in the name of her holy forbears.

Suddenly the black one inside her pushed with all his might. A piercing scream tore itself from Hindele's throat and she was swallowed in darkness. Bells were ringing as on a gentile holiday. A hellish fire flared up. It was as red as blood, as scarlet as leprosy. The earth opened like in the time of Korah, and Hindele's canopied bed began to sink into the abyss. Hindele had lost everything, this world and the world to come. In the distance she heard the crying of women, the clapping of hands, blessings and good wishes, while she flew straight into the castle of Asmodeus where Lilith, Namah, Machlath, Hurmizah rule.

In Tzivkev and in the neighborhood the tidings spread that Hindele had given birth to a male child by Reb Simon of Yampol. The mother had died in childbirth.

Translated by Martha Glicklich

A Tale of Two Liars

A LIE can only thrive on truth; lies, heaped one upon another, lack substance. Let me tell you how I manipulated two liars by pulling the strings, making them dance to my tune.

The woman of the pair, Glicka Genendel, arrived in Janov several weeks before Passover, claiming to be the widow of the Zosmir rabbi; she was childless, she said, and anxious to remarry. She was not required to participate first in the levirate marriage ceremony, she explained, since her husband had been an only son. She was settling in Janov because a soothsayer had prophesied that she would meet a mate in this town. She boasted that her late husband had studied the Talmud with her, and, to prove it, she sprinkled her conversation with quotations. She was a source of constant wonder to the townspeople. True, she was no beauty. Her nose sloped like a ram's horn, but she did have a pleasantly pale complexion, and large, dark eyes; in addition, her chin was pointed and her tongue glib. There was a bounce to her walk, and she scattered witticisms wherever she went.

No matter what occurred, she could remember a similar experience; for every sorrow, she offered comfort, for every illness, a remedy. She was dazzling in her high-buttoned shoes, woolen dress, fringed silk shawl, and head-band festooned with precious gems. There was slush on the ground, and so she skipped nimbly from stone to stone and plank to plank, holding her skirt daintily in one hand, and her satchel in the other. She brought joy wherever she went, although she did solicit donations, but the donations were not for herself, God forbid. What she got, she turned over to poor brides and indigent mothers-to-be. Because she was such a doer of good deeds, she boarded at the inn free of charge. The guests enjoyed her quips and yarns, and, you may be sure, the innkeeper lost nothing by the arrangement.

She was immediately showered with proposals, and she accepted them all. In almost no time, the town's widowers and divorcees were at each other's throats, each determined to have this remarkable "catch" for himself. Meanwhile, she ran up bills for dresses and underclothing, and dined well on roast squab and egg-noodles. She was also active in community affairs, helping in the preparation of the mill for Passover, examining the sheaves of Pashcal wheat, assisting in the baking of the matzoths, joking with the bakers as they kneaded, rolled, perforated, poured, and cut. She even went to the rabbi so that the ceremony of selling the leavened bread which she had left behind in Zosmir could be performed. The rabbi's wife invited Glicka Genendel to the Seder. She came adorned in a white satin gown and heavy with jewelry, and chanted the Haggadah as fluently as any man. Her coquetry made the rabbi's daughters and daughters-in-law jealous. The widows and divorcees of Janov were simply consumed with rage. It seemed as if this crafty woman would snare for herself the wealthiest widower in town, and, without as much as a by-your-leave, become the richest matron in Janov. But it was I, the Arch-Devil, who saw to it that she was supplied with a mate.

He showed up in Janov during Passover, arriving in an ornate *britska* which had been hired for the occasion. His story was that he had come from Palestine to solicit charity, and he, like Glicka, had also recently lost his spouse His trunk was banded with brass; he smoked a hookah, and the bag in which he carried his prayer shawl was made of leather. He put on two sets of phylacteries when he prayed, and his conversation was sprinkled with Aramaic. His name was Reb Yomtov, he said. He was a tall, thin man, with a pointed beard, and though he dressed like any other townsman in caftan, fur cap, breeches, and high hose, his swarthy face and burning eyes brought to mind a Sephardic Jew from Yemen or Persia. He insisted that he had seen with his own eyes Noah's Ark on Mount Ararat, and that the splinters he sold at six farthings a piece had been carved from one of its planks. He also had in his possession coins over which Yehudah the Chassid had cast a spell, along with a sack of chalky earth from Rachel's grave. This sack, apparently, had no bottom as it never grew empty.

He too put up at the inn, and soon he and Glicka Genendel were friends, to their mutual delight. When they traced back their ancestry, they discovered that they were distant relatives, both descended from some saint or other. They would chat with each other and plot deep into the night. Glicka Genendel hinted that she found Reb Yomtov attractive. She didn't have to spell it out for him—they understood each other.

Those two were in a hurry. That is—I, Sammael, spurred them on. So the Articles of Engagement were drawn up, and after the prospective bride had signed, her husband-to-be gave as his gifts an engagement ring and a necklace of pearls. He had received them, he said, from his first wife who had been an heiress in Baghdad. In return, Glicka Genendel presented to her betrothed a sapphire-studded cover for the Sabbath loaf which she had inherited from her late father, the famous philanthropist.

Then, just at the end of Passover, there was a great to-do in town. One of the very substantial citizens, a Reb Kathriel Abba, complained to the rabbi that Glicka Genendel was engaged to him and that he had given her thirty gulden for a trousseau.

The widow was enraged at these allegations.

"It's just spite," she said, "because I wouldn't sin with him."

She demanded that her slanderer pay her thirty gulden as restitution. But Reb Kathriel Abba stood by the truth of his accusation, and offered to take an oath before the Holy Scroll. Glicka Genendel was just as determined to defend her statement in front of the Black Candles. However an epidemic was raging in the town at the time and the women were fearful that all this oath-taking would end up costing them the lives of their children, and so the rabbi finally ruled that Glicka was obviously a good woman and he commanded that Reb Kathriel Abba apologize and pay the settlement.

Immediately after that, a beggar arrived from Zosmir and surprised everyone by explaining that the late rabbi's wife could not be visiting in Janov, since she was in Zomir, God be praised, with her husband who was not the least bit dead. There was great excitement and the townspeople rushed to the inn to punish the fraudulent widow for her infamous lie. She was not at all upset and merely explained that she had said "Kosmir," not "Zosmir." Once more all was well, and the preparations for the wedding continued. The wedding had been set for the thirty-third day of the Feast of Omer.

But there was one additional incident before the wedding. For one reason or another, Glicka Genendel thought it wise to consult a goldsmith about the pearls which Reb Yomtov had given her. The jeweler weighed and examined the pearls and declared them to be paste. The wedding was off, Glicka Genendel announced, and informed the bridegroom to that effect. He speedily rose to his own defense; in the first place, the jeweler was incompetent; there couldn't be any doubt of that since he, Reb Yomtov, had personally paid ninety-five drachmas for the pearls in Stamboul; in the second place, immediately after the ceremony, God willing, he would replace the counterfeits with the genuine article, and finally he wanted to point out, just in passing, that the cover Glicka Genedel had given him was not embroidered with sapphires, but with beads, and beads, mind you, that sold for three groshen a dozen in the market. Therefore the two liars were quits, and with their differences patched up, stood under the marriage canopy together.

However, later that night, the delegate from the Holy Land discovered that he had not married a spring chicken. She took off her wig, releasing a mass of gray hair. A hag stood before him, and he ransacked his brain to find a solution. But since he was a professional he didn't show his irritation. Nevertheless, Glicka Genendel was taking no chances; to make sure of her husband's love, she fashioned a love charm. She plucked hair from a private place and wove it around a button of her dear one's dressing gown; in addition, she washed her breasts in water which she then poured into a potion for him to drink. As she went about performing this significant business, she sang:

> *As a tree has its shadow,*
> *Let me have my love.*
> *As wax melts in a fire,*
> *Let him burn to my touch.*
> *Now and forever,*
> *In me be his trust,*
> *Trapped in desire*
> *Until all turn to dust.*
> *Amen. Selah.*

II

"Is there any reason why we should stay in Janov?" Reb Yomtov asked when the seven days of nuptial benediction were over. "I would prefer to return to Jerusalem. After all we have a fine house waiting for us near the Wailing Wall. But first I must visit a few towns in Poland to make collections. There are my yeshiva students to think of and then also funds are required to erect a prayer house on the grave of Reb Simon Bar Johai. The last is a very expensive project and will require a good deal of money."

"What towns will you visit? And how long will you be away?" Glicka Genendel asked.

"I intend to stop off at Lemberg, Brod, and some of the other towns in their immediate vicinity. I should be back by midsummer, God willing. We should be in Jerusalem in time to celebrate the High Holy days."

"That's fine," she said. "I'll use the time to visit the graves of my dear ones and to say goodbye to my relatives in Kalish. God speed, and don't forget the way home."

They embraced warmly, and she presented him with some preserves and cookies, and a jar of chicken fat. She also gave him an amulet to protect him from highwaymen, and he set off on his journey.

When he arrived at the River San he halted, turned his carriage around, and drove off on the Lublin road. His destination was Piask, a small town on the outskirts of Lublin. The inhabitants of Piask had a fine reputation. It was said that you did not put on a prayer shawl there, if you didn't want your phylacteries stolen; the point being that in Piask you dared not cover your eyes even that long. Well, it was in that splendid place that the legate sought out the assistant rabbi and had the scribe write out a Bill of Divorcement for Glicka Genendel. He then sent the papers by messenger to Janov. The whole thing cost Reb Yomtov five gulden, but he considered it money well spent.

This done, Reb Yomtov rode into Lublin and preached at the famous Marshall Synagogue. He had a tongue of silver, and chose a Lithuanian accent for his sermon. Beyond the Cossack Steppes and the land of the Tartars, he explained, dwelt the last of the Chazars. This ancient people were cave-dwellers, fought with bow and arrow, sacrificed in the Biblical manner, and spoke Hebrew. He had in his possession a letter from their chieftain, Yedidi Ben Achitov, a grandson of the Chazar king, and he exhibited a parchment scroll which bore the name of many witnesses. These distant Jews who were waging such a stubborn war against the enemies of Israel and who were the only ones who knew the secret road to the river Sambation, were in dire need of funds, he pointed out, and he went through the crowd collecting money for them.

As he circulated among the people, he was approached by a blond-haired young man who asked him his name.

"Solomon Simeon," Reb Yomtov replied, merely lying out of habit.

The young man wished to know where he was staying, and when he heard that it was at the inn, he shook his head.

"Such a needless expense," he said. "And why associate with riff-raff? I have a large house, God be praised. In it there is a guest room and holy books to spare. I am at business all day, and I have no children (may you be spared my fate), so you won't be disturbed. My wife would be honored to have a scholar in the house, and my mother-in-law, who is visiting us, is a learned woman, and a matchmaker in the bargain. Should you need a wife, she will find you one, and a real catch, I can assure you."

"Alas, I am a widower," the spurious Reb Solomon Simeon said, putting on a glum expression, "but I cannot think of marriage at this time. My dear wife was a true grandchild of Rabbi Sabbatai Kohen, and though she is gone three years now, I cannot forget her." And Reb Yomtov continued to sigh mournfully.

"Who are we to question the wisdom of the Almighty?" the young man asked. "It is written in the Talmud that one must not grieve too long."

On their way to the young man's house, the two carried on a lively discussion concerning the Torah, with occasional digressions to more worldly matters. The young man was amazed at his guest's knowledge and intellect.

As he mounted the steps of the young man's house, Reb Yomtov was almost overcome by the odors he smelled. His mouth watered. Fowl was being roasted, cabbage boiled. "Praised be His name," he thought to himself, "Lublin looks like it will be very satisfactory. If his wife wants a learned man, she will certainly have one. And who can tell, I may be strong enough to produce a miracle, and they may yet have a son and heir. Nor if a rich bride becomes available, will I turn her down either."

The door swung open, admitting Reb Yomtov to a kitchen whose walls were covered with copper pans. An oil lamp hung from the ceiling. In the room were two women, the lady of the house and a servant girl; they stood at the stove in which a goose was being roasted. The young man introduced his guest (it was obvious that he was proud to have brought home such a man) and his wife smiled warmly at Reb Yomtov.

"My husband does not praise everyone so highly," she said. "You must be a very unusual man. It is good to have you here. My mother is in the dining room, and will make you welcome. Should you want anything, don't hesitate to let her know."

Reb Yomtov thanked his hostess, and walked in the direction she had indicated, but his host lingered for a moment in the kitchen, no doubt anxious to amplify further on what a distinguished visitor they were entertaining.

Piously Reb Yomtov kissed the *mezuzah*, and opened the door to the adjoining room. What lay beyond was even better than what had gone before. The room which he was entering was most elegantly furnished. But then he stopped. What was this he saw? His heart dropped, and words failed him. No, it couldn't be, he was dreaming. He was seeing a mirage. No, it was witchcraft. For there stood his former bride, his Janov sweetheart. There could be no doubt about it. This was Glicka Genedel.

"Yes, it is me," she said, and once more he heard that familiar shrewish voice.

"What are you doing here?" he asked. "You said you were going to Kalish."

"I have come to visit my daughter."

"Your daughter? You told me you had no children."

"I thought you were on your way to Lemberg," she said. "Didn't you get the divorce papers?"

"What divorce papers?"

"Those I sent by messenger."

"I tell you I've received nothing. May all my bad dreams be visited on your head."

Reb Yomtov saw how things were: he had fallen into a trap; there was no means of escape. His host would enter at any moment, and he would be exposed.

"I have been guilty of a great foolishness," he said, summoning up all of his courage. "These people are under the impression that I am a traveler just returned from the land of the Chazars. It's to your interest to protect me. You don't want to have me driven out of town and remain a deserted wife forever. Don't say anything, and I swear by my beard and earlocks that I'll make it worthwhile for you."

Glicka Genendel had a good many abusive things that she was longing to say, but just then her son-in-law entered. He was beaming.

"We have a most distinguished guest in the house," he said. "This is Reb Solomon Simeon of Lithuania. He has just returned from a visit to the Chazars, who, as you know, live very close to the Lost Ten Tribes." And to Reb Yomtov he explained, "My mother-in-law is to depart shortly for the Holy Land. She is married to a Reb Yomtov, a delegate from Jerusalem and a descendant of the house of David. Possibly you've heard of him?"

"I most certainly have," Reb Yomtov said.

By this time, Glicka Genendel had recovered her composure sufficiently to say, "Do be seated, Reb Solomon Simeon, and tell us all about the Lost Ten Tribes. Did you actually see the River Sambation hurling stones? Were you able to cross over safely and meet the king?"

But the moment her son-in-law left the room, she was on her feet hissing, "Well, what about it, Reb Solomon Simeon? Where is my payment?"

Before he had a chance to say anything, she grabbed him by his lapels and thrust her hand into the inside pocket of his coat. There she found a pouch of ducats, and it took only a very few seconds for her to transfer them to her stocking. For good measure, she pulled a handful of hair from his beard.

"I'm going to teach you a lesson," she said. "Don't think that you're going to get away from here in one piece. Your descendants to the tenth generation will beware of being such an outrageous liar." And she spat in his face. He took out his handkerchief and wiped himself off. Then the lady of the house and the servant girl came in and set the table for supper. In honor of the visitor, the host descended to the wine cellar to fetch a bottle of dry wine.

III

After supper, Glicka Genendel made up a bed for the guest.

"Now get in there," she said, "and I don't want you to do so much as stir a whisker. After the others are asleep, I'll be back for a little chat."

And to prevent him from escaping she impounded his overcoat, cap, and shoes. Reb Yomtov said his prayers and went to bed. He lay there trying to think of some way out of his predicament; and it was at this point that I, the Evil One, materialized.

"Why hang around here like a trussed calf awaiting the slaughterer?" I said. "Open the window and run."

"Just how am I to manage that," he asked, "with no clothes or shoes?"

"It's warm enough outside," I told him. "You're not going to get sick. Just find your way to Piask, and once there, you'll make out all right. Anything is better than remaining with this termagant."

As usual he heeded my counsel. He rose from the bed, threw open the window, and began the descent. I saw to it, however, that there was an obstacle in his path, and he lost his footing and fell, spraining his ankle. For a moment he lay on the ground unconscious. But I revived him.

He forced himself to his feet. It was a very dark night. Barefoot, half-naked, limping, he started off down the Piask road.

While this was going on, Glicka Genendel was occupied otherwise. She could hear the snores of her daughter and son-in-law coming from their bedroom, and so she got up, put on her wrapper, and tiptoed to the chamber of her best beloved. To her astonishment she saw that the bed was unoccupied and the window open. Before she could scream, however, I appeared to her.

"Now what's the sense of that?" I asked her. "It's not a crime for a man to get out of bed, is it? He hasn't stolen anything. The fact is it's you who've done the stealing, and if he's caught, he'll tell about the money you took from him. You're the one who'll suffer."

"Well, what shall I do?" she asked me.

"Don't you see? Steal your daughter's jewel box; then begin to yell. If he's apprehended he'll be the one who's thrown in jail. That way your revenge is certain."

The idea appealed to her and she took my advice. A few shrieks and she had awakened the household. Right away it was discovered that the jewelry was missing, and the ensuing din brought in the neighbors. A posse of men, equipped with lanterns and cudgels, took off after the thief.

I saw that the noble young altruist was quite shaken by what his guest had done, and so I took the opportunity to taunt him.

"You see what happens when you bring a guest home," I pointed out.

"So long as I live there'll be no more poor strangers in this house," he promised.

By this time the posse was busy searching the streets for the fugitive. They were joined by the night watch and the magistrate's constables. It wasn't very difficult to hunt down Reb Yomtov, lame and half-clothed as he was. They found him seated under a balcony, futilely attempting to set his dislocated ankle. Immediately they began to beat him with their clubs despite his protestations of innocence.

"Of course," they laughed, "innocent men always leave a house by the window in the middle of the night."

His hostess followed, screaming invectives at every step. "Thief! Murderer! Criminal! My jewels! My jewels!"

He kept repeating that he knew nothing about the robbery, but to no avail. The guards threw him into a cell and wrote down the names of the witnesses.

Glicka Genendel returned to bed. It was sweet to lie under the warm comforter while one's enemy rotted in jail. She thanked God for the favor he had bestowed upon her, and promised to donate eighteen groshen to charity. All the running about had exhausted her, and she longed for sleep, but I came to her and would not permit her to rest.

"Why such great elation?" I inquired. "Yes, he's in jail all right, but now you won't get a divorce from him. He'll tell everyone whose husband he is, and you and your whole family will be disgraced."

"What should I do?" she asked.

"He sent you a divorce by a messenger to Janov. Go to Janov and get the papers. First of all, you'll be rid of him. Secondly, if you're not here, you can't be called as a witness. And if you're not at the trial, who will believe his story? When the excitement is over, you can return."

My argument convinced her, and the very next morning she arose at sunrise, and explained to her daughter that she was off to Warsaw to meet her husband, Reb Yomtov. Her daughter was still in a state of shock and so did not put up much resistance. Actually Glicka Genendel wanted to put back the jewelry she had stolen from her daughter, but I talked her out of it.

"What's the rush?" I asked. "If the jewels are found, they'll let the liar out, and who's that going to harm, but you? Let him stay behind bars. He'll learn that one doesn't trifle with such a fine, upstanding woman as you."

So to make a long story short, Glicka Genendel set out for Janov, with the intention of either meeting the messenger there in person, or at least getting some clue as to his whereabouts. When she walked into the market place, everyone stared at her. They all knew about the messenger and the divorce papers. She sought out the rabbi and the rabbi's wife snubbed her; his daughter, who was the one who let her in, did not bid her welcome, nor ask her to sit down. But, at any rate, the rabbi gave her the facts: a messenger had come to Janov to present her with divorce papers, but not being able to locate her in town, had left. He remembered that the messenger was named Leib and that he came from Piask. Leib, he recalled, had yellow hair and a red beard. When Glicka Genendel heard this, she immediately engaged a carriage to take her to Piask. There was no point in staying in Janov any longer as the townspeople avoided her.

Reb Yomtov was still in jail. He sat surrounded by thieves and murderers. Vermin-infested rags were his only clothing. Twice daily he fed on bread and water.

And then, at length, the day of his trial rolled round, and he stood before the judge, who turned out to be an irascible man who was hard of hearing.

"Well, what about the jewels?" the judge growled. "Did you steal them?"

Reb Yomtov pleaded not guilty. He was no thief.

"All right, you're no thief. But why did you run out of the house in the middle of the night?"

"I was running away from my wife," Reb Yomtov explained.

"What wife?" the judge asked angrily.

Patiently Reb Yomtov began his elucidation: The mother-in-law of the man at whose house he had been staying was none other than his, Reb Yomtov's wife, but the judge did not allow him to proceed further.

"That's a fine story," he shouted. "You certainly are a brazen-faced liar."

Nevertheless, he did send for Glicka Genendel. Since she had already left town, her daughter came in her place, and testified that it was quite true that her mother was married, but that it was to a highly respectable man from Jerusalem, the famous scholar Reb Yomtov. As a matter of fact, she was even then on her way to meet him.

The prisoner lowered his eyes and cried out, "I am Reb Yomtov."

"You Reb Yomtov," the woman shouted. "Everyone knows you are Reb Solomon Simeon." And she began to curse him with the choicest oaths at her command.

"The farce is over," the judge said sternly. "We have enough scoundrels here already. We don't need any foreign importations." And he decreed that the prisoner be given twenty-five lashes, and then hanged.

It did not take long for the Jews of Lublin to hear of the decree; one of their own, and a scholar at that, was to be hanged, and immediately they sent a delegation to intercede with the governor in the prisoner's behalf. But this time they could accomplish nothing.

"Why are you Jews always so anxious to buy back your

criminals?" the governor asked. "We know how to deal with ours, but you let yours off scot free. No wonder there are so many crooks among you." And he had the delegation chased off by dogs, and Reb Yomtov remained in jail.

He lay in his cell, chained hand and foot, awaiting execution. As he tossed about on his bundle of straw, mice darted out from chinks in the wall, and gnawed at his limbs. He cursed them and sent them scurrying back to cover. Outside the sun shone, but in his dungeon all was black as night. His situation, he saw, was comparable to that of the Prophet Jonah when he had been deep inside the stomach of the whale. He opened his lips to pray, but I, Satan the Destroyer, came to him and said, "Are you stupid enough to still believe in the power of prayer? Remember how the Jews prayed during the Black Plague, and, nevertheless, how they perished like flies? And what about the thousands the Cossacks butchered? There was enough prayer, wasn't there, when Chmielnicki came? How were those prayers answered? Children were buried alive, chaste wives raped—and later their bellies ripped open and cats sewed inside. Why should God bother with your prayers? He neither hears nor sees. There is no judge. There is no judgment."

This is the way I spoke to him, after the fashion of the philosophers, and shortly his lips had lost their inclination to pray.

"How can I save myself?" he asked. "What is your advice?"

"Become a convert," I told him. "Let the priests sprinkle a little holy water over you. That way you can stay alive and have revenge in the bargain. You do want to revenge yourself, don't you, on your enemies? And who are your enemies but the Jews, the Jews who are quite willing to see you hang because of the lies that a Jewess has invented to destroy you?"

He listened carefully to these words of wisdom and when the turnkey brought him his food, told him that he had a desire to be converted. This news was brought to the priests, and a monk was dispatched to interview the prisoner.

"What is your motive in wanting to become a Christian?" the monk inquired. "Is it merely to save your skin? Or has Jesus Christ entered your heart?"

It had happened while he was asleep, Reb Yomtov explained. His grandfather had come to him in a vision. Jesus, the saintly man had told him, was among the most exalted in Heaven, and sat with the Patriarchs in Paradise. No sooner did Reb Yomtov's words reach the bishop, than the prisoner was taken out of his cell, and washed and combed. Dressed in clean raiment, he was put in the company of a friar who instructed him in the catechism; and while he learned of the significance of the host and the cross, he dined on delicious food. What is more, the best families in the neighborhood came to visit him. Then, at last, he was led at the head of a procession to the monastery and converted to Christianity. Now he was certain that his troubles were over, and that he would shortly be a free man, but instead he was led back to his cell.

"When one is sentenced to death," the priest told him, "there's no way out. But don't be sorrowful; you will go with a clean soul into the next world."

Now Reb Yomtov realized that he had cut himself off from all of his worlds. His sorrow was so extreme that he lost his power of speech and spoke not one word as the hangman tightened the noose around his neck.

IV

On her way from Janov to Piask, Glicka Genendel stopped to visit a relative. She spent the Sabbath and Pentecost in the small village in which this relative lived. As she helped her hostess decorate the windows for the holiday, she munched on butter-cookies. And then the day after Pentecost she resumed her journey to Piask.

Of course, it never entered her mind that she was already a widow. Nor did it occur to her, you may be sure, that she was walking into a trap, a trap that I had baited. She traveled leisurely, stopping at all the inns on the way, stuffing herself with egg-cookies and brandy. She did not forget the coachman, but bought him egg-cookies and brandy as well, and to show his gratitude, he arranged a comfortable seat for her in the wagon, and helped her to mount and alight. He looked her over lecherously, but she couldn't bring herself to lie with so low a fellow.

The weather was mild. The fields were green with wheat. Storks circled overhead; frogs croaked, crickets chirped;

butterflies were everywhere. At night as the wagon rolled through the deep forest, Glicka Genendel stretched herself out on the matting like a queen, and loosened her blouse, and permitted the soft breezes to cool her skin. She was well along in years, but her body had resisted old age, and passion still burnt in her as brightly as ever. Already she was making plans to get a new husband.

Then early one morning she arrived in Piask, just as the merchants were opening their shops. The grass was still wet with dew. Troops of barefoot girls, carrying ropes and baskets, were on their way into the forest to gather firewood and mushrooms. Glicka Genendel sought out the assistant rabbi and asked him what he knew of her divorce. He received her cordially, explaining that the Bill of Divorcement had been drawn up by him personally and signed in his presence. The papers were now in the hands of Leib the Coachman. When Glicka Genendel suggested that the beadle be sent to fetch the man, the assistant rabbi made a counter proposal.

"Why don't you go to his house yourself?" he said. "Then you can settle the whole thing with him personally."

So Glicka Genendel went to Leib's house which was a hut that squatted on a hilltop behind the slaughterhouses. The roof of the building was made of rotting straw, and the windows were covered with cow-bladders instead of glass. Although it was summer, the earth around the house was wet and slimy, but this did not bother the ragged, half-naked children who were entertaining themselves there with worn-out brooms and poultry feathers. Scrawny goats, as grimy as pigs, scurried about this way and that.

Leib the Coachman had neither wife nor children. He was a short, broad-shouldered man, with large hands and feet; there was a growth on his forehead and his beard was a fiery red. He was dressed in a short jacket and straw shoes; on his head he wore the lining of a cap which could not quite conceal his bristling tufts of yellow hair.

The sight of him repelled Glicka Genendel, but, nevertheless, she said, "Are you Leib?"

"Well, we can be sure of one thing, you're not Leib," he answered insolently

"Do you have the divorce papers?"

"What business is that of yours?" he wanted to know.

"I am Glicka Genendel. The divorce was drawn up for me."

"That's your story," he said. "How do I know you're telling me the truth? I don't see your name written on your forehead."

Glicka Genendel realized that this was going to be a difficult man to deal with, and she asked, "What's the matter? Are you after money?—Don't worry I'll give you a handsome tip."

"Come back tonight," he said.

And when she inquired why that was necessary, he told her that one of his horses was dying, and he couldn't bear any further conversation. He conducted her into an alleyway. There lay an emaciated nag with a mangy skin, foam frothing from its mouth, its stomach rising and falling like a bellows. Droves of flies buzzed around the dying creature, and overhead were circling crows, cawing as they waited.

"Very well, I'll come back this evening," Glicka Genendel said, now thoroughly disgusted. And her high buttoned shoes moved as fast as she could make them go, taking her away from the ruin and poverty.

It just happened that the night before the Piask thieves had been out on business; they had invaded Lenchic with carts and covered wagons, and had emptied the stores. It had been the evening before market day and so there had been more than enough goods to take. But this rich haul had not been sufficient to satisfy the raiders; they had also broken into the church and had divested it of its gold chains, crowns, plates, and jewels. The holy statues had been left naked. Then they had beaten a hasty retreat homewards, and, as a matter of fact, the horse that Glicka Genendel had seen expiring had been a casualty of the expedition; it had been whipped so mercilessly during the withdrawal that it had collapsed as soon as the robbers had reached home.

Of course, Glicka Genendel knew nothing of this. She went to an inn and ordered a roast chicken. To get the sight of the dying horse out of her mind, she drank a pint of mead. Inevitably, she made friends with all the male guests, inquiring of each his name, home town, and business in this vicinity. Inevitably also, she spoke of her background: her noble descent, her knowledge of Hebrew, her wealth, her jewels, her skill at cooking, sewing, and crocheting. Then when dinner was finished she went to her room and took a nap.

She awoke to find that the sun was setting and that the cows were being driven home from pasture. From the chimneys of the village smoke was issuing as the housewives prepared the evening meal.

Once more Glicka Genendel took the path that led to Leib's. When she entered the house she left behind the purple dusk, and found herself in a night that was almost as black as the inside of a chimney. There was only one small candle burning—inside of a shard. She could just make out Leib who sat astride an inverted bucket. He was mending a saddle. Leib was not a thief himself; he just drove for the thieves.

Glicka Genendel began to talk business immediately, and he took up his old complaint. "How do I know that it's your divorce?"

"Here take these two gulden and stop this nonsense," she said.

"It's not a question of money," he grumbled.

"What's eating you, anyway?" she wanted to know.

He hesitated for a moment.

"I am a man too," he said, "not a dog. I like the same things everyone else does." And he winked lecherously and pointed toward a bench-bed heaped with straw. Glicka Genendel was almost overcome with disgust, but I, the Prince of Darkness, hastened to whisper in her ear, "It doesn't pay to haggle with such an ignoramus."

She begged him to give her the divorce papers first. It was merely a question of lessening the sin. Didn't he see that it would be better for all concerned if he went to bed with a divorcee rather than a married woman? But he was too shrewd for that.

"Oh, no," he said, "as soon as I serve you with the papers, you'll change your mind."

He bolted the door and put out the candle. She wanted to scream but I muffled her voice. Oddly enough she was only half afraid; the other half of her was alive with lust. Leib pulled her down onto the straw; he stank of leather and horses. She lay there in silence and astonishment.

That such a thing should happen to me! she marveled to herself.

She did not know that it was I, the Arch-Fiend, who stoked her blood and muddled her reason. Outside destruction already lay in wait for her.

Suddenly there was the sound of horsemen. The door was splintered open as if by a hurricane, and dragoons and guardsmen, carrying torches, burst into the room. All this happened so quickly that the adulterers did not even get a chance to stop what they were doing. Glicka Genendel screamed and fainted.

This foray had been led by the Lenchic squire himself who came with his troops to punish the thieves. His men broke into the homes of all known criminals. An informer accompanied the platoon. Leib wilted at the first blow and confessed that he was a driver for the gang. Two soldiers hustled him out, but before they left one of them asked Glicka Genendel, "Well, whore, who are you?"

And he ordered that she be searched.

Of course, she protested that she knew nothing of the sacking of Lenchic, but the informer said, "Don't listen to that tart!" He thrust his hand inside her bosom and drew out a treasure trove: her daughter's jewelry and Reb Yomtov's pouch of gold. Under the glow of the torches, the ducats, diamonds, sapphires, and rubies gleamed wickedly. Now Glicka Genendel could not doubt that misfortune had overtaken her, and she threw herself at the squire's feet, begging for mercy. But despite her entreaties she was clapped into irons and taken along with the other thieves to Lenchic.

At her trial, she swore that the jewels were her own. But the rings did not fit her fingers, nor the bracelets her wrists. She was asked how much money was in the pouch, but she did not know because Reb Yomtov had coins from Turkey in his hoard. When the prosecutor wanted to know where she had obtained the ducats, she replied, "From my husband."

"And where is your husband?"

"In Lublin," she blurted out in her confusion, "in prison."

"The husband is a jailbird," the prosecutor said. "And she is a whore. The jewelry is obviously not hers, and she doesn't even know how much money is in her possession. Is there any doubt about the conclusion?"

Everyone agreed that there was not.

Now Glicka Genendel saw that her chances were indeed slim, and it occurred to her that her only hope was to announce that she had a daughter and son-in-law in Lublin, and that the jewelry belonged to her daughter. But I said to her, "First of all, no one's going to believe you. And suppose they do, look what happens. They fetch your daughter here and she finds out that not only have you stolen her jewelry, but also that you've fornicated with that scab-head like a common harlot. The disgrace will kill her, and so you'll have your punishment anyway. Incidentally, Reb Yomtov will be released, and believe me, he'll find your situation amusing. No, better keep quiet. Rather perish than yield to your enemies."

And although my advice led to the abyss, she did not object, for it is well known that my people are vain and will lay down their lives for their vanity. For what is the pursuit of pleasure but pride and delusion?

So Glicka Genendel was sentenced to the gallows.

The night before the execution I came to her and urged her to become a convert, just as I had in the case of the late, unlamented Reb Yomtov, but she said, "Is it any greater honor to have a convert for a mother than a prostitute? No, I'll go to my death a good Jewess."

Don't think I didn't do my best! I pleaded with her over and over again, but, as it is written: A female has nine measures of stubbornness.

The following day, a gallows was erected in Lenchic. When the town's Jews learned that a daughter of Israel was to be hanged, they became frantic and petitioned the Squire. But a church had been pillaged, and he would not grant mercy. And so from the surrounding areas the peasants and gentry drove in, converging on the place of execution in coaches and wagons. Hog-butchers hawked salamis. Beer and whiskey were guzzled.

A darkness fell upon the Jews, and they closed their shutters at mid-day. Just before the execution, there was a near-riot among the peasants as to who would stand closest to the gallows in order to get a piece of the rope for a good luck charm.

First they hanged the thieves, Leib the Coachman among them. Then Glicka Genendel was led up the steps. Before the hood was placed over her head, they asked her if she had a final request, and she begged that the rabbi be summoned to hear her confession. He came, and she told him the true story. It was probably the first time in her life she had ever told the truth. The rabbi recited the Confession for her and promised her Paradise.

It seems, however, that the Lenchic rabbi had little influence in Heaven because before Glicka Genendel and Reb Yomtov were admitted to Paradise, they had to atone for every last sin. No allowances are made up there for anything.

When I told this story to Lilith, she found it very amusing and decided to see these two sinners in Gehenna. I flew with her to purgatory and showed her how they hung suspended by their tongues, which is the prescribed punishment for liars.

Under their feet were braziers of burning hot coals. Devils flogged their bodies with fiery rods. I called out to the sinners, "Now, tell me whom did you fool with those lies? Well, you have only yourselves to thank. Your lips spun the thread, and your mouths wove the net. But be of good cheer. Your stay in Gehenna lasts only for twelve months, including Sabbaths and holidays."

Translated from the Yiddish by Cecil Hemley and June Ruth Flaum

The Shadow of a Crib

Dr. Yaretzky's Arrival

ALL of a sudden, one day, a new doctor came to town. He arrived in a hired wagon, with a basket of possessions, a stack of books bound with a thong, a parrot in a cage and a poodle. In his thirties, short, swarthy, with black eyes and mustache, he might have looked Jewish, if his nose had not had its Polish tilt. He wore an elegant, old-fashioned fur-lined overcoat, gaiters, and a broad-brimmed hat like those of gypsies, magicians and tinkers. Standing amid his things in the center of the market place, he addressed the Jews in the halting Yiddish a gentile occasionally acquires: "Hey there, Jews, I want to live here. Me, Doctor. Doctor Yaretzky. . . . Head hurt, eh? See tongue!"

"Where are you from?" the Jews asked.

"Far, far away! . . ."

"A madman!" the Jews decided, "A mad doctor!"

He settled in a house on a side street, near the fields. He had neither wife, nor furniture. He bought an iron bed and a rickety table. The old doctor, Chwaschinski, charged fifty groszy per visit and a half-ruble for outside calls, but Dr. Yaretzky took what was offered, jamming it uncounted into his pocket. He liked to joke with his patients. Soon two factions formed in town—those who insisted he was a quack who did not know his foot from his elbow, and others who swore he was a master physician. One glance at a patient, his admirers claimed, and diagnosis was complete. He restored the dying to life.

The apothecary, the mayor appointed by the Russians, the notary public and the Russian authorities were all partisan to Dr. Chwaschinski. Since Yaretzky did not attend church, the priest maintained that the doctor was no Christian but an infidel, perhaps a Tartar—and a heathen. Some suggested that he might even poison people. He could be a sorcerer. But the destitute Jews of Bridge Street and the sand flats patronized Dr. Yaretzky. And the peasants too began to consult him, and Dr. Yaretzky furnished an office and hired a maid. But he still wore disheveled clothes and remained friendless. Alone, he strolled down oak-lined Zamosc Avenue. Alone he shopped for groceries, since his maid was a deaf-mute who could neither write nor haggle. In fact, she rarely left the house at all.

The maid was rumored pregnant. Her belly began to expand —but eventually flattened again. Yaretzky was blamed for both the pregnancy and the miscarriage. The authorities at their club spoke of putting the doctor on trial, but the prosecutor was a timid man, afraid of the piercing black eyes and satanic smile beneath Yaretzky's bristling mustache. Yaretzky had, moreover, a medical diploma from Petersburg, and, since he feared no one, possibly had influence with the aristocracy. When visiting Jewish homes, he derided Dr. Chwaschinski, called the apothecary a sucking leech, maligned the County Natchalnik, the Town Natchalnik, the Post Natchalnik, branded them thieves, boot-lickers, lackeys. He even taught obscenities to the parrot. How could anyone start a feud with him? Toward what end? Difficult childbirths were his stock in trade. If necessary, he operated. He lanced abscesses and malignancies unceremoniously, with a knife. They called him a butcher; nevertheless, they recovered. Dr. Chwaschinski was old—his hands trembled, his head shook from side to side, and he had grown deaf. His frequent illnesses forced people to go to Yaretzky. When the mayor was his patient, Dr. Yaretzky addressed him in Yiddish as if that dignitary were a Jew.

"Head hurt? Aah—tongue!" and he tickled the mayor under the arm.

The Doctor conducted himself even more outrageously with the women. Before they could say what was wrong, he made them disrobe. Pipe in mouth, he blew smoke into their faces. Once during conscription time, when Dr. Chwaschinski was sick, Dr. Yaretzky became the assistant to the military doctor, and elderly colonel from Lublin, who was forever drunk. Dr. Yaretzky let the Jewish population know that for one hundred rubles he would issue a blue certificate, signifying rejection during peacetime, for two hundred—a white, meaning absolute rejection, and for a five-and-twenty note, a green—a postponement for at least a year's duration. Mothers of indigent recruits came weeping to Yaretzky and he'd lower the price for them. That year, scarcely a Jew was drafted into the service. An informer was sent to Lublin and a military commission arrived to investigate, but Dr. Yaretzky was exonerated. No doubt he bribed the commission or fooled them completely. In Jewish homes he would say: "Mother Russia is a pig, no? She stinks!"

After Dr. Chwaschinski's death the gentry began to try to please Dr. Yaretzky. The mayor pledged a truce with him, the apothecary invited him to a party. The ladies praised his gifts as an *accoucheur*.

Mrs. Woychehovska, a stout person who, morning and evening walked to church wearing a black shawl over her head and carrying a gold-embossed prayer book, was a gentile marriage broker in the town. Mrs. Woychehovska kept a roster of eligible bachelors and maidens. She frequented the better homes. She boasted that her matches were arranged in dreams by an angel who appeared revealing who was destined for whom. To date, not one of her couples had ever quarreled, separated or proved childless.

Mrs. Woychehovska came to Dr. Yaretzky proposing a highly advantageous match. The young lady came from one of the noblest families in Poland. Her widowed mother owned an estate just outside town. Although Helena was no longer in the first flush of youth, she was single; not from lack of suitors, but from overdiscrimination, Mrs. Woychehovska assured Dr. Yaretzky. She had picked and chosen for so long, that she had been left a maiden. Helena was an accomplished pianist, could converse in French and read poetry. She was known for her love of animals, she kept an aquarium of goldfish in her blue room, and had raised a pair of parrots on the farm. A donkey purchased from a licorice-selling Turk was in her stable. Mrs. Woychehovska swore to Dr. Yaretzky that in her dream she had seen him kneeling alongside Helena before the altar in church. Over their heads hung a halo emanating rays of light—a sure omen that they'd been destined for each other. Dr. Yaretzky heard her out, patiently.

"Who sent you?" he asked her after she'd finished, "the mother or the daughter?"

"For the love of Jesus, neither of them even suspects."

"Why bring Jesus into this?" Dr. Yaretzky said. "Jesus was nothing but a lousy Jew . . ."

Mrs. Woychehovska's face immediately flooded with tears. "Kind sir, what are you saying? May God forgive you! . . ."

"There is no God!"

"Then what is there?"

"Worms. . . ."

"Poor soul, I pity you! And may God pity you! He is merciful. He has compassion even for those who profane Him. . . ."

Mrs. Woychehovska left and crossed Dr. Yaretzky's name off her list. Soon afterwards she suffered an attack of hiccups and it was some time before the spasms subsided.

II

Helena Seeks Revenge

Mrs. Woychehovska repeated the incident to her crony, a Mrs. Markewich who told it secretly to her in-law, a Mrs. Krul. Mrs. Krul's servant girl repeated it to a milkmaid who worked at the estate, and she in turn told it to Helena as her mistress was feeding bread and sugar to her pet donkey. Helena, normally pale, turned white as the lumps of sugar when she learned of the incident. She ran to her mother screaming: "Mama, I'll never forgive you for this, not even on my deathbed!"

The widow denied any knowledge of the affair, but Helena was unconvinced. She flew to her blue room and ordered the chamber maid to remove the aquarium. She wanted to be alone, without the presence of even the goldfish. Bolting the door, closing the shutters, she began to pace up and down. Helena had suffered much. The day her father hanged himself from an apple tree in the orchard was the most terrible day of her life, but even that had been easier to bear than this. Dr. Yaretzky, that barbarian, that anti-Christ, that worm, had slapped her face, sullied her soul. If her servant knew, it must be common gossip by now. True, her mother swore she had not sent the matchmaker, but who would believe it? She, Helena, had been disgraced. The entire neighborhood was probably laughing at her.

But what could she do about it? Should she vanish so completely no one would ever hear of her again? Should she drown herself in the pond? Should she revenge herself upon that charlatan, Yaretzky?—But how? Were she a man, she would challenge him to a duel, but what could a mere female do? Fury raged in Helena's heart. Her honor had been the only thing left of her pride. Now, that too had been taken away. She'd been debased. There was nothing to do but die.

She stopped eating. She no longer fed the parrots and the donkey. She neglected to change the water in the fish tank. Naturally slim, she grew emaciated: a tall pale girl with a white face, a high forehead, and faded hair, once the color of gold, now like straw. White hairs became evident. Her skin grew transparent, networks of bluish veins covered her temples. Malnutrition and vexation sapped her strength, and she spent her days on the divan. Even Slowacki's divine poetry ceased to interest her.

When her mother realized that her only daughter was de-clining, she decided to act. But Helena refused to visit an aunt in Pietrkow Province. Nor would she consult doctors in Lublin or vacation at the Nalenchow spa. Every night she tossed sleepless in bed, seeking ways to revenge herself on Yaretzky. The hot blood of her father, the squire, and other noble ancestors tormented her. She fancied herself an aveng-ing knight, stripping Yaretzky and lashing him in the market-square. After the scourging, she bound him to the tail of a pack horse and had him dragged off to the turnpike. And then, after all this torture, she gouged bits of flesh from his body and poured acid into the wounds. And while she was at it, she had that accused matchmaker, that Woychehovska slut hanged.

But what good were fantasies? They merely fatigued the mind and intensified one's helplessness.

III
Helena Attends a Ball

Who can understand the feminine soul? Even an angelic woman shelters within herself devils, imps, and goblins. The evil ones act perversely, mock human feelings, profane holi-ness. For example, in Shebreshin during a funeral oration over a deceased landlord, a Squire Woyski, his widow suddenly burst out laughing. She stood over the coffin and laughed so intemperately that all the mourners and even the deceased's relatives began to laugh with her. Another time in Zamosc the wife of a brewer went to a barber-surgeon to have a tooth pulled, and when the man put his finger in her mouth to test the tooth, the woman bit it. Afterwards she began to wail and suffered an epileptic fit. Such things happen frequently. It is all part of the perversity so characteristic of the female's nature.

It happened this way. The Post Natchalnik, a Russian married to a Pole, the daughter of a squire near Hrubyeshov, gave a ball to celebrate his wife's birthday. He invited the entire officialdom, as well as the better Polish townspeople and the neighboring gentry, Helena and her mother included. In the past, Helena had always found some excuse to avoid these social functions. Years passed without a single formal appearance on her part. But this time she decided to go. Her mother was overjoyed. She summoned Aaron-Leib, the most successful ladies' tailor in town, and gave him a bolt of silk from which to fashion a ball gown for her daughter. The material had been lying around for years. Aaron-Leib took Helena's measurements and complimented her on her slenderness. Most of the ladies were squat and chunky and the clothes looked baggy on them. This was the first time Helena had permitted a man to touch her. In the past, it had been almost impossible to take her measurements, but this time she cooperated. She was even amiable to this Jew, Aaron-Leib, and asked about his family. Before he left, she gave him a coin for his youngest daughter. Aaron-Leib thanked God for having left him off so easily. Helena's reputation was that of an eccentric.

Customarily Helena accepted an invitation only after having made a full inquiry into the lists of guests. She kept a mental dossier on everybody. This one didn't please her, the other was beneath her station, a third had done a disservice to her father, or grandfather—she found fault with everyone. Quite often, if the hostess wanted Helena to attend, she was forced to scratch some prospective guests off her list, but, if on the other hand, she refused to give in, Helena grew enraged and severed all relations with the person. This time, however, Helena made no stipulations. She seemed to have forgotten her previous misanthropy; her feminine vanity had awakened. She insisted on several fittings of her gown, she ordered dancing slippers from Lublin, and each day she tried on a new item of jewelry to see what would be most appropriate. She grew sprightlier, more talkative, her appetite sharpened, she slept more easily. Her mother was delighted. How long, after all, should a girl sulk and isolate herself? Perhaps God had heeded the widow's supplications and turned her daughter's heart towards conventional behavior. The widow's hopes for the ball were high. Besides the married men, several eligible bachelors were to attend. Two orchestras had been engaged, one military, the other civilian.

Helena, when younger, had been considered an excellent dancer, but she hadn't danced in years, and new dances were in vogue. She asked her mother to hire the town dancemaster, Professor Rayanc. He came and gave Helena lessons. The servants stared as Mistress Helena whirled around the salon with the lanky Professor, who it was said, was ill with consumption and wore a wig to cover his bald head. He was astonished at how quickly Helena learned the new steps. His black eyes filled with tears of admiration, and he suffered a coughing spell, spitting blood into a silken handkerchief. The widow offered him a glass of cherry brandy and a bit of pastry. He licked his fingers and raised the glass: "To your health, esteemed Ladies! May you soon dance at Lady Helena's wedding!"

And he artfully twirled the button on his highly lacquered shoe to make sure the toast would become a reality.

The gown turned out more beautiful than expected. It fit Helena as if she'd been made for it. The flower on the shoulder strap and the gold tasseled bow about the waist lent the gown a chic and elegance rare even in the large cities.

The day of the ball was sunny and the evening mild. Britzskas, carriages and phaetons pulled up before the officer's club where the balls were held. Horses and vehicles filled the parade ground where the soldiers drilled. Liveried footmen mingled with common coachmen. Ladies in sweeping gowns splendid with tucks and ribbons, escorted by gentlemen in dress-uniforms and civilian evening attire with rows of medals on their chests, tried to outshine each other. An old Polish nobleman with mustachios extending to his shoulders accompanied his small round wife, who carried a fringed umbrella even though the sky was clear. Regimental caps and swords hung in the hall. Many young people of the town had assembled around the club to watch the guests and listen to the dance music. The horses behaved as always—chewing their oats and swishing their tails. Occasionally one would whinny but the others disregarded him. What did a horse's whinny mean? Nothing—even to horses.

Helena and her mother arrived late, after the music had started. When the coachman opened the carriage door and Helena stepped down she was greeted by the admiring shrieks of the girls and whistles of the young hoodlums. She was like a portrait come alive.

IV
A Kiss on the Hand

Helena and her mother were welcomed by the Post Natchalnik and his wife. Other guests came to greet them. The men kissed their hands, the ladies paid them compliments. Helena felt as if she were floating. She spoke, not knowing what she said, or why. Her eyes searched, not knowing for whom. Suddenly she spied Dr. Yaretzky. He was surrounded by young, attractive ladies—the wives and daughters of the gentry and the authorities. He might have been the only man in the ballroom who wore no medals. The days when Yaretzky had been branded gypsy, Jew-barber and Devil were long past. The town's ladies, particularly the young and prominent ones, adored him. They repeated his piquant witticisms, they lauded his medical ability. They even forgave him his bachelorhood and his living with the deaf-mute servant girl. He was bold with the ladies, having delivered the children of some and seen others undressed in his office.

When Helena saw him, she was stunned momentarily. She had almost forgotten about him—or had she made herself forget? He seemed so dashing now in his dress coat and highly polished shoes. The black eyes seemed wise and humorous. A young woman tried coquettishly to place a flower in his lapel where apparently there was no buttonhole. The women laughed and clapped their hands, as Dr. Yaretzky undoubtedly offered a riposte, one of his impertinent sallies, which no other man present would have dared utter in mixed company. "Do I still hate him?" Helena asked herself, and even as she asked it, she knew the answer. Her antagonism had mysteriously dissolved—and been replaced by a curiosity as strong as her enmity—perhaps even stronger. She realized something else: she had not forgotten about Dr. Yaretzky at all but had thought of him constantly, possessed as if in a dream, when one thinks with every tissue of the brain without being aware of it. "Will someone introduce us?" she wondered. "I must speak with him, dance with him."

She was jealous of the fawning women who flirted with him so casually. As if he'd been reading her mind, the Natchalnik said: "Is the esteemed Lady Helena acquainted with our Doctor Yaretzky? One moment, if you please. . . ."

He trotted over to Yaretzky, whispered something in his ear, took him by the arm and good-naturedly led him over to Helena.

The other ladies protested, half jestingly, that he was appropriating their cavalier. A few of them even trailed along, not sure of how to react. The balmy evening, the scintillating music, the fragrance of the flowers and perfumes and the drinks the ladies had had, all contributed to an atmosphere of frivolity; Yaretzky bowed to Helena, his smoldering eyes seemed to imply: "Yes, it's about time we two got together. I've anticipated this meeting!" and he offered his hand.

And then there occurred one of those mysteries, one of those imponderables, which confound human reason. Helena lifted Dr. Yaretzky's hand to her mouth—and kissed it. It happened so quickly, that she did not realize what she had done until afterwards. She laughed strangely. Her mother choked off a scream. The ladies were struck dumb. The Natchalnik looked paralyzed—his mouth remained open. Only two young officers began to hoot and clap their palms along their striped trousers. Dr. Yaretzky himself turned pale, but quickly recovered and said: "If Mohammed does not come to the mountain, the mountain comes to Mohammed. . . . Since I neglected to kiss Lady Helena's hand, the Lady kissed mine," and he took Helena's hand and kissed it three times, twice on the glove and once on the exposed wrist. Only now did the ladies begin to titter, prattle. In a second, the story had spread through the ballroom. The guests found it incredible. Everyone was overcome with curiosity and a sense of scandal. The town would have something to gossip about for months to come. Even the lackeys, coachmen and servant girls outside quickly learned of the incident. Their eyes widened. Was she insane? Was she madly infatuated with him? Had someone bewitched her? The musicians came to life, as if revived by the indiscretion and both orchestras began to play with the renewed vigor. The violins sang, the bass fiddles buzzed, the cellos shrieked, the trumpets wailed, the drums throbbed. The dancers' feet grew light, reacting with satisfaction to the spectacle of another's downfall. A debauched mood infected everyone. Couples previously inhibited now danced into the corridors or the courtyard and openly embraced. If Helena could kiss Dr. Yaretzky's hand before everyone, what need was there for decorum?

In ten minutes the widow and Helena had left the ball. Her mother held her train in one hand and pulled Helena along with the other. Helena did not walk but shuffled slightly. The coachmen snickered, pointed, whispered a muffled innuendo. The widow's coachman quickly came up to help the ladies into their carriage The widow could not raise her feet and the coachman had to lift her up by her hips. Helena collapsed into the carriage. The driver mounted, cracked his whip and a great cry came up from everyone—catcalls, hooting. Children who should have been asleep mingled with the adults, running behind the carriage, screaming frenziedly, flinging stones and horse dung. Someone at the ball had overheard the widow admonish Helena: "Wretched girl, what can you do now but dig a grave and lie down in it?"

After the widow and Helena had left, the ladies flocked around Dr. Yaretzky with increased enthusiasm. They chattered, smiled, lured him with their eyes, as if each were Helena's mortal enemy, and savored her disgrace. They tried to extract from Dr. Yaretzky a word, an explanation, a passing remark, even a jest—anything that could be repeated later. Dr. Yaretzky seemed perturbed, his face pallid. Without either answering or apologizing, he forced his way past those who surrounded him. He left the ballroom, not through the main entrance, but through a side door. Since he lived near the club, he'd come on foot, and now he headed home. Someone against whom he happened to stumble maintained that the Doctor had not been walking, but running.

Alone at last in his office, Dr. Yaretzky asked aloud: "Now, what sort of nonsense was that?"

He did not light his kerosene lamp, but sat on the couch in the dark. Since his arrival in town he'd enjoyed many triumphs, but today's conquest was not to his taste. Obviously, Helena was madly in love with him, but to what end? She was no eager matron, simply an old maid. He had no desire to saddle himself with a wife, to become a father and to raise sons and daughters—to perpetrate all that absurdity. He had his share of money and affairs. On this same couch he'd experienced adventures which would have been branded pathological lies by him, had they been claimed by someone else. Long ago he had concluded that family life was a fraud, a swamp to mire fools—since deceit is as essential to women as violence to men. It was not too likely that Helena would deceive him, but what use was she to him? He appealed to women because he was single. As soon as a man marries, other women treat him like a leper. "I'll ignore the incident," Dr. Yaretzky decided. "They'll gossip about it until they forget it. Every scandal grows stale eventually."

He went into the bedroom and lay down—but sleep would not come. He could still hear the music from the ball—polkas, mazurkas, military marches. Distant laughter and sounds of violence drifted towards him. A warm breeze bore the scents of grass, leaves, flowers from beneath his window. Crickets chirped, frogs croaked. The night swarmed with myriads of creatures, each of them calling. Dogs bayed, cats caterwauled. A neighbor's child awoke in its crib. The moon, obscured earlier, now appeared, suspended miraculously in the sky. Stars of many colors sparkled around it. "What is it she sees in me? Why is her love so strong?" mused Dr. Yaretzky. "It's only that old urge to reproduce." The Doctor considered himself a follower of Schopenhauer. No one understood the truth as well as that pessimistic philosopher. His collected works, bound in leather, tooled in gold, stood in Dr. Yaretzky's bookcase. Yes, it was only the blind will to propagate, to perpetuate suffering, the eternal human tragedy. But for what purpose? Why give in to the will if one were aware of its blindness? Man was given his drop of intellect so that he might expose the instincts and their devices.

The Doctor realized that it was useless to try to sleep. He was even out of the sleeping pills he had taken on similar nights. He put on his clothes. He suddenly felt like walking. It might help him sleep later.

V

A Window in the Rabbi's Study

Dr. Yaretzky walked without knowing where. Did it matter? He felt unusually alert and agile. His feet hadn't seemed this light in years. He observed that although this day's triumph had only embarrassed him, his nervous system reacted as it had to previous triumphs. His body felt buoyant as if Helena's kiss on his hand had diminished the effect of gravity. He breathed more deeply. His senses grew keener. "If I were to go hunting right now," he thought, "I could trap a stag with my bare hands. I'd grab him by his antlers and snap his spine." He felt an urge to fire a gun but had left his revolver at home. He wanted to rap on a shutter and frighten a Jew—but controlled himself. After all, a doctor couldn't behave like a wanton boy.

Yaretzky grew more serious. He recalled that afternoon, years ago, when, having divided a sheet of paper into many slips, each bearing the name of a county seat, he had picked from a hat the name of this town. What if he had picked another town? Would his life have been different? Consequently, everything that had happened to him had been pure chance. But what, actually, was chance? If everything was predetermined, no such thing as chance existed. And then again, if causality was nothing but a category of reason, then there certainly was no such thing as chance. The thought swiftly went further. Conceding that Schopenhauer was right, then that which Kant called "The thing in itself" was will. But how did it follow that the will was blind? If the world-will could bring out Schopenhauer's intellect, why couldn't the world-will itself be endowed with intelligence? "I'll have to consult 'The

World as Will and Idea'," Dr. Yaretzky decided. "There's bound to be some sort of an answer in there. I've neglected my reading shamelessly."

He realized that he was in the street, near the rabbi's house. A shutter in the rabbi's study was open. On the table near the stove, a candle flickered in a brass candleholder. Books and manuscripts were heaped on the table. The venerable rabbi, his white beard distended, a skull cap above his high forehead, an unbuttoned gabardine over a yellow-gray fringed garment, sat engrossed in a book, glass of tea in hand. On one side of him was a samovar, on the other, a fan of chicken feathers, used no doubt to fan the coals. Everything, it seemed, was precisely where it should be. The old rabbi was pouring over one of his theological volumes, but Dr. Yaretzky watched, amazed. Did the rabbi keep such late hours, or had he already risen for the day? And what in that book engrossed him so much? The rabbi seemed withdrawn from the world. The Doctor knew the old man. He had treated him for catarrh and hemorrhoids. He, Yaretzky, had handled the rabbi with more respect than the other patients, had not said: "Say aah—," had not asked: "Head hurt, eh? . . ." The Jews of the town deified their rabbi, spoke of his erudition. His large gray eyes, his high forehead, his entire appearance suggested knowledge, under- standing, character—and yet something else, reminiscent of an alien, impenetrable culture. It was too bad that the rabbi knew neither Polish nor Russian, for Yaretzky, while he had learned a little Yiddish in his youth, did not understand it sufficiently to converse with the rabbi. The old man seemed more spiritual than ever now. Blending with the night, he resembled an an- cient sage, both saint and philosopher—a Hebrew Socrates or Diogenes. His shadow extended to the ceiling. "Where do they get such huge foreheads?" Yaretzky wondered. He re- membered what the other Jews had told him—that the rabbi was a *gaon*, a genius. But what kind of a genius? Only in line with prescribed dogma? And how could he have made peace with a world full of sorrow? "I'd give one hundred rubles to know what the old man is reading!" Yaretzky said to himself. "One thing is certain—he doesn't even know there's a ball tonight. Physically they dwell side by side with us, but spiritu- ally they are somewhere in Palestine, on Mount Sinai or God knows where. He may not even be aware that this is the Nineteenth Century. Surely he doesn't know that he is in Europe. He exists beyond time and space. . . ."

Yaretzky recalled something he'd read in a periodical: The Jews do not record their history, they have no sense of chronology. It would seem that instinctively they know that time and space are mere illusion. If that were so, perhaps they could break through the categories of pure reason and conceive the thing-in-itself, that which is behind phenomena?

Yaretzky's urge to communicate with the rabbi increased. He stopped himself just as he was about to tap on the window. He knew beforehand that he would be unable to speak with the old man.—Who knows? Perhaps it was their desire to remain apart that kept them from learning other languages. Judaism could be summed up in one word:—isolation. If not driven into a ghetto, Jews formed a ghetto voluntarily; if not compelled to display a yellow patch, they wore the kind of clothes that their neighbors found odd.

On the other hand, the Jews who did learn other languages and mingled with the Christians were bores.

VI
A Scene of Love

Just as he was about to walk on, something else caught his eye. The door opened from a back room and an old woman entered, tiny, with bent shoulders, dressed in a wide housecoat and battered slippers. Rather than walk, she scraped along—the bent head bound in a kerchief, the face puckered as a cabbage leaf, the ancient eyes hung with pouches. She crept towards the table, silently picked up the chicken feather fan and fanned the coals under the samovar. Dr. Yaretzky knew her well. It was the rabbi's wife. Strange, that the rabbi did not address her and kept his eyes on the book. But his face grew gentler as he half-concentrated on his reading, half-listened to his wife's movements. He raised his eyebrows and on the ceiling the shadow trembled. Dr. Yaretzky stood there, unable to move. He was convinced that he witnessed a love-scene, an old, pious, love ritual between husband and wife. She'd roused herself in the middle of the night to tend the coals of the rabbi's samovar. He, the rabbi, did not dare interrupt his holy studies but, aware of her nearness, he offered silent gratitude. How different all this was! How oriental!—"They've lived for no one knows how many years in Europe. Their great-great-great-grandfathers were born here, but they conduct themselves as if only yesterday they'd been exiled from Jerusalem. How is this possible? Is such behavior hereditary? Or is this an expression of deep faith? How can they be so certain that everything inscribed in several ancient volumes is absolutely true?

"Well, and what of me? How can I guarantee that the world is blind will? Let us say, for the sake of argument that 'The thing in itself' is not blind will, but a seeing will. Then the whole concept of the cosmos changes. Because, if the universal powers are capable of seeing, then they see all—every person, every worm, every atom, every thought. Then the slip of paper that I ostensibly chose by pure chance was not chosen by chance at all but was simply part of a plan, a decree that I experience everything that I've experienced here. If this is so, everything has a purpose: every insect, every blade of grass, every embryo in every mother's womb. It would then follow that that which Helena did tonight was no idle caprice, but part of a scheme of the all-seeing will. But just what is this scheme? Was I destined to become a father?"

It suddenly struck Dr. Yaretzky that while he'd been philosophizing, someone had lowered the curtain—he'd undoubtedly been observed. He felt ashamed. It would be gossiped about among the Jews that he loitered at windows.

He began to stride away hastily, almost running. His thoughts ran with him. He remembered that when he'd first come to town, the rabbi's beard had been blond, not white, and the rabbi's wife?—she'd still had a houseful of youngsters to raise. Had so many years passed? Does one change this quickly from youth to old age? And how old was he, Yaretzky? Would he too soon grow gray? And how long does life last? If it were true what he'd recently read in a medical magazine, he had fourteen years of life left. But how long is fourteen years? The past fourteen years had flown by like a dream. He couldn't exactly say where.

Something within Dr. Yaretzky began to rebel. "Is this my fate? Is this my purpose? Fourteen more years to creep to patients, then fall dead like a dray horse? How can I resign myself to this? No, better a bullet in the temple! But, conceding that the world-will is not blind—this opens innumerable possibilities. An all-seeing Will—is God. The rabbi, this would mean, is no fanatic at all. He has his philosophy. He believes in a seeing universe, rather than a blind one. All the rest is tradition, folklore. Apparently the powers of creation try to achieve variety in the shapes of their creatures, as well as in their behavior.

"Assuming this to be true, what must I do? Return to the church? Become a Jew? Stop seducing my patients? Because if the cosmos sees all, it can also punish. . . . No, I must put all this nonsense out of my head. From here on, it's but one more step to religious positivism.—But why am I running like this? And where?" All at once Dr. Yaretzky saw that he was at the widow's estate. His feet seemed to have brought him here of their own volition. "What am I doing? What am I looking for? Someone will surely see me! Am I going out of my mind?" But even while cautioning himself, he walked up to the gate leading into the courtyard. There was no watchman about, and the gate was unlocked. Unhesitatingly, he pushed it open and walked inside. "Suppose the dogs attack me? They'll mistake me for a prowler." Incautious, abandoned, he was like a drunk to whom awareness of his condition does not bring sobriety. He walked stealthily, like a boy raiding an orchard. He was searching for something, he did not know what.

Why were the dogs so still? Were they sleeping? Everything had been left unattended . . . The house emerged, its windows black. "She isn't here!" something within him said. He followed the path which led to the back of the house, the garden and the fields. Dr. Yaretzky had once visited the estate to treat an ailing farm hand, a long time ago. Although the moon was still shining, there was a pre-dawn silence in the air. The frogs and crickets grew still. The trees seemed petrified. The world held its breath, awaiting daybreak. Dr. Yaretzky felt as if everything within him had also ceased to function. He moved like a phantom. He was awake, but dreaming. He walked past a barn, sheds, a stack of hay. Suddenly he heard a moan and at that instant a shallow pit materialized. He forgot to be surprised: In the pit lay Helena.

Only afterwards did everything become clear. Helena had taken her mother's suggestion to dig herself a grave literally. After everyone was asleep she'd taken a shovel, gone into the orchard where her father had hanged himself, and dug a grave. Then she'd lain down in it and swallowed half a bottle of iodine. As it happened, everyone had been in a deep sleep that night, even the dogs in the kennel.

Dr. Yaretzky thrust his finger down Helena's windpipe, forced her to retch. He roused her mother and the servants, poured half a pitcher of milk down Helena's throat. The widow embraced Dr. Yaretzky, attempting to kiss him. The court echoed with loud voices, barking, cries. Helena's tongue was burned from the poison, her hair matted with mud and clay. She was barefoot and in her nightgown. Dr. Yaretzky carried her into her room and put her to bed.

The widow tried to keep the incident secret but the town learned all about it. Dr. Yaretzky had asked Helena for her hand. Before the widow and the servants he'd kissed Helena's seared lips. She'd raised her lids, taken Yaretzky's hand, put it to her mouth, and for the second time that day—kissed it.

VII

Between Yes and No

The town prepared itself for a splendid wedding. At the estate tailors sewed Helena's trousseau, seamstresses embroidered lingerie. The town merchants imported numerous items from Lublin and Warsaw to supplement the bride's outfit. The orchestra tuned up its instruments. A ball was scheduled at the Military Club in honor of the engaged couple. Dr. Yaretzky, however, knew no peace He felt as if he were at the edge of disaster. Precisely at one o'clock every night he would awaken with the sensation that someone was blowing into his ear. He would sit up trembling, sweating—heavyhearted. "What am I doing?" he would ask himself. "How have I managed to ensnare myself? Why am I suddenly getting married?"

The ardor that he'd felt towards Helena the night he'd found her poisoned, had deserted him. Only apprehension remained. He was well aware of the pitfalls of married life. "Have I lost my senses?" he wondered, "have I been bewitched? But there is no such thing as black magic!"

Dr. Yaretzky recalled how he had stared through the rabbi's window. "Could the scene between the rabbi and his wife actually have unbalanced me, deprived me of my convictions, my resolutions? If so, I have no character at all!" he said aloud.

He would get up and wander like a sleepwalker from room to room in the dark. Various remedies occurred to him: To run away while there was still time; perhaps put a bullet through his brain . . . or write Helena a note breaking the engagement. He could not forget Schopenhauer's description of woman: That narrow-waisted, high-breasted, wide-hipped vessel of sex, which blind will has formed for its own purposes—to perpetuate the eternal suffering and tedium. "No! I won't do it!" he would shout. "I won't stumble into a ditch like some blind horse! Yes, I made a promise—but what is a promise? What is honor?" Yaretzky knew Schopenhauer's essay on dueling and his whole concept of honor. It was waste, refuse—a relic of the days of knighthood, an absurd anachronism! "A curse on the whole damned thing?" Yaretzky would say to himself.

After considerable struggle with himself, Dr. Yaretzky decided to run away. What ties did he have in this God-forsaken hole? Neither friends nor relatives, a house which was not his own, furniture not worth a kopeck. His money was hidden in a secret place, he could hitch up his britzska in the middle of the night, load it with clothes, books, and instruments—and be gone. What code ordained that a man must endure the human comedy to the end? No one could force him to swear faithfulness to a wife, to raise sons and daughters, to blend his seed with the seed of those who served blind will like slaves, celebrated its weddings, wailed at its funerals, grew old, broken, crushed, forgotten. It was true that he felt compassion for Helena; he agreed with Schopenhauer—pity was the basis of morality; but what of the generations he and Helena would spawn? It was worse for them. Their anguish would persist eternally. How does it go: The luckiest child is the one not born?

He had little time left, he'd have to move quickly. His maid was deaf and mute and in addition, a heavy sleeper. His coachman spent his nights with a sweetheart in a nearby village. The only obstacle was the dog. He would bark and raise a rumpus. "I'll have to give him something!" Dr. Yaretzky decided. He had various poisons in his cabinet. Would it matter whether he lived twelve years—or nine? Death was unavoidable. It was everywhere—in the bed of a woman in labor, in a child's cradle, it trailed life like a shadow. Those who are familiar with death smell the stench of shrouds even in the diapers of an infant.

When Dr. Yaretzky finally arrived at his decision it was too late. A gray dawn had appeared. Dew was on the orchard grass but he sat in it. He did not believe in colds. He leaned against the trunk of an apple tree and inhaled the aromas of dawn. He felt ravaged by the struggle that had gone on within him for almost two weeks. Insufficient sleep, inner doubt and lack of food had exhausted him. His body felt hollow inside, his skull seemed stuffed with sand. He was Dr. Yaretzky, yet, he was not Yaretzky at all. He fought alien, mysterious forces, listening as they met for the final battle, the outcome of which he could not determine until the last second. But the powers that said, "No," were nevertheless the stronger. They marshaled their arguments like armies, dispatched them to the most strategic positions, overwhelmed the affirmative faction, throttled it, pelted it with logic, mockery, blasphemy.

Dr. Yaretzky looked up at the sky. The stars shone against the dawn, divinely luminous, filled with unearthly joy. The heavenly spheres appeared festive. But was it truly so?—No, it was a deception. If there was life on other planets, it was the same pattern of gluttony and violence as on earth. Our planet also appeared shining and glorious if viewed from Mars or the Moon. Even the town slaughterhouse looked like a temple from the distance.

He spat at the sky but the spittle landed on his own knee.

VIII
Shadows of the Past

The following night, Dr. Yaretzky made his escape. Three months later Helena left to take the nun's vows at the convent of Saint Ursula. Dressed entirely in black, she took a black trunk, much like a coffin. The widow died soon afterwards, reportedly of a broken heart. Her steward must have been a thief for the estate was left badly in debt and quickly deteriorated. Some of the property was divided among the peasants; the house was abandoned. Everyone knows that an unoccupied house quickly goes to ruin. Moss and nests covered the roof, the walls sprouted mold and toadstools, an owl perched on the chimney and hooted in the night as if mourning an old misery.

Time passed. The town now had a new doctor, a new rabbi. The new rabbi was not a sage like the other but he persevered assiduously. After the evening services he went directly to bed. At midnight, he was in his study poring over the holy books. He also wrote interpretations of the Talmud.

Fourteen years had gone by. One midnight, the rabbi raised his eyes from his book and saw someone looking into his window—a swarthy individual with black eyes, a high forehead and black mustache. At first the rabbi thought his wife had forgotten to close the shutter and some gentile was spying on him, but suddenly he realized that the shutter was indeed closed. In the pane, along with the lamp, the table and the samovar, the face was reflected. Terrified, the rabbi's cry for help choked in his throat. After a while he rose and with trembling knees went to his wife in the bedroom.

Since there is a measure of doubt even in the most pious, the rabbi himself decided that he had only fancied what he had seen and he told no one of the incident. In the morning, he ordered the scribe to examine the *Mezuzah* and that night, as a good luck charm, he placed a volume of the Zohar and a prayer shawl with phylacteries on the table. He was determined never to interrupt his prayers or look up at the window again. Deeply engrossed in his writing, having forgotten his fear, he suddenly looked up and saw the face again in the window, real and yet unreal, insubstantial, not of the world. The rabbi cried out and fainted. Hearing the thud of his body, his wife let out a mournful wail.

They revived the rabbi but he no longer could nor would deny what he had seen. He sent the beadle to summon the elders of the community, and secretly recounted his experience. After long discussion and much supposition, it was decided that three of the men would sit up with the rabbi to observe.

The first night, the three guardians sat until sunrise and saw nothing. Sensing he was suspected of fabrication and hallucinations, the rabbi swore that he had seen either a phantom or the devil. The next night the three men again kept the vigil. When the roosters had crowed and no one had appeared at the window, two of the citizens stretched out on the benches to sleep. Only one remained awake, leafing through a copy of the Mishnah. Suddenly he leaped from his seat. The rabbi, who'd been working on one of his tracts, was so startled that he overturned the inkhorn. He, himself, had seen nothing, but the other man told, with a tremor in his voice, of having seen the image in the window and furthermore, that he had recognized the face as Dr. Yaretzky's.

The other two men were astounded. Why, of all people, would Dr. Yaretzky's ghost manifest itself here? Why should the spirit of such a rogue linger at the rabbi's window?

Although the elders promised to keep the story secret, it soon became common knowledge. The rabbi was unable to continue his studies—he was constantly attended by guardians —and each time, Dr. Yaretzky revealed himself to another witness. At times he materialized within one second and immediately afterwards dissolved. Other times he lingered a moment or two. Often the upper part of his clothing was likewise visible: a thin blouse, an opened collar, a sash around his waist. He would appear in the window like a portrait in a frame, absorbed, lost in meditation, the widely opened eyes focused on one point.

Within a short time, Dr. Yaretzky began to appear in other places. One night when a peasant awoke and went to see about his horse, which, tethered, grazed in the pasture outside, he saw the figure of a man bending over the grass holding his hands as if he were lifting some weight. The peasant thought the man a thief or a gypsy and he advanced, brandishing his whip, but at that moment, the other vanished as if the earth had swallowed him. According to the peasant's description it was evident that it was the spirit of Dr. Yaretzky. The invisible something which he'd been supposedly lifting must have been Helena since an old woman swore that it was the exact spot where Helena had dug the grave after she'd swallowed the poison, and it was from there that Dr. Yaretzky had carried her into the house.

Another time, the present doctor (who'd moved into Yaretzky's old residence) was preparing to ride off in the middle of the night to visit a dying patient. His coachman went out to the stall to hitch up the britzska, and spied someone sitting in the orchard under an apple tree, his head leaning against the tree-trunk, his legs drawn up, a strange dog at his side. He was, to all appearances, asleep. The coachman was puzzled. The man did not look like a vagrant who slept under open skies, but like a gentleman. "He's probably drunk!" the coachman said to himself. He walked over to wake the other, but in that moment the figure disintegrated. Neither was there a trace left of the dog. From sheer terror the coachman began to hiccup and kept on hiccupping for three days. Only after the attack subsided was he able to tell what he'd seen.

The town separated into two camps. The faithful believed that the soul of Dr. Yaretzky wandered through all the tortures of hell and could find no resting place. The wordly citizens on the other hand, maintained that since there was no such thing as a soul, the entire thing was simply hysteria and superstition. The priest wrote a letter to the convent of Saint Ursula and an answer came back stating that Sister Helena had passed away. Dr. Yaretzky was apparently no longer alive either, since the spirits of living people do not roam about in the night. One thing remained a topic of discussion even among the believers: Why would the soul of Dr. Yaretzky hover in the window of the rabbi's study? Why should a Christian heretic seek the house of a rabbi?

Soon there was talk that lights could be seen at night in the windows of the crumbling estate. An old crone who walked past the ruin swore that she'd heard a thin voice as if that of a mother crooning lullabies to her infant and the old woman had recognized it as Helena's voice. Another woman confirmed this and added that on moonlit nights one could see on the wall of Helena's room, the shadow of a crib. . . .

After a while the ruin was demolished and a granary erected on the site. The rabbi's house was rebuilt. The doctor added a wing to his house and ordered the apple trees chopped down. Heaven and earth conspire that everything which has been, be rooted out and reduced to dust. Only the dreamers, who dream while awake, call back the shadows of the past and braid from unspun threads—unwoven nets.

Translated by Elaine Gottlieb and June Ruth Flaum

Shiddah and Kuziba

SHIDDAH and her child, Kuziba, a schoolboy, were sitting nine yards inside the earth at a place where two ledges of rock came together and an underground stream was flowing. Shiddah's body was made of cobwebs; her hair reached to her anklebones; her feet were like those of a chicken; and she had the wings of a bat. Kuziba, who looked like his mother, had, in addition, donkey ears and wax horns. Kuziba was sick with a high fever. Every half hour his mother gave him medicine made of devil's dung mixed with copper juice, the darkness of a ditch, and the droppings of a red crow. Shiddah, leaning over her son, licked his navel with her long tongue. Kuziba was sleeping the restless sleep of the sick. Suddenly the boy woke up.

"I'm frightened, mother," he said.

"Of what, dear?"

"Of light. Of human beings."

Shiddah trembled; and then spat on her son to ward off such evils.

"What are you talking about, child? We're safe here—far from light and far from human beings. It's as dark as Egypt here, thank God, and as silent as a cemetery. We're protected by nine yards of solid rock."

"But they say men can break rocks," said the boy.

"Old wives' tales!" countered his mother. "The power of man is only on the surface. The heights are for angels. The depths are for us. The lot of man is to creep on the skin of the earth like a louse."

"But what *are* human beings, mother? Tell me."

"What are they? They're the waste of creation, offal; where sin is brewed in a kettle, mankind is the foam. Man is the mistake of God."

"How can God the Almighty make a mistake?" asked Kuziba.

"That is a secret, my child," answered Shiddah. "For when God created the last of all the worlds, the earth, his love for our mistress, Lilith, was stronger than ever. Only for an instant his gaze wandered, and in that instant he produced man—an evil mixture of flesh, love, dung, and lust.

"Man!" Shiddah spat. "He has a white skin but inside he is red. He shouts as if he were strong, but really he is weak and shaky. Throw a stone and he breaks; use a thong and he bleeds. In heat he melts. In cold he freezes. There is a bellows in his chest which has to contract and expand constantly. In his left side is a small sac which must throb and quiver all the time. He stuffs himself with mildew of a kind which grows in mud or sand. This mildew he has to swallow constantly and after it passes through his body he must drop it out. He depends on a thousand accidents, and that's why he is so nasty and angry."

"But what do human beings do, mother?"

"Evil," Shiddah answered her son, "only evil. But that keeps them busy so that they leave us in peace. Why, some of them even deny our existence. They think life can only breed on the surface of the earth. Like all fools they consider themselves clever.

"Imagine! They study wisdom on crushed wood pulp smeared with blotches of ink. And their ideas come from a slimy matter which they carry in a bony skull on their necks. They can't even run the way animals can: their legs are too feeble. But one thing they do possess in great measure: insolence. If God the Omnipotent did not have so much patience he would have destroyed such rabble long ago."

Kuziba, who had listened intently to his mother's words, was not reassured. He stared at his mother feverishly.

"I'm afraid of them, mother. I'm afraid."

"Don't be, Kuziba. They can't come here."

"In my sleep I dream about them." Kuziba trembled.

"Don't shake so, my darling little devil." Shiddah caressed her son. "Dreams are silly. They too come from the surface where chaos rules."

II

Kuziba, who had lain for some time in a deep sleep, suddenly cried out. His mother awakened him.

"What's the matter, my son?"

"I'm frightened."

"Again?"

"I was dreaming about a man."

"What did he look like, my child?"

"So fierce. He made a noise that almost made me go deaf. And he had a light that was blinding me. I would have died from fear if you hadn't waked me."

"Be still, my son. I will chant a spell for you."

And Shiddah murmured:

> *Lord of the Depths*
> *Curse the evil surface.*
> *Lord of all Silence*
> *Destroy the Din.*
>
> *Save us great Father*
> *From Light, from Words,*
> *From Man his Deceit.*
> *Save us, Lord God.*

For a while it was quiet. Kuziba dozed off. Shiddah cradled her only son, swaying rhythmically above him. She thought of her husband, Hurmiz, who did not live at home. He went to the Yeshivah of Chittim and Tachtim which was thousands of yards deeper, nearer the center of the earth. There he studied the secret of silence. Because silence has many degrees. As Shiddah knew, no matter how quiet it is, it can be even quieter. Silence is like fruits which have pits within pits, seeds within seeds. There is a final silence, a last point so small that it is nothing, yet so mighty that worlds can be created from it. This last point is the essence of all essences. Everything else is external, nothing but skin, peel, surface. He who has reached the final point, the last degree of silence, knows nothing of time and space, of death and lust. There male and female are forever united; will and deed are the same. This last silence is God. But God himself keeps on penetrating deeper into Himself. He descends into his depths. His nature is like a cave without bottom. He keeps on investigating his own abyss.

Kuziba had fallen asleep. Shiddah, too, rested her head against a stone pillow. She imagined dreamily how Kuziba would grow up and become a big devil; how he would marry and become a father, and how she, Shiddah, would serve her daughter-in-law and her grandchildren. The babies would begin to call her grandma; and she would delouse their heads. She would braid the girls' hair, clean the boys' noses, take them to *Cheder*, feed them, put them to sleep. Then the grandchildren themselves would grow up and be led under black canopies to marry the sons and daughters of the most reputable and well-established demons.

Her husband, Hurmiz, would become a rabbi of the netherworld, giving out amulets, reciting incantations. He would teach imps the chapter of curses on Mount Ebal, and the curses which Balaam should have used on the Israelites; he would teach them the prophecies of the false prophets, the words of temptation which the primeval snake used in the Garden of Eden; he would teach them the cunning of the fallen angels, the confusion of tongues of those who built the tower of Babel; he would instruct them in the perversities of men at the time of the flood, in the vanities of Jeroboam and Ahab, Jezebel and Vashti. Then Hurmiz would become King of the Demons. He would be offered the throne in the Abyss of the Great Female, a thousand miles away from the surface where no one had ever heard of man and his insanity.

Suddenly Shiddah's daydreaming was interrupted. There was a terrible thundering. Shiddah leapt to her feet. A racketing clamor filled the cave as if a thousand hammers were beating. Everything shook. Kuziba woke up with a scream.

"Mother, mother," yelled the boy. "Run, run."

"Help, demons! Help!" Shiddah shouted.

She caught up Kuziba in her arms and tried to flee. But where to? From all sides came a rumbling and cracking. Rocks were crashing down; stones were flying about. The narrow hole which led further underground to the homes of the richer demons was already clogged. A rain of dust, sparks, stone splinters struck the mother and son. Then a light, awful, glaring, a thing with no name in the netherworld, blinded them with its approach. Presently, a monstrous, spiraling machine plunged through the ledge of rock in front of them. Shiddah fell back to the opposite wall, but at that moment it too shattered into a thousand pieces. A second light appeared and another gigantic screw, twisting round and round, pushing with a strange and overwhelming power, ready to crush and grind everything with a cruelty beyond good and evil, broke into their home.

Kuziba, with a terrible sigh, fainted. He hung in Shiddah's arms as if he were dead. Shiddah saw a crevice among some stones and crawled in. She huddled there stiff with fear. What she saw was more horrible than all the horror stories she had ever heard from all the old grandmothers and great-grand-mothers. The drills turned a last time and then were silent. The stones stopped falling and in the smoke and dust men appeared—tall, two-legged, dirty, stinking, with white teeth in faces black with tar, and with eyes from which glared iniquity, malice, and pride. They spoke in ugly gibberish; laughed with abandonment; danced; stretched out their paws to one an-other. Then they began to drink a poisonous beverage, the sheer smell of which made Shiddah faint. She wanted to rouse Kuziba, but she was afraid, if he came to, he would begin screaming, or even might die at the sight of such monsters. The only thing Shiddah could do now was pray. She prayed to Satan, to Asmodeus, to Lilith, and to all the other powers which maintain creation. Help us, she called from the cranny in which she was hiding, help us, not because of my merit but because of the merit of my scholarly husband, because of my innocent child and my worthy ancestors. Long, long, Shiddah knelt in the crack in the stones and prayed and wept. When she again opened her eyes, the ugly images had gone and the noise had subsided. What remained was garbage, a stench, and a ball of light which hung above her head like fire from Gehenna. Only now did she wake up her son.

"Kuziba, Kuziba. Wake up!" Shiddah called to her son. "We are in great danger!"

Kuziba opened his eyes.

"What is this? Oh mother. Light!"

The boy trembled and screamed. For a long while Shiddah comforted him, kissing him and caressing him. But they could not stay there any more. They had to find refuge. But where? The road down to Hurmiz was cut off. Shiddah was now a grass widow, Kuziba a fatherless child. There was only one way to go. Shiddah had heard the saying that if you cannot go down you have to go up. Mother and son began to climb to the surface. Up there, there would also be caves, marshes, graves, dark rocky crevices; there too, she had heard, there were dense forests and empty deserts. Man had not covered the whole surface with his greed. There, too, lived demons, imps, shades, hobgoblins. True, they were refugees, exiles from the netherworld. But still, exile is better than slavery.

For Shiddah knew that the last victory would be to darkness. Until then, demons who were forsaken or driven-out would have to suffer patience. But a time would come when the light of the Universe would be extinguished. All the stars would be snuffed out; all voices, silenced; all surfaces, cut off. God and Satan would be one. The remembrance of man and his abominations would be nothing but a bad dream which God had spun out for a while to distract himself in his eternal night.

Translated by Elizabeth Pollet

Caricature

THE WALLS of the study where Dr. Boris Margolis sat reading his manuscript were lined with books and on the floor and sofa was a litter of newspapers, magazines, discarded envelopes. In addition, there were two wastepaper baskets crammed with papers which the doctor had forbidden anyone to discard until he had one more look at them. Books, their pages still uncut, manuscripts, his own as well as other people's, letters which remained unopened, had become a curse in the apartment. They were dust collectors; bugs were to be seen crawling on them. The smell of print, sealing wax, cigar smoke, was omnipresent in the place, an acrid and musty odor. Every day Dr. Margolis argued with his wife, Mathilda, about cleaning the room but the ash trays remained filled with cigar butts and pieces of food. Mathilda kept him on a diet and hunger was forever assaulting the doctor. He was constantly nibbling egg-cookies, halva, chocolate; he also liked a taste of brandy. He had been warned about scattering ashes, but, nevertheless, there were small gray heaps on the window sill and armchairs. The doctor had ordered that no window be opened; the wind might blow his papers away. Nothing could be discarded without his agreement and Dr. Margolis never agreed. He would peer at the paper in question from beneath his bushy eyebrows and plead, "No, I'd better keep this around just a little bit longer."

"How much longer is that?" Mathilda would ask. "Until the coming of the Messiah?"

"Indeed, how much longer?" Dr. Margolis would say with a sniff. When you are sixty-nine years old and have a weak heart, you can't postpone things forever. He had taken on so many obligations the day was too short. Scholars kept writing to him here in Warsaw from England and America, even from Germany where that maniac Hitler had come to power. Since Dr. Margolis published criticism in an academic journal from time to time, authors sent him their books to review. He had once subscribed to several philosophical magazines and, though he had long since given up renewing his subscriptions, the issues continued to arrive along with demands for payment. Most of the scholars of his generation had died. He himself, for a while, had been as good as forgotten. But the new generation had rediscovered him, and he was now showered with letters of praise as well as all sorts of requests. Just when he had at last resigned himself to never seeing his masterpiece in print (the work had been the labor of twenty-five years), a Swiss publisher had got in touch with him. He had gone as far as to give Dr. Margolis a five hundred franc advance. But now that the publisher was waiting for the manuscript, the realization had come to Dr. Margolis that the work was full of mistakes and inaccuracies, even contradictions. He was uncertain whether his philosophy, a return to metaphysics, had any value. At sixty-nine he no longer had the need to see his name in print. If he could not bring out a consistent system, it was better to keep silent.

Now Dr. Margolis sat, small, broad-shouldered, his head bent forward, his white hair blowing about his head like foam. His goatee pointed upward and to the side of his gray moustache, singed from the cigars he had smoked down to the butt, his cheeks hung limp. Between the thick, bushy eyebrows and the pouchlike bags underlining the eyes, were the eyes themselves, dark, and despite their keen, penetrating gaze, good-natured. The retinas were covered with brown, hornlike specks; cataracts had begun to form and sooner or later the doctor would have to undergo an operation. A small beard sprouted from the doctor's nose and wisps of hair protruded from his ears. Every morning Mathilda reminded him to put on a dressing gown and slippers, but as soon as he arose, he dressed in his black suit, his spats and a stiff collar and black tie. He heeded neither his wife nor his doctors. He poured the medicines which had been prescribed down the drain, threw away the pills, smoked continually, consumed every variety of sweet and fatty foods. Now he sat reading and grimacing. He pulled at his beard, sniffed and grunted.

"Rubbish. Tripe. Just no good."

Mathilda appeared at the door, small and round as a barrel, wearing a silk kimono and open sandals which left her twisted toes exposed. Whenever Dr. Margolis looked at her, he was astonished. Was this really the woman he had fallen in love with and taken from another man thirty-two years ago? She had grown smaller and smaller and puffier and puffier; her stomach stuck out like a man's. Since she had practically no neck, her large square head just sat on her shoulders. Her nose was flat and her thick lips and jowls made him think of a bulldog. Her scalp showed through her hair. Worst of all she had begun to grow a beard, and though she had tried to cut, shave, singe off the hair, it had merely grown denser. The skin of her face was covered with roots from each of which sprouted a few prickly shoots of a nondescript color. Rouge peeled from the creases on her face like plaster. Her eyes stared with a masculine severity. Dr. Margolis remembered a saying of Schopenhauer: Woman has the appearance and mentality of a child. If she becomes intellectually mature, she develops the face of a man.

"What do you want, eh?" Dr. Margolis asked.

"Open a window. It stinks in here."

"All right, let it stink."

"What about the manuscript? They're waiting for it in Berne."

"Let them wait."

"How long are they supposed to wait? Such opportunities don't come every day."

Dr. Margolis laid down his pen. He half-turned towards Mathilda and blew a cloud of smoke at her. He took a last pull and spat out a small fragment of tobacco which was still smoldering.

"I'll send back the five hundred francs, Mathilda."

Mathilda edged away.

"Send back the money? You're mad."

"It's no use. I can't publish something I don't even like. It doesn't matter if others tear me to pieces. But I must be convinced the work has merit."

"All these years you've insisted it's a work of genius."

"I said no such thing. I hoped it might be worth something but at home they used to say: Hoping and having are worlds apart." Dr. Margolis groped for another cigar.

"I won't return one franc," Mathilda cried.

"Come now, do you want me to become a thief in my old age?"

"Send them the manuscript then. It's the best thing you've done. What crazy idea has got into you? And anyway, how can you be your own judge?"

"Who can, then? You?"

"Yes, I. Other people publish a book a year, but you brood over your wretched scribblings like a hen over her eggs. . . . You fiddle around and spoil everything. . . . I don't have the money; I've spent it. . . . The less you tinker with it, the better off you'll be. I'm beginning to think you're getting senile."

"Maybe—maybe I am."

"I don't have the money any longer."

"Well, well, it'll be all right," Dr. Margolis grunted half to Mathilda and half to himself. For days he had been preparing to tell her his decision, but he had feared a scene. Now the worst was over. One way or another he'd manage to dig up the five hundred francs. If everything else failed, he'd borrow from a bank. Morris Traybitcher would sign for him. And as for his so-called immortality, that was lost anyway. He had squandered his last years (the years in Berlin as well as those in Warsaw) on lectures and articles and Zionist conferences. And indeed what if the work were published and several professors praised it? Now philosophy had become nothing but the history of human illusions. Hume had given it the *coup de grace* and had buried it. Kant's attempts at resurrection had failed. Those who had followed the German had written merely afterthoughts. With his tobacco-stained fingers Dr. Margolis began to search for a match. He had an overpowering desire to smoke. Then once more he turned toward the door.

"Still here, eh?"

"I just want you to know that I intend to send the manuscript tomorrow whether you like it or not."

"So you're in command now? No, today it goes out with the garbage."

"You wouldn't dare. What will we do in our old age? Go begging?"

Dr. Margolis grinned.

"Our old age is already here. Do you think we'll live as long as Methuselah?"

"I don't expect to die just yet."

"All right, all right, close the door and leave me in peace. Just don't interfere in my affairs."

He heard the door slam, found his matches and lit a cigar. He inhaled the bitter smoke deeply and read three more sentences which he also disliked. The very last statement he couldn't even recognize as his. If it hadn't been in his handwriting, he would have assumed someone else had written it. It sounded trite. The syntax was faulty. The words had no relevance to what was under discussion. Dr. Margolis sat with his mouth open. Had it been a *dybbuk* who was responsible? He began to shake his head as though there was something supernatural involved. He recalled a sentence from Ecclesiastes: "And further, by these, my son, be admonished: of making books there is no end." Evidently even then there had been too much scribbling. He remembered the bottle of cognac in his bookcase.

"I think I'll have a sip. At this point it can't do me any harm."

Days passed and Dr. Margolis could not decide what to do. The more he worked on the manuscript, the more confused he became. It had some good ideas in it, but the structure was poor and there was a general limpness to the work. He tried cutting, but there was no cohesion to the paragraphs he kept. The book should be entirely rewritten, but he no longer had the required energy. Recently his hands had begun to tremble. His pen skipped and blotted; he omitted letters and words. He even found misspellings and apparently he had forgotten German. Occasionally he caught himself using Yiddish idioms. What was more, he had developed the habit of dozing off as soon as he sat down to work. At night he would lie awake for hours, his brain strangely alert. He would make imaginary speeches, think up strange puns, and argue with such celebrities as Wundt, Kuno Fischer and Professor Bauch. But during the day he tired quickly. His shoulders would sag and his head would nod. He would dream he was in Switzerland— penniless, hungry, homeless, about to be deported by the authorities. "Perhaps, Mathilda is right after all and I am getting senile," Dr. Margolis said to himself. "The brain is indeed a machine and it does wear out. Possibly the materialists are correct after all." The perverse thought crossed his mind. In a world where everything was topsy-turvy, Feuerbach might even be the Messiah.

That evening Dr. Margolis went to a meeting. It concerned a Hebrew encyclopedia which had been begun years before in Berlin. Now that Hitler had become Chancellor, the editorial board had moved to Warsaw. The truth was that the entire undertaking was absurd. Neither the funds nor the contributors were available. In addition, Hebrew still lacked the technical terminology for a modern encyclopedia. But the board would not give up the plan. They had found a rich patron willing to contribute money. And so a few refugees supported themselves through the enterprise. Well, it was all just a question of sponging, Dr. Margolis remarked to himself. . . . But, nevertheless, there could be no harm in spending a few hours in such a gathering. The meeting was to be held in the donor's house and Dr. Margolis traveled there by taxi. He rode upstairs in a paneled elevator, and once inside he found himself seated at the head of the table. The host, Morris Traybitcher, a small man with a bald head, pink cheeks, and a pointed belly, introduced him first to his giant of a wife and then to his daughters, bleached blondes in dresses with low necklines. Dr. Margolis conversed with the wife and daughters in broken Polish. Tea, jam, pastries, liqueurs were served and, though Dr. Margolis had already had his dinner, these delicacies stimulated his appetite. He smoked his wealthy host's Havana cigars, ate, drank, meanwhile trying to clarify the difficulties involved in publishing such an encyclopedia.

"Forgetting the other problems for a moment, there's Hitler himself who isn't going to stay in Berchtesgaden. One of these days he'll be on his way here. . . ."

"You may have to eat your words, Dr. Margolis," Traybitcher said, interrupting him.

"Spengler was right. Europe is committing suicide."

"We survived Haman and we'll also survive Hitler."

"May it be so. Jews build everything on their faith in survival, but what is the basis of that faith? Oh, let's go ahead and publish the encyclopedia. It won't kill any children."

Of those present some spoke Yiddish, and others a kind of German. One man who had a short white beard and gold-rimmed glasses spoke in Hebrew with a Sephardic accent. There was also a refugee professor from Berlin who wore a monocle in his left eye and looked like a Junker. He bore himself more stiffly than any Prussian Dr. Margolis had ever met and alluded to the *Ost-Juden*. Dr. Margolis listened with only half an ear. Each of these calculating individuals had his ambitions and his idiosyncrasies. They were after a few zlotys and the tiny bit of prestige the encyclopedia offered. The philanthropist went as far as to suggest that the work be named after him: The Traybitcher Encyclopedia. Yet he had only contributed a negligible part of the expenses. Microbes, Dr. Margolis thought, nothing but microbes. A glob of matter, a breath of spirit. The whole business lasted but an instant, as the prayer book said. Ah, but the rent must be paid and when money was lacking, life could be very bitter. The forces that had created man hadn't stinted on suffering. . . . It was getting late, and Morris Traybitcher began to yawn. As usual, the decision was to call another meeting. The guests took their leave, each kissing their hostess' heavy braceleted hands. The elevator was so crowded Dr. Margolis tried to pull in his stomach, and when they arrived at the courtyard, they found the gate locked. The janitor growled at them; a dog barked. Dr. Margolis looked about for a cab, but couldn't find one. The professor from Berlin was becoming impatient.

"Ach," he said, "Warsaw is nothing but an Asiatic town."

But finally a cab did stop for him and he drove away. Dr. Margolis waited so long that he gave up and went in search of a streetcar. He felt bloated, could hardly see in the badly lit street, and went tapping his cane before him like a blind man. At first it seemed that he was sliding downhill, and then he got the impression that it was the sidewalk that was slanting. He sought to find out from a passerby in which direction to go, but the man didn't answer. —I'm going to catch it from Mathilda, he thought. She never stopped preaching to him about the necessity of going to bed early. He began to meditate about her. In the old days she had never interfered in his affairs. She had had her home and her clothes and her spas where she went to drink mineral water. When he attempted to speak to her about philosophy, she had refused to listen; nor had she read the reviews of his work he had showed her. She had avoided everything intellectual. Now that he had lost his ambition, she had become ambitious for him. She read his early writings, and whenever they were invited out, she called him professor, praised him, even sought to explain his philosophy. She repeated his jokes, maligned his enemies, took over his mannerisms. He was shamed by her ignorance and her exaggerated loyalty. Yet none of this prevented her from scolding him at home in the coarsest language. As the Polish proverb says: Old age is no joy. No, old age was merely a parody of one's youth.

Finally, Dr. Margolis found the proper streetcar and rode home. He had to wait interminably for the janitor to open the gate. Panting heavily, he mounted the dark steps and then stopped to rest. His heart pounded, every now and again missed a beat. There was a tugging sensation at his knees as if he were climbing a mountain. He could hear his breath coming in snorts. He wiped the sweat from his brow, unlocked the door, and entered on tiptoes so as not to awake Mathilda. He took off his clothes in the living room leaving only his underpants on. The mirror reflected his unclothed body—his chest covered with white hair, his bulging stomach, his excessively short legs and his yellow toenails. Thank the Lord we don't go around naked, Dr. Margolis meditated. No animal was as ugly as homo sapiens. . . . He walked into the bedroom and saw in the semi-darkness that Mathilda's bed was empty. This frightened him and he switched on the light.

"What kind of nonsense is this?" Dr. Margolis asked out loud. "She can't have thrown herself out of the window?" He went back to the hall and noticed a light on in his study. What could she be doing in there so late? He walked to the door and threw it open: There sat Mathilda clad in his dressing gown and slippers asleep at the desk. The manuscript lay open in front of her. A half-smoked cigar was propped against the ash tray and a bottle of cognac and a glass stood among the litter of papers. Never before had her beard seemed to him so grotesquely long and thick; it was as though during the few hours he had been absent it had been growing wildly. Her head was almost bald. She was snoring heavily. In sleep her eyebrows were drawn together, and her hairy, masculine nose protruded; her nostrils were clotted with small tufts of hair. In some mysterious way she had grown to resemble him—she was like the image he had just seen in the mirror. Man and wife share a pillow so long that their heads grow alike, Dr. Margolis quoted to himself, recalling the proverb. But, no, there was more to it than that. This was a biological imitation, like those creatures that simulate being trees and bushes or the bird whose bill looks like a banana. But what was the purpose of this imitation in old age? How could it benefit the species? He felt both compassion and disgust. Evidently she wished to convince herself that the book was worth publishing. On her tightly shut lids was stamped disappointment, the look of disillusionment that sometimes lingers on the face of a corpse. He started to wake her:

"Mathilda. Mathilda."

She stirred, then awoke and rose to her feet. Man and wife viewed each other, silent and amazed, with that strangeness which sometimes follows a life of intimacy. Dr. Margolis wanted to scold her, but he could not. It wasn't her fault. This was apparently that last stage of declining femininity.

"Come to sleep," he said. "It's late, you ninny."

Mathilda shook herself and pointed to the manuscript. "It's a great book, a work of genius."

Translated by Shulamith Charney and Cecil Hemley

The Beggar Said So

ONE hot summer day a big wagon, drawn by one horse, lumbered into the market place of Yanov. It was piled high with motley rags and bedding, laden with cans and buckets, and from the axle between the rear wheels a lantern hung. On top of everything a flower pot and a cage with a little yellow bird swayed precariously. The driver of the wagon was dark, with a pitch-black beard. He wore a cap with a leather visor and a coat not cut in the usual style. At first glance one could have taken him for an ordinary Russian. But the woman with him wore on her head the familiar Jewish coif. Jews, then, after all. Instantly, from all the little shops round about, the Jews of the town rushed out to meet the new arrivals. The stranger stood there in the market place with his whip in his hand.

"Wher-r-re's your magistr-r-rate?" he demanded. He pronounced his "r's" in the dialect of Great Poland, hard and sharp.

"And what would you need the magistrate for?"

"I want to be a chimney sweep," said the newcomer.

"And why should a Jew want to be a chimney sweep?"

"I served in the Army for twenty-five years. I have my working papers."

"There's a chimney sweep in town already."

"But the beggar said there wasn't," the newcomer insisted.

"What beggar?"

"Why, the one that came to our town."

It seemed that the man—his name was Moshe—had been a chimney sweep in some small town on the other side of the river Vistula, not far from the Russian border. One day a beggar who traveled from place to place had come to that town and had said something about a chimney sweep being needed in Yanov. Moshe and his wife had lost no time; they had loaded all their worldly goods onto a wagon and set out for Yanov.

The young men watched them smiled, nudged each other and exchanged meaningful glances. The older householders shrugged their shoulders.

"Why didn't you write a letter first?" they asked Moshe.

"I can't w-r-rite," was the answer.

"So you can get someone else to write for you. Beggars have made up stories before."

"But the beggar said. . . ."

All talk and counter-arguments proved vain. To every question the man had only one answer: "The beggar said so." One might have thought his wife would have had more sense, but she, too, had the same stock rejoinder: "The beggar said so." The crowd of townspeople grew swiftly and the strange tale passed from mouth to mouth. The onlookers began to whisper to each other about it; they shook their heads and made crude puns. One of the men, a flour dealer, called out:

"Just think, believing a poor tramp like that!"

"Maybe the beggar was the Prophet Elijah in disguise," jeered another.

The school children came out from the *Cheder* and mimicked the new arrivals. "The beggar said so," they hooted after them. The young girls giggled while the older women wrung their hands and lamented the lot of these poor fools from Great Poland. In the meantime Moshe the chimney sweep filled one of his cans with water at the town pump and gave his horse a drink. Then he proceeded to fasten a bag of oats around the animal's jaws. From the horse's collar which was studded with bits of brass two pine branches protruded stiffly. The shaft was painted blue. Everyone soon saw that the two travelers had with them, besides the horse and the bird, an odd assortment of geese, ducks, chickens, and one black rooster with a red comb—all in one big cage.

In Yanov at the time there were no vacant dwellings; temporarily, therefore, the two strangers were put up at the poorhouse. A coachman took their horse into his own stable, and someone else bought the fowl. Moshe's spouse, Mindel, immediately joined the other *shnorrers'* wives in the kitchen of the poorhouse where she cooked some porridge. Moshe, himself, went off to the study house to recite a few chapters from the Book of Psalms. And a new byword became fashionable in Yanov: "But the beggar said so." The schoolboys never tired of questioning Moshe and of laughing up their sleeves.

"Tell us," they would query, "just what did he look like, that beggar?"

"Like all other beggars," Moshe would reply.

"What kind of a beard did he have?"

"Yellow."

"Don't you know that men who grow yellow hair are cheaters?"

"How should I know?" Moshe would report. "I'm a simple man. The beggar said so, and I believed him."

"If he had told you that the rabbi's wife lays eggs, would you have believed that too?"

Moshe did not answer. He was a man well into his fifties, though still without one grey hair. His face was tanned like that of a gypsy. His back was straight; his shoulders and chest, broad. He produced for the school teacher's inspection two medals which he had gotten in the Tsar's service for proficiency in riding and marksmanship, and he told of his experiences as a soldier. He had been one of the young boys inducted by force. His father had been a blacksmith. He, Moshe, had still been a student at the *Cheder* when a child-snatcher from the Tsar's army had taken him away. But he, Moshe, had refused to eat forbidden foods and had fasted until he was faint with hunger. The village priest had tried to convert him, but he had a *mezuzah* which his mother had given him as well as the fringed ritual garment worn next to the body to remind him of his God at all times. Yes, they had whipped him, flogged him too with wet switches, but he had not given in. He had remained a Jew. When they tortured him, he had cried out, "Hear, O Israel, the Lord our God is One."

Moshe also told about the time, years later, when he had fallen asleep while on sentry duty and his gun had slipped from his hand. If he had been caught napping, he would have been sent to Siberia. But lo, his dead grandfather had appeared to him in a dream and awakened him. He had had another close call: while crossing a frozen river, he had been stranded on an ice floe. Once too he had been attacked by a wild ox. But he had managed to grab the beast by its horns—he still bore the scar on his wrist. The Tsar's veterans had a reputation for telling tall tales, but everyone believed Moshe; it was clear from the way he told his stories that he had not made them up.

Not long after the arrival of Moshe and his wife, a room was found for them to live in and a stable for the horse. Just at that time one of the Yanov water carriers died; Moshe procured a wooden yoke and became a water carrier. His wife, Mindel, went every Thursday to knead dough in the baking troughs and, besides that job, she stripped feathers for the bedding of new brides. Gradually the two newcomers grew accustomed to Yanov. Yet one question still burrowed deep in the heart of Moshe. Why should the beggar have deceived him so? Had not he, Moshe, given his guest, the beggar, his own bed while he himself tossed about on the ground all night? Not to brag about it, but on that Sunday morning, hadn't he given his guest a loaf of bread and a slab of cheese to take on the way? Why, then, should the beggar have wanted to make a fool of him? Moshe often discussed the riddle with his wife. But she did not know the answer either, and each time he broached the subject, she would say:

"Moshe, take my advice and stop thinking about it."

"But . . . why should the beggar have said so if it wasn't true?" he would persist.

Moshe knew that wandering beggars can turn up anywhere. Every Sabbath he looked over the transients gathered at the synagogue entrance to see if this one beggar was among them. But the years passed and the beggar never came. Was the man afraid that Moshe might take revenge? Or, perhaps, Moshe thought, God had punished him and he had died on the road. In time, the odd thing was that Moshe was not even angry any longer. He had made up his mind that he would not even give the beggar a beating if he were to meet him again. He would simply take him by the neck and say:

"Why did you make a fool of me, contemptible creature?"

Several coachmen tried to persuade Moshe to sell his horse. The wells from which water was drawn for the town of Yanov were nearby so that a water carrier had no need of a horse. And why, they argued, should he have to feed an animal for nothing? But Moshe refused to part with his old mare. He and his wife were fond of animals. God had not granted them any children, but a variety of living things—stray dogs, cats, birds that could no longer fly—had joined their household. The wife would buy a live carp for the Sabbath, but instead of cleaning it and chopping it up she would let it swim about in a washtub for weeks until it finally died of natural causes. Even though one beggar had misused their kindness, these two did not take out their chagrin on other little people. Moshe's wife carried groats to the poorhouse, and every Friday night Moshe would take a wayfarer home as his guest for the Sabbath. To every one of them he would tell the story of what had happened to him and at the end he would ask, "Now why should the beggar have said so?"

II

Late one winter night, Moshe was sitting in his chair soaking his feet in a tub of water. His wife had opened the door of a little cage and a tiny yellow bird was flying about the room. They had taught it a number of tricks. For instance, Moshe would place some millet seeds between his fingers and the bird would take them. Or else he would put one single grain on his lips and the bird would snatch it with its beak, exchanging a kiss with the master.

The oven was warm and the door locked tightly against the cold outside. The woman sat in a corner darning socks. Suddenly, Moshe's head sank down on his chest; he fell asleep and at once began to dream. He dreamed that the soot in the chimney of the poorhouse had caught fire. A bright flame shot out from the chimney and was melting all the snow on the shingle roof. Moshe awoke with a start.

"Mindel," he called to his wife. "There's a fire at the poorhouse."

"How do you know?"

"I saw it in a dream."

"A dream can fool."

"No, it's true," said Moshe.

In vain did his wife argue that it was bitter outside and that he might catch cold—Heaven forbid—if he went out so soon after soaking his feet. Hurrying, Moshe put on his boots, his fur coat and his sheepskin cap. In his closet he still had his chimney sweep's broom, with the rope and iron plummet. He took them with him now as he left the house. He walked through Lublin Street and the Street of the Synagogue and then arrived at the poorhouse. There he saw everything exactly as it had been in his dream. The chimney spouted fiery sparks. The snow near it had melted. Moshe began to shout as hard as he could but the people in the poorhouse did not hear him. Indeed, even if they had waked immediately, they would hardly have been able to save themselves for all of them were old, sick and lame. There was no ladder. Moshe attempted to scale the wall. He caught hold of a giant icicle but that broke off. Then he clung to a shingle but it, too, fell from the eaves before he could climb up. Already, a part of the roof was on fire. In desperation, Moshe grabbed his broom with the iron plummet and with a forceful heave aimed it at the chimney. Amazingly, at the first try it landed in the chimney. The rope hung out; Moshe grasped it and, like an acrobat, he swung himself onto the roof. There was no water; quickly he scooped up snow and patting it into balls threw them into the chimney, all the while bellowing at the top of his voice. But no one heard him. The poorhouse was some distance away from the town; besides, the wind was howling. And the people of Yanov were sound sleepers.

When Moshe failed to return home, his wife put on her boots and padded jacket and went to the poorhouse to see what was keeping him. The dream was true: there he was, standing on the roof. The fire was out but the chimney was still smoking. Pale moonlight shone on the eery scene. By now some of the old people inside had waked and come out, carrying a scoop and shovel. They crowded around. All declared that had it not been for Moshe, the building would have burned to cinders and they would all have perished inside. What with the wind blowing in the direction of the town, the fire could have spread to the synagogue, the bathhouse, the study house and, yes, even to the houses in the market place. And then not only would the houses have been burned-out shells, but there would have been more deaths from cold and exposure.

By the next day the report of the feat of Moshe the water carrier had spread through the town. The mayor appointed a commission to inspect all the chimneys, and the investigation revealed that the town chimney sweep had not done his job in months. They found him in his room, dead drunk, with a straw in his mouth, still sipping vodka from a cask. He was sent packing and, in his place, Moshe became the official chimneysweep of the town of Yanov.

And now a marvelous thing came to pass.

A few days later, when Moshe went to the poorhouse and the inmates crowded round him to thank him and to shower him with blessings, he noticed someone whose features seemed familiar. The man's beard was a mixture of yellow and gray. He was lying on a straw sack covered with rags. The face from which the eyes bulged out was yellow with jaundice. Moshe stopped short and thought in wonder: Where have I met him before? I could swear that I know this man. And then he clasped his hands together in amazement. Why, this was none other than the beggar, the very same one who, years ago, had told him that they needed a chimney sweep in Yanov. A stream of tears gushed forth from Moshe's eyes.

Yes, it was the beggar. He had long forgotten his words but he did recall that in that year and at that time he had spent the Sabbath in that village in Great Poland. He even recalled that he had stayed with some chimney sweep there.

And what was the fruit of all this questioning, of this investigation? Why, it had become quite clear to Moshe that the whole chain of events had been directed from On High. Years ago, this one beggar had been ordained to find a man who would one day save him and all the other people of Yanov from death. It was plain, then, that this beggar had been an instrument of God. Besides, his words had come true after all. Not at the time he said them, to be sure, but much later, for now Moshe had indeed become the official chimney sweep of Yanov. The longer Moshe thought about it, the more clearly did he see the hand of Divine Providence in it all. It was beyond his grasp. Imagine! Holy angels in Heaven thinking of Moshe the Chimney Sweep and sending him messengers with prophecies, just as in the story of Father Abraham!

Moshe was overcome by awe and humility. Had the poorhouse floor not been so dirty he would have fallen upon his face right there and prostrated himself and given thanks to the Almighty. A sob came from his throat and his beard grew sodden with his tears. After he had recovered his composure, he lifted the beggar's frail body in his arms and bore him home upon his shoulders. He washed him, bathed him, dressed him in a clean shirt and laid him on his bed. Mindel immediately went to the stove and made some soup. And the people of the town who for so many years had poked fun at Moshe and had dubbed him "But-The-Beggar-Said-So" took the events to heart and told their children to stop using that name.

III

For over three months the beggar lay in Moshe's bed while Moshe slept on the floor. Gradually the poor man regained some of his strength and wanted to go on the road again, but Moshe and his wife would not hear of it. The beggar had neither wife nor child and he was much too old and weak to wander about. He remained with the pair. Regularly he went to the study house to pray and recite psalms. His eyes failed and he grew almost blind. Other wayfarers told story after story of noblemen, merchants and rabbis, but this beggar was silent. When he finished his reading of the Book of Psalms, he would immediately start all over again. He had also memorized whole passages from the Mishnah. When the Talmud students came to him to inquire why, so many years ago, he had told Moshe that there was no chimney sweep in Yanov, he would raise his eyebrows, shrug his shoulders and answer:

"I really don't know."

"And where do you come from?" they would ask him.

He would give some sort of reply, but his words did not come out clearly. The people thought he was deaf. And yet he had no trouble at all hearing the Reader's prayers from his remote corner of the study house. Mindel catered to him, pampering him with chicken and oatmeal, but he ate less and less as time went by. He would absently raise a spoonful of soup to his lips and then forget to put it in his mouth. The little bird which Moshe had brought with him to Yanov had long since died, but his wife had bought another bird from the gypsies. The cage was never closed, and the bird would fly out and perch on the beggar's shoulder for hours on end.

After some time had passed, the beggar was taken ill again. Moshe and his wife sent for a doctor who spared neither time nor remedies, but apparently the man had no more years left.

He died during the Passover month and was buried on a Friday. The burial society set aside a plot for him among the graves of residents of long standing. Half of Yanov followed the funeral procession. When Moshe and Mindel returned home from the cemetery they found that their bird had gone. It never came back. And in Yanov the word went around that the old beggar who had died had been a *Lamed-Vavnik*, one of the Thirty-Six Righteous Men who, living out their days in obscurity, were keeping the world from destruction by the strength of their virtues.

One night, not long after the beggar's death, Moshe and his wife could not sleep. They began to speak of all sorts of things, talking on till sunrise. That morning Moshe announced in the study house that he and his wife wanted to have a new Scroll of the Law made for the community.

The scribe of Yanov labored over the Scroll for three years, and during all that time Moshe and Mindel talked of their Scroll as if it had been their only daughter. Mindel skimped and saved on household expenses, but for the Scroll she bought remnants of silk and velvet, golden thread, and she hired poor maidens to fashion these into embroidered mantelets. Moshe went all the way to Lublin to order the rollers, a crown with bells, a breastplate and a silver pointer, all to adorn the Scroll. Both the mantelets and the rollers bore the beggar's name—Abraham, the son of Chaim.

On the day the Scroll was dedicated, Moshe gave a festive meal for all the poor of Yanov. Just before dusk the guests assembled in the courtyard of the synagogue. The final sheet of the Scroll had been left incomplete, and after evening services the respected citizens of the community each bought the privilege of having one letter on the last sheet inscribed in their behalf. When all the ink had dried on the parchment and the sheet had been sewn into place, the festive procession began. A wedding canopy was spread out on its poles, and held aloft by four of the most distinguished members of the congregation. Beneath the canopy marched the rabbi, carrying the new Scroll in his arms. The little bells on the shining crown tinkled softly. The men and boys sang; the maidens held up braided candles. Waxen tapers had been lit. Moshe and his wife shone in their holiday best. Simple man that he was, Moshe had pinned his two Russian medals to his lapel. Some of the more learned congregants took this amiss and wanted to tell him in no uncertain terms to take them off, but the rabbi would not allow them to humiliate Moshe in public.

Not even the very old in the congregation could recall ever having witnessed a dedication feast like this one. Two bands played without pause. The night was mild and the moon shone brightly. The sky looked like a star-studded curtain for a Heavenly Ark. The girls and the women danced together, apart from the men. One young man strode about merrily on stilts, and a jester serenaded the host and hostess—Moshe and his wife. There was plenty of wine and ginger cake, supplied by Moshe and Mindel. The band played a real wedding march, a Shear Dance, an Angry Dance, and a Good Morning Dance; it was all just like a regular wedding feast. And then Moshe hitched up his coattails and Mindel her skirts and they danced a *Kasatzke* together, bumping fronts and backsides as they pranced about.

Moshe called out:

"The Beggar-r-r's right next to God!"

And Mindel sang out in reply:

"We are not worthy even of the dust of his feet."

Moshe and Mindel still lived on for quite a few years after this celebration. Before he died, Moshe reserved a burial place for himself next to the grave of the beggar, and he asked to have the broom, the rope and the plummet, with which he had saved the old people at the poorhouse, placed in his coffin.

And as for Mindel—each day she went to the study house and drew aside the velvet curtain of the Ark to bestow a reverent kiss upon her own beloved Scroll. Early every morning without fail, until the last day of her life, she performed this ritual. And in her last will and testament she stipulated that she be buried next to her husband and the beggar who had, after all, spoken the truth.

Translated by Gertrude Hirschler

The Man Who Came Back

You may not believe it but there are people in the world who were called back. I myself knew such a one, in our town of Turbin, a rich man. He was taken with a mortal illness, the doctors said a lump of fat had formed under his heart, God forbid it should happen to any of us. He made a journey to the hot springs, to draw off the fat, but it didn't help. His name was Alter, and his wife's name was Shifra Leah; I can see them both, as if they were standing right before my eyes.

She was lean as a stick, all skin and bones, and black as a spade; he was short and fair, with a round paunch and a small round beard. A rich man's wife, but she wore a pair of broken-down clodhoppers and a shawl thrown over her head, and was forever looking out for bargains. When she heard of a village where one could pick up cheap a measure of corn or a pot of buckwheat, she would go all the way on foot and haggle there with the peasant until he let her have it for next to nothing. I beg her pardon—but the family she came from was scum. He was a lumber merchant, a partner in the sawmill; half the town bought their lumber from him. Unlike his wife, he was fond of good living, dressing like a count, always in a shortcoat and fine leather boots. You could count each hair in his beard, it was so carefully combed and brushed.

He liked a good meal too. His old woman stinted on everything for herself—but for him no delicacy was too dear. Because he favored rich broths, with circlets of fat floating on top, she bullied the butcher, demanding fat meat, with a marrow bone thrown in, for her husband's broth with the gold coins in it, as she explained. In my time, when people got married they loved each other; who ever thought of divorce? But this Shifra Leah was so wrapped up in her Alter that people laughed in their fists. My husband this, and my husband that; heaven and earth and Alter. They had no children, and it's well known that when a woman is childless she turns all her love on her husband. The doctor said he was to blame, but who can be sure about such things?

Well, to make the story short. The man took sick and it

looked bad. The biggest doctors came to see him—it didn't help; he lay in bed and sank from day to day. He still ate well, she feeding him roast pigeons and marzipans and all sorts of other delicacies, but his strength was ebbing away. One day I came to bring him a prayer book that my father—rest in peace—had sent over to him. There he lay on the sofa in a green dressing gown and white socks, a handsome figure. He looked healthy, except that his paunch was blown up like a drum, and when he spoke he puffed and he panted. He took the prayer book from me, and gave me a cookie together with a pinch on the cheek.

A day or two later the news was that Alter was dying. The menfolk gathered; the burial society waited at the door. Well, listen to what happened. When she saw that Alter was at his final gasp, Shifra Leah ran for the doctor. But by the time she got back with the doctor in tow, there was Leizer Godl, the elder of the burial society, holding a feather to her Alter's nostrils. It was all over, they were ready to lift him off the bed, as the custom is. The instant Shifra Leah took it in, she flew into a frenzy; God help us, her screaming and wailing could be heard at the edge of town. "Beasts, murderers, thugs! Out of my house! He'll live! He'll live!" She seized a broom and began to lay about her—everybody thought she had gone out of her mind. She knelt by the corpse: "Don't leave me! Take me with you!" and ranting and raving, she shook and jostled him with lamentations louder than those you'd hear on Yom Kippur.

You know you are not allowed to shake a corpse, and they tried to restrain her, but she threw herself prone on the dead man and screeched into his ear: "Alter, wake up! Alter! Alter!" A living man couldn't have stood it—his eardrums would have burst. They were just making a move to pull her away when suddenly the corpse stirred and let out a deep sigh. She had called him back. You should know that when a person dies his soul does not go up to heaven at once. It flutters at the nostrils and longs to enter the body again, it's so used to being there. If someone screams and carries on, it may take fright and fly back in, but it seldom remains long, because it cannot stay inside a body ruined by disease. But once in a great while it does, and when that happens, you have a person who was called back.

Oh, it's forbidden. When the time comes for a man to die, he should die. Besides, one who has been called back is not like other men. He wanders about, as the saying goes, between worlds; he is here, and yet he isn't here; he would be better off in the grave. Still, the man breathes and eats. He can even live with his wife. Only one thing, he casts no shadow. They say there was a man once in Lublin who had been called back. He sat all day in the prayer house and never said a word, for twelve years; he did not even recite the Psalms. When he died at last, all that was left of him was a sack of bones. He had been rotting all those years and his flesh had turned to dust. Not much was left to bury.

Alter's case was different. He immediately began to recover, talking and wisecracking as if nothing had happened. His belly shrank, and the doctor said that the fat was gone from his heart. All Turbin was agog, people even coming from other towns to get a look at him. There was muttering that the burial society put living men into the ground; for if it was possible to call Alter back, then why not others? Perhaps others were also merely cataleptic?

Shifra Leah soon drove everyone away, she allowed no one to enter her house, not even the doctor. She kept the door locked and the curtains drawn, while she tended and watched over her Alter. A neighbor reported he was already sitting up, taking food and drink, and even looking into his account books.

Well, my dear people, it wasn't a month before he showed up at the market place, with his cane and his pampered beard and his shiny boots. Folks greeted him, gathering round and wishing him health, and he answered, "So you thought you were rid of me, eh? Not so soon! Plenty of water will yet run under the bridge before I go." People asked, "What happened after you stopped breathing?" And he said: "I ate of the Leviathan and dipped it in mustard." He was always ready with the usual wisecrack. It was said that the Rabbi summoned him and they were locked up together in the judgment chamber. But no one ever knew what talk passed between them.

Anyhow, it was Alter, only now he had a nickname: the One

Who Was Called Back. He was soon back at his trading in boards and logs. The gravediggers' brethren went about with long faces; they had hoped to pick up a juicy bone at the funeral. At first people were a bit afraid of him. But what was there to be afraid of? He was the same merchant. His illness had cost quite a sum, but he had enough left over. On Saturdays he came to prayer, he was called to the reading, offered thanksgiving. He was also expected to contribute to the poorhouse and to give a feast for the townsfolk, but Alter played dumb. As for his wife, Shifra Leah, she strutted like a peacock, looking down her nose at everyone. A small matter?—she had brought a dead man back to life! Ours was quite a big town. Other men fell ill and other wives tried to call them back, but no one had a mouth like hers. If everybody could be recalled, the Angel of Death would have to put aside his sword.

Well, things took a turn. Alter had a partner in his mill, Falik Weingarten; in those days people were not called by their family names, but Falik was a real aristocrat. One day Falik came to the rabbi with a queer story: Alter, his partner, had become a swindler. He stole money from the partnership, he pulled all sorts of tricks and was trying to push him, Falik, out of the business. The rabbi couldn't believe it: when a man had gone through such an ordeal, would he suddenly become a crook? It didn't stand to reason. But Falik was not one to make up tales, and they sent for Alter. He went into a song and dance—black was white, and white was black. He dug up ancient bills and accounts all the way back from King Sobieski's time. He showed bundles of claims. To hear him tell it, his partner still owed *him* a small fortune, and what's more, he threatened to start court action.

The townspeople tried arguing with Alter: "You've done business together for so many years, what's gone wrong all of a sudden?" But Alter was a changed man—he seemed to be looking for quarrels. He started litigation, and the case dragged on and cost a fortune. Falik took it so to heart that he died. Who won, I don't remember, I only remember that the sawmill went over to creditors, and Falik's widow was left penniless. The rabbi rebuked Alter: "Is this how you thank the Lord for putting you back on your feet and raising you from the dead?" Alter's answer was no better than the barking of a

dog: "It was not God who did it. It was Shifra Leah." And he
said further: "There is no other world. I was good and dead,
and I can tell you there is nothing—no hell and no paradise."
The rabbi decided he had lost his mind—perhaps so. But wait,
hear the rest.

His wife, Shifra Leah, was the worst kind of draggletail—
people said that a pile of dirt sprang up wherever she stood.
Suddenly Alter began to demand that she should dress up,
deck herself out. "A wife's place," he said, "is not only under
the quilt. I want you to go promenading with me on Lublin
Street." The whole town buzzed. Shifra Leah ordered a new
cotton dress made, and on Sabbath afternoon, after the *cholent*
meal, there were Alter and his wife Shifra Leah on the prome-
nade, along with the tailors' helpers and shoemakers' apprentices. It was a sight—whoever had the use of his limbs ran out
to look.

Alter even trimmed his beard. He became—what's it called?
an atheist. Nowadays, they're all over the place; every fool puts
on a short jacket and shaves his chin. But in my time we had
only one atheist—the apothecary. People began to say that
when Shifra Leah called Alter back with her screams, the soul
of a stranger had entered his body. Souls come flying when
someone dies, souls of kinsfolk and others, and, who knows,
evil souls too, ready to take possession. Reb Arieh Vishnitzer, a
pupil of the old rabbi, declared that Alter was no longer Alter.
True, it was not the same Alter. He talked differently, he
laughed differently, he looked at you differently. His eyes were
like a hawk's, and when he stared at a woman, it was enough
to make a shudder pass through you. He hung out with the
musicians and all sorts of riffraff. At first his wife said amen to
everything, whatever Alter said or did was all right with her. I
beg her pardon, but she was a cow. But then a certain female
arrived in our town, from Warsaw. She came to visit her sister,
who wasn't much to boast of and whose husband was a barber;
on market days he shaved the peasants, and he also bled them.
You can expect anything from such people: he had a cage full
of birds, twittering all day long, and he also had a dog. His
own wife had never shaved off her hair, and the sister from
Warsaw was a divorcee—no one knew who her husband was.
She came among us bedecked and bejeweled, but who ever

looked at her twice? A broomstick can be dressed up too. She showed the women the long stockings she was wearing, hooked, if you'll pardon the word, to her drawers. It was not hard to guess that she had come to trap some man. And who do you think fell into her clutches? Alter. When the townsfolk heard that Alter was running around with the barber's sister-in-law, they couldn't believe it; even coopers and skinners, in those days, had some regard for decency. But Alter was a changed man. God forbid, he had lost all shame. He strolled with the divorcee in the market place, and people looked from all the windows, shaking their heads and spitting in disgust. He went with her to the tavern, for all the world like a peasant with his woman. There they sat, in the middle of the week, guzzling wine.

When Shifra Leah heard it, she knew she was in trouble. She came running to the tavern, but her husband turned on her with the vilest abuse. The newcomer, the slut, also jeered at her and taunted her. Shifra Leah tried to appeal to him: "Have you no shame before the world?" "The world can kiss what we sit on," says he. Shifra Leah cried to the other one: "He is my husband!" "Mine, also," answers she. The tavern keeper tried to put a word in, but Alter and the slut belabored him too; a woman depraved is worse than the worst man. She opened such a mouth that she shocked even the tavern keeper. People said she grabbed a pitcher and threw it at him. Turbin is not Warsaw. The town was in an uproar. The rabbi sent the sexton to summon Alter to him, but Alter refused to come. Then the community threatened him with the three letters of excommunication. It didn't help, he had connections with the authorities and defied one and all.

After a couple of weeks, the divorced slut left town, and people thought things would quiet down. Before the week was out, the man who was called back from the dead came to his wife with a tale. He had an opportunity, he said, to buy a wood in Wolhynia, an unusual bargain, and he must leave at once. He collected all his money, and told Shifra Leah that he had to pawn her jewelry too. He bought a barouche and two horses. People suspected he was up to something crooked and warned his wife, but the faith she had in him, he could have been a wonder rabbi. She packed his suits and underwear; roasted chickens and prepared jams for him for the journey. Just before he set off he handed her a small box: "In here," he said, "are three promissory notes. On Thursday, eight days from today, take the notes to the rabbi. The money was left with him." He spun her a story, and she swallowed it. Then he was off.

Thursday, eight days later, she opened the box and discovered a writ of divorce. She let out a scream and fell into a faint. When she came to, she ran to the Rabbi, but he took one look at the paper and said: "There is nothing to be done. A writ of divorce can be hung on your doorknob, or it can be slipped under your door." You can imagine what went on in Turbin that day. Shifra Leah pulled at her cheeks, screaming: "Why didn't I let him croak? May he drop dead wherever he is!" He had cleaned her out—even her holiday kerchief was gone. The house was there still, but it was mortgaged to the barber. In olden times, runners would have been sent after such a shameless betrayer. The Jews once had power and authority, and there was a pillory in the synagogue court, to which a wretch would have been bound. But among our Gentile officials a Jew was of small consequence—they couldn't care less. Besides, Alter had taken care to bribe his way.

Well, Shifra Leah took sick, climbed into her bed and refused to get up. She would take nothing to eat, and kept cursing him with the deadliest curses. Then suddenly she started beating her breast and lamenting: "It's all my fault. I did not do enough to please him." She wept and she laughed —she was like one possessed by an evil spirit. The barber, who claimed now to be the legal owner of the house, wanted to throw her out of her home, but the community wouldn't let him, and she remained, in a room in the attic.

In time, after a few weeks, she recovered, and she went out with a peddler's pack, like a man, to trade among the peasants. She turned out to be a good hand at buying and selling; soon the matchmakers were approaching her with proposals of marriage. She wouldn't hear of it; all she talked about, she bent your ear if you would listen, was her Alter. "You wait," she said, "he'll come back to me. The other one didn't want him, she was after his money. She'll clean him out and leave him flat." "And you'd take such riffraff back again?" folks asked her, to which she answered: "Only let him come. I'll wash his feet and drink the water." She still had a trunk left and she collected linens and woolens, like a bride. "This will be my dowry for when he returns," she boasted. "I'll marry him again." Nowadays you call it infatuation; we called it plumb crazy.

Whenever people came from the big cities, she ran to them: "Have you run into my Alter?" But no one had seen him: it was rumored that he had become an apostate. Some said he had married a she-demon. Such things happen. The years went by, the people began to think that Alter would never be heard of again.

One Sabbath afternoon, when Shifra Leah was dozing on her bench-bed (she had never learned to read the Holy Book, as the women do), the door opened and in stepped a soldier. He took out a sheet of paper. "Are you Shifra Leah, the wife of the scoundrel Alter?" She turned white as chalk; she could not understand Russian, and an interpreter was brought in. Well, Alter was in prison, a serious crime, because he was sentenced to life. He was being kept in the Lublin jail, and he had managed to bribe the soldier, who was going home on leave, to bring a letter to Shifra Leah. Who knows where Alter got the money to bribe in prison? He must have hidden it somewhere in his cot when he was first brought in. Those who read the letter said that it would have melted a stone; he wrote to his former wife: "Shifra Leah, I have sinned against you. Save me! Save me! I am going under. Death is better than such a life." The other one, the slut, the barber's sister-in-law, had stripped him of everything and left him only his shirt. She probably informed on him too.

The town buzzed with excitement. But what could anyone do to help him?—you may be sure he was not put away for reading the Holy Book. But Shifra Leah ran to all the important people in town. "It is not his fault," she cried, "it comes from his sickness." She was not yet sobered up, the old cow. People asked her: "What do you need that lecher for?" She would not allow a speck to fall on his name. She sold everything, even her Passover dishes; she borrowed money, she got what she could from high and low. Then she took herself off to Lublin, and there she must have turned heaven and earth, for she finally got him freed from jail.

Back she came to Turbin with him, and young and old ran out to meet them. When he stepped out from the covered wagon, you couldn't recognize him: without a beard, only a thick mustache, and he had on a short caftan and high boots. It was a *goy*, not Alter. On looking closer, you saw that it was Alter after all: the same walk, the same swagger. He called each man by his name and asked about all kinds of detail. He wisecracked and said things to make the women blush. They asked him: "Where's your beard?" He answers: "I pawned it with a moneylender." They asked him: "How does a Jew take up such ways?" He replies: "Are you any better? Everybody is a thief." On the spot he gave a recital of everybody's secret sins. It was plain to see that he was in the hands of the Evil One.

Shifra Leah tried to make excuses for him and to restrain him; she fluttered over him like a mother hen. She forgot that they were divorced and wanted to take him home, but the rabbi sent word that they must not live under the same roof; it was even wrong for her, he said, to have traveled with him in the same wagon. Alter might scoff at Jewishness, but the law still remained. The women took a hand. The pair were separated for twelve days, while she took the prescribed ablutions, and then they were led under the wedding canopy. A bride must go to the ritual bath even if she is taking back her own husband.

Well, a week after the wedding he started thieving. On market days he was among the carts, picking pockets. He went off to the villages to steal horses. He was no longer plump, but lean as a hound. He clambered over roofs, forced locks, broke open stable doors. He was strong as iron and nimble as a devil. The peasants got together and posted a watch with dogs and lanterns. Shifra Leah was ashamed to show her face and kept her window shuttered; you can imagine what must have gone on between man and wife. Soon Alter became the leader of a band of roughnecks. He guzzled at the tavern with them, and they sang a Polish song in his honor; I remember the words to this day: "Our Alter is a decent sort, he hands out beer by the quart."

There is a saying: a thief will end up on the gallows.

One day, as Alter was drinking with his toughs, a squadron of Cossacks came riding up to the tavern with drawn swords.

Orders had come from the governor to throw him into irons and bring him to the jail. Alter saw at once that this was the end, and he grabbed a knife; his drinking pals ran off—they left him to fight it out alone. The tavern keeper said afterwards that he fought with the strength of a demon, chopping away at the Cossacks as though they were a field of cabbages. He turned over tables and threw barrels at them; he was no longer a young man, but for a while it almost looked as though he might get the better of them all. Still, as the saying goes, one is none. The Cossacks slashed and hacked at him till there was no more blood left in his veins. Someone brought the bad news to Shifra Leah, and she came running like crazy to his side. There he lay, and she wanted to call him back again, but he said one word to her: "Enough!" Shifra Leah fell silent. The Jews ransomed his body from the officials.

I didn't see him dead. But those who did swore that he looked like an old corpse that had been dug up from the grave. Pieces were dropping from his body. The face could not be recognized, it was a shapeless pulp. It was said that when he was being cleansed for burial, an arm came off, and then a foot; I wasn't there, but why should people lie? Men who are called back rot while they are alive. He was buried in a sack outside the graveyard fence, at midnight. After his death, an epidemic struck our town, and many innocent children died. Shifra Leah, that deluded woman, put up a stone for him and went to visit his grave. What I mean to say is—it is not proper to recall the dying. If she had let him go at his appointed hour, he would have left behind a good name. And who knows how many men who were called back are out in the world today? All our misfortunes come from them.

Translated by Mirra Ginsburg

A Piece of Advice

TALK about a holy man! Our powers are not theirs; their ideas are not for us to understand! But let me tell you what happened to my own father-in-law.

At the time, I was still a young man, a mere boy, and a follower of the rabbi of Kuzmir—who was there more worthy? My father-in-law lived in Rachev, where I boarded with him. He was a wealthy man and ran his house in a grand manner. For instance, look at what happened at meal times. Only *after* I had washed my hands and said the blessing, did my mother-in-law take the rolls from the oven. So that they were still hot and fresh! She timed it to the very second. In my soup, she put hardboiled eggs. I wasn't accustomed to such luxuries. In my own home the loaves of bread were baked two weeks in advance. I used to rub garlic on a slice, and wash it down with cold well water.

But at my father-in-law's everything was fancy—brass door latches, copper pans. You had to wipe your boots on a straw mat before crossing the threshold. And the fuss that was made about brewing coffee with chicory! My mother-in-law was descended from a family of Misnagids—the enemies of the Hasids—and to Misnagids the pleasures of this world mean something.

My father-in-law was an honest Jew, a Talmudic scholar; also a dealer in timber, and a mathematician of sorts. He used to have his own hut in the forest; and took a gun and two dogs when he went there, because of robbers. He knew logarithms; and by tapping the bark of a tree with his hammer, could tell if the tree were as sound inside as out. He knew how to play a game of chess with a Gentile squire. Whenever he had a free moment, he read one of the Holy Books. He carried the "Duty of the Heart" about with him in his pocket. He smoked a long pipe with an amber mouthpiece and a silver cover. He kept his prayer shawl in a hide bag, and for his phylacteries he owned silver cases.

He had two faults. First of all, he was a fervent Misnagid. What a Misnagid—he burned like fire! He called the Hasids

264

"the heretics" and he was not ashamed to speak evil of the saintly Baal Shem himself. The first time I heard him talk like that I shuddered. I wanted to pack up and run away. But the rabbi of Kuzmir was against divorce. You married your wife, not your father-in-law. And he told me Jethro, Moses' father-in-law, hadn't been a Hasid either. I was amazed. Jethro later became a holy man. But that's putting the cart before the horse. . . .

My father-in-law's second fault was his uncontrollable anger. He had been able to conquer all his other moral weaknesses, but not that one. If a merchant did not repay a debt on time and to the penny, he called him a swindler and refused to have any further dealings with him. If the town shoemaker made him a pair of boots, and they were a little too tight or too loose, he harangued him heartlessly.

Everything had to be just so. He had gotten it into his head that Jewish homes had to be as clean as those of the Christian squires, and he insisted that his wife let him inspect the pots and pans. If there was a spot on them, he was furious. There was a joke about him: that he had discovered a hole in a potato grater! His family loved him; the town respected him. But how much bad temper can people take? Everybody became his enemy. His business partners left him. Even my mother-in-law couldn't stand it any more.

Once I borrowed a pen from him. I forgot to return it immediately, and when he wanted to write a letter to Lublin, he began hunting. Remembering that I had it, I hastened to give it back. But he had fallen into such a rage that he struck me in the face. Well, if one's own father does a thing like that, it's his privilege. But for a father-in-law to strike a son-in-law: it's unheard of! My mother-in-law became sick from what had happened; my wife wept bitterly. I myself wasn't that upset: What was the tragedy? But I saw that my father-in-law was eating his heart out, regretting it. So I went to him. "Father-in-law," I said. "Don't take it to heart. I forgive you."

As a rule he spoke very little to me. Because if he was particular about everything, I was lax. When I took off my coat, I never remembered where I had put it. If I was given some coins, I promptly misplaced them. And though Rachev was a tiny village, when I went beyond the market place, I could no longer find my way back. The houses were all alike, and I never looked at the women within. When I got lost, I would open a cottage door and ask, "Doesn't my father-in-law live here?" Those inside would always begin to titter and laugh. Finally I took a vow never to walk anywhere except straight from my home to the study house and back again. —Only later did it occur to me that near my father-in-law's house stood a landmark: a thick tree with deep roots, which must have been two hundred years old.

Anyway, for one reason or another, my father-in-law and I were always quarreling, and he avoided me. But after the incident of the pen, he talked to me. "Baruch, what shall I do?" he said. "I'm a bad-tempered man. I know the sin of anger is as evil as that of idolatry. For years I've tried to control my temper, yet it only gets worse. I'm sinking into hell. In worldly matters too, it's very bad. My enemies want to destroy me. I'm afraid I'll end up without bread in the house."

I answered: "Father-in-law, come with me to Rabbi Chazkele of Kuzmir."

He turned pale. "Have you gone mad?" he shouted. "You know I don't believe in wonder-rabbis!"

I held my tongue. First, because I didn't want him to scold me as he always regretted it later. And, second, I didn't want him to go on slandering a holy man.

Imagine then: After the evening prayer, he came over to me and said: "Baruch, we're going to Kuzmir." I was stupefied. But why go into that. . . . He had decided to go, and we began to prepare for the journey immediately. As it was winter, we had to hire a sleigh. A deep snow had fallen and the road was far from safe; the forests were full of wolves; nor was there any lack of highwaymen. But we had to go right away. Such was my father-in-law's nature! My mother-in-law thought— heaven forbid—that he had lost his mind. He put on his fur coat, a pair of straw overshoes, and said the special prayer for a journey. I found the whole thing a great adventure. Wasn't I going to Kuzmir and taking my father-in-law with me? Who could be happier than I? Yet I trembled with fear, for who knew what would happen there!

On the journey, my father-in-law didn't utter a word. It snowed the whole way. The fields as we passed were full of swirling snowflakes. Philosophers say the shape of each flake is unique. But snow is a subject in itself. It comes from Heaven and lets us experience the peace of the other world. White is the color of mercy according to the cabala, while red signifies the law.

Nowadays snow is a trifle: it falls for a day or two at most. But in those days! Often it snowed for a month without stopping! Huge snowdrifts piled up; houses were buried; and everyone had to dig their way out. Heaven and earth merged and became one. Why does the beard of an old man turn white? Such things are all related. —At night, we heard the howling of beasts . . . or perhaps it was only the sound of the wind.

We arrived in Kuzmir on a Friday afternoon. My father-in-law went to the rabbi's study to greet him. He was permitted to go in immediately. Since it was the middle of winter, few of the rabbi's disciples had come. I waited in the study house, my skin tingling. My father-in-law was by nature such a bull-headed man. He might very well talk back to Rabbi Chazkele. It was three-quarters of an hour before he came out, his face white as chalk above his long beard, his eyes burning like coals beneath his bushy eyebrows.

"If it wasn't the eve of the Sabbath, I would go home immediately," he said.

"What happened, father-in-law?" I asked.

"Your wonder-rabbi is a fool! An ignoramus! If he weren't an old man, I would tear off his sidelocks."

The taste of gall was strong in my mouth; and I regretted the whole affair. To talk this way about Rabbi Chazkele of Kuzmir!

"Father-in-law," I asked, "what did the rabbi say to you?"

"He told me to become a flatterer," my father-in-law answered. "For eight days I must flatter everyone I meet, even the worst scoundrel. If your rabbi had an ounce of sense he would know that I hate flattery like the plague. It makes me sick even to come in contact with it. For me, a flatterer is worse than a murderer."

"Well, father-in-law," said I, "do you think the rabbi doesn't know that flattery is bad? Believe me, he knows what he's doing."

"What does he know? One sin cannot wipe out another. He knows nothing about the law."

I went away completely crushed. I had not yet been to the ritual bath, so I went there. I have forgotten to mention that my father-in-law never went to the ritual bath. I don't know why. I guess it's the way of the Misnagids. He was haughty perhaps. It was beneath his dignity to undress among other men. When I came out of the ritual bath, the Sabbath candles were already lit. Rabbi Chazkele used to bless the Sabbath candles long before dark—he himself, not his wife. His wife lit her own candles. But that's another matter. . . .

I entered the study house. The rabbi was standing in his white gabardine and his white hat. His face shone like the sun. One could see clearly he was in a higher world. When he sang out, "Give thanks unto the Lord for He is good for His mercy endureth forever," the walls shook. While praying the rabbi clapped his hands and stamped his feet.

Only a few disciples were present. But they were the elite, men of holy deeds, every one of them a personal friend of the rabbi. As they chanted, I felt their prayers reaching the heavens. Never, not even at Kuzmir, had I experienced such a beginning of the holy Sabbath. The rejoicing was so real that you could touch it. All their eyes were shining. My mind became so light that I could barely keep my feet on the ground. I happened to be praying near a window. Snow had covered everything—no road, no path, no cottages. Candles seemed to burn in the snow. Heaven and earth were one. The moon and the stars touched the roofs. Those who were not in Kuzmir that Friday evening will never know what this world can be. . . . I'm not speaking now of the world to come. . . .

I glanced at my father-in-law. He stood in a corner, his head bent. As a rule, his sternness was visible in his face, but now he looked humble, quite a different person. After the prayers we went to eat at the rabbi's table.

The rabbi had put on a white robe of silk, with silver fasteners, and embroidered with flowers. As his custom was before the Sabbath meal, he now sat alone in his library, reciting chapters of the Mishnah and of the Zohar. The older disciples sat down on benches; the younger men, I among them, stood about.

When the rabbi came out of his study, he intoned the verses, "Peace be with you," and "A woman of worth, who can find?" Then he blessed the wine and said a prayer over the white bread of the Sabbath. He ate a morsel no bigger than an olive. Immediately thereafter, he began the Sabbath table chants. But this wasn't mere chanting! His body swayed; he cooed like a dove; it sounded like the singing of angels. His communion with God was so complete that his soul almost left his body. Everybody could see that the holy man was not here but high up in heaven.

Who knows what heights he reached? How can one describe it? As the Talmud says, "He who has not seen joy like this has never seen joy at all." He was at the same time at the court in Kuzmir, and high above in God's temples, in the Nest of the Bird, at the Throne of Glory. Such rapture is impossible to imagine. I forgot about my father-in-law and even about myself. I was no longer Baruch from Rachev—but bodiless, sheer nothing. It was one o'clock in the morning before we left the rabbi's table. Such a Sabbath service never happened before and never will again—maybe, when the Messiah comes.

But I am forgetting the main thing. The rabbi commented on the law. And what he said was connected with what he had told my father-in-law at their meeting. "What should a Jew do if he is not a pious man?" the Rabbi asked. And answered: "Let him play the pious man. The Almighty does not require good intentions. The deed is what counts. It is what you do that matters. Are you angry perhaps? Go ahead and be angry, but speak gentle words and be friendly at the same time. Are you afraid of being a dissembler? So what if you pretend to be something you aren't? For whose sake are you lying? For your Father in Heaven. His Holy Name, blessed be He, knows the intention and the intention behind the intention, and it is this that is the main thing."

How can one convey the rabbi's lesson? Pearls fell from his mouth and each word burned like fire and penetrated the heart. It wasn't so much the words themselves, but his gestures and his tone. The evil spirit, the rabbi said, cannot be conquered by sheer will. It is known that the evil one has no body, and works mainly through the power of speech. Do not lend him a mouth—that is the way to conquer him. Take, for example, Balaam, the son of Beor. He wanted to curse the children of Israel but forced himself to bless them instead, and because of this, his name is mentioned in the Bible. When one doesn't lend the evil one a tongue, he must remain mute.

Why should I ramble on? My father-in-law attended all three Sabbath meals. And when, on the Sabbath night, he went to the rabbi to take leave of him, he stayed in his study for a whole hour.

On the way home, I said, "Well, father-in-law?" And he answered: "Your rabbi is a great man."

The road back to Rachev was full of dangers. Though it was still midwinter, the ice on the Vistula had cracked—ice-blocks were floating downstream the way they do at Passover time. In the midst of all the cold, thunder and lightning struck. No doubt about it, only Satan could be responsible for this! We were forced to put up at an inn until Tuesday—and there were many Misnagids staying there. No one could travel further. A real blizzard was raging outside. The howling in the chimney made you shiver.

Misnagids are always the same. These were no exception. They began to heap ridicule upon Hasids—but my father-in-law maintained silence. They tried to provoke him but he refused to join in. They took him to task: "What about this one? What about that one?" He put them off good-naturedly with many tricks. "What change has come over you?" they asked. If they had known that he was coming from Rabbi Chazkele, they would have devoured him.

What more can I tell you? My father-in-law did what the Rabbi had prescribed. He stopped snapping at people. His eyes glowed with anger but his speech was soft. And if at times he lifted his pipe about to strike someone, he always stopped himself and spoke with humility. It wasn't long before the people of Rachev realized that my father-in-law was a changed man. He made peace with his enemies. He would stop any little brat in the street and give him a pinch on the cheek. And if the water carrier splashed water entering our house, though I knew this just about drove my father-in-law crazy, he never showed it. "How are you, Reb Yontle?" he would say. "Are you cold, eh?" One could feel that he did this only with great effort. That's what made it noble.

In time, his anger disappeared completely. He began to visit Rabbi Chazkele three times a year. He became a kindly man, so good-natured it was unbelievable. But that is what a habit is like—if you break it, it becomes the opposite. One can turn the worst sin into a good deed. The main thing is to act, not to ponder. He even began to visit the ritual bath. And when he grew old, he acquired disciples of his own. This was after the death of Rabbi Chazkele. My father-in-law always used to say, "If you can't be a good Jew, act the good Jew, because if you act something, you *are* it. Otherwise why does any man try to act at all? Take, for example, the drunk in the tavern. Why doesn't he try to act differently?"

The rabbi once said: "Why is 'Thou Shalt Not Covet' the very last of the Ten Commandments? Because one must first avoid doing the wrong things. Then, later on, one will not desire to do them. If one stopped and waited until all the passions ceased, one could never attain holiness."

And so it is with all things. If you are not happy, act the happy man. Happiness will come later. So also with faith. If you are in despair, act as though you believed. Faith will come afterwards.

Translated by Martha Glicklich and Joel Blocker

In the Poorhouse

THERE was a warm, homelike feeling about the poorhouse today. The rich man of the town, Reb Leizer Lemkes, married off his youngest daughter, Altele. And he gave a feast for the poor. In addition to gorging themselves on carp, *kreplach* with soup, *chalah*, beef and carrot stew, and washing it all down with wine, each of the paupers was given something to take home: a slice of honey cake, a chicken drumstick, an apple, a piece of pastry. Everyone had eaten his fill. Most of them had overeaten. The poorhouse overseer had also had his share and did not stint today: he piled the stove full of firewood. Such heat came from its iron door that Hodele the beggar asked someone to open the chimney, she was in such a sweat.

After the feast everybody fell asleep. Night descended quickly. None of the men had prayed that evening. But after some hours of sleep, the little family began to wake. First to open his eyes was Leibush Scratch. He had hidden a roast chicken in the straw. And he began to put it away now, for fear that someone might steal it during the long night, or else the mice might get at it.

The second to wake up was Jonah the Thief. He had slipped under his pillow a head of a carp wrapped in cabbage leaves— a present from Serele the servant girl. Bashe the Whore, who had hidden three macaroons in her stocking, could not sleep either. The sounds of munching, chewing, gnawing mingled with the snuffling and snoring of the sleepers. Outside, fresh snow had fallen, and the moon was bright. After a while, Leibush Scratch asked:

"Jonah, my friend, are you eating or sleeping on it?"

"Chewing is no sin," Jonah the Thief retorted smartly.

"Leave him alone, Reb Leibush," put in Bashe the Whore, "or he may swallow a bone."

"What are you crunching there?" asked Leibush. "Last Passover's matzos?"

"A bit of a macaroon."

"I thought you had something. Who gave it to you, eh?"

"The little Tsipele."

"Give me a piece. . . ."

Bashe did not answer.

Jonah the Thief laughed: "Her kind doesn't give anything for nothing."

"I can give her my bellyache."

"If you have an ache, you can keep it to yourself," replied Bashe.

"I have plenty to spare for you too."

"Don't curse, Reb Leibush, I am cursed enough," said Bashe. At any other time she would not trouble to talk to Leibush, but the food and the wine and the glowing stove softened all hearts. People forgot their quarrels for a while. Besides, the night was long, and they could not go back to sleep.

For a while it was quiet again. Leibush could be heard cracking the chicken bones and sucking the marrow. Then he asked:

"I wonder how late it is?"

"I sent my watch for repair," joked Jonah the Thief.

"Once upon a time I had no need for watches. In the daytime I could tell the hour by the sun. At night I looked at the stars, or sniffed the wind. But you can't tell anything in this stench. Why are no roosters crowing?"

"All the roosters were slaughtered for the wedding," said Bashe.

"Tell us a story, Reb Leibush," asked Jonah the Thief.

"What story? I've told you everything. Old Getsl makes up his stories, but I don't like to make them up. What's the good of that? I can tell you that I was Count Pototsky once upon a time, or that Radziwill used to heat the bath house for me. What will come of that? Did I ever tell you about the mannikin?"

"In the glass of whiskey? With the magician?"

"Yes."

"You told us that one."

"And about the hail?"

"The hail too."

"And the ox?"

"The way the ox attacked you on the way to night prayers?"

"Yes."

"You did, you told us that one too."

"Well, what can I tell you, then? You are a thief, you have many stories to tell. I spent my life over the grindstone."

"Hey, you, Bashe, why don't you ever tell us anything?" asked Jonah.

Bashe was silent. They no longer expected her to answer. Suddenly her voice was heard:

"What can I tell you?"

"Tell us how you became a whore, and all the rest of it."

"The moment I open my mouth, the women begin to curse."

"The women are asleep."

"They'll wake soon enough. They don't let me live. God has forgiven long ago, but they won't forgive. What harm have I done them? I am not from these parts. I have never sinned with their husbands. I lie here and never hurt a fly, but they eat me up alive with their eyes. They spit into my face. Whenever anyone brings a plate of soup or a bowl of *kashe*, they begin to hiss like snakes: 'Not for her! Not for her!' If it were up to them, I would have died of hunger long ago. But kind people have pity. If I had my legs, I'd not be lying here. I'd run from here to where black pepper grows."

"But you have none."

"And that's my bitter misfortune. I long for death, but it doesn't come. Healthy people go, but I lie here and rot alive. It's lucky they put me here. The women used to pinch me, they used to tear out lumps of my flesh. They threw garbage at me. They spilled their night slops over me. . . ."

"We know, we know it all."

"You don't know one thousandth of it. When a man hits someone, everybody sees it and there's a hullabaloo. But women can dig your heart out on the sly. Now they cannot reach me with their hands, so they stick needles into me with their eyes. They can't forgive me that I lie here among the men. When I lie dead, with my feet toward the door and a straw under my head, they will still envy me."

"I thought you were going to tell us a story."

"What have I to tell? I've had troubles from my childhood on. My mother, may she intercede for me, had three daughters before me. My father wanted a boy. He made a journey to a rabbi, and the rabbi promised him a boy. When the midwife told him it was a girl, he would not believe her. He demanded to be shown. . . . My father was a Hasid, and it was a custom in the study house that a man whose wife gave birth to one daughter after another was given a whipping. The Hasidim stretched my father out on the table, and whipped him with their sashes. He never wanted to look at me. He would not even call me by my name. He never hit me either. Just as if I were a step-child. When I called him 'father,' he pretended he did not hear me. Was it my fault? My mother used to say: 'You were born in a black hour.' When I was nine, I left home."

"Why did you leave home?"

"Because I slaughtered three ducks."

"What? You slaughtered ducks?"

"Yes, I was growing up a wild thing. Whatever I saw, I imitated. One day my mother sent me to the *shochet*, to have him slaughter a hen. I saw him standing there with the knife slaughtering the fowl, and I liked it. We had three ducks locked in the pantry. I took a pocket knife, spit on a stone, sharpened it, and cut the throats of the three ducks. Suddenly the door opened, and my father came in. He turned white as chalk. He ran to my mother, screaming: 'Either she goes, or I do . . .' On the following day they packed a few things into a bundle and sent me into service in Lublin."

"But how did you become a whore?"

"How did you become a horse thief? Little by little. A young fellow promises to lead you under the bridal canopy. Then he tells you to go and whistle."

"Who was the first one?"

"A teacher's helper."

"A teacher's helper, eh? And then?"

"He went away, and that was the last of him. Try and find a teacher's helper in God's world. After him came a tailor's assistant, and after the tailor, a hat-maker. When a girl loses her virtue, she is anybody's game. Whoever wants to, has the use of her. A bridal canopy is only a few lengths of velvet and four posts. But without it, a girl is less than the dirt under your nail."

"We know that. When did you enter a brothel?"

"When I got a belly full."

"And what happened there?"

"What could happen there? Nothing."

"And the child, what became of it?"

"It was left on the church steps."

"One child?"

"Three."

"And then what?"

"Nothing."

"This is no story."

"The story comes later."

"What happened?"

"I'm ashamed to tell it before Reb Leibush."

"What? But he's sleeping."

"He fell asleep?"

"Don't you hear him snoring?"

"Yes. But he was talking just now!"

"At his age you can talk one minute, doze off the next, and a minute later you make bye-bye, and it's all over. And with me you don't have to feel ashamed."

"No."

"Let's hear it, then."

"I'm afraid the women are listening."

"They're sleeping like the dead. Talk quietly. I am not deaf."

"There are times when you want to talk. I was already in Warsaw at that time. I was with a madam. She had three of us, and I was the prettiest. Don't look at me today. I am a broken vessel. I have no legs, my hair is gone, my teeth are gone. I am an old scarecrow. But in my young days I was a beauty. The queen! That's what they called me. People could not look into my face—it dazzled like the sun. Whenever a guest had me, he never wanted anyone else. The other two stood at the gate all night, but I sat on my bed and they came to me as if I were a doctor. The madam had a tongue like a whip, but when she spoke to me, it was as through a silken cloth. I had a fiancé— that's what we called them—Yankel, and he was crazy about me. He bought me whatever I wanted. If the madam said an unkind word to me, right away he'd pull the knife out of his boot. He was a wild one, too. A guest is a guest, after all. But suddenly he'd get jealous. He'd grab the man by the collar and throw him down the whole flight of stairs, if he just dared to kiss me. The madam would yell murder, but he'd yell back: 'Shut up, or I'll knock out all your teeth.' He wanted to marry me, too, but his years were short. He caught the smallpox and was covered with blisters all over. They took him in an ambulance to the hospital, and there they poisoned everybody."

"Poisoned? Why?"

"Just so."

"And then what?"

"He died and was buried. After that my luck changed. I was taken over by another fellow, but that one had only money on his mind. Sender was his name, Senderl the Bum. He did not care for me, and I did not care for him. When the madam saw that things were going badly with me, she began to lord it over me. I could not run away because I had a yellow passport. And where can our kind escape? Only to the grave. The madam began to abuse me, and the other two sluts made my life miserable. A woman must have someone to protect her, or else she's nine feet deep in trouble.

"Once in two weeks we had our day off. When Yankel was alive, he used to take me everywhere. We even drove out in a *droshky*. He bought me chocolates, marmalade, halvah and licorice from a Turk—whatever my heart desired. There was a carousel in Voiny Place, and we used to go round and round in it. But when Yankel was gone, I was all alone. The madam lived on Nizka Street, and I went out walking along the Dzhika. Were you ever in Warsaw? I had nothing to do. So I leaned on a lamp-post, cracking sunflower seeds. I was not out to catch anyone. I put on a cotton dress and a shawl over my shoulders, like an honest girl.

"I stand there, and think about my life. Suddenly a tall young man comes over to me, in a wide-brimmed hat, with a shock of long hair and a cape down to the sidewalk. I was so startled, I cried out. He looked strange, pale and disheveled like a free-thinker. In those years workers were organizing unions and throwing bombs at the Tsar. I thought he was one of that company. I wanted to get away, but he put out a long hand and grabbed me. 'Fraulein,' says he, 'do not run away. I do not eat people.' 'What does the gentleman want?' I ask. And he says: 'Do you want to earn some money?' 'Who doesn't want money?' I say, 'But I have no time. I must be back at the old woman's in an hour.' 'It won't take an hour,' says he. He starts talking so fast that I cannot understand anything at first. He is in love, he tells me, with a girl, and she is making him sweat. So he wants me to come with him and he'll introduce me as his fiancée. 'What will come of it?' I ask, '—besides, I must get back very soon.' And he says: 'I want to test her.' 'How do you know who I am?' I ask. So he tells me he lives across the street and he sees me at the gate. It seems he followed me.

"I was afraid because I could not stay out long, and Sender was free with his fists. Anything not to his liking, and he could beat you to death. But before I could say a word, I was sitting in a *droshky*. 'Take off your shawl,' says he. On Nalewki Street there was a milliner. He tells the droshky to wait and picks out a hat for me, with a wide brim, for three roubles. I put it on, and I don't know my own face in the mirror. He takes my shawl and hides it under his cloak. We drive out on Mead Street, and there he buys me a handbag. All the customers haggle. They bargain the shopkeeper down to half the asking price. But he doesn't bargain, he pays whatever they ask. The salesgirls laugh at him and pinch one another. My mother used to say: 'Send a fool to market, and the shopkeepers rejoice.' To make it short and sweet, I was now a lady from Marshalkovski Street.

"From Mead Street we drove back to Franciscan Boulevard. The driver was already beginning to grumble that it was more than a single fare zone. So the man takes a half a rouble from his pocket and hands it to him. He is throwing money around like a lord.

"Then we come to a leather goods store, and there's a girl inside. There are no customers. He lets me walk ahead and then follows me in. Respect for the ladies, we called it in Warsaw. She was an ordinary girl. I could not tell what he saw in her. Her eyes were black and sharp. You could tell she was a shrew. She took one look at him and turned white as chalk. He takes me under the arm and leads me to the counter. 'Leah, my dear,' he says, 'this is my fiancée.' I thought the jade would catch apoplexy on the spot. If she could, she would have swallowed me up alive. 'Why did you bring your fiancée here?' she asked, 'Do you want me to congratulate her?' 'No,' he answers, 'this wasn't the reason. I want a pair of shoes made for her, and I know your father sells the best leather. Give her first-class goods. The price is no object.' If the girl did not catch a stroke, she was stronger than iron. 'You cannot buy leather without a shoemaker,' she says. 'You have to know the size and the trimmings.' 'You can take her size,' says he, and tells me to sit down on the stool. He lifts up my dress, tears off a strip of paper and measures my foot. And he says: 'Leah my dear, did you ever see such a foot? It's the smallest foot in Warsaw.' I really had small feet. He tickles me with his long fingers, and I can hardly keep a straight face. The girl says: 'Don't think you are fooling me. You could have gotten your leather somewhere else. You came here to tease me. So I can tell you: whoever begrudges you, let him have nothing himself. And she isn't your fiancée either. You picked someone up in the street. I know your tricks. I don't need your trade. Get out of here and don't come back. If you show up again, alone or with her, I'll call the policeman!' My gentleman turns white and says nothing. He drops my foot, and I sit there with one shoe and one stocking. And then he cries out: 'Yes, you are right. She is a girl from the street, but I swear to God I'll marry her this very day! Tonight she'll be my wife, and I'll forget all about you. I'll tear you from my heart. I'll love her with my whole soul. Even if she is an unfortunate one, she has more decency than you. . . .' Those were his words. He started abusing her in the vilest language. He caught me by the hand and screamed:

" 'Come to the rabbi, my bride! Tonight we shall be man and wife.'

"I was so mixed up that I left one shoe in the store."

II

Leibush Scratch woke up.

"You're talking? Talk. What happened after that?"

"Have you heard it, then?" Jonah the Thief asked. "But you were sleeping!"

"I dozed off, but I heard. At my age sleep isn't what it used to be. I dream I am at a fair, and I know I am lying here at the poorhouse. I am here, and I am there. I am Leibush, and I am the rabbi. Why did you leave your shoe, eh?"

"I was afraid a crowd would gather."

"How could you walk around in one shoe?"

"Just as I stood there, the shoe flew after me from the store. I ran to catch it, and a cart almost knocked me over. My fine gentleman dropped down on his knees in the middle of the gutter and put the shoe on my foot. Just like a play in the theatre. The whole street laughed. The *droshky* was gone, and he pulled me and yelled: 'Where do you find a rabbi around here?' People pointed out a house across the street. And then, my friends, I saw that I had no luck. We were already in front of the steps, when I was suddenly afraid. I said to him: 'You love the other girl, not me.' 'I'll love you, I'll love you,' he answers. 'I am a trained pharmacist. I can live in Petersburg, in Moscow, anywhere in Russia. We'll leave this city, and I'll pluck her out of my heart. I'll love and cherish you, and you will be the mother of my children.' I remember every word as if it happened yesterday. I did not know what a pharmacist was. Later someone explained to me it meant a druggist. An educated man. But I say: 'Do you know what I do?' 'I know,' he cries, 'but I don't want to know. I'll forgive you everything . . .' 'But you don't even know me,' I say, but he screams: 'I do not need to know you. You are more pure than she is . . .' I looked at him: he is foaming at the mouth. His eyes are like a madman's. I suddenly felt sick. I broke away and began to run. I ran out of the gates, and heard him running after me and calling: 'Where are you running? Where are you running? Come back! . . .' I ran as if he were a murderer. I came to the butcher stalls in the market, and there I got away from him. The place was so crowded that you could not drop a needle. It was only after I cooled off that I realized that I was done for. Where was I running, woe is me? Back to the mire.

"When I came home and they saw me with the stylish hat and handbag, there was an uproar. The old woman asks: 'Where is the shawl?' And I don't have the shawl. He hid it under his cape. Well, there was no end to talk and laughter. They wouldn't believe me, either. When Sender came and they told him everything, he took away the hat and the handbag. He gave me a punch too, into the bargain. He had a fiancée somewhere, and he took everything to her. And, my dear people, I'll tell you something else: the old woman deducted from my wages for the shawl, or may I never have a holy burial."

For a long while everyone was silent. Then Leibush Scratch asked:

"You are sorry now, eh?"

"Why not? I wouldn't be rotting here today."

"If he lived across the street, why didn't you seek him out?" asked Jonah the Thief.

"They would not give me any days off after that. I thought he would come, but he never did."

"Perhaps he made up with the girl from the leather store?"

"Perhaps."

"There is a saying: forge the iron while it's hot," Leibush Scratch said reflectively.

"That's true."

"And yet, if it is not written for you, it isn't. Was it you, then, who was running? Your feet carried you. Or take me. Did I have to end up lying here on a bundle of straw? Not more than you have to dance on the roof. I was not rich, but I was a man of some property. I owned a house, a small mill. I had a wife . . . But if they want it up in heaven that a man should fall, they find a way. First my wife sickened and died. Then the house went up in smoke. Nobody knew how it started. A few splinters were smoldering under the tripod. Then suddenly there was a burst of fire as though hell itself had opened. There wasn't even any wind. My house stood right next to Chaim the Cooper's, but never a spark touched his place, while I was ruined. Can anyone understand that?"

"No."

"Someone saw a little flame sit on the bed. It rolled over and made somersaults. It was all from the evil ones."

"What did the evil ones have against you?"

"I was destined to take up a beggar's sack. . . ."

Jonah the Thief began to crack his knuckles, first one hand, then the other.

"Isn't it the truth, though? That night when I went to the village of Bysht I knew well enough that I should not go. The peasants had heard of me. I was warned that they were sleeping in the stables. Wojciech the village elder had posted a watch with a rattle. I needed the whole business like a hole in the head. Just a few days before that I pulled in a big haul. Zeldele, may she rest in peace, begged me: 'Jonah, don't try to grab the whole world. I'd rather eat dry bread than see you making this kind of a living.' And what did we need? There were only the two of us. Zelig the horse merchant wanted to hire me as a driver. I could have become a horse dealer myself. Sometimes you earn more, sometimes less, but it's honest money. I was already going to bed that night. I closed the shutters and pulled off my boots. Suddenly I put them on again and started out for Bysht. I walked with a heavy heart. I kept stopping and wanting to turn back. But I never walked back—they brought me home in a wheelbarrel."

"What did they do it with? Sticks?" asked Leibush.

"Whatever they could lay their hands on. A whole village against one man. . . ."

"I'll tell you the truth—it's a wonder you came out alive. This was before your day. There was a certain Itchele Nonie —that's what they called him because he had a long nose— and he went to Boyares to steal a horse. The peasants ambushed him and burned him alive. All that was left of him was a heap of ashes. The gravediggers' brotherhood had nothing to bury . . ."

"I know. I've heard of it. He had better luck than I."

"When did your wife die? I don't remember any more."

"Six months later."

"From all that trouble, eh?"

"No, from pleasure."

"Well, everything is destined. Everything is written for us above, to the last breath. As my grandmother used to say: Nobody is mightier than the Almighty."

"Who writes it all? God?"

"Not you."

"Where does he get so much paper?"

"Don't let your brains dry up in worrying about that."

"Man has his share of responsibility too."

"No, he hasn't. . . ."

It became quiet at the poorhouse. Hodele the beggar moaned in her sleep, muttered unintelligible words. A cricket chirped once. Leibush Scratch resumed his snoring, whistling through his nose. Jonah the Thief asked:

"Do you still have a piece of macaroon? I have a bitter taste in my mouth. . . ."

Bashe did not answer.

Translated by Mirra Ginsburg

The Destruction of Kreshev

Reb Bunim Comes to Kreshev

I AM the Primeval Snake, the Evil One, Satan. The cabala refers to me as Samael and the Jews sometimes call me merely, "that one."

It is well-known that I love to arrange strange marriages, delighting in such mismatings as an old man with a young girl, an unattractive widow with a youth in his prime, a cripple with a great beauty, a cantor with a deaf woman, a mute with a braggart. Let me tell you about one such "interesting" union I contrived in Kreshev, which is a town on the river San, that enabled me to be properly abusive and gave me the opportunity to perform one of those little stunts that forces the forsaking of both this world and the next between the saying of a "yes" and a "no."

Kreshev is about as large as one of the smallest letters in the smallest prayer books. On two sides of the town there is a thick pine forest and on the third the river San. The peasants in the neighboring villages are poorer and more isolated than any others in the Lublin district and the fields are the most barren. During a good part of the year the roads leading to the larger towns are merely broad trenches of water; one travels by wagon at one's peril. Bears and wolves lurk at the edge of the settlement in winter and often attack a stray cow or calf, occasionally even a human being. And, finally, so that the peasants shall never be rid of their wretchedness, I have instilled in them a burning faith. In that part of the country there is a church in every other village, a shrine at every tenth house. The Virgin stands with rusty halo, holding in her arms Jesus, the infant son of the Jewish carpenter Yossel. To her the aged come—and in the depth of winter kneel down, thus acquiring rheumatism. When May comes we have daily processions of the half-starved chanting with hoarse voices for rain. The incense gives off an acrid odor, and a consumptive drummer beats with all his might to frighten me away. Nevertheless, the rains don't come. Or if they do, they are never in time. But that doesn't prevent the people from believing. And so it has continued from time immemorial.

The Jews of Kreshev are both somewhat better informed and more prosperous than the peasants. Their wives are shop-keepers and are skilled in giving false weight and measure. The village peddlers know how to get the peasant women to pur-chase all sorts of trinkets and thus earn for themselves corn, potatoes, flax, chickens, ducks, geese—and sometimes a little extra. What won't a woman give for a string of beads, a deco-rated feather duster, a flowered calico, or just a kind word from a stranger? So it is not entirely surprising that here and there among the flaxen-haired children one comes across a curly-haired, black-eyed imp with a hooked nose. The peasants are extremely sound sleepers but the devil does not permit their young women to rest but leads them down backpaths to barns where the peddlers wait in the hay. Dogs bay at the moon, roosters crow, frogs croak, the stars in heaven look down and wink, and God himself dozes among the clouds. The Almighty is old; it is no easy task to live forever.

But let us return to the Jews of Kreshev.

All year round, the market place is one deep marsh, for the very good reason that the women empty their slops there. The houses don't stand straight; they are half-sunk into the earth and have patched roofs; their windows are stuffed with rags or covered with ox bladders. The homes of the poor have no floors; some even lack chimneys. In such houses the smoke from the stove escapes through a hole in the roof. The women marry when they are fourteen or fifteen and age quickly from too much childbearing. In Kreshev the cobblers at their low benches have only worn-out, scuffed shoes on which to prac-tice their trade. The tailors have no alternative but to turn the ragged furs brought to them to their third side. The brush-makers comb hog bristles with wooden combs and hoarsely sing fragments of ritual chants and wedding tunes. After mar-ket day there is nothing for the storekeepers to do and so they hang around the study house, scratching themselves and leafing through the Talmud or else telling each other amazing stories of monsters and ghosts and werewolves. Obviously in such a town there isn't much for me to do. One is just very hard put to come across a real sin thereabouts. The inhabitants lack both the strength and the inclination. Now and again a seamstress gossips about the rabbi's wife or the water bearer's girl grows large with child, but those are not the sort of things that amuse me. That is why I rarely visit Kreshev.

But at the time I am speaking about there were a few rich men in the town and in a prosperous home anything can happen. So whenever I turned my eyes in that direction, I made sure to see how things were going in the household of Reb Bunim Shor, the community's richest man. I would take too long to explain in detail how Reb Bunim happened to settle in Kreshev. He had originally lived in Zholkve which is a town near Lemberg. He had left there for business reasons. His interest was lumber and for a very small sum he had purchased a nice tract of woods from the Kreshev squire. In addition, his wife, Shifrah Tammar (a woman of distinguished family, granddaughter of the famous scholar Reb Samuel Edels) suffered from a chronic cough which made her spit blood, and a Lemberg doctor had recommended that she live in a wooded area. At any rate, Reb Bunim had moved to Kreshev with all his possessions, bringing along with him also a grown son and Lise, his ten-year-old daughter. He had built a house set apart from all the other dwellings at the end of the synagogue street; and several wagonloads of furniture, crockery, clothing, books and a host of other things had been crammed into the building. He had also brought with him a couple of servants, an old woman and a young man called Mendel, who acted as Reb Bunim's coachman. The arrival of the new inhabitant restored life to the town. Now there was work for the young men in Reb Bunim's forests and Kreshev's coachmen had logs to haul. Reb Bunim repaired the town's bath and he constructed a new roof for the almshouse.

Reb Bunim was a tall, powerful, large-boned man. He had the voice of a cantor and a pitch-black beard that ended in two points. He wasn't much of a scholar and could scarcely get through a chapter of the Midrash, but he always contributed generously to charity. He could sit down to a meal and finish at one sitting a loaf of bread and a six-egg omelet, washing it all down with a quart of milk. Fridays at the bath, he would climb to the highest perch and would have the attendant beat him with a bundle of twigs until it was time to light the candles. When he went into the forest he was accompanied by two fierce hounds, and he carried a gun. It was said that he could tell at a glance whether a tree was healthy or rotten. When necessary, he could work eighteen hours on end and walk for miles on foot. His wife, Shifrah Tammar, had once been very handsome, but between running to doctors and worrying about herself, she'd managed to become prematurely old. She was tall and thin, almost flat-chested, and she had a long, pale face and a beak of a nose Her thin lips stayed forever closed and her gray eyes looked belligerently out at the world. Her periods were painful and when they came she would take to her bed as though she were mortally ill. In fact she was a constant sufferer—one moment it would be a headache, the next an abscessed tooth or pressure on her abdomen. She was not a fit mate for Reb Bunim but he was not the sort who complained. Very likely he was convinced that that was the way it was with all women since he had married when he was fifteen years old.

There isn't very much to say about his son. He was like his father—a poor scholar, a voracious eater, a powerful swimmer, an aggressive businessman. He had married a girl from Brody before his father had even moved to Kreshev and had immediately immersed himself in business. He very seldom came to Kreshev. Like his father he had no lack of money. Both of the men were born financiers. They seemed to draw money to them. The way it looked, there didn't appear to be any reason why Reb Bunim and his family would not live out their days in peace as so often happens with ordinary people who because of their simplicity are spared bad luck and go through life without any real problems.

II

The Daughter

But Reb Bunim also had a daughter, and women, as it is well known, bring misfortune.

Lise was both beautiful and well brought-up. At twelve she was already as tall as her father. She had blond, almost yellow, hair and her skin was as white and smooth as satin. At times her eyes appeared to be blue and at other times green. Her behavior was a mixture, half Polish lady, half pious Jewish maiden. When she was six her father had engaged a governess to instruct her in religion and grammar. Later Reb Bunim had sent her to a regular teacher and from the very beginning she had shown a great interest in books. On her own she had studied the Scriptures in Yiddish, and dipped into her mother's Yiddish commentary on the Pentateuch. She had also been through "The Inheritance of the Deer," "The Rod of Punishment," "The Good Heart," "The Straight Measure," and other similar books that she had found in the house. After that she had managed all by herself to pick up a smattering of Hebrew. Her father had told her repeatedly that it was not proper for a girl to study Torah and her mother cautioned her that she would be left an old maid since no one wanted a learned wife, but these warnings made little impression on the girl. She continued to study, read "The Duty of the Heart," and Josephus, familiarized herself with the tales of the Talmud, and in addition learned all sorts of proverbs of the Tanaites and Amorites. She put no limit to her thirst for knowledge. Every time a book peddler wandered into Kreshev she would invite him to the house and buy whatever he had in his sack. After the Sabbath meal her contemporaries, the daughters of the best families of Kreshev, would drop in for a visit. The girls would chatter, play odds and evens, set each other riddles to answer and act as giddily as young girls generally do. Lise was always very polite to her friends, would serve them Sabbath fruits, nuts, cookies, cakes, but she never had much to say—her mind was concerned with weightier matters than dresses and shoes. Yet her manner was always friendly, without the slightest trace of haughtiness in it. On holidays Lise went to the women's synagogue although it was not customary for girls of her age to attend services. On more than one occasion, Reb Bunim, who was devoted to her, would say sorrowfully: "It's a shame that she's not a boy. What a man she would have made."

Shifrah Tammar's feelings were otherwise.

"You're just ruining the girl," she would insist. "If this continues she won't even know how to bake a potato."

Since there was no competent teacher of secular subjects in Kreshev (Yakel, the community's only teacher, could just about write a single line of legible Yiddish), Reb Bunim sent his daughter to study with Kalman the Leech. Kalman was highly esteemed in Kreshev. He knew how to burn out elf-locks, apply leeches, and do operations with just an ordinary breadknife. He owned a caseful of books and manufactured his own pills from the herbs in the field. He was a short, squat man with an enormous belly and as he walked his great weight seemed to make him totter. He looked like one of the local gentry in his plush hat, velvet caftan, knee-length trousers and shoes with buckles. It was the custom in Kreshev to have the procession, taking the bride to the ritual bath, stop for a moment in front of Kalman's porch to serenade him gaily. "Such a man," it was said in town, "must be kept in a good humor. All one can hope is that one never needs him."

But Reb Bunim did need Kalman. The Leech was in perpetual attendance upon Shifrah Tammar, and not only did he treat the mother's ailments, but he permitted the daughter to borrow books from his library. Lise read through his whole collection: tomes about medicine, travel books describing distant lands and savage peoples, romantic stories of the nobility, how they hunted and made love, the brilliant balls they gave. Nor was this all. In Kalman's library were also marvelous yarns about sorcerers and strange animals, about knights, kings and princes. Yes, every line of all this Lise read.

Well, now it is time for me to speak about Mendel, Mendel the man-servant—Mendel the Coachman. No one in Kreshev knew quite where this Mendel had come from. One story was that he'd been a love child who'd been abandoned in the streets. Others said he was the child of a convert. Whatever his origins, he was certainly an ignoramus and was famous not only in Kreshev but for miles around. He literally didn't know his Alef Beth, nor had he ever been seen to pray, although he did own a set of phylacteries. On Friday night all the other men would be at the House of Prayer but Mendel would be loitering in the market place. He would help the servant girls draw water from the well and would hang around the horses in the stables. Mendel shaved, had discarded his fringed garment, offered no benedictions; he had completely emancipated himself from Jewish custom. On his first appearance in Kreshev, several people had interested themselves in him. He'd been offered free instruction. Several pious ladies had warned him that he'd end up reclining on a bed of nails in Gehenna. But the young man had ignored everyone. He just puckered up his lips and whistled impudently. If some woman assailed him too vigorously, he would snarl back arrogantly: "O you cossack of God, you. Anyway you won't be in my Gehenna."

And he would take the whip that he always carried with him and use it to hike up the woman's skirt. There would be a great deal of commotion and laughter and the pious lady would vow never again to tangle with Mendel the Coachman.

Though he was a heretic that didn't prevent him from being handsome. No, he was very good-looking, tall and lithe, with straight legs and narrow hips and dense black hair which was a little bit curly and a little kinky and in which there were always a few stalks of hay and straw. He had heavy eyebrows which joined together over his nose. His eyes were black, his lips thick. As for his clothing, he went around dressed like a gentile. He wore riding breeches and boots, a short jacket and a Polish hat with a leather visor which he pulled down in the back until it touched the nape of his neck. He carved whistles from twigs and he also played the fiddle. Another of his hobbies was pigeons and he'd built a coop on top of Reb Bunim's house and occasionally he'd be seen scampering up to the roof to exercise the birds with a long stick. Although he had a room of his own and a perfectly adequate bench-bed, he preferred to sleep in the hay loft, and when he was in the mood he was capable of sleeping for fourteen hours at a stretch. Once there had been so bad a fire in Kreshev that the people had decided to flee the town. At Reb Bunim's house everyone had been looking for Mendel so that he might help pack and carry things away. But there had been no Mendel to be found anywhere. Only after the fire had been put out at last and the excitement had died down had he been discovered in the courtyard snoring under an apple tree as if nothing had happened.

But Mendel the Coachman wasn't only a sleeper. It was well-known that he chased the women. One thing, however, could be said for him: he didn't go after the Kreshev maidens. His escapades were always with young peasant girls from the neighboring villages. The attraction that he had for these women seemed almost unnatural. The beer drinkers at the local tavern maintained that Mendel had only to gaze at one of these girls and she would immediately come to him. It was known that more than one had visited him in his attic. Naturally the peasants didn't like this and Mendel had been warned that one of these days they would chop off his head, but he ignored these threats and wallowed deeper and deeper in carnality. There wasn't a village that he had visited with Reb Bunim where he didn't have his "wives" and families. It almost seemed true that a whistle from him was sufficient sorcery to bring some girl flying to his side. Mendel, however, didn't discuss his power over women. He drank no whiskey, avoided fights, and stayed away from the shoemakers, tailors, hoopers and brushmakers that comprised the poorer population of Kreshev. Nor did they regard him as one of them. He didn't even bother much about money. Reb Bunim, it was said, supplied him with room and board only. But when a Kreshev teamster wanted to hire him and pay him real wages, Mendel remained loyal to the house of Reb Bunim. He apparently did not mind being a slave. His horses and his boots, his pigeons and his girls were the only things that concerned him. So the townspeople gave up on Mendel the Coachman.

"A lost soul," they commented.—"A Jewish gentile."

And gradually they became accustomed to him and then forgot him.

III
The Articles of Engagement

As soon as Lise turned fifteen, conjecture began about whom she would marry. Shifrah Tammar was sick, and relations between her and Reb Bunim were strained, so Reb Bunim decided to discuss the matter with his daughter. When the subject was mentioned Lise became shy and would reply that she would do what her father thought best.

"You have two possibilities," Reb Bunim said during one of these conversations. "The first is a young man from Lublin who comes of a very wealthy family but is no scholar. The other is from Warsaw and a real prodigy. But I must warn you that he doesn't have a cent. Now speak up, girl. The decision is up to you. Which would you prefer?"

"Oh, money," Lise said scornfully. "What value does it have? Money can be lost, but not knowledge." And she turned her gaze downward.

"Then, if I understand you correctly, you prefer the boy from Warsaw?" Reb Bunim said, stroking his long, black beard.

"You know best, Father. . . ." Lise whispered.

"One thing in addition that I should mention," he went on, "is that the rich man is very handsome—tall and with blond hair. The scholar is extremely short—a full head shorter than you."

Lise grasped both of her braids and her face turned red and then quickly lost all color. She bit her lip.

"Well, what have you decided, daughter?" Reb Bunim demanded. "You mustn't be ashamed to speak."

Lise began to stammer and her knees trembled from shame.

"Where is he?" she asked. "I mean, what does he do? Where is he studying?"

"The Warsaw boy? He is, may God preserve us, an orphan, and he is at present studying at the Zusmir Yeshiva. I am told that he knows the entire Talmud by heart and that he is also a philosopher and a student of the cabala. He has already written a commentary on Maimonides, I believe."

"Yes," Lise mumbled.

"Does that mean that you want him?"

"Only if you approve, Father."

And she covered her face with both of her hands and ran from the room. Reb Bunim followed her with his eyes. She delighted him—her beauty, chastity, intelligence. She was closer to him than to her mother, and although almost fully grown, would cuddle close to him and run her fingers through his beard. Fridays before he went off to the bath house she would have a clean shirt ready for him and on his return before the lighting of the candles she would serve him freshly-baked cake and plum stew. He never heard her laughing raucously as did the other young girls nor did she ever go barefoot in his presence. After the Sabbath meal when he napped, she would walk on tiptoe so as not to wake him. When he was ill, she would put her hand on his forehead to see whether he had fever and would bring all sorts of medicine and tidbits. On more than one occasion Reb Bunim had envied the happy young man who would have her as a wife.

Some days later the people of Kreshev learned that Lise's prospective husband had arrived in town. The young man came in a wagon by himself and he stayed at the house of Rabbi Ozer. Everyone was surprised to see what a scrawny fellow he was, small and thin, with black tousled sidelocks, a pale face and a pointed chin which was barely covered by a few sparse whiskers. His long gabardine reached to below the ankles. His back was bent and he walked rapidly and as if he didn't know where he was going. The young girls crowded to the windows and watched him pass by. When he arrived at the study house, the men came up to greet him and he immediately began to expatiate in the cleverest possible way. There was no mistaking that this man was a born city dweller.

"Well, you really have some metropolis here," the young man observed.

"No one's claiming that it's Warsaw," one of the town boys commented.

The young cosmopolitan smiled.

"One place is pretty much like another," he pointed out. "If they're on the face of the earth, they're all the same."

This said, he began to quote liberally from the Babylonian Talmud and the Talmud of Jerusalem, and when he was finished with that he entertained everyone with news about what was going on in the great world beyond Kreshev. He wasn't himself personally acquainted with Radziwill but he had seen him and he did know a follower of Sabbatai Zevi, the false Messiah. He also had met a Jew who came from Shushan which was the ancient capital of Persia and another Jew who had become a convert and studied the Talmud in secret. As if this weren't enough, he began to ask those assembled the most difficult of riddles and, when he tired of that, amused himself by repeating anecdotes of Rabbi Heshl. Somehow or other he managed to convey the additional information that he knew how to play chess, could paint murals employing the twelve signs of the zodiac, and write Hebrew verse which could be read either backwards or forwards and said exactly the same thing no matter how you read it. Nor was this all. This young prodigy, in addition, had studied philosophy and the cabala, and was an adept in mystical mathematics, being able even to work out the fractions which are to be found in the treatise of Kilaim. It goes without saying that he had had a look at the Zohar and "The Tree of Life" and he knew "The Guide to the Perplexed" as well as his own first name.

He had come to Kreshev looking ragged, but several days after his arrival Reb Bunim outfitted him in a new gabardine, new shoes and white stockings, and presented him with a gold watch. And now the young man began to comb his beard and curl his sidelocks. It was not until the signing of the contract that Lise saw the bridegroom but she had received reports of how learned he was and she was happy that she had chosen him and not the rich young man from Lublin.

The festivities to celebrate the signing of the Engagement Contract were as noisy as a wedding. Half the town had been invited. As always the men and women were seated separately and Shloimele, the groom-to-be, made an extremely clever speech and then signed his name with a brilliant flourish. Several of the town's most learned men tried to converse with him on weighty subjects, but his rhetoric and wisdom were too much for them. While the celebration was still going on, and before the serving of the banquet, Reb Bunim broke the usual custom that the bride and groom must not meet before the marriage and let Shloimele into Lise's chamber since the true interpretation of the law is that a man not take a wife unless he has seen her. The young man's gabardine was unbuttoned, exposing his silk vest and gold watch chain. He appeared a man of the world with his brightly polished shoes and velvet skull cap perched on the top of his head. There was moisture on his high forehead and his cheeks were flushed. Inquisitively, bashfully, he gazed about him with his dark eyes, and his index finger kept twining itself nervously around a fringe of his sash. Lise turned a deep red when she saw him. She had been told that he was not at all good-looking but to her he seemed handsome. And this was the view of the other girls who were present. Somehow or other Shloimele had become much more attractive.

"This is the girl you are to marry," Reb Bunim said. "There's no need for you to be bashful."

Lise had on a black silk dress and around her neck was a string of pearls which was the present she had been given for this occasion. Her hair appeared almost red under the glow of candlelight, and on the finger of her left hand she wore a ring with the letter "M" inscribed upon it, the first letter of the word *mazeltov*. At the moment of Shloimele's entrance she had been holding an embroidered handkerchief in her hand but upon seeing him it had fallen from her fingers. One of the girls in the room walked over and picked it up.

"It's a very fine evening," Shloimele said to Lise.

"And an excellent summer," answered the bride and her two attendants.

"Perhaps it's a trifle hot," Shloimele observed.

"Yes, it is hot," the three girls answered again in unison.

"Do you think the fault is mine?" Shloimele asked in a sort of singsong. "It is said in the Talmud. . . ."

But Shloimele didn't get any further as Lise interrupted him.

"I know very well what the Talmud says, 'A donkey is cold even in the month of Tammuz.'"

"Oh, a Talmudic scholar!" Shloimele exclaimed in surprise, and the tips of his ears reddened.

Very soon after that the conversation ended and everyone began to crowd into the room. But Rabbi Ozer did not approve of the bride and groom meeting before the wedding, and he ordered them to be separated. So Shloimele was once more surrounded only by men and the celebration continued until daybreak.

IV

Love

From the very first moment that she saw him Lise loved Shloimele deeply. At times she believed that his face had been shown to her in a dream before the marriage. At other times she was certain that they had been married before in some other existence. The truth was that I, the Evil Spirit, required so great a love for the furtherance of my schemes.

At night when Lise slept I sought out his spirit and brought it to her and the two of them spoke and kissed and exchanged love tokens. All of her waking thoughts were of him. She held his image within her and addressed it, and this fiction within her replied to her words. She bared her soul to it, and it consoled her and uttered the words of love that she longed to hear. When she put on a dress or a nightgown she imagined that Shloimele was present, and she felt shy and was pleased that her skin was pale and smooth. Occasionally she would ask this apparition those questions which had baffled her since childhood: "Shloimele, what is the sky? How deep is the earth? Why is it hot in summer and cold in the winter? Why do corpses gather at night to pray in the synagogue? How can one see a demon? Why does one see one's reflection in a mirror?"

And she even imagined that Shloimele answered each of these questions. There was one other question that she asked the shadow in her mind: "Shloimele, do you really love me?"

Shloimele reassured her that no other girl was equal to her in beauty. And in her daydreams she saw herself drowning in the river San and Shloimele rescued her. She was abducted by evil spirits and he saved her. Indeed, her mind was all daydreams, so confused had love made her.

But as it happened, Reb Bunim postponed the wedding until the Sabbath after Pentecost and so Lise was forced to wait nearly three quarters of a year longer. Now through her impatience she understood what misery Jacob had undergone when he had been forced to wait seven years before marrying Rachel. Shloimele remained at the Rabbi's house and would not be able to visit Lise again until Chanukah. The young girl often stood at the window in a vain attempt to catch a glimpse of him, for the path from the Rabbi's to the study house did not pass Reb Bunim's. The only news that Lise received of him was from the girls who came to see her. One reported that he had grown slightly taller and another said that he was studying the Talmud with the other young men at the study house. A third girl observed that obviously the Rabbi's wife was not feeding Shloimele properly as he had become quite thin. But out of modesty Lise refrained from questioning her friends too closely; nevertheless she blushed each time her beloved's name was mentioned. In order to make the winter pass more quickly she began to embroider for her husband-to-be a phylactery bag and a cloth to cover the Sabbath loaf. The bag was of black velvet upon which she sewed in gold thread a star of David along with Shloimele's name and the date of the month and year. She took even greater pains with the tablecloth on which were stitched two loaves of bread and a goblet. The words "Holy Sabbath" were done in silver thread, and in the four corners the heads of a stag, a lion, a leopard, and an eagle were embroidered. Nor did she forget to line the seams of the cloth with beads of various colors and she decorated the edges with fringes and tassels. The girls of Kreshev were overwhelmed by her skill and begged to copy the pattern she had used.

Her engagement had altered Lise: she had become even more beautiful. Her skin was white and delicate; her eyes gazed off into space. She moved through the house with the silent step of a somnambulist. From time to time she would smile for no reason at all, and she would stand in front of the mirror for hours on end, arranging her hair and speaking to her reflection as though she had been bewitched. Now if a beggar came to the house she received him graciously and gladly offered him alms. After every meal she went to the poorhouse, bringing soup and meat to the ill and indigent. The poor unfortunates would smile and bless her: "May God grant that you soon eat soup at your wedding."

And Lise quietly added her own "Amen."

Since time continued to hang heavy on her hands, she often browsed among the books in her father's library. There she came across one entitled "The Customs of Marriage" in which it was stated that the bride must purify herself before the ceremony, keep track of her periods and attend the ritual bath. The book also enumerated the wedding rites, told of the period of the seven nuptial benedictions, admonished husband and wife on their proper conduct, paying particular attention to the woman and setting forth a myriad of details. Lise found all of this very interesting since she already had some idea of what went on between the sexes and had even witnessed the love-play of birds and animals. She began to meditate carefully on what she had read, and spent several sleepless nights deep in thought. Her modesty became more intense than it had ever been before, and her face grew flushed and she became feverish; her behavior was so strange that the servant thought she had been bewitched by the evil eye, and sang incantations to cure her. Every time the name of Shloimele was mentioned, she blushed—whether she was included in the reference or not; and whenever anyone approached, she concealed the book of instructions she was forever reading. What was more, she became anxious and suspicious and soon she had got herself into such a state that she both looked forward to the day of marriage and turned away in dread. But Shifrah Tammar just went on preparing her daughter's trousseau. Though estranged from her daughter, she nevertheless wanted the wedding to be so magnificent that the event would live on for years in the minds of the people of Kreshev.

V

The Wedding

The wedding was indeed a grand one. Dressmakers from Lublin had made the bride's garments. For weeks there had been seamstresses at Reb Bunim's house, embroidering and stitching lace on nightgowns, lingerie, and shirtwaists. Lise's wedding gown had been made of white satin and its train was a full four cubits in length. As for food, the cooks had baked a Sabbath loaf which was almost the size of a man and was braided at both ends. Never before had such a bread been seen in Kreshev. Reb Bunim had spared no expense; at his order, sheep, calves, hens, geese, ducks, capons had been slaughtered for the wedding feast. There was also fish from the river San and Hungarian wines and mead supplied by the local innkeeper. The day of the wedding Reb Bunim commanded that the poor of Kreshev be fed, and when word got around an assortment of riffraff from the neighboring district drifted into town to surfeit themselves also. Tables and benches were set up in the street and the beggars were served white Sabbath loaves, stuffed carp, meat stewed in vinegar, gingerbread and tankards of ale. Musicians played for the vagrants and the traditional wedding jester entertained them. The tattered multitude formed circles in the center of the market place and danced and jigged delightedly. Everyone was singing and bellowing and the noise was deafening. At evening, the wedding guests began to assemble at Reb Bunim's house. The women wore beaded jackets, headbands, furs, all of their jewelry. The girls had on silk dresses and pointed shoes made especially for the occasion, but inevitably the dressmakers and cobblers had been unable to fill all orders and there were quarrels. There was more than one girl who stayed home, huddling close to the stove the night of the wedding and, unlucky one, weeping her eyes out.

That day Lise fasted and when it was prayer time confessed her sins. She beat her breast as though it were the Day of Atonement for she knew that on one's wedding day all one's transgressions are forgiven. Although she was not particularly pious, and at time even wavered in her faith, as is common with those who are reflective, on this occasion she prayed with great fervor. She also offered up prayers for the man who by the end of the day would have become her husband. When Shifrah Tammar came into the room and saw her daughter standing in a corner with tears in her eyes and beating herself with her fists, she blurted out, "Look at the girl! A real saint!"—and she demanded that Lise stop crying or her eyes would look red and puffy when she stood beneath the canopy.

But you can take my word for it, it was not religious fervor that was causing Lise to weep. For days and weeks before the wedding I had been busy applying myself. All sorts of strange and evil thoughts had been tormenting the girl. One moment she feared that she might not be a virgin at all, and the next she would dream about the instant of deflowering and would burst into tears, fearful that she would not be able to stand the pain. At other times she would be torn by shame, and the very next second would fear that on her wedding night she would perspire unduly, or become sick to her stomach, or wet the bed, or suffer worse humiliation. She also had a suspicion that an enemy had bewitched her, and she searched through her clothing, looking for hidden knots. She wanted to be done with these anxieties but she couldn't control them. "Possibly," she said to herself on one occasion, "I am only dreaming this and I am not to be married at all. Or, perhaps, my husband is some sort of a devil who has materialized in human form and the wedding ceremony will be only a fantasy and the guests, spirits of evil."

This was only one of the nightmares she suffered. She lost

her appetite, became constipated, and though she was envied by all the girls in Kreshev, none knew the agony she
was undergoing.

Since the bridegroom was an orphan, his father-in-law, Reb
Bunim, took care of supplying him with a wardrobe. He ordered for his son-in-law two coats made of fox fur, one for
everyday and one for the Sabbath, two gabardines, one of silk
and one of satin, a cloth overcoat, a couple of dressing gowns,
several pairs of trousers, a thirteen-pointed hat edged with
skunk, as well as a Turkish prayer shawl with three ornaments.
Included in the gifts to the bridegroom were a silver spice box
upon which a picture of the wailing wall was engraved, a
golden citron container, a breadknife with a mother-of-pearl
handle, a tobacco box with an ivory lid, a silk-bound set of the
Talmud, and a prayer book with silver covers. At the bachelor
dinner Shloimele spoke brilliantly. First of all he propounded
ten questions which seemed to be absolutely basic, and then
he answered all ten with a single statement. But after having
disposed of these essential questions, he turned around and
showed that the questions he had asked were not really questions at all, and the enormous facade of erudition he had
erected tumbled to nothing. His audience was left amazed and
speechless.

I won't linger too long over the actual ceremony. Suffice it
to say that the crowd danced, sang and jumped about the
way crowds always do at a wedding, particularly when the
richest man in town marries off his daughter. A couple of tailors and shoemakers tried to dance with the serving girls, but
were chased away. Several of the guests became drunk and
started to jig, shouting "Sabbath, Sabbath." Several of the
others sang Yiddish songs which began with words like
"What does a poor man cook? Borscht and potatoes . . ."
The musicians sawed away on their fiddles, blared with their
trumpets, clanged their cymbals, pounded their drums, piped
on their flutes and bagpipes. Ancient crones lifted their trains,
pushed back their bonnets, and danced, facing each other and
clapping hands, but then when their faces almost touched they
turned away as if in rage, all of which made the onlookers
laugh even more heartily. Shifrah Tammar, despite her usual
protestations of bad health (she could scarcely lift her foot

from the floor), was recruited by one of the bands of merry-makers and forced to perform both a cossatzke and a scissor dance. As is usual at weddings, I the Arch-Fiend arranged the customary number of jealous spats, displays of vanity and outbursts of wantonness and boasting. When the girls performed the water dance they pulled their skirts up over their ankles as though they were actually wading in the water and the idlers peering in through the windows could not help having their imaginations inflamed. And so anxious was the wedding jester to entertain that he sang countless songs of love for the guests, and corrupted the meaning of Scriptures by interpolating obscenities into the midst of sacred phrases as do the clowns on Purim, and hearing all this, the girls and young matrons clapped their hands and squealed with joy. Suddenly the entertainment was interrupted by a woman's scream. She had lost her brooch and had fainted from anxiety. Though everyone searched high and low, the piece could not be found. A moment later there was more excitement when one of the girls claimed that a young man had pricked her thigh with a needle. This outburst over, it was time for the virtue dance, and while this dance was going on, Shifrah Tammar and the bridesmaids led Lise off to the bridal chamber which was on the ground floor and so heavily draped and curtained that no light could shine through. On their way to the room the women gave her advice on how to conduct herself, and cautioned her not to be afraid when she saw the groom since the first commandment bids us to propagate and multiply. Shortly after that, Reb Bunim and another man escorted the groom to his bride.

Well, this is one instance when I'm not going to satisfy your curiosity and tell you what went on in the wedding chamber. It is enough to say that when Shifrah Tammar entered the room in the morning, she found her daughter hiding under the quilt and too ashamed to speak to her. Shloimele was already out of bed and in his own room. It took a good deal of coaxing before Lise would permit her mother to examine the sheets, and indeed, there was blood on them.

"Mazeltov, daughter," Shifrah Tammar exclaimed. "You are now a woman and share with us all the curse of Eve."

And weeping, she threw her arms about Lise's neck and kissed her.

VI
Strange Behavior

Immediately after the wedding Reb Bunim rode off into the woods to tend to some business, and Shifrah Tammar returned to her sickbed and medicines. The young men at the study house had been of the opinion that once Shloimele was married he would become the head of a Yeshiva and dedicate himself to the affairs of the community, which seemed appropriate for a prodigy who was also the son-in-law of a wealthy man. But Shloimele did no such thing. He turned out to be a stay-at-home. He couldn't seem to get to the morning services on time and as soon as the concluding "On Us" was said, he was out the door and on his way home. Nor did he think of hanging around after evening prayers. The women around town said that Shloimele went to bed right after supper, and there could be no doubt that the green shutter on his bedroom stayed closed until late in the day. There were also reports from Reb Bunim's maid. She said that the young couple carried on in the most scandalous ways. They were always whispering together, telling each other secrets, consulting books together, and calling each other odd nicknames. They also ate from the same dish, drank from the same goblet, and held hands the way young men and women of the Polish aristocracy did. Once the maid had seen Shloimele hitch up Lise with a sash as if she were a dray horse and then proceed to whip her with a twig. Lise had cooperated in this game by simulating the whinny and gait of a mare. Another game the maid had seen them play was one in which the winner pulls the earlobes of the loser, and she swore that they had continued this nonsense until the ears of both of them had been a blood red.

Yes, the couple was in love and each day only increased their passion. When he went off to pray she stood at the window watching him disappear as if he were off on some long journey; and when she retired to the kitchen to prepare some broth or a dish of oat grits, Shloimele tagged along or else he immediately called, demanding that she hurry out. On Sabbath, Lise forgot to pray at the synagogue but stood behind the lattice and watched Shloimele in his prayer shawl going about his devotions at the eastern wall. And he, in turn, would gaze upwards at the women's section to catch a glimpse of her. This display also set vicious tongues wagging, but none of this bothered Reb Bunim who was most gratified to learn how well his daughter and son-in-law got on. Each time he returned from a trip he came bearing presents. But, on the other hand, Shifrah Tammar was very far from pleased. She did not approve of this eccentric behavior, these whispered words of endearment, these perpetual kisses and caresses. Nothing like this had ever happened in her father's house, nor had she even seen such goings-on among ordinary people. She felt disgraced and began rebuking both Lise and Shloimele. This was a kind of conduct that she could not tolerate.

"No, I won't stand for it," she would complain. "The mere thought of it makes me sick." Or she would cry out suddenly: "Not even the Polish nobility make such an exhibition of themselves."

But Lise knew how to answer her.

"Wasn't Jacob permitted to show his love for Rachel?" the erudite Lise asked her mother. "Didn't Solomon have a thousand wives?"

"Don't you dare to compare yourself to those saints!" Shifrah Tammar shouted back. "You're not fit to mention their names."

Actually, in her youth Shifrah Tammar had not been very strict in her observances but now she watched over her daughter closely and saw to it that she obeyed all the laws of purity, and would even accompany Lise to the ritual bath to make sure that her immersions were conducted in the prescribed manner. Now and again mother and daughter would quarrel on Friday nights because Lise was late lighting the candles. After the wedding ceremony the bride had had her hair shaved off and begun wearing the customary silk kerchief, but Shifrah Tammar discovered that Lise's hair had grown back and that she would often sit before a mirror now, combing and braiding her curling locks. Shifrah Tammar also exchanged sharp words with her son-in-law. She was displeased that he went so seldom to the study house and spent his time strolling through orchards and fields. Then it became apparent that he had a taste for food and was extremely lazy. He wanted stuffed derma with fritters daily and he made Lise add honey to his milk. As if this were not enough, he'd have plum stews and seed cookies along with raisins and cherry juice sent to his bedroom. At night when they retired, Lise would lock and bolt the bedroom door and Shifrah Tammar would hear the young couple laughing. Once she thought she heard the pair running barefoot across the floor; plaster fell from the ceiling; the chandeliers trembled. Shifrah Tammar had been forced to send a maid upstairs to knock on the door and bid the young lovers be quiet.

Shifrah Tammar's wish had been that Lise would become pregnant quickly and endure the agonies of labor. She had hoped that when Lise became a mother she would be so busy nursing the child, changing its diapers, tending it when it became ill, that she would forget her silliness. But months passed and nothing happened. Lise's face grew more wan, and her eyes burned with a strange fire. The gossip in Kreshev was that the couple were studying the cabala together.

"It's all very strange," people whispered to each other. "Something weird is going on there."

And the old women sitting on their porches and darning socks or spinning flax had a perpetually interesting topic of conversation. And they listened sharply with their half-deafened ears and shook their heads in indignation.

VII
Secrets of the Chamber

It is now time to reveal the secrets of that bed chamber. There are some for whom it is not enough to satisfy their desires; they must, in addition, utter all sorts of vain words and let their minds wallow in passion. Those who pursue this iniquitous path are inevitably led to melancholy and they enter the Forty-nine Gates of Uncleanliness. The wise men long ago pointed out that everyone knows why a bride steps under the wedding canopy but he who dirties this act through words loses his place in the world to come. The clever Shloimele because of his great learning and his interest in philosophy began to delve more and more into the questions of "he and she." For example, he would suddenly ask while caressing his wife, "Suppose you had chosen that man from Lublin instead of me, do you think you would be lying with him here now?" Such remarks first shocked Lise and she would reply, "But I didn't make that choice. I chose you." Shloimele, however, would not be denied an answer and he would go on talking and proposing even more obscene questions until Lise would finally be forced to admit that if indeed she had picked her husband from Lublin she would unquestionably be lying in his arms and not in those of Shloimele. As if this weren't enough he would also nag her about what she would do if he were to die. "Well," he wanted to know, "would you marry again?" No, no other man could possibly interest her, Lise would insist, but Shloimele would slyly argue with her and through skillful sophistry would undermine her convictions.

"Look, you're still young and attractive. Along would come the matchmaker and shower you with proposals and your father would just not hear of your staying single. So there would be another wedding canopy and another celebration and off you'd be to another marriage bed."

It was useless for Lise to beg him not to talk in such a way since she found the whole subject painful and, in addition, of no value, since it was impossible to foresee the future. No matter what she said, Shloimele continued his sinful words, for they stimulated his passion and at length she grew to enjoy them too, and they were soon spending half their nights whispering questions and answers and wrangling over matters that were beyond anyone's knowledge. So Shloimele wanted to know what she would do if she were shipwrecked on a desert island with only the captain, how she would behave herself if she were among African savages. Suppose she were captured by eunuchs and taken to a sultan's harem, what then? Imagine herself Queen Esther brought before Ahasuerus! And these were only a small part of his imaginings. When she reproached him for being so engrossed in frivolous matters, he undertook the study of cabala with her, the secrets of intimacy between man and woman and the revelation of conjugal union. Found in Reb Bunim's house were the books "The Tree of Life," "The Angel Raziel," and still other volumes of the cabala and Shloimele told Lise how Jacob, Rachel, Leah, Bilhah, and Zilpah copulate in the higher world, face to face and rump to rump, and the matings of the Holy Father and the Holy

Mother, and there were words in these books that simply seemed profane.

And if this were not enough, Shloimele began to reveal to Lise the powers possessed by evil spirits—that they were not only satans, phantoms, devils, imps, hobgoblins and harpies, but that they also held sway over the higher worlds, as for example Nogah, a blend of sanctity and impurity. He produced alleged evidence that the Evil Host had some connection with the world of emanations, and one could infer from Shloimele's words that Satan and God were two equal powers and that they waged constant combat and neither could defeat the other. Another claim of his was that there was no such thing as a sin, since a sin, just as a good deed, can be either big or small and if it is elevated it rises to great heights. He assured her that it is preferable for a man to commit a sin with fervor, than a good deed without enthusiasm, and that yea and nay, darkness and light, right and left, heaven and hell, sanctity and degradation were all images of the divinity and no matter where one sank one remained in the shadow of the Almighty, for beside His light, nothing else exists. He proffered all this information with such rhetoric and strengthened his argument with so many examples that it was a delight to hear him. Lise's thirst to share his company and absorb such revelations increased. Occasionally she felt that Shloimele was luring her from the path of righteousness. His words terrified her and she no longer felt mistress of herself; her soul seemed captive and she thought only what he wanted her to think. But she hadn't the will to stand up to him and she said to herself: "I will go where he leads no matter what happens." Soon he gained such mastery over her that she obeyed him implicitly. And he ruled her at will. He commanded her to strip naked before him, crawl on all fours like an animal, dance before him, sing melodies that he composed half in Hebrew, half in Yiddish, and she obeyed him.

By this time it is quite obvious that Shloimele was a secret disciple of Sabbatai Zevi. For even though the False Messiah was long dead, secret cults of his followers remained in many lands. They met at fairs and markets, recognized each other through secret signs and thus remained safe from the wrath of the other Jews who would excommunicate them. Many rabbis, teachers, ritual slaughterers and other ostensibly respectable folk were included in this sect. Some of them posed as miracle workers, wandering from town to town passing out amulets into which they had introduced not the sacred name of God but unclean names of dogs and evil spirits, Lilith and Asmodeus as well as the name of Sabbatai Zevi himself. All this they managed with such cunning that only the members of the brotherhood could appreciate their handiwork. It provided them great satisfaction to deceive the pious and create havoc. Thus, one disciple of Sabbatai Zevi arrived at a settlement, announced that he was a thaumaturgist and soon many people came to him with chits upon which they'd written their pleas for advice, their problems and requests. Before the counterfeit miracle worker left town, he played his joke and scattered the notes all over the market place where they were found by the town rogues, causing disgrace to many. Another cultist was a scribe and placed into the phylacteries, not the passages of law on parchment as prescribed, but filth and goat dung as well as a suggestion that the wearer kiss the scribe's behind. Others of the sect tortured themselves, bathed in icy water, rolled in snow in the winter, subjected themselves to poison ivy in the summer and fasted from Sabbath-day to Sabbath-day. But these were depraved as well, they sought to corrupt the principles of the Torah and of the cabala and each of them in his own fashion paid homage to the forces of evil—and Shloimele was one of them.

VIII
Shloimele and Mendel the Coachman

One day, Shifrah Tammar, Lise's mother, died. After the seven days of mourning, Reb Bunim returned to his business affairs and Lise and Shloimele were left to themselves. Having purchased a tract of lumber somewhere in Wolhynia, Reb Bunim maintained horses and oxen there as well as peasants to work them, and, when he left, did not take Mendel the Coachman with him. The youth remained in Kreshev. It was summertime and Shloimele and Lise often rode through the countryside in the carriage with Mendel driving. When Lise was busy, the two men went out alone. The fresh pine scent invigorated Shloimele. Also, he enjoyed bathing in the river San, and Mendel would wait on him after they drove to a spot where the water was shallow, for eventually Shloimele would be master of the entire estate.

Thus they became friends. Mendel was nearly two heads taller than Shloimele, and Shloimele admired the coachman's worldly knowledge. Mendel could swim face-up or -down, tread water, catch a fish in the stream with his bare hands and climb the highest trees by the riverbank. Shloimele was afraid of a single cow, but Mendel would chase a whole herd of cattle and had no fear of bulls. He boasted that he could spend a whole night in a cemetery and spoke of having overpowered bears and wolves which attacked him. He claimed victory over a highwayman who had accosted him. In addition, he could play all sorts of tunes on a fife, imitate a crow's cawing, a woodpecker's pecking, cattle's lowing, sheep's and goats's bleating, cat's mewling, and the chirping of crickets. His stunts amused Shloimele who enjoyed his company. Also he promised to teach Shloimele horseback riding. Even Lise, who used to ignore Mendel, treated him amiably now, sent him on all sorts of errands and offered him honeycake and sweet brandy, for she was a kindly young woman.

Once when the two men were bathing in the river, Shloimele noticed Mendel's physique and admired its masculine attractiveness. His long legs, slim hips, and broad chest all exuded power. After dressing, Shloimele conversed with Mendel who spoke unrestrainedly of his success among the peasant women, bragging of the women he'd had from nearby villages and the many bastards he had sired. He also numbered among his lovers aristocrats, town women, and prostitutes. Shloimele doubted none of this. When he asked Mendel if he had no fear of retribution, the young man asked what could be done to a corpse. He didn't believe in life after death. He went on expressing himself heretically. Then, puckering his lips and whistling shrilly, he scampered agilely up a tree, knocking down cones and birds' nests. While doing this he roared like a lion, so powerfully that the sound carried for miles, echoing from tree to tree as though hundreds of evil spirits responded to his call.

That night Shloimele told Lise everything that had happened. They discussed the incident in such detail that both of them grew aroused. But Shloimele was not equipped to satisfy his wife's passion. His ardor was greater than his capability and they had to content themselves with lewd talk. Suddenly Shloimele blurted: "Tell me the truth, Lise my love, how would you like to go to bed with Mendel the Coachman?"

"God save us, what kind of evil talk is this?" she countered. "Have you lost your mind?"

"Well—? He is a strong and handsome young man—the girls are wild about him. . . ."

"Shame on you!" Lise cried. "You defile your mouth!"

"I love defilement!" Shloimele cried, his eyes ablaze. "I am going all the way over to the side of the Host!"

"Shloimele, I'm afraid for you!" Lise said after a long pause. "You're sinking deeper and deeper!"

"One dares everything!" Shloimele said, his knees trembling. " 'Since this generation cannot become completely pure, let it grow completely impure!' "

Lise seemed to shrink and for a long while she was silent. Shloimele could scarcely tell whether she slept or was thinking.

"Were you serious then?" she asked curiously, her voice muffled.

"Yes, serious."

"And it wouldn't anger you at all?" she demanded.

"No. . . . If it brought you pleasure, it would please me as well. You could tell me about it afterwards."

"You're an infidel!" Lise cried out. "A heretic!"

"Yes, so I am! Elisha the son of Abijah was also a heretic! Whoever looks into the vineyard must suffer the consequences."

"You quote the Talmud in answer to everything—watch out, Shloimele! Be on your guard! You're playing with fire!"

"I love fire! I love a holocaust . . . I would like the whole world to burn and Asmodeus to take over the rule."

"Be still!" Lise cried, "Or I shall scream for help."

"What are you afraid of, foolish one?" Shloimele soothed her. "The thought is not the deed. I study with you, I unfold to you the secrets of the Torah, and you remain naïve. Why do you suppose God ordered Hosea to marry a harlot? Why did

King David take Bathsheba from Uriah the Hittite and Abigail from Nabal? Why did he, in his old age, order Abeishag the Shunammite brought to him? The noblest ancients practiced adultery. Sin is cleansing! Ah, Lise love, I wish you would obey every whim of mind. I think only of your happiness. . . . Even while I guide you to the abyss . . . !"

And he embraced her, caressed and kissed her. Lise lay exhausted and confused by his oratory. The bed beneath her vibrated, the walls shook and it seemed to her that she was already swaying in the net that I, the Prince of Darkness, had spread to receive her.

IX

Adonijah, the Son of Haggith

Strange events followed. Usually Lise did not see very much of Mendel the Coachman. She paid little attention to him when they did meet. But since the day Shloimele had spoken to her about Mendel, she seemed to run into him everywhere. She'd walk into the kitchen and find him fooling around with the maid. Confronting Lise, he would grow silent. Soon she began to see him everywhere, in the barn, on horseback, riding toward the river San. Erect as a Cossack he sat, disdainful of saddle or reins. Once when Lise needed water and could not find the maid, she took the pitcher and headed for the well. Suddenly, out of nowhere, Mendel the Coachman materialized to help her draw water. One evening as Lise strolled through the meadow (Shloimele happened to be at the study house), the old communal billy goat met her. Lise tried to walk past him, but when she turned off to the right, he blocked her path again. When she turned to the left, he leaped to the left also. At the same time he lowered his pointed horns as if to gore her. Suddenly, rising on his hind legs, he leaned his front legs against her. His eyes were a fiery red, blazing with fury, as if possessed. Lise began to struggle to free herself but he was more powerful than she and almost up-ended her. She screamed and was about to faint when suddenly a loud whistle and the crack of a whip were heard. Mendel the Coachman had come upon them, and seeing the struggle, slashed the billy goat across its back with his whip. The thickly knotted thong almost broke the animal's spine. With a choking bleat, he ran off haphazardly. His legs were thickly tufted, tangled with hair. He resembled a wild beast more than a billy goat. Lise was left stunned. For a while, she stared at Mendel silently. Then she shook herself as if waking from a nightmare and said: "Many thanks."

"Such a stupid goat!" Mendel exclaimed. "If ever I get my hands on him again I'll tear his guts out!"

"What was he after?" Lise asked.

"Who knows? Sometimes goats will attack a person. But they'll always go after a woman, never a man!"

"Why is that?—you must be joking!"

"No, I'm serious. . . . In a village where I went with the master, there was a billy goat who used to wait for the women as they returned from the ritual bath and attack them. The people asked the rabbi what to do and he ordered the goat slaughtered. . . ."

"Really? Why did he have to be killed?"

"So he could no longer gore the women. . . ."

Lise thanked him again and thought it miraculous that he had come when he did. In his gleaming boots and riding breeches, whip in hand, the young man faced her with knowing and insolent eyes. Lise was uncertain whether to continue her stroll or return home, since by this time she was afraid of the goat and imagined that it plotted revenge. And the young man, as if reading her mind, offered to escort and protect her. He walked behind her like a guard. After a while, Lise decided to return to the house. Her face was burning, and as she sensed Mendel's eyes upon her, her ankles rubbed together and she stumbled. Sparks were dancing in front of her.

Later when Shloimele came home, Lise wanted to tell him everything at once, but she restrained herself. Not until that night after putting out the light, did she tell him. Shloimele's astonishment was boundless and he questioned Lise in detail. He kissed and caressed her and the incident seemed to please him immensely. Suddenly he said: "That damned billy goat wanted you—", and Lise asked: "How could a goat possibly want a woman?" He explained that beauty as great as hers could arouse even a goat. At the same time he praised the coachman for his loyalty and argued that his appearance at the propitious moment had been no accident but a manifestation of love, and that he was ready to go through fire for her. When Lise wondered how Shloimele could know all this, he promised to reveal a secret to her. He directed her to place her hand under his thigh in accordance with ancient custom, imploring her never to reveal a word of this.

When she had obliged him, he began, "Both you and the coachman are reincarnations and descended from a common spiritual source. You, Lise, were in your first existence Abeishag the Shunammite, and he was Adonijah, the son of Haggith. He desired you and sent Bathsheba to King Solomon so that he might surrender you to him for a wife, but since according to the law you were David's widow, his wish was punishable by death and the Horns of the Altar could not protect him, for he was taken away and killed. But law applies only to the body, not the soul. Thus, when one soul lusts for another, the heavens decree that they can find no peace until that lust is gratified. It is written that the Messiah will not come until all passions have been consummated, and because of this, the generations before the Messiah will be completely impure! And when a soul cannot consummate its desire in one existence, it is reincarnated again and again and thus it was with you two. Almost three thousand years now your souls have wandered naked and cannot enter the World of Emanations from where they stem. The forces of Satan have not allowed you two to meet, for then redemption would come. So it happened that when he was a prince, you were a handmaiden, and when you were a princess, he was a slave. In addition, you were separated by oceans. When he sailed to you, the Devil created a storm and sank the ship. There were other obstacles too, and your grief was intense. Now you are both in the same house, but since he is an ignoramus, you shun him. Actually, holy spirits inhabit your bodies, crying out in the dark and longing for union. And you are a married woman because there is a kind of cleansing that can be accomplished through adultery alone. Thus Jacob consorted with two sisters and Jehudah lay with Tamar, his daughter-in-law, and Reuben violated the bed of Bilhah, his own father's concubine, and Hosea took a wife from a brothel, and that is how it was with the rest of them. And know also that the goat was no common goat, but a devil, one of Satan's own and if Mendel hadn't come when he did, the beast would have, God forbid, done you injury."

When Lise inquired if he, Shloimele, were also a reincarnation, he said that he was King Solomon and that he'd returned to earth to nullify the error of his earlier existence, that because of the sin of having Adonijah executed, he was not able to enter the Mansion due him in Paradise. When Lise asked what would follow the correction of the error, if they would all then have to leave the earth, Shloimele replied that he and Lise would subsequently enjoy a long life together but he said nothing of Mendel's future, intimating only that the young man's stay on earth would be a short one. And he made all these statements with the dogmatic absoluteness of the cabalist to whom no secret is inviolate.

When Lise heard his words, a tremor shook her and she lay there numbed. Lise, familiar with the Scriptures, had often felt a compassion for Adonijah, King David's errant son, who'd lusted for his father's concubine and wished to be king and paid with his head for his rebelliousness. More than once she had wept with pity on reading this chapter in the Book of Kings. She had also pitied Abeishag the Shunammite, the fairest maiden in the land of Israel, who although carnally not known to the king was forced to remain a widow for the rest of her life. It was a revelation to hear that she, Lise, was actually Abeishag the Shunammite and that Adonijah's soul dwelt in Mendel's body.

Suddenly it occurred to her that Mendel indeed resembled Adonijah as she had fancied him in her imagination, and she considered this astonishing. She realized now why his eyes were so black and strange, his hair so thick, why he avoided her and kept himself apart from people and why he gazed at her with such desire. She began to imagine that she could remember her earlier existence as Abeishag the Shunammite and how Adonijah had driven past the palace in a chariot, fifty men running before him, and although she served King Solomon, she'd felt a strong desire to give herself to Adonijah. . . . It was as if Shloimele's explanation had unfolded a deep riddle to her and released within her the skein of secrets long past.

That night, the couple did not sleep. Shloimele lay next to

her and they conversed quietly until morning. Lise asked questions and Shloimele answered them all reasonably, for my people are notoriously glib, and in her innocence, she believed everything. Even a cabalist could have been fooled into thinking that these were the words of the living God and that Elijah the Prophet revealed himself to Shloimele. Shloimele's words aroused him to such enthusiasm that he tossed and jerked and his teeth chattered as if he were feverish and the bed swayed beneath him and rivulets of sweat coursed from his body. When Lise realized what she was destined to do, and that Shloimele had to be obeyed, she wept bitterly and soaked her pillow with tears. And Shloimele comforted her and caressed her and divulged to her the innermost secrets of the cabala. At dawn she lay in a stupor, her strength evaporated, more dead than alive. And thus the power of a false cabalist and the corrupt words of a disciple of Sabbatai Zevi caused a modest woman to stray from the path of righteousness.

In truth, Shloimele, the villain, devised this whim merely to satisfy his own depraved passions, since he had grown perverse from too much thinking, and what gratified him would make the average person suffer intensely. From an overabundance of lust he had become impotent. Those who understand the complexities of human nature know that joy and pain, ugliness and beauty, love and hate, mercy and cruelty and other conflicting emotions often blend and cannot be separated from each other. Thus I am able not only to make people turn away from the Creator, but to damage their own bodies, all in the name of some imaginary cause.

X

The Repentance

That summer was hot and dry. Reaping their meager corn crop, the peasants sang as though they were keening. Corn grew stunted and half-shriveled. I brought in locusts and birds from the other bank of the river San and what the farmers had labored for the insects devoured. Many cows went dry, probably from spells cast by witches. In the village of Lukoff, not far from Kreshev, a witch was seen riding a hoop and brandishing a broom. Before her ran something with black elflocks, a furry hide and a tail. The millers complained that imps scattered devil's dung in their flour. A herder of horses who tended his animals at night near the marshes, saw hovering in the sky a creature with a crown of thorns and Christians considered this an omen that their Day of Judgment was not far off.

It was the month of Elul. A blight struck the leaves which tore loose from the trees and whirled about in circles in the wind. The heat of the sun blended with the frigid breeze from the Congealed Sea. The birds that migrate to distant lands, held a meeting on the rooftop of the synagogue, chirped, twittered and argued in avian language. Bats swooped about at evening and girls feared leaving their homes, for if a bat got tangled in someone's hair, that person would not live out the year. As usual at this season my disciples, the Shades, began to perpetrate their own brand of mischief. Children were struck down by the measles, the pox, diarrhea, croup and rashes, and although the mothers took the usual protections, measured graves and lit memorial candles, their offspring perished. In the prayer house the ram's horn was sounded several times each day. Blowing the ram's horn, is, as is well known, an effort to drive me away, for when I hear the horn I am supposed to imagine that the Messiah is coming and that God, praised be His name, is about to destroy me. But my ears are not that insensitive that I cannot distinguish between the blast of the Great Shofar and the horn of a Kreshev ram. . . .

So you can see I remained alert and arranged a treat for the people of Kreshev that they would not forget in a hurry.

It was during services on a Monday morning. The prayer house was crowded. The sexton was about to take out the Scroll of the Law. He had already turned back the curtain before the Holy Ark and opened the door when suddenly a tumult erupted through the entire chamber. The worshipers stared at the place where the noise had come from. Through the opened doors burst Shloimele. His appearance was shocking. He wore a ragged capote, its lining torn, the lapel ripped as if he were in mourning; he was in stockinged feet as if it were the Ninth day of Ab, and about his hips was a rope instead of a sash. Ashen, his beard was tousled, his sidelocks askew. The worshipers could not believe their eyes. He moved quickly to the copper laver and washed his hands. Then he stepped to the reading desk, struck it and cried out in a trembling voice: "Men! I bear evil tidings! . . . Something terrible has happened." In the suddenly still prayer house, the flames in the memorial candles crackled loudly. Presently as in a forest before a storm, a rustle passed through the crowd. Everyone surged closer to the lectern. Prayer books fell to the floor and no one bothered to pick them up. Youngsters climbed up on benches and tables, upon which lay the sacred prayer books, but no one ordered them off. In the women's section there was a commotion and a scuffling. The women were crowding the grate to see what went on below amongst the menfolk.

The aged rabbi, Reb Ozer, was still amongst the living and ruled his flock with an iron hand. Although he wasn't inclined to interrupt the services, he now turned from his place along the eastern wall where he worshiped in prayer shawl and phylacteries and shouted angrily: "What do you want? Speak up!"

"Men, I am a transgressor! A sinner who causes others to sin. Like Jerobom, the son of Nebat!" Shloimele exclaimed and pounded his breast with his fist. "Know ye that I forced my wife into adultery. I confess to everything, I bare my soul!"

Although he spoke quietly, his voice echoed as if the hall were now empty. Something like laughter emanated from the women's section of the synagogue and then it turned to the kind of low wailing that is heard at the evening prayers on the eve of the Day of Atonement. The men seemed petrified. Many thought Shloimele had lost his reason. Others had already heard gossip. After a while Reb Ozer, who had long suspected that Shloimele was a secret follower of Sabbatai Zevi, raised the prayer shawl from his head with trembling hands and draped it about his shoulders. His face with its patches of white beard and sidelocks became a corpse-like yellow.

"What did you do?" the patriarch asked with a cracked voice full of foreboding. "With whom did your wife commit this adultery?"

"With my father-in-law's coachman, that Mendel. . . . It's all my fault. . . . She did not want to do it, but I persuaded her. . . ."

"You?" Reb Ozer seemed about to charge at Shloimele.

"Yes, Rabbi—I."

Reb Ozer stretched out his arm for a pinch of snuff as if to fortify his wasted spirit, but his hand trembled and the snuff slipped from between his fingers. Knees shaking, he was forced to support himself on a stand.

"Why did you do this thing?" he asked feebly.

"I don't know, Rabbi. . . . Something came over me!" cried Shloimele, and his puny figure seemed to shrink. "I committed a grave error. . . . A grave error!"

"An error?" Reb Ozer demanded and raised one eye. It seemed as if the single eye held a laughter not of this world.

"Yes, an error!" Shloimele said, forlorn, bewildered.

"Oi, *vei*—Jews, a fire rages, a fire from Gehenna!" a man with a pitch-black beard and long, disheveled sidelocks cried suddenly. "Our children are dying because of them! Innocent infants who knew nothing of sin!"

With the mention of children, a lament arose from the women's synagogue. It was the mothers remembering their babies who had perished. Since Kreshev was a small town the news spread quickly and a terrible excitement followed. Women mingled with the men, phylacteries fell to the ground, prayer shawls were torn loose. When the crowd quieted, Shloimele started his confession again. He told how he had joined the ranks of the cult of Sabbatai Zevi while still a boy, how he had studied with his fellow disciples, how he had been taught that an excess of degradation meant greater sanctity and that the more heinous the wickedness the closer the day of redemption.

"Men, I am a traitor to Israel!" he wailed. "A heretic from sheer perversity and a whoremonger! I secretly desecrated the Sabbath, ate dairy with meat, neglected my prayers, profaned my prayer books and indulged in every possible iniquity. . . . I forced my own wife into adultery! I fooled her into thinking that that bum, Mendel the Coachman, was in truth Adonijah the son of Haggith and that she was Abeishag the Shunammite and that they could obtain salvation only through union . . . ! I even convinced her that, by sinning, she'd commit a good deed! I have trespassed, been faithless, spoken basely, wrought unrighteousness, been presumptuous and counseled evil."

He screamed in a shrill voice and, each time, beat his bosom.

"Spit upon me, Jews. . . . Flail me! Tear me to bits! Judge me!" he cried. "Let me pay for my sins with death."

"Jews, I am not the rabbi of Kreshev but of Sodom!" shouted Reb Ozer—"Sodom and Gomorrah!"

"Oi—Satan dances in Kreshev!" wailed the black Jew and clapped his head in both hands, "Satan the Destroyer!"

The man was right. All that day and through the following night I ruled over Kreshev. No one prayed or studied that day, no ram's horn was blown. The frogs in the marshes croaked: "Unclean! Unclean! Unclean!" Crows heralded evil tidings. The community goat went berserk and attacked a woman returning from the ritual bath. In every chimney a demon hovered. From every woman a hobgoblin spoke. Lise was still in bed when the mob over-ran her house. After shattering the windows with rocks, they stormed her bedroom. When Lise saw the crowds she grew white as the sheet beneath her. She asked to be allowed to dress but they tore the bedding and shredded the silk nightgown from her body, and in such disarray, barefoot and in tatters, her head uncovered, she was dragged off to the house of the rabbi. The young man, Mendel, had just arrived from a village where he had spent several days. Before he even knew what was happening, he was set upon by the butcher boys, tied with ropes, beaten severely and spirited away to the community jail in the anteroom of the synagogue. Since Shloimele had confessed voluntarily, he got away with several facial blows, but of his own free will he stretched out on the threshold of the study house and told everyone who entered or left to spit and walk over him, which is the first penance for the sin of adultery.

XI
The Punishment

Late into the night Reb Ozer sat in the chamber of justice with the ritual slaughterer, the trustee, the seven town elders and other esteemed citizens, listening to the sinners' stories. Although the shutters were closed and the door locked, a curious crowd gathered and the beadle had to keep going out to drive them away. It would take too long to tell all about the shame and depravities detailed by Shloimele and Lise. I'll repeat only a few particulars. Although everyone had supposed Lise would weep and protest her innocence, or simply fall into a faint, she maintained her composure. She answered with clarity every question that the rabbi asked her. When she admitted fornicating with the young man, the rabbi asked how it was possible for a good and intelligent Jewish daughter to do such a thing, and she replied that the blame was all hers, she had sinned and was reconciled to any punishment now. "I know that I've forsaken this world and the next," she said, "and there's no hope for me." She said this as calmly as if the entire chain of events had been a common occurrence, thus astonishing everyone. And when the rabbi asked if she were in love with the young man or if she had sinned under duress she replied that she had acted willingly and of her own accord.

"Perhaps an evil spirit bewitched you?" the rabbi suggested. "Or a spell was cast upon you? Or some dark force compelled you? You could have been in a trance and forgotten the teachings of the Torah and that you were a good Jewish daughter? If this is so—do not deny it!"

But Lise maintained that she knew of no evil spirits, nor demons nor magic nor illusions.

The other men probed further, asked if she'd found knots in her clothing or elflocks in her hair or a yellow stain on the mirror, or a black and blue mark on her body, and she announced that she had encountered nothing. When Shloimele insisted that he had spurred her on and that she was pure of heart, she bowed her head and would neither admit nor deny this. And when the rabbi asked if she regretted her trespasses, she was silent at first, then said: "What's the use of regretting?" and added: "I wish to be judged according to the law—unmercifully." Then she grew silent and it was difficult to get another word out of her.

Mendel confessed that he'd lain with Lise, the daughter of his master, many times; that she'd come to him in his garret and in the garden between the flower beds and that he'd also visited her several times in her own bedroom. Although he had been beaten and his clothing was in shreds, he remained defiant—for as it is written: "Sinners do not repent even at the very gates of Gehenna . . ." and he made uncouth remarks.

When one well-respected citizen asked him: "How could you possibly do such a thing?" Mendel snarled: "And why not? She is better than your wife."

At the same time he vilified his inquisitors, called them thieves, gluttons and usurers, claimed that they gave false weight and measure. He also spoke derogatorily of their wives and daughters. He told one worthy that his wife left a trail of refuse behind her; another—that he was too smelly even for his wife, who refused to sleep with him; and made similar observations full of arrogance, mockery and ridicule.

When the rabbi asked him: "Have you no fear? Do you expect to live forever?" he replied that there was no difference between a dead man and a dead horse. The men were so infuriated that they whipped him again and the crowds outside heard his curses while Lise, covering her face with both her hands, sobbed.

Since Shloimele had confessed his sins voluntarily and was prepared to do immediate penance, he was spared and some of the people even addressed him with kindness. Again before the court he related how the disciples of Sabbatai Zevi had ensnarled him in their net when he was a boy and how he had secretly studied their books and manuscripts and come to believe that the deeper one sank in the dregs, the closer one came to the End of Days. And when the rabbi asked why he had not chosen another expression of sin rather than adultery and whether even a man steeped in evil would want his wife defiled, he replied that this particular sin gave him pleasure, that after Lise came to him from the arms of Mendel and they made love, he probed for all the details and this gratified him more than if he had participated in the act himself. When a citizen observed that this was unnatural, Shloimele replied that that was the way it was, all the same. He related that only after she'd lain with Mendel many times and had begun to turn away from him, had he realized that he was losing his beloved wife, and his delight had changed to deep sorrow. He had then tried to change her ways but it was already too late, for she had grown to love the youth, yearned for him and spoke of him day and night. Shloimele also divulged that Lise had given Mendel presents and taken money from her dowry for her lover, who had then bought himself a horse, a saddle and all sorts of trappings. And one day, Lise had told him that Mendel had advised her to divorce her husband and suggested that the two of them flee to a foreign land. Shloimele had still more to reveal. He said that before the affair, Lise had always been truthful, but afterwards, she began to protect herself with all sorts of lies and deceptions and finally it came to the point where she put off telling Shloimele about being with Mendel. This statement provoked argument and even violence. The citizens were shocked at these revelations; it was difficult to conceive how so small a town as Kreshev could hide such scandalous actions. Many members of the community were afraid the whole town would suffer God's vengeance and that, Heaven forbid, there would be drought, a Tartar attack, or a flood. The rabbi announced that he would decree a general fast immediately.

Afraid that the townspeople might attack the sinners, or even shed blood, the rabbi and town elders kept Mendel in prison until the following day. Lise, in custody of the women of the Burial Society, was led to the almshouse and locked in a separate room for her own safety. Shloimele remained at the rabbi's house. Refusing to lie in bed, he stretched out on the woodshed floor. Having consulted the elders, the rabbi gave his verdict. The sinners would be led through the town the following day to exemplify the humiliation of those who have forsaken God. Shloimele would then be divorced from Lise, who according to the law was now forbidden to him. Nor would she be permitted to marry Mendel the Coachman.

Sentence was executed very early the next morning. Men, women, boys and girls began to assemble in the synagogue courtyard. Truant children climbed to the roof of the study house and the balcony of the women's synagogue in order to see better. Pranksters brought stepladders and stilts. Despite the beadle's warning that the spectacle was to be watched gravely, without jostling or mirth, there was no end of clowning. Although this was their busy pre-holiday season, seamstresses left their work to gloat over the downfall of a daughter of the rich. Tailors, cobblers, barrelmakers and hog-bristle combers clustered about, joked, nudged each other and flirted with the women. In the manner of funeral guests, respectable girls draped shawls about their heads. Women wore double aprons, one before, one behind, as if they were present at the exorcizing of a dybbuk or participating in a levirate marriage ceremony. Merchants closed their shops, artisans left their workbenches. Even the gentiles came to see the Jews punish their sinners. All eyes were fixed upon the old synagogue from which the sinners would be led to suffer public shame.

The oaken door swung open, accompanied by a humming from the spectators. The butchers led out Mendel—with tied hands, a tattered jacket and the lining of a skullcap on his head. A bruise discolored his forehead. A dark stubble covered his unshaven chin. Arrogantly, he faced the mob and puckered his lips as if to whistle. The butchers held him fast by the elbows for he had already attempted to escape. Catcalls greeted him. Although Shloimele had repented willingly and been spared by the tribunal, he demanded that his punishment be the same as the others. Whistling, shouting and laughter arose when he appeared. He had changed beyond recognition. His face was dead-white. Instead of a gabardine, a fringed garment and trousers—bits of rag hung from him. One cheek was swollen. Shoeless, holes in his stockings, his bare toes showed. They placed him beside Mendel, and he stood there, bent and stiff as a scarecrow. Many women began to weep at the spectacle as if lamenting one who had died. Some complained that the town elders were cruel and that if Reb Bunim were around such a thing could never take place.

Lise did not appear for a long time. The mob's great curiosity about her caused a terrible crush. Women, in the excitement, lost their headbands. When Lise appeared in the doorway escorted by the Burial Society women, the crowd seemed to freeze. A cry was torn from every throat. Lise's attire had not been altered—but a pudding-pot sat upon her head, around her neck hung a necklace of garlic cloves and a dead goose; in one hand she held a broom, in the other a goose-wing duster. Her loins were girdled by a rope of straw. It was plain that the ladies of the Burial Society had toiled with diligence to cause the daughter of a noble and wealthy home to suffer the highest degree of shame and degradation. According to the sentence the sinners were to be led through all the streets in town, to halt before each house where every man and woman was to spit and heap abuse upon them. The procession began at the house of the rabbi and worked its way down to the homes of the lowest members of the community. Many feared that Lise would collapse and spoil their fun but she was apparently determined to accept her punishment in all its bitterness.

For Kreshev it was like the Feast of Omer in the middle of the month of Elul. Armed with pine cones, bows and arrows, the Cheder boys brought food from home, ran wild, screamed and bleated like goats all day. Housewives let their stoves grow cold, the study house was empty. Even the ailing and indigent almshouse occupants came out to attend the Black Feast.

Women whose children were sick or those who still observed the seven days of mourning ran outside their houses to berate the sinners with cries, laments, oaths and clenched fists. Being afraid of Mendel the Coachman who could easily exact revenge, and feeling no real hatred against Shloimele, whom they considered addled, they expressed their fury on Lise. Although the beadle had warned against violence, some of the women pinched and mishandled her. One woman doused her with a bucket of slops, another pelted her with chicken entrails and she was splattered with all sorts of slime. Because Lise had told the story of the goat and it had made her think of Mendel, town wags had snared the goat and with it in tow followed the procession. Some people whistled, others sang mocking songs. Lise was called: "Harlot, whore, strumpet, wanton, tart, streetwalker, stupid ass, doxie, bitch," and similar names. Fiddlers, a drummer, and a cymbalist played a wedding march alongside the procession. One of the young men, pretending to be the wedding jester, declaimed verses, ribald and profane. The women who escorted Lise tried to humor and comfort her, for this march was her atonement and by repenting she could regain her decency—but she made no response. No one saw her shed a single tear. Nor did she loose her hold on the broom and duster. To Mendel's credit, let me state that he did not oppose his tormentors either. Silently, making no reply to all the abuse, he walked on. As for Shloimele, from the faces he made, it was hard to tell whether he laughed or cried. He walked unsteadily, constantly stopping, until he was pushed and had to go on. He began to limp. Since he had only made others sin, but had not done so himself, he was soon allowed to drop out. A guard accompanied him for protection. Mendel was returned to prison that night. At the rabbi's house, Lise and Shloimele were divorced. When Lise raised both her hands and Shloimele placed the Bill of Divorcement in them, the women lamented. Men had tears in their eyes. Then Lise was led back to her father's house in the company of the women of the Burial Society.

XII
The Destruction of Kreshev

That night a gale blew as if (as the saying goes) seven witches had hanged themselves. Actually, only one young woman hanged herself—Lise. When the old servant came into her mistress' room in the morning, she found an empty bed. She waited, thinking that Lise was attending to her personal needs, but after a long time had gone by without Lise appearing, the maid went looking for her. She soon found Lise in the attic—hanging from a rope with nothing on her head, barefoot and in her nightgown. She had already grown cold.

The town was shocked. The same women who the day previous had thrown stones at Lise and expressed indignation over her mild punishment, wailed now that the community elders had killed a decent Jewish daughter. The men split into two factions. The first faction said that Lise had already paid for her transgressions and that her body should be buried in the cemetery beside her mother's and considered respectable; the second faction argued that she be buried outside the cemetery proper, behind the fence—like other suicides. Members of the second faction maintained that from everything Lise said and did at the chamber of justice, she had died rebellious and unrepentant. The rabbi and community elders were members of the second faction, and they were the ones who triumphed. She was buried at night, behind the fence, by the light of a lantern. Women sobbed, choking. The noise wakened crows nesting in the graveyard trees and they began to caw. Some of the elders asked Lise for forgiveness. Shards were placed over her eyes, according to custom, and a rod between her fingers, so that when the Messiah came she would be able to dig a tunnel from Kreshev to the Holy Land. Since she was a young woman, Kalman the Leech was summoned to find out if she was pregnant, for it would have been bad luck to bury an unborn child. The gravedigger said what is said at funerals: "The Rock, His work is perfect, for all His ways are judgment: a God of faithfulness and without iniquity, just and right is He." Handfuls of grass were plucked and thrown over shoulders. The attendants each threw a spadeful of earth into the grave. Although Shloimele no longer was Lise's husband, he walked behind the stretcher and said the Kaddish over her grave. After the funeral he flung himself upon the mound of earth and refused to rise and had to be dragged away by force. And although, according to law, he was exempt from observing the seven days of mourning, he retired to his father-in-law's house and observed all the prescribed rites.

During the period of mourning, several of the townspeople came to pray with Shloimele and offer their condolences, but as though he had vowed eternal silence, he made no response. Ragged and threadbare, peering into the Book of Job, he sat on a footstool, his face waxen, his beard and sidelocks disheveled. A candle flickered in a shard of oil. A rag lay soaking in a glass of water. It was for the soul of the deceased, that she might immerse herself therein. The aged servant brought food for Shloimele but he would take no more than a slice of stale bread with salt. After the seven days of mourning, Shloimele, staff in hand and a pack on his back, went into exile. The townspeople trailed him for a while, trying to dissuade him or to make him wait at least until Reb Bunim returned, but he did not speak, merely shook his head and went on until those who had spoken grew weary and turned back. He was never seen again.

Reb Bunim, meanwhile, detained somewhere in Woliny, had been absorbed in business affairs and knew nothing of his misfortune. A few days before Rosh Hashonah he had a peasant with a wagon take him to Kreshev. He carried numerous gifts for his daughter and son-in-law. One night he stopped at an inn. He asked for news of his family, but although everyone knew what had happened, no one had the courage to tell him. They declared they had heard nothing. And when Reb Bunim treated some of them to whiskey and cake, they reluctantly ate and drank, avoiding his eyes as they offered toasts. Reb Bunim was puzzled by so much reticence.

The town seemed abandoned in the morning, when Reb Bunim rode into Kreshev. The residents had actually fled him. Riding to his house, he saw the shutters closed and barred in midday, and he was frightened. He called Lise, Shloimele and Mendel, but no one answered. The maid too had left the house and lay ill at the Almshouse. Finally an old woman appeared from nowhere and told Reb Bunim the terrible news.

"Ah, there is no Lise anymore!" the old woman cried, wringing her hands.

"When did she die?" Reb Bunim asked, his face white and frowning.

She named the day.

"And where is Shloimele?"

"Gone into exile!" the woman said. "Immediately after the seventh day of mourning. . . ."

"Praised be the true Judge!" Reb Bunim offered the benediction for the dead. And he added the sentence from the Book of Job: " 'Naked I came from my mother's womb and naked I will return therein.' "

He went to his room, tore a rent in his lapel, removed his boots and seated himself on the floor. The old woman brought bread, a hard-boiled egg and a bit of ash, as the law decrees. Gradually she explained to him that his only daughter hadn't died a natural death but had hanged herself. She also explained the reason for her suicide. But Reb Bunim was not shattered by the information for he was a God-fearing man and accepted whatever punishment came from above, as it is written: "Man is obliged to be grateful for the bad as well as the good," and he maintained his faith and held no resentment against the Lord of the Universe.

On Rosh Hashonah Reb Bunim prayed at the prayer house and chanted his prayers vigorously. Afterwards he ate the holiday meal alone. A maid served him the head of a sheep, apples with honey and a carrot, and he chewed and swayed and sang the table chants. I, the Evil Spirit, tried to tempt the grief-stricken father from the path of righteousness and to fill his spirit with melancholy, for that is the purpose for which the

Creator sent me down to earth. But Reb Bunim ignored me and fulfilled the phrase from the proverb: "Thou shalt not answer the fool according to his foolishness." Instead of disputing with me, he studied and prayed, and soon after the Day of Atonement began to construct a Sukkoth booth, and thus occupied his time with the Torah and holy deeds. It is known that I have power only over those who question the ways of God, not those who do holy deeds. And so the holy days passed. He also asked that Mendel the Coachman be released from prison so that he might go his own way. Thus Reb Bunim left the town like the saint of whom it is written: "When a saint leaves town, gone is its beauty, its splendor, its glory."

Immediately after the holidays, Reb Bunim sold his house and other possessions for a pittance and left Kreshev, because the town reminded him too much of his misfortune. The rabbi and everyone else accompanied him to the road and he left a sum for the study house, the poorhouse and for other charitable purposes.

Mendel the Coachman lingered for a while in neighboring villages. The Kreshev peddlers spoke of how the peasants feared him and of how often he quarreled with them. Some said he had become a horse thief, others a highwayman. There was gossip also that he had visited Lise's grave; his boot marks were discovered in the sand. There were other stories about him. Some people feared that he would exact revenge upon the town—and they were correct. One night a fire broke out. It started in several places at once and despite the rain, flames leaped from house to house until nearly three-quarters of Kreshev was destroyed. The community goat lost its life also. Witnesses swore that Mendel the Coachman had started the fire. Since it was bitter cold at the time and many people were left without a roof over their heads, quite a few fell ill, a plague followed, men, women and children perished, and Kreshev was truly destroyed. To this day the town has remained small and poor; it has never been rebuilt to its former size. And this was all because of a sin committed by a husband, a wife, and a coachman. And although it is not customary among Jews to make supplications over the grave of a suicide, the young women who came to visit their parents' graves often stretched out on the mound of earth behind the fence and wept and offered prayers, not only for themselves and their families, but for the soul of the fallen Lise, daughter of Shifrah Tammar. And the custom remains to this day.

Translated by Elaine Gottlieb and June Ruth Flaum

SHORT FRIDAY

AND OTHER STORIES

Contents

Author's Note

I wish to express my gratitude to Robert Giroux for editing the whole manuscript, and to Cecil Hemley, now head of Ohio University Press, for revising parts of the translation in collaboration with me. Mirra Ginsburg, Elizabeth Pollet, Elaine Gottlieb, Ruth Whitman, Marion Magid, Chana Faerstein, Martha Glicklich, Joel Blocker, Roger Klein, and my nephew, Joseph Singer, all deserve my thanks for their devotion in bringing this collection to the American reader.

I dedicate these pages to the blessed memory of my brother, I. J. Singer, author of *The Brothers Ashkenazi*, *Yoshe Kalb* etc. who helped me to come to this country and was my teacher and master in literature. I am still learning from him and his work.

Isaac Bashevis Singer

Taibele and Her Demon

I N the town of Lashnik, not far from Lublin, there lived a man and his wife. His name was Chaim Nossen, hers Taibele. They had no children. Not that the marriage was barren; Taibele had borne her husband a son and two daughters, but all three had died in infancy—one of whooping cough, one of scarlet fever, and one of diphtheria. After that Taibele's womb closed up, and nothing availed: neither prayers, nor spells, nor potions. Grief drove Chaim Nossen to withdraw from the world. He kept apart from his wife, stopped eating meat, and no longer slept at home, but on a bench in the prayer house. Taibele owned a dry-goods store, inherited from her parents, and she sat there all day, with a yardstick on her right, a pair of shears on her left, and the Women's Prayer Book in Yiddish in front of her. Chaim Nossen, tall, lean, with black eyes and a wedge of a beard, had always been a morose, silent man even at the best of times. Taibele was small and fair, with blue eyes and a round face. Although punished by the Almighty, she still smiled easily, the dimples playing on her cheeks. She had no one else to cook for now, but she lit the stove or the tripod every day and cooked some porridge or soup for herself. She also went on with her knitting—now a pair of stockings, now a vest; or else she would embroider something on canvas. It wasn't in her nature to rail at fate or cling to sorrow.

One day Chaim Nossen put his prayer shawl and phylacteries, a change of underwear, and a loaf of bread into a sack and left the house. Neighbors asked where he was going; he answered: "Wherever my eyes lead me."

When people told Taibele that her husband had left her, it was too late to catch up with him. He was already across the river. It was discovered that he had hired a cart to take him to Lublin. Taibele sent a messenger to seek him out, but neither her husband nor the messenger was ever seen again. At thirty-three, Taibele found herself a deserted wife.

After a period of searching, she realized that she had nothing more to hope for. God had taken both her children and her husband. She would never be able to marry again; from now on she would have to live alone. All she had left was her house, her store, and her belongings. The townspeople pitied her, for she was a quiet woman, kind-hearted and honest in her business dealings. Everyone asked: how did she deserve such misfortunes? But God's ways are hidden from man.

Taibele had several friends among the town matrons whom she had known since childhood. In the daytime housewives are busy with their pots and pans, but in the evening Taibele's friends often dropped in for a chat. In the summer, they would sit on a bench outside the house, gossiping and telling each other stories.

One moonless summer evening when the town was as dark as Egypt, Taibele sat with her friends on the bench, telling them a tale she had read in a book bought from a peddler. It was about a young Jewish woman, and a demon who had ravished her and lived with her as man and wife. Taibele recounted the story in all its details. The women huddled closer together, joined hands, spat to ward off evil, and laughed the kind of laughter that comes from fear. One of them asked:

"Why didn't she exorcise him with an amulet?"

"Not every demon is frightened of amulets," answered Taibele.

"Why didn't she make a journey to a holy rabbi?"

"The demon warned her that he would choke her if she revealed the secret."

"Woe is me, may the Lord protect us, may no one know of such things!" a woman cried out.

"I'll be afraid to go home now," said another.

"I'll walk with you," a third one promised.

While they were talking, Alchonon, the teacher's helper who hoped one day to become a wedding jester, happened to be passing by. Alchonon, five years a widower, had the reputation of being a wag and a prankster, a man with a screw loose. His steps were silent because the soles of his shoes were worn through and he walked on his bare feet. When he heard Taibele telling the story, he halted to listen. The darkness was so thick, and the women so engrossed in the weird tale, that they did not see him. This Alchonon was a dissipated fellow,

full of cunning goatish tricks. On the instant, he formed a mischievous plan.

After the women had gone, Alchonon stole into Taibele's
yard. He hid behind a tree and watched through the window.
When he saw Taibele go to bed and put out the candle, he
slipped into the house. Taibele had not bolted the door;
thieves were unheard of in that town. In the hallway, he took
off his shabby caftan, his fringed garment, his trousers, and
stood as naked as his mother bore him. Then he tiptoed to
Taibele's bed. She was almost asleep, when suddenly she saw a
figure looming in the dark. She was too terrified to utter a
sound.

"Who is it?" she whispered, trembling.

Alchonon replied in a hollow voice: "Don't scream,
Taibele. If you cry out, I will destroy you. I am the demon
Hurmizah, ruler over darkness, rain, hail, thunder, and wild
beasts. I am the evil spirit who espoused the young woman
you spoke about tonight. And because you told the story with
such relish, I heard your words from the abyss and was filled
with lust for your body. Do not try to resist, for I drag away
those who refuse to do my will beyond the Mountains of
Darkness—to Mount Sair, into a wilderness where man's foot
is unknown, where no beast dares to tread, where the earth is
of iron and the sky of copper. And I roll them in thorns and in
fire, among adders and scorpions, until every bone of their
body is ground to dust, and they are lost for eternity in the
nether depths. But if you comply with my wish, not a hair of
your head will be harmed, and I will send you success in every
undertaking. . . ."

Hearing these words, Taibele lay motionless as in a swoon.
Her heart fluttered and seemed to stop. She thought her end
had come. After a while, she gathered courage and murmured:

"What do you want of me? I am a married woman!"

"Your husband is dead. I followed in his funeral procession
myself." The voice of the teacher's helper boomed out. "It is
true that I cannot go to the rabbi to testify and free you to remarry, for the rabbis don't believe our kind. Besides, I don't
dare step across the threshold of the rabbi's chamber—I fear
the Holy Scrolls. But I am not lying. Your husband died in an

epidemic, and the worms have already gnawed away his nose. And even were he alive, you would not be forbidden to lie with me, for the laws of the *Shulchan Aruch* do not apply to us."

Hurmizah the teacher's helper went on with his persuasions, some sweet, some threatening. He invoked the names of angels and devils, of demonic beasts and of vampires. He swore that Asmodeus, King of the Demons, was his step-uncle. He said that Lilith, Queen of the Evil Spirits, danced for him on one foot and did every manner of thing to please him. Shibtah, the she-devil who stole babies from women in childbed, baked poppyseed cakes for him in Hell's ovens and leavened them with the fat of wizards and black dogs. He argued so long, adducing such witty parables and proverbs, that Taibele was finally obliged to smile, in her extremity. Hurmizah vowed that he had loved Taibele for a long time. He described to her the dresses and shawls she had worn that year and the year before; he told her the secret thoughts that came to her as she kneaded dough, prepared her Sabbath meal, washed herself in the bath, and saw to her needs at the outhouse. He also reminded her of the morning when she had wakened with a black and blue mark on her breast. She had thought it was the pinch of a ghoul. But it was really the mark left by a kiss of Hurmizah's lips, he said.

After a while, the demon got into Taibele's bed and had his will of her. He told her that from then on he would visit her twice a week, on Wednesdays and on Sabbath evenings, for those were the nights when the unholy ones were abroad in the world. He warned her, though, not to divulge to anyone what had befallen her, or even hint at it, on pain of dire punishment: he would pluck out the hair from her skull, pierce her eyes, and bite out her navel. He would cast her into a desolate wilderness where bread was dung and water was blood, and where the wailing of Zalmaveth was heard all day and all night. He commanded Taibele to swear by the bones of her mother that she would keep the secret to her last day. Taibele saw that there was no escape for her. She put her hand on his thigh and swore an oath, and did all that the monster bade her.

Before Hurmizah left, he kissed her long and lustfully, and

since he was a demon and not a man, Taibele returned his kisses and moistened his beard with her tears. Evil spirit though he was, he had treated her kindly. . . .

When Hurmizah was gone, Taibele sobbed into her pillow until sunrise.

Hurmizah came every Wednesday night and every Sabbath night. Taibele was afraid that she might find herself with child and give birth to some monster with tail and horns—an imp or a mooncalf. But Hurmizah promised to protect her against shame. Taibele asked whether she need go to the ritual bath to cleanse herself after her impure days, but Hurmizah said that the laws concerning menstruation did not extend to those who consorted with the unclean host.

As the saying goes, may God preserve us from all that we can get accustomed to. And so it was with Taibele. In the beginning she had feared that her nocturnal visitant might do her harm, give her boils or elflocks, make her bark like a dog or drink urine, and bring disgrace upon her. But Hurmizah did not whip her or pinch her or spit on her. On the contrary, he caressed her, whispered endearments, made puns and rhymes for her. Sometimes he pulled such pranks and babbled such devil's nonsense, that she was forced to laugh. He tugged at the lobe of her ear and gave her love-bites on the shoulder, and in the morning she found the marks of his teeth on her skin. He persuaded her to let her hair grow under her cap and he wove it into braids. He taught her charms and spells, told her about his night-brethren, the demons with whom he flew over ruins and fields of toadstools, over the salt marshes of Sodom, and the frozen wastes of the Sea of Ice. He did not deny that he had other wives, but they were all she-devils; Taibele was the only human wife he possessed. When Taibele asked him the names of his wives, he enumerated them: Namah, Machlath, Aff, Chuldah, Zluchah, Nafkah, and Cheimah. Seven altogether.

He told her that Namah was black as pitch and full of rage. When she quarreled with him, she spat venom and blew fire and smoke through her nostrils.

Machlath had the face of a leech, and those whom she touched with her tongue were forever branded.

Aff loved to adorn herself with silver, emeralds, and diamonds. Her braids were of spun gold. On her ankles she wore bells and bracelets; when she danced, all the deserts rang out with their chiming.

Chuldah had the shape of a cat. She meowed instead of speaking. Her eyes were green as gooseberries. When she copulated, she always chewed bear's liver.

Zluchah was the enemy of brides. She robbed bridegrooms of potency. If a bride stepped outside alone at night during the Seven Nuptial Benedictions, Zluchah danced up to her and the bride lost the power of speech or was taken by a seizure.

Nafkah was lecherous, always betraying him with other demons. She retained his affections only by her vile and insolent talk, which delighted his heart.

Cheimah should have, according to her name, been as vicious as Namah should have been mild, but the reverse was true: Cheimah was a she-devil without gall. She was forever doing charitable deeds, kneading dough for housewives when they were ill, or bringing bread to the homes of the poor.

Thus Hurmizah described his wives, and told Taibele how he disported himself with them, playing tag over roofs and engaging in all sorts of pranks. Ordinarily, a woman is jealous when a man consorts with other women, but how can a human be jealous of a female devil? Quite the contrary. Hurmizah's tales amused Taibele, and she was always plying him with questions. Sometimes he revealed to her mysteries no mortal may know—about God, his angels and seraphs, his heavenly mansions, and the seven heavens. He also told her how sinners, male and female, were tortured in barrels of pitch and cauldrons of fiery coals, on beds studded with nails and in pits of snow, and how the Black Angels beat the bodies of the sinners with rods of fire.

The greatest punishment in hell was tickling, Hurmizah said. There was a certain imp in hell by the name of Lekish. When Lekish tickled an adulteress on her soles or under the arms, her tormented laughter echoed all the way to the island of Madagascar.

In this way, Hurmizah entertained Taibele all through the night, and soon it came about that she began to miss him when he was away. The summer nights seemed too short, for

Hurmizah would leave soon after cockcrow. Even winter nights were not long enough. The truth was that she now loved Hurmizah, and though she knew a woman must not lust after a demon, she longed for him day and night.

2

Although Alchonon had been a widower for many years, matchmakers still tried to marry him off. The girls they proposed were from mean homes, widows and divorcees, for a teacher's helper was a poor provider, and Alchonon had besides the reputation of being a shiftless ne'er-do-well. Alchonon dismissed the offers on various pretexts: one woman was too ugly, the other had a foul tongue, the third was a slattern. The matchmakers wondered: how could a teacher's helper who earned nine groschen a week presume to be such a picker and chooser? And how long could a man live alone? But no one can be dragged by force to the wedding canopy.

Alchonon knocked around town—long, lean, tattered, with a red disheveled beard, in a crumpled shirt, with his pointed Adam's apple jumping up and down. He waited for the wedding jester Reb Zekele to die, so that he could take over his job. But Reb Zekele was in no hurry to die; he still enlivened weddings with an inexhaustible flow of quips and rhymes, as in his younger days. Alchonon tried to set up on his own as a teacher for beginners, but no householder would entrust his child to him. Mornings and evenings, he took the boys to and from the *cheder*. During the day he sat in Reb Itchele the Teacher's courtyard, idly whittling wooden pointers, or cutting out paper decorations which were used only once a year, at Pentecost, or modeling figurines from clay. Not far from Taibele's store there was a well, and Alchonon came there many times a day, to draw a pail of water or to take a drink, spilling the water over his red beard. At these times, he would throw a quick glance at Taibele. Taibele pitied him: why was the man knocking about all by himself? And Alchonon would say to himself each time: "Woe, Taibele, if you knew the truth! . . ."

Alchonon lived in a garret, in the house of an old widow who was deaf and half-blind. The crone often chided him for not going to the synagogue to pray like other Jews. For as soon as Alchonon had taken the children home, he said a hasty evening prayer and went to bed. Sometimes the old woman thought she heard the teacher's helper get up in the middle of the night and go off somewhere. She asked him where he wandered at night, but Alchonon told her that she had been dreaming. The women who sat on benches in the evenings, knitting socks and gossiping, spread the rumor that after midnight Alchonon turned into a werewolf. Some women said he was consorting with a succubus. Otherwise, why should a man remain so many years without a wife? The rich men would not trust their children to him any longer. He now escorted only the children of the poor, and seldom ate a spoonful of hot food, but had to content himself with dry crusts.

Alchonon became thinner and thinner, but his feet remained as nimble as ever. With his lanky legs, he seemed to stride down the street as though on stilts. He must have suffered constant thirst, for he was always coming down to the well. Sometimes he would merely help a dealer or peasant to water his horse. One day, when Taibele noticed from the distance how his caftan was torn and ragged, she called him into her shop. He threw a frightened glance and turned white.

"I see your caftan is torn," said Taibele. "If you wish, I will advance you a few yards of cloth. You can pay it off later, five pennies a week."

"No."

"Why not?" Taibele asked in astonishment. "I won't haul you before the Rabbi if you fall behind. You'll pay when you can."

"No."

And he quickly walked out of the store, fearing she might recognize his voice.

In summertime it was easy to visit Taibele in the middle of the night. Alchonon made his way through back lanes, clutching his caftan around his naked body. In winter, the dressing and undressing in Taibele's cold hallway became increasingly painful. But worst of all were the nights after a fresh snowfall. Alchonon was worried that Taibele or one of the neighbors might notice his tracks. He caught cold and began to cough. One night he got into Taibele's bed with his teeth chattering; he could not warm up for a long time. Afraid that she might discover his hoax, he invented explanations and excuses. But Taibele neither probed nor wished to probe too closely. She had long discovered that a devil had all the habits and frailties of a man. Hurmizah perspired, sneezed, hiccuped, yawned. Sometimes his breath smelled of onion, sometimes of garlic. His body felt like the body of her husband, bony and hairy, with an Adam's apple and a navel. At times, Hurmizah was in a jocular mood, at other times a sigh broke from him. His feet were not goose feet, but human, with nails and frost-blisters. Once Taibele asked him the meaning of these things, and Hurmizah explained:

"When one of us consorts with a human female, he assumes the shape of a man. Otherwise, she would die of fright."

Yes, Taibele got used to him and loved him. She was no longer terrified of him or his impish antics. His tales were inexhaustible, but Taibele often found contradictions in them. Like all liars, he had a short memory. He had told her at first that devils were immortal. But one night he asked:

"What will you do if I die?"

"But devils don't die!"

"They are taken to the lowest abyss. . . ."

That winter there was an epidemic in town. Foul winds came from the river, the woods, and the swamps. Not only children, but adults as well were brought down with the ague. It rained and it hailed. Floods broke the dam on the river. The storms blew off an arm of the windmill. On Wednesday night, when Hurmizah came into Taibele's bed, she noticed that his body was burning hot, but his feet were icy. He shivered and moaned. He tried to entertain her with talk of she-devils, of how they seduced young men, how they cavorted with other devils, splashed about in the ritual bath, tied elflocks in old men's beards, but he was weak and unable to possess her. She had never seen him in such a wretched state. Her heart misgave her. She asked:

"Shall I get you some raspberries with milk?"

Hurmizah replied: "Such remedies are not for our kind."

"What do you do when you get sick?"

"We itch and we scratch. . . ."

He spoke little after that. When he kissed Taibele, his breath was sour. He always remained with her until cockcrow, but this time he left early. Taibele lay silent, listening to his movements in the hallway. He had sworn to her that he flew out of the window even when it was closed and sealed, but she heard the door creak. Taibele knew that it was sinful to pray for devils, that one must curse them and blot them from memory; yet she prayed to God for Hurmizah.

She cried out in anguish: "There are so many devils, let there be one more. . . ."

On the following Sabbath Taibele waited in vain for Hurmizah until dawn; he never came. She called him inwardly and muttered the spells he had taught her, but the hallway was silent. Taibele lay benumbed. Hurmizah had once boasted that he had danced for Tubal-cain and Enoch, that he had sat on the roof of Noah's Ark, licked the salt from the nose of Lot's wife, and plucked Ahasuerus by the beard. He had prophesied that she would be reincarnated after a hundred years as a princess, and that he, Hurmizah, would capture her, with the help of his slaves Chittim and Tachtim, and carry her off to the palace of Bashemath, the wife of Esau. But now he was probably lying somewhere ill, a helpless demon, a lonely orphan—without father or mother, without a faithful wife to care for him. Taibele recalled how his breath came rasping like a saw when he had been with her last; when he blew his nose, there was a whistling in his ear. From Sunday to Wednesday Taibele went about as one in a dream. On Wednesday she could hardly wait until the clock struck midnight, but the night went, and Hurmizah did not appear. Taibele turned her face to the wall.

The day began, dark as evening. Fine snow dust was falling from the murky sky. The smoke could not rise from the chimneys; it spread over the roofs like ragged sheets. The rooks cawed harshly. Dogs barked. After the miserable night, Taibele had no strength to go to her store. Nevertheless, she dressed and went outside. She saw four pallbearers carrying a stretcher. From under the snow-swept coverlet protruded the blue feet of a corpse. Only the sexton followed the dead man. Taibele asked who it was, and the sexton answered:

"Alchonon, the teacher's helper."

A strange idea came to Taibele—to escort Alchonon, the feckless man who had lived alone and died alone, on his last journey. Who would come to the store today? And what did she care for business? Taibele had lost everything. At least, she would be doing a good deed. She followed the dead on the long road to the cemetery. There she waited while the grave-digger swept away the snow and dug a grave in the frozen earth. They wrapped Alchonon the teacher's helper in a prayer shawl and a cowl, placed shards on his eyes, and stuck between his fingers a myrtle twig that he would use to dig his way to the Holy Land when the Messiah came. Then the grave was closed and the gravedigger recited the Kaddish. A cry broke from Taibele. This Alchonon had lived a lonely life, just as she did. Like her, he left no heir. Yes, Alchonon the teacher's helper had danced his last dance. From Hurmizah's tales, Taibele knew that the deceased did not go straight to heaven. Every sin creates a devil, and these devils are a man's children after his death. They come to demand their share. They call the dead man Father and roll him through forest and wilderness until the measure of his punishment is filled and he is ready for purification in hell. . . .

From then on Taibele remained alone, doubly deserted—by an ascetic and by a devil. She aged quickly. Nothing was left to her of the past except a secret that could never be told and would be believed by no one. There are secrets that the heart cannot reveal to the lips. They are carried to the grave. The willows murmur of them, the rooks caw about them, the gravestones converse about them silently, in the language of stone. The dead will awaken one day, but their secrets will abide with the Almighty and His Judgment until the end of all generations.

Translated by Mirra Ginsburg

Big and Little

You say—big, little, what's the difference? Man is not measured by a yardstick. The main thing is the head, not the feet. Still, if a person gets hold of some foolish notion, you never know where it may lead. Let me tell you a story. There was a couple in our town. He was called Little Motie, and she, Motiekhe. No one ever used her real name. He was not just little; he was hardly bigger than a midget. The idle jokers—and there are always plenty of them around—amused themselves at the poor man's expense. The teacher's assistant, they said, took him by the hand and led him off to Reb Berish, who taught the youngest children at the *cheder*. On Simkhas Torah the men got drunk and called him up with the small boys to the reading of the Torah. Someone gave him a holiday flag—with an apple and a candle on the flagstick. When a woman gave birth, the wags would come to tell him that a boy was needed for the childbed prayer, to ward off the evil spirits. If, at least, he'd had a decent beard! But no, it was only a wisp—a few hairs here and there. He had no children and, to tell the truth, he did look like a schoolboy himself. His wife, Motiekhe, wasn't a beauty either, but there was a whole lot of her. Well, be that as it may, the two of them lived together, and Motie became something of a rich man. He was a grain merchant and owned a storehouse. Our local landowner took a liking to him, though he'd also make fun of the man's size now and then. Still, it was a living. What's the good of being big if the hole in your pocket is even bigger?

But the worst of it was that Motiekhe (may she be forgiven!) was forever teasing him. Tiny do this, Tiny do that. She always had something for him to do in places he could not reach. "Put a nail in the wall, up there!" "Take the copper pan down from the shelf!" She ridiculed him in front of strangers, too, and the stories were carried all over town afterwards. One day she even said (can you imagine such talk from an honest Jewish wife?) that he needed a footstool to get into bed with her. You can guess what the gossips did with that! If someone came to ask for him when he was out, she'd say: "Take a look under the table."

There was a teacher with a wicked tongue who told how he had once mislaid his pointer. He looked around—and there, said he, was Motie, using his pointer as a walking stick. In those years, people had time on their hands, and nothing better to do than wag their tongues. Motie himself took these mean jokes with a smile, as the saying goes, but they hurt. After all, what is so funny about being small? What if a man has longer legs, is he worth more in the eyes of God? All this, mind you, went on only among the riffraff. Pious folk shun evil gossip.

This Motie was no scholar, just an ordinary man. He liked to listen to the parables of visiting preachers at the synagogue. On Saturday mornings he chanted Psalms with the rest of the congregation. He was also fond of an occasional glass of whisky. Sometimes he came to our house. My father (may he rest in peace!) bought oats from him. You'd hear Motie scraping at the latch like a cat asking to be let in. We girls were small then, and we'd greet him with bursts of laughter. Father would draw up a chair for him and address him as Reb Motie, but our chairs were high and he'd have difficulty climbing up. When tea was served, he would fidget and stretch, unable to reach the rim of the glass with his lips. Evil tongues said that he padded his heels, and that he had fallen once into a wooden bucket, such as people use for showering themselves at the bath house. But all this aside, he was a clever merchant. And Motiekhe had a life of ease and comfort with him. He owned a handsome house, and the cupboard shelves were always filled with the best of everything.

Now listen to this. One day man and wife had a disagreement. One word led to another, and soon there was a real quarrel. It happens in a family. But, as luck would have it, a neighbor was present. Motiekhe (may she not hold this against me!) had a mouth on hinges, and when she flew into a rage she forgot God himself. She screamed at her husband: "You midget! You little stinker! What kind of a man are you? No bigger than a fly. I am ashamed to be seen walking to the synagogue with such an undersized tot!" And she went on and on, heaping coal upon ashes till all the blood drained out of his face. He said nothing, and this drove her altogether wild. She shrieked: "What do I want with such a midget of a man? I'll buy you a stepping stool and put you into a cradle. If my mother had loved me, she would have found me a man, not a newborn infant!" She was in such a frenzy, she no longer knew what she was saying. He was red-haired, with a ruddy face, but now he turned white as chalk and he said to her: "Your second husband will be big enough to make up for me." And as he said it, he broke down and cried, for all the world like a small child. No one had ever seen him cry, not even on Yom Kippur. His wife was stricken dumb at once. I do not know what happened afterwards, I wasn't there. They must have patched it up. But as the proverb says, a blow heals, but a word abides.

Before a month had passed, the townspeople had something new to talk about. Motie had brought home an assistant from Lublin. What did he want with an assistant? He had managed his business well enough by himself all these years. The newcomer walked down the street and everyone turned to look at him: a giant of a man, black as pitch, with a pair of black eyes and a black beard. The other merchants asked Motie: "What do you need an assistant for?" And he replied: "The business has grown, thank God! I can no longer carry the whole burden by myself." Well, they thought, he must know what he is doing. But in a small town everybody sees what's cooking in his neighbor's pot. The man from Lublin—his name was Mendl—didn't seem to be much of a merchant. He hung about the yard, gawking and rolling his black eyes this way and that. On market days he stood like a post among the carts, towering over the peasants and chewing at a straw.

When he came to the prayer house, people asked him: "What did you do in Lublin?" He answered: "I am a wood-chopper." "Do you have a wife?" "No," he said, he was a widower. The Brick Street idlers had something to prattle and gossip about. And it was strange. The man was as big as Motie was little. When they talked to each other, the newcomer had to bend down to his waist, and Motie raised himself up on tiptoe. When they walked down the street, everyone ran to the window to look. The big fellow strode ahead, and Motie had to run after him at a trot. When the man raised his arm, he could have touched the roof. It was like that story of the Bible, when the Israelite spies looked like grasshoppers, and the others like giants. The assistant lived at Motie's house and Motiekhe served him his meals. The women asked her: "Why did Motie bring home such a Goliath?" And she replied: "I should know of evil as I know why. If he were, at least, good at business. But he can't tell wheat from rye. He eats like a horse and snores like an ox. And on top of it all, he's an oaf—so sparing of a word as if it were a gold coin."

Motiekhe had a sister to whom she poured out her bitter heart. Motie needed a helper, she said, like a hole in the head. It was all done out of spite. The man didn't do a stitch of work. He would eat them out of house and home. Those were her words. In our town there were no secrets. Neighbors listened at your window and bent their ears to your keyhole. "Why spite?" asked the sister, and Motiekhe burst out weeping: "Because I called him a premature baby."

The story was immediately all over town, but people found it difficult to believe. What kind of spite was it? Whom was he hurting with such a Turkish trick? It was his own money, not hers. But when a man takes a foolish notion into his head, God pity him! That's the truth, as it is written—I forget just where.

Two weeks hadn't passed before Motiekhe came weeping to the rabbi.

"Rebe," said she, "my husband's taken leave of his senses. He's brought an idle glutton into our home. And if that's not enough, he's turned over all the money to him." The stranger, she said, held the purse, and whenever she, Motiekhe, needed anything, she had to go to him. He was the cashier. "Holy Rebe," she cried, "Motie has done all this only to spite me, because I called him a puppet." The rabbi could not quite make out what she wanted. He was a holy man, but helpless in worldly matters. And he said: "I cannot interfere in your husband's business." "But Rebe," she cried, "this will be the ruin of us!"

The rabbi sent for Motie, but the man insisted: "I've carried enough grain sacks. I can permit myself to hire a helper." In the end, the rabbi dismissed them both with the command: "Let there be peace!" What else could he say?

Then suddenly Little Motie fell ill. Nobody knew what ailed him, but he lost color. Small as he was, he shrank still more. He came to the synagogue to pray and hovered in the corner like a shadow. On market day he was not out among the carts. His wife asked: "What's wrong with you, my husband?" But he replied: "Nothing, nothing at all." She sent for the healer, but what does a healer know? He prescribed some herbs, but they did not help. In the middle of the day, Motie would go to bed and lie there. Motiekhe asked: "What hurts you?" And he answered: "Nothing hurts." "Why, then, are you lying in bed like a sick man?" And he said: "I have no strength." "How can you have strength," she wanted to know, "when you eat like a bird?" But he only said: "I have no appetite."

What shall I tell you? Everyone saw that Motie was in a bad way. He was going out like a light. Motiekhe wanted him to go to Lublin to see the doctors but he refused. She began to wail and moan: "What's to become of me? With whom are you leaving me?" And he answered: "You will marry the big fellow." "Wretch! Murderer!" she cried. "You are dearer to me than any giant. Why must you torment me? What if I said a few words? It was only out of affection. You are my husband, my child, you are everything in the world to me. Without you my life isn't worth a pinch of dust." But all he said to her was: "I am a withered branch. With him you will have children."

If I wanted to tell you everything that went on, I'd have to stay here a day and a night. The town's leading citizens came and talked to him. The rabbi paid a sickbed visit. "What is this madness you've taken into your head? It is God's world, not man's." But Motie pretended he did not understand. When his wife saw that things were going from bad to worse, she raised a row and ordered the stranger to leave her house. But Motie said: "No, he stays. As long as I breathe, I am master here."

Nevertheless, the man went to sleep at the inn. But in the morning he was back and took full charge of the business. Everything was now in his hands—the money, the keys, every last scrap. Motie had never written anything down but the assistant entered everything in a long ledger. He was miserly too. Motiekhe demanded money for the household, but he made her account for every kopek. He weighed and measured every ounce and every crumb. She screamed: "You're a stranger, and it's none of your business! Go to all the black devils, you robber, you murderer, you highwayman out of the woods." His answer was: "If your husband dismisses me, I will go." But most of the time he said nothing at all, merely grunted like a bear.

While the summer was warm, Little Motie still managed to be up on his feet some of the time. He even fasted on Yom Kippur. But soon after Succoth he began to fail rapidly. He went to bed and did not get up. His wife brought a doctor from Zamosc, but the doctor could do nothing for him. She went to witch-healers, measured graves with a wick and made candles for the synagogue as an offering, sent messengers to holy rabbis, but Motie grew weaker from day to day. He lay on his back and stared at the ceiling. It was now necessary to help him put on his prayer shawl and phylacteries in the morning; he no longer had the strength to do it himself. He ate nothing but a spoonful of oatmeal now and then. He no longer said the benediction over the wine on Sabbath. The tall one would come from the synagogue, bless the angels, and recite the benediction.

When Motiekhe saw where all this was leading, she called in three Jews and brought out the Bible. She washed her hands, picked up the Holy Book and cried: "Be my witnesses, I swear by the Holy Book and by God Almighty that I will not marry this man, even if I remain a widow to the age of ninety!" And after she had said this, she spat at the big fellow—right in the eye. He wiped his face with a handkerchief and went out. Motie said: "It doesn't matter. You'll be absolved of your oath . . ."

A week later Motie lay dying. It did not take long, and Motie was no more. He was laid out on the ground, with candles at his head and his feet pointing to the door. Motiekhe pinched her cheeks and screamed: "Murderer! You took your own life! You have no right to a holy Jewish burial! You should be buried outside the cemetery fence!" She was not in her right mind.

The tall one took himself off somewhere and stayed out of sight. The burial society wanted money for the funeral but

Motiekhe didn't have a kopek. She had to pawn her jewelry. Those who prepared Motie for burial said afterwards that he was as light as a bird. I saw them carry out the body. It looked as if there was a child under the cloth. On the coverlet lay the dipper which he had used to pour out the grain. He had ordered it to be laid there as a reminder that he had always given good measure. They dug a grave and buried him. Suddenly the giant turned up, as if from out of the ground. He began to say the Kaddish, and the widow shrieked: "You Angel of Death, it was you who drove him from this world!" And she threw herself upon him with her fists. People barely managed to hold her back.

The day was short. Evening came, and Motiekhe seated herself on a low stool to begin her seven days of mourning. And all the while the tall one was in and out of the yard, carrying things, doing this and that. He sent a boy to the widow with some money for her needs. And so it went from day to day. Finally the community took a hand in the affair and called the man before the rabbi. "What's all this?" they argued. "Why have you fastened on to that house?" At first he was silent as if he didn't think the words were addressed to him. Then he pulled a paper from his breast pocket and showed them. Motie had made him guardian over all his worldly goods. He left his wife only the household belongings. The townsfolk read the will and were stunned. "How did he come to do such a thing?" the rabbi asked . . . Well, it was simple enough: Motie had gone to Lublin, sought out the biggest man he could find, and made him his heir and executor. Before that, the man had been a foreman of a lumbering gang.

The rabbi gave his instructions: "The widow has sworn an oath, and so you must not enter the house. Return her property to her, for the whole thing is unholy." But the giant said: "You don't get things back from the graveyard." Those were his words. The leaders of the community reviled him, threatened him with the three letters of excommunication and a beating. But he was not easily scared. He was tall as an oak, and, when he spoke, his voice boomed out as from a barrel. In the meantime, Motiekhe kept to her vow. Each time a visitor came with condolences, she renewed her oath—over candles, over prayer books, over anything she could think of. On the

Sabbath, a quorum of men came to the house to pray. She ran up to the Holy Scrolls and swore by them. She wouldn't do what Motie wanted, she screamed, he wouldn't have his way.

And she cried so bitterly that everyone wept with her.

Well, dear people, she married him. I don't remember how long it took—six months, or nine . . . It was less than a year. The big fellow had everything and she had nothing. She put aside her pride and went to the rabbi. "Holy Rebe, what should I do? Motie wanted it so. He haunts my dreams. He pinches me. He cries into my ear that he will choke me." She rolled up her sleeve, right there in the rabbi's study chamber, and showed him an arm covered with black and blue marks. The rabbi did not want to take the decision upon himself and wrote to Lublin. Three rabbis arrived and pored over the Talmud for three days. In the end they gave her—what do you call it?—a release.

The wedding was a quiet one, but the crowd made enough noise to make up for it. You can imagine all the jeering and hooting! Before the marriage, Motiekhe had been lean as a board and looked green and yellow. But soon after the wedding she began to blossom like a rose. She was no longer young, but she became pregnant. The town was agog. Just as she had called her first husband "the small one," so she called her second, "the tall one." It was the tall one this, and the tall one that. She hung on his every look and became altogether silly over him. After nine months she gave birth to a boy. The child was so big that she suffered in labor for three days. People thought she would die, but she pulled through. Half the town came to the circumcision. Some came to rejoice, others to laugh. It was quite an occasion.

At first everything seemed fine. After all, it's no small matter—a son in one's old age! But just as Motie had been lucky in every venture, so Mendl was unlucky. The landowner took a dislike to him. The other merchants shunned him. The warehouse was invaded by mice as big as cats, and they devoured the grain. Everyone agreed that this was a punishment from on high, and it didn't take long before Mendl was finished as a merchant. He went back to being a foreman in the woods. And now listen to this. He goes up to a tree and taps the bark with his mallet. And the tree falls over, right on top of him. There was not even any wind. The sun was shining. He didn't have time to cry out.

Motiekhe lasted a while longer, but she seemed to have gone out of her mind. All she did was mutter endlessly—short, tall, tall, short . . . Every day she rushed off to the cemetery to wail over the graves, running back and forth, from one grave to the other. By the time she died, I was no longer in town. I had gone to live with my husband's parents.

As I was saying—spite . . . One shouldn't tease. Little is little, and big is big. It's not our world. We didn't make it. But for a man to do such an unnatural thing! Did you ever hear the like of it? Surely, the evil one must have gotten into him. I shudder every time I think of it.

Translated by Mirra Ginsburg

Blood

THE cabalists know that the passion for blood and the passion for flesh have the same origin, and this is the reason "Thou shalt not kill" is followed by "Thou shalt not commit adultery."

Reb Falik Ehrlichman was the owner of a large estate not far from the town of Laskev. He was born Reb Falik but because of his honesty in business his neighbors had called him *ehrlichman* for so long that it had become a part of his name. By his first wife Reb Falik had had two children, a son and a daughter, who had both died young and without issue. His wife had died too. In later years he had married again, according to the Book of Ecclesiastes: "In the morning sow thy seed, and in the evening withhold not thy hand." Reb Falik's second wife was thirty years younger than he and his friends had tried to dissuade him from the match. For one thing Risha had been widowed twice and was considered a man-killer. For another, she came of a coarse family and had a bad name. It was said of her that she had beaten her first husband with a stick, and that during the two years her second husband had lain paralyzed she had never called in a doctor. There was other gossip as well. But Reb Falik was not frightened by warnings or whisperings. His first wife, peace be with her, had been ill for a long time before she died of consumption. Risha, corpulent and strong as a man, was a good housekeeper and knew how to manage a farm. Under her kerchief she had a full head of red hair and eyes as green as gooseberries. Her bosom was high and she had the broad hips of a childbearer. Though she had not had children by either of her first two husbands, she contended it was their fault. She had a loud voice and when she laughed one could hear her from far off. Soon after marrying Reb Falik, she began to take charge: she sent away the old bailiff who drank and hired in his place a young and diligent one; she supervised the sowing, the reaping, the cattle breeding; she kept an eye on the peasants to make sure they did not steal eggs, chickens, honey from the hives. Reb Falik hoped Risha would bear him a son to recite Kaddish after his death, but the years passed without her becoming pregnant. She said he was too old. One day she took him with her to Laskev to the notary public where he signed all his property over to her.

Reb Falik gradually ceased to attend to the affairs of the estate at all. He was a man of moderate height with a snowy white beard and rosy cheeks flushed with that half-faded redness of winter apples characteristic of affluent and meek old men. He was friendly to rich and poor alike and never shouted at his servants or peasants. Every spring before Passover he sent a load of wheat to Laskev for the poor, and in the fall after the Feast of Tabernacles he supplied the poorhouse with firewood for the winter as well as sacks of potatoes, cabbages, and beets. On the estate was a small study house which Reb Falik had built and furnished with a bookcase and Holy Scroll. When there were ten Jews on the estate to provide a quorum, they could pray there. After he had signed over all his possessions to Risha, Reb Falik sat almost all day long in this study house, reciting psalms, or sometimes dozing on the sofa in a side room. His strength began to leave him; his hands trembled; and when he spoke his head shook sidewise. Nearly seventy, completely dependent on Risha, he was, so to speak, already eating the bread of mercy. Formerly, the peasants could come to him for relief when one of their cows or horses wandered into his fields and the bailiff demanded payment for damages. But now that Risha had the upper hand, the peasant had to pay to the last penny.

On the estate there lived for many years a ritual slaughterer named Reb Dan, an old man who acted as beadle in the study house, and who, together with Reb Falik, studied a chapter of the Mishnah every morning. When Reb Dan died, Risha began to look about for a new slaughterer. Reb Falik ate a piece of chicken every evening for supper; Risha herself liked meat. Laskev was too far to visit every time she wanted an animal killed. Moreover, in both fall and spring, the Laskev road was flooded. Asking around, Risha heard that among the Jews in the nearby village of Krowica there was a ritual slaughterer named Reuben whose wife had died giving birth to their first child and who, in addition to being a butcher, owned a small tavern where the peasants drank in the evenings.

One morning Risha ordered one of the peasants to harness the britska in order to take her to Krowica to talk to Reuben. She wanted him to come to the estate from time to time to do their slaughtering. She took along several chickens and a gander in a sack so tight it was a wonder the fowl did not choke.

When she reached the village, they pointed out Reuben's hut near the smithy. The britska stopped and Risha, followed by the driver carrying the bag of poultry, opened the front door and went in. Reuben was not there but looking out a window into the courtyard behind she saw him standing by a flat ditch. A barefooted woman handed him a chicken which he slaughtered. Unaware he was being watched from his own house, Reuben was being playful with the woman. Jokingly, he swung the slaughtered chicken as if about to toss it into her face. When she handed him the penny fee, he clasped her wrist and held it. Meanwhile the chicken, its throat slit, fell to the ground where it fluttered about, flapping its wings in its attempt to fly and spattering Reuben's boots with blood. Finally the little rooster gave a last start and then lay still, one glassy eye and its slit neck facing up to God's heaven. The creature seemed to say: "See, Father in Heaven, what they have done to me. And still they make merry."

2

Reuben, like most butchers, was fat with a big stomach and a red neck. His throat was short and fleshy. On his cheeks grew bunches of pitchblack hair. His dark eyes held the cold look of those born under the sign of Mars. When he caught sight of Risha, mistress of the large neighboring estate, he became confused and his face turned even redder than it was. Hurriedly, the woman with him picked up the slaughtered bird and scurried away. Risha went into the courtyard, directing the peasant to set the sack with the fowl near Reuben's feet. She could see that he did not stand on his dignity, and she spoke to him lightly, half-jokingly, and he answered her in kind. When she asked if he would slaughter the birds in the sack for her, he answered: "What else should I do? Revive dead ones?" And when she remarked how important it was to her husband that his food be strictly kosher, he said: "Tell him he shouldn't worry. My knife is as smooth as a fiddle!"—and to show her he drew the bluish edge of the blade across the nail of his index finger. The peasant untied the sack and handed Reuben a yellow chicken. He promptly turned back its head, pulled a tuft of down from the center of its throat and slit it. Soon he was ready for the white gander.

"He's a tough one," said Risha. "All the geese were afraid of him."

"He won't be tough much longer," Reuben answered.

"Don't you have any pity?" Risha teased. She had never seen a slaughterer who was so deft. His hands were thick with short fingers matted with dense black hair.

"With pity, one doesn't become a slaughterer," answered Reuben. A moment later, he added, "When you scale a fish on the Sabbath, do you think the fish enjoys it?"

Holding the fowl, Reuben looked at Risha intently, his gaze traveling up and down her and finally coming to rest on her bosom. Still staring at her, he slaughtered the gander. Its white feathers grew red with blood. It shook its neck menacingly and suddenly went up in the air and flew a few yards. Risha bit her lip.

"They say slaughterers are destined to be born murderers but become slaughterers instead," Risha said.

"If you're so soft-hearted, why did you bring me the birds?" Reuben asked.

"Why? One has to eat meat."

"If someone has to eat meat, someone has to do the slaughtering."

Risha told the peasant to take away the fowl. When she paid Reuben, he took her hand and held it for a moment in his. His hand was warm and her body shivered pleasurably. When she asked him if he would be willing to come to the estate to slaughter, he said yes if in addition to paying him she would send a cart for him.

"I won't have any herd of cattle for you," Risha joked.

"Why not?" Reuben countered. "I have slaughtered cattle before. In Lublin I slaughtered more in one day than I do here in a month," he boasted.

Since Risha did not seem to be in any hurry, Reuben asked her to sit down on a box and he himself sat on a log. He told her of his studies in Lublin and explained how he had happened to come to this God-forsaken village where his wife, peace be with her, had died in childbirth due to the lack of an experienced midwife.

"Why haven't you remarried?" Risha questioned. "There's no shortage of women—widows, divorcees, or young girls."

Reuben told her the matchmakers were trying to find him a wife but the destined one had not yet appeared.

"How will you know the one who is destined for you?" Risha asked.

"My stomach will know. She will grab me right here"—and Reuben snapped his fingers and pointed at his navel. Risha would have stayed longer, except that a girl came in with a duck. Reuben arose. Risha returned to the britska.

On the way back Risha thought about the slaughterer Reuben, his levity and his jocular talk. Though she came to the conclusion that he was thick-skinned and his future wife would not lick honey all her life, still she could not get him out of her mind. That night, retiring to her canopied bed across the room from her husband's, she tossed and turned sleeplessly. When she finally dozed off, her dreams both frightened and excited her. She got up in the morning full of desire, wanting to see Reuben as quickly as possible, wondering how she might arrange it, and worried that he might find some woman and leave the village.

Three days later Risha went to Krowica again even though the larder was still full. This time she caught the birds herself, bound their legs, and shoved them into the sack. On the estate was a black rooster with a voice clear as a bell, a bird famous for its size, its red comb, and its crowing. There was also a hen that laid an egg every day and always at the same spot. Risha now caught both of these creatures, murmuring, "Come, children, you will soon taste Reuben's knife," and as she said these words a tremor ran down her spine. She did not order a peasant to drive the britska but, harnessing the horse herself, went off alone. She found Reuben standing at the threshold of his house as if he were waiting impatiently for her, as in fact he was. When a male and a female lust after each other, their thoughts meet and each can foresee what the other will do.

Reuben ushered Risha in with all the formality due a guest. He brought her a pitcher of water, offered her liqueur and a slice of honey cake. He did not go into the courtyard but untrussed the fowl indoors. When he took out the black rooster, he exclaimed, "What a fine cavalier!"

"Don't worry. You will soon take care of him," said Risha.

"No one can escape my knife," Reuben assured her. He slaughtered the rooster on the spot. The bird did not exhale its spirit immediately but finally, like an eagle caught by a bullet, it slumped to the floor. Then Reuben set the knife down on the whetstone, turned, and came over to Risha. His face was pale with passion and the fire in his dark eyes frightened her. She felt as if he were about to slaughter her. He put his arms around her without a word and pressed her against his body.

"What are you doing? Have you lost your mind?" she asked.

"I like you," Reuben said hoarsely.

"Let me go. Somebody might come in," she warned.

"Nobody will come," Reuben assured her. He put up the chain on the door and pulled Risha into a windowless alcove.

Risha wrangled, pretending to defend herself, and exclaimed, "Woe is me. I'm a married woman. And you—a pious man, a scholar. We'll roast in Gehenna for this . . ." But Reuben paid no attention. He forced Risha down on his bench-bed and she, thrice married, had never before felt desire as great as on that day. Though she called him murderer, robber, highwayman, and reproached him for bringing shame to an honest woman, yet at the same time she kissed him, fondled him, and responded to his masculine whims. In their amorous play, she asked him to slaughter her. Taking her head, he bent it back and fiddled with his finger across her throat. When Risha finally arose, she said to Reuben: "You certainly murdered me that time."

"And you, me," he answered.

3

Because Risha wanted Reuben all to herself and was afraid he might leave Krowica or marry some younger woman, she determined to find a way to have him live on the estate. She could not simply hire him to replace Reb Dan, for Reb Dan had been a relative whom Reb Falik would have had to provide for in any case. To keep a man just to slaughter a few chickens every week did not make sense and to propose it would arouse her husband's suspicions. After puzzling for a while, Risha found a solution.

She began to complain to her husband about how little profit the crops were bringing; how meagre the harvests were; if things went on this way, in a few years they would be ruined. Reb Falik tried to comfort his wife saying that God had not forsaken him hitherto and that one must have faith, to which Risha retorted that faith could not be eaten. She proposed that they stock the pastures with cattle and open a butcher shop in Laskev—that way there would be a double profit both from the dairy and from the meat sold at retail. Reb Falik opposed the plan as impractical and beneath his dignity. He argued that the butchers in Laskev would raise a commotion and that the community would never agree to him, Reb Falik, becoming a butcher. But Risha insisted. She went to Laskev, called a meeting of the community elders, and told them that she intended to open a butcher shop. Her meat would be sold at two cents a pound less than the meat in the other shops. The town was in an uproar. The rabbi warned her he would prohibit the meat from the estate. The butchers threatened to stab anyone who interfered with their livelihood. But Risha was not daunted. In the first place she had influence with the government, for the *starosta* of the neighborhood had received many fine gifts from her, often visited her estate and went hunting in her woods. Moreover, she soon found allies among the Laskev poor who could not afford to buy much meat at the usual high prices. Many took her side, coachmen, shoemakers, tailors, furriers, potters, and they announced that if the butchers did her any violence, they would retaliate by burning the butcher shops. Risha invited a mob of them to the estate, gave them bottles of homemade beer from her brewery, and got them to promise her their support. Soon afterwards she rented a store in Laskev and employed Wolf Bonder, a fearless man known as a horse-thief and brawler. Every other day, Wolf Bonder drove to the estate with his horse and buggy to cart meat to the city. Risha hired Reuben to do the slaughtering.

For many months the new business lost money, the rabbi having proscribed Risha's meat. Reb Falik was ashamed to look the townspeople in the face, but Risha had the means and strength to wait for victory. Since her meat was cheap, the number of her customers increased steadily, and soon because of competition several butchers were forced to close their shops and of the two Laskev slaughterers, one lost his job. Risha was cursed by many.

The new business provided the cover Risha needed to conceal the sins she was committing on Reb Falik's estate. From the beginning it was her custom to be present when Reuben slaughtered. Often she helped him bind an ox or a cow. And her thirst to watch the cutting of throats and the shedding of blood soon became so mixed with carnal desire that she hardly knew where one began and the other ended. As soon as the business became profitable, Risha built a slaughtering shed and gave Reuben an apartment in the main house. She bought him fine clothes and he ate his meals at Reb Falik's table. Reuben grew sleeker and fatter. During the day he seldom slaughtered but wandered about in a silken robe, soft slippers on his feet, a skullcap on his head, watching the peasants working in the fields, the shepherds caring for the cattle. He enjoyed all the pleasures of the outdoors and, in the afternoons, often went swimming in the river. The aging Reb Falik retired early. Late in the evening Reuben, accompanied by Risha, went to the shed where she stood next to him as he slaughtered and while the animal was throwing itself about in the anguish of its death throes she would discuss with him their next act of lust. Sometimes she gave herself to him immediately after the slaughtering. By then all the peasants were in their huts asleep except for one old man, half deaf and nearly blind, who aided them at the shed. Sometimes Reuben lay with her on a pile of straw in the shed, sometimes on the grass just outside, and the thought of the dead and dying creatures near them whetted their enjoyment. Reb Falik disliked Reuben. The new business was repulsive to him but he seldom said a word in opposition. He accepted the annoyance with humility, thinking that he would soon be dead anyway and what was the point of starting a quarrel? Occasionally it occurred to him that his wife was overly familiar with Reuben, but he pushed the suspicion out of his mind since he was by nature honest and righteous, a man who gave everyone the benefit of the doubt.

One transgression begets another. One day Satan, the father of all lust and cunning, tempted Risha to take a hand in the slaughtering. Reuben was alarmed when she first suggested this. True, he was an adulterer, but nevertheless he was also a believer as many sinners are. He argued that for their sins they would be whipped, but why should they lead other people into iniquity, causing them to eat non-kosher carcasses? No, God forbid he and Risha should do anything like that. To become a slaughterer it was necessary to study the *Shulchan Aruch* and the Commentaries. A slaughterer was responsible for any blemish on the knife, no matter how small, and for any sin one of his customers incurred by eating impure meat. But Risha was adamant. What difference did it make? she asked. They would both toss on the bed of needles anyhow. If one committed sins, one should get as much enjoyment as possible out of them. Risha kept after Reuben constantly, alternating threats and bribes. She promised him new excitements, presents, money. She swore that if he would let her slaughter, immediately upon Reb Falik's death she would marry him and sign over all her property so that he could redeem some part of his iniquity through acts of charity. Finally Reuben gave in. Risha took such pleasure in killing that before long she was doing all the slaughtering herself, with Reuben acting merely as her assistant. She began to cheat, to sell tallow for kosher fat, and she stopped extracting the forbidden sinews in the thighs of the cows. She began a price war with the other Laskev butchers until those who remained became her hired employees. She got the contract to supply meat to the Polish army barracks, and since the officers took bribes, and the soldiers received only the worst meat, she earned vast sums. Risha became so rich that even she did not know how large her fortune was. Her malice grew. Once she slaughtered a horse and sold it as kosher beef. She killed some pigs too, scalding them in boiling water like the pork butchers. She managed never to be caught. She got so much satisfaction from deceiving the community that this soon became as powerful a passion with her as lechery and cruelty.

Like all those who devote themselves entirely to the pleasures of the flesh, Risha and Reuben grew prematurely old. Their bodies became so swollen they could barely meet. Their hearts floated in fat. Reuben took to drink. He lay all day long on his bed, and when he woke drank liquor from a carafe with a straw. Risha brought him refreshments and they passed their time in idle talk, chattering as do those who have sold their souls for the vanities of this world. They quarreled and kissed, teased and mocked, bemoaned the fact that time was passing and the grave coming nearer. Reb Falik was now sick most of the time but, though it often seemed his end was near, somehow his soul did not forsake his body. Risha toyed with ideas of death and even thought of poisoning Reb Falik. Another time, she said to Reuben: "Do you know, already I am satiated with life! If you want, slaughter me and marry a young woman."

After saying this, she transferred the straw from Reuben's lips to hers and sucked until the carafe was empty.

4

There is a proverb: Heaven and earth have sworn together that no secret can remain undivulged. The sins of Reuben and Risha could not stay hidden forever. People began to murmur that the two lived too well together. They remarked how old and feeble Reb Falik had become, how much oftener he stayed in bed than on his feet, and they concluded that Reuben and Risha were having an affair. The butchers Risha had forced to close their businesses had been spreading all kinds of calumny about her ever since. Some of the more scholarly housewives found sinews in Risha's meat which, according to the Law, should have been removed. The Gentile butcher to whom Risha had been accustomed to sell the forbidden flanken complained that she had not sold him anything for months. With this evidence, the former butchers went in a body to the rabbi and community leaders and demanded an investigation of Risha's meat. But the council of elders was hesitant to start a quarrel with her. The rabbi quoted the Talmud to the effect that one who suspects the righteous deserves to be lashed, and added that, as long as there were no witnesses to any of Risha's transgression, it was wrong to shame her, for the one who shames his fellow man loses his portion in the world to come.

The butchers, thus rebuffed by the rabbi, decided to hire a spy and they chose a tough youth named Jechiel. This young man, a ruffian, set out from Laskev one night after dark, stole into the estate, managing to avoid the fierce dogs Risha kept, and took up his position behind the slaughtering shed. Putting his eye to a large crack, he saw Reuben and Risha inside and watched with astonishment as the old servant led in the hobbled animals and Risha, using a rope, threw them one by one to the ground. When the old man left, Jechiel was amazed in the torchlight to see Risha catch up a long knife and begin to cut the throats of the cattle one after the other. The steaming blood gurgled and flowed. While the beasts were bleeding, Risha threw off all her clothes and stretched out naked on a pile of straw. Reuben came to her and they were so fat their bodies could barely join. They puffed and panted. Their wheezing mixed with the death-rattles of the animals made an unearthly noise; contorted shadows fell on the walls; the shed was saturated with the heat of blood. Jechiel was a hoodlum, but even he was terrified because only devils could behave like this. Afraid that fiends would seize him, he fled.

At dawn, Jechiel knocked on the rabbi's shutter. Stammering, he blurted out what he had witnessed. The rabbi roused the beadle and sent him with his wooden hammer to knock at the windows of the elders and summon them at once. At first no one believed Jechiel could be telling the truth. They suspected he had been hired by the butchers to bear false witness and they threatened him with beating and excommunication. Jechiel, to prove he was not lying, ran to the Ark of the Holy Scroll which stood in the Judgment Chamber, opened the door, and before those present could stop him swore by the Scroll that his words were true.

His story threw the town into a turmoil. Women ran out into the streets, striking their heads with their fists, crying and wailing. According to the evidence, the townspeople had been eating non-kosher meat for years. The wealthy housewives carried their pottery into the market place and broke it into shards. Some of the sick and several pregnant women fainted. Many of the pious tore their lapels, strewed their heads with ashes, and sat down to mourn. A crowd formed and ran to the butcher shops to punish the men who sold Risha's meat. Refusing to listen to what the butchers said in their own defense, they beat up several of them, threw whatever carcasses were on hand outdoors, and overturned the butcher blocks. Soon voices arose suggesting they go to Reb Falik's estate and the mob began to arm itself with bludgeons, rope, and knives. The rabbi, fearing bloodshed, came out into the street to stop them, warning that punishment must wait until the sin had been proved intentional and a verdict had been passed. But the mob wouldn't listen. The rabbi decided to go with them, hoping to calm them down on the way. The elders followed. Women trailed after them, pinching their cheeks and weeping as if at a funeral. Schoolboys dashed alongside.

Wolf Bonder, to whom Risha had given gifts and whom she had always paid well to cart the meat from the estate to Laskev, remained loyal to her. Seeing how ugly the temper of the crowd was becoming, he went to his stable, saddled a fast horse, and galloped out toward the estate to warn Risha. As it happened, Reuben and Risha had stayed overnight in the shed and were still there. Hearing hoofbeats, they got up and came out and watched with surprise as Wolf Bonder rode up. He explained what had happened and warned them of the mob on its way. He advised them to flee, unless they could prove their innocence; otherwise the angry men would surely tear them to pieces. He himself was afraid to stay any longer lest before he could get back the mob turn against him. Mounting his horse, he rode away at a gallop.

Reuben and Risha stood frozen with shock. Reuben's face turned a fiery red, then a deadly white. His hands trembled and he had to clutch at the door behind him to remain on his feet. Risha smiled anxiously and her face turned yellow as if she had jaundice, but it was Risha who moved first. Approaching her lover, she stared into his eyes. "So, my love," she said, "the end of a thief is the gallows."

"Let's run away." Reuben was shaking so violently that he could hardly get the words out.

But Risha answered that it was not possible. The estate had only six horses and all of them had been taken early that morning by peasants going to the forest for wood. A yoke of oxen would move so slowly that the rabble could overtake them. Besides, she, Risha, had no intention of abandoning her property and wandering like a beggar. Reuben implored her to flee with him, since life is more precious than all possessions, but Risha remained stubborn. She would not go. Finally they went into the main house where Risha rolled some linen up into a bundle for Reuben, gave him a roast chicken, a loaf of bread, and a pouch with some money. Standing outdoors, she watched as he set out, swaying and wobbling across the wooden bridge that led into the pine woods. Once in the forest he would strike the path to the Lublin road. Several times Reuben turned about-face, muttered and waved his hand as if calling her, but Risha stood impassively. She had already learned he was a coward. He was only a hero against a weak chicken and a tethered ox.

5

As soon as Reuben was out of sight, Risha moved towards the fields to call in the peasants. She told them to pick up axes, scythes, shovels, explained to them that a mob was on its way from Laskev, and promised each man a gulden and a pitcher of beer if he would help defend her. Risha herself seized a long knife in one hand and brandished a meat cleaver in the other. Soon the noise of the crowd could be heard in the distance and before long the mob was visible. Surrounded by her peasant guard, Risha mounted a hill at the entrance to the estate. When those who were coming saw peasants with axes and scythes, they slowed down. A few even tried to retreat. Risha's fierce dogs ran among them snarling, barking, growling.

The rabbi, seeing that the situation could lead only to bloodshed, demanded of his flock that they return home, but the tougher of the men refused to obey him. Risha called out taunting them: "Come on, let's see what you can do! I'll cut your heads off with this knife—the same knife I used on the horses and pigs I made you eat." When a man shouted that no one in Laskev would buy her meat anymore and that she would be excommunicated, Risha shouted back: "I don't need your money. I don't need your God either. I'll convert. Immediately!" And she began to scream in Polish, calling the

Jews cursed Christ-killers and crossing herself as if she were already a Gentile. Turning to one of the peasants beside her, she said: "What are you waiting for, Maciek? Run and summon the priest. I don't want to belong to this filthy sect anymore." The peasant went and the mob became silent. Everyone knew that converts soon became enemies of Israel and invented all kinds of accusations against their former brethren. They turned away and went home. The Jews were afraid to instigate the anger of the Christians.

Meanwhile Reb Falik sat in his study house and recited the Mishnah. Deaf and half-blind, he saw nothing and heard nothing. Suddenly Risha entered, knife in hand, screaming: "Go to your Jews. What do I need a synagogue here for?" When Reb Falik saw her with her head uncovered, a knife in her hand, her face contorted by abuse, he was seized by such anguish that he lost his tongue. In his prayer shawl and phylacteries, he rose to ask her what had happened, but his feet gave way and he collapsed to the floor dead. Risha ordered his body placed in an ox cart and she sent his corpse to the Jews in Laskev without even linen for a shroud. During the time the Laskev Burial Society cleansed and laid out Reb Falik's body, and while the burial was taking place and the rabbi speaking the eulogy, Risha prepared for her conversion. She sent men out to look for Reuben, for she wanted to persuade him to follow her example, but her lover had vanished.

Risha was now free to do as she pleased. After her conversion she reopened her shops and sold non-kosher meats to the Gentiles of Laskev and to the peasants who came in on market days. She no longer had to hide anything. She could slaughter openly and in whatever manner she pleased pigs, oxen, calves, sheep. She hired a Gentile slaughterer to replace Reuben and went hunting with him in the forest and shot deer, hares, rabbits. But she no longer took the same pleasure in torturing creatures; slaughtering no longer incited her lust; and she got little satisfaction from lying with the pig butcher. Fishing in the river, sometimes when a fish dangled on her hook or danced in her net, a moment of joy came to her heart imbedded in fat and she would mutter: "Well, fish, you are worse off than I am . . . !"

The truth was that she yearned for Reuben. She missed their lascivious talk, his scholarship, his dread of reincarnation, his terror of Gehenna. Now that Reb Falik was in his grave, she had no one to betray, to pity, to mock. She had bought a pew in the Christian church immediately upon conversion and for some months went every Sunday to listen to the priest's sermon. Going and coming, she had her driver take her past the synagogue. Teasing the Jews gave her some satisfaction for a while, but soon this too palled.

With time Risha became so lazy that she no longer went to the slaughtering shed. She left everything in the hands of the pork butcher and did not even care that he was stealing from her. Immediately upon getting up in the morning, she poured herself a glass of liqueur and crept on her heavy feet from room to room talking to herself. She would stop at a mirror and mutter: "Woe, woe, Risha. What has happened to you? If your saintly mother should rise from her grave and see you— she would lie down again!" Some mornings she tried to improve her appearance but her clothes would not hang straight, her hair could not be untangled. Frequently she sang for hours in Yiddish and in Polish. Her voice was harsh and cracked and she invented the songs as she went along, repeating meaningless phrases, uttering sounds that resembled the cackling of fowl, the grunting of pigs, the death-rattles of oxen. Falling onto her bed she hiccuped, belched, laughed, cried. At night in her dreams, phantoms tormented her: bulls gored her with their horns; pigs shoved their snouts into her face and bit her; roosters cut her flesh to ribbons with their spurs. Reb Falik appeared dressed in his shroud, covered with wounds, waving a bunch of palm leaves, screaming: "I cannot rest in my grave. You have defiled my house."

Then Risha, or Maria Pawlowska as she was now called, would start up in bed, her limbs numb, her body covered with a cold sweat. Reb Falik's ghost would vanish but she could still hear the rustle of the palm leaves, the echo of his outcry. Simultaneously she would cross herself and repeat a Hebrew incantation learned in childhood from her mother. She would force her bare feet down to the floor and would begin to stumble through the dark from one room to another. She had thrown out all Reb Falik's books, had burned his Holy Scroll. The study house was now a shed for drying hides. But in the dining room there still remained the table on which Reb Falik had eaten his Sabbath meals, and from the ceiling hung the candelabra where his Sabbath candles had once burned. Sometimes Risha remembered her first two husbands whom she had tortured with her wrath, her greed, her curses and shrewish tongue. She was far from repenting, but something inside her was mourning and filling her with bitterness. Opening a window, she would look out into the midnight sky full of stars and cry out: "God, come and punish me! Come Satan! Come Asmodeus! Show your might. Carry me to the burning desert behind the dark mountains!"

6

One winter Laskev was terrified by a carnivorous animal lurking about at night and attacking people. Some who had seen the creature said it was a bear, others a wolf, others a demon. One woman, going outdoors to urinate, had her neck bitten. A yeshiva boy was chased through the streets. An elderly night-watchman had his face clawed. The women and children of Laskev were afraid to leave their houses after nightfall. Everywhere shutters were bolted tight. Many strange things were recounted about the beast: someone had heard it rave with a human voice; another had seen it rise on its hind legs and run. It had overturned a barrel of cabbage in a courtyard, had opened chicken coops, thrown out the dough set to rise in the wooden trough in the bakery, and it had defiled the butcher blocks in the kosher shops with excrement.

One dark night the butchers of Laskev gathered with axes and knives determined either to kill or capture the monster. Splitting up into small groups they waited, their eyes growing accustomed to the darkness. In the middle of the night there was a scream and running toward it they caught sight of the animal making for the outskirts of town. A man shouted that he had been bitten in the shoulder. Frightened, some of the men dropped back, but others continued to give chase. One of the hunters saw it and threw his axe. Apparently the animal was hit, for with a ghastly scream it wobbled and fell. A horrible howling filled the air. Then the beast began to curse in Polish and Yiddish and to wail in a high-pitched voice like a woman in labor. Convinced that they had wounded a she-devil, the men ran home.

All that night the animal groaned and babbled. It even dragged itself to a house and knocked at the shutters. Then it became silent and the dogs began to bark. When day dawned, the bolder people came out of their houses. They discovered to their amazement that the animal was Risha. She lay dead dressed in a skunk fur coat wet with blood. One felt boot was missing. The hatchet had buried itself in her back. The dogs had already partaken of her entrails. Nearby was the knife she had used to stab one of her pursuers. It was now clear that Risha had become a werewolf. Since the Jews refused to bury her in their cemetery and the Christians were unwilling to give her a plot in theirs, she was taken to the hill on the estate where she had fought off the mob, and a ditch was dug for her there. Her wealth was confiscated by the city.

Some years later a wandering stranger lodged in the poorhouse of Laskev became sick. Before is death, he summoned the rabbi and the seven elders of the town and divulged to them that he was Reuben the slaughterer, with whom Risha had sinned. For years he had wandered from town to town, eating no meat, fasting Mondays and Thursdays, wearing a shirt of sack cloth, and repenting his abominations. He had come to Laskev to die because it was here his parents were buried. The rabbi recited the confession with him and Reuben revealed many details of the past which the townspeople had not known.

Risha's grave on the hill soon became covered with refuse. Yet long afterwards it remained customary for the Laskev schoolboys on the thirty-third day of Omer, when they went out carrying bows and arrows and a provision of hard-boiled eggs, to stop there. They danced on the hill and sang:

Risha slaughtered
Black horses
Now she's fallen
To evil forces.

A pig for an ox
Sold Risha the witch
Now she's roasting
In sulphur and pitch.

Before the children left, they spat on the grave and recited:

Thou shalt not suffer a witch to live
A witch to live thou shalt not suffer
Suffer a witch to live thou shalt not.

Translated by The Author and Elizabeth Pollet

Alone

M ANY TIMES in the past I have wished the impossible to happen—and then it happened. But though my wish came true, it was in such a topsy-turvy way that it appeared the Hidden Powers were trying to show me I didn't understand my own needs. That's what occurred that summer in Miami Beach. I had been living in a large hotel full of South American tourists who had come to Miami to cool off, as well as with people like myself who suffered from hay fever. I was fed up with the whole business—splashing about in the ocean with those noisy guests; hearing Spanish all day long; eating heavy meals twice each day. If I read a Yiddish newspaper or book, the others looked at me with astonishment. So it happened that taking a walk one day, I said out loud: "I wish I were alone in a hotel." An imp must have overheard me for immediately he began to set a trap.

When I came down to breakfast the next morning, I found the hotel lobby in confusion. Guests stood about in small groups, their voices louder than usual. Valises were piled all over. Bellboys were running about pushing carts loaded with clothing. I asked someone what was the matter. "Didn't you hear the announcement over the public address system? They've closed the hotel." "Why?" I asked. "They're bankrupt." The man moved away, annoyed at my ignorance. Here was a riddle: the hotel was closing! Yet so far as I knew, it did a good business. And how could you suddenly close a hotel with hundreds of guests? But in America I had decided it was better not to ask too many questions.

The air conditioning had already been shut off and the air in the lobby was musty. A long line of guests stood at the cashier's desk to pay their bills. Everywhere there was turmoil. People crushed out cigarettes on the marble floor. Children tore leaves and flowers off the potted tropical plants. Some South Americans, who only yesterday had pretended to be full-blooded Latins, were now talking loudly in Yiddish. I myself had very little to pack, only one valise. Taking it, I went in search of another hotel. Outside the burning sun reminded me of the Talmudic story of how, on the plains of Mamre, God had removed the sun from its case so that no strangers would bother Abraham. I felt a little giddy. The days of my bachelorhood came back when, carefree, I used to pack all my belongings in one valise, leave, and within five minutes find myself another room. Passing a small hotel, which looked somewhat run-down, I read the sign: "Off-Season Rates from $2 a Day." What could be cheaper? I went inside. There was no air conditioning. A hunchbacked girl with black piercing eyes stood behind the desk. I asked her if I could have a room.

"The whole hotel," she answered.

"No one is here?"

"Nobody." The girl laughed, displaying a broken row of teeth with large gaps between. She spoke with a Spanish accent.

She had come from Cuba, she told me. I took a room. The hunchback led me into a narrow elevator, which took us up to the third floor. There we walked down a long, dark corridor meagerly lit by a single bulb. She opened a door and let me into my room, like a prisoner into his cell. The window, covered by mosquito netting, looked out over the Atlantic. On the walls the paint was peeling, and the rug on the floor was threadbare and colorless. The bathroom smelled of mildew, the closet of moth repellent. The bed linen, though clean, was damp. I unpacked my things and went downstairs. Everything was mine alone: the swimming pool, the beach, the ocean. In the patio stood a group of dilapidated canvas chairs. All around the sun beat down. The sea was yellow, the waves low and lazy, barely moving, as if they too were fatigued by the stifling heat. Only occasionally, out of duty, they tossed up a few specks of foam. A single seagull stood on the water trying to decide whether or not to catch a fish. Here before me, drenched in sunlight, was a summer melancholy—odd, since melancholy usually suggests autumn. Mankind, it seemed, had perished in some catastrophe, and I was left, like Noah—but in an empty ark, without sons, without a wife, without any animals. I could have swum naked, nevertheless I put on my bathing suit. The water was so warm, the ocean might have been a bathtub. Loose bunches of seaweed floated about. Shyness had held me back in the first hotel—here it was solitude.

Who can play games in an empty world? I could swim a little, but who would rescue me if something went wrong? The Hidden Powers had provided me with an empty hotel—but they could just as easily provide me with an undertow, a deep hole, a shark, or a sea serpent. Those who toy with the unknown must be doubly careful.

After a while I came out of the water and lay down on one of the limp canvas beach chairs. My body was pale, my skull bare, and though my eyes were protected by tinted glasses, the sun's rays glared through. The light-blue sky was cloudless. The air smelled of salt, fish, and mangoes. There was no division, I felt, between the organic and the inorganic. Everything around me, each grain of sand, each pebble, was breathing, growing, lusting. Through the heavenly channels, which, says the Cabala, control the flow of Divine Mercy, came truths impossible to grasp in a northern climate. I had lost all ambition; I felt lazy; my few wants were petty and material—a glass of lemonade or orange juice. In my fancy a hot-eyed woman moved into the hotel for a few nights. I hadn't meant I wanted a hotel completely to myself. The imp had either misunderstood or was pretending to. Like all forms of life, I, too, wanted to be fruitful, wanted to multiply—or at least to go through the motions. I was prepared to forget any moral or aesthetic demands. I was ready to cover my guilt with a sheet and to give way wholly, like a blind man, to the sense of touch. At the same time the eternal questions tapped in my brain: Who is behind the world of appearance? Is it Substance with its Infinite Attributes? Is it the Monad of all Monads? Is it the Absolute, Blind Will, the Unconscious? Some kind of superior being has to be hidden in back of all these illusions.

On the sea, oily-yellow near the shore, glassy-green farther out, a sail walked over the water like a shrouded corpse. Bent forward, it looked as if it were trying to call something up from the depths. Overhead flew a small airplane trailing a sign: MARGOLIES' RESTAURANT—KOSHER, 7 COURSES, $1.75. So the Creation had not yet returned to primeval chaos. They still served soup with kasha and kneidlach, knishes and stuffed derma at Margolies' restaurant. In that case perhaps tomorrow I would receive a letter. I had been promised my mail would be forwarded. It was my only link, in Miami, with the outside world. I'm always amazed that someone has written me, taken the trouble to stamp and mail the envelope. I look for cryptic meanings, even on the blank side of the paper.

2

When you are alone, how long the day can be! I read a book and two newspapers, drank a cup of coffee in a cafeteria, worked a crossword puzzle. I stopped at a store that auctioned Oriental rugs, went into another where Wall Street stocks were sold. True, I was on Collins Avenue in Miami Beach, but I felt like a ghost, cut off from everything. I went into the library and asked a question—the librarian grew frightened. I was like a man who had died, whose space had already been filled. I passed many hotels, each with its special decorations and attractions. The palm trees were topped by half-wilted fans of leaves, and their coconuts hung like heavy testicles. Everything seemed motionless, even the shiny new automobiles gliding over the asphalt. Every object continued its existence with that effortless force which is, perhaps, the essence of all being.

I bought a magazine, but was unable to read past the first few lines. Getting on a bus, I let myself be taken aimlessly over causeways, islands with ponds, streets lined with villas. The inhabitants, building on a wasteland, had planted trees and flowering plants from all parts of the world; they had filled up shallow inlets along the shore; they had created architectural wonders and had worked out elaborate schemes for pleasure. A planned hedonism. But the boredom of the desert remained. No loud music could dispel it, no garishness wipe it out. We passed a cactus plant whose blades and dusty needles had brought forth a red flower. We rode near a lake surrounded by groups of flamingos airing their wings, and the water mirrored their long beaks and pink feathers. An assembly of birds. Wild ducks flew about, quacking—the swampland refused to give way.

I looked out the open window of the bus. All that I saw was new, yet it appeared old and weary: grandmothers with dyed hair and rouged cheeks, girls in bikinis barely covering their shame, tanned young men guzzling Coca-Cola on water skis.

An old man lay sprawled on the deck of a yacht, warming his

rheumatic legs, his white-haired chest open to the sun. He smiled wanly. Nearby, the mistress to whom he had willed his fortune picked at her toes with red fingernails, as certain of her charms as that the sun would rise tomorrow. A dog stood at the stern, gazing haughtily at the yacht's wake, yawning.

It took a long time to reach the end of the line. Once there, I got on another bus. We rode past a pier where freshly caught fish were being weighed. Their bizarre colors, gory skin wounds, glassy eyes, mouths full of congealed blood, sharp-pointed teeth—all were evidence of a wickedness as deep as the abyss. Men gutted the fishes with an unholy joy. The bus passed a snake farm, a monkey colony. I saw houses eaten up by termites and a pond of brackish water in which the descendants of the primeval snake crawled and slithered. Parrots screeched with strident voices. At times, strange smells blew in through the bus window, stenches so dense they made my head throb.

Thank God the summer day is shorter in the South than in the North. Evening fell suddenly, without any dusk. Over the lagoons and highways, so thick no light could penetrate, hovered a jungle darkness. Automobiles, headlamps on, slid forward. The moon emerged extraordinarily large and red; it hung in the sky like a geographer's globe bearing a map not of this world. The night had an aura of miracle and cosmic change. A hope I had never forsaken awoke in me: Was I destined to witness an upheaval in the solar system? Perhaps the moon was about to fall down. Perhaps the earth, tearing itself out of its orbit around the sun, would wander into new constellations.

The bus meandered through unknown regions until it returned to Lincoln Road and the fancy stores, half-empty in summer but still stocked with whatever a rich tourist might desire—an ermine wrap, a chinchilla collar, a twelve-carat diamond, an original Picasso drawing. The dandified salesmen, sure in their knowledge that beyond nirvana pulses karma, conversed among themselves in their air-conditioned interiors. I wasn't hungry; nevertheless I went into a restaurant where a waitress with a newly bleached permanent served me a full meal, quietly and without fuss. I gave her a half-dollar. When I left, my stomach ached and my head was heavy. The late-evening air, baked by the sun, choked me as I came out. On a nearby building a neon sign flashed the temperature—it was ninety-six, and the humidity almost as much! I didn't need a weatherman. Already, lightning flared in the glowing sky, although I didn't hear thunder. A huge cloud was descending from above, thick as a mountain, full of fire and of water. Single drops of rain hit my bald head. The palm trees looked petrified, expecting the onslaught. I hurried back toward my empty hotel, wanting to get there before the rain; besides, I hoped some mail had come for me. But I had covered barely half the distance when the storm broke. One gush and I was drenched as if by a huge wave. A fiery rod lit up the sky and, the same moment, I heard the thunder crack—a sign the lightning was near me. I wanted to run inside somewhere, but chairs blown from nearby porches somersaulted in front of me, blocking my way. Signs were falling down. The top of a palm tree, torn off by the wind, careened past my feet. I saw a second palm tree sheathed in sackcloth, bent to the wind, ready to kneel. In my confusion I kept on running. Sinking into puddles so deep I almost drowned, I rushed forward with the lightness of boyhood. The danger had made me daring, and I screamed and sang, shouting to the storm in its own key. By this time all traffic had stopped, even the automobiles had been abandoned. But I ran on, determined to escape such madness or else go under. I had to get that special delivery letter, which no one had written and I never received.

I still don't know how I recognized my hotel. I entered the lobby and stood motionless for a few moments, dripping water on the rug. In the mirror across the room, my half-dissolved image reflected itself like a figure in a cubist painting. I managed to get to the elevator and ride up to the third floor. The door of my room stood ajar: inside, mosquitoes, moths, fireflies, and gnats fluttered and buzzed about, sheltering from the storm. The wind had torn down the mosquito net and scattered the papers I had left on the table. The rug was soaked. I walked over to the window and looked at the ocean. The waves rose like mountains in the middle of seas—monstrous billows ready once and for all to overflow the shores and float the land away. The waters roared with spite and sprayed white foam into the darkness of the night. The waves were barking at the Creator like packs of hounds. With all the strength I had left, I pulled the window down and lowered the blind. I squatted to put my wet books and manuscripts in order. I was hot. Sweat poured from my body, mingling with rivulets of rain water. I peeled off my clothes and they lay near my feet like shells. I felt like a creature who has just emerged from a cocoon.

3

The storm had still not reached its climax. The howling wind knocked and banged as if with mighty hammers. The hotel seemed like a ship floating on the ocean. Something came off and crashed down—the roof, a balcony, part of the foundation. Iron bars broke. Metal groaned. Windows tore loose from their casements. The windowpanes rattled. The heavy blind on my window billowed up as easily as a curtain. The room was lit with the glare of a great conflagration. Then came a clap of thunder so strong I laughed in fear. A white figure materialized from the darkness. My heart plummeted, my brain trembled in its socket. I always knew that sooner or later one of that brood would show himself to me bodily, full of horrors that are never told because no one who has seen them has survived to tell the story. I lay there silently, ready for the end. Then I heard a voice:

"Excuse please, Señor, I am much afraid. You are asleep?" It was the Cuban hunchback.

"No, come in," I answered her.

"I shake. I think I die with fear," the woman said. "A hurricane like this never come before. You are the only one in this hotel. Please excuse that I disturb you."

"You aren't disturbing me. I would put on the light but I'm not dressed."

"No, no. It is not necessary . . . I am afraid to be alone. Please let me stay here until the storm is over."

"Certainly. You can lie down if you want. I'll sit on the chair."

"No, I will sit on the chair. Where is the chair, Señor? I do not see it."

I got up, found the woman in the darkness, and led her to the armchair. She dragged herself after me, trembling. I wanted to go to the closet and get some clothing. But I stumbled into the bed and fell on top of it. I covered myself quickly with the sheet so that the stranger would not see me naked when the lightning flashed. Soon after there was another bolt and I saw her sitting in the chair, a deformed creature in an overlarge nightgown, with a hunched back, disheveled hair, long hairy arms, and crooked legs, like a tubercular monkey. Her eyes were wide with an animal's fear.

"Don't be afraid," I said. "The storm will soon be over."

"Yes, yes."

I rested my head on the pillow and lay still with the eerie feeling that the mocking imp was fulfilling my last wish. I had wanted a hotel to myself—and I had it. I had dreamed of a woman coming, like Ruth to Boaz, to my room—a woman had come. Each time the lightning flashed, my eyes met hers. She stared at me intently, as silent as a witch casting a spell. I feared the woman more than I did the hurricane. I had visited Havana once and, there, found the forces of darkness still in possession of their ancient powers. Not even the dead were left in peace—their bones were dug up. At night I had heard the screams of cannibals and the cries of maidens whose blood was sprinkled on the altars of idolaters. She came from there. I wanted to pronounce an incantation against the evil eye and pray to the spirits who have the final word not to let this hag overpower me. Something in me cried out: *Shaddai*, destroy Satan. Meanwhile, the thunder crashed, the seas roared and broke with watery laughter. The walls of my room turned scarlet. In the hellish glare the Cuban witch crouched low like an animal ready to seize its prey—mouth open, showing rotted teeth; matted hair, black on her arms and legs; and feet covered with carbuncles and bunions. Her nightgown had slipped down, and her wrinkled breasts sagged weightlessly. Only the snout and tail were missing.

I must have slept. In my dream I entered a town of steep, narrow streets and barred shutters, under the murky light of an eclipse, in the silence of a Black Sabbath. Catholic funeral processions followed one after the other endlessly, with crosses and coffins, halberds and burning torches. Not one but many corpses were being carried to the graveyard—a complete tribe annihilated. Incense burned. Moaning voices cried a song of utter grief. Swiftly, the coffins changed and took on the form of phylacteries, black and shiny, with knots and thongs. They divided into many compartments—coffins for twins, triplets, quadruplets, quintuplets . . .

I opened my eyes. Somebody was sitting on my bed—the Cuban woman. She began to talk thickly in her broken English.

"Do not fear. I won't hurt you. I am a human being, not a beast. My back is broken. But I was not born this way. I fell off a table when I was a child. My mother was too poor to take me to the doctor. My father, he no good, always drunk. He go with bad women, and my mother, she work in a tobacco factory. She cough out her lungs. Why do you shake? A hunchback is not contagious. You will not catch it from me. I have a soul like anyone else—men desire me. Even my boss. He trust me and leave me here in the hotel alone. You are a Jew, eh? He is also a Jew . . . from Turkey. He can speak—how do you say it?—Arabic. He marry a German Señora, but she is a Nazi. Her first husband was a Nazi. She curse the boss and try to poison him. He sue her but the judge is on her side. I think she bribe him—or give him something else. The boss, he has to pay her—how do you call it?—alimony."

"Why did he marry her in the first place?" I asked, just to say something.

"Well, he love her. He is very much a man, red blood, you know. You have been in love?"

"Yes."

"Where is the Señora? Did you marry her?"

"No. They shot her."

"Who?"

"Those same Nazis."

"Uh-huh . . . and you were left alone?"

"No, I have a wife."

"Where is your wife?"

"In New York."

"And you are true to her, eh?"

"Yes, I'm faithful."

"Always?"

"Always."

"One time to have fun is all right."

"No, my dear, I want to live out my life honestly."

"Who cares what you do? No one see."

"God sees."

"Well, if you speak of God, I go. But you are a liar. If I not a cripple, you no speak of God. He punish such lies, you pig!"

She spat on me, then got off the bed, and slammed the door behind her. I wiped myself off immediately, but her spittle burned me as if it were hot. I felt my forehead puffing up in the darkness, and my skin itched with a drawing sensation, as if leeches were sucking my blood. I went into the bathroom to wash myself. I wet a towel for a compress and wrapped it around my forehead. I had forgotten about the hurricane. It had stopped without my noticing. I went to sleep, and when I woke up again it was almost noon. My nose was stopped up, my throat was tight, my knees ached. My lower lip was swollen and had broken out in a large cold sore. My clothes were still on the floor, soaking in a huge puddle. The insects that had come in for refuge the night before were clamped to the wall, dead. I opened the window. The air blowing in was cool, though still humid. The sky was an autumn gray and the sea leaden, barely rocking under its own heaviness. I managed to dress and go downstairs. Behind the desk stood the hunchback, pale, thin, with her hair drawn back, and a glint in her black eyes. She wore an old-fashioned blouse edged with yellowed lace. She glanced at me mockingly. "You have to move out," she said. "The boss call and tell me to lock up the hotel."

"Isn't there a letter for me?"

"No letter."

"Please give me my bill."

"No bill."

The Cuban woman looked at me crookedly—a witch who had failed in her witchcraft, a silent partner of the demons surrounding me and of their cunning tricks.

Translated by Joel Blocker

Esther Kreindel the Second

A TALMUD teacher named Meyer Zissl lived in the town of Bilgoray. He was a short, broad-shouldered man with a round face, black beard, red cheeks, cherry-black eyes, a mouth full of jutting teeth, and a furry head with hair that blanketed his neck. Meyer Zissl like to eat well; he could drink down half a pint of brandy at one draught, and he liked to sing and dance at weddings until dawn. He had no patience for teaching, but still the wealthy sent him their sons as pupils.

When Meyer Zissl was thirty-six years old his wife died, leaving him with six children. Half a year later he married a widow, Reitze, from the village of Krashnik, a tall, lean, silent woman with a long nose and many freckles. This Reitze had been a milkmaid before marrying a rich man of seventy, Reb Tanchum Izhbitzer, by whom she had one daughter, Simmele. Before his death, Reb Tanchum had gone bankrupt leaving his widow with nothing but their one beloved child. Simmele knew how to write and she could read the Bible in Yiddish. Her father, returning from business trips, had always brought her gifts—a shawl, an apron, slippers, an embroidered hand-kerchief, and a new storybook. Simmele, bringing all her possessions, came to live with her mother and stepfather in Bilgoray.

Meyer Zissl's brood, four girls and two boys, were a greedy, ragged lot, fighters, gluttons, screamers, full of spiteful tricks, always ready to beg or steal. They immediately attacked Simmele, robbed her of all her treasures, and nicknamed her Miss Stuck-up. Simmele was delicate. She had a narrow waist, long legs, a thin face, white skin, black hair, gray eyes. She was afraid of the dogs in the courtyard, shrank at the way the family snatched food from each other's plates, and was ashamed to undress before her stepsisters. Before long she stopped talking to Meyer Zissl's children, nor did she make friends with any of the girls in the neighborhood. When she went into the street, the urchins threw stones after her and called her a fraidy-cat. Simmele stayed home, read books, and wept.

From childhood on Simmele had liked to listen to stories. Her mother had always been able to calm her so, and when Reb Tanchum was alive he had regularly put her to sleep with a fairytale. A ready subject for storytelling was Reb Zorach Lipover, a great friend of Reb Tanchum's who lived in Zamosc. Reb Zorach was known throughout half of Poland for his wealth. His wife, Esther Kreindel, also came from a rich home. Simmele loved to hear about this famous family, their wealth, and well-bred children.

One day Meyer Zissl came home for lunch with the news that Zorach Lipover's wife had died. Simmele opened her eyes wide. The name brought back memories of Krashnik, of her dead father, of the time when she had had her own room, a bed with two pillows, a silken coverlet in an embroidered linen case, a maid to serve refreshments. Now she sat here in an untidy room, wore a torn dress, ripped shoes; her hair had chicken feathers in it; she went unwashed; and she was surrounded by nasty brats who watched for every opportunity to do her mischief. Hearing of Esther Kreindel's death, Simmele covered her face with both hands and wept. The girl didn't know herself whether she was bemoaning Esther Kreindel's fate or her own, the fact that the pampered Esther Kreindel was now rotting in the grave or that her own, Simmele's, life had come to a dismal end.

2

When Simmele slept alone on her bench-bed, Meyer Zissl's children tormented her, so Reitze often took Simmele into her own bed to sleep. This was not a good arrangement because Meyer Zissl often wanted to come to his wife and then Simmele, though she understood well enough what the adults were up to, had to pretend to sleep through it all.

One night when Simmele was in bed with her mother, Meyer Zissl returned from a wedding drunk. He lifted the sleeping girl from his wife's side, only to discover that Reitze had left a heap of wet wash on the bench-bed. Because his desire was so strong, Meyer Zissl set his stepdaughter down on top of the oven among the rags. Simmele dozed off. Some

time later she awoke to hear Meyer Zissl snoring. She pulled a
flour sack over herself to keep warm. Then she heard a rustling
sound as if somebody's fingers were scratching at a board.
Lifting her head, she was astonished to see a bright spot of
light on the wall nearest her. The shutters were closed; the fire
in the oven was long since extinct; no lamp was lit. Where
could it come from? As Simmele stared the brightness began
to shake and tremble, the rings of light to coagulate. Simmele,
bewildered, forgot to be afraid. A woman began to materialize, forehead first, then eyes, nose, chin, throat. The woman
opened her mouth and began to speak, words that sounded as
if they came from the Yiddish Bible.

"Simmele, my daughter," the voice said, "be it known to
you that I am Esther Kreindel, the spouse of Reb Zorach
Lipover. It is not usual for the dead to break their slumber, but
because my husband longs for me endlessly day and night, I
am unable to remain in peace. Though the thirty days of
mourning have passed, he does not cease his lamentations and
cannot put me out of his mind. If I could throw off death, I
would gladly rise and return to him. But my body is buried under seven feet of ground, my eyes have already been consumed
by the worms. Therefore, I, the spirit of Esther Kreindel have
been permitted to find myself another body. Because your
father, Reb Tanchum, was like a brother to my Zorach, I have
chosen you, Simmele. You are indeed no stranger to me but almost a relative. Simmele, I will enter your body soon, and you
will become me. Have no fear, for nothing evil will befall you.
In the morning rise, cover your head, and announce to your
family and to the townspeople what has happened. The wicked
will contradict you and accuse you, but I will protect you.
Heed my words, Simmele, for you must do all that I bid you.
Go to Zamosc to my sorrowing husband, and be a wife to
him. Lie in his lap and serve him faithfully as I have done for
forty years. Zorach may doubt at first that I have returned to
him, but I will give you signs with which to convince him. You
must not tarry because Zorach is consumed with longing and
soon, God forbid, it may be too late. God willing, when the
time comes for you to pass away, both you and I will be Zorach's footstools in Paradise. He will rest his right foot on me

and his left on you; we will be like Rachel and Leah; my children will be yours. It will be as if they had issued from your womb . . ."

Esther Kreindel went on speaking, telling Simmele those intimacies only a wife can know. Not until the rooster in the coop crowed and the midnight moon was visible through the chinks of the shutters did she stop. Then Simmele felt something hard like a pea enter her nostrils and penetrate her skull. For a moment her head ached, but then the pain ceased and she felt her hands and feet stretching, her belly, her breasts ripening. Her mind was maturing too, her thoughts becoming those of a wife, a mother, a grandmother, who is used to commanding a large house with menservants, maids, cooks. It was all too wonderful. "I put myself into Thy hands," Simmele murmured. Soon she sank into sleep, and immediately Esther Kreindel reappeared in her dream and stayed with her until Simmele opened her eyes in the morning.

3

The delicate Simmele usually stayed in bed late but that morning she awoke with the rest of the family. Her stepbrothers and stepsisters, seeing her on top of the oven with a meal sack pulled over her, began to laugh, to spray water up at her, to tickle her bare feet with straws. Reitze drove them away. Simmele, sitting up, smiled benignly and recited, "I thank Thee." And though it is not the custom to set a pitcher of water near a girl's bed for morning ablutions, Simmele asked her mother for water and a basin. Reitze shrugged her shoulders. When Simmele was dressed, Reitze handed her a slice of bread and a cup of chickory, but Simmele said she wanted to pray first, and taking out her Saturday kerchief, she covered her head. Meyer Zissl watched the conduct of his stepdaughter with amazement. Simmele recited from the prayer book, bowed down, beat her breast, and after the words, "He makes peace on high," retreated three steps. Then, before eating, she washed her hands up to the wrists and recited the Benediction. The children flocked around, mimicking, mocking, but she only smiled in a motherly fashion and called out, "Please, children, let me say my prayers." She kissed the smallest girl on the head, pinched the youngest boy in the cheek, and made the older boy wipe his nose on her apron. Reitze gaped. Meyer Zissl scratched his head.

"What sort of stunts are these? I scarcely recognize the girl," said Meyer Zissl.

"She's matured overnight," said Reitze.

"She shakes like Yentl the Pious One," scoffed the oldest boy.

"Simmele, what's going on?" Reitze asked.

The girl didn't answer immediately, but went on chewing slowly the bread in her mouth. It was not like her to act with such quiet deliberation. When she had swallowed the last crumb, she said:

"I am no longer Simmele."

"Then who are you?" Meyer Zissl inquired.

"I am Esther Kreindel, the wife of Reb Zorach Lipover. Last night her soul entered me. Take me to Zamosc to my husband and children. My home is being neglected. Zorach needs me."

The older children burst out laughing; the younger gawked. Reitze turned white. Meyer Zissl clutched his beard, and said, "The girl is possessed by a dybbuk."

"No, not a dybbuk, but the sacred soul of Esther Kreindel has entered me. She could not remain in her grave because her husband, Zorach Lipover, is expiring of grief. His affairs are topsy-turvy. His fortune is disappearing. She has told me all her secrets. If you don't believe me, I will furnish proof." And Simmele began to repeat some of the things Esther Kreindel had confided to her while she was awake and while asleep. As Simmele's mother and Meyer Zissl listened, they became more and more amazed. Simmele's words, phrases, her whole style, were those of an experienced woman, of one who is accustomed to running a business and a large household. She referred to matters that it was impossible for one as young as Simmele to know. She described Esther Kreindel's final illness, told how the doctors had made her worse with their pills and salves, bleeding her by cupping and leeches.

The neighbors were soon aware that something strange was happening as people are wont in a town where they listen behind doors and peer through keyholes. The story spread and a crowd began to gather at Meyer Zissl's. When the rabbi heard what had happened, he sent a message ordering the girl to be brought to him. At the rabbi's the council of elders was assembled along with the most distinguished matrons of the community. After Simmele's arrival, the rabbi's wife chained the door and the interrogation began. It was necessary to find out if the girl was trying to deceive them, if she was possessed by a devil or by one of those insolent demons who try to outsmart the righteous and entrap them. After hours of interrogation, everyone was convinced that Simmele was telling the truth. They had all met Esther Kreindel and not only did Simmele talk like the dead woman but her gestures, her smile, the way she tossed her head and brushed her brow with her kerchief was exactly like the deceased. Her manner too was certainly that of someone who had always been accustomed to affluence. Moreover, if an evil spirit had possessed the girl, it would have become abusive whereas Simmele was respectful and answered all questions politely and judiciously. Soon, the men began tugging at their beards; the women wrung their hands, straightened their bonnets, and tightened their aprons. The members of the Burial Society, usually so tough and unemotional, wiped tears from their eyes. Even a blind man could see that Esther Kreindel's soul had returned.

While the interrogation was still in process, Zeinvel the coachman harnessed his horse and buggy and taking several witnesses with him set out for Zamosc to bring Reb Zorach Lipover the news. Reb Zorach wept when he was informed. He ordered the coachman to bring a four-horse carriage and he, a son and two daughters got in. The coachman did not spare the whip. The road was dry, the horses galloped, and by nightfall Zorach Lipover and his family had arrived in Bilgoray. Simmele was staying at the rabbi's and was being cared for by the rabbi's wife to escape the morbid and the curious. She sat in the kitchen knitting, something Reitze swore she had never known how to do before. Simmele had been reminiscing to those present of long forgotten events: dreadful winters three decades past, heat waves following the Feast of Tabernacles, snows in summer, winds that broke windmills, hails that shattered roofs, rainfalls of fish and toads. She had also chattered of roasting, baking; the illnesses women were susceptible to in pregnancy; she had discussed the rituals pertaining to cohabitation and the menstrual period. The women in the kitchen sat in stunned silence. To them it was like listening to a corpse speak. Suddenly there was the noise of wheels as Reb Zorach's carriage rolled into the courtyard. When Zorach entered, Simmele, having put down her knitting, rose and announced:

"Zorach, I have returned."

The women burst into a wail. Zorach just kept on staring. The questioning began again and continued until past midnight. Later there were many conflicting statements about what was said, and these disagreements led to protracted quarrels. But from the very beginning everyone admitted that the woman who received Zorach was no one but Esther Kreindel. Soon Zorach began to cry in a heartrending voice; Zorach's son called Simmele mother. The daughters did not give in so quickly but sought to prove that Simmele was a liar, anxious to assume their mother's prerogatives. Slowly they too realized that the matter was not that simple. First the younger became silent and then the older one bowed her head. Before daybreak both daughters had uttered the word they had been avoiding for hours: Mother!

4

According to the law, Zorach Lipover could have married Simmele immediately, but Reb Zorach had a third daughter, Bina Hodel, who remained stubbornly unconvinced. She argued that Simmele could have learned all about Esther Kreindel from her own parents or from some maid Esther Kreindel had dismissed. Or Simmele might be a witch or could be in league with an imp.

Bina Hodel was not the only one who suspected Simmele. In Zamosc there were widows and divorcees who thought of Reb Zorach as a catch. None of these had any intention of letting Simmele grab Zorach without opposition, and they went around town saying that she was a sly fox, a scheming wanton, a pig trying to put its snout into someone else's garden. When the rabbi of Zamosc heard of Simmele's claim he ordered her to be brought before him for examination. Suddenly Zamosc found itself divided. The wealthy, the scholarly, and those with sharp tongues were dubious of Simmele's claims and wanted to examine her closely. Esther Kreindel's neighbors and friends also wanted to interrogate the girl.

When Reitze heard how things stood in Zamosc and how her daughter was likely to be treated, she protested that she did not want her child dragged around and made the talk of the town and that Simmele was not interested in Reb Zorach Lipover's fortune. But Meyer Zissl had different plans. He was tired of teaching, and he had long wanted to move to Zamosc, a larger and gayer city than Bilgoray, full of rich men, gay youths, handsome women, taverns and wine cellars. Meyer Zissl persuaded Reitze to let him take Simmele to Zamosc. He had already received a sum of money from Zorach Lipover.

In Zamosc a large crowd gathered outside the rabbi's house to watch Simmele arrive with Meyer Zissl. Meyer Zissl and those on his side saw to it that only the most influential citizens were admitted. Simmele was dressed in Reitze's holiday dress and had a silk kerchief on her head. In recent weeks, she had grown taller, plumper, and more mature. Attacked from all sides with questions, she answered with so much good taste and breeding that finally even those who had come to mock her became silent. Esther Kreindel herself could not have given better answers. At the beginning, she was asked much about the other world. Simmele told of her death agony, the cleansing of her body, her burial; she described how the Angel Dumah had approached the grave with his fiery rod and asked her her name; then how evil spirits and hobgoblins had tried to fasten themselves to her and how she had been saved by the Kaddish of her pious sons. Her good deeds and transgressions were weighed against each other on the scale at her trial in heaven. Satan had plotted against her, but holy angels defended her. She told of her encounter with her parents, her grandparents, her great grandparents and other souls who had long been residing in Paradise. But on her way to judgment she had been permitted to look at Gehenna through a window. When she spoke of the terrors of Gehenna, the torture beds, the piles of snow and beds of coals whereon the wicked were turned, the glowing hooks on which the spiteful were hung by their tongues or breasts, the whole assemblage sighed. Even the scornful and the impenitent trembled. Simmele identified by name many residents of Zamosc who were being punished, some by immersion in barrels of boiling pitch, others by being forced to gather wood for the pyres on which they were burned; still others were poisoned by snakes, or eaten by vipers and hedgehogs. A stranger would never have heard of most of these people, nor of their crimes.

Next Simmele described the diamond pillars of Paradise among which the just sit on golden chairs with crowns on their heads, feasting on Leviathan and the Wild Ox, drinking the wine which God keeps for his beloved ones while angels divulge to them the secrets of the Torah. Simmele explained that the righteous don't use their wives as footstools; rather the holy women sit near their husbands, but on chairs whose gold heads are somewhat lower than those of the men. The women of Zamosc, gladdened by this news, began to cry and laugh. Reb Zorach Lipover covered his face with both hands and tears ran down his beard.

After the interrogation at the rabbi's house, Simmele was taken to Reb Zorach's where his children, relatives, and neighbors had gathered. There she was closely questioned again, this time about Esther Kreindel's friends, merchants, and servants. Simmele knew everything and remembered everybody. Reb Zorach's daughters pointed to drawers in the closets and sideboards and Simmele listed the linens and other objects contained within. She remarked of one embroidered table cloth that Zorach had bought it for her as a gift in Leipzig; of an incense box that he had purchased it at a fair in Prague. She spoke familiarly to all the aging women, Esther Kreindel's contemporaries. "Treina, do you still have heartburn after meals? . . . Riva Gutah, has the boil on your left breast healed?" And she joked good naturedly with Reb Zorach's daughters, remarking to one, "Do you still hate radishes?" and to another, "Do you remember the day I took you to Doctor Palecki and a pig frightened you?" She recalled the words the women of the Burial Society had spoken while cleansing her. When the questioning slackened, Simmele repeated that the yearning of her husband Zorach had not allowed her to rest in peace, and that the Lord of the living, taking pity on Zorach had sent her back to him. She explained that when Zorach died she would die also for all of her years were used up, and she was living now only for his sake. No one took this prediction seriously, so young and healthy did she seem.

Zamosc had expected Simmele's interrogation to last many days but most of those who questioned her at the rabbi's and then later at Reb Zorach's were soon satisfied that she was truly the reincarnation of Esther Kreindel. Even the cat recognized her old mistress, meowing excitedly and running to rub its head against her ankles. By the end of the day, only a small group still held out. Esther Kreindel's friends covered Simmele with kisses; all Zorach's daughters except for Bina Hodel wept and embraced their mother; his sons did her honor. The grandchildren kissed her fingers. Everyone ignored the scoffers. Reb Zorach Lipover and Meyer Zissl set the marriage day.

The wedding was noisy. For though the soul was Esther Kreindel's, the body was that of a virgin.

5

Esther Kreindel had returned. But nevertheless it was hard for Zorach and the town to believe in the occurrence of such a miracle. When Esther Kreindel the second went to the market place, followed by her maid, girls peeped at her from the windows and those on the street stopped to stare. In the half-holidays of Passover and of the Feast of Tabernacles young people from all over traveled to Zamosc to see the woman who had returned from the grave. Crowds gathered in front of Reb Zorach's house and the door had to be chained to keep out the intruders. Zorach Lipover himself went around in a trance; his children, in the presence of their resurrected mother, blushed and stammered.

The town sceptics constantly reverted to the subject, referring to Zorach as an old goat; they asserted that he had arranged the miracle with Reitze, and speculated on how much he had paid—some said a thousand guldens—for her young daughter. One night two pranksters stealthily set a ladder against the wall of Zorach's house and peered through the shutter into his bedroom. In the tavern later they told how they had watched Esther Kreindel the second recite her prayers, bring a pitcher of water for the morning ablutions; how they had seen her herself remove Zorach's boots, tickle his soles, he lasciviously pulling at her earlobes. Even the Gentiles in their winehouse discussed the matter, several of them predicting that the court would enter the case and investigate the imposter, who was very likely a witch and in league with Lucifer.

For many months the new couple spent their nights talking. Zorach did not stop questioning Esther Kreindel about her departure from this world and what she had seen in the hereafter. He kept on looking for irrefutable proofs that she was what she claimed. He told her many times of the anguish he had endured while she lay sick and dying, and of the despair he felt while sitting *shiva* and during the thirty days of mourning. Esther Kreindel affirmed again and again that she had longed for him in her grave, that his agony had not let her rest, that she had gone as a supplicant before the Throne of Glory, while cherubim sang her praise and demons howled accusations. She kept on adding particulars about her encounters with dead relatives, their adventures in their graves, in Tophet, and later in the garden of Eden. When daybreak came, husband and wife were still talking.

On those nights that Esther Kreindel went to the ritual bath and Zorach came to her bed, he proclaimed that her body was more beautiful than it had been even in the first weeks of their first marriage. He said to her: "Perhaps I too will die and reappear as a young man." Esther Kreindel scolded him good-naturedly, assured him that she loved him more than she could possibly love any young fellow, and her only wish was to have him live to be a hundred and twenty.

Gradually everyone grew accustomed to the situation. Soon after the wedding Reitze and her stepchildren came to live in Zamosc in a house that Reb Zorach gave them. Reb Zorach took Meyer Zissl into his business, and put him in charge of loans to the local gentry. Meyer Zissl's boys who had so recently slapped, kicked, and spat on Simmele, now came to bid Esther Kreindel a good Sabbath and to be treated to almond bread and wine. The name Simmele was soon forgotten. Even Reitze no longer called her daughter Simmele.

Esther Kreindel had been nearly sixty when she died; Simmele now treated Reitze like one of her daughters. It was strange to hear the younger woman calling Reitze child, giving her advice on baking, cooking, and bringing up children. The second Esther Kreindel like the first had a talent for business and her husband, Zorach, would make no decisions without consulting her.

In the community too the second Esther Kreindel assumed the position of the first. She was invited to accompany brides to the synagogue, to be the matron of honor at weddings, to hold the babies at circumcisions. And she conducted herself as if she had been accustomed to such honors for years. At first the younger women tried to make her their friend, but she treated them as if they belonged to another generation. At the wedding people had predicted that Esther Kreindel the second would soon conceive, but when several years passed and she did not, everyone began to remark that the returned Esther Kreindel was aging prematurely, her flesh shrinking, her skin drying up. Moreover she dressed like an old woman, wearing a cape with raised shoulders and a ribboned bonnet when she went out. She often wore tucked tops and pleated skirts with long trains. Every morning she entered the women's section of the synagogue carrying a gold-rimmed prayer book and a book of supplications. On the day before the new moon she fasted and attended the prayers to which only the old women went. During the months of Elul and Nissan when it is customary to visit the graves of relatives, the second Esther Kreindel visited the cemetery and, prostrated herself on the grave of the first Esther Kreindel, weeping and begging forgiveness. It seemed then as if the corpse buried within had emerged to mourn and eulogize itself.

The years passed and Zorach grew older and weaker. Both his stomach and his feet pained him. Having stopped attending to his business, he sat all day long in an armchair, reading. Esther Kreindel brought him food and medicines. Sometimes she played "goat and wolf" or even cards with him; other times she read aloud to him. She took over the entire management of the business since his sons were lazy and incompetent. Every day she reported to him what had happened. Husband and wife talked of the old days as if they were really the same age. He reminded her of their early struggles, when the children were small. They recalled family worries and business complications with creditors, nobles, competitors. Esther Kreindel knew and remembered all the details. Often she reminded him of things he had forgotten. Other times they sat in silence for hours, Esther Kreindel knitting socks, Zorach Lipover watching her in amazement. The second Esther Kreindel had grown more and more like the first, had developed her high bosom, the wrinkles and folds in the face, the double chin, the bags under the eyes. Like the former Esther Kreindel, the present one wore her glasses on the point of her nose, scratched her ear with a knitting needle, refreshed herself with cherry wine and jam while muttering to herself or to the cat. Even her smell of fresh linen and lavender was that of the first Esther Kreindel. When she stopped going to the ritual bath everyone assumed she was undergoing her meno-pause. Even Reitze her mother could recognize nothing of the former Simmele.

Some of the first Esther Kreindel's contemporaries hinted that not only had their friend's soul returned from the grave but her body as well. The shoemaker insisted that the feet of the reincarnated woman were duplicates of the first. A wart had sprouted on the throat of the second in exactly the same spot where one had been on the throat of the first. There were those in Zamosc who said that if the grave of Esther Kreindel were opened, God forbid that anyone should commit such a sacrilege, the body exhumed would be not of Esther Kreindel but Simmele's.

Because a female cannot completely take over the place of a male, much of the responsibility for running Zorach Lipover's business passed to Meyer Zissl. The former Talmud teacher be-gan to spend money lavishly. He got up late, drank wine from a silver goblet, sported a pipe with an amber bowl. Reb Zorach had always bowed and raised his hat to the squires but Meyer Zissl tried to be their equal. He dressed in a squire's costume with silver buttons, wore a sable hat with a feather, dined with the nobles, went hunting with them. When he was tipsy he threw coins to the peasants. His sons were sent to study in Italy, his daughters were married off to rich boys in Bohemia. After a while the Gentiles of Zamosc addressed him as Pan.

Esther Kreindel reproached him, said it was not good for a Jew to indulge in worldly pleasures, that it made the Christians jealous, and that the money was being squandered, but Meyer Zissl paid no attention. There came a time when he ceased to go into Reitze's bedroom. Gossips spread the rumor that he had begun an affair with a Countess Zamoyska. There was a scandal over a woman of pleasure. Meyer Zissl and a noble fought a duel and the latter was wounded in the thigh. Meyer Zissl finally stopped coming to the synagogue except on the High Holidays.

Reb Zorach Lipover had become extremely feeble. His final illness was long and protracted. Esther Kreindel sat up with her husband for many nights, refusing to let others watch him. When he died, she fell on the corpse in her anguish and would not allow it to be laid out. The men of the Burial Society had to pull her away. Following the funeral, Esther Kreindel returned home surrounded by all of Zorach's sons and daughters who had come to sit the seven days of mourning with her. Because Zorach had been so old when he died, his children sat on small stools in their stocking feet and babbled of everyday matters. There were frequent references to his will: they all knew he had made one but what it contained they could not say. They assumed Zorach had left his widow a fortune and were already preparing to haggle with her. These men and women who had called the second Esther Kreindel mother for years now avoided looking her in the face. Esther Kreindel took her Bible and opened it to the Book of Job. Weeping, she read the words of Job and his companions. Bina Hodel, who hadn't cried once during her father's final illness, muttered loud enough to be heard: "God's thief."

Esther Kreindel closed the Bible and stood up. "Children, I want to take leave of you."

"Are you going somewhere?" Bina Hodel asked, lifting her brows.

"Tonight I will be with your father," Esther Kreindel replied.

"Tell us that next year," quipped Bina Hodel.

At supper that night Esther Kreindel hardly touched the food on her plate. Afterwards she stood at the east wall. She bowed, beat her breast and confessed her sins as if it were Yom

Kippur. Reitze washed dishes in the kitchen. Meyer Zissl had gone to a ball. When Esther Kreindel was finished, she went to the bedroom and ordered the maid to make up the bed there. The maid demurred, muttering that the lady should sleep elsewhere. The master had died in that room. A wick was still burning in a shard, and the customary glass of water stood on the night table with the piece of linen inside prepared for the soul to cleanse itself. Who would spend the night in a room from which a corpse had so recently been taken out? But Esther Kreindel bade the girl do as she had been told.

Esther Kreindel undressed. The instant she stretched out on the bed her face began to change, and became yellow and sunken. The maid ran to summon the family. A doctor was sent for. Those who watched Esther Kreindel die testified later that she looked exactly like the first Esther Kreindel in her death throes. Her eyes remained open but opaque and unseeing. She was addressed but did not answer. A spoonful of chicken soup poured into her mouth dribbled out. All at once she heaved a sigh and the soul left the body. Bina Hodel threw herself down at the foot of the bed calling out, "My good mother. My sacred mother."

The funeral was a large one. Esther Kreindel the second was buried near Esther Kreindel the first. The most venerable woman of the town sewed her shroud. The rabbi delivered a eulogy. When the funeral was over, Meyer Zissl presented to the rabbi two wills. In one Zorach Lipover willed his wife three-quarters of his fortune; in the other Esther Kreindel left a third of her inheritance to charity and two-thirds to Reitze and her children. Meyer Zissl was the executor.

Not many months later Bina Hodel died and Meyer Zissl, without Esther Kreindel's stabilizing influence, became reckless. He gave credit to insolvent merchants, accepted mortgages without evaluating the property, and continued to lose large sums of money. He was forever initiating law suits. More and more often he had to hide from his creditors and from the King's tax collectors. One day a group of squires accompanied by marshals, bailiffs, and soldiers came to Meyer Zissl's palace. The governor of Lublin had authorized a public auction of all his property. Meyer Zissl was arrested, shackled, and thrown into prison. Reitze tried to raise money from the community to get him released, but because he had ignored the Jews and Jewishness, the elders refused him assistance. The squires with whom he had drunk and caroused did not even bother to answer his letters of supplication. One morning nine months later when the jailer entered Meyer Zissl's cell with a loaf of bread and a bowl of hot water he found the prisoner hanging from the window grating. Meyer Zissl had torn his shirt into strips and braided it into a rope. The Jews took away the corpse and buried it behind the fence.

6

Years later the people in Zamosc, in Bilgoray, in Krashnik, even in Lublin continued to discuss the case of the girl who went to sleep Simmele and woke up Esther Kreindel. Reitze had long since died in the poorhouse. Her children who lived in foreign lands had completely forsaken their faith. Of Zorach Lipover's great fortune nothing was left. But the controversy still went on. A wedding jester wrote a poem about Simmele. Seamstresses sang a ballad about her. On long winter nights girls and women, plucking feathers, chopping cabbage, knitting jackets, reviewed the facts. Even *cheder* boys told one another the story of how the soul of Esther Kreindel was reincarnated. Some contended that the whole thing had been mere fraud. What fools Reb Zorach Lipover and his family had been to let themselves be tricked by a girl. They claimed that the mastermind was Meyer Zissl. He had wanted to give up teaching and enjoy Zorach's wealth. One man concluded after much thought that Meyer Zissl had copulated with his step-daughter and persuaded her to be a party in the plot. Another said Reitze had initiated the conspiracy and had primed her daughter for the part. In Zamosc there was a Dr. Ettinger who argued that miraculous though it was for a woman to rise from her grave and return to her husband, it was an even greater miracle for a fourteen-year-old girl to deceive the elders of Zamosc. After all Zamosc, unlike Chelm, was not a town of fools. In addition, how had it happened that Simmele had not become pregnant and had died the night after her husband's burial? No one can make a contract with the Angel of Death.

In any case, there is a birch tree growing from Zorach Lipover's grave. Birds nest in its branches. The leaves never stop trembling and their perpetual rustle rings like tiny bells. The tombstones of Esther Kreindel the first and Esther Kreindel the second lean against each other and have been made almost one by time. The world is full of puzzles. It is possible that not even Elijah will be able to answer all our questions when the Messiah comes. Even God in seventh Heaven may not have solved all the mysteries of His Creation. This may be the reason He conceals His face.

Translated by The Author and Elizabeth Pollet

Jachid and Jechidah

I N A PRISON where souls bound for Sheol—Earth they call it there—await destruction, there hovered the female soul Jechidah. Souls forget their origin. Purah, the Angel of Forgetfulness, he who dissipates God's light and conceals His face, holds dominion everywhere beyond the Godhead. Jechidah, unmindful of her descent from the Throne of Glory, had sinned. Her jealousy had caused much trouble in the world where she dwelled. She had suspected all female angels of having affairs with her lover Jachid, had not only blasphemed God but even denied him. Souls, she said, were not created but had evolved out of nothing: they had neither mission nor purpose. Although the authorities were extremely patient and forgiving, Jechidah was finally sentenced to death. The judge fixed the moment of her descent to that cemetery called Earth.

The attorney for Jechidah appealed to the Superior Court of Heaven, even presented a petition to Metatron, the Lord of the Face. But Jechidah was so filled with sin and so impenitent that no power could save her. The attendants seized her, tore her from Jachid, clipped her wings, cut her hair, and clothed her in a long white shroud. She was no longer allowed to hear the music of the spheres, to smell the perfumes of Paradise and to meditate on the secrets of the Torah, which sustain the soul. She could no longer bathe in the wells of balsam oil. In the prison cell, the darkness of the nether world already surrounded her. But her greatest torment was her longing for Jachid. She could no longer reach him telepathically. Nor could she send a message to him, all of her servants having been taken away. Only the fear of death was left to Jechidah.

Death was no rare occurrence where Jechidah lived but it befell only vulgar, exhausted spirits. Exactly what happened to the dead, Jechidah did not know. She was convinced that when a soul descended to Earth it was to extinction, even though the pious maintained that a spark of life remained. A dead soul immediately began to rot and was soon covered with a slimy stuff called semen. Then a grave digger put it into a

womb where it turned into some sort of fungus and was
henceforth known as a child. Later on, began the tortures of
Gehenna: birth, growth, toil. For according to the morality
books, death was not the final stage. Purified, the soul returned to its source. But what evidence was there for such be-
liefs? So far as Jechidah knew, no one had ever returned from
Earth. The enlightened Jechidah believed that the soul rots
for a short time and then disintegrates into a darkness of no
return.

Now the moment had come when Jechidah must die, must
sink to Earth. Soon, the Angel of Death would appear with his
fiery sword and thousand eyes.

At first Jechidah had wept incessantly, but then her tears had
ceased. Awake or asleep she never stopped thinking of Jachid.
Where was he? What was he doing? Whom was he with? Jechidah was well aware he would not mourn for her for ever. He
was surrounded by beautiful females, sacred beasts, angels,
seraphim, cherubs, ayralim, each one with powers of seduc-
tion. How long could someone like Jachid curb his desires?
He, like she, was an unbeliever. It was he who had taught her
that spirits were not created, but were products of evolution.
Jachid did not acknowledge free will, nor believe in ultimate
good and evil. What would restrain him? Most certainly he already lay in the lap of some other divinity, telling those stories
about himself he had already told Jechidah.

But what could she do? In this dungeon all contact with the
mansions ceased. All doors were closed: neither mercy, nor
beauty entered here. The one way from this prison led down
to Earth, and to the horrors called flesh, blood, marrow,
nerves, and breath. The God-fearing angels promised resurrection. They preached that the soul did not linger forever on
Earth, but that after it had endured its punishment, it returned
to the Higher Sphere. But Jechidah, being a modernist, regarded all of this as superstition. How would a soul free itself
from the corruption of the body? It was scientifically impossible. Resurrection was a dream, a silly comfort of primitive
and frightened souls.

2

One night as Jechidah lay in a corner brooding about Jachid and the pleasures she had received from him, his kisses, his caresses, the secrets whispered in her ear, the many positions and games into which she had been initiated, Dumah, the thousand-eyed Angel of Death, looking just as the Sacred Books described him, entered bearing a fiery sword.

"Your time has come, little sister," he said.

"No further appeal is possible?"

"Those who are in this wing always go to Earth."

Jechidah shuddered. "Well, I am ready."

"Jechidah, repentance helps even now. Recite your confession."

"How can it help? My only regret is that I did not transgress more," said Jechidah rebelliously.

Both were silent. Finally Dumah said, "Jechidah, I know you are angry with me. But is it my fault, sister? Did I want to be the Angel of Death? I too am a sinner, exiled from a higher realm, my punishment to be the executioner of souls. Jechidah, I have not willed your death, but be comforted. Death is not as dreadful as you imagine. True, the first moments are not easy. But once you have been planted in the womb, the nine months that follow are not painful. You will forget all that you have learned here. Coming out of the womb will be a shock; but childhood is often pleasant. You will begin to study the lore of death, clothed in a fresh, pliant body, and soon will dread the end of your exile."

Jechidah interrupted him. "Kill me if you must, Dumah, but spare me your lies."

"I am telling you the truth, Jechidah. You will be absent no more than a hundred years, for even the wickedest do not suffer longer than that. Death is only the preparation for a new existence."

"Dumah, please. I don't want to listen."

"But it is important for you to know that good and evil exist there too and that the will remains free."

"What will? Why do you talk such nonsense?"

"Jechidah, listen carefully. Even among the dead there are laws and regulations. The way you act in death will determine what happens to you next. Death is a laboratory for the rehabilitation of souls."

"Make an end of me, I beseech you."

"Be patient, you still have a few more minutes to live and must receive your instructions. Know, then, that one may act well or evilly on Earth and that the most pernicious sin of all is to return a soul to life."

This idea was so ridiculous that Jechidah laughed despite her anguish.

"How can one corpse give life to another?"

"It's not as difficult as you think. The body is composed of such weak material that a mere blow can make it disintegrate. Death is no stronger than a cobweb; a breeze blows and it disappears. But it is a great offense to destroy either another's death or one's own. Not only that, but you must not act or speak or even think in such a way as to threaten death. Here one's object is to preserve life, but there it is death that is succoured."

"Nursery tales. The fantasies of an executioner."

"It is the truth, Jechidah. The Torah that applies to Earth is based on a single principle: Another man's death must be as dear to one as one's own. Remember my words. When you descend to Sheol, they will be of value to you."

"No, no, I won't listen to any more lies." And Jechidah covered her ears.

3

Years passed. Everyone in the higher realm had forgotten Jechidah except her mother who still continued to light memorial candles for her daughter. On Earth Jechidah had a new mother as well as a father, several brothers and sisters, all dead. After attending a high school, she had begun to take courses at the university. She lived in a large necropolis where corpses are prepared for all kinds of mortuary functions.

It was spring, and Earth's corruption grew leprous with blossoms. From the graves with their memorial trees and cleansing waters arose a dreadful stench. Millions of creatures, forced to descend into the domains of death, were becoming flies, butterflies, worms, toads, frogs. They buzzed, croaked, screeched, rattled, already involved in the death struggle. But since Jechidah was totally inured to the habits of Earth, all this seemed to her part of life. She sat on a park bench staring up at the moon, which from the darkness of the nether world is sometimes recognized as a memorial candle set in a skull. Like all female corpses, Jechidah yearned to perpetuate death, to have her womb become a grave for the newly dead. But she couldn't do that without the help of a male with whom she would have to copulate in the hatred which corpses call love.

As Jechidah sat staring into the sockets of the skull above her, a white-shrouded corpse came and sat beside her. For a while the two corpses gazed at each other, thinking they could see, although all corpses are actually blind. Finally the male corpse spoke:

"Pardon, Miss, could you tell me what time it is?"

Since deep within themselves all corpses long for the termination of their punishment, they are perpetually concerned with time.

"The time?" Jechidah answered. "Just a second." Strapped to her wrist was an instrument to measure time but the divisions were so minute and the symbols so tiny that she could not easily read the dial. The male corpse moved nearer to her.

"May I take a look? I have good eyes."

"If you wish."

Corpses never act straightforwardly but are always sly and devious. The male corpse took Jechidah's hand and bent his head toward the instrument. This was not the first time a male corpse had touched Jechidah but contact with this one made her limbs tremble. The stared intently but could not decide immediately. Then he said: "I think it's ten minutes after ten."

"Is it really so late?"

"Permit me to introduce myself. My name is Jachid."

"Jachid? Mine is Jechidah."

"What an odd coincidence."

Both hearing death race in their blood were silent for a long while. Then Jachid said: "How beautiful the night is!"

"Yes, beautiful!"

"There's something about spring that cannot be expressed in words."

"Words can express nothing," answered Jechidah.

As she made this remark, both knew they were destined to lie together and to prepare a grave for a new corpse. The fact is, no matter how dead the dead are there remains some life in them, a trace of contact with that knowledge which fills the universe. Death only masks the truth. The sages speak of it as a soap bubble that bursts at the touch of a straw. The dead, ashamed of death, try to conceal their condition through cunning. The more moribund a corpse the more voluble it is.

"May I ask where you live?" asked Jachid.

Where have I seen him before? How is it his voice sounds so familiar to me? Jechidah wondered. *And how does it happen that he's called Jachid? Such a rare name.*

"Not far from here," she answered.

"Would you object to my walking you home?"

"Thank you. You don't have to. But if you want . . . It is still too early to go to bed."

When Jachid rose, Jechidah did, too. Is this the one I have been searching for? Jechidah asked herself, the one destined for me? But what do I mean by destiny? According to my professor, only atoms and motion exist. A carriage approached them and Jechidah heard Jachid say:

"Would you like to take a ride?"

"Where to?"

"Oh, just around the park."

Instead of reproving him as she intended to, Jechidah said: "It would be nice. But I don't think you should spend the money."

"What's money? You only live once."

The carriage stopped and they both got in. Jechidah knew that no self-respecting girl would go riding with a strange young man. What did Jachid think of her? Did he believe she would go riding with anyone who asked her? She wanted to explain that she was shy by nature, but she knew she could not wipe out the impression she had already made. She sat in silence, astonished at her behavior. She felt nearer to this stranger than she ever had to anyone. She could almost read his mind. She wished the night would continue for ever. Was this love? Could one really fall in love so quickly? And am I happy? she asked herself. But no answer came from within her. For the dead are always melancholy, even in the midst of gaiety. After a while Jechidah said: "I have a strange feeling I have experienced all this before."

"*Déjà vu*—that's what psychology calls it."

"But maybe there's some truth to it . . ."

"What do you mean?"

"Maybe we've known each other in some other world."

Jachid burst out laughing. "In what world? There is only one, ours, the earth."

"But maybe souls do exist."

"Impossible. What you call the soul is nothing but vibrations of matter, the product of the nervous system. I should know, I'm a medical student." Suddenly he put his arm around her waist. And although Jechidah had never permitted any male to take such liberties before, she did not reprove him. She sat there perplexed by her acquiescence, fearful of the regrets that would be hers tomorrow. I'm completely without character, she chided herself. But he is right about one thing. If there is no soul and life is nothing but a short episode in an eternity of death, then why shouldn't one enjoy oneself without restraint? If there is no soul, there is no God, free will is meaningless. Morality, as my professor says, is nothing but a part of the ideological superstructure.

Jechidah closed her eyes and leaned back against the upholstery. The horse trotted slowly. In the dark all the corpses, men and beasts, lamented their death—howling, laughing, buzzing, chirping, sighing. Some of the corpses staggered, having drunk to forget for a while the tortures of hell. Jechidah had retreated into herself. She dozed off, then awoke again with a start. When the dead sleep they once more connect themselves with the source of life. The illusion of time and space, cause and effect, number and relation ceases. In her dream Jechidah had ascended again into the world of her origin. There she saw her real mother, her friends, her teachers. Jachid was there, too. The two greeted each other, embraced, laughed and wept with joy. At that moment, they both recognized the truth, that death on Earth is temporary and illusory, a trial and a means of purification. They traveled together past heavenly mansions, gardens, oases for convalescent souls, forests for divine beasts, islands for heavenly birds. No, our meeting was not an accident, Jechidah murmured to herself. There is a God. There is a purpose in creation. Copulation, free will, fate—all are part of His plan. Jachid and Jechidah passed by a prison and gazed into its window. They saw a soul condemned to sink down to Earth. Jechidah knew that this soul would become her daughter. Just before she woke up, Jechidah heard a voice:

"The grave and the grave digger have met. The burial will take place tonight."

Translated by The Author and Elizabeth Pollet

Under the Knife

LEIB opened his one good eye, but it was dark in the cellar. He couldn't tell whether it was day or still night. He fumbled for the matches and pack of cigarettes he had left on a stool near the iron cot. Every time he waked in the windowless room in which he'd been living lately, the same doubt assailed him: what if his other eye had gone blind too? He struck a match and watched the flame glow. Lighting his cigarette, he inhaled deeply, and with the little blue fire that remained on the match lit a small kerosene lamp which had lost its glass chimney. Its trembling light fell on the peeling walls, on the floor that was completely rotted away. But if you don't have to pay rent, even a living grave is a bargain. Thank God, he still had some vodka left over from yesterday. The bottle stood on an egg crate, stopped up with paper. Thoughtfully, Leib lowered his bare feet, took a few steps towards the crate. Well, I'll just rinse my mouth, he joked to himself.

He put the bottle to his lips, drank it to the bottom, and then threw it aside. He sat for a while feeling the fumes rise from his stomach into his brain. All right, so I'm a fallen man, he muttered. Usually there were mice rustling around the room, but now the cold had driven them away. The place smelled of mould and subterranean odors. The air was damp. A fungus grew on the remains of the woodwork.

Leib leaned back against the wall, surrendering himself to the alcohol. When he drank, he stopped reasoning. His thoughts ran on by themselves, without his head so to speak. He had lost everything: his left eye, his job, his wife, Rooshke. He, Leib, who at one time had been the second warden in the Society of Loving Friends was now a drunkard, a bum. I'll kill her, I'll kill her, Leib muttered to himself. She's done for. I'll kill her and then take my own life. Every day she survives is a gift to her. In a week she'll be in her grave, that whore, packed up to travel. . . . If there is a God, he'll deal with her in the next world. . . .

Leib had long since planned everything. He went over it again, only he thought he would postpone the end for a little while. The knife he was going to stick in tough Rooshke's belly was hidden in the straw mattress. He had sharpened it recently until it could cut a hair. He would thrust it in her belly and twist it twice to slash her guts. Then he would stamp his foot on Rooshke's breast and while she was in her death throes shout at her: Well, Rooshke, are you still tough? Eh? And he would spit in her face. After that he would go to the cemetery and, near Chaye's grave, slash his wrists.

Growing tired of sitting up, Leib stretched out on the cot again, covered himself with the black blanket scarred with cigarette burns, and blew out the lamp. The right moment would come. He had been waiting for it for a long time. First he had sold all his possessions; then he had borrowed from his friends. Now it took miracles to survive at all. He ate in soup kitchens. His old friends gave him a few pennies, a worn shirt, shorts, a pair of discarded boots. He was living like an animal, like one of the cats, dogs, rats which swarmed through the neighborhood. In the dark, Leib returned to his cherished vision: Rooshke, deathly pale, lay there, dress up, legs stretched out, the yellow-blonde hair in disorder, the knife in her stomach with only the metal handle sticking out. She began to scream in an agonized voice, pleading, gurgling, opening her blue eyes wide. He, Leib, holding his boot firmly on her chest, asked: Well, are you still tough, eh?

2

Leib awoke. During the last few days he had drowsed like a man in a fever. He no longer knew whether it was night or day, Tuesday or Thursday. It might even be Saturday already. There was no more vodka and he had smoked his last cigarette. He had been having a long dream, all about Rooshke, a strange one for he had been slitting her throat and at the same time making love to her, as if there were two Rooshkes. Remembering the senseless dream for a moment, he tried to interpret it, but soon let it go. Am I sick? he wondered. Perhaps I'll die in this hole and Rooshke will attend my funeral. But even in death I'll come and strangle her. . . .

Some time later he shuddered and woke again. He touched his forehead, but it felt cool. His tiredness had evaporated; his strength had returned; he felt a need to dress and go out to the street. Enough of this rotting alive! Leib said to himself. He wanted to light the lamp but he couldn't find any matches. So I'll dress in the dark, he thought. His clothes were damp and stiff. Blindly he pulled on his trousers, put on his padded jacket, boots, his cap with the wide peak. Judging by the cold indoors Leib guessed it must be snowing outside. He went up the flight of stairs to the yard and saw that it was night. It wasn't raining or snowing, but the cobblestones were wet. Some of the windows were lit up so it couldn't be after midnight as he had at first thought. Well, I skipped a few days, Leib said to himself. Walking with shaky steps, as though after an attack of typhus, he went through the gates and outside. The stores were all closed, boarded up with shutters. Above the metal roofs the sky was heavy, reddish with cold, saturated with snow. As Leib stood there hesitating, the janitor closed the gates behind him. I wonder what Rooshke is doing now? Leib asked himself. He knew what she was doing. She would be sitting with Lemkin the barber eating a second supper of fresh rolls that crackled under the teeth, of cold cuts with mustard washed down with tea and preserves. The stove would be lit, the phonograph playing, the telephone ringing. Her friends would be gathering there: Leizer Tsitrin the apothecary, Kalman from the non-kosher butcher shop, Berele Bontz the fisherman, Shmuel Zeinvel the musician from the orchestra in the Vienna Wedding Hall. Rooshke would smile at everyone with her generous mouth, show her dimples, push up her skirt so that they could see her round knees, her red garters, the lace on her panties. She wouldn't give one thought to him, Leib. Such a thief, such a whore . . . one death was not enough for her. . . .

Leib felt something in his boot top and reached down. I took the knife with me, he thought, surprised. But to have it with him made him feel more at ease. He had bought a leather sheath for it. The knife was his only friend now; with it he would pay off all his accounts. Leib pushed the knife deeper into his boot top so it would not bump against his ankle. Maybe I ought to pay her that visit now, he told himself. But he was just toying with the idea. He had to find her alone. The best time to go would be in the morning after Lemkin had gone to the barbershop and when the maid Tsipeh had gone out to shop in the market. Rooshke would still be in bed, dozing, or listening to her canaries singing. She loved to sleep in the nude. He would open the apartment door with the passkey he had had duplicated, enter her room quietly, pull the blanket off her, and ask: Well, Rooshke, are you still tough? Eh?

Leib stopped, overpowered by the idea of revenge. Enough waiting, his inner voice commanded. This voice usually ordered him about like a superior officer—left, right, attention, forward march! And Leib never did anything until the voice commanded it. Now he knew why he had slept so much the past week. The invisible power directing him had been preparing him for action. While he slept the decision had been hatching inside him like a disease drawing to its crisis. A chill spread over his spine. Yes, he had delayed long enough. The time had come. . . . He was not afraid but his ribs felt icy. His mind was amazingly clear, but he realized that he must think everything out to the last detail. He hadn't a penny, no vodka, no cigarettes. All the gates were closed now and there was nowhere he could go. Thinking about Rooshke's second supper had made him hungry. He too would like to swallow a few fresh rolls with salami or hot sausages. He felt a rumbling and gnawing in his intestines. For the first time in years Leib was seized with self-pity. Suddenly he recalled the words to a song he had sung as a child while acting in the Purim play. His friend Berish, wearing a tricornered hat shaped like a Purim cake and the black-mustached mask of the villain, had come at him, wanting to kill him, swinging a cardboard sword covered with silver paper. He, Leib, masquerading as a merchant with a red beard, had sung:

> *Take away my one piece of bread,*
> *But give me an hour before I'm dead;*
> *Take my bit of challah beside,*
> *But give me an hour with my bride.*

Berish was long since dead—he had been kicked by a horse. It was he, Leib, who was going to be the murderer, and who hadn't even a piece of bread to redeem one hour from death. . . .

Leib walked slowly, taking short steps. He put his trust in the power commanding him. He would have to have help. Without a drink, without cigarettes, without food in his stomach, he could not carry out the murder. With his one eye he stared into the semi-darkness surrounding him. Several people walked by but he did not really see them. Everything in him was listening; everything hung in the balance; something would happen. If nothing happens, thought Leib, I'll go home—deciding this, he felt as if he were flinging a challenge to the power that had ruled him for so many years and was about to lead him to the final step. He screwed up his eyes. Fiery straws seemed to radiate from the dim gaslights. A few raindrops hit his head. He felt drowsy. Simultaneously he felt that he had lived through this same experience before. At that moment Leib heard a voice which startled him even though he had expected it.

"Are you cold, Leibele? Come in and warm up . . ."

Leib looked around. A whore was standing near the gate of Number 6. Leib did not know her, but apparently she knew him. Under the light of the gas lamp, he saw that she was small, thin, had sunken cheeks smeared with rouge, eyes smudged with mascara. Her red hair was half-covered by a shawl and she was wearing a red dress and red boots that were wet and caked with mud. Leib stopped.

"You know me?"

"Yes, I know you."

"Can I really warm up with you? You're an old hag already," Leib said, knowing it wasn't so.

"My enemies should die so young . . ."

"Maybe I can spend the night in your place?"

"For money you can do anything."

Leib was silent for a moment.

"I don't have any money."

"The only thing you get for nothing is death," the woman answered.

Leib thought it over.

"Maybe you'll take something on account?"

"What on account? A gold watch?"

Leib knew it was foolish, but he put his hand into his boot top and took out the knife in its leather sheath.

"What's that—a knife?"

"Yes, a knife."

"Why should I need a knife? I don't want to stab anyone."

"It's worth three rubles. Take a look at the handle . . ."

Leib stepped under the gaslight and pulled the blade from the sheath. It shone like a flame and the girl moved back a step.

"With the sheath it's worth four rubles."

"I don't need it."

"Well then . . . forget it."

But Leib did not move. He waited as if he expected the girl to change her mind. She wrapped herself deeper in her shawl.

"Why do you carry a knife with you? Do you want to kill someone?"

"Maybe."

"Who? Tough Rooshke?"

Leib froze.

"What makes you say that?"

"People talk. They know all about you."

"What do they say?"

"That Rooshke jilted you, that because of her you became a drunkard."

Something tugged at Leib's heart. People knew about him, talked about him. And he thought the street had forgotten him as though he were dead. His eyes filled with tears.

"Let me come with you. I'll pay you tomorrow."

The girl lifted her head. She looked at him searchingly, with a reserved smile as though all this talk were just a game and a test. She seemed to belong to his life as if she were a relative of his who had waited for him, ready to help him in his need.

"You're lucky the madame isn't here. If she finds out, she'll eat me alive. . . ."

3

Her room was in the basement. The passageway to it was so narrow that only one person could pass at a time. The girl walked ahead and Leib followed. On both sides brick walls hemmed them in; the ground was uneven; and Leib had to bend down in order not to hit his head. He felt as if he were already dead, wandering somewhere in subterranean caves amid devils from the nether world. A lamp glimmered in her room and the walls were painted pink. In the stove the coals glowed; on top a teakettle bubbled. A cat sat on a footstool squinting its green eyes. The bed had only a straw mattress with a dirty sheet, no other bedding. But that was for the guests. A pillow and a blanket were set on a chair in the corner. On the table lay half a loaf of bread. Leib saw himself reflected in the mirror: a large man with a pockmarked face, a long nose, a sunken mouth, a hole and a slit in place of a left eye. In the greenish glass, cracked, covered with dust, his image was refracted as if the glass were a murky pool. He hadn't shaved in over a week and a straw-colored beard covered his chin. The girl took off her shawl and for the first time Leib could really see her. She was small, flat-chested, with scrawny arms and bony shoulders. Her neck, too long, had a white spot on it. She had yellow eyebrows, yellow eyes, a crooked nose, a pointed chin. Her face was still youthful, but around her mouth there were two deep wrinkles, as though the mouth had aged all by itself. From her accent, she came from the country. Leib stared, vaguely recognizing her.

"Are you the only one here?" he asked.

"The other one is in the hospital."

"Where's the madame?"

"Her brother died. She's sitting *shiva*."

"You could steal everything."

"There's nothing to steal."

Leib sat down on the edge of the bed. He no longer looked at the girl, but at the bread. Though he was not hungry, he could not take his eyes off the loaf. The girl took off her boots but left on her red stockings.

"I wouldn't let a dog stay out in such weather," she said.

"Are you going back out in front of the gate tonight?" Leib asked.

"No, I'll stay here."

"Then we can talk."

"What is there to talk about with me? I've ruined my life. My father was an honorable man. Do you really want to stab Rooshke?"

"She doesn't deserve anything better."

"If I wanted to stab everyone who'd hurt me, I'd have to go around with six knives in each hand."

"Women are different."

"Yes? One should wait and let God judge. Half of my enemies are already rotting in their graves and the other half will end badly too. Why spill blood? God waits a long time but he punishes well."

"He doesn't punish Rooshke."

"Just wait. Nothing lasts forever. She'll get hers sooner than you think."

"Sooner than *you* think," he answered with a laugh like a bark. Then he said: "As long as I'm here, give me something to chew on."

The girl blinked.

"Here. Have some bread. Pull up a chair to the table."

Leib sat down. She brought him a glass of watery tea and with her bony fingers dug out two cubes of sugar from a tin box. She busied herself about him like a wife. Leib took the knife from his boot top and cut off a piece of bread. The girl, watching him, laughed, showing her sparse teeth that were rusty and crooked. In her yellow eyes shone something sisterly and cunning as if she were an accomplice of his.

"The knife is not for bread," she observed.

"What is it for then, eh? Flesh?"

She brought him a piece of salami from the cupboard and he sliced it in half with his knife. The cat jumped off her footstool and began to rub against his leg, meowing.

"Don't give her any. Let her eat the mice."

"Are there enough mice?"

"Enough for ten cats."

Leib cut his piece of salami in two and threw a slice to the cat. The girl looked at him crookedly, half-curiously, half-mockingly as though his whole visit were nothing but a joke. For a long while both of them were silent. Then Leib opened his mouth and asked without thinking:

"Would you like to get married?"

The girl laughed.

"I'll marry the Angel of Death."

"I'm not joking."

"As long as a woman breathes she wants to get married."

"Would you marry me?"

"Even you—"

"Well then, let's get married."

The girl was pouring water into the teakettle.

"Do you mean in bed or at the rabbi's?"

"First in bed, then at the rabbi's."

"Whatever you want. I don't believe anybody any more, but what do I care if they pull my leg? If you say so, it's so. If you back out, nothing is lost. What's a word? Every third guest wants to marry me. Afterwards, they don't even want to pay the twenty kopecks."

"I'll marry you. I've got nothing left to lose."

"And what have I got to lose? Only my life."

"Don't you have any money?"

The girl smiled familiarly, grimacing slightly as though she had expected Leib to ask this. Her whole face became aged, knowing, good-naturedly wrinkled like that of an old crone. She hesitated, glanced about, looked up at the small window covered with a black curtain. Her face seemed to laugh and at the same time to ponder something sorrowful and ancient. Then she nodded.

"My whole fortune is here in my stocking."

She pointed with her finger to her knee.

4

Next morning Leib waited until the janitor opened the gates. Then he walked outside. Everything had gone smoothly. It was still dark but on this side of the Vistula, in the east, a piece of sky showed pale blue with red spots. Smoke was rising from chimneys. Peasant carts with meat, fruit, vegetables came by, the horses plodding along still half asleep. Leib breathed deeply. His throat felt dry. His guts were knotted up. Where could he get food and drink at this hour? He remembered Chaim Smetene's restaurant, which opened up when God was still asleep. Leib, shaking his head like a horse, set off in that direction. Well, it's all destined: I'm fulfilling my fate, he thought. Chaim Smetene's restaurant, smelling of tripe, beer, and goose gravy, was already open, its gaslights lit. Men who had been awake all night were sitting there eating but whether a meat breakfast or the remains of last night's supper was hard to know. Leib sat down at an empty table and ordered a bottle of vodka, onions with chicken fat, and an omelette. He drank three shots straight off on his empty stomach. Well, it's my last meal, he muttered to himself. Tomorrow by this time I'll be a martyr . . . ! The waiters were suspicious of him, thought maybe he was trying to get a free meal. The owner Chaim Smetene himself came over and asked:

"Leib, have you any money?"

Leib wanted to swing the bottle and hit him in his fat stomach which was draped with a chain of silver rubles.

"I'm no beggar."

And Leib took a packet of banknotes tied with a red string from his pocket.

"Well, don't get mad."

"Drop dead!"

Leib wanted to forget the insult. He tossed off one shot after another, became so engrossed in his drinking that he even forgot about the omelette. He took out a paper bill, gave it to the waiter for a tip, and ordered another bottle of vodka, not forty or sixty proof this time but ninety proof. The place was filling up with customers, growing thick with haze, noisy with voices. Someone threw sawdust over the stone floor. Near Leib men were talking, but though he heard the separate words, he could not grasp the connections between them. His ears felt as if filled with water. He leaned his head on the chair, snored, but at the same time kept his hand on the bottle to make sure it was not taken away. He was not asleep, but neither was he awake. He dreamed but the dream itself seemed far away. Someone was making a long speech to him, without interruption, like a preacher's sermon, but who was speaking and what he was saying, Leib could not understand. He opened his one eye, then closed it again.

After a while he sat up. It was bright day and the gaslights were out. The clock on the wall showed a quarter to nine. The room was full of people, but although he knew everyone on the street, he didn't recognize anyone. There was still some vodka in the bottle and he drank it. He tasted the cold omelette, grimaced, and began to bang his spoon on the plate for the waiter. Finally he left, walking out with unsteady legs.

In front of his one eye hung a fog with something in the middle of it tossing about like jelly. I'm going completely blind, Leib said to himself. He went into Yanosh's bazaar, looking for Tsipeh, Rooshke's maid, who he knew came there every morning to shop. The bazaar was already packed with customers. Market women shouted their wares; fishmongers bent over tubs filled with fish; three slaughterers were killing fowl over a marble sink that glowed from the light of a kerosene lamp, handing them to pluckers who plucked and packed them, still alive, into baskets. Whoever has a knife uses it, Leib thought. God doesn't mind. Going towards the exit he spotted Tsipeh. She had just arrived with an empty basket. Well, now's the time!

He walked out of the bazaar and turned towards Rooshke's yard. He was not afraid of being seen. He entered the gate, climbed up the stairs to the second floor where an engraved plaque said, "Lemkin—Master Barber." What will I do if the key doesn't fit? Leib asked himself. I'll break down the door, he answered. He could feel his strength; he was like Samson now. Taking the key from his breast pocket as if he were the owner of the flat, he put it into the keyhole and opened the door. The first thing he saw was a gas meter. A top hat was hanging on a hatrack and he tapped it playfully. Through the half-open kitchen door he saw a coffee grinder, a brass mortar and pestle. Smells of coffee grounds and fried onions came from there. Well, Rooshke, your time is up! He stepped quietly along the carpet in the corridor, moving, head forward, as adroitly and carefully as a dogcatcher trying to catch a dog. Something like laughter seized him as he drew out the knife leaving the sheath in his boot top. Leib threw open the bedroom door. There was Rooshke, asleep under a red blanket, her bleached blonde hair spread out on a white pillow, her face yellowish, flabby, smeared with cream. Eyeballs protruded against her closed lids and a double chin covered her wrinkled throat. Leib stood gaping. He almost didn't recognize her. In the few months since he had last seen her, she had grown fat and bloated, had lost her girlish looks, become a matron. Gray hair was visible near the scalp. On a night table a set of false teeth stood in a glass of water. So that's it, Leib muttered. She was right. She really has become an old hag. He recalled her words before they parted: "I've been used enough. I'm not getting any younger, only older. . . ."

He couldn't go on standing there. Any minute someone would knock at the door. But neither could he leave. What must be must be, Leib said to himself. Approaching the bed, he pulled off the blanket. Rooshke was not sleeping naked, but in an unbuttoned nightgown which exposed a pair of flabby breasts like pieces of dough, a protruding stomach, thick, unusually wide hips. Leib would never have imagined Rooshke could have such a fat belly, that her skin could have become so yellowish, withered, and scarred. Leib expected her to scream, but she opened her eyes slowly as if, until now, she had been only pretending she was asleep. Her eyes stared at him seriously, sadly, as if she were saying: Woe unto you, what has become of you? Leib trembled. He wanted to say the words he had rehearsed to himself so often, but he had forgotten them. They hung on the tip of his tongue. Rooshke herself had apparently lost her voice. She examined him with a strange calmness.

Suddenly she let out a scream. Leib raised the knife.

5

Well, it's really very easy, Leib muttered to himself. He closed the door and walked down the stairs slowly, banging his heels, as if he were looking for a witness, but he met no one either on the stairs or in the yard. Leaving, he stood for a while at the gates. The sky, which at sunrise had started out so blue, had turned dark and rainy. A porter passed by carrying a sack full of coal on his back. A hunchback shouted out, peddling pickled herring. At the dairy they were unloading milk cans. At the grocery a delivery man was piling loaves on his arm. The two horses in harness had put their heads together as if sharing a secret. Yes, it's the same street, nothing has changed, Leib thought. He yawned, shook himself. Then he remembered the words he had forgotten: Well, Rooshke, are you still tough, eh? He felt no fear, only an emptiness. It is morning but it looks like dusk, he mused. He felt in his pocket for cigarettes but had lost them somewhere. He passed the stationery shop. At the butcher's he looked in. Standing at his block, Leizer the butcher was cutting a side of beef with a wide cleaver. A throng of pushing, shoving women were bargaining and stretching out their hands for marrowbones. He'll cut off some woman's finger yet, Leib muttered. Suddenly he found himself in front of Lemkin's barber shop and he looked in through the glass door. The assistant hadn't arrived yet. Lemkin was alone, a small man, fat and pink, with a naked skull, short legs, and a pointed stomach. He was wearing striped pants, shoes with spats, a collar and bowtie, but no jacket, and his suspenders were short like those of a child. Standing there, he was thumbing through a Polish newspaper. He doesn't even know yet that he is a widower, Leib said to himself. He watched him, baffled. It was hard to believe that he, Leib, had brooded about this swinish little man for so long and had hated him so terribly. Leib pushed open the door and Lemkin looked at him sideways, startled, even frightened. I'll fix him too, Leib decided. He bent down to draw the knife from his boot top, but some force held him back. An invisible power seemed to have grabbed his wrist. Well, he's destined to live, Leib decided. He spoke:

"Give me a shave."

"What? Sure, sure . . . sit down."

Cheerfully, Lemkin put on his smock which lay ready on a chair, wrapped Leib in a fresh sheet, and poured warm water into a bowl. Soaping Leib, he half patted, half tickled his throat. Leib leaned his head back, closed the lid on his one eye, relaxed in the darkness. I think I'll take a nap, he decided. I'll tell him to cut my hair too. Leib felt a little dizzy and belched. A chill breeze ran through the barber shop and he sneezed. Lemkin wished him *Gesundheit*. The chair was too high and Lemkin lowered it. Taking a razor from its sheath, he stropped it on a leather strap and then began to scrape. Tenderly, as if they were relatives, he pinched Leib's cheek between his thick fingertips. Leib could feel the barber's breath as Lemkin said confidentially:

"You're a friend of Rooshke's . . . I know, I know . . . she told me everything."

Lemkin waited for a reply from Leib. He even stopped scraping with his razor. After a while he began again.

"Poor Rooshke is sick."

Leib was silent for a time.

"What's wrong with her?"

"Gallstones. The doctors say she should have an operation. She's been in the hospital two weeks now. But you don't go under the knife so easily."

Leib lifted his head.

"In the hospital? Where?"

"In Chista. I go there every day."

"Who's at home then?"

"A sister from Praga."

"An older one, eh?"

"A grandmother already."

Leib lowered his head. Lemkin lifted it up again.

"Believe me, Rooshke's not your enemy," he whispered in Leib's ear. "She talks about you all the time. After all, what happened happened. We would like to do something for you, but you keep yourself a stranger. . . ."

Lemkin was bending so near Leib as almost to touch him with his forehead. He smelled of mouth rinse and a brotherly warmth. Leib wanted to say something, but outside there was a scream and people began to run. Lemkin straightened up.

"I'll see what all the excitement's about."

He walked outside, still in his smock, with the razor in his right hand and the left smeared with soap and beard. He lingered a minute or two, questioning someone. He came back in cheerfully.

"A whore's dead. Ripped open with a knife. The little redhead at Number 6."

Translated by Ruth Whitman and Elizabeth Pollet

The Fast

ITCHE NOKHUM was always a small eater, but after Roise Genendel had left him and his father, may he live long, had ordered him to send her a writ of divorce, Itche Nokhum had given himself over to fasting. It was easy to fast in the house of the Bekhever rebbe. The rebbetsin, his wife, was dead. Aunt Peshe, who kept house, never paid attention to whether one ate or didn't. The servant, Elke Dobe, often forgot to bring Itche Nokhum his meals. Under his window there was a pit where refuse was dumped. Itche Nokhum threw the food out of the window. Dogs, cats and birds ate the scraps. It was only now, at the age of forty, that Itche Nokhum understood why the sages of old had fasted from Sabbath to Sabbath. An empty stomach, a pure bowel, is an exquisite pleasure. The body is light as though freed of gravity; the mind is clear. At first there is a slight gnawing at the stomach and the mouth waters, but after the first two days all hunger ceases. Itche Nokhum had long felt a repugnance to eating meat or anything that came from living creatures. Ever since he had seen Leizer the *shokhet* slaughter an ox at the slaughterhouse, meat made him nauseous. Even milk, drawn from udders, and eggs, laid by hens, were repellent. All of these had to do with blood, veins, gut. True, the Holy Books permitted the eating of meat, but only to saints, who have the power to deliver the sinful souls incarnated in kine and fowl. Itche Nokhum would have none of it.

Even bread, potatoes and greens were too much. It was enough to eat just to sustain life. And for that, a bite or two sufficed for several days. Anything more was self-indulgence. Why yield to gluttony? Since Roise Genendel, daughter of the Bialer rebbe, had left Itche Nokhum, he had discovered that a man can curb every desire. There is something in the heart that lusts, but one can thumb his nose at it. It wants to think carnal thoughts, but one compels it to pore over the Holy Book. It tempts one into longings and imaginings, but just to thwart it one recites the Psalms. In the morning it wants to sleep till nine, but one awakens it at daybreak. What this enemy within hates most of all is a cold ritual bath.

But there is a little spot in the brain that has the final word, and when it commands the feet to go, they go, be the water cold as ice. In time, opposing this lusting creature becomes a habit. One bends it, gags it, or else one lets it babble on without answering—as it is written: "Answer not a fool according to his folly."

Itche Nokhum paced his room, back and forth—small, lean, with a wispy straw-colored beard, a face white as chalk, with a reddish, pointed nose and watery-blue eyes under shaggy yellow eyebrows. Over his forehead sat a crumpled skullcap with bits of straw and feathers clinging to it. Since Itche Nokhum had lost weight, everything hung loosely on his body: his trousers, held up by a sash, his gabardine, down to his ankles, his creased, unbuttoned shirt. Even his slippers and white socks were now too big. He did not walk, but shuffled. When the tempter became too strong, Itche Nokhum fooled him with a pinch of snuff or a pipe. Tobacco dulls the appetite. Itche Nokhum grappled with the enemy without respite. One moment he was seized with lust for Roise Genendel, the next—with anger at his father, may he live long, for urging him to divorce her; now he wanted to sleep under a quilt, and now he was consumed with thirst for a cup of coffee. When he tired of pacing, he lay down on a bench, with his handkerchief under his head in place of a pillow. The boards pressed against his ribs, made it impossible to remain long in one position. If Itche Nokhum managed to doze off, he was immediately attacked by dreams—not one after another, as in the past, but in a swarm, like locusts, as though the visions and delusions had hovered over him, just waiting till he closed his eyes. Roise Genendel appeared to him, as naked as mother Eve, spoke perverse words, laughed shamelessly. Itche Nokhum ate pastries, marzipans, drank wine, swooped through the air like a bat. Musicians played, drums pounded. It was both Purim and Simkhas Torah. "How can this be?" Itche Nokhum wondered. "The Messiah must have come—Sabbati Zevi himself . . ."

He woke with a start, drenched with perspiration. For a while he still remembered all the apparitions, absurdities and delusions, but soon they vanished from his mind, leaving only the image of Roise Genendel. Her body dazzled. He heard the echo of her laughter. "I shouldn't have divorced her!" Itche

Nokhum muttered to himself. "I should have left her and disappeared, so that she wouldn't know where my bones were resting. Too late now . . ." People were saying in Bekhev that she was about to become the daughter-in-law of a Galician, the wife of the Komarner rebbe. A Hassid who knew the Komarner rebbe said that he was tall up to the ceiling, black as a Gypsy and three times a widower . . .

Itche Nokhum caught himself in a sin. Why did he want to leave her a deserted wife? Out of revenge. He had mentally broken the Mosaic precept: Thou shalt not avenge nor bear any grudge. Itche Nokhum took *The Beginning of Wisdom* from the bookshelf. What were the penances for vengefulness? He turned the yellowed pages, scanning them. There was a long list of sins, but revenge was not among them. Itche Nokhum grimaced. This was not the first time that he cursed Roise Genendel in his mind, wishing her ill. He had imagined her sick, dying, dead. He knew that he was consumed with rancor, hatred, evil thoughts. The stiff-necked body refused to yield. It was full of spite.

Itche Nokhum opened a drawer where he had put a handful of pebbles collected in the courtyard, some nettles he had gathered by the fence, and burrs, such as the urchins throw on Tishe b'Ov. Itche Nokhum latched the door, removed his slippers and put in the pebbles: let them cut his soles. He held the nettles against his arms and neck, and rubbed his chest with them. They stung, but not too badly. The blisters would come later. "And now I'll treat you to a cold immersion!" he said to himself. "Come along! . . ." He unlocked the door and started down the stairs. Itche Nokhum was no longer one man, but two. One meted out punishment, and the other resisted. One Itche Nokhum dragged the other to the ritual bath, and the other babbled obscenities, cursed, blasphemed. Itche Nokhum raised his hand and gave himself a slap on the face:

"Wanton!"

2

It was the fifth day of Itche Nokhum's fast. He had begun the fast on Sabbath evening, and now it was Thursday night.

At first, Itche Nokhum had wanted to prove to himself that what the men of old could do, could also be done today. If Rabbi Zadock of Jerusalem had been able to nourish himself for forty years by sucking at a fig, he, Itche Nokhum, could surely abstain from glutting for a week. Secondly, the other one, the adversary, had become altogether too obstreperous. He sat in Itche Nokhum like a dybbuk, forever doing spite. One Itche Nokhum prayed, and the other gabbled rhymes like a clown. One applied the phylacteries, and the other belched, hiccuped, spat. One recited the Eighteen Benedictions, and the other conjured pictures of the Komarner disporting himself with Roise Genendel. Itche Nokhum no longer knew what he was doing. He repeated the same prayer three times. He was no longer in a wrestling bout, but in a fight for life or death. Itche Nokhum stopped sleeping. If a man cannot overcome the enemy by fasting, by lying on thorns, by cold immersions, then how is he to drive him out? By destroying himself? But that is forbidden! A man is expected to break the casket without spilling the wine. Yet how could this be done? Itche Nokhum lay on the bench in his trousers and socks, with a stone for a pillow, like the patriarch Jacob. His skin tingled, but he refused to scratch. Beads of sweat trickled down his neck, but he would not wipe it. The evil one thought of a different trick every minute. Itche Nokhum's hair pricked his skull. His ear buzzed as if a gnat had gotten into it. His nostrils itched to sneeze, his mouth tried to yawn. His knees ached. His belly swelled as though overstuffed with food. Itche Nokhum felt ants running up and down his back. He muttered in the dark:

"Go on, torment me, tear at my flesh! . . ."

For a while the other relented and Itche Nokhum dozed off. A huge frog opened its maw, ready to swallow him. The church bell rang out. Itche Nokhum started up, trembling. Was there a fire or some other disaster? He waited for the bell to ring again. But there was only a distant, hollow echo. Itche Nokhum felt a need to urinate. He stood by the pail, but nothing came. He washed his hands, preparing to say the prayer proper for the occasion, but the urge returned. He felt a burning and a throbbing. His entrails contracted with cramps. A bitterness flooded his mouth, as on the verge of vomiting. "Shall I take a drink of water?" Itche Nokhum asked himself. He went to the stool, where a pitcher stood, half-filled with water for ritual hand-washing, and turned it over reluctantly. One of his socks became wet. "I'll not give in to him!" Itche Nokhum whispered. "Show a dog a finger and he'll snap up the whole hand . . ."

Itche Nokhum stretched out again on his bench, his limbs numb. The pains and aches, the gnawing hunger, the dryness of thirst had suddenly vanished. He was neither asleep nor awake. The brain was thinking, but Itche Nokhum did not know what it thought. The other, the spiteful one, was gone, and there was once again only one Itche Nokhum. He was no longer divided. "Am I dying?" he asked himself. All fear of death had disappeared. He was ready to go. When a funeral is held on Friday afternoon, he thought, the newly dead is spared interrogation and torture by the Black Angel. Itche Nokhum watched his strength ebbing away. His mind slipped over a stretch of time, leaving a blank. It was as if Purah, the Angel of Forgetfulness, had plucked out a piece of Itche Nokhum's memory. He marveled at it in the dark. The lapse may have lasted a minute, an hour, or a day and a night. Itche Nokhum had once read a story about a bewitched young man who bent over a barrel to dip some water, and when he straightened up it was seventy years later.

Suddenly Itche Nokhum was petrified. Something began to stir in the dark by the door—a coiling wisp of vapor, airy and misty. Itche Nokhum was so astonished that he forgot to be frightened. A figure loomed up, an apparition with head and shoulders, neck and hair—a woman. Her face seemed to glow with its own light. Itche Nokhum recognized her: Roise Genendel! The upper part of her body was now quite distinct; the face swayed as if trying to speak. The eyesockets grinned. Below, the phantasm trailed off in ragged wisps and shreds. Itche Nokhum heard his own voice:

"What do you want?"

He tried to rise, but his legs were numb and heavy. The specter flowed toward him, dragging its tail of slime like a chick prematurely breaking out of the shell. "The Primeval Substance!" something cried in Itche Nokhum. He recalled the Psalm: "Thine eyes did see my substance, yet being unperfect." He wanted to speak to the night-creature, but he was robbed of the power of speech. For a time he watched dumbly as she approached, half woman, half shapeless ooze, a monstrous fungus straining to break away from its root, a creature put together in haste. After a while she began to melt away. Pieces dropped from her. The face dissolved, the hair scattered, the nose stretched out and became a snout, as in the manikins that people put on their window sills in winter to mock the frost. She spat out her tongue. Roise Genendel vanished, and the sun flashed in the east sharp as a knife. Bloody stains spattered the walls, the ceilings, the floor. The morning had slaughtered Roise Genendel and splashed her blood. A last bubble of life had burst, and everything returned to the void. Itche Nokhum sat up and rocked as men do over a corpse.

"Roise Genendel! . . . Woe is me! . . ."

3

They were blowing the ram's horn in Bekhev. Elul breezes blew in from the willows in the cemetery. Bright gossamer floated high in the air over the courtyard. Ripe fruit dropped from the trees in the rebbe's orchard. Desolation rustled in the prayer house. Sparrows skipped over the tables. The community goat wandered into the antechamber, leaned against the box with torn, discarded prayerbooks and tried to chew at the corner of a psalm-book. It was Thursday again, and Itche Nokhum had not tasted food since the Sabbath evening meal, but no one paid any attention. When a man fasts all year, he does not begin to eat in Elul, the month of repentance. Itche Nokhum sat in his room, turning the pages of *The Covenant of Rest*. He mumbled for a while. Then he leaned his head on the back of the chair and dozed off.

Suddenly Itche Nokhum heard steps and loud voices. Someone was coming rapidly upstairs to him. The door was flung open and Itche Nokhum saw Roise Genendel and behind her, Yente, her maidservant. It was not the Roise Genendel who revealed herself to him in the nights and through whom he could see as through the weave of his sash, but Roise Genendel in the living flesh: tall, narrow, with a crooked nose, fiery black eyes, thick lips and a long neck. She was dressed in a black shawl, a silk cloak and high-heeled shoes. She was scolding her servant and made her a sign to follow her no further. Roise Genendel entered Itche Nokhum's room, leaving the door open—evidently in order not to remain alone with him. Yente remained standing half-way up the stairs. Itche Nokhum was astounded. "Have I already attained such power?" the thought flashed through his brain. For a long while she stood upon the threshold, holding up her skirt, appraising him with a sidelong stare, in which anger mingled with silent pity. Then she said:

"White as a corpse!"

"What do you want?" asked Itche Nokhum in a faint voice that he could scarcely hear himself.

"What are you doing? Fasting, eh?" Roise Genendel asked mockingly.

Itche Nokhum did not answer.

"Itche Nokhum, I must speak to you!"

Roise Genendel slammed the door to.

"What is it?"

"Itche Nokhum, leave me in peace!" Roise Genendel almost shouted. "We were divorced, we are strangers now. I want to marry, and you can also marry. Everything must have an end!"

"I don't know what you mean."

"You know, you know. You're sitting here and casting spells. I was already on the eve of marriage, and I had to postpone it. Why don't you let me be? You'll drive me from this world. I'll throw myself into the well!"

Roise Genendel stamped her foot. She truculently placed her hand on the doorpost. A diamond ring flashed on her finger. She breathed both fear and strength. Itche Nokhum raised his eyebrows. His heart knocked once and seemed to stop.

"I swear, I don't know . . ."

"You wake me up! You scream into my ear! What do you want of me? It wasn't right between us. From the very first. Forgive me, but you're not a man. Why do you torment me, then? Will you tell me?"

"What am I doing?"

"You come to me, you pinch me, you flay me. I hear your

steps. I don't eat and I don't sleep because of you. I am losing weight. People see you in our courtyard, they see you, I'm not mad! . . . Yente almost died of fright. I'll call her in, she will tell you herself. She was going, if you will pardon me, to the outhouse, and you floated toward her. She raised such screams that everybody in the yard came running . . . Just before sunrise you came and sat on my bed, and I could not move my feet. What are you, a devil?"

Itche Nokhum was silent.

"We've kept it secret," Roise Genendel went on. "But I can't suffer forever. I'll tell the whole world who you are and what you're doing. You will be excommunicated. I'm only sorry for your old father . . ."

Itche Nokhum wanted to answer, but he could not utter a single word. Everything in him shrank and dried up. He began to gasp and croak like a grandfather clock before striking. Something inside him leaped like a snake. Itche Nokhum was filled with a strange fluttering. An icy feather brushed down his spine. He shook his head from side to side, as if to say, "No."

"I've come to warn you! Swear that you will release me. If not, I'll raise such a commotion that all Bekhev will come running. I'll put aside all shame. Come down to the prayer house and swear upon the Holy Scrolls. It's either my death or yours! . . ."

Itche Nokhum made another effort and began to mumble in a choked voice, as if he were being strangled.

"I swear to you, I am not to blame."

"Who is then? You're using Sacred Names. You've plunged yourself into the Cabala. You've lost this world—you'll lose the next one too. My father, may he live long, has sent me to you. He also has intercessors in heaven. You're dealing with the evil ones, woe is me. You'll be driven behind the Black Mountains! You'll be thrown into the Hollow of the Sling! Mooncalf! . . ."

"Roise Genendel!"

"Fiend! Satan! Asmodeus!"

Roise Genendel was suddenly stricken mute. She stared at Itche Nokhum with her enormous black eyes, recoiling from him. The room became so still that one could hear the buzzing of a single fly. Itche Nokhum strained to speak. His throat contracted as if he had swallowed something.

"Roise Genendel, I cannot . . . I cannot forget you!"

"Miserable leech! I'm in your power . . ."

Roise Genendel's mouth twisted. She covered her face with both hands and broke into a hoarse wail.

Translated by Mirra Ginsburg

The Last Demon

I, A DEMON, bear witness that there are no more demons left. Why demons, when man himself is a demon? Why persuade to evil someone who is already convinced? I am the last of the persuaders. I board in an attic in Tishevitz and draw my sustenance from a Yiddish storybook, a leftover from the days before the great catastrophe. The stories in the book are pablum and duck milk, but the Hebrew letters have a weight of their own. I don't have to tell you that I am a Jew. What else, a Gentile? I've heard that there are Gentile demons, but I don't know any, nor do I wish to know them. Jacob and Esau don't become in-laws.

I came here from Lublin. Tishevitz is a God-forsaken village; Adam didn't even stop to pee there. It's so small that a wagon goes through town and the horse is in the market place just as the rear wheels reach the toll gate. There is mud in Tishevitz from Succoth until Tishe b'Ov. The goats of the town don't need to lift their beards to chew at the thatched roofs of the cottages. Hens roost in the middle of the streets. Birds build nests in the women's bonnets. In the tailor's synagogue a billy goat is the tenth in the quorum.

Don't ask me how I managed to get to this smallest letter in the smallest of all prayer books. But when Asmodeus bids you go, you go. After Lublin the road is familiar as far as Zamosc. From there on you are on your own. I was told to look for an iron weathercock with a crow perched upon its comb on the roof of the study house. Once upon a time the cock turned in the wind, but for years now it hasn't moved, not even in thunder and lightning. In Tishevitz even iron weathercocks die.

I speak in the present tense as for me time stands still. I arrive. I look around. For the life of me I can't find a single one of our men. The cemetery is empty. There is no outhouse. I go to the ritual bathhouse, but I don't hear a sound. I sit down on the highest bench, look down on the stone on which the buckets of water are poured each Friday, and wonder. Why am I needed here? If a little demon is wanted, is it necessary to import one all the way from Lublin? Aren't there enough devils in Zamosc? Outside the sun is shining—it's close to the summer solstice—but inside the bathhouse it's gloomy and cold. Above me is a spider web, and within the web a spider wiggling its legs, seeming to spin but drawing no thread. There's no sign of a fly, not even the shell of a fly. "What does the creature eat?" I ask myself, "its own insides?" Suddenly I hear it chanting in a Talmudic singsong: "A lion isn't satisfied by a morsel and a ditch isn't filled up with dirt from its own walls."

I burst out laughing.

"Is that so? Why have you disguised yourself as a spider?"

"I've already been a worm, a flea, a frog. I've been sitting here for two hundred years without a stitch of work to do. But you need a permit to leave."

"They don't sin here?"

"Petty men, petty sins. Today someone covets another man's broom; tomorrow he fasts and puts peas in his shoes. Ever since Abraham Zalman was under the illusion that he was Messiah, the son of Joseph, the blood of the people has congealed in their veins. If I were Satan, I wouldn't even send one of our first-graders here."

"How much does it cost him?"

"What's new in the world?" he asks me.

"It's not been so good for our crowd."

"What's happened? The Holy Spirit grows stronger?"

"Stronger? Only in Tishevitz is he powerful. No one's heard of him in the large cities. Even in Lublin he's out of style."

"Well, that should be fine."

"But it isn't," I say. " 'All Guilty is worse for us than All Innocent.' It has reached a point where people want to sin beyond their capacities. They martyr themselves for the most trivial of sins. If that's the way it is, what are we needed for? A short while ago I was flying over Levertov Street, and I saw a man dressed in a skunk's coat. He had a black beard and wavy sidelocks; an amber cigar holder was clamped between his lips. Across the street from him an official's wife was walking, so it occurs to me to say, 'That's quite a bargain, don't you think, Uncle?' All I expected from him was a thought. I had my handkerchief ready if he should spit on me. So what does the man do? 'Why waste your breath on me?' he calls out angrily. 'I'm willing. Start working on her.' "

"What sort of a misfortune is this?"

"Enlightenment! In the two hundred years you've been sitting on your tail here, Satan has cooked up a new dish of kasha. The Jews have now developed writers. Yiddish ones, Hebrew ones, and they have taken over our trade. We grow hoarse talking to every adolescent, but they print their *kitsch* by the thousands and distribute it to Jews everywhere. They know all our tricks—mockery, piety. They have a hundred reasons why a rat must be kosher. All that they want to do is to redeem the world. Why, if you could corrupt nothing, have you been left here for two hundred years? And if you could do nothing in two hundred years, what do they expect from me in two weeks?"

"You know the proverb, 'A guest for a while sees a mile.'"

"What's there to see?"

"A young rabbi has moved here from Modly Bozyc. He's not yet thirty, but he's absolutely stuffed with knowledge, knows the thirty-six tractates of the Talmud by heart. He's the greatest Cabalist in Poland, fasts every Monday and Thursday, and bathes in the ritual bath when the water is ice cold. He won't permit any of us to talk to him. What's more he has a handsome wife, and that's bread in the basket. What do we have to tempt him with? You might as well try to break through an iron wall. If I were asked my opinion, I'd say that Tishevitz should be removed from our files. All I ask is that you get me out of here before I go mad."

"No, first I must have a talk with this rabbi. How do you think I should start?"

"You tell me. He'll start pouring salt on your tail before you open your mouth."

"I'm from Lublin. I'm not so easily frightened."

2

On the way to the rabbi, I ask the imp, "What have you tried so far?"

"What haven't I tried?" he answers.

"A woman?"

"Won't look at one."

"Heresy?"

"He knows all the answers."

"Money?"

"Doesn't know what a coin looks like."

"Reputation?"

"He runs from it."

"Doesn't he look backwards?"

"Doesn't even move his head."

"He's got to have some angle."

"Where's it hidden?"

The window of the rabbi's study is open, and in we fly. There's the usual paraphernalia around: an ark with the Holy Scroll, bookshelves, a mezuzah in a wooden case. The rabbi, a young man with a blond beard, blue eyes, yellow sidelocks, a high forehead, and a deep widow's peak sits on the rabbinical chair peering in the Gemara. He's fully equipped: *yarmulka*, sash, and fringed garment with each of the fringes braided eight times. I listen to his skull: pure thoughts! He sways and chants in Hebrew, *"Rachel t'unah v'gazezah,"* and then translates, "a wooly sheep fleeced."

"In Hebrew Rachel is both a sheep and a girl's name," I say. "So?"

"A sheep has wool and a girl has hair."

"Therefore?"

"If she's not androgynous, a girl has pubic hair."

"Stop babbling and let me study," the rabbi says in anger.

"Wait a second," I say, "Torah won't get cold. It's true that Jacob loved Rachel, but when he was given Leah instead, she wasn't poison. And when Rachel gave him Bilhah as a concubine, what did Leah do to spite her sister? She put Zilpah into his bed."

"That was before the giving of Torah."

"What about King David?"

"That happened before the excommunication by Rabbi Gershom."

"Before or after Rabbi Gershom, a male is a male."

"Rascal. *Shaddai kra Satan*," the rabbi exclaims. Grabbing both of his sidelocks, he begins to tremble as if assaulted by a bad dream. "What nonsense am I thinking?" He takes his ear lobes and closes his ears. I keep on talking but he doesn't listen; he becomes absorbed in a difficult passage and there's no longer anyone to speak to. The little imp from Tishevitz says, "He's a hard one to hook, isn't he? Tomorrow he'll fast and roll in a bed of thistles. He'll give away his last penny to charity."

"Such a believer nowadays?"

"Strong as a rock."

"And his wife?"

"A sacrificial lamb."

"What of the children?"

"Still infants."

"Perhaps he has a mother-in-law?"

"She's already in the other world."

"Any quarrels?"

"Not even half an enemy."

"Where do you find such a jewel?"

"Once in awhile something like that turns up among the Jews."

"This one I've got to get. This is my first job around here. I've been promised that if I succeed, I'll be transferred to Odessa."

"What's so good about that?"

"It's as near paradise as our kind gets. You can sleep twenty-four hours a day. The population sins and you don't lift a finger."

"So what do you do all day?"

"We play with our women."

"Here there's not a single one of our girls." The imp sighs. "There was one old bitch but she expired."

"So what's left?"

"What Onan did."

"That doesn't lead anywhere. Help me and I swear by Asmodeus' beard that I'll get you out of here. We have an opening for a mixer of bitter herbs. You only work Passovers."

"I hope it works out, but don't count your chickens."

"We've taken care of tougher than he."

3

A week goes by and our business has not moved forward; I find myself in a dirty mood. A week in Tishevitz is equal to a year in Lublin. The Tishevitz imp is all right, but when you sit two hundred years in such a hole, you become a yokel. He cracks jokes that didn't amuse Enoch and convulses with laughter; he drops names from the Haggadah. Every one of his stories wears a long beard. I'd like to get the hell out of here, but it doesn't take a magician to return home with nothing. I have enemies among my colleagues and I must beware of intrigue. Perhaps I was sent here just to break my neck. When devils stop warring with people, they start tripping each other.

Experience has taught that of all the snares we use, there are three that work unfailingly—lust, pride, and avarice. No one can evade all three, not even Rabbi Tsots himself. Of the three, pride has the strongest meshes. According to the Talmud a scholar is permitted the eighth part of an eighth part of vanity. But a learned man generally exceeds his quota. When I see that the days are passing and that the rabbi of Tishevitz remains stubborn, I concentrate on vanity.

"Rabbi of Tishevitz," I say, "I wasn't born yesterday. I come from Lublin where the streets are paved with exegeses of the Talmud. We use manuscripts to heat our ovens. The floors of our attics sag under the weight of Cabala. But not even in Lublin have I met a man of your eminence. How does it happen," I ask, "that no one's heard of you? True saints should hide themselves, perhaps, but silence will not bring redemption. You should be the leader of this generation, and not merely the rabbi of this community, holy though it is. The time has come for you to reveal yourself. Heaven and earth are waiting for you. Messiah himself sits in the Bird Nest looking down in search of an unblemished saint like you. But what are you doing about it? You sit on your rabbinical chair laying down the law on which pots and which pans are kosher. Forgive me the comparison, but it is as if an elephant were put to work hauling a straw."

"Who are you and what do you want?" the rabbi asks in terror. "Why don't you let me study?"

"There is a time when the service of God requires the neglect of Torah," I scream. "Any student can study the Gemara."

"Who sent you here?"

"I was sent; I am here. Do you think they don't know about you up there? The higher-ups are annoyed with you. Broad shoulders must bear their share of the load. To put it in rhyme: the humble can stumble. Hearken to this: Abraham Zalman was Messiah, son of Joseph, and you are ordained to prepare the way of Messiah, son of David, but stop sleeping. Get ready for battle. The world sinks to the forty-ninth gate of uncleanliness, but you have broken through to the seventh firmament. Only one cry is heard in the mansions, the man from Tishevitz. The angel in charge of Edom has marshalled a clan of demons against you. Satan lies in wait also. Asmodeus is undermining you. Lilith and Namah hover at your bedside. You don't see them, but Shabriri and Briri are treading at your heels. If the Angels were not defending you, that unholy crowd would pound you to dust and ashes. But you do not stand alone, Rabbi of Tishevitz. Lord Sandalphon guards your every step. Metratron watches over you from his luminescent sphere. Everything hangs in the balance, man of Tishevitz; you can tip the scales."

"What should I do?"

"Mark well all that I tell you. Even if I command you to break the law, do as I bid."

"Who are you? What is your name?"

"Elijah the Tishbite. I have the ram's horn of the Messiah ready. Whether the redemption comes, or we wander in the darkness of Egypt another 2,689 years is up to you."

The rabbi of Tishevitz remains silent for a long time. His face becomes as white as the slips of paper on which he writes his commentaries.

"How do I know you're speaking the truth?" he asks in a trembling voice. "Forgive me, Holy Angel, but I require a sign."

"You are right. I will give you a sign."

And I raise such a wind in the rabbi's study that the slip of paper on which he is writing rises from the table and starts flying like a pigeon. The pages of the Gemara turn by themselves. The curtain of the Holy Scroll billows. The rabbi's *yarmulka* jumps from his head, soars to the ceiling, and drops back onto his skull.

"Is that how Nature behaves?" I ask.

"No."

"Do you believe me now?"

The rabbi of Tishevitz hesitates.

"What do you want me to do?"

"The leader of this generation must be famous."

"How do you become famous?"

"Go and travel in the world."

"What do I do in the world?"

"Preach and collect money."

"For what do I collect?"

"First of all collect. Later on I'll tell you what to do with the money."

"Who will contribute?"

"When I order, Jews give."

"How will I support myself?"

"A rabbinical emissary is entitled to a part of what he collects."

"And my family?"

"You will get enough for all."

"What am I supposed to do right now?"

"Shut the Gemara."

"Ah, but my soul yearns for Torah," the rabbi of Tishevitz groans. Nevertheless he lifts the cover of the book, ready to shut it. If he had done that, he would have been through. What did Joseph de la Rinah do? Just hand Samael a pinch of snuff. I am already laughing to myself, "Rabbi of Tishevitz, I have you all wrapped up." The little bathhouse imp, standing in a corner, cocks an ear and turns green with envy. True, I have promised to do him a favor, but the jealousy of our kind is stronger than anything. Suddenly the rabbi says, "Forgive me, my Lord, but I require another sign."

"What do you want me to do? Stop the sun?"

"Just show me your feet."

The moment the rabbi of Tishevitz speaks these words, I know everything is lost. We can disguise all the parts of our body but the feet. From the smallest imp right up to Ketev Meriri we all have the claws of geese. The little imp in the corner bursts out laughing. For the first time in a thousand years I, the master of speech, lose my tongue.

"I don't show my feet," I call out in rage.

"That means you're a devil. *Pik*, get out of here," the rabbi cries. He races to his bookcase, pulls out the *Book of Creation* and waves it menacingly over me. What devil can withstand the *Book of Creation*? I run from the rabbi's study with my spirit in pieces.

To make a long story short, I remain stuck in Tishevitz. No more Lublin, no more Odessa. In one second all my stratagems turn to ashes. An order comes from Asmodeus himself, "Stay in Tishevitz and fry. Don't go further than a man is allowed to walk on the Sabbath."

How long am I here? Eternity plus a Wednesday. I've seen it all, the destruction of Tishevitz, the destruction of Poland. There are no more Jews, no more demons. The women don't pour out water any longer on the night of the winter solstice. They don't avoid giving things in even numbers. They no longer knock at dawn at the antechamber of the synagogue. They don't warn us before emptying the slops. The rabbi was martyred on a Friday in the month of Nisan. The community was slaughtered, the holy books burned, the cemetery desecrated. The *Book of Creation* has been returned to the Creator. Gentiles wash themselves in the ritual bath. Abraham Zalman's chapel has been turned into a pig sty. There is no longer an Angel of Good nor an Angel of Evil. No more sins, no more temptations! The generation is already guilty seven times over, but Messiah does not come. To whom should he come? Messiah did not come for the Jews, so the Jews went to Messiah. There is no further need for demons. We have also been annihilated. I am the last, a refugee. I can go anywhere I please, but where should a demon like me go? To the murderers?

I found a Yiddish storybook between two broken barrels in the house which once belonged to Velvel the Barrelmaker. I sit there, the last of the demons. I eat dust. I sleep on a feather duster. I keep on reading gibberish. The style of the book is in our manner: Sabbath pudding cooked in pig's fat: blasphemy rolled in piety. The moral of the book is: neither judge, nor judgment. But nevertheless the letters are Jewish. The alphabet they could not squander. I suck on the letters and feed myself. I count the words, make rhymes, and tortuously interpret and reinterpret each dot.

Aleph, the abyss, what else waited?
Bet, the blow, long since fated.

Geemel, God, pretending he knew,
Dalet, death, its shadow grew.
Hey, the hangman, he stood prepared;
Wov, wisdom, ignorance bared.
Zayeen, the zodiac, signs distantly loomed;
Chet, the child, prenatally doomed.
Tet, the thinker, an imprisoned lord;
Jod, the judge, the verdict a fraud.

Yes, as long as a single volume remains, I have something to sustain me. As long as the moths have not destroyed the last page, there is something to play with. What will happen when the last letter is no more, I'd rather not bring to my lips.

When the last letter is gone,
The last of the demons is done.

Translated by Martha Glicklich and Cecil Hemley

Yentl the Yeshiva Boy

AFTER her father's death, Yentl had no reason to remain in Yanev. She was all alone in the house. To be sure, lodgers were willing to move in and pay rent; and the marriage brokers flocked to her door with offers from Lublin, Tomashev, Zamosc. But Yentl didn't want to get married. Inside her, a voice repeated over and over: "No!" What becomes of a girl when the wedding's over? Right away she starts bearing and rearing. And her mother-in-law lords it over her. Yentl knew she wasn't cut out for a woman's life. She couldn't sew, she couldn't knit. She let the food burn and the milk boil over; her Sabbath pudding never turned out right, and her *challah* dough didn't rise. Yentl much preferred men's activities to women's. Her father Reb Todros, may he rest in peace, during many bedridden years had studied Torah with his daughter as if she were a son. He told Yentl to lock the doors and drape the windows, then together they pored over the Pentateuch, the Mishnah, the Gemara, and the Commentaries. She had proved so apt a pupil that her father used to say:

"Yentl—you have the soul of a man."

"So why was I born a woman?"

"Even Heaven makes mistakes."

There was no doubt about it, Yentl was unlike any of the girls in Yanev—tall, thin, bony, with small breasts and narrow hips. On Sabbath afternoons, when her father slept, she would dress up in his trousers, his fringed garment, his silk coat, his skull-cap, his velvet hat, and study her reflection in the mirror. She looked like a dark, handsome young man. There was even a slight down on her upper lip. Only her thick braids showed her womanhood—and if it came to that, hair could always be shorn. Yentl conceived a plan and day and night she could think of nothing else. No, she had not been created for the noodle board and the pudding dish, for chattering with silly women and pushing for a place at the butcher's block. Her father had told her so many tales of yeshivas, rabbis, men of letters! Her head was full of Talmudic disputations, questions and answers, learned phrases. Secretly, she had even smoked her father's long pipe.

Yentl told the dealers she wanted to sell the house and go to live in Kalish with an aunt. The neighborhood women tried to talk her out of it, and the marriage brokers said she was crazy, that she was more likely to make a good match right here in Yanev. But Yentl was obstinate. She was in such a rush that she sold the house to the first bidder, and let the furniture go for a song. All she realized from her inheritance was one hundred and forty rubles. Then late one night in the month of Av, while Yanev slept, Yentl cut off her braids, arranged sidelocks at her temples, and dressed herself in her father's clothes. Packing underclothes, phylacteries, and a few books into a straw suitcase, she started off on foot for Lublin.

On the main road, Yentl got a ride in a carriage that took her as far as Zamosc. From there, she again set out on foot. She stopped at an inn along the way, and gave her name there as Anshel, after an uncle who had died. The inn was crowded with young men journeying to study with famous rabbis. An argument was in progress over the merits of various yeshivas, some praising those of Lithuania, others claiming that study was more intensive in Poland and the board better. It was the first time Yentl had ever found herself alone in the company of young men. How different their talk was from the jabbering of women, she thought, but she was too shy to join in. One young man discussed a prospective match and the size of the dowry, while another, parodying the manner of a Purim rabbi, declaimed a passage from the Torah, adding all sorts of lewd interpretations. After a while, the company proceeded to contests of strength. One pried open another's fist; a second tried to bend a companion's arm. One student, dining on bread and tea, had no spoon and stirred his cup with his penknife. Presently, one of the group came over to Yentl and poked her in the shoulder:

"Why so quiet? Don't you have a tongue?"

"I have nothing to say."

"What's your name?"

"Anshel."

"You *are* bashful. A violet by the wayside."

And the young man tweaked Yentl's nose. She would have given him a smack in return, but her arm refused to budge. She turned white. Another student, slightly older than the rest, tall and pale, with burning eyes and a black beard, came to her rescue.

"Hey, you, why are you picking on him?"

"If you don't like it, you don't have to look."

"Want me to pull your sidelocks off?"

The bearded young man beckoned to Yentl, then asked where she came from and where she was going. Yentl told him she was looking for a yeshiva, but wanted a quiet one. The young man pulled at his beard.

"Then come with me to Bechev."

He explained that he was returning to Bechev for his fourth year. The yeshiva there was small, with only thirty students, and the people in the town provided board for them all. The food was plentiful and the housewives darned the students' socks and took care of their laundry. The Bechev rabbi, who headed the yeshiva, was a genius. He could pose ten questions and answer all ten with one proof. Most of the students eventually found wives in the town.

"Why did you leave in the middle of the term?" Yentl asked.

"My mother died. Now I'm on my way back."

"What's your name?"

"Avigdor."

"How is it you're not married?"

The young man scratched his beard.

"It's a long story."

"Tell me."

Avigdor covered his eyes and thought a moment.

"Are you coming to Bechev?"

"Yes."

"Then you'll find out soon enough anyway. I was engaged to the only daughter of Alter Vishkower, the richest man in town. Even the wedding date was set when suddenly they sent back the engagement contract."

"What happened?"

"I don't know. Gossips, I guess, were busy spreading tales. I had the right to ask for half the dowry, but it was against my nature. Now they're trying to talk me into another match, but the girl doesn't appeal to me."

"In Bechev, yeshiva boys look at women?"

"At Alter's house, where I ate once a week, Hadass, his daughter, always brought in the food. . . ."

"Is she good-looking?"

"She's blond."

"Brunettes can be good-looking too."

"No."

Yentl gazed at Avigdor. He was lean and bony with sunken cheeks. He had curly sidelocks so black they appeared blue, and his eyebrows met across the bridge of his nose. He looked at her sharply with the regretful shyness of one who has just divulged a secret. His lapel was rent, according to the custom for mourners, and the lining of his gabardine showed through. He drummed restlessly on the table and hummed a tune. Behind the high furrowed brow his thoughts seemed to race. Suddenly he spoke:

"Well, what of it. I'll become a recluse, that's all."

2

It was strange, but as soon as Yentl—or Anshel—arrived in Bechev, she was allotted one day's board a week at the house of that same rich man, Alter Vishkower, whose daughter had broken off her betrothal to Avigdor.

The students at the yeshiva studied in pairs, and Avigdor chose Anshel for a partner. He helped her with the lessons. He was also an expert swimmer and offered to teach Anshel the breast stroke and how to tread water, but she always found excuses for not going down to the river. Avigdor suggested that they share lodgings, but Anshel found a place to sleep at the house of an elderly widow who was half blind. Tuesdays, Anshel ate at Alter Vishkower's and Hadass waited on her. Avigdor always asked many questions: "How does Hadass look? Is she sad? Is she gay? Are they trying to marry her off? Does she ever mention my name?" Anshel reported that Hadass upset dishes on the tablecloth, forgot to bring the salt, and dipped her fingers into the plate of grits while carrying it. She ordered the servant girl around, was forever engrossed in storybooks, and changed her hairdo every week. Moreover, she must consider herself a beauty, for she was always in front of the mirror, but, in fact, she was not that good-looking.

"Two years after she's married," said Anshel, "she'll be an old bag."

"So she doesn't appeal to you?"

"Not particularly."

"Yet if she wanted you, you wouldn't turn her down."

"I can do without her."

"Don't you have evil impulses?"

The two friends, sharing a lectern in a corner of the study house, spent more time talking than learning. Occasionally Avigdor smoked, and Anshel, taking the cigarette from his lips, would have a puff. Avigdor liked baked flatcakes made with buckwheat, so Anshel stopped at the bakery every morning to buy one, and wouldn't let him pay his share. Often Anshel did things that greatly surprised Avigdor. If a button came off Avigdor's coat, for example, Anshel would arrive at the yeshiva the next day with needle and thread and sew it back on. Anshel bought Avigdor all kinds of presents: a silk handkerchief, a pair of socks, a muffler. Avigdor grew more and more attached to this boy, five years younger than himself, whose beard hadn't even begun to sprout. Once Avigdor said to Anshel:

"I want you to marry Hadass."

"What good would that do *you*?"

"Better you than a total stranger."

"You'd become my enemy."

"Never."

Avigdor liked to go for long walks through the town and Anshel frequently joined him. Engrossed in conversation, they would go off to the water mill, or to the pine forest, or to the crossroads where the Christian shrine stood. Sometimes they stretched out on the grass.

"Why can't a woman be like a man?" Avigdor asked once, looking up at the sky.

"How do you mean?"

"Why couldn't Hadass be just like you?"

"How like me?"

"Oh—a good fellow."

Anshel grew playful. She plucked a flower and tore off the petals one by one. She picked up a chestnut and threw it at Avigdor. Avigdor watched a ladybug crawl across the palm of his hand. After a while he spoke up:

"They're trying to marry me off."

Anshel sat up instantly.

"To whom?"

"To Feitl's daughter, Peshe."

"The widow?"

"That's the one."

"Why should you marry a widow?"

"No one else will have me."

"That's not true. Someone will turn up for you."

"Never."

Anshel told Avigdor such a match was bad. Peshe was neither good-looking nor clever, only a cow with a pair of eyes. Besides, she was bad luck, for her husband died in the first year of their marriage. Such women were husband-killers. But Avigdor did not answer. He lit a cigarette, took a deep puff, and blew out smoke rings. His face had turned green.

"I need a woman. I can't sleep at night."

Anshel was startled.

"Why can't you wait until the right one comes along?"

"Hadass was my destined one."

And Avigdor's eyes grew moist. Abruptly he got to his feet.

"Enough lying around. Let's go."

After that, everything happened quickly. One day Avigdor was confiding his problem to Anshel, two days later he became engaged to Peshe, and brought honey cake and brandy to the yeshiva. An early wedding date was set. When the bride-to-be is a widow, there's no need to wait for a trousseau. Everything is ready. The groom, moreover, was an orphan and no one's advice had to be asked. The yeshiva students drank the brandy and offered their congratulations. Anshel also took a sip, but promptly choked on it.

"Oy, it burns!"

"You're not much of a man," Avigdor teased.

After the celebration, Avigdor and Anshel sat down with a volume of the Gemara, but they made little progress, and their conversation was equally slow. Avigdor rocked back and forth, pulled at his beard, muttered under his breath.

"I'm lost," he said abruptly.

"If you don't like her, why are you getting married?"

"I'd marry a she-goat."

The following day Avigdor did not appear at the study house. Feitl the Leatherdealer belonged to the Hasidim and he wanted his prospective son-in-law to continue his studies at the Hasidic prayer house. The yeshiva students said privately that though there was no denying the widow was short and round as a barrel, her mother the daughter of a dairyman, her father half an ignoramus, still the whole family was filthy with money. Feitl was part-owner of a tannery; Peshe had invested her dowry in a shop that sold herring, tar, pots and pans, and was always crowded with peasants. Father and daughter were outfitting Avigdor and had placed orders for a fur coat, a cloth coat, a silk *kapote*, and two pair of boots. In addition, he had received many gifts immediately, things that had belonged to Peshe's first husband: the Vilna edition of the Talmud, a gold watch, a Chanukah candelabra, a spice box. Anshel sat alone at the lectern. On Tuesday when Anshel arrived for dinner at Alter Vishkower's house, Hadass remarked:

"What do you say about your partner—back in clover, isn't he?"

"What did you expect—that no one else would want him?"

Hadass reddened.

"It wasn't my fault. My father was against it."

"Why?"

"Because they found out a brother of his had hanged himself."

Anshel looked at her as she stood there—tall, blond, with a long neck, hollow cheeks, and blue eyes, wearing a cotton dress and a calico apron. Her hair, fixed in two braids, was flung back over her shoulders. A pity I'm not a man, Anshel thought.

"Do you regret it now?" Anshel asked.

"Oh, yes!"

Hadass fled from the room. The rest of the food, meat dumplings and tea, was brought in by the servant girl. Not until Anshel had finished eating and was washing her hands for the Final Blessings did Hadass reappear. She came up to the table and said in a smothered voice:

"Swear to me you won't tell him anything. Why should he know what goes on in my heart! . . ."

Then she fled once more, nearly falling over the threshold.

3

The head of the yeshiva asked Anshel to choose another study partner, but weeks went by and still Anshel studied alone. There was no one in the yeshiva who could take Avigdor's place. All the others were small, in body and in spirit. They talked nonsense, bragged about trifles, grinned oafishly, behaved like shnorrers. Without Avigdor the study house seemed empty. At night Anshel lay on her bench at the widow's, unable to sleep. Stripped of gaberdine and trousers she was once more Yentl, a girl of marriageable age, in love with a young man who was betrothed to another. Perhaps I should have told him the truth, Anshel thought. But it was too late for that. Anshel could not go back to being a girl, could never again do without books and a study house. She lay there thinking outlandish thoughts that brought her close to madness. She fell asleep, then awoke with a start. In her dream she had been at the same time a man and a woman, wearing both a woman's bodice and a man's fringed garment. Yentl's period was late and she was suddenly afraid . . . who knew? In *Medrash Talpioth* she had read of a woman who had conceived merely through desiring a man. Only now did Yentl grasp the meaning of the Torah's prohibition against wearing the clothes of the other sex. By doing so one deceived not only others but also oneself. Even the soul was perplexed, finding itself incarnate in a strange body.

At night Anshel lay awake; by day she could scarcely keep her eyes open. At the houses where she had her meals, the women complained that the youth left everything on his plate. The rabbi noticed that Anshel no longer paid attention to the lectures but stared out the window lost in private thoughts. When Tuesday came, Anshel appeared at the Vishkower house for dinner. Hadass set a bowl of soup before her and waited, but Anshel was so disturbed she did not even say thank you. She reached for a spoon but let it fall. Hadass ventured a comment:

"I hear Avigdor has deserted you."

Anshel awoke from her trance.

"What do you mean?"

"He's no longer your partner."

"He's left the yeshiva."

"Do you see him at all?"

"He seems to be hiding."

"Are you at least going to the wedding?"

For a moment Anshel was silent as though missing the meaning of the words. Then she spoke:

"He's a big fool."

"Why do you say that?"

"You're beautiful, and the other one looks like a monkey."

Hadass blushed to the roots of her hair.

"It's all my father's fault."

"Don't worry. You'll find someone who's worthy of you."

"There's no one I want."

"But everyone wants you. . . ."

There was a long silence. Hadass' eyes grew larger, filling with the sadness of one who knows there is no consolation.

"Your soup is getting cold."

"I, too, want you."

Anshel was astonished at what she had said. Hadass stared at her over her shoulder.

"What are you saying!"

"It's the truth."

"Someone might be listening."

"I'm not afraid."

"Eat the soup. I'll bring the meat dumpling in a moment."

Hadass turned to go, her high heels clattering. Anshel began hunting for beans in the soup, fished one up, then let it fall. Her appetite was gone; her throat had closed up. She knew very well she was getting entangled in evil, but some force kept urging her on. Hadass reappeared, carrying a platter with two meat dumplings on it.

"Why aren't you eating?"

"I'm thinking about you."

"What are you thinking?"

"I want to marry you."

Hadass made a face as though she had swallowed something.

"On such matters, you must speak to my father."

"I know."

"The custom is to send a matchmaker."

She ran from the room, letting the door slam behind her. Laughing inwardly, Anshel thought: "With girls I can play as I please!" She sprinkled salt on the soup and then pepper. She sat there lightheaded. What have I done? I must be going mad. There's no other explanation. . . . She forced herself to eat, but could taste nothing. Only then did Anshel remember that it was Avigdor who had wanted her to marry Hadass. From her confusion, a plan emerged: she would exact vengeance for Avigdor, and at the same time, through Hadass, draw him closer to herself. Hadass was a virgin: what did she know about men? A girl like that could be deceived for a long time. To be sure, Anshel too was a virgin but she knew a lot about such matters from the Gemara and from hearing men talk. Anshel was seized by both fear and glee, as a person is who is planning to deceive the whole community. She remembered the saying: "The public are fools." She stood up and said aloud: "Now I'll really start something."

That night Anshel didn't sleep a wink. Every few minutes she got up for a drink of water. Her throat was parched, her forehead burned. Her brain worked away feverishly of its own volition. A quarrel seemed to be going on inside her. Her stomach throbbed and her knees ached. It was as if she had sealed a pact with Satan, the Evil One who plays tricks on human beings, who sets stumbling blocks and traps in their paths. By the time Anshel fell asleep, it was morning. She awoke more exhausted than before. But she could not go on sleeping on the bench at the widow's. With an effort she rose and, taking the bag that held her phylacteries, set out for the study house. On the way whom should she meet but Hadass' father. Anshel bade him a respectful good morning and received a friendly greeting in return. Reb Alter stroked his beard and engaged her in conversation:

"My daughter Hadass must be serving you leftovers. You look starved."

"Your daughter is a fine girl, and very generous."

"So why are you so pale?"

Anshel was silent for a minute.

"Reb Alter, there's something I must say to you."

"Well, go ahead, say it."

"Reb Alter, your daughter pleases me."

Alter Vishkower came to a halt.

"Oh, does she? I thought yeshiva students didn't talk about such things."

His eyes were full of laughter.

"But it's the truth."

"One doesn't discuss these matters with the young man himself."

"But I'm an orphan."

"Well . . . in that case the custom is to send a marriage broker."

"Yes. . . ."

"What do you see in her?"

"She's beautiful . . . fine . . . intelligent. . . ."

"Well, well, well. . . . Come along, tell me something about your family."

Alter Vishkower put his arm around Anshel and in this fashion the two continued walking until they reached the courtyard of the synagogue.

4

Once you say "A," you must say "B." Thoughts lead to words, words lead to deeds. Reb Alter Vishkower gave his consent to the match. Hadass' mother Freyda Leah held back for a while. She said she wanted no more Bechev yeshiva students for her daughter and would rather have someone from Lublin or Zamosc; but Hadass gave warning that if she were shamed publicly once more (the way she had been with Avigdor) she would throw herself into the well. As often happens with such ill-advised matches, everyone was strongly in favor of it—the rabbi, the relatives, Hadass' girl friends. For some time the girls of Bechev had been eyeing Anshel longingly, watching from their windows when the youth passed by on the street. Anshel kept his boots well polished and did not drop his eyes in the presence of women. Stopping in at Beila the Baker's to buy a *pletzl*, he joked with them in such a worldly fashion that they marveled. The women agreed there was something special about Anshel: his sidelocks curled like nobody else's and he tied his neck scarf differently; his eyes, smiling yet distant, seemed always fixed on some faraway point. And the fact that Avigdor had become betrothed to Feitl's daughter Peshe, forsaking Anshel, had endeared him all the more to the people of the town. Alter Vishkower had a provisional contract drawn up for the betrothal, promising Anshel a bigger dowry, more presents, and an even longer period of maintenance than he had promised Avigdor. The girls of Bechev threw their arms around Hadass and congratulated her. Hadass immediately began crocheting a sack for Anshel's phylacteries, a *challah* cloth, a matzoh bag. When Avigdor heard the news of Anshel's betrothal, he came to the study house to offer his congratulations. The past few weeks had aged him. His beard was disheveled, his eyes were red. He said to Anshel:

"I knew it would happen this way. Right from the beginning. As soon as I met you at the inn."

"But it was you who suggested it."

"I know that."

"Why did you desert me? You went away without even saying goodbye."

"I wanted to burn my bridges behind me."

Avigdor asked Anshel to go for a walk. Though it was already past Succoth, the day was bright with sunshine. Avigdor, friendlier than ever, opened his heart to Anshel. Yes, it was true, a brother of his had succumbed to melancholy and hanged himself. Now he too felt himself near the edge of the abyss. Peshe had a lot of money and her father was a rich man, yet he couldn't sleep nights. He didn't want to be a store-keeper. He couldn't forget Hadass. She appeared in his dreams. Sabbath night when her name occurred in the Hav-dala prayer, he turned dizzy. Still it was good that Anshel and no one else was to marry her. . . . At least she would fall into decent hands. Avigdor stopped and tore aimlessly at the shriveled grass. His speech was incoherent, like that of a man possessed. Suddenly he said:

"I have thought of doing what my brother did."

"Do you love her *that* much?"

"She's engraved in my heart."

The two pledged their friendship and promised never again to part. Anshel proposed that, after they were both married, they should live next door or even share the same house. They would study together every day, perhaps even become partners in a shop.

"Do you want to know the truth?" asked Avigdor. "It's like the story of Jacob and Benjamin: my life is bound up in your life."

"Then why did you leave me?"

"Perhaps for that very reason."

Though the day had turned cold and windy, they continued to walk until they reached the pine forest, not turning back until dusk when it was time for the Evening Prayer. The girls of Bechev, from their posts at the windows, watched them going by with their arms around each other's shoulders and so engrossed in conversation that they walked through puddles and piles of trash without noticing. Avigdor looked pale, disheveled, and the wind whipped one sidelock about; Anshel chewed his fingernails. Hadass, too, ran to the window, took one look, and her eyes filled with tears. . . .

Events followed quickly. Avigdor was the first to marry. Because the bride was a widow, the wedding was a quiet one, with no musicians, no wedding jester, no ceremonial veiling of the bride. One day Peshe stood beneath the marriage canopy, the next she was back at the shop, dispensing tar with greasy hands. Avigdor prayed at the Hasidic assembly house in his new prayer shawl. Afternoons, Anshel went to visit him and the two whispered and talked until evening. The date of Anshel's wedding to Hadass was set for the Sabbath in Chanukah week, though the prospective father-in-law wanted it sooner. Hadass had already been betrothed once. Besides, the groom was an orphan. Why should he toss about on a makeshift bed at the widow's when he could have a wife and home of his own?

Many times each day Anshel warned herself that what she was about to do was sinful, mad, an act of utter depravity. She was entangling both Hadass and herself in a chain of deception and committing so many transgressions that she would never be able to do penance. One lie followed another. Repeatedly Anshel made up her mind to flee Bechev in time, to put an end to this weird comedy that was more the work of an imp than a human being. But she was in the grip of a power she could not resist. She grew more and more attached to Avigdor, and could not bring herself to destroy Hadass' illusory happiness. Now that he was married, Avigdor's desire to study was greater than ever, and the friends met twice each day: in the mornings they studied the Gemara and the Commentaries, in the afternoons the Legal Codes with their glosses. Alter Vishkower and Feitl the Leatherdealer were pleased and compared Avigdor and Anshel to David and Jonathan. With all the complications, Anshel went about as though drunk. The tailors took her measurements for a new wardrobe and she was forced into all kinds of subterfuge to keep them from discovering she was not a man. Though the imposture had lasted many weeks, Anshel still could not believe it: How was it possible? Fooling the community had become a game, but how long could it go on? And in what way would the truth come to the surface? Inside, Anshel laughed and wept. She had turned into a sprite brought into the world to mock people and trick them. I'm wicked, a transgressor, a Jeroboam ben Nabat, she told herself. Her only justification was that she had taken all these burdens upon herself because her soul thirsted to study Torah. . . .

Avigdor soon began to complain that Peshe treated him badly. She called him an idler, a schlemiel, just another mouth to feed. She tried to tie him to the store, assigned him tasks for which he hadn't the slightest inclination, begrudged him pocket money. Instead of consoling Avigdor, Anshel goaded him on against Peshe. She called his wife an eyesore, a shrew, a miser, and said that Peshe had no doubt nagged her first husband to death and would Avigdor also. At the same time, Anshel enumerated Avigdor's virtues: his height and manliness, his wit, his erudition.

"If I were a woman and married to you," said Anshel, "I'd know how to appreciate you."

"Well, but you aren't. . . ."

Avigdor sighed.

Meanwhile Anshel's wedding date drew near.

On the Sabbath before Chanukah Anshel was called to the pulpit to read from the Torah. The women showered her with raisins and almonds. On the day of the wedding Alter Vishkower gave a feast for the young men. Avigdor sat at Anshel's right hand. The bridegroom delivered a Talmudic discourse, and the rest of the company argued the points, while smoking cigarettes and drinking wine, liqueurs, tea with lemon or raspberry jam. Then followed the ceremony of veiling the bride, after which the bridegroom was led to the wedding canopy that had been set up at the side of the synagogue. The night was frosty and clear, the sky full of stars. The musicians struck up a tune. Two rows of girls held lighted tapers and braided wax candles. After the wedding ceremony the bride and groom broke their fast with golden chicken broth. Then the dancing began and the announcement of the wedding gifts, all according to custom. The gifts were many and costly. The wedding jester depicted the joys and sorrows that were in store for the bride. Avigdor's wife Peshe was one of the guests but, though she was bedecked with jewels, she still looked ugly in a wig that sat low on her forehead, wearing an enormous fur cape, and with traces of tar on her hands that no amount of washing could ever remove. After the Virtue Dance the bride and groom were led separately to the marriage chamber. The wedding attendants instructed the couple in the proper conduct and enjoined them to "be fruitful and multiply."

At daybreak Anshel's mother-in-law and her band descended upon the marriage chamber and tore the bedsheets from beneath Hadass to make sure the marriage had been consummated. When traces of blood were discovered, the company grew merry and began kissing and congratulating the bride. Then, brandishing the sheet, they flocked outside and danced a Kosher Dance in the newly fallen snow. Anshel had found a way to deflower the bride. Hadass in her innocence was unaware that things weren't quite as they should have been. She was already deeply in love with Anshel. It is commanded that the bride and groom remain apart for seven days after the first intercourse. The next day Anshel and Avigdor took up the study of the Tractate on Menstruous Women. When the other men had departed and the two were left to themselves in the synagogue, Avigdor shyly questioned Anshel about his night with Hadass. Anshel gratified his curiosity and they whispered together until nightfall.

5

Anshel had fallen into good hands. Hadass was a devoted wife and her parents indulged their son-in-law's every wish and boasted of his accomplishments. To be sure, several months went by and Hadass was still not with child, but no one took it to heart. On the other hand, Avigdor's lot grew steadily worse. Peshe tormented him and finally would not give him enough to eat and even refused him a clean shirt. Since he was always penniless, Anshel again brought him a daily buckwheat cake. Because Peshe was too busy to cook and too stingy to hire a servant, Anshel asked Avigdor to dine at his house. Reb Alter Vishkower and his wife disapproved, arguing that it was wrong for the rejected suitor to visit the house of his former fiancée. The town had plenty to talk about. But Anshel cited precedents to show that it was not prohibited by the Law. Most of the townspeople sided with Avigdor and blamed Peshe for everything. Avigdor soon began pressing Peshe for a divorce, and, because he did not want to have a child by such a fury, he acted like Onan, or, as the Gemara translates it: he threshed on the inside and cast his seed without. He confided in Anshel, told him how Peshe came to bed unwashed and snored like a buzz saw, of how she was so occupied with the cash taken in at the store that she babbled about it even in her sleep.

"Oh, Anshel, how I envy you," he said.

"There's no reason for envying me."

"You have everything. I wish your good fortune were mine—with no loss to you, of course."

"Everyone has troubles of his own."

"What sort of troubles do *you* have? Don't tempt Providence."

How could Avigdor have guessed that Anshel could not sleep at night and thought constantly of running away? Lying with Hadass and deceiving her had become more and more painful. Hadass' love and tenderness shamed her. The devotion of her mother- and father-in-law and their hopes for a grandchild were a burden. On Friday afternoons all of the townspeople went to the baths and every week Anshel had to find a new excuse. But this was beginning to awake suspicions. There was talk that Anshel must have an unsightly birthmark, or a rupture, or perhaps was not properly circumcised. Judging by the youth's years, his beard should certainly have begun to sprout, yet his cheeks remained smooth. It was already Purim and Passover was approaching. Soon it would be summer. Not far from Bechev there was a river where all the yeshiva students and young men went swimming as soon as it was warm enough. The lie was swelling like an abscess and one of these days it must surely burst. Anshel knew she had to find a way to free herself.

It was customary for the young men boarding with their in-laws to travel to nearby cities during the half-holidays in the middle of Passover week. They enjoyed the change, refreshed themselves, looked around for business opportunities, bought books or other things a young man might need. Bechev was not far from Lublin and Anshel persuaded Avigdor to make a journey with her at her expense. Avigdor was delighted at the prospect of being rid for a few days of the shrew he had at home. The trip by carriage was a merry one. The fields were turning green; storks, back from the warm countries, swooped across the sky in great arcs. Streams rushed toward the valleys. The birds chirped. The windmills turned. Spring flowers were beginning to bloom in the fields. Here and there a cow was already grazing. The companions, chatting, ate the fruit and little cakes that Hadass had packed, told each other jokes, and exchanged confidences until they reached Lublin. There they went to an inn and took a room for two. On the journey, Anshel had promised to reveal an astonishing secret to Avigdor in Lublin. Avigdor had joked: what sort of secret could it be? Had Anshel discovered a hidden treasure? Had he written an essay? By studying the Cabala, had he created a dove? . . . Now they entered the room and while Anshel carefully locked the door, Avigdor said teasingly:

"Well, let's hear your great secret."

"Prepare yourself for the most incredible thing that ever was."

"I'm prepared for anything."

"I'm not a man but a woman," said Anshel. "My name isn't Anshel, it's Yentl."

Avigdor burst out laughing.

"I knew it was a hoax."

"But it's true."

"Even if I'm a fool, I won't swallow this."

"Do you want me to show you?"

"Yes."

"Then I'll get undressed."

Avigdor's eyes widened. It occurred to him that Anshel might want to practice pederasty. Anshel took off the gaberdine and the fringed garment, and threw off her underclothes. Avigdor took one look and turned first white, then fiery red. Anshel covered herself hastily.

"I've done this only so that you can testify at the courthouse. Otherwise Hadass will have to stay a grass widow."

Avigdor had lost his tongue. He was seized by a fit of trembling. He wanted to speak, but his lips moved and nothing came out. He sat down quickly, for his legs would not support him. Finally he murmured:

"How is it possible? I don't believe it!"

"Should I get undressed again?"

"No!"

Yentl proceeded to tell the whole story: how her father, bedridden, had studied Torah with her; how she had never had the patience for women and their silly chatter; how she had sold the house and all the furnishings, left the town, made her way disguised as a man to Lublin, and on the road met Avigdor. Avigdor sat speechless, gazing at the storyteller. Yentl was by now wearing men's clothes once more. Avigdor spoke:

"It must be a dream."

He pinched himself on the cheek.

"It isn't a dream."

"That such a thing should happen to me . . . !"

"It's all true."

"Why did you do it? *Nu*, I'd better keep still."

"I didn't want to waste my life on a baking shovel and a kneading trough."

"And what about Hadass—why did you do that?"

"I did it for your sake. I knew that Peshe would torment you and at our house you would have some peace. . . ."

Avigdor was silent for a long time. He bowed his head, pressed his hands to his temples, shook his head.

"What will you do now?"

"I'll go away to a different yeshiva."

"What? If you had only told me earlier, we could have . . ." Avigdor broke off in the middle.

"No—it wouldn't have been good."

"Why not?"

"I'm neither one nor the other."

"What a dilemma I'm in!"

"Get a divorce from that horror. Marry Hadass."

"She'll never divorce me and Hadass won't have me."

"Hadass loves you. She won't listen to her father again."

Avigdor stood up suddenly but then sat down.

"I won't be able to forget you. Ever. . . ."

6

According to the Law Avigdor was now forbidden to spend another moment alone with Yentl; yet dressed in the gaberdine and trousers, she was again the familiar Anshel. They resumed their conversation on the old footing:

"How could you bring yourself to violate the commandment every day: 'A woman shall not wear that which pertaineth to a man'?"

"I wasn't created for plucking feathers and chattering with females."

"Would you rather lose your share in the world to come?"

"Perhaps. . . ."

Avigdor raised his eyes. Only now did he realize that Anshel's cheeks were too smooth for a man's, the hair too abundant, the hands too small. Even so he could not believe that such a thing could have happened. At any moment he expected to wake up. He bit his lips, pinched his thigh. He was seized by shyness and could not speak without stammering. His friendship with Anshel, their intimate talk, their confidences, had been turned into a sham and delusion. The thought even occurred to him that Anshel might be a demon. He shook himself as if to cast off a nightmare; yet that power which knows the difference between dream and reality told him it was all true. He summoned up his courage. He and Anshel could never be strangers to one another, even though Anshel was in fact Yentl. . . . He ventured a comment:

"It seems to me that the witness who testifies for a deserted woman may not marry her, for the Law calls him 'a party to the affair.' "

"What? That didn't occur to me!"

"We must look it up in Eben Ezer."

"I'm not even sure that the rules pertaining to a deserted woman apply in this case," said Anshel in the manner of a scholar.

"If you don't want Hadass to be a grass widow, you must reveal the secret to her directly."

"That I can't do."

"In any event, you must get another witness."

Gradually the two went back to their Talmudic conversation. It seemed strange at first to Avigdor to be disputing holy writ with a woman, yet before long the Torah had reunited them. Though their bodies were different, their souls were of one kind. Anshel spoke in a singsong, gesticulated with her thumb, clutched her sidelocks, plucked at her beardless chin, made all the customary gestures of a yeshiva student. In the heat of argument she even seized Avigdor by the lapel and called him stupid. A great love of Anshel took hold of Avigdor, mixed with shame, remorse, anxiety. If I had only known this before, he said to himself. In his thoughts he likened Anshel (or Yentl) to Bruria, the wife of Reb Meir, and to Yalta, the wife of Reb Nachman. For the first time he saw clearly that this was what he had always wanted: a wife whose mind was not taken up with material things. . . . His desire for Hadass was gone now, and he knew he would long for Yentl, but he dared not say so. He felt hot and knew that his face was burning. He could no longer meet Anshel's eyes. He began to enumerate Anshel's sins and saw that he too was implicated, for he had sat next to Yentl and had touched her during her unclean days. *Nu*, and what could be said about her marriage to Hadass? What a multitude of transgressions there! Wilful deception, false vows, misrepresentation!—Heaven knows what else. He asked suddenly:

"Tell the truth, are you a heretic?"

"God forbid!"

"Then how could you bring yourself to do such a thing?"

The longer Anshel talked, the less Avigdor understood. All Anshel's explanations seemed to point to one thing: she had the soul of a man and the body of a woman. Anshel said she had married Hadass only in order to be near Avigdor.

"You could have married me," Avigdor said.

"I wanted to study the Gemara and Commentaries with you, not darn your socks!"

For a long time neither spoke. Then Avigdor broke the silence:

"I'm afraid Hadass will get sick from all this, God forbid!"

"I'm afraid of that too."

"What's going to happen now?"

Dusk fell and the two began to recite the evening prayer. In his confusion Avigdor mixed up the blessings, omitted some and repeated others. He glanced sideways at Anshel who was rocking back and forth, beating her breast, bowing her head. He saw her, eyes closed, lift her face to Heaven as though beseeching: You, Father in Heaven, know the truth. . . . When their prayers were finished, they sat down on opposite chairs, facing one another yet a good distance apart. The room filled with shadows. Reflections of the sunset, like purple embroidery, shook on the wall opposite the window. Avigdor again wanted to speak but at first the words, trembling on the tip of his tongue, would not come. Suddenly they burst forth:

"Maybe it's still not too late? I can't go on living with that accursed woman. . . . You. . . ."

"No, Avigdor, it's impossible."

"Why?"

"I'll live out my time as I am. . . ."

"I'll miss you. Terribly."

"And I'll miss you."

"What's the sense of all this?"

Anshel did not answer. Night fell and the light faded. In the darkness they seemed to be listening to each other's thoughts. The Law forbade Avigdor to stay in the room alone with Anshel, but he could not think of her just as a woman. What a strange power there is in clothing, he thought. But he spoke of something else:

"I would advise you simply to send Hadass a divorce."

"How can I do that?"

"Since the marriage sacraments weren't valid, what difference does it make?"

"I suppose you're right."

"There'll be time enough later for her to find out the truth."

The maidservant came in with a lamp but as soon as she had gone, Avigdor put it out. Their predicament and the words which they must speak to one another could not endure light. In the blackness Anshel related all the particulars. She answered all Avigdor's questions. The clock struck two, and still they talked. Anshel told Avigdor that Hadass had never forgotten him. She talked of him frequently, worried about his health, was sorry—though not without a certain satisfaction— about the way things had turned out with Peshe.

"She'll be a good wife," said Anshel. "I don't even know how to bake a pudding."

"Nevertheless, if you're willing. . . ."

"No, Avigdor. It wasn't destined to be. . . ."

7

It was all a great riddle to the town: the messenger who arrived bringing Hadass the divorce papers; Avigdor's remaining in Lublin until after the holidays; his return to Bechev with slumping shoulders and lifeless eyes as if he had been ill. Hadass took to her bed and was visited by the doctor three times a day. Avigdor went into seclusion. If someone ran across him by chance and addressed him, he did not answer. Peshe complained to her parents that Avigdor paced back and forth smoking all night long. When he finally collapsed from sheer fatigue, in his sleep he called out the name of an unknown female—Yentl. Peshe began talking of a divorce.

The town thought Avigdor wouldn't grant her one or would demand money at the very least, but he agreed to everything.

In Bechev the people were not used to having mysteries stay mysteries for long. How can you keep secrets in a little town where everyone knows what's cooking in everyone else's pots? Yet, though there were plenty of persons who made a practice of looking through keyholes and laying an ear to shutters, what happened remained an enigma. Hadass lay in her bed and wept. Chanina the herb doctor reported that she was wasting away. Anshel had disappeared without a trace. Reb Alter Vishkower sent for Avigdor and he arrived, but those who stood straining beneath the window couldn't catch a word of what passed between them. Those individuals who habitually pry into other people's affairs came up with all sorts of theories, but not one of them was consistent.

One party came to the conclusion that Anshel had fallen into the hands of Catholic priests, and had been converted. That might have made sense. But where could Anshel have found time for the priests, since he was always studying in the yeshiva? And apart from that, since when does an apostate send his wife a divorce?

Another group whispered that Anshel had cast an eye on another woman. But who could it be? There were no love affairs conducted in Bechev. And none of the young women had recently left town—neither a Jewish woman nor a Gentile one.

Somebody else offered the suggestion that Anshel had been carried away by evil spirits, or was even one of them himself. As proof he cited the fact that Anshel had never come either to the bathhouse or to the river. It is well known that demons have the feet of geese. Well, but had Hadass never seen him barefoot? And who ever heard of a demon sending his wife a divorce? When a demon marries a daughter of mortals, he usually lets her remain a grass widow.

It occurred to someone else that Anshel had committed a major transgression and gone into exile in order to do penance. But what sort of transgression could it have been? And why had he not entrusted it to the rabbi? And why did Avigdor wander about like a ghost?

The hypothesis of Tevel the Musician was closest to the truth. Tevel maintained that Avigdor had been unable to forget Hadass and that Anshel had divorced her so that his friend would be able to marry her. But was such friendship possible in this world? And in that case, why had Anshel divorced Hadass even before Avigdor divorced Peshe? Furthermore, such a thing can be accomplished only if the wife has been informed of the arrangement and is willing, yet all signs pointed to Hadass' great love for Anshel, and in fact she was ill from sorrow.

One thing was clear to all: Avigdor knew the truth. But it was impossible to get anything out of him. He remained in seclusion and kept silent with an obstinancy that was a reproof to the whole town.

Close friends urged Peshe not to divorce Avigdor, though they had severed all relations and no longer lived as man and wife. He did not even, on Friday night, perform the kiddush blessing for her. He spent his nights either at the study house or at the widow's where Anshel had found lodgings. When Peshe spoke to him he didn't answer, but stood with bowed head. The tradeswoman Peshe had no patience for such goings-on. She needed a young man to help her out in the store, not a yeshiva student who had fallen into melancholy. Someone of that sort might even take it into his head to depart and leave her deserted. Peshe agreed to a divorce.

In the meantime Hadass had recovered, and Reb Alter Vishkower let it be known that a marriage contract was being drawn up. Hadass was to marry Avigdor. The town was agog. A marriage between a man and a woman who had once been engaged and their betrothal broken off was unheard of. The wedding was held on the first Sabbath after Tishe b'Ov, and included all that is customary at the marriage of a virgin: the banquet for the poor, the canopy before the synagogue, the musicians, the wedding jester, the Virtue Dance. Only one thing was lacking: joy. The bridegroom stood beneath the marriage canopy, a figure of desolation. The bride had recovered from her sickness, but had remained pale and thin. Her tears fell into the golden chicken broth. From all eyes the same question looked out: why had Anshel done it?

After Avigdor's marriage to Hadass, Peshe spread the rumor that Anshel had sold his wife to Avigdor for a price, and that the money had been supplied by Alter Vishkower. One young man pondered the riddle at great length until he finally arrived at the conclusion that Anshel had lost his beloved wife to Avigdor at cards, or even on a spin of the Chanukah *dreidl*. It is a general rule that when the grain of truth cannot be found, men will swallow great helpings of falsehood. Truth itself is often concealed in such a way that the harder you look for it, the harder it is to find.

Not long after the wedding, Hadass became pregnant. The child was a boy and those assembled at the circumcision could scarcely believe their ears when they heard the father name his son Anshel.

Translated by Marion Magid and Elizabeth Pollet

Three Tales

THERE were three in the circle: Zalman the glazier, Meyer the eunuch, and Isaac Amshinover. Their meeting place was the Radzyminer study house where they visited daily to tell each other stories. Meyer was only present two weeks out of every month; being one of those whom the Talmud called periodic madmen, he was out of his mind the other two. On nights when the full moon shone, Meyer paced up and down in the study house, rubbing his hands together, and muttering to himself. Though tall, his shoulders were so stooped he looked like a hunchback. His bony face was as smooth, or perhaps even smoother than a woman's. He had a long chin, high forehead, crooked nose. His eyes were those of a scholar. It was said that he knew the Talmud by heart. When he was not deranged, he peppered his talk with Hassidic proverbs and quotations from learned books. He had known the old rabbi of Kotsk and remembered him well. Both summer and winter, he dressed in an alpaca gaberdine that reached to his ankles, wore mules and white stockings on his feet, and two skullcaps, one in the front and one in the back on his head; on top of them he put his silk hat. Though already an old man, Meyer had straight-hanging earlocks and a head of black hair. When he was in his sick periods, he apparently didn't eat, but the other half of the month fed on oatmeal porridge and chicken soup brought to the study house by pious women. He slept in a dark alcove at the house of a teacher.

It being the end of the month and a moonless night, Meyer the eunuch was rational. Opening a bone snuffbox, he took a pinch of tobacco mixed with ether and alcohol. He then offered pinches to Zalman the glazier and Isaac Amshinover, even though they had their own snuffboxes. So absorbed was he in his own thoughts that he scarcely heard what Zalman was saying. Wrinkling his brow, he pulled with his thumb and index finger at his beardless chin.

Isaac Amshinover's hair had not turned entirely gray; here and there traces of red were still to be seen in his eyebrows, earlocks and beard. Reb Isaac suffered from trachoma and wore dark glasses; he supported himself on a cane that had once belonged to Rabbi Chazkele of Kuzmir. Reb Isaac swore that he had been offered a large sum of money for the cane. But who would think of selling a stick that had known the hand of so saintly a rabbi? Reb Isaac earned his living with that cane. Women who were having difficult pregnancies borrowed it; it was also used to cure children suffering from scarlet fever, whooping cough, and croup, and was reputed to be helpful in exorcising dybbuks, stopping hiccups, and locating buried treasures. Reb Isaac did not lay the cane down even when praying. Saturdays and holidays, however, he locked it in the lectern. At the moment it was firmly clasped in his hairy, blue-veined hands. Reb Isaac had a weak heart, bad lungs, and defective kidneys. The Hasidim remarked that he would have been dead if he hadn't had Reb Chazkele's cane.

Zalman the glazier, a tall, broad-shouldered man, had a bushy beard the color of pepper and eyebrows as thick as brushes. Though eighty years old, he still drank two tumblers of vodka daily. For breakfast he had an onion, a radish, a two pound loaf of bread, and a pitcher of water. Zalman's wife, born crippled, was half mute, and could use neither her arms nor her legs. In her youth, Zalman had transported her to the ritual bath in a wheelbarrow. This broken shell of a woman had borne him eight sons and daughters. Zalman no longer worked at his craft because he received a pension of twelve rubles a month from his oldest son, a wealthy man. He and his wife lived in a small room which had a balcony that was reached by a ladder. Zalman did his own cooking and fed his wife like a baby. He even emptied the chamber pots.

Tonight he was telling of the time when he had lived in Radoshitz and traveled from village to village bearing a wooden frame loaded with glass on his back.

"Are there any real frosts today?" he inquired. "I wouldn't give you two kopeks for what they consider a freeze now. They think it's winter when there's ice on the Vistula. In my day the cold began just after the Feast of Tabernacles and at Passover you could still cross the river on foot. It was so cold then the trunks of oak trees burst. Wolves used to steal into Radoshitz at night and run off with chickens. Their eyes shone like candles. Their howling would drive you crazy. Once it hailed stones as big as goose eggs. They broke the shingles on the roofs. Some of the hail fell through the chimneys into the pots. I remember a storm when living fish and little animals fell from the sky. You could see them crawling in the gutters."

"How come there was fish in the sky?" Isaac Amshinover asked.

"Don't the clouds drink from the rivers? In one of the villages near Radoshitz a snake dropped down. The fall killed it, but before it died it crawled into a well. The peasants were afraid to touch it; the rotting carcass made the most awful stink."

"There are many similar occurrences mentioned in the *Midrash Talpioth*," interrupted Meyer the eunuch.

"What do I need the *Midrash Talpioth* for? I've seen it all with my own eyes. Nowadays there aren't many highwaymen. But in my time the forests were infested with them. They lived in caves. My father remembered seeing the king of them all, the notorious bandit Dobosh. Everyone was scared stiff of him. But he was only a figurehead; his mother was the power behind the throne. She was ninety years old, and she planned out everything, told them where and how to rob, how to hide the loot and where to get rid of it. She was also a witch and that's why everyone was frightened of her. She'd see someone, mumble a few words and down he fell with a burning fever. You probably never heard what happened between her and Rabbi Leib Saras. She was still young and lusty at the time, a shameless harlot. Well, the rabbi liked to go into the woods and immerse himself in a pool there before saying his prayers. One morning he looked up and saw the Dobosh woman standing naked before him with her unloosened hair falling down her back. When he cried out the Holy Name, a whirlwind caught hold of her and carried her to the top of a tree. 'Rabbi, marry me,' she called out from the branch from which she was sitting, 'and we'll rule the world together.'"

"What a brazen female," Isaac Amshinover said.

"There's no mention of the story in the *Community of the Hasidim*," Meyer the eunuch remarked.

"*The Community of the Hasidim* doesn't contain everything. I had an encounter with a warlock myself. It happened in a forest just outside one of the villages near Radoshitz. It was a clear day and I'd been toting glass as usual. The night before I'd sleep in a granary. But I always went home for the Sabbath. I was walking along deep in thought when suddenly I saw the tiniest man; he was even smaller than a dwarf. I swear he wasn't any bigger than my arm. I looked at him and I couldn't figure out what he was. He was dressed like the gentry in a green coat, feathered hat, and red boots. In his hand he carried a hunter's leather bag. It seems to me that he was also bearing a rifle—you know the small kind boys carry on the Feast of Omer. I just stood and gawked. Even if he was a midget or a freak what was he doing walking by himself? I stopped to let him pass by, but he stopped, too. When I started to walk, he walked beside me. How could he take such long steps with such short legs, I asked myself. Well, it was clear enough that he was one of the devil's people. I recited, 'Hear, O Israel,' and '*Shaddai*, destroy Satan,' but it didn't do any good. Laughing, he aimed his rifle at me. Things looked bad, and so when I caught sight of a stone, I picked it up and heaved it at him. The guffaw he let loose made me shiver. Then he stuck out his tongue. You know how long it was? Right down to his navel."

"Didn't he hurt you?"

"No, he ran away."

"Were you wearing a charm?"

"I had a bag around my neck in which there was the tooth of a wolf and a talisman blessed by the saintly rabbi of Kozhenitz. I started wearing it when I was a child."

"Well, that must have been helpful."

"How do you know that it was a warlock?" Meyer the eunuch asked. "It could have been an imp or a mock demon."

"I found out his story later. His father, a rich landowner, left him his manor, but the boy got interested in witchcraft. He knew how to make himself small or large, could change himself into a cat or dog or whatever he pleased. He lived with an old servant who was deaf as a wall and did his cooking for him. He had more money than he knew what to do with. It was his wife's death that drove him to magic. Sometimes he used his sorcery to help people. But not often. He preferred to make fun of the villagers and frighten them."

"What happened to him?" Isaac Amshinover asked.

"I don't know. He was still alive when I moved away from Radoshitz. You know what happens to such people. In the end they fall into the bottomless pit."

2

There was silence when Zalman the glazier finished speaking. Then Isaac Amshinover, having taken out his pipe and lit it, inquired: "What's so amazing about a Gentile sorcerer? There were sorcerers even in Egypt. Didn't the Egyptian magicians vie with Moses? But I knew of a Jewish one. Well, maybe not really a sorcerer, but someone who did business with the evil ones. His father-in-law was an acquaintance of mine, Mordecai Liskover. A very wealthy man and learned, too. He had five sons and a daughter. The girl was named Pesha and he was crazy about her. His sons all married well. Half the town belonged to them. He had a watermill that was always busy. The peasants came there from miles around to line up with their carts. They thought that flour ground in his mill was blessed. Mordecai wanted to find Pesha—she was his youngest—the finest possible husband. He gave her a large dowry and promised to support her husband and her for the rest of their lives. So he went to a yeshiva and asked the principal to show him his smartest student. 'That's him,' the principal said, indicating a not very large boy. 'His name is Zeinvele. He may look small but he has more brains than all the scholars of Poland put together.' What more could one want? The boy was an orphan and was supported by the town. He was taken to Reb Mordecai's house, dressed up like a king, and given the betrothal papers to sign. Then Zeinvele was put up at an inn because it is forbidden for a man to live in the same house as his fiancée. He fed on squabs and marzipan. When he came to the study house, all the other boys tried to engage him in learned conversation, but he didn't say much. He was the sort of person to whom a word is like a gold coin. But what he did say was worth hearing. I can still see him as he was then, small, light-skinned, and beardless, standing in the study house reeling off an entire page of the Commentaries from memory. Reb Mordecai gave him clothes a size too large for him expecting him to grow into them.

His gaberdine dragged along the floor. Actually he never did get any bigger, but that's another story. When he discussed learned matters, he spoke very softly; he didn't speak about worldly matters at all, merely said yes or no when he was asked something. Sometimes he just nodded his head. He always sat by himself in some remote corner of the study house. The boys complained that he wasn't friendly. When he prayed, he stood looking out the window and didn't turn his head until he was finished. The window faced Synagogue Street and overlooked the cemetery.

"Well, so he wasn't interested in the world. The town respected him. Why shouldn't they have? He was to be Reb Mordecai's son-in-law. Then an odd thing happened. One night a boy walked into the study house looking as white as chalk. 'What's happened to you?' the others asked. 'Who scared you?' At first the fellow refused to answer. Then he took three of his friends aside, and after swearing them to secrecy, told them the following: While he was walking in the synagogue yard, he'd caught sight of Zeinvele standing near the poorhouse making curious motions with his hands. He knew that Zeinvele never studied at night. And anyway what was he doing near the poorhouse? Everyone knew the poorhouse was a dangerous place; the cleansing board on which the corpses were washed was kept leaning against its door. Two paths led to it; one from the town's outskirts and the other from the cemetery. The boy thought that perhaps Zeinvele being a stranger had lost his way, and called out, 'Zeinvele, what are you doing there?' No sooner did he say this than Zeinvele began to shrink until he became so small there was nothing left of him but a puff of smoke. Finally, even the smoke disappeared. The amazing thing was that the boy hadn't died of fright. 'Are you sure the tassels on your ritual garment are all there?' the other fellows asked. 'Maybe one of the letters in your mezuzah is missing?' It was clear to all of them that it was really one of the evil ones in disguise as Zeinvele. The incident was kept a secret. The town would have been saved a lot of trouble had it not been.

"The wedding was a noisy one. Musicians were brought from Lublin, Yukele the jester from far away Kovle. But Zeinvele didn't participate in the usual discussion of the Torah with his fellow students, nor pass around the cookies and drinks. He just sat at the head of the table as if he weren't there. He had such thick eyebrows it was difficult to tell whether he was meditating or asleep. There were those who even thought he was deaf. But all things pass away quickly. Zeinvele was married and moved in with his father-in-law. Now he sat in his corner of the study house reading the Tractate on Ablutions prescribed for newly married men. It wasn't very long, however, before Pesha started complaining that he didn't act like a young husband should. Though he did come to her bed after she had been to the ritual bath, he acted as cold as ice. Early one morning, Pesha ran weeping into her mother's bedroom. 'What's happened, daughter?' Well, according to Pesha, she'd been to the ritual bath the evening before and Zeinvele had gotten in bed with her. But when she'd glanced over at his bed expecting to find it empty, she'd found a second Zeinvele lying there. She'd become so frightened that she'd crawled under the featherbed and refused to come out. As soon as it was light, Zeinvele had gotten up and gone to his study. 'Daughter, you're imagining things,' her mother told her. But Pesha solemnly swore that she was telling the truth. 'Mother, I'm terrified,' she screamed. And her anxiety was so great that she fainted.

"How long can such matters be concealed? There really were two Zeinveles. Everybody realized it. Grabovitz did have a few sceptics who as usual with that sort made light of the matter. You know their sort of explanation: it was a hallucination, a fantasy, a morbid tendency, but for all of that, they were just as scared as everyone else. Zeinvele would be locked in his room lying asleep in his bed, but also he'd be wandering around the synagogue yard, or the market place. Sometimes he'd appear in the antechamber of the study house and stand there motionless near the wash basin until somebody realized that he was only the false Zeinvele. When that happened, he floated off and disintegrated like a cobweb.

"For some time no one said anything about this to Zeinvele. He may have had no idea himself of what was going on. But finally his wife Pesha refused to be quiet any longer. She announced that she would not sleep in the same room with him. They had to hire a night watchman. His father-in-law, thinking that Zeinvele would become alarmed and deny everything, confronted him with the facts, but he just stood there like a statue, not saying a word. So Reb Mordecai took him to the rabbi of Turisk who completely covered Zeinvele's body with talismans. But when Zeinvele returned home, nothing had changed. At night his mother-in-law locked the bedroom door from the outside and propped a heavy chair against it, but in spite of this Zeinvele continued to wander. At the sight of him dogs growled and horses reared in terror. The women didn't dare go out at night without putting on two aprons—one in the front and one in the rear. One evening a young townswoman went to the ritual bath and, after being washed down by the attendant in the anteroom, entered the bath chamber itself. As she descended the steps, she saw someone splashing around in the water. The candle in the room was flickering so badly she couldn't make out who it was. When she came closer and saw it was Zeinvele, she screamed and fainted. If the attendant hadn't been nearby, she would have drowned. The real Zeinvele happened to be in the study house at the moment. I was there myself and saw him. But actually it had become impossible to know which was the real Zeinvele and which the phantom. The townsboys now began to say that Zeinvele visited the ritual bath to peek at the naked women. Pesha said that she would no longer live with him. If he had had parents they would have shipped him home, but where can you send an orphan? His father-in-law took him to the rabbi and gave him a hundred gulden to divorce Pesha. I was one of the witnesses to the divorce papers. Pesha couldn't stop crying but Zeinvele sat quietly on the bench as if none of this concerned him. He seemed to be sleeping. The rabbi looked at the wall to make sure that Zeinvele was casting a shadow. Demons don't, you know. After the divorce Zeinvele was put in a cart Reb Mordecai had hired and taken to a yeshiva. The cart was driven by a Gentile, no Jew being willing to accept the job. When the coachman returned he clamed the Jews had bewitched him. His horses, though he had kept on whipping them, had refused to pull the wagon. He pointed to his team. They had left the marketplace healthy and had returned sick and wasted. Mordecai Liskover had to pay him damages. I was told that both horses died soon after.

"Even though Zeinvele was gone, people still continued to see him. They met him after dark at the flour mill, at the river where the women washed their linens, near the outhouse. Several times he was seen in the middle of the night standing like a chimney sweep on top of a roof. Students stopped studying in the evening knowing that Zeinvele liked to wander in the synagogue yard. Then when Pesha remarried, he disappeared. No one knows what happened to him. Somebody who visited the yeshiva he was supposed to have been taken to, said he never got there."

"Do you mean to imply by your story that the talismans of the rabbi of Turisk are ineffective?" Zalman the glazier asked.

"Not every talisman works."

"All of the rabbi of Kozhenitz's talismans do."

"How many such rabbis are there?"

3

Meyer the eunuch pulled at his naked chin. His left eye shut tightly and his right eye stared. Though he was now in his good period, he laughed insanely.

"What's so terribly novel about all that? We all know sorcerers exist. Maybe Zeinvele was innocent. He could have been bewitched. He might have been a mooncalf or a freak. Besides when a man sleeps, his spirit leaves him. Usually you can't see the spirit leaving the body, but sometimes it's visible. There was a woman in Krasnotstav who emitted a green light when she slept. When they put out the lamp, the wall near her bed lit up. I also know of a cat which after it had been drowned by a coachman came back to bite his nose. Everyone recognized the creature. It started to spit and mew and would have clawed out his eyes if he hadn't covered his face with his hands. The body dies but the spirit lives on. I speak of the spirit not the soul. Not everything has a soul. One has to have a certain merit to be worthy of having a soul. But even animals possess a spirit.

"Let me tell you about the Jenukah. You may not know it, Reb Zalman, but Jenukah means child in Aramaic. The Jenukah, as he was called, was the sixth child of Zekele, an ordinary water carrier. There didn't seem to be anything unusual

about him when he was born. He was circumcised just like his
brothers. His real name was Zaddock, after his grandfather.
However his mother began to complain that the baby was
growing too fast. But who listens to such talk from a woman?
Every mother thinks her child is the most wonderful. But three
months later, the whole town was gossiping about Zekele's
amazing child. At five months the boy was talking; at six
months he walked. When he was a year old, they wrapped him
in a prayer shawl and took him to school. We have newspapers
nowadays; in those times the Jews didn't. The boy was written
up in one of the Gentile papers. The governor sent a delegation to interview him and make a report. The town doctor
sent copies of his findings to Warsaw and Petersburg. All kinds
of university professors and experts visited the town. They
didn't believe that little Zaddock was only fifteen months old,
but there were plenty of witnesses. The birth had been registered at the town hall and the midwife had kept her own
record. The man who performed the circumcision, the rabbi
who held the baby at the ceremony, and the woman who had
handed the child to the latter, gave corroborating evidence.
Zaddock had to be taken out of school. To begin with, all of
the furor interrupted the classroom routine, and in the second
place he was just too bright for the other children. He took
one look at the alphabet and knew it by heart. When he was
eighteen months old, he was deep in the study of the Pentateuch and the Commentaries of Rashi. At two, he began his
study of the Gemara.

"I know it's hard to believe but I myself can attest to its
truth. Zekele, who was our water carrier, used to bring the boy
to our house to show him off. At three, Zaddock preached in
the synagogue. He opened his mouth and out spouted the
Torah. Anyone who wasn't present on that great Sabbath before Passover doesn't know what a miracle is. Even a blind
man could see that the child must be the reincarnation of
some ancient saint. At four he was as tall as an adolescent and
began to sprout a beard. That was when they started calling
him the Jenukah after the holy child in the *Zohar*. But we'd sit
here all night, if I told you everything about him. Why elaborate? At five Zaddock had a long beard. It was time for him to
have a wife but who would marry his daughter to a five-year-

old boy? Anyway, Zaddock was completely immersed in the Cabala. The community gave him a room and Zaddock spent his time there studying the *Zohar*, the *Tree of Life*, the *Book of Creation*, and the *Book of the Esoterics*. People offered to give him money to pray for them, but he refused. There are unbelievers everywhere, but whoever looked at Zaddock no longer doubted. On the Sabbath he sat at the head of the table presiding like a rabbi, and only a few select people were allowed to be with him. Even these learned men found it difficult to understand his profound exegesis. He had a special genius for translating the alphabet into numbers and creating acrostics. Sometimes, when he was in a forgetful mood, he would speak entirely in Aramaic. His handwriting was such that what he wrote had to be read in a mirror.

"Then suddenly the news came that the Jenukah was engaged. It seemed that in the neighboring town there was a rich man, seven of whose children had died before they were three. His only surviving child was a girl whom he dressed in white linen and called Altele, Little Old One, to fool the Angel of Death. I don't remember the man's name but he was advised by some rabbi to marry his daughter to the Jenukah. The girl was fourteen. The Jenukah at five looked like a man of forty. They didn't think he would consent, but he did. I went to the engagement party myself. The girl looked as if she were marrying her father. They signed the contract and broke plates for good luck. Throughout the ceremony, the Jenukah kept mumbling to himself. He was probably receiving instructions from Heaven. I don't know why, but both sides were anxious to get the wedding over with quickly. The engagement took place on Chanukah and the wedding was set for the Sabbath after Pentecost. It took place not in the bride's town, as was the custom, but in the bridegroom's, because it was feared that the sight of the Jenukah would be too much for people not accustomed to him. Eighty rabbis, all specialists in miracles, were invited. They came not only from Poland proper, but also from Volhynia and Galicia. Many freethinkers, doctors, and philosophers also attended. Among the guests were the governor of Lublin and I think the vice governor, too. Barren women came, hoping that their presence there would cure them. Someone brought a girl whose hiccups sounded like the barking of a dog. She recited whole chapters from the Mishnah and when she sang from the prayer book, her voice was deep as a cantor's. The inns were packed, word having got about that whoever attended the wedding would never be condemned to the fires of Gehenna. Many visitors had to sleep in the streets. The stores were emptied so quickly of food that wagons had to be sent to Lublin for more provisions.

"Now listen to this. Three days before the wedding the Jenukah's mother entered his room to bring him a cup of tea. She took one look and saw that his beard was as white as snow. His face was yellow and as lined as parchment. She called the rest of the family. Though a child not yet six-years-old, he had turned into a hoary sage. A crowd gathered, but was not let into the house. Someone informed the bride's parents of what had happened. But they didn't dare break the engagement.

"The day of his wedding at the feast for the young men, the Jenukah divulged mystery upon mystery. When the time came to lift the veil from the bride, the crowd surged forward wildly. The groom's attendants did not escort, but carried him. He seemed to be completely debilitated. When the bride saw that the Jenukah was an old man, she began to weep and protest, but finally was quieted. I was there myself and saw everything. When the bride and groom were served the golden soup, they scarcely touched it, though both had fasted. The musicians were afraid to play. The jester didn't open his mouth. The Jenukah sat at the head of the table, holding his hands over his eyes. I don't remember whether he danced with the bride or not. He lived only three months more. Each day he became whiter and more shrunken. He drooped and melted like a wax candle. The last few days of his life no strangers were allowed in his room, not even the doctor. The Jenukah, dressed in a white robe, and wearing his prayer shawl and phylacteries, sat like an ancient saint not of this world. He stopped eating. When they gave him a spoonful of soup, he couldn't swallow it. I happened to be out of town when the Jenukah died, but I was told that at the moment of death his face shone like the sun. You couldn't pass near the house without feeling the heat of his saintly radiance. An apothecary who came to ridicule him became a believer and put peas in his boots as penance. A priest was converted. Those who were at the deathbed heard the beating of an angel's wings. The Jenukah had ordered that his shroud be made while he was still living. He died with the finishing of the last stitch.

"When the men from the Burial Society came, they found almost no body left to wash. With such saints, even matter turns into spirit. The pallbearers said that the corpse was lighter than a bird's. The eulogies took three days to complete. Afterwards, the community raised money to build a chapel on the grave in which was to burn an eternal light. Zekele was provided with a pension. One should receive something for being the father of such a son."

"What happened to the widow?" Zalman the glazier asked.

"She never remarried."

"Was there a child?"

"Ridiculous."

"Did she live long?"

"She's still alive."

"Who was the Jenukah really?" Isaac Amshinover wanted to know.

"How can you tell? Sometimes a soul is sent down from Heaven which has to fulfill its mission in a hurry. Why are some babies born who live only one day? Every soul descends to earth to correct some error. It's the same with souls as with manuscripts; there may be few or many errors. Everything that's wrong on this earth has to be corrected. The world of evil is the world of correction. This is the answer to all questions."

Translated by Ruth Whitman and Cecil Hemley

Zeidlus the Pope

I N ancient times there always lived a few men in every generation whom I, the Evil One, could not corrupt in the usual
manner. It was impossible to tempt them to murder, lechery,
robbery. I could not even get them to cease studying the Law.
In one way only could the inner passions of these righteous
souls be reached: through their vanity.

Zeidel Cohen was such a man. In the first place, he had the
protection of noble ancestors: he was a descendant of Rashi
whose genealogy reached back to King David. In the second
place, he was the greatest scholar in the whole province of
Lublin. At five he had studied the Gemara and Commentaries;
at seven he had memorized the Laws of Marriage and Divorce;
at nine, he had preached a sermon, quoting from so many
books that even the oldest among the scholars were confounded. He was completely at home in the Bible; in Hebrew
grammar he had no equal. What is more he studied constantly:
summer and winter alike he rose with the morning star and
began to read. As he seldom left his rooms for air and did no
physical labor, he had little appetite and slept lightly. He had
neither the desire nor the patience to converse with friends.
Zeidel loved only one thing: books. The moment he entered
the study house, or his own home for that matter, he ran
straight to the shelves and began to leaf through volumes,
sucking into his lungs the dust from ancient pages. So strong
was his power of memory that one look at some passage in the
Talmud, at some new interpretation in a Commentary and he
could remember it forever.

Nor could I gain power over Zeidel through his body. His
limbs were hairless; by seventeen his pointed skull was bald;
only a few hairs grew on his chin. His face was long and stiff;
three or four drops of perspiration always hung on the high
forehead; his crooked nose was strangely naked, like that of a
man who is accustomed to wearing glasses but has just taken
them off. He had reddish eyelids behind which lay a pair of
yellow, melancholy eyes. His hands and feet were small and
white as a woman's, though as he never visited the ritual bath

it was not known if he was a eunuch or an androgyne. But since his father, Reb Sander Cohen, was extremely rich, himself a scholar and a man of some note, he saw to it that his son made a match befitting the family. The bride came from a rich Warsaw family and was a beauty. Until the day of the wedding she had never seen the groom, and when she did set eyes upon him, just before he covered her face with the veil, it was already too late. She married him and was never able to conceive. She spent her time sitting in the rooms her father-in-law had allotted to her, knitting stockings, reading storybooks, listening to the large wall-clock with its gilded chains and weights ring out the half-hours—patiently waiting, it seemed, for the minutes to become days, the days years, until the time should come for her to go to sleep in the old Janov cemetery.

Zeidel possessed such intensity that all his surroundings acquired his character. Though a servant took care of his rooms, the furniture was always covered with dust; the windows, hung with heavy drapes, seemed never to have been opened; thick rugs covered the floors muffling his footsteps so that it sounded as if a spirit, not a man, were walking there. Zeidel received regularly an allowance from his father, but he never spent a penny on himself. He hardly knew what a coin looked like, yet he was a miser and never took a poor man home for a Sabbath meal. He never took the trouble to make friends, and since neither he nor his wife ever invited a guest, no one knew what the interior of their house looked like.

Untroubled by passions or the need to make a living, Zeidel studied diligently. He first devoted himself to the Talmud and the Commentaries. Then he delved into the Cabala and soon became an expert on the occult, even writing tracts on *The Angel Raziel* and *The Book of Creation*. Naturally he was well acquainted with *The Guide for the Perplexed*, the *Kuzari*, and other philosophical works. One day he happened to acquire a copy of the Vulgate. Soon he had learned Latin, and he began to read extensively in the forbidden literature, borrowing many books from a scholarly priest who lived in Janov. In short, just as his father had accumulated gold coins all his life, so Zeidel accumulated knowledge. By the time he was thirty-five no one in all Poland could equal him in learning. Just then I was ordered to tempt him to sin.

"Persuade Zeidel to sin?" I asked. "What kind of sin? He doesn't enjoy food, is indifferent to women, and never has anything to do with business." I have tried heresy before, without success. I remembered our last conversation:

"Let's assume that, God forbid, there is no God," he had answered me. "So what? Then His non-being itself is divine. Only God, the Cause of all Causes, could have the power not to exist."

"If there is no Creator, why do you pray and study?" I continued.

"What else should I do?" he asked in return. "Drink vodka and dance with Gentile girls?"

To tell the truth I had no answer to that, so I left him in peace. His father had since died, and now I was ordered to devote myself to him again. With not the slightest idea of how to begin, I descended to Janov with a heavy heart.

2

I discovered after some time that Zeidel possessed one human weakness: haughtiness. He had much more than that sliver of vanity which the Law permits the scholar.

I laid my plans. In the middle of one night, I woke him from his slumber and said: "Do you know, Zeidel, that you are better versed than any rabbi in Poland in the fine print of the Commentaries?"

"Certainly I know it," he replied. "But who else does? Nobody."

"Do you know, Zeidel, that you outshine all other grammarians in your knowledge of Hebrew?" I continued. "Are you aware that you know more of the Cabala than was divulged to Reb Chaim Vital? Do you know that you are a greater philosopher than Maimonides?"

"Why are you telling me these things?" Zeidel asked, wondering.

"I'm telling you because it's not right that a great man such as you, a master of the Torah, an encyclopedia of knowledge, should be buried in a God-forsaken village such as this where no one pays the slightest attention to you, where the townspeople are coarse and the rabbi an ignoramus, with a wife who has no understanding of your true worth. You are a pearl lost in sand, Reb Zeidel."

"Well?" he asked. "What can I do? Should I go about singing my own praises?"

"No, Reb Zeidel. That wouldn't help you. The town would only call you a madman."

"What do you advise, then?"

"Promise me not to interrupt and I'll tell you. You know the Jews have never honored their leaders: They grumbled about Moses; rebelled against Samuel; threw Jeremiah into a ditch; and murdered Zacharias. The Chosen People hate greatness. In a great man, they sense a rival to Jehovah, so they love only the petty and mediocre. Their thirty-six saints are all shoe-makers and water-carriers. The Jewish laws are concerned mainly with a drop of milk falling into a pot of meat or with an egg laid on a holiday. They have deliberately corrupted Hebrew, degraded the ancient texts. Their Talmud makes King David into a provincial rabbi advising women about menstruation. The way they reason, the smaller the greater, the uglier the prettier. Their rule is: The closer one is to dust, the nearer one is to God. So you can see, Reb Zeidel, why they find you a thumb in the eye—you with your erudition, wealth, fine breeding, brilliant perceptions, and extraordinary memory."

"Why do you tell me all these things?" Zeidel asked.

"Reb Zeidel, listen to me: what you must do is become a Christian. The Gentiles are the antithesis of the Jews. Since their God is a man, a man can be a God to them. Gentiles admire greatness of any kind and love the men who possess it: men of great pity or great cruelty, great builders or great destroyers, great virgins or great harlots, great sages or great fools, great rulers or great rebels, great believers or great infidels. They don't care what else a man is: if he is great, they idolize him. Therefore, Reb Zeidel, if you want honor, you must embrace their faith. And don't worry about God. To One so mighty and sublime the earth and its inhabitants are no more than a swarm of gnats. He doesn't care whether men pray to Him in a synagogue or a church, fast from Sabbath to Sabbath or bloat themselves with pork. He is too exalted to notice these puny creatures who delude themselves thinking that they are the crown of Creation."

"Does that mean God did not give the Torah to Moses at Sinai?" Zeidel asked.

"What? God open His heart to a man born of woman?"

"And Jesus was not His son?"

"Jesus was a bastard from Nazareth."

"Is there no reward or punishment?"

"No."

"Then what is there?" Zeidel asked me, fearful and confused.

"There is something that exists, but it has no existence," I answered in the manner of the philosophers.

"Is there no hope then ever to know the truth?" Zeidel asked in despair.

"The world is not knowable and there is no truth," I replied, turning his question around. "Just as you can't learn the taste of salt with your nose, the smell of balsam with your ear, or the sound of a violin with your tongue, it's impossible for you to grasp the world with your reason."

"With what can you grasp it?"

"With your passions—some small part of it. But you, Reb Zeidel, have only one passion: pride. If you destroy that too, you'll be hollow, a void."

"What should I do?" Zeidel asked, baffled.

"Tomorrow, go to the priest and tell him that you want to become one of them. Then sell your goods and property. Try to convince your wife to change her religion—if she's willing, good; if not, the loss is small. The Gentiles will make you a priest and a priest is not allowed to have a wife. You'll continue to study, to wear a long coat and skullcap. The only difference will be that instead of being stuck away in a remote village among Jews who hate you and your accomplishments, praying in a sunken hole of a study house where beggars scratch themselves behind the stove, you will live in a large city, preach in a luxurious church where an organ will play, and where your congregation will consist of men of stature whose wives will kiss your hand. If you excel and throw together some hodgepodge about Jesus and his mother the Virgin, they will make you a bishop, and later a cardinal—and God willing, if everything goes well, they'll make you Pope one day. Then the Gentiles will carry you on a gilded chair like an idol and burn incense around you; and they'll kneel before your image in Rome, Madrid, and Crackow."

"What will my name be?" asked Zeidel.

"Zeidus the First."

So great an impression did my words make that Zeidel started violently and sat up in bed. His wife awoke and asked why he wasn't sleeping. With some hidden instinct, she knew he was possessed by a great desire, and thought: Who knows, perhaps a miracle has happened. But Zeidel had already made up his mind to divorce her, so he told her to keep still and not ask any more questions. Putting on his slippers and robe, he went to his study, where he lit a wax candle and sat until dawn re-reading the Vulgate.

3

Zeidel did as I advised. He went to the priest and let him know that he wished to speak about matters of faith. Of course the Gentile was more than willing. What better merchandise is there for a priest than a Jewish soul? Anyway, to cut a long story short, priests and noblemen from the entire province promised Zeidel a great career in the Church; he quickly sold all his possessions, divorced his wife, let himself be baptized with holy water, and became a Christian. For the first time in his life, Zeidel was honored: the ecclesiastics made a big fuss over him, the noblemen lavished praise on him, their wives smiled benignly at him, and he was invited to their estates. The Bishop of Zamosc was his godfather. His name was changed from Zeidel son of Sander to Benedictus Janovsky—the surname in honor of the village where he had been born. Although Zeidel was not yet a priest or even a deacon, he ordered a black cassock from a tailor and hung a rosary and cross around his neck. For the time being, he lived in the priest's rectory, seldom venturing out because when he did Jewish schoolboys ran after him in the streets shouting, "Convert! Apostate!"

His Gentile friends had many different plans for him. Some advised him to go to a seminary and study; others recommended that he enter the Dominican priory in Lublin. Still others suggested he marry a wealthy local woman and become a squire. But Zeidel had little inclination to travel the usual road. He wanted greatness immediately. He knew that in the past many Jewish converts to Christianity had become famous by writing polemics against the Talmud—Petrus Alfonzo, Fablo Christiani of Montpelier, Paul de Santa Maria, Johann Baptista, Johann Pfefferkorn, to mention only a few. Zeidel decided to follow in their footsteps. Now that he had converted and Jewish children abused him in the streets, he suddenly discovered that he had never loved the Talmud. Its Hebrew was debased by Aramaic; its pilpul was dull, its legends improbable, and its Biblical Commentaries were far-fetched and full of sophistries.

Zeidel traveled to the seminary libraries in Lublin and Crackow to study the treatises written by Jewish converts. He soon discovered they were all much alike. The authors were ignorant, plagiarized from one another liberally, and all cited the same few anti-Gentile passages from the Talmud. Some of them had not even used their own words, had copied the work of others and signed their names. The real *Apologia Contra Talmudum* had yet to be written, and no one was better prepared to do such a work than he with his knowledge of philosophy and the Cabalistic mysteries. At the same time, Zeidel undertook to find fresh proofs in the Bible that the prophets had foreseen Jesus' birth, martyrdom, and resurrection; and to discover corroborative evidence for the Christian religion in logic, astronomy, and natural science. Zeidel's treatise would be for Christianity what Maimonides' *The Strong Hand* was for Judaism—and it would carry its author from Janov directly to the Vatican.

Zeidel studied, thought, wrote, sitting all day and half the night in libraries. From time to time he met Christian scholars and conversed with them in Polish and Latin. With the same fervor that he had studied Jewish books, he now studied the Christian texts. Soon he could recite whole chapters of the New Testament. He became an expert Latinist. After a while he was so thoroughly versed in Christian theology that the priests and monks were afraid to talk to him for with his erudition he found mistakes everywhere. Many times he was promised a seminary appointment but somehow he never got one. A post as librarian in Crackow which was to be his went to a relative of the governor instead. Zeidel began to realize that even among the Gentiles things were far from perfect. The clergy cared more for gold than for their God. Their sermons were full of errors. Most of the priests did not know Latin, but even in Polish their quotations were incorrect.

For years Zeidel worked on his treatise, but still it was not finished. His standards were so high that he was continually finding flaws, yet the more changes he made, the more he found were necessary. He wrote, crossed out, rewrote, threw away. His drawers were stuffed with manuscript pages, notes, references, but he could not bring his work to a conclusion. After years of effort, he was so fatigued that he could no longer distinguish between right and wrong, sense and non-sense, between what would please and what displease the Church. Nor did he believe any more in what is called truth and falsehood. Nevertheless he continued to ponder, to come up occasionally with a few new ideas. He consulted the Talmud so often in his work that once more he delved into its depths, scribbling notes on the margins of the pages, comparing all the different texts, hardly knowing whether he did so to find new accusations or simply out of habit. At times, he read books about witch trials, accounts of young women possessed by the devil, documents of the Inquisitions, whatever manuscripts he could find that described such events in various countries and epochs.

Gradually, the bag of gold coins that hung around his neck became lighter. His face turned yellow as parchment. His eyes dimmed. His hands trembled like an old man's. His cassock was stained and torn. His hope to become famous among the nations vanished. He came to regret his conversion. But the way back was blocked: first because he doubted all faiths now; second because it was the law of the land that a Christian who returned to Judiasm should be burned at the stake.

One day while Zeidel was sitting, studying a faded manuscript in the library in Crackow, everything went dark before his eyes. At first he thought dusk had fallen and asked why the candles had not been lit. But when a monk told him that the day was still bright, he realized he had gone blind. Unable to return home alone, Zeidel had to be led by the monk. From that time on Zeidel lived in darkness. Fearing that his money would soon run out and he would be left without a groschen as well as without eyes, Zeidel decided, after much hesitation, to become a beggar outside the church of Crackow. "I have lost both this world and the world to come," he reasoned, "so why be haughty? If there is no way up, one must go down." Thus Zeidel son of Sander, or Benedictus Janovsky, took his place among the beggars on the steps of the great cathedral of Crackow.

In the beginning the priests and canons tried to help him. They wanted to put him into a cloister. But Zeidel had no wish to become a monk. He wanted to sleep alone in his garret, and to continue to carry his money bag under his shirt. Nor was he inclined to kneel before an altar. Occasionally a seminary student would stop to talk with him for a few minutes on scholarly matters. But in a short while, everyone forgot him. Zeidel hired an old woman to lead him to the church in the morning and home at night. She also brought him a bowl of groats each day. Good-hearted Gentiles threw him alms. He was even able to save some money, and the bag around his neck became heavy again. The other mendicants mocked him, but Zeidel never replied. For hours he kneeled on the steps, his bald skull uncovered, his eyes closed, his black robe buttoned to the chin. His lips never ceased shaking and murmuring. Passers-by thought he was praying to the Christian saints, but actually he was reciting the Gemara, the Mishnah, and the Psalms. The Gentile theology he had forgotten as quickly as he had learned it; what remained was what he had acquired in his youth. The street was full of tumult: wagons rolled by on the cobblestones; horses neighed; coachmen screamed with hoarse voices and cracked their whips; girls laughed and screeched; children cried; women quarreled, called one another names, uttered obscenities. Every once in a while Zeidel stopped murmuring, but only to doze with his head sunken into his chest. He no longer had any earthly desire, but one yearning still plagued him: to know the truth. Was there a Creator or was the world nothing but atoms and their combinations? Did the soul exist or was all thought mere reverberations of the brain? Was there a final accounting with reward and punishment? Was there a Substance or was the whole of existence nothing but imagination? The sun burned down on him, the rains soaked him, pigeons soiled him with their droppings, but he was impervious to everything. Now that he had lost his only passion, pride, nothing material mattered to him. Sometimes he asked himself: Is it possible that I am Zeidel the prodigy? Was my father Reb Sander, the leader of the community? Did I really have a wife once? Are there still some who knew me? It seemed to Zeidel that none of these things could be true. Such events had never happened, and if they had not, reality itself was one great illusion.

One morning when the old woman came to Zeidel's attic room to take him to the church, she found him ill. Waiting until he dozed off, she stealthily cut the bag of money from around his neck and left. In his stupor Zeidel knew he was being robbed, but he didn't care. His head lay as heavy as a stone on the straw pillow. His feet ached. His joints were filled with pain. His emaciated body was hot and hollow. Zeidel fell asleep, awoke, dozed off; then he awoke again with a start, unable to tell whether it was night or day. Out in the streets he heard voices, screams, stamping hoofs, ringing bells. It seemed to him some pagan multitude was celebrating a holiday with trumpets and drums, torches and wild beasts, lascivious dances, idolatrous sacrifices. "Where am I?" he asked himself. He could not remember the name of the city; he had even forgotten he was in Poland. He thought he might be in Athens, or Rome, or perhaps he was in Carthage. "In what age do I live?" he wondered. His fevered brain made him think it was hundreds of years before the Christian era. Soon he tired from too much thought. Only one question remained to perplex him: Are the Epicureans right? Am I really dying without any revelation? Am I about to be extinguished forever?

Suddenly I, the Tempter, materialized. Although blind, he saw me. "Zeidel," I said, "prepare yourself. The last hour has come."

"Is it you, Satan, Angel of Death?" Zeidel exclaimed joyously.

"Yes, Zeidel," I replied, "I have come for you. And it won't help you to repent or confess, so don't try."

"Where are you taking me?" he asked.

"Straight to Gehenna."

"If there is a Gehenna, there is also a God," Zeidel said, his lips trembling.

"This proves nothing," I retorted.

"Yes it does," he said. "If Hell exists, everything exists. If you are real, He is real. Now take me to where I belong. I am ready."

Drawing my sword I finished him off, took hold of his soul in my claws and, accompanied by a band of demons, flew to the nether world. In Gehenna the Angels of Destruction were raking up the coals. Two mocking imps stood at the threshold, half-fire and half-pitch, each with a three-cornered hat on his head, a whipping rod on his loins. They burst out laughing.

"Here comes Zeidlus the First," one said to the other, "the yeshiva boy who wanted to become Pope."

Translated by Joel Blocker and Elizabeth Pollet

A Wedding in Brownsville

THE WEDDING had been a burden to Dr. Solomon Margolin from the very beginning. True, it was to take place on a Sunday, but Gretl had been right when she said that was the only evening in the week they could spend together. It always turned out that way. His responsibilities to the community made him give away the evenings that belonged to her. The Zionists had appointed him to a committee; he was a board member of a Jewish scholastic society; he had become co-editor of an academic Jewish quarterly. And though he often referred to himself as an agnostic and even an atheist, nevertheless for years he had been dragging Gretl to Seders at Abraham Mekheles', a *Landsman* from Sencimin. Dr. Margolin treated rabbis, refugees, and Jewish writers without charge, supplying them with medicines and, if necessary, a hospital bed. There had been a time when he had gone regularly to the meetings of the Senciminer Society, had accepted positions in their ranks, and had attended all the parties. Now Abraham Mekheles was marrying off his youngest daughter, Sylvia. The minute the invitation arrived, Gretl had announced her decision: she was not going to let herself be carted off to a wedding somewhere out in the wilds of Brownsville. If he, Solomon, wanted to go and gorge himself on all kinds of greasy food, coming home at three o'clock in the morning, that was his prerogative.

Dr. Margolin admitted to himself that his wife was right. When would he get a chance to sleep? He had to be at the hospital early Monday morning. Moreover he was on a strict fat-free diet. A wedding like this one would be a feast of poisons. Everything about such celebrations irritated him now: the Anglicized Yiddish, the Yiddishized English, the ear-splitting music and unruly dances. Jewish laws and customs were completely distorted; men who had no regard for Jewishness wore skullcaps; and the reverend rabbis and cantors aped the Christian ministers. Whenever he took Gretl to a wedding or Bar Mitzvah, he was ashamed. Even she, born a Christian, could see that American Judaism was a mess. At least this time he would be spared the trouble of making apologies to her.

Usually after breakfast on Sunday, he and his wife took a walk in Central Park, or, when the weather was mild, went to the Palisades. But today Solomon Margolin lingered in bed. During the years, he had stopped attending the functions of the Senciminer Society; meanwhile the town of Sencimin had been destroyed. His family there had been tortured, burned, gassed. Many Senciminers had survived, and, later, come to America from the camps, but most of them were younger people whom he, Solomon, had not known in the old country. Tonight everyone would be there: the Senciminers belonging to the bride's family and the Tereshpolers belonging to the groom's. He knew how they would pester him, reproach him for growing aloof, drop hints that he was a snob. They would address him familiarly, slap him on the back, drag him off to dance. Well, even so, he had to go to Sylvia's wedding. He had already sent out the present.

The day had dawned, gray and dreary as dusk. Overnight, a heavy snow had fallen. Solomon Margolin had hoped to make up for the sleep he was going to lose, but unfortunately he had waked even earlier than usual. Finally he got up. He shaved himself meticulously at the bathroom mirror and also trimmed the gray hair at his temples. Today of all days he looked his age: there were bags under his eyes, and his face was lined. Exhaustion showed in his features. His nose appeared longer and sharper than usual; there were deep folds at the sides of his mouth. After breakfast he stretched out on the living-room sofa. From there he could see Gretl, who was standing in the kitchen, ironing—blonde, faded, middle-aged. She had on a skimpy petticoat, and her calves were as muscular as a dancer's. Gretl had been a nurse in the Berlin hospital where he had been a member of the staff. Of her family, one brother, a Nazi, had died of typhus in a Russian prison camp. A second, who was a Communist, had been shot by the Nazis. Her aged father vegetated at the home of his other daughter in Hamburg, and Gretl sent him money regularly. She herself had become almost Jewish in New York. She had made friends with Jewish women, joined Hadassah, learned to cook Jewish dishes. Even her sigh was Jewish. And she lamented continually over the Nazi catastrophe. She had her plot waiting for her beside his in that part of the cemetery that the Senciminers had reserved for themselves.

Dr. Margolin yawned, reached for the cigarette that lay in an ashtray on the coffee table beside him, and began to think about himself. His career had gone well. Ostensibly he was a success. He had an office on West End Avenue and wealthy patients. His colleagues respected him, and he was an important figure in Jewish circles in New York. What more could a boy from Sencimin expect? A self-taught man, the son of a poor teacher of Talmud? In person he was tall, quite handsome, and he had always had a way with women. He still pursued them— more than was good for him at his age and with his high blood pressure. But secretly Solomon Margolin had always felt that he was a failure. As a child he had been acclaimed a prodigy, reciting long passages of the Bible and studying the Talmud and Commentaries on his own. When he was a boy of eleven, he had sent for a Responsum to the rabbi of Tarnow who had referred to him in his reply as "great and illustrious." In his teens he had become a master in the *Guide for the Perplexed* and the Kuzari. He had taught himself algebra and geometry. At seventeen he had attempted a translation of Spinoza's *Ethics* from Latin into Hebrew, unaware that it had been done before. Everyone predicted he would turn out to be a genius. But he had squandered his talents, continually changing his field of study; and he had wasted years in learning languages, in wandering from country to country. Nor had he had any luck with his one great love, Raizel, the daughter of Melekh the watchmaker. Raizel had married someone else and later had been shot by the Nazis. All his life Solomon Margolin had been plagued by the eternal questions. He still lay awake at night trying to solve the mysteries of the universe. He suffered from hypochondria and the fear of death haunted even his dreams. Hitler's carnage and the extinction of his family had rooted out his last hope for better days, had destroyed all his faith in humanity. He had begun to despise the matrons who came to him with their petty ills while millions were devising horrible deaths for one another.

Gretl came in from the kitchen.

"What shirt are you going to put on?"

Solomon Margolin regarded her quietly. She had had her own share of troubles. She had suffered in silence for her two brothers, even for Hans, the Nazi. She had gone through a prolonged change of life. She was tortured by guilt feelings toward him, Solomon. She had become sexually frigid. Now her face was flushed and covered with beads of sweat. He earned more than enough to pay for a maid, yet Gretl insisted on doing all the housework herself, even the laundry. It had become a mania with her. Every day she scoured the oven. She was forever polishing the windows of their apartment on the sixteenth floor and without using a safety belt. All the other housewives in the building ordered their groceries delivered, but Gretl lugged the heavy bags from the supermarket herself. At night she sometimes said things that sounded slightly insane to him. She still suspected him of carrying on with every female patient he treated.

Now husband and wife sized each other up wryly, feeling the strangeness that comes of great familiarity. He was always amazed at how she had lost her looks. No one feature had altered, but something in her aspect had given way: her pride, her hopefulness, her curiosity. He blurted out:

"What shirt? It doesn't matter. A white shirt."

"You're not going to wear the tuxedo? Wait, I'll bring you a vitamin."

"I don't want a vitamin."

"But you yourself say they're good for you."

"Leave me alone."

"Well, it's your health, not mine."

And slowly she walked out of the room, hesitating as if she expected him to remember something and call her back.

2

Dr. Solomon Margolin took a last look in the mirror and left the house. He felt refreshed by the half-hour nap he had had after dinner. Despite his age, he still wanted to impress people with his appearance—even the Senciminers. He had his illusions. In Germany he had taken pride in the fact that he looked like a *Junker*, and in New York he was often aware that he could pass for an Anglo-Saxon. He was tall, slim, blond, blue-eyed. His hair was thinning, had turned somewhat gray, but he managed to disguise these signs of age. He stooped a little, but in company was quick to straighten up. Years ago in Germany he had worn a monocle and though in New York that would have been too pretentious, his glance still retained a European severity. He had his principles. He had never broken the Hippocratic Oath. With his patients he was honorable to an extreme, avoiding every kind of cant; and he had refused a number of dubious associations that smacked of careerism. Gretl claimed his sense of honor amounted to a mania. Dr. Margolin's car was in the garage—not a Cadillac like that of most of his colleagues—but he decided to go by taxi. He was unfamiliar with Brooklyn and the heavy snow made driving hazardous. He waved his hand and at once a taxi pulled over to the curb. He was afraid the driver might refuse to go as far as Brownsville, but he flicked the meter on without a word. Dr. Margolin peered through the frosted window into the wintry Sunday night but there was nothing to be seen. The New York streets sprawled out, wet, dirty, impenetrably dark. After a while, Dr. Margolin leaned back, shut his eyes, and retreated into his own warmth. His destination was a wedding. Wasn't the world, like this taxi, plunging away somewhere into the unknown toward a cosmic destination? Maybe a cosmic Brownsville, a cosmic wedding? Yes. But why did God—or whatever anyone wanted to call Him—create a Hitler, a Stalin? Why did He need world wars? Why heart attacks, cancers? Dr. Margolin took out a cigarette and lit it hesitantly. What had they been thinking of, those pious uncles of his, when they were digging their own graves? Was immortality possible? Was there such a thing as the soul? All the arguments for and against weren't worth a pinch of dust.

The taxi turned onto the bridge across the East River and for the first time Dr. Margolin was able to see the sky. It sagged low, heavy, red as glowing metal. Higher up, a violet glare suffused the vault of the heavens. Snow was sifting down gently, bringing a winter peace to the world, just as it had in the past—forty years ago, a thousand years ago, and perhaps a million years ago. Fiery pillars appeared to glow beneath the East River; on its surface, through black waves jagged as rocks, a tugboat was hauling a string of barges loaded with cars. A front window in the cab was open and icy gusts of wind blew in, smelling of gasoline and the sea. Suppose the weather never changed again? Who then would ever be able to imagine a summer day, a moonlit night, spring? But how much imagination—for what it's worth—does a man actually have? On Eastern Parkway the taxi was jolted and screeched suddenly to a stop. Some traffic accident, apparently. The siren on a police car shrieked. A wailing ambulance drew nearer. Dr. Margolin grimaced. Another victim. Someone makes a false turn of the wheel and all a man's plans in this world are reduced to nothing. A wounded man was carried to the ambulance on a stretcher. Above a dark suit and blood-spattered shirt and bow tie the face had a chalky pallor; one eye was closed, the other partly open and glazed. Perhaps he, too, had been going to a wedding, Dr. Margolin thought. He might even have been going to the same wedding as I. . . .

Some time later the taxi started moving again. Solomon Margolin was now driving through streets he had never seen before. It was New York, but it might just as well have been Chicago or Cleveland. They passed through an industrial district with factory buildings, warehouses of coal, lumber, scrap iron. Negroes, strangely black, stood about on the sidewalks, staring ahead, their great dark eyes full of a gloomy hopelessness. Occasionally the car would pass a tavern. The people at the bar seemed to have something unearthly about them, as if they were being punished here for sins committed in another incarnation. Just when Solomon Margolin was beginning to suspect that the driver, who had remained stubbornly silent the whole time, had gotten lost or else was deliberately taking him out of his way, the taxi entered a thickly populated neighborhood. They passed a synagogue, a funeral parlor, and there, ahead, was the wedding hall, all lit up, with its neon Jewish sign and Star of David. Dr. Margolin gave the driver a dollar tip and the man took it without uttering a word.

Dr. Margolin entered the outer lobby and immediately the comfortable intimacy of the Senciminers engulfed him. All the faces he saw were familiar, though he didn't recognize individuals. Leaving his hat and coat at the checkroom, he put on a skullcap and entered the hall. It was filled with people and music, with tables heaped with food, a bar stacked with bottles. The musicians were playing an Israeli march that was a hodgepodge of American jazz with Oriental flourishes. Men were dancing with men, women with women, men with women. He saw black skullcaps, white skullcaps, bare heads. Guests kept arriving, pushing their way through the crowd, some still in their hats and coats, munching hors d'oeuvres, drinking schnapps. The hall resounded with stamping, screaming, laughing, clapping. Flash bulbs went off blindingly as the photographers made their rounds. Seeming to come from nowhere, the bride appeared, briskly sweeping up her train, followed by a retinue of bridesmaids. Dr. Margolin knew everybody, and yet knew nobody. People spoke to him, laughed, winked, and waved, and he answered each one with a smile, a nod, a bow. Gradually he threw off all his worries, all his depression. He became half-drunk on the amalgam of odors: flowers, sauerkraut, garlic, perfume, mustard, and that nameless odor that only Senciminers emit. "Hello, Doctor!" "Hello, Schloime-Dovid, you don't recognize me, eh? Look, he forgot!" There were the encounters, the regrets, the reminiscences of long ago. "But after all, weren't we neighbors? You used to come to our house to borrow the Yiddish newspaper!" Someone had already kissed him: a badly shaven snout, a mouth reeking of whiskey and rotten teeth. One woman was so convulsed with laughter that she lost an earring. Margolin tried to pick it up, but it had already been trampled underfoot. "You don't recognize me, eh? Take a good look! It's Zissl, the son of Chaye Beyle!" "Why don't you eat something?" "Why don't you have something to drink? Come over here. Take a glass. What do you want? Whiskey? Brandy? Cognac? Scotch? With soda? With Coca Cola? Take some, it's good. Don't let it stand. So long as you're here, you might as well enjoy yourself." "My father? He was killed. They were all killed. I'm the only one left of the entire family." "Berish the son of Feivish? Starved to death in Russia—they sent him to Kazakhstan. His wife? In Israel. She married a Lithuanian." "Sorele? Shot. Together with her children." "Yentl? Here at the wedding. She was standing here just a moment ago. There she is, dancing with that tall fellow." "Abraham Zilberstein? They burned him in the synagogue with twenty others. A mound of charcoal was all that was left, coal and ash." "Yosele Budnik? He passed away years ago. You must mean Yekele Budnik. He has a delicatessen store right here in Brownsville —married a widow whose husband made a fortune in real estate."

"*Lechayim*, Doctor! *Lechayim*, Schloime-Dovid! It doesn't offend you that I call you Schloime-Dovid? To me you're still the same Schloime-Dovid, the little boy with the blond side-curls who recited a whole tractate of the Talmud by heart. You remember, don't you? It seems like only yesterday. Your father, may he rest in peace, was beaming with pride. . . ." "Your brother Chayim? Your Uncle Oyzer? They killed everyone, everyone. They took a whole people and wiped them out with German efficiency: *gleichgeschaltet!*" "Have you seen the bride yet? Pretty as a picture, but too much make-up. Imagine, a grandchild of Reb Todros of Radzin! And her grandfather used to wear two skullcaps, one in front and one in back." "Do you see that young woman dancing in the yellow dress? It's Riva's sister—their father was Moishe the candlemaker. Riva herself? Where all the others ended up: Auschwitz. How close we came ourselves! All of us are really dead, if you want to call it that. We were exterminated, wiped out. Even the survivors carry death in their hearts. But it's a wedding, we should be cheerful." "*Lechayim*, Schloime-Dovid! I would like to congratulate you. Have you a son or daughter to marry off? No? Well, it's better that way. What's the sense of having children if people are such murderers?"

3

It was already time for the ceremony, but someone still had not come. Whether it was the rabbi, the cantor, or one of the in-laws who was missing, nobody seemed able to find out. Abraham Mekheles, the bride's father, rushed around, scowled, waved his hand, whispered in people's ears. He looked strange in his rented tuxedo. The Tereshpol mother-in-law was wrangling with one of the photographers. The musicians never stopped playing for an instant. The drum banged, the bass fiddle growled, the saxophone blared. The dances became faster, more abandoned, and more and more people were drawn in. The young men stamped with such force that it seemed the dance floor would break under them. Small boys romped around like goats, and little girls whirled about wildly together. Many of the men were already drunk. They shouted boasts, howled with laughter, kissed strange women. There was so much commotion that Solomon Margolin could no longer grasp what was being said to him and simply nodded yes to everything. Some of the guests had attached themselves to him, wouldn't move, and kept pulling him in all directions, introducing him to more and more people from Sencimin and Tereshpol. A matron with a nose covered with warts pointed a finger at him, wiped her eyes, called him Schloimele. Solomon Margolin inquired who she was and somebody told him. Names were swallowed up in the tumult. He heard the same words over and over again: died, shot, burned. A man from Tereshpol tried to draw him aside and was shouted down by several Senciminers calling him an intruder who had no business there. A latecomer arrived, a horse and buggy driver from Sencimin who had become a millionaire in New York. His wife and children had perished, but, already, he had a new wife. The woman, weighted with diamonds, paraded about in a low-cut gown that bared a back, covered with blotches, to the waist. Her voice was husky. "Where did she come from? Who was she?" "Certainly no saint. Her first husband was a swindler who amassed a fortune and then dropped dead. Of what? Cancer. Where? In the stomach. First you don't have anything to eat, then you don't have anything to eat with. A man is always working for the second husband." "What is life anyway? A dance on the grave." "Yes, but as long as you're playing the game, you have to abide by the rules." "Dr. Margolin, why aren't you dancing? You're not among strangers. We're all from the same dust. Over there you weren't a doctor. You were only Schloime-Dovid, the son of the Talmud teacher. Before you know it, we'll all be lying side by side."

Margolin didn't recall drinking anything but he felt intoxicated all the same. The foggy hall was spinning like a carousel; the floor was rocking. Standing in a corner, he contemplated the dance. What different expressions the dancers wore. How many combinations and permutations of being, the Creator had brought together here. Every face told its own story. They were dancing together, these people, but each one had his own philosophy, his own approach. A man grabbed Margolin and for a while he danced in the frantic whirl. Then, tearing himself loose, he stood apart. Who was that woman? He found his eye caught by her familiar form. He knew her! She beckoned to him. He stood baffled. She looked neither young nor old. Where had he known her—that narrow face, those dark eyes, that girlish smile? Her hair was arranged in the old manner, with long braids wound like a wreath around her head. The grace of Sencimin adorned her—something he, Margolin, had long since forgotten. And those eyes, he was in love with those eyes and had been all his life. He half smiled at her and the woman smiled back. There were dimples in her cheeks. She too appeared surprised. Margolin, though he realized he had begun to blush like a boy, went up to her.

"I know you—but you're not from Sencimin?"

"Yes, from Sencimin."

He had heard that voice long ago. He had been in love with that voice.

"From Sencimin—who are you, then?"

Her lips trembled.

"You've forgotten me already?"

"It's a long time since I left Sencimin."

"You used to visit my father."

"Who was your father?"

"Melekh the watchmaker."

Dr. Margolin shivered.

"If I'm not out of my mind then I'm seeing things."

"Why do you say that?"

"Because Raizel is dead."

"I'm Raizel."

"You're Raizel? Here? Oh my God, if that's true—then anything is possible! When did you come to New York?"

"Some time ago."

"From where?"

"From over there."

"But everyone told me that you were all dead."

"My father, my mother, my brother Hershl . . ."

"But you were married!"

"I was."

"If that's true, then anything is possible!" repeated Dr. Margolin, still shaken by the incredible happening. Someone must have purposely deceived him. But why? He was aware there was a mistake somewhere but could not determine where.

"Why didn't you let me know? After all . . ."

He fell silent. She too was silent for a moment.

"I lost everything. But I still had some pride left."

"Come with me somewhere quieter—anywhere. This is the happiest day of my life!"

"But it's night . . ."

"Then the happiest night! Almost—as if the Messiah had come, as if the dead had come to life!"

"Where do you want to go? All right, let's go."

Margolin took her arm and felt at once the thrill, long forgotten, of youthful desire. He steered her away from the other guests, afraid that he might lose her in the crowd, or that someone would break in and spoil his happiness. Everything had returned on the instant: the embarrassment, the agitation, the joy. He wanted to take her away, to hide somewhere alone with her. Leaving the reception hall, they went upstairs to the chapel where the wedding ceremony was to take place. The door was standing open. Inside, on a raised platform stood the permanent wedding canopy. A bottle of wine and a silver goblet were placed in readiness for the ceremony. The chapel with it empty pews and only one glimmering light was full of shadows. The music, so blaring below, sounded soft and distant up here. Both of them hesitated at the threshold. Margolin pointed to the wedding canopy.

"We could have stood there."

"Yes."

"Tell me about yourself. Where are you now? What are you doing?"

"It is not easy to tell."

"Are you alone? Are you attached?"

"Attached? No."

"Would you never have let me hear from you?" he asked. She didn't answer.

Gazing at her, he knew his love had returned with full force.

Already, he was trembling at the thought that they might soon have to part. The excitement and the expectancy of youth filled him. He wanted to take her in his arms and kiss her, but at any moment someone might come in. He stood beside her, ashamed that he had married someone else, that he had not personally confirmed the reports of her death. "How could I have suppressed all this love? How could I have accepted the world without her? And what will happen now with Gretl?— I'll give her everything, my last cent." He looked round toward the stairway to see if any of the guests had started to come up. The thought came to him that by Jewish law he was not married, for he and Gretl had had only a civil ceremony. He looked at Raizel.

"According to Jewish law, I'm a single man."

"Is that so?"

"According to Jewish law, I could lead you up there and marry you."

She seemed to be considering the import of his words.

"Yes, I realize . . ."

"According to Jewish law, I don't even need a ring. One can get married with a penny."

"Do you have a penny?"

He put his hand to his breast pocket, but his wallet was gone. He started searching in his other pockets. Have I been robbed? he wondered. But how? I was sitting in the taxi the whole time. Could someone have robbed me here at the wedding? He was not so much disturbed as surprised. He said falteringly:

"Strange, but I don't have any money."

"We'll get along without it."

"But how am I going to get home?"

"Why go home?" she said, countering with a question. She smiled with that homely smile of hers that was so full of mystery. He took her by the wrist and gazed at her. Suddenly it occurred to him that this could not be his Raizel. She was too young. Probably it was her daughter who was playing along with him, mocking him. For God's sake, I'm completely confused! he thought. He stood bewildered, trying to untangle the years. He couldn't tell her age from her features. Her eyes were deep, dark, and melancholy. She also appeared confused, as if she, too, sensed some discrepancy. The whole thing is a mistake, Margolin told himself. But where exactly was the mistake? And what had happened to the wallet? Could he have left it in the taxi after paying the driver? He tried to remember how much cash he had had in it, but was unable to. "I must have had too much to drink. These people have made me drunk—dead drunk!" For a long time he stood silent, lost in some dreamless state, more profound than a narcotic trance. Suddenly he remembered the traffic collision he had witnessed on Eastern Parkway. An eerie suspicion came over him: Perhaps he had been more than a witness? Perhaps he himself had been the victim of that accident! That man on the stretcher looked strangely familiar. Dr. Margolin began to examine himself as though he were one of his own patients. He could find no trace of pulse or breathing. And he felt oddly deflated as if some physical dimension were missing. The sensation of weight, the muscular tension of his limbs, the hidden aches in his bones, all seemed to be gone. It can't be, it can't be, he murmured. Can one die without knowing it? And what will Gretl do? He blurted out:

"You're not the same Raizel."

"No? Then who am I?"

"They shot Raizel."

"Shot her? Who told you that?"

She seemed both frightened and perplexed. Silently she lowered her head like someone receiving the shock of bad news. Dr. Margolin continued to ponder. Apparently Raizel didn't realize her own condition. He had heard of such a state—what was it called? Hovering in the World of Twilight. The Astral Body wandering in semi-consciousness, detached from the flesh, without being able to reach its destination, clinging to the illusions and vanities of the past. But could there be any truth to all this superstition? No, as far as he was concerned, it was nothing but wishful thinking. Besides, this kind of survival would be less than oblivion. "I am most probably in a drunken stupor," Dr. Margolin decided. "All this may be one long hallucination, perhaps a result of food poisoning. . . ."

He looked up, and she was still there. He leaned over and whispered in her ear:

"What's the difference? As long as we're together."

"I've been waiting for that all these years."

"Where have you been?"

She didn't answer, and he didn't ask again. He looked around. The empty hall was full, all the seats taken. A ceremonious hush fell over the audience. The music played softly. The cantor intoned the benedictions. With measured steps, Abraham Mekheles led his daughter down the aisle.

Translated by Chana Faerstein and Elizabeth Pollet

I Place My Reliance on No Man

F ROM the day people began to talk about his becoming
the rabbi at Yavrov, Rabbi Jonathan Danziger of Yampol
didn't have a minute's peace. His Yampol enemies begrudged his going to the bigger city, though they couldn't
wait for him to leave Yampol because they already had someone to take his place. The Yampol elders wanted the rabbi to
leave Yampol without being able to go to Yavrov. They tried
to ruin his chances for the Yavrov appointment by spreading
rumors about him. They intended to treat him the way they
had treated the previous rabbi: he was to leave town in disgrace riding in an ox-drawn cart. But why? What evil had he
done? He had hurt no one's honor; he was invariably
friendly to everyone. Yet they all had private grudges against
him. One claimed that the rabbi gave a wrong interpretation
of the Talmud; another had a son-in-law who wanted to take
over the rabbi's position; a third thought Rabbi Jonathan
should follow a Hasidic leader. The butchers whined that the
rabbi found too many cows unkosher, the ritual slaughterer
that the rabbi asked to check his knife twice a week. The
bathhouse attendant complained because once, on the eve of
a holy day, the rabbi had declared the ritual bath impure,
and thus the women could not copulate with their husbands.

On Bridge Street the mob insisted that the rabbi spent too
much time at his books, that he didn't pay attention to the
common people. In taverns ruffians made fun of the way the
rabbi shouted when reciting "Hear, O Israel," and how he
spat when he mentioned the idols. The enlightened proved
that the rabbi made mistakes in Hebrew grammar. The rabbi's
wife was mocked by the ladies because she spoke in the accent
of Great Poland and because she drank her chicory and coffee
without sugar. There was nothing they didn't make fun of.
They didn't like it when the rabbi's wife baked bread every
Thursday rather than once every three weeks. They looked
askance at the rabbi's daughter, Yentl the widow, who, they
said, spent too much time knitting and embroidering. Before
each Passover there was a row because of the Passover mat-

zohs, and the rabbi's enemies ran to his house to break his windows. After Succoth, when many children fell ill, the pious matrons screamed that the rabbi hadn't cleansed the town of sins, that he had allowed the young women to go about with uncovered hair, and that the Angel of Death was thus punishing innocent infants with his sword. One way or another, every faction carped and found fault. With all this, the rabbi received the lowly salary of five gulden a week; he lived in the direst need.

As if he wasn't burdened enough with enemies, even his friends behaved like enemies. They relayed every petty accusation to him. The rabbi told them that this was a sin, quoting from the Talmud that gossip hurts all three parties: the gossiper, the one who receives the gossip, and the one gossiped about. It breeds anger, hatred, desecration of the Holy Name. The rabbi begged his followers not to trouble him with slander; but every word his enemies uttered was reported to him. If the rabbi expressed disapproval of the messenger of evil, then that person would immediately defect to the hostile camp. The rabbi could no longer pray and study in peace. He would plead with God: How long can I endure this Gehenna? Even condemned men don't suffer more than twelve months. . . .

Now that Rabbi Jonathan was about to take over the office in Yavrov, he could see that it was very much like Yampol. There was already an opposition in Yavrov, too. There, as well, was a rich man whose son-in-law coveted the rabbi's post. Besides, though the Yavrov rabbi made his living by selling candles and yeast, a few merchants had taken the forbidden merchandise into their stores, even after being threatened with excommunication.

The rabbi was barely fifty, but he was already gray. His tall figure was bent. The beard which once had been the color of straw had become white and sparse like that of an old man. His eyebrows were bushy, and below his eyes hung mossy, brownish-blue bags. He suffered from all sorts of ailments. He coughed, winter and summer. His body was mere skin and bone; he was so light that when he walked in the wind, his coattails almost lifted him into the air. His wife lamented that he didn't eat enough, drink enough, sleep enough.

Racked by nightmares he would wake from sleep with a start. He dreamed of persecutions and pogroms, and because of these he often had to fast. The rabbi believed that he was being punished for his sins. Sometimes he would say harsh words against his tormentors; he would question the ways of God and even doubt His mercy. He would put on his prayer shawl and phylacteries and the thought would suddenly flash through his mind: Suppose there is no Creator? After such blasphemy, the rabbi would not allow himself to taste food all day, until the stars came out. "Woe is me, where shall I run?" the rabbi sighed, "I'm a lost man."

In the kitchen sat mother and daughter and each one kept her own counsel. Ziporah, the rabbi's wife, came from a wealthy family. As a girl she had been considered beautiful, but the years of poverty had ruined her looks. In her unbecoming old-fashioned bonnet and dress from the time of King Sobieski, she seemed stooped and emaciated; her face was wrinkled and had taken on the rustiness of an unripe pear. Her hands had grown large and full of veins like those of a man. But Ziporah found one consolation in all her misery: work. She washed, chopped wood, carried water from the well, scoured the floors. People in Yampol joked that she scrubbed the dishes so hard that she made holes in them. She darned the table cloths and sheets so thickly that not a thread remained of the original weave. She even repaired the rabbi's slippers. Of the six children to which she had given birth, only Yentl had survived.

Yentl took after her father: her hair was yellowish, she was tall, fair-skinned, freckled, flat-chested. Yentl was no less diligent than her mother, but her mother would not allow her to touch any housework. Yentl's husband Ozer, a yeshiva student, had died of consumption. Yentl now sewed, knitted, read books which she borrowed from peddlers. At first she had received many marriage offers, but she managed to discourage the matchmakers. She never stopped mourning her husband. As soon as someone began arranging a match for her, she suddenly began to suffer from cramps. People in Yampol spread the rumor that she had given Ozer an oath on his deathbed that she would never marry again. She didn't have a single girl friend in Yampol. Summers she would take a basket, a rope, and go off into the woods to pick berries and mushrooms. Such behavior was considered highly improper for a rabbi's daughter.

The move to Yavrov seemed a good prospect, but the rabbi's wife and Yentl worried more than they rejoiced. Neither mother nor daughter had a decent stitch of clothing or piece of jewelry. During the years at Yampol, they had become so destitute that the rabbi's wife wailed to her husband that she had forgotten to speak to people. She prayed at home, avoided escorting brides to the synagogue or taking part in a circumcision ceremony. But Yavrov was a different matter. There, ladies decked themselves out in fashionable dresses, costly furs, silken wigs, shoes with high heels and pointed toes. The young married women went to the synagogue in feathered hats. Each had a golden chain or brooch. How could one come to such a place in rags, with broken-down furniture and patched linen? Yentl simply refused to move. What would she do in Yavrov? She was neither a girl nor a married woman; at least in Yampol she had a mound of earth and a gravestone.

Rabbi Jonathan listened and shook his head. He had been sent a contract from Yavrov, but had not as yet received any advance. Was that the custom, or were they treating him this way because they considered him naive? He was ashamed to ask for money. It went against his nature to use the Torah for profit. The rabbi paced back and forth in his study; "Father in heaven, save me. 'I am come into deep waters, where the floods overflow me!'"

2

It was the rabbi's custom to pray in the synagogue rather than in the study house, for among the poor Jews he had fewer enemies. He prayed at sunrise with the first quorum. It was after Pentecost. At three-thirty the morning star rose. At four the sun was already shining. The rabbi loved the stillness of the morning when most of the townfolk were still sleeping behind closed shutters. He never tired of watching the sun come up: purple, golden, washed in the waters of the Great Sea. The rising sun always brought the same thought to his mind: unlike the sun, the son of man never renews himself; that is why he is doomed to death. Man has memories, regrets, resentments. They collect like dust, they block him up so he can't receive the light and life that descends from heaven. But God's creation is constantly renewing itself. If the sky becomes cloudy, it clears up again. The sun sets, but is reborn every morning. There is no blemish of the past on the moon or stars. The ceaselessness of nature's creation is never so obvious as at dawn. Dew is falling, the birds twitter, the river catches fire, the grass is moist and fresh. Happy is the man who can renew himself together with creation "when all the stars of the morning sing together."

This morning was like any other morning. The rabbi rose early in order to be first in the synagogue. He knocked on the oak door to warn the spirits who pray there of his arrival. Then he went into the dark antechamber. The synagogue was hundreds of years old, but it remained almost as it was on the day it was built. Everything exuded eternity: the gray walls, the high ceilings the brass candelabras, the copper wash basin, the lectern with the four pillars, the carved high Ark with the tables of the Commandments and the two gilded lions. Streams of sun motes passed through the oval, stained-glass windows. Even though the ghosts who pray there usually leave it at cockcrow to make room for the living, there remained behind them a breathlessness and stillness. The rabbi began to pace up and down and to recite the "Lord of the Universe." The rabbi repeated the words, "And after all things shall have had an end, He alone shall reign," several times. The rabbi imagined the family of man perishing, houses crumbling, everything evil melting away and God's light again inhabiting all space. The shrinking of His power, the unholy forces, everything mean and filthy would cease. Time, accidents, passions, struggles would vanish, for these were but illusion and deception. The real truth was sheer goodness.

The rabbi said his prayers, contemplating the inner meaning of the words. Little by little the worshipers began to arrive: the first quorum was of hardworking men who rise at the rooster's crow—Leibush the carter, Chaim Jonah the fish merchant, Avrom the saddlemaker, Shloime Meyer who grows orchards outside Yampol. They greeted the rabbi, then put on their phylacteries and prayer shawls. It occurred to the rabbi that his enemies in the town were either the rich or the lazy idlers. The poor and hardworking, all those who made an honest living, were on his side. "Why didn't it ever occur to me?" the rabbi wondered. "Why didn't I realize it?" He felt a sudden love for these Jews who deceived no one, who knew nothing of swindling and grabbing, but followed God's sentence: "From the sweat of thy brow thou shalt eat bread . . ." Now they thoughtfully wrapped the phylactery thongs around their arms, kissed the fringes of the prayer shawls, and assumed the heavy yoke of the Kingdom of Heaven. A morning tranquility rested on their faces and beards. Their eyes shone with the mildness of those who have been burdened from childhood on.

It was Monday. After confession the scroll was taken from the Ark while the rabbi recited "Blessed be Thy Name." The opening of the Holy Ark always moved him. Here they stood, the pure scrolls, the Torah of Moses, silken-skirted and decorated with chains, crowns, silver plates—all similar, but each with its separate destiny. Some scrolls were read on weekdays, others on the Sabbath, still others were taken out only on the Day of the Rejoicing of the Law. There were also several worn books of the Law with faded letters and mouldering parchment. Every time the rabbi thought about these holy ruins, he felt a pain in his heart. He swayed back and forth, mumbling the Aramaic words, "Thou rulest over all . . . I, the servant of the Holy One, blessed be He, bow down before Him and the splendor of His law . . ." When the rabbi came to the words, "I place my reliance on no man," he stopped. The words stuck in his throat.

For the first time he realized that he was lying. No one relied on people more than he. The whole town gave him orders, he depended on everyone. Anyone could do him harm. Today it happened in Yampol, tomorrow it would happen in Yavrov. He, the rabbi, was a slave to every powerful man in the community. He must hope for gifts, for favors, and must always seek supporters. The rabbi began to examine the other worshipers. Not one of them needed allies. No one else worried about who might be for or against him. No one cared a penny for the tales of rumor-mongers. "Then what's the use of lying?" the rabbi thought. "Whom am I cheating?

The Almighty?" The rabbi shuddered and covered his face in shame. His knees buckled. They had already put the scroll on the reading table, but the rabbi had not noticed this. Suddenly something inside the rabbi laughed. He lifted his hand as if swearing an oath. A long forgotten joy came over him, and he felt an unexpected determination. In one moment everything became clear to him. . . .

They called the rabbi to the reading and he mounted the steps to the lectern. He placed a fringe on the parchment, touched it to his brow and kissed it. He recited the benediction in a loud voice. Then he listened to the reader. It was the chapter, "Send thou men . . ." It told of the spies who went to search the land of Canaan and who returned frightened by the sons of Anak. Cowardice had destroyed the generation of the desert, Rabbi Jonathan said to himself. And if they were not supposed to fear giants, why should I tremble before midgets? It's worse than cowardice; it's nothing but pride. I'm afraid to lose my rabbinical vestments. The co-worshipers gaped at the rabbi. He seemed transformed. A mysterious strength emanated from him. It's probably because he's moving to Yavrov, they explained to themselves.

After praying, the men began to disperse. Shloime Meyer took his prayer shawl, ready to leave. He was a small man, wide-boned, with a yellow beard, yellow eyes, yellow freckles. His canvas cap, his gabardine coat and his coarse boots were parched yellow by the sun. The rabbi made a sign to him. "Shloime Meyer, please wait a minute."

"Yes, Rabbi."

"How are the orchards?" the rabbi asked. "Is the harvest good?"

"Thank God. If there are no winds, then it will be good."

"Do you have men to do the picking?"

Shloime Meyer thought it over for a moment. "They're hard to get, but we manage."

"Why are they hard to get?"

"The work isn't easy. They have to stand on ladders all day and sleep in the barn at night."

"How much do you pay?"

"Not much."

"Enough to live on?"

"I feed them."

"Shloime Meyer, take me on. I'll pick fruit for you."

Shloime Meyer's yellow eyes filled with laughter. "Why not?"

"I'm not joking."

Shloime Meyer's eyes saddened. "I don't know what the Rabbi means."

"I'm not a rabbi any more."

"What? Why is that?"

"If you have a minute, I'll tell you."

Shloime Meyer listened while the rabbi spoke. The quorum had left and the two men remained alone. They stood near the pulpit. Although the rabbi spoke quietly, each word echoed back as though someone unseen were repeating it after him.

"What do you say, Shloime Meyer?" the rabbi finally asked.

Shloime Meyer made a face as though he had swallowed something sour. He shook his head from side to side.

"What can I say? I'm afraid I'll be excommunicated."

"You must not fear anyone. 'Ye shall not fear the face of man.' That's the essence of Jewishness."

"What will your wife say?"

"She'll help me with my work."

"It's not for the likes of you."

"They that wait on the Lord shall renew their strength."

"Well, well . . ."

"You agree, then?"

"If the Rabbi wants . . ."

"Don't call me Rabbi anymore. From now on I'm your employee. And I'll be an honest worker."

"I'm not worried about that."

"When do you leave for the orchards?"

"In a couple of hours."

"Come by with your cart. I'll be waiting."

"Yes, Rabbi."

Shloime Meyer waited a while longer and then left. Near the door to the antechamber he glanced back. The rabbi stood alone, his hands clasped, his gaze wandering from wall to wall. He would make his departure from the synagogue where he had prayed for so many years. It was all so familiar: the twelve signs of the zodiac, the seven stars, the figures of the lion, the stag, the leopard and the eagle, the unutterable Name of God, painted in red. The gilded lions on the top of the Ark stared at the rabbi with their amber eyes while their curved tongues supported the tables with the Ten Commandments. It seemed to the rabbi that these sacred beasts were asking: Why did you wait so long? Couldn't you see from the start that one cannot serve God and man at the same time? Their open mouths seemed to laugh with benign ferocity. The rabbi clutched at his beard. "Well, it is never too late. Eternity is still before one . . ." He walked backwards until he reached the threshold. There is no mezuzah in a synagogue, but the rabbi touched the jamb with his index finger and then his lips.

In Yampol, in Yavrov, the strange news soon spread. Rabbi Jonathan, his wife, and Yentl his daughter, had gone off to pick fruit in Shloime Meyer's orchards.

Translated by Ruth Whitman

Cunegunde

TOWARD evening a breeze arose from the swamps beyond the village. The sky clouded and the lime tree rattled its last leaves on a single rust-spotted branch. Out of a window-less structure resembling a toadstool, its mossy thatch roof hung with fibres, walked old Cunegunde. A hole in one wall served as a chimney, and her doorway was slanted like the cavity of a tree struck by lightning. Small and thick, she had a snout and eyes like a bull dog's, and a broad, gristly chin. White hairs sprouted from the warts on her cheeks. The few strands of hair remaining on her head had twisted themselves into the semblance of a horn. Corns and bunions crowded her nailless toes. Leaning on a stick and carrying a mattock, Cunegunde looked about her, sniffed the wind, frowned. "It's from the swamps," she murmured. "All pestilence and evil come from there. Foul weather. Cursed land. There'll be a bad harvest this year. The wind will blow everything away. With nothing but chaff left for the peasants, their bastards will swell from hunger. Death will come often."

Around Cunegunde's hut, isolated at the edge of the forest, weeds grew, brambles, hairy leaves with scales like scabs, poisonous berries, and thorns that seemed to bite at one's clothing. Mothers forbade their children to pass Cunegunde's snake-infested shack. Even the goats, the villagers said, avoided it. Larks built their nests on other roofs, but none was heard singing from Cunegunde's hut. Cunegunde appeared to be waiting for the storm. Her frog-like mouth croaked, "It's a plague, a plague. Sickness always comes from there. Evil will strike someone. This foul air will bring death."

The old woman had come out with her mattock not to dig up potatoes, but to unearth wild roots and herbs necessary for her sorcery. There was an entire apothecary in her hovel: devil's dung and snake venom, wormy cabbage and the rope with which a man had been hung, adder's meat and elves' hair, leeches and amulets, wax and incense. Cunegunde needed all this, not only for those who sought her help, but for her own defense. The evil powers had tormented her since the moment she took her first step. Her mother, may she rot in hell, had hit and pinched her. When drunk, her father beat her. She was teased by her brother Joziek, frightened by his stories of Dziad and Babuk. The tales of her sister Tekla worried her as well. Why did they torment her? While other children played on the grass, Cunegunde, barely six, had to feed the geese. Once, hailstones large as eggs fell upon her, almost fracturing her skull, killing a gander—for which Cunegunde was flogged. She was stalked by all kinds of animals—wolves, foxes, martens, skunks, wild dogs, and hunchbacked, unearthly creatures with pouches, flapping ears, knotty tails and protruding teeth. They ambushed themselves behind trees and bushes, growling at her, dogging her footsteps, more terrifying than the hobgoblins described by Tekla. A chimney-sweep descended from the sky, attempting to bind Cunegunde to his broom, to drag her upward. In the pasture where she herded geese, a tiny, elf-woman appeared, in a black kerchief, a pack on her back and a basket on her hip, floating over the field. Cunegunde tossed a pebble, but the elf-woman struck her so fiercely in the breast that she fainted. At night imps came to her bed, mocking her, wetting her sheet, calling her names, poking and biting her, braiding her hair. Mice dung and vermin remained after they had gone.

If Cunegunde had not acquired witchcraft, she might have been destroyed. She soon learned that what harmed others was propitious for her. When men and animals suffered, she was at peace. She began to wish sickness, strife and misery on the village. Although other girls abhorred the dead, Cunegunde liked to study a corpse, chalky or clay yellow, prostrated with candles at its head. The wails of the mourners comforted her. She enjoyed seeing hogs killed by peasants, hacked with knives and seared alive in boiling water. Cunegunde herself liked to torture creatures. She strangled a bird, and cut up worms to watch each segment wriggle. Stabbing a frog with a thorn, she observed its contortions. Soon she realized that curses had their value. Cunegunde cursed to death a woman who villified her. When a boy threw a pine cone into her eyes, she wished him blind; some weeks later, while he was chopping wood, a splinter flew into his eye, and its sight was lost. She made use of incantations and spells. Close to the swamp, a par-

alyzed woman living in a hovel, prattled continually about
warlocks, black mirrors, one-eyed giants, dwarves who dwelt
among toadstools, danced by the light of the moon, and lured
girls into caves. This woman advised Cunegunde on how to
exorcise demons, protect herself against vicious men, jealous
women, and false friends; taught her to interpret dreams and
recall the spirits of the dead.

While she was still young, Cunegunde's parents died. Her
brother took a wife from another village. Her sister Tekla, after
marrying a widower, finally died in childbirth. At Cunegunde's age, other girls were betrothed, but she saw in men
only the purveyors of miscarriage, birth pains and hemor-
rhages. A little hut and three-quarters of an acre of land were
left to her, but she refused to till it. Since everyone cheated—
the miller, the grain merchant, the priest, the village elder—
why labor?

It didn't take much to satisfy her: a radish, a raw potato, the
heart of a cabbage. Although the peasants found them repulsive, she savored the flesh of cats and dogs. Hunger could be
glutted by a dead mouse found in a field. Despite many days of
fasting, one could still remain alive. Even on Easter and
Christmas, Cunegunde stayed away from church; she did not
care to be insulted by the women or ridiculed by the men, nor
did she have any money for shoes, clothes, or the alms box.

Shamed by the mockery of others, Cunegunde would lock
herself into her hut for days, not even emerging to take care of
her needs. She was never invited to harvest festivals, when the
cabbage was chopped and pickles prepared, nor to any weddings, confirmations, or wakes. As if she were excommunicated, the entire village opposed this one orphan. Sitting in
the dark, she would dole out curses. Hearing laughter outside,
she would spit. Cries of joy pained her. Irritated by the cows
lowing as they returned from pasture, she discovered an incantation that prevented their giving milk. Yes, Cunegunde was in
debt to no one. All her enemies died. She learned to give the
Evil Eye, to conceal a charm in granary or stable, to lure rats
to grain, to close the womb of a woman in labor, to form
someone's image in clay and pierce it with pins, and to produce growths of chickens' beaks. Long ago Cunegunde had
stopped beseeching God to secure her from her enemies; He

was not interested in the prayers of an orphan. While the powerful ruled, He obscured himself in heaven. The Devil was whimsical, but one could bargain with him.

Cunegunde's generation had almost entirely disappeared. She had grown old. She was no longer laughed at; her rages were dreaded, and she was called The Witch. Every Saturday night, the villagers said, she rode a broom to meet other witches at the Black Mass. The unfortunate came knocking at her door, from all over the village—women with womb-tumors, mothers of monsters, hiccuping girls, abandoned wives. But of what value were the loaves of bread they brought, the bags of buckwheat, slabs of butter, the money? From having eaten too little, Cunegunde's stomach had shrunk; also, her teeth had fallen out, and because of varicose veins, she could barely walk. Half-deaf from having been silent for years and raving to herself, she had almost forgotten human speech. She had sent all her enemies to their graves, and there seemed to be no enemies in the new generation. However, accustomed to cursing, Cunegunde could not stop grumbling: *death and afflictions . . . fire and the plague . . . a pox on their tongues . . . blisters in their throats. . . .*

Storms rarely arose in midsummer, but during the winter Cunegunde had predicted a summer of catastrophes. She could sniff death; misfortune wafted toward her. The wind was not yet especially potent, but Cunegunde knew where it had come from. She could smell cinders, rot, and flesh, and something else oily and rancid, whose source she alone could perceive. Her toothless mouth grimaced. "It's a pestilence, a pestilence. The approach of death. . . ."

2

Despite the increasing wind, Cunegunde continued digging. Each root growing near her hut had a singular power. Occasionally, Cunegunde would gather herbs near the swamps, which extended over a vast region, as far as the eye could reach. Flowers and leaves floated amid the slime of the mossy water. Strange birds, and unusual large flies with golden-green bellies, flew about. Although she had sent all her foes to the other world, she could not banish them completely. Their spirits hovered over the swamps, spinning nets of vengeance. Sometimes the walls of her hut, her thatched roof, resounded with their noises; the straw fibres trembled as they hung from her eaves. Cunegunde had to be constantly alert to the potential evil-doings of the dead. Even a strangled cat could be nasty. More than once, at night, a murdered cat had come to claw her. Cunegunde could hear the scratching of a familiar spirit that had settled amidst the rags beneath her bench-bed. Sometimes he was good to her, bringing a rabbit, a sick bird, or some other animal that might be roasted and eaten, but at other times he was malicious. Objects disappeared after she had put them away. He confused her herbs, concealed her salves, and muddied her food. Once Cunegunde had covered and placed in a corner a pitcher of borscht that a young peasant woman had brought to her. The next day there was a thick skin on the borscht, smelling like axle grease. In a pot of buckwheat, sand and pebbles from some unknown region had been cast. When Cunegunde bent down to scold the spirit, he whispered, "Old bogy!"

The swirling wind became a gale as she dug, and seemed to shriek wildly around her. Later, within her hut, Cunegunde peered through a chink in the wall. In the field, unable to withstand the blasts, ears of wheat were leveled. Hay ricks were blown apart. Torn-off shingles flew over the village. Trying to attach their roofs, protect their walls, tether horses and cattle in the barns, peasants were met by a burst of rain and wind together. One downpour flooded the village. Lightning flashed like hell fire. Thunder exploded so close to Cunegunde that the brains in her skull shook like the kernel in a nut. Barring the door, Cunegunde sat on a footstool, unable to do anything but mutter. Of all the huts, hers was the most frail. It quivered when a pig rubbed against it. Calling out the names of Satan and Lucifer, Baba Yaga and Kadik, Malfas and Pan Twardowski, she had placed a ball of wax and goat turds in every corner. To improve her protection, she had opened the oaken chest where she kept the knee bone of a virgin, a hare's foot, the horn of a black ox, wolves' teeth, a rag soaked in menstrual blood, and (most efficacious of all) the rope with which a criminal had been hanged. She murmured:

"Strong is the leopard,
Angry the lizard;
Hudak and Gudak
Come in with the blizzard.
Blood is red,
Dark is the night;
Magister and Djabel
Lend me your might."

Although it shook and swayed, the hut remained undamaged. From the tremulous roof, the fibres waved without loosening. In a moment of blinding light, Cunegunde could see clearly the sooty wall, the clay floor, the pot on the tripod, the spinning wheel. Then it became dark again, rain striking like whips, thunder hammering. Trying to comfort herself, Cunegunde thought she had to die some day; sooner or later everyone must rot in the grave. But each time the hut vibrated, Cunegunde shivered. Finding the footstool uncomfortable, she lay on her bed, her head on a pillow stuffed with straw. This was no accidental storm; it had been gathering for months. Among the peasants in the village there was much corruption and injustice. Cunegunde had heard stories of goblins, werewolves and other vicious beings. Bastards were born to girls from union with their fathers. Widows copulated with their sons, herdsmen with their cows, mares, pigs. Over the swamps at night tiny flames appeared. Human bones were extricated from the earth by peasants ploughing or digging ditches for potato storage. There was much incitement against Cunegunde in the netherworld. Until now the Powers had been on her side, but they could desert at any time to those who plotted against her. She closed her eyes. Previously her stubbornness had conquered each plotter; a miracle always occurred and the other side went down. But she was frightened by this pre-harvest storm. Perhaps she had left a corner exposed. The hostile demons lay in wait, baying like hounds, clawing beneath the floor. Dozing off, Cunegunde dreamed of a tom cat as huge as a barrel, with black fur, green eyes, and a fiery moustache. Thrusting out his tongue, it meowed like a ringing bell. Suddenly Cunegunde started. Someone tugged at the barred door. In an apprehensive voice she asked, "Who is it, eh?"

There was no answer.

It is Topiel—Cunegunde thought. She had never settled accounts with that demon. But she could not remember a spell to drive him off. All she could say was, "Go away to all the deserted forests where neither men nor cattle will pass. In the name of Amadai, Sagratanas, Belial, Barrabas, I implore you . . ."

There was no sound outside.

> *"Naked-boned, in smoke and fire,*
> *Water-bellied, feet in brier,*
> *Without teeth, without air,*
> *Break your neck, run from here. . . ."*

The door opened. A figure entered with the wind.

"Little Mother," Cunegunde gasped.

"Are you Cunegunde, The Witch?" a man's voice asked harshly.

Frozen, Cunegunde replied, "Who are you? Have pity."

"I am Stach, Yanka's fiance."

Disguising himself as a man! Cunegunde whispered, "What do you want, Stach?"

"I know everything, you old bitch. You gave her a poison to finish me. She told me. Now . . ."

Although Cunegunde wanted to scream, she knew it was useless, for even without the raging storm, her voice was too small to be heard. She began mumbling, "No poison, no poison. If you really are Stach, I want you to know that I bear malice to no one. Yanka cried that she was dying of love, and that you, my hero, took no notice of her. I gave her a potion to forget you. She swore to God to keep it a secret."

"A potion, eh? Snake venom."

"No venom, my lord and master. If you long for her, take her. I'll give you a gift. I'll come to the wedding and bless you, even if she did betray me."

"Who wants your blessing? Cursed bitch, bloodthirsty beast."

"Help! Mercy!"

"No."

Overturning the dishes before him, he strode to the bench bed, lifted and beat her powerfully. Cunegunde scarcely groaned. Dragging her along the floor, he stamped on her. Cunegunde heard a rooster flapping its wings. Soon she found herself among rocks, ditches, and leafless trees, in a dusky land with no sky. She viewed a magic show that was simultaneously a Gehenna. Moving through the air like bats, black men climbed ladders, swung from ropes, somersaulted. Others, with millstones around their necks, were dumped into barrels of pitch. Women were suspended by their hair, their breasts, their nails. There was a wedding, and cupping their hands, the guests drank spirits from a trough. From nowhere, Cunegunde's enemies materialized, a lusty mob carrying axes, pitchforks and spears. A covey of horned devils ran alongside them. Everyone had joined up against her: Beezlebub, Baba Yaga, Babuk, Kulas, Balwochwalec. Torches aloft, neighing, they ran at her with a vengeful joy. "Holy Mother, save me," Cunegunde screamed for the last time.

The next day, peasants who came in search of The Witch found her hut collapsed. From among the beams and the rotten thatch, her crushed body was brought forth, the skull emptied of brains, and nothing left but a cluster of bones. A boat conveyed the body to the chapel. Despite the great damage inflicted by the storm, only one person had died—Cunegunde.

Yanka moved in the cortege, knelt and said, "Grandmother, a good fortune came to me. At dawn today Stach showed up. He will marry me at the altar. Your potion purified his heart. Next week we go to the priest. My mother has already started baking."

There was no wind now but heavy clouds still lingered in the sky, dimming the day to a kind of twilight. Flocks of crows flew in from the swamps. Odors of smoke permeated the air. Half the village had been blown down, the other half flooded. In the muddy waters the dismantled roofs, caved-in walls and maimed trunks were reflected. With skirts lifted above their knees, three peasant women rummaged all day in Cunegunde's flooded room, seeking the rope with which a murderer had been hanged.

Translated by The Author and Elaine Gottlieb

Short Friday

IN the village of Lapschitz lived a tailor named Shmul-Leibele with his wife, Shoshe. Shmul-Leibele was half tailor, half furrier, and a complete pauper. He had never mastered his trade. When filling an order for a jacket or a gaberdine, he inevitably made the garment either too short or too tight. The belt in the back would hang either too high or too low, the lapels never matched, the vent was off center. It was said that he had once sewn a pair of trousers with the fly off to one side. Shmul-Leibele could not count the wealthy citizens among his customers. Common people brought him their shabby garments to have patched and turned, and the peasants gave him their old pelts to reverse. As is usual with bunglers, he was also slow. He would dawdle over a garment for weeks at a time. Yet despite his shortcomings, it must be said that Shmul-Leibele was an honorable man. He used only strong thread and none of his seams ever gave. If one ordered a lining from Shmul-Leibele, even one of common sackcloth or cotton, he bought only the very best material, and thus lost most of his profit. Unlike other tailors who hoarded every last bit of remaining cloth, he returned all scraps to his customers.

Had it not been for his competent wife, Shmul-Leibele would certainly have starved to death. Shoshe helped him in whatever way she could. On Thursdays she hired herself out to wealthy families to knead dough, and on summer days went off to the forest to gather berries and mushrooms, as well as pinecones and twigs for the stove. In winter she plucked down for brides' featherbeds. She was also a better tailor than her husband, and when he began to sigh, or dally and mumble to himself, an indication that he could no longer muddle through, she would take the chalk from his hand and show him how to continue. Shoshe had no children, but it was common knowledge that it wasn't she who was barren, but rather her husband who was sterile, since all of her sisters had borne children, while his only brother was likewise childless. The townswomen repeatedly urged Shoshe to divorce him, but she turned a deaf ear, for the couple loved one another with a great love.

Shmul-Leibele was small and clumsy. His hands and feet were too large for his body, and his forehead bulged on either side as is common in simpletons. His cheeks, red as apples, were bare of whiskers, and but a few hairs sprouted from his chin. He had scarcely any neck at all; his head sat upon his shoulders like a snowman's. When he walked, he scraped his shoes along the ground so that every step could be heard far away. He hummed continuously and there was always an amiable smile on his face. Both winter and summer he wore the same caftan and sheepskin cap with earlaps. Whenever there was any need for a messenger, it was always Shmul-Leibele who was pressed into service, and however far away he was sent, he always went willingly. The wags saddled him with a variety of nicknames and made him the butt of all sorts of pranks, but he never took offense. When others scolded his tormentors, he would merely observe: "What do I care? Let them have their fun. They're only children, after all. . . ."

Sometimes he would present one or another of the mischief makers with a piece of candy or a nut. This he did without any ulterior motive, but simply out of good-heartedness.

Shoshe towered over him by a head. In her younger days she had been considered a beauty, and in the households where she worked as a servant they spoke highly of her honesty and diligence. Many young men had vied for her hand, but she had selected Shmul-Leibele because he was quiet and because he never joined the other town boys who gathered on the Lublin road at noon Saturdays to flirt with the girls. His piety and retiring nature pleased her. Even as a girl Shoshe had taken pleasure in studying the Pentateuch, in nursing the infirm at the almshouse, in listening to the tales of the old women who sat before their houses darning stockings. She would fast on the last day of each month, the Minor Day of Atonement, and often attended the services at the women's synagogue. The other servant girls mocked her and thought her old-fashioned. Immediately following her wedding she shaved her head and fastened a kerchief firmly over her ears, never permitting a stray strand of hair from her matron's wig

to show as did some of the other young women. The bath attendant praised her because she never frolicked at the ritual
bath, but performed her ablutions according to the laws. She
purchased only indisputably kosher meat, though it was a half-
cent more per pound, and when she was in doubt about the
dietary laws she sought out the rabbi's advice. More than once
she had not hesitated to throw out all the food and even to
smash the earthen crockery. In short, she was a capable, God-
fearing woman, and more than one man envied Shmul-Leibele
his jewel of a wife.

Above all of life's blessings the couple revered the Sabbath.
Every Friday noon Shmul-Leibele would lay aside his tools
and cease all work. He was always among the first at the ritual
bath, and he immersed himself in the water four times for the
four letters of the Holy Name. He also helped the beadle set
the candles in the chandeliers and the candelabra. Shoshe
scrimped throughout the week, but on the Sabbath she was
lavish. Into the heated oven went cakes, cookies and the Sabbath loaf. In winter, she prepared puddings made of chicken's
neck stuffed with dough and rendered fat. In summer she
made puddings with rice or noodles, greased with chicken fat
and sprinkled with sugar or cinnamon. The main dish consisted of potatoes and buckwheat, or pearl barley with beans,
in the midst of which she never failed to set a marrowbone. To
insure that the dish would be well cooked, she sealed the oven
with loose dough. Shmul-Leibele treasured every mouthful,
and at every Sabbath meal he would remark: "Ah, Shoshe love,
it's food fit for a king! Nothing less than a taste of Paradise!"
to which Shoshe replied, "Eat hearty. May it bring you good
health."

Although Shmul-Leibele was a poor scholar, unable to mem-
orize a chapter of the Mishnah, he was well versed in all the
laws. He and his wife frequently studied *The Good Heart* in
Yiddish. On half-holidays, holidays, and on each free day, he
studied the Bible in Yiddish. He never missed a sermon, and
though a pauper, he bought from peddlers all sorts of books
of moral instructions and religious tales, which he then read
together with his wife. He never wearied of reciting sacred
phrases. As soon as he arose in the morning he washed his
hands and began to mouth the preamble to the prayers. Then

he would walk over to the study house and worship as one of the quorum. Every day he recited a few chapters of the Psalms, as well as those prayers which the less serious tended to skip over. From his father he had inherited a thick prayer book with wooden covers, which contained the rites and laws pertaining to each day of the year. Shmul-Leibele and his wife heeded each and every one of these. Often he would observe to his wife: "I shall surely end up in Gehenna, since there'll be no one on earth to say Kaddish over me." "Bite your tongue, Shmul-Leibele," she would counter, "For one, everything is possible under God. Secondly, you'll live until the Messiah comes. Thirdly, it's just possible that I will die before you and you will marry a young woman who'll bear you a dozen children." When Shoshe said this, Shmul-Leibele would shout: "God forbid! You must remain in good health. I'd rather rot in Gehenna!"

Although Shmul-Leibele and Shoshe relished every Sabbath, their greatest satisfaction came from the Sabbaths in wintertime. Since the day before the Sabbath evening was a short one, and since Shoshe was busy until late Thursday at her work, the couple usually stayed up all of Thursday night. Shoshe kneaded dough in the trough, covering it with cloth and a pillow so that it might ferment. She heated the oven with kindling-wood and dry twigs. The shutters in the room were kept closed, the door shut. The bed and bench-bed remained unmade, for at daybreak the couple would take a nap. As long as it was dark Shoshe prepared the Sabbath meal by the light of a candle. She plucked a chicken or a goose (if she had managed to come by one cheaply), soaked it, salted it and scraped the fat from it. She roasted a liver for Shmul-Leibele over the glowing coals and baked a small Sabbath loaf for him. Occasionally she would inscribe her name upon the loaf with letters of dough, and then Shmul-Leibele would tease her: "Shoshe, I am eating you up. Shoshe, I have already swallowed you." Shmul-Leibele loved warmth, and he would climb up on the oven and from there look down as his spouse cooked, baked, washed, rinsed, pounded and carved. The Sabbath loaf would turn out round and brown. Shoshe braided the loaf so swiftly that it seemed to dance before Shmul-Leibele's eyes. She bustled about efficiently with spatulas, pokers, ladles and goosewing dusters, and at times even snatched up a live coal with her bare fingers. The pots perked and bubbled. Occasionally a drop of soup would spill and the hot tin would hiss and squeal. And all the while the cricket continued its chirping. Although Shmul-Leibele had finished his supper by this time, his appetite would be whetted afresh, and Shoshe would throw him a knish, a chicken gizzard, a cookie, a plum from the plum stew or a chunk of the pot-roast. At the same time she would chide him, saying that he was a glutton. When he attempted to defend himself she would cry: "Oh, the sin is upon me, I have allowed you to starve . . ."

At dawn they would both lie down in utter exhaustion. But because of their efforts Shoshe would not have to run herself ragged the following day, and she could make the benediction over the candles a quarter of an hour before sunset.

The Friday on which this story took place was the shortest Friday of the year. Outside, the snow had been falling all night and had blanketed the house up to the windows and barricaded the door. As usual, the couple had stayed up until morning, then had lain down to sleep. They had arisen later than usual, for they hadn't heard the rooster's crow, and since the windows were covered with snow and frost, the day seemed as dark as night. After whispering, "I thank Thee," Shmul-Leibele went outside with a broom and shovel to clear a path, after which he took a bucket and fetched water from the well. Then, as he had no pressing work, he decided to lay off for the whole day. He went to the study house for the morning prayers, and after breakfast wended his way to the bathhouse. Because of the cold outside, the patrons kept up an eternal plaint: "A bucket! A bucket!" and the bath attendant poured more and more water over the glowing stones so that the steam grew constantly denser. Shmul-Leibele located a scraggly willow-broom, mounted to the highest bench and whipped himself until his skin glowed red. From the bathhouse, he hurried over to the study house where the beadle had already swept and sprinkled the floor with sand. Shmul-Leibele set the candles and helped spread the tablecloths over the tables. Then he went home again and changed into his Sabbath clothes. His boots, resoled but a few days before, no longer let the wet through. Shoshe had done her washing for the week, and had given him a fresh shirt, underdrawers, a fringed garment, even a clean pair of stockings. She had already performed the benediction over the candles, and the spirit of the Sabbath emanated from every corner of the room. She was wearing her silk kerchief with the silver spangles, a yellow and gray dress, and shoes with gleaming, pointed tips. On her throat hung the chain that Shmul-Leibele's mother, peace be with her, had given her to celebrate the signing of the wedding contract. The marriage band sparkled on her index finger. The candlelight reflected in the window panes, and Shmul-Leibele fancied that there was a duplicate of this room outside and that another Shoshe was out there lighting the Sabbath candles. He yearned to tell his wife how full of grace she was, but there was no time for it, since it is specifically stated in the prayer book that it is fitting and proper to be amongst the first ten worshipers at the synagogue; as it so happened, going off to prayers he was the tenth man to arrive. After the congregation had intoned the Song of Songs, the cantor sang, "Give thanks," and "O come, let us exult," Shmul-Leibele prayed with fervor. The words were sweet upon his tongue, they seemed to fall from his lips with a life of their own, and he felt that they soared to the eastern wall, rose above the embroidered curtain of the Holy Ark, the gilded lions, and the tablets, and floated up to the ceiling with its painting of the twelve constellations. From there, the prayers surely ascended to the Throne of Glory.

2

The cantor chanted, "Come, my beloved," and Shmul-Leibele trumpeted along in accompaniment. Then came the prayers, and the men recited, "It is our duty to praise . . ." to which Shmul-Leibele added a "Lord of the Universe." Afterwards, he wished everyone a good Sabbath: the rabbi, the ritual slaughterer, the head of the community, the assistant rabbi, everyone present. The *cheder* lads shouted, "Good Sabbath, Shmul-Leibele," while they mocked him with gestures and grimaces, but Shmul-Leibele answered them all with a smile, even occasionally pinched a boy's cheek affectionately. Then he was off for home. The snow was piled high so that one could barely make out the contours of the roofs, as if the entire settlement had been immersed in white. The sky, which had hung low and overcast all day, now grew clear. From among white clouds a full moon peered down, casting a day-like brilliance over the snow. In the west, the edge of a cloud still held the glint of sunset. The stars on this Friday seemed larger and sharper, and through some miracle Lapschitz seemed to have blended with the sky. Shmul-Leibele's hut, which was situated not far from the synagogue, now hung suspended in space, as it is written: "He suspendeth the earth on nothingness." Shmul-Leibele walked slowly since, according to law, one must not hurry when coming from a holy place. Yet he longed to be home. "Who knows?" he thought. "Perhaps Shoshe has become ill? Maybe she's gone to fetch water and, God forbid, has fallen into the well? Heaven save us, what a lot of troubles can befall a man."

On the threshold he stamped his feet to shake off the snow, then opened the door and saw Shoshe. The room made him think of Paradise. The oven had been freshly whitewashed, the candles in the brass candelabras cast a Sabbath glow. The aromas coming from the sealed oven blended with the scents of the Sabbath supper. Shoshe sat on the bench-bed apparently awaiting him, her cheeks shining with the freshness of a young girl's. Shmul-Leibele wished her a happy Sabbath and she in turn wished him a good year. He began to hum, "Peace upon ye ministering angels . . ." and after he had said his farewells to the invisible angels that accompany each Jew leaving the synagogue, he recited: "The worthy woman." How well he understood the meaning of these words, for he had read them often in Yiddish, and each time reflected anew on how aptly they seemed to fit Shoshe.

Shoshe was aware that these holy sentences were being said in her honor, and thought to herself, "Here am I, a simple woman, an orphan, and yet God has chosen to bless me with a devoted husband who praises me in the holy tongue."

Both of them had eaten sparingly during the day so that they would have an appetite for the Sabbath meal. Shmul-Leibele said the benediction over the raisin wine and gave Shoshe the cup so that she might drink. Afterwards, he rinsed his fingers from a tin dipper, then she washed hers, and they both dried their hands with a single towel, each at either end. Shmul-Leibele lifted the Sabbath loaf and cut it with the bread knife, a slice for himself and one for his wife.

He immediately informed her that the loaf was just right, and she countered: "Go on, you say that every Sabbath."

"But it happens to be the truth," he replied.

Although it was hard to obtain fish during the cold weather, Shoshe had purchased three-fourths of a pound of pike from the fishmonger. She had chopped it with onions, added an egg, salt and pepper, and cooked it with carrots and parsley. It took Shmul-Leibele's breath away, and after it he had to drink a tumbler of whiskey. When he began the table chants, Shoshe accompanied him quietly. Then came the chicken soup with noodles and tiny circlets of fat which glowed in the surface like golden ducats. Between the soup and the main course, Shmul-Leibele again sang Sabbath hymns. Since goose was cheap at this time of year, Shoshe gave Shmul-Leibele an extra leg for good measure. After the dessert, Shmul-Leibele washed for the last time and made a benediction. When he came to the words: "Let us not be in need either of the gifts of flesh and blood nor of their loans," he rolled his eyes upward and brandished his fists. He never stopped praying that he be allowed to continue to earn his own livelihood and not, God forbid, become an object of charity.

After grace, he said yet another chapter of the Mishnah, and all sorts of other prayers which were found in his large prayer book. Then he sat down to read the weekly portion of the Pentateuch twice in Hebrew and once in Aramaic. He enunciated every word and took care to make no mistake in the difficult Aramaic paragraphs of the Onkelos. When he reached the last section, he began to yawn and tears gathered in his eyes. Utter exhaustion overcame him. He could barely keep his eyes open and between one passage and the next he dozed off for a second or two. When Shoshe noticed this, she made up the bench-bed for him and prepared her own featherbed with clean sheets. Shmul-Leibele barely managed to say the retiring prayers and began to undress. When he was already lying on his bench-bed he said: "A good Sabbath, my pious wife. I am very tired . . ." and turning to the wall, he promptly began to snore.

Shoshe sat a while longer gazing at the Sabbath candles which had already begun to smoke and flicker. Before getting into bed, she placed a pitcher of water and a basin at Shmul-Leibele's bedstead so that he would not rise the following morning without water to wash with. Then she, too, lay down and fell asleep.

They had slept an hour or two or possibly three—what does it matter, actually?—when suddenly Shoshe heard Shmul-Leibele's voice. He waked her and whispered her name. She opened one eye and asked, "What is it?"

"Are you clean?" he mumbled.

She thought for a moment and replied, "Yes."

He rose and came to her. Presently he was in bed with her. A desire for her flesh had roused him. His heart pounded rapidly, the blood coursed in his veins. He felt a pressure in his loins. His urge was to mate with her immediately, but he remembered the law which admonished a man not to copulate with a woman until he had first spoken affectionately to her, and he now began to speak of his love for her and how this mating could possibly result in a male-child.

"And a girl you wouldn't accept?" Shoshe chided him, and he replied, "Whatever God deigns to bestow would be welcome."

"I fear this privilege isn't mine anymore," she said with a sigh.

"Why not?" he demanded. "Our mother Sarah was far older than you."

"How can one compare oneself to Sarah? Far better you divorce me and marry another."

He interrupted her, stopping her mouth with his hand. "Were I sure that I could sire the twelve tribes of Israel with another, I still would not leave you. I cannot even imagine myself with another woman. You are the jewel of my crown."

"And what if I were to die?" she asked.

"God forbid! I would simply perish from sorrow. They would bury us both on the same day."

"Don't speak blasphemy. May you outlive my bones. You are a man. You would find somebody else. But what would I do without you?"

He wanted to answer her, but she sealed his lips with a kiss.

He went to her then. He loved her body. Each time she gave herself to him, the wonder of it astonished him anew. How was it possible, he would think, that he, Shmul-Leibele, should have such a treasure all to himself? He knew the law, one dared not surrender to lust for pleasure. But somewhere in a sacred book he had read that it was permissible to kiss and embrace a wife to whom one had been wed according to the laws of Moses and Israel, and he now caressed her face, her throat and her breasts. She warned him that this was frivolity. He replied, "So, I'll lie on the torture rack. The great saints also loved their wives." Nevertheless, he promised himself to attend the ritual bath the following morning, to intone psalms and to pledge a sum to charity. Since she loved him also and enjoyed his caresses, she let him do his will.

After he had satiated his desire, he wanted to return to his own bed, but a heavy sleepiness came over him. He felt a pain in his temples. Shoshe's head ached as well. She suddenly said, "I'm afraid something is burning in the oven. Maybe I should open the flue?"

"Go on, you're imagining it," he replied. "It'll become too cold in here."

And so complete was his weariness that he fell asleep, as did she.

That night Shmul-Leibele suffered an eerie dream. He imagined that he had passed away. The Burial-Society brethren came by, picked him up, lit candles by his head, opened the windows, intoned the prayer to justify God's ordainment. Afterwards, they washed him on the ablution board, carried him on a stretcher to the cemetery. There they buried him as the gravedigger said Kaddish over his body.

"That's odd," he thought, "I hear nothing of Shoshe lamenting or begging forgiveness. Is it possible that she would so quickly grow unfaithful? Or has she, God forbid, been overcome by grief?"

He wanted to call her name, but he was unable to. He tried to tear free of the grave, but his limbs were powerless. All of a sudden he awoke.

"What a horrible nightmare!" he thought. "I hope I come out of it all right."

At that moment Shoshe also awoke. When he related his dream to her, she did not speak for a while. Then she said, "Woe is me. I had the very same dream."

"Really? You too?" asked Shmul-Leibele, now frightened. "This I don't like."

He tried to sit up, but he could not. It was as if he had been shorn of all his strength. He looked towards the window to see if it were day already, but there was no window visible, nor any windowpane. Darkness loomed everywhere. He cocked his ears. Usually he would be able to hear the chirping of a cricket, the scurrying of a mouse, but this time only a dead silence prevailed. He wanted to reach out to Shoshe, but his hand seemed lifeless.

"Shoshe," he said quietly, "I've grown paralyzed."

"Woe is me, so have I," she said. "I cannot move a limb."

They lay there for a long while, silently, feeling their numbness. Then Shoshe spoke: "I fear that we are already in our graves for good."

"I'm afraid you're right," Shmul-Leibele replied in a voice that was not of the living.

"Pity me, when did it happen? How?" Shoshe asked. "After all, we went to sleep hale and hearty."

"We must have been asphyxiated by the fumes from the stove," Shmul-Leibele said.

"But I said I wanted to open the flue."

"Well, it's too late for that now."

"God have mercy upon us, what do we do now? We were still young people . . ."

"It's no use. Apparently it was fated."

"Why? We arranged a proper Sabbath. I prepared such a tasty meal. An entire chicken neck and tripe."

"We have no further need of food."

Shoshe did not immediately reply. She was trying to sense her own entrails. No, she felt no appetite. Not even for a chicken neck and tripe. She wanted to weep, but she could not.

"Shmul-Leibele, they've buried us already. It's all over."

"Yes, Shoshe, praised be the true Judge! We are in God's hands."

"Will you be able to recite the passage attributed to your name before the Angel Dumah?"

"Yes."

"It's good that we are lying side by side," she muttered.

"Yes, Shoshe," he said, recalling a verse: *Lovely and pleasant in their lives, and in their death they were not divided.*

"And what will become of our hut? You did not even leave a will."

"It will undoubtedly go to your sister."

Shoshe wished to ask something else, but she was ashamed. She was curious about the Sabbath meal. Had it been removed from the oven? Who had eaten it? But she felt that such a query would not be fitting of a corpse. She was no longer Shoshe the dough-kneader, but a pure, shrouded corpse with shards covering her eyes, a cowl over her head, and myrtle twigs between her fingers. The Angel Dumah would appear at any moment with his fiery staff, and she would have to be ready to give an account of herself.

Yes, the brief years of turmoil and temptation had come to an end. Shmul-Leibele and Shoshe had reached the true world. Man and wife grew silent. In the stillness they heard the flapping of wings, a quiet singing. An angel of God had come to guide Shmul-Leibele the tailor and his wife, Shoshe, into Paradise.

Translated by Joseph Singer and Roger Klein

THE SÉANCE

AND OTHER STORIES

In memory of my beloved sister

HINDE ESTHER

Contents

Author's Note

Most of these stories were written in recent years—*The Dead Fiddler*, for example, was written only last year. However, one story, *Two Corpses Go Dancing*, was published in Yiddish in 1943. I am glad that three of the stories—the title story, *The Lecture*, and *The Letter Writer*—deal with events in the United States or Canada. I am grateful to the following translators: Mirra Ginsburg, Cecil Hemley, Ellen Kantarov, Roger Klein, J. M. Lask, Elizabeth Pollet, Alizah Shevrin, Elizabeth Shub, Joseph Singer, Dorothea Straus, Ruth Whitman, Alma Singer. As the reader will see, I was often the co–translator of the stories, all of which were edited by Robert Giroux and some of them by Cecil Hemley, Rachel MacKenzie, and Elizabeth Shub, to all of whom I wish to express my gratitude.

I.B.S.

The Séance

IT WAS during the summer of 1946, in the living room of Mrs. Kopitzky on Central Park West. A single red bulb burned behind a shade adorned with one of Mrs. Kopitzky's automatic drawings—circles with eyes, flowers with mouths, goblets with fingers. The walls were all hung with Lotte Kopitzky's paintings, which she did in a state of trance and at the direction of her control—Bhaghavar Krishna, a Hindu sage supposed to have lived in the fourth century. It was he, Bhaghavar Krishna, who had painted the peacock with the golden tail, in the middle of which appeared the image of Buddha; the otherworldly trees hung with elflocks and fantastic fruits; the young women of the planet Venus with their branch-like arms and their ears from which stretched silver nets—organs of telepathy. Over the pictures, the old furniture, the shelves with books, there hovered reddish shadows. The windows were covered with heavy drapes.

At the round table on which lay a Ouija board, a trumpet, and a withered rose, sat Dr. Zorach Kalisher, small, broad-shouldered, bald in front and with sparse tufts of hair in the back, half yellow, half gray. From behind his yellow bushy brows peered a pair of small, piercing eyes. Dr. Kalisher had almost no neck—his head sat directly on his broad shoulders, making him look like a primitive African statue. His nose was crooked, flat at the top, the tip split in two. On his chin sprouted a tiny growth. It was hard to tell whether this was a remnant of a beard or just a hairy wart. The face was wrinkled, badly shaven, and grimy. He wore a black corduroy jacket, a white shirt covered with ash and coffee stains, and a crooked bow tie.

When conversing with Mrs. Kopitzky, he spoke an odd mixture of Yiddish and German. "What's keeping our friend Bhaghavar Krishna? Did he lose his way in the spheres of heaven?"

"Dr. Kalisher, don't rush me," Mrs. Kopitzky answered. "We cannot give them orders . . . they have their motives and their moods. Have a little patience."

535

"Well, if one must, one must."

Dr. Kalisher drummed his fingers on the table. From each finger sprouted a little red beard. Mrs. Kopitzky leaned her head on the back of the upholstered chair and prepared to fall into a trance. Against the dark glow of the red bulb, one could discern her freshly dyed hair, black without luster, waved into tiny ringlets; her rouged face, the broad nose, high cheekbones, and eyes spread far apart and heavily lined with mascara. Dr. Kalisher often joked that she looked like a painted bulldog. Her husband, Leon Kopitzky, a dentist, had died eighteen years before, leaving no children. The widow supported herself on an annuity from an insurance company. In 1929 she had lost her fortune in the Wall Street crash, but had recently begun to buy securities again on the advice of her Ouija board, planchette, and crystal ball. Mrs. Kopitzky even asked Bhaghavar Krishna for tips on the races. In a few cases, he had divulged in dreams the names of winning horses.

Dr. Kalisher bowed his head and covered his eyes with his hands, muttering to himself as solitary people often do. "Well, I've played the fool enough. This is the last night. Even from kreplach one has enough."

"Did you say something, Doctor?"

"What? Nothing."

"When you rush me, I can't fall into the trance."

"Trance-shmance," Dr. Kalisher grumbled to himself. "The ghost is late, that's all. Who does she think she's fooling? Just crazy—meshugga."

Aloud, he said: "I'm not rushing you, I've plenty of time. If what the Americans say about time is right, I'm a second Rockefeller."

As Mrs. Kopitzky opened her mouth to answer, her double chin, with all its warts, trembled, revealing a set of huge false teeth. Suddenly she threw back her head and sighed. She closed her eyes, and snorted once. Dr. Kalisher gaped at her questioningly, sadly. He had not yet heard the sound of the outside door opening, but Mrs. Kopitzky, who probably had the acute hearing of an animal, might have. Dr. Kalisher began to rub his temples and his nose, and then clutched at his tiny beard.

There was a time when he had tried to understand all things

through his reason, but that period of rationalism had long passed. Since then, he had constructed an anti-rationalistic philosophy, a kind of extreme hedonism which saw in eroticism the *Ding an sich*, and in reason the very lowest stage of being, the entropy which led to absolute death. His position had been a curious compound of Hartmann's idea of the Unconscious with the Cabala of Rabbi Isaac Luria, according to which all things, from the smallest grain of sand to the very Godhead itself, are Copulation and Union. It was because of this system that Dr. Kalisher had come from Paris to New York in 1939, leaving behind in Poland his father, a rabbi, a wife who refused to divorce him, and a lover, Nella, with whom he had lived for years in Berlin and later in Paris. It so happened that when Dr. Kalisher left for America, Nella went to visit her parents in Warsaw. He had planned to bring her over to the United States as soon as he found a translator, a publisher, and a chair at one of the American universities.

In those days Dr. Kalisher had still been hopeful. He had been offered a cathedra in the Hebrew University in Jerusalem; a publisher in Palestine was about to issue one of his books; his essays had been printed in Zurich and Paris. But with the outbreak of the Second World War, his life began to deteriorate. His literary agent suddenly died, his translator was inept and, to make matters worse, absconded with a good part of the manuscript, of which there was no copy. In the Yiddish press, for some strange reason, the reviewers turned hostile and hinted that he was a charlatan. The Jewish organizations which arranged lectures for him cancelled his tour. According to his own philosophy, he had believed that all suffering was nothing more than negative expressions of universal eroticism: Hitler, Stalin, the Nazis who sang the Horst Wessel song and made the Jews wear yellow armbands, were actually searching for new forms and variations of sexual salvation. But Dr. Kalisher began to doubt his own system and fell into despair. He had to leave his hotel and move into a cheap furnished room. He wandered about in shabby clothes, sat all day in cafeterias, drank endless cups of coffee, smoked bad cigars, and barely managed to survive on the few dollars that a relief organization gave him each month. The refugees whom he met spread all sorts of rumors about visas for those left behind in

Europe, packages of food and medicines that could be sent them through various agencies, ways of bringing over relatives from Poland through Honduras, Cuba, Brazil. But he, Zorach Kalisher, could save no one from the Nazis. He had received only a single letter from Nella.

Only in New York had Dr. Kalisher realized how attached he was to his mistress. Without her, he became impotent.

2

Everything was exactly as it had been yesterday and the day before. Bhaghavar Krishna began to speak in English with his foreign voice that was half male and half female, duplicating Mrs. Kopitzky's errors in pronunciation and grammar. Lotte Kopitzky came from a village in the Carpathian Mountains. Dr. Kalisher could never discover her nationality—Hungarian, Rumanian, Galician? She knew no Polish or German, and little English; even her Yiddish had been corrupted through her long years in America. Actually she had been left languageless and Bhaghavar Krishna spoke her various jargons. At first Dr. Kalisher had asked Bhaghavar Krishna the details of his earthly existence but had been told by Bhaghavar Krishna that he had forgotten everything in the heavenly mansions in which he dwelt. All he could recall was that he had lived in the sub-urbs of Madras. Bhaghavar Krishna did not even know that in that part of India Tamil was spoken. When Dr. Kalisher tried to converse with him about Sanskrit, the Mahabharata, the Ramayana, the Sakuntala, Bhaghavar Krishna replied that he was no longer interested in terrestrial literature. Bhaghavar Krishna knew nothing but a few theosophic and spiritualistic brochures and magazines which Mrs. Kopitzky subscribed to.

For Dr. Kalisher it was all one big joke; but if one lived in a bug-ridden room and had a stomach spoiled by cafeteria food, if one was in one's sixties and completely without family, one became tolerant of all kinds of crackpots. He had been intro-duced to Mrs. Kopitzky in 1942, took part in scores of her séances, read her automatic writings, admired her automatic paintings, listened to her automatic symphonies. A few times he had borrowed money from her which he had been unable to return. He ate at her house—vegetarian suppers, since Mrs.

Kopitzky touched neither meat, fish, milk, nor eggs, but only fruit and vegetables which mother earth produces. She specialized in preparing salads with nuts, almonds, pomegranates, avocados.

In the beginning, Lotte Kopitzky had wanted to draw him into a romance. The spirits were all of the opinion that Lotte Kopitzky and Zorach Kalisher derived from the same spiritual origin: *The Great White Lodge*. Even Bhaghavar Krishna had a taste for matchmaking. Lotte Kopitzky constantly conveyed to Dr. Kalisher regards from the Masters, who had connections with Tibet, Atlantis, the Heavenly Hierarchy, the Shambala, the Fourth Kingdom of Nature and the Council of Sanat Kumara. In heaven as on the earth, in the early forties, all kinds of crises were brewing. The Powers having realigned themselves, the members of the Ashrams were preparing a war on Cosmic Evil. The Hierarchy sent out projectors to light up the planet Earth, and to find esoteric men and women to serve special purposes. Mrs. Kopitzky assured Dr. Kalisher that he was ordained to play a huge part in the Universal Rebirth. But he had neglected his mission, disappointed the Master. He had promised to telephone, but didn't. He spent months in Philadelphia without dropping her a postcard. He returned without informing her. Mrs. Kopitzky ran into him in an automat on Sixth Avenue and found him in a torn coat, a dirty shirt, and shoes worn so thin they no longer had heels. He had not even applied for United States citizenship, though refugees were entitled to citizenship without going abroad to get a visa.

Now, in 1946, everything that Lotte Kopitzky had prophesied had come true. All had passed over to the other side— his father, his brothers, his sisters, Nella. Bhaghavar Krishna brought messages from them. The Masters still remembered Dr. Kalisher, and still had plans for him in connection with the Centennial Conference of the Hierarchy. Even the fact that his family had perished in Treblinka, Maidanek, Stutthof was closely connected with the Powers of Light, the Development of Karma, the New Cycle after Lemuria, and with the aim of leading humanity to a new ascent in Love and a new Aquatic Epoch.

During the last few weeks, Mrs. Kopitzky had become dissatisfied with summoning Nella's spirit in the usual way. Dr.

Kalisher was given the rare opportunity of coming into contact with Nella's materialized form. It happened in this way: Bhaghavar Krishna would give a sign to Dr. Kalisher that he should walk down the dark corridor to Mrs. Kopitzky's bedroom. There in the darkness, near Mrs. Kopitzky's bureau, an apparition hovered which was supposed to be Nella. She murmured to Dr. Kalisher in Polish, spoke caressing words into his ear, brought him messages from friends and relatives. Bhaghavar Krishna had admonished Dr. Kalisher time and again not to try to touch the phantom, because contact could cause severe injury to both, to him and Mrs. Kopitzky. The few times that he sought to approach her, she deftly eluded him. But confused though Dr. Kalisher was by these episodes, he was aware that they were contrived. This was not Nella, neither her voice nor her manner. The messages he received proved nothing. He had mentioned all these names to Mrs. Kopitzky and had been questioned by her. But Dr. Kalisher remained curious: Who was the apparition? Why did she act the part? Probably for money. But the fact that Lotte Kopitzky was capable of hiring a ghost proved that she was not only a self-deceiver but a swindler of others as well. Every time Dr. Kalisher walked down the dark corridor, he murmured, "Crazy, meshugga, a ridiculous woman."

Tonight Dr. Kalisher could hardly wait for Bhaghavar Krishna's signal. He was tired of these absurdities. For years he had suffered from a prostate condition and now had to urinate every half hour. A Warsaw doctor who was not allowed to practice in America, but did so clandestinely nonetheless, had warned Dr. Kalisher not to postpone an operation, because complications might arise. But Kalisher had neither the money for the hospital nor the will to go there. He sought to cure himself with baths, hot-water bottles, and with pills he had brought with him from France. He even tried to massage his prostate gland himself. As a rule, he went to the bathroom the moment he arrived at Mrs. Kopitzky's, but this evening he had neglected to do so. He felt a pressure on his bladder. The raw vegetables which Mrs. Kopitzky had given him to eat made his intestines twist. "Well, I'm too old for such pleasures," he murmured. As Bhaghavar Krishna spoke, Dr. Kalisher could scarcely listen. "What is she babbling, the idiot? She's not even a decent ventriloquist."

The instant Bhaghavar Krishna gave his usual sign, Dr. Kalisher got up. His legs had been troubling him greatly but had never been as shaky as tonight. "Well, I'll go to the bathroom first," he decided. To reach the bathroom in the dark was not easy. Dr. Kalisher walked hesitantly, his hands outstretched, trying to feel his way. When he had reached the bathroom and opened the door, someone inside pulled the knob back. It is she, the girl, Dr. Kalisher realized. So shaken was he that he forgot why he was there. "She most probably came here to undress." He was embarrassed both for himself and for Mrs. Kopitzky. "What does she need it for, for whom is she playing this comedy?" His eyes had become accustomed to the dark. He had seen the girl's silhouette. The bathroom had a window giving on to the street, and the shimmer of the street lamp had fallen on to it. She was small, broadish, with a high bosom. She appeared to have been in her underwear. Dr. Kalisher stood there hypnotized. He wanted to cry out, "Enough, it's all so obvious," but his tongue was numb. His heart pounded and he could hear his own breathing.

After a while he began to retrace his steps, but he was dazed with blindness. He bumped into a clothes tree and hit a wall, striking his head. He stepped backwards. Something fell and broke. Perhaps one of Mrs. Kopitzky's otherworldly sculptures! At that moment the telephone began to ring, the sound unusually loud and menacing. Dr. Kalisher shivered. He suddenly felt a warmth in his underwear. He had wet himself like a child.

3

"Well, I've reached the bottom," Dr. Kalisher muttered to himself. "I'm ready for the junkyard." He walked toward the bedroom. Not only his underwear, his pants also had become wet. He expected Mrs. Kopitzky to answer the telephone; it happened more than once that she awakened from her trance to discuss stocks, bonds, and dividends. But the telephone kept on ringing. Only now he realized what he had done—he

had closed the living-room door, shutting out the red glow
which helped him find his way. "I'm going home," he resolved. He turned toward the street door but found he had
lost all sense of direction in that labyrinth of an apartment. He
touched a knob and turned it. He heard a muffled scream.
He had wandered into the bathroom again. There seemed to
be no hook or chain inside. Again he saw the woman in a
corset, but this time with her face half in the light. In that split
second he knew she was middle-aged.

"Forgive, please." And he moved back.

The telephone stopped ringing, then began anew. Suddenly
Dr. Kalisher glimpsed a shaft of red light and heard Mrs. Kopitzky walking toward the telephone. He stopped and said,
half statement, half question: "Mrs. Kopitzky!"

Mrs. Kopitzky started. "Already finished?"

"I'm not well, I must go home."

"Not well? Where do you want to go? What's the matter?
Your heart?"

"Everything."

"Wait a second."

Mrs. Kopitzky, having approached him, took his arm and
led him back to the living room. The telephone continued to
ring and then finally fell silent. "Did you get a pressure in your
heart, huh?" Mrs. Kopitzky asked. "Lie down on the sofa, I'll
get a doctor."

"No, no, not necessary."

"I'll massage you."

"My bladder is not in order, my prostate gland."

"What? I'll put on the light."

He wanted to ask her not to do so, but she had already
turned on a number of lamps. The light glared in his eyes. She
stood looking at him and at his wet pants. Her head shook
from side to side. Then she said, "This is what comes from
living alone."

"Really, I'm ashamed of myself."

"What's the shame? We all get older. Nobody gets younger.
Were you in the bathroom?"

Dr. Kalisher didn't answer.

"Wait a moment, I still have *his* clothes. I had a premonition
I would need them someday."

Mrs. Kopitzky left the room. Dr. Kalisher sat down on the edge of a chair, placing his handkerchief beneath him. He sat there stiff, wet, childishly guilty and helpless, and yet with that inner quiet that comes from illness. For years he had been afraid of doctors, hospitals, and especially nurses, who deny their feminine shyness and treat grownup men like babies. Now he was prepared for the last degradations of the body. "Well, I'm finished, *kaput*," . . . He made a swift summation of his existence. "Philosophy? what philosophy? Eroticism? whose eroticism?" He had played with phrases for years, had come to no conclusions. What had happened to him, in him, all that had taken place in Poland, in Russia, on the planets, on the far-away galaxies, could not be reduced either to Schopenhauer's blind will or to his, Kalisher's, eroticism. It was explained neither by Spinoza's substance, Leibnitz's monads, Hegel's dialectic, or Heckel's monism. "They all just juggle words like Mrs. Kopitzky. It's better that I didn't publish all that scribbling of mine. What's the good of all these preposterous hypotheses? They don't help at all. . . ." He looked up at Mrs. Kopitzky's pictures on the wall, and in the blazing light they resembled the smearings of school children. From the street came the honking of cars, the screams of boys, the thundering echo of the subway as a train passed. The door opened and Mrs. Kopitzky entered with a bundle of clothes: a jacket, pants, and shirt, and underwear. The clothes smelled of mothballs and dust. She said to him, "Have you been in the bedroom?"

"What? No."

"Nella didn't materialize?"

"No, she didn't materialize."

"Well, change your clothes. Don't let me embarrass you."

She put the bundle on the sofa and bent over Dr. Kalisher with the devotion of a relative. She said, "You'll stay here. Tomorrow I'll send for your things."

"No, that's senseless."

"I knew that this would happen the moment we were introduced on Second Avenue."

"How so? Well, it's all the same."

"*They* tell me things in advance. I look at someone, and I know what will happen to him."

"So? When am I going to go?"

"You still have to live many years. You're needed here. You have to finish your work."

"My work has the same value as your ghosts."

"There *are* ghosts, there are! Don't be so cynical. They watch over us from above, they lead us by the hand, they measure our steps. We are much more important to the Cyclic Revival of the Universe than you imagine."

He wanted to ask her: "Why then, did you have to hire a woman to deceive me?" but he remained silent. Mrs. Kopitzky went out again. Dr. Kalisher took off his pants and his underwear and dried himself with his handkerchief. For a while he stood with his upper part fully dressed and his pants off like some mad jester. Then he stepped into a pair of loose drawers that were as cool as shrouds. He pulled on a pair of striped pants that were too wide and too long for him. He had to draw the pants up until the hem reached his knees. He gasped and snorted, had to stop every few seconds to rest. Suddenly he remembered! This was exactly how as a boy he had dressed himself in his father's clothes when his father napped after the Sabbath pudding: the old man's white trousers, his satin robe, his fringed garment, his fur hat. Now his father had become a pile of ashes somewhere in Poland, and he, Zorach, put on the musty clothes of a dentist. He walked to the mirror and looked at himself, even stuck out his tongue like a child. Then he lay down on the sofa. The telephone rang again, and Mrs. Kopitzky apparently answered it, because this time the ringing stopped immediately. Dr. Kalisher closed his eyes and lay quietly. He had nothing to hope for. There was not even anything to think about.

He dozed off and found himself in the cafeteria on Forty-second Street, near the Public Library. He was breaking off pieces of an egg cookie. A refugee was telling him how to save relatives in Poland by dressing them up in Nazi uniforms. Later they would be led by ship to the North Pole, the South Pole, and across the Pacific. Agents were prepared to take charge of them in Tierra del Fuego, in Honolulu and Yokohama. . . . How strange, but that smuggling had something to do with his, Zorach Kalisher's, philosophic system, not with his former version but with a new one, which blended eroticism with memory. While he was combining all these images, he asked himself in astonishment: "What kind of relationship can there be between sex, memory, and the redemption of the ego? And how will it work in infinite time? It's nothing but casuistry, casuistry. It's a way of explaining my own impotence. And how can I bring over Nella when she has already perished? Unless death itself is nothing but a sexual amnesia." He awoke and saw Mrs. Kopitzky bending over him with a pillow which she was about to put behind his head.

"How do you feel?"

"Has Nella left?" he asked, amazed at his own words. He must still be half asleep.

Mrs. Kopitzky winced. Her double chin shook and trembled. Her dark eyes were filled with motherly reproach.

"You're laughing, huh? There is no death, there isn't any. We live forever, and we love forever. This is the pure truth."

Translated by Roger H. Klein and Cecil Hemley

The Slaughterer

YOINEH MEIR should have become the Kolomir rabbi. His father and his grandfather had both sat in the rabbinical chair in Kolomir. However, the followers of the Kuzmir court had set up a stubborn opposition: this time they would not allow a Hassid from Trisk to become the town's rabbi. They bribed the direct official and sent a petition to the governor. After long wrangling, the Kuzmir Hassidim finally had their way and installed a rabbi of their own. In order not to leave Yoineh Meir without a source of earnings, they appointed him the town's ritual slaughterer.

When Yoineh Meir heard of this, he turned even paler than usual. He protested that slaughtering was not for him. He was softhearted; he could not bear the sight of blood. But everybody banded together to persuade him—the leaders of the community; the members of the Trisk synagogue; his father-in-law, Reb Getz Frampoler; and Reitze Doshe, his wife. The new rabbi, Reb Sholem Levi Halberstam, also pressed him to accept. Reb Sholem Levi, a grandson of the Sondz rabbi, was troubled about the sin of taking away another's livelihood; he did not want the younger man to be without bread. The Trisk rabbi, Reb Yakov Leibele, wrote a letter to Yoineh Meir saying that man may not be more compassionate than the Almighty, the Source of all compassion. When you slaughter an animal with a pure knife and with piety, you liberate the soul that resides in it. For it is well known that the souls of saints often transmigrate into the bodies of cows, fowl, and fish to do penance for some offense.

After the rabbi's letter, Yoineh Meir gave in. He had been ordained a long time ago. Now he set himself to studying the laws of slaughter as expounded in the *Grain of the Ox*, the *Shulchan Aruch*, and the Commentaries. The first paragraph of the *Grain of the Ox* says that the ritual slaughterer must be a God-fearing man, and Yoineh Meir devoted himself to the Law with more zeal than ever.

Yoineh Meir—small, thin, with a pale face, a tiny yellow beard on the tip of his chin, a crooked nose, a sunken mouth, and yellow frightened eyes set too close together—was renowned for his piety. When he prayed, he put on three pairs of phylacteries: those of Rashi, those of Rabbi Tam, and those of Rabbi Sherira Gaon. Soon after he had completed his term of board at the home of his father-in-law, he began to keep all fast days and to get up for midnight service.

His wife, Reitze Doshe, already lamented that Yoineh Meir was not of this world. She complained to her mother that he never spoke a word to her and paid her no attention, even on her clean days. He came to her only on the nights after she had visited the ritual bath, once a month. She said that he did not remember the names of his own daughters.

After he agreed to become the ritual slaughterer, Yoineh Meir imposed new rigors upon himself. He ate less and less. He almost stopped speaking. When a beggar came to the door, Yoineh Meir ran to welcome him and gave him his last groschen. The truth is that becoming a slaughterer plunged Yoineh Meir into melancholy, but he did not dare to oppose the rabbi's will. It was meant to be, Yoineh Meir said to himself; it was his destiny to cause torment and to suffer torment. And only heaven knew how much Yoineh Meir suffered.

Yoineh Meir was afraid that he might faint as he slaughtered his first fowl, or that his hand might not be steady. At the same time, somewhere in his heart, he hoped that he would commit an error. This would release him from the rabbi's command. However, everything went according to rule.

Many times a day, Yoineh Meir repeated to himself the rabbi's words: "A man may not be more compassionate than the Source of all compassion." The Torah says, "Thou shalt kill of thy herd and thy flock as I have commanded thee." Moses was instructed on Mount Sinai in the ways of slaughtering and of opening the animal in search of impurities. It is all a mystery of mysteries—life, death, man, beast. Those that are not slaughtered die anyway of various diseases, often ailing for weeks or months. In the forest, the beasts devour one another. In the seas, fish swallow fish. The Kolomir poorhouse is full of cripples and paralytics who lie there for years, befouling themselves. No man can escape the sorrows of this world.

And yet Yoineh Meir could find no consolation. Every tremor of the slaughtered fowl was answered by a tremor in

Yoineh Meir's own bowels. The killing of every beast, great or small, caused him as much pain as though he were cutting his own throat. Of all the punishments that could have been visited upon him, slaughtering was the worst.

Barely three months had passed since Yoineh Meir had become a slaughterer, but the time seemed to stretch endlessly. He felt as though he were immersed in blood and lymph. His ears were beset by the squawking of hens, the crowing of roosters, the gobbling of geese, the lowing of oxen, the mooing and bleating of calves and goats; wings fluttered, claws tapped on the floor. The bodies refused to know any justification or excuse—every body resisted in its own fashion, tried to escape, and seemed to argue with the Creator to its last breath.

And Yoineh Meir's own mind raged with questions. Verily, in order to create the world, the Infinite One had had to shrink His light; there could be no free choice without pain. But since the beasts were not endowed with free choice, why should they have to suffer? Yoineh Meir watched, trembling, as the butchers chopped the cows with their axes and skinned them before they had heaved their last breath. The women plucked the feathers from the chickens while they were still alive.

It is the custom that the slaughterer receives the spleen and tripe of every cow. Yoineh Meir's house overflowed with meat. Reitze Doshe boiled soups in pots as huge as cauldrons. In the large kitchen there was a constant frenzy of cooking, roasting, frying, baking, stirring, and skimming. Reitze Doshe was pregnant again, and her stomach protruded into a point. Big and stout, she had five sisters, all as bulky as herself. Her sisters came with their children. Every day, his mother-in-law, Reitze Doshe's mother, brought new pastries and delicacies of her own baking. A woman must not let her voice be heard, but Reitze Doshe's maidservant, the daughter of a water carrier, sang songs, pattered around barefoot, with her hair down, and laughed so loudly that the noise resounded in every room.

Yoineh Meir wanted to escape from the material world, but the material world pursued him. The smell of the slaughterhouse would not leave his nostrils. He tried to forget himself in the Torah, but he found that the Torah itself was full of earthly matters. He took to the Cabala, though he knew that no man may delve into the mysteries until he reaches the age of forty. Nevertheless, he continued to leaf through the *Treatise of the Hassidim*, *The Orchard*, the *Book of Creation*, and *The Tree of Life*. There, in the higher spheres, there was no death, no slaughtering, no pain, no stomachs and intestines, no hearts or lungs or livers, no membranes, and no impurities.

This particular night, Yoineh Meir went to the window and looked up into the sky. The moon spread a radiance around it. The stars flashed and twinkled, each with its own heavenly secret. Somewhere above the World of Deeds, above the constellations, Angels were flying, and Seraphim, and Holy Wheels, and Holy Beasts. In Paradise, the mysteries of the Torah were revealed to souls. Every holy zaddik inherited three hundred and ten worlds and wove crowns for the Divine Presence. The nearer to the Throne of Glory, the brighter the light, the purer the radiance, the fewer the unholy host.

Yoineh Meir knew that man may not ask for death, but deep within himself he longed for the end. He had developed a repugnance for everything that had to do with the body. He could not even bring himself to go to the ritual bath with the other men. Under every skin he saw blood. Every neck reminded Yoineh Meir of the knife. Human beings, like beasts, had loins, veins, guts, buttocks. One slash of the knife and those solid householders would drop like oxen. As the Talmud says, all that is meant to be burned is already as good as burned. If the end of man was corruption, worms, and stench, then he was nothing but a piece of putrid flesh to start with.

Yoineh Meir understood now why the sages of old had likened the body to a cage—a prison where the soul sits captive, longing for the day of its release. It was only now that he truly grasped the meaning of the words of the Talmud: "Very good, this is death." Yet man was forbidden to break out of his prison. He must wait for the jailer to remove the chains, to open the gate.

Yoineh Meir returned to his bed. All his life he had slept on a feather bed, under a feather quilt, resting his head on a pillow; now he was suddenly aware that he was lying on feathers and down plucked from fowl. In the other bed, next to Yoineh

Meir's, Reitze Doshe was snoring. From time to time a whistle came from her nostrils and a bubble formed on her lips. Yoineh Meir's daughters kept going to the slop pail, their bare feet pattering on the floor. They slept together, and sometimes they whispered and giggled half the night.

Yoineh Meir had longed for sons who would study the Torah, but Reitze Doshe bore girl after girl. While they were small, Yoineh Meir occasionally gave them a pinch on the cheek. Whenever he attended a circumcision, he would bring them a piece of cake. Sometimes he would even kiss one of the little ones on the head. But now they were grown. They seemed to have taken after their mother. They had spread out in width. Reitze Doshe complained that they ate too much and were getting too fat. They stole tidbits from the pots. The eldest, Bashe, was already sought in marriage. At one moment, the girls quarreled and insulted each other, at the next they combed each other's hair and plaited it into braids. They were forever babbling about dresses, shoes, stockings, jackets, panties. They cried and they laughed. They looked for lice, they fought, they washed, they kissed.

When Yoineh Meir tried to chide them, Reitze Doshe cried, "Don't butt in! Let the children alone!" Or she would scold, "You had better see to it that your daughters shouldn't have to go around barefoot and naked!"

Why did they need so many things? Why was it necessary to clothe and adorn the body so much, Yoineh Meir would wonder to himself.

Before he had become a slaughterer, he was seldom at home and hardly knew what went on there. But now he began to stay at home, and he saw what they were doing. The girls would run off to pick berries and mushrooms; they associated with the daughters of common homes. They brought home baskets of dry twigs. Reitze Doshe made jam. Tailors came for fittings. Shoemakers measured the women's feet. Reitze Doshe and her mother argued about Bashe's dowry. Yoineh Meir heard talk about a silk dress, a velvet dress, all sorts of skirts, cloaks, fur coats.

Now that he lay awake, all those words reechoed in his ears. They were rolling in luxury because he, Yoineh Meir, had begun to earn money. Somewhere in Reitze Doshe's womb a new child was growing, but Yoineh Meir sensed clearly that it would be another girl. "Well, one must welcome whatever heaven sends," he warned himself.

He had covered himself, but now he felt too hot. The pillow under his head became strangely hard, as though there were a stone among the feathers. He, Yoineh Meir, was himself a body: feet, a belly, a chest, elbows. There was a stabbing in his entrails. His palate felt dry.

Yoineh Meir sat up. "Father in heaven, I cannot breathe!"

2

Elul is a month of repentance. In former years, Elul would bring with it a sense of exalted serenity. Yoineh Meir loved the cool breezes that came from the woods and the harvested fields. He could gaze for a long time at the pale-blue sky with its scattered clouds that reminded him of the flax in which the citrons for the Feast of Tabernacles were wrapped. Gossamer floated in the air. On the trees the leaves turned saffron yellow. In the twittering of the birds he heard the melancholy of the Solemn Days, when man takes an accounting of his soul.

But to a slaughterer Elul is quite another matter. A great many beasts are slaughtered for the New Year. Before the Day of Atonement, everybody offers a sacrificial fowl. In every courtyard, cocks crowed and hens cackled, and all of them had to be put to death. Then comes the Feast of Booths, the Day of the Willow Twigs, the Feast of Azereth, the Day of Rejoicing in the Law, the Sabbath of Genesis. Each holiday brings its own slaughter. Millions of fowl and cattle now alive were doomed to be killed.

Yoineh Meir no longer slept at night. If he dozed off, he was immediately beset by nightmares. Cows assumed human shape, with beards and side locks, and skullcaps over their horns. Yoineh Meir would be slaughtering a calf, but it would turn into a girl. Her neck throbbed, and she pleaded to be saved. She ran to the study house and spattered the courtyard with her blood. He even dreamed that he had slaughtered Reitze Doshe instead of a sheep.

In one of his nightmares, he heard a human voice come from a slaughtered goat. The goat, with his throat slit, jumped on Yoineh Meir and tried to butt him, cursing in Hebrew and Aramaic, spitting and foaming at him. Yoineh Meir awakened in a sweat. A cock crowed like a bell. Others answered, like a congregation answering the cantor. It seemed to Yoineh Meir that the fowl were crying out questions, protesting, lamenting in chorus the misfortune that loomed over them.

Yoineh Meir could not rest. He sat up, grasped his side locks with both hands, and rocked.

Reitze Doshe woke up. "What's the matter?"

"Nothing, nothing."

"What are you rocking for?"

"Let me be."

"You frighten me!"

After a while Reitze Doshe began to snore again. Yoineh Meir got out of bed, washed his hands, and dressed. He wanted to put ash on his forehead and recite the midnight prayer, but his lips refused to utter the holy words. How could he mourn the destruction of the Temple when a carnage was being readied here in Kolomir, and he, Yoineh Meir, was the Titus, the Nebuchadnezzar!

The air in the house was stifling. It smelled of sweat, fat, dirty underwear, urine. One of his daughters muttered something in her sleep, another one moaned. The beds creaked. A rustling came from the closets. In the coop under the stove were the sacrificial fowls that Reitze Doshe had locked up for the Day of Atonement. Yoineh Meir heard the scratching of a mouse, the chirping of a cricket. It seemed to him that he could hear the worms burrowing through the ceiling and the floor. Innumerable creatures surrounded man, each with its own nature, its own claims on the Creator.

Yoineh Meir went out into the yard. Here everything was cool and fresh. The dew had formed. In the sky, the midnight stars were glittering. Yoineh Meir inhaled deeply. He walked on the wet grass, among the leaves and shrubs. His socks grew damp above his slippers. He came to a tree and stopped. In the branches there seemed to be some nests. He heard the twittering of awakened fledglings. Frogs croaked in the swamp beyond the hill. "Don't they sleep at all, those frogs?" Yoineh Meir asked himself. "They have the voices of men."

Since Yoineh Meir had begun to slaughter, his thoughts were obsessed with living creatures. He grappled with all sorts of questions. Where did flies come from? Were they born out of their mother's womb, or did they hatch from eggs? If all the flies died out in winter, where did the new ones come from in summer? And the owl that nested under the synagogue roof—what did it do when the frosts came? Did it remain there? Did it fly away to warm countries? And how could anything live in the burning frost, when it was scarcely possible to keep warm under the quilt?

An unfamiliar love welled up in Yoineh Meir for all that crawls and flies, breeds and swarms. Even the mice—was it their fault that they were mice? What wrong does a mouse do? All it wants is a crumb of bread or a bit of cheese. Then why is the cat such an enemy to it?

Yoineh Meir rocked back and forth in the dark. The rabbi may be right. Man cannot and must not have more compassion than the Master of the universe. Yet he, Yoineh Meir, was sick with pity. How could one pray for life for the coming year, or for a favorable writ in Heaven, when one was robbing others of the breath of life?

Yoineh Meir thought that the Messiah Himself could not redeem the world as long as injustice was done to beasts. By rights, everything should rise from the dead: every calf, fish, gnat, butterfly. Even in the worm that crawls in the earth there glows a divine spark. When you slaughter a creature, you slaughter God. . . .

"Woe is me, I am losing my mind!" Yoineh Meir muttered.

A week before the New Year, there was a rush of slaughtering. All day long, Yoineh Meir stood near a pit, slaughtering hens, roosters, geese, ducks. Women pushed, argued, tried to get to the slaughterer first. Others joked, laughed, bantered. Feathers flew, the yard was full of quacking, gabbling, the screaming of roosters. Now and then a fowl cried out like a human being.

Yoineh Meir was filled with a gripping pain. Until this day he had still hoped that he would get accustomed to slaughtering. But now he knew that if he continued for a hundred years his suffering would not cease. His knees shook. His belly felt distended. His mouth was flooded with bitter fluids. Reitze Doshe and her sisters were also in the yard, talking with the women, wishing each a blessed New Year, and voicing the pious hope that they would meet again next year.

Yoineh Meir feared that he was no longer slaughtering according to the Law. At one moment, a blackness swam before his eyes; at the next, everything turned golden green. He constantly tested the knife blade on the nail of his forefinger to make sure it was not nicked. Every fifteen minutes he had to go to urinate. Mosquitoes bit him. Crows cawed at him from among the branches.

He stood there until sundown, and the pit became filled with blood.

After the evening prayers, Reitze Doshe served Yoineh Meir buckwheat soup with pot roast. But though he had not tasted any food since morning, he could not eat. His throat felt constricted, there was a lump in his gullet, and he could scarcely swallow the first bite. He recited the Shema of Rabbi Isaac Luria, made his confession, and beat his breast like a man who was mortally sick.

Yoineh Meir thought that he would be unable to sleep that night, but his eyes closed as soon as his head was on the pillow and he had recited the last benediction before sleep. It seemed to him that he was examining a slaughtered cow for impurities, slitting open its belly, tearing out the lungs and blowing them up. What did it mean? For this was usually the butcher's task. The lungs grew larger and larger; they covered the whole table and swelled upward toward the ceiling. Yoineh Meir ceased blowing, but the lobes continued to expand by themselves. The smaller lobe, the one that is called "the thief," shook and fluttered, as if trying to break away. Suddenly a whistling, a coughing, a growling lamentation broke from the windpipe. A dybbuk began to speak, shout, sing, pour out a stream of verses, quotations from the Talmud, passages from the Zohar. The lungs rose up and flew, flapping like wings. Yoineh Meir wanted to escape, but the door was barred by a black bull with red eyes and pointed horns. The bull wheezed and opened a maw full of long teeth.

Yoineh Meir shuddered and woke up. His body was bathed in sweat. His skull felt swollen and filled with sand. His feet lay on the straw pallet, inert as logs. He made an effort and sat up. He put on his robe and went out. The night hung heavy and impenetrable, thick with the darkness of the hour before sunrise. From time to time a gust of air came from somewhere, like a sigh of someone unseen.

A tingling ran down Yoineh Meir's spine, as though someone brushed it with a feather. Something in him wept and mocked. "Well, and what if the rabbi said so?" he spoke to himself. "And even if God Almighty had commanded, what of that? I'll do without rewards in the world to come! I want no Paradise, no Leviathan, no Wild Ox! Let them stretch me on a bed of nails. Let them throw me into the Hollow of the Sling. I'll have none of your favors, God! I am no longer afraid of your Judgment! I am a betrayer of Israel, a willful transgressor!" Yoineh Meir cried. "I have more compassion than God Almighty—more, more! He is a cruel God, a Man of War, a God of Vengeance. I will not serve Him. It is an abandoned world!" Yoineh Meir laughed, but tears ran down his cheeks in scalding drops.

Yoineh Meir went to the pantry where he kept his knives, his whetstone, the circumcision knife. He gathered them all and dropped them into the pit of the outhouse. He knew that he was blaspheming, that he was desecrating the holy instruments, that he was mad, but he no longer wished to be sane.

He went outside and began to walk toward the river, the bridge, the wood. His prayer shawl and phylacteries? He needed none! The parchment was taken from the hide of a cow. The cases of the phylacteries were made of calf's leather. The Torah itself was made of animal skin. "Father in Heaven, Thou art a slaughterer!" a voice cried in Yoineh Meir. "Thou art a slaughterer and the Angel of Death! The whole world is a slaughterhouse!"

A slipper fell off Yoineh Meir's foot, but he let it lie, striding on in one slipper and one sock. He began to call, shout, sing. I am driving myself out of my mind, he thought. But this is itself a mark of madness. . . .

He had opened a door to his brain, and madness flowed in, flooding everything. From moment to moment, Yoineh Meir grew more rebellious. He threw away his skullcap, grasped his prayer fringes and ripped them off, tore off pieces of his vest. A strength possessed him, the recklessness of one who had cast away all burdens.

Dogs chased him, barking, but he drove them off. Doors were flung open. Men ran out barefoot, with feathers clinging to their skullcaps. Women came out in their petticoats and nightcaps. All of them shouted, tried to bar his way, but Yoineh Meir evaded them.

The sky turned red as blood, and a round skull pushed up out of the bloody sea as out of the womb of a woman in childbirth.

Someone had gone to tell the butchers that Yoineh Meir had lost his mind. They came running with sticks and rope, but Yoineh Meir was already over the bridge and was hurrying across the harvested fields. He ran and vomited. He fell and rose, bruised by the stubble. Shepherds who take the horses out to graze at night mocked him and threw horse dung at him. The cows at pasture ran after him. Bells tolled as for a fire.

Yoineh Meir heard shouts, screams, the stamping of running feet. The earth began to slope and Yoineh Meir rolled downhill. He reached the wood, leaped over tufts of moss, rocks, running brooks. Yoineh Meir knew the truth: this was not the river before him; it was a bloody swamp. Blood ran from the sun, staining the tree trunks. From the branches hung intestines, livers, kidneys. The forequarters of beasts rose to their feet and sprayed him with gall and slime. Yoineh Meir could not escape. Myriads of cows and fowls encircled him, ready to take revenge for every cut, every wound, every slit gullet, every plucked feather. With bleeding throats, they all chanted, "Everyone may kill, and every killing is permitted."

Yoineh Meir broke into a wail that echoed through the wood in many voices. He raised his fists to heaven: "Fiend! Murderer! Devouring beast!"

For two days the butchers searched for him, but they did not find him. Then Zeinvel, who owned the watermill, arrived in town with the news that Yoineh Meir's body had turned up in the river by the dam. He had drowned.

The members of the burial society immediately went to bring the corpse. There were many witnesses to testify that

Yoineh Meir had behaved like a madman, and the rabbi ruled that the deceased was not a suicide. The body of the dead man was cleansed and given burial near the graves of his father and his grandfather. The rabbi himself delivered the eulogy.

Because it was the holiday season and there was danger that Kolomir might remain without meat, the community hastily dispatched two messengers to bring a new slaughterer.

Translated by Mirra Ginsburg

The Dead Fiddler

I N THE TOWN of Shidlovtse, which lies between Radom and
Kielce, not far from the Mountains of the Holly Cross,
there lived a man by the name of Reb Sheftel Vengrover. This
Reb Sheftel was supposedly a grain merchant, but all the
buying and selling was done by his wife, Zise Feige. She
bought wheat, corn, barley, and buckwheat from the landowners and the peasants and sent it to Warsaw. She also had some
of the grain milled and sold the flour to stores and bakeries.
Zise Feige owned a granary and had an assistant, Zalkind, who
helped her in the business and did all the work that required a
man's hand; he carried sacks, looked after the horses, and
served as coachman whenever Zise Feige drove out to a fair or
went to visit a landowner.

Reb Sheftel held to the belief that the Torah is the worthiest
merchandise of all. He rose at dawn and went to the study
house to pore over the Gemara, the Annotations and Commentaries, the Midrash, and the Zohar. In the evenings, he
would read a lesson from the Mishnah with the Mishnah Society. Reb Sheftel also devoted himself to community affairs and
was an ardent Radzymin Hassid.

Red Sheftel was not much taller than a midget, but he had
the longest beard in Shidlovtse and the surrounding district.
His beard reached down to his knees and seemed to contain
every color: red, yellow, even the color of hay. At Tishah b'Av,
when the mischiefmakers pelted everyone with burs, Reb Sheftel's beard would be full of them. At first Zise Feige had tried
to pull them out, but Reb Sheftel would not allow it, for she
pulled out the hairs of the beard too, and a man's beard is a
mark of his Jewishness and a reminder that he was created in
the image of God. The burs remained in his beard until they
dropped out by themselves. Reb Sheftel did not curl his sidelocks, considering this a frivolous custom. They hung down to
his shoulders. A tuft of hair grew on his nose. As he studied, he
smoked a long pipe.

When Reb Sheftel stood at the lectern in the synagogue in
his prayer shawl and phylacteries, he looked like one of the

ancients. He had a high forehead, and under shaggy eyebrows, eyes that combined the sharp glance of a scholar with the humility of a God-fearing man. Reb Sheftel imposed a variety of penances upon himself. He drank no milk unless he had been present at the milking. He ate no meat except on the Sabbath and on holidays and only if he had examined the slaughtering knife in advance. It was told of him that on the eve of Passover he ordered that the cat wear socklets on its feet, lest it bring into the house the smallest crumb of unleavened bread. Every night, he faithfully performed the midnight prayers. People said that although he had inherited his grain business from his father and grandfather he still could not distinguish between rye and wheat.

Zise Feige was a head taller than her husband and in her younger days had been famous for her good looks. The land-lords who sold her grain showered her with compliments, but a good Jewish woman pays no attention to idle talk. Zise Feige loved her husband and considered it an honor to help him serve the Almighty.

She had borne nine children, but only three remained: a married son, Jedidiah, who took board with his father-in-law in Wlodowa; a boy Tsadock Meyer, who was still in heder; and a grown daughter, Liebe Yentl. Liebe Yentl had been engaged and about to be married, but her fiancé, Ozer, caught a cold and died. This Ozer had a reputation as a prodigy and a scholar. His father was the president of the community in Opola. Although Liebe Yentl had seen Ozer only during the signing of the betrothal papers, she wept bitterly when she heard the bad news. Almost at once she was besieged with marriage offers, for she was already a ripe girl of seventeen, but Zise Feige felt that it was best to wait until she got over her misfortune.

Liebe Yentl's betrothed, Ozer, departed this world just after Passover. Now it was already the month of Heshvan. Succoth is usually followed by rains and snow, but this fall was a mild one. The sun shone. The sky was blue, as after Pentecost. The peasants in the villages complained that the winter crops were beginning to sprout in the fields, which could lead to crop fail-ure. People feared that the warm weather might bring epi-demics. In the meantime, grain prices rose by three groschen on the pood, and Zise Feige had higher profits. As was the custom between man and wife, she gave Reb Sheftel an accounting of the week's earnings every Sabbath evening, and he immediately deducted a share—for the study house, the prayer house, the mending of sacred books, for the inmates of the poorhouse, and for itinerant beggars. There was no lack of need for charity.

Since Zise Feige had a servant girl, Dunya, and was herself a fine housekeeper, Liebe Yentl paid little attention to household matters. She had her own room, where she would often sit, reading storybooks. She copied letters from the letter book. When she had read through all the storybooks, she secretly took to borrowing from her father's bookcase. She was also good at sewing and embroidery. She was fond of fine clothes. Liebe Yentl inherited her mother's beauty, but her red hair came from her father's side. Like her father's beard, her hair was uncommonly long—down to her loins. Since the mishap with Ozer, her face, always pale, had grown paler still and more delicate. Her eyes were green.

Reb Sheftel paid little attention to his daughter. He merely prayed to the Lord to send her the right husband. But Zise Feige saw that the girl was growing up as wild as a weed. Her head was full of whims and fancies. She did not allow herring or radishes to be mentioned in her presence. She averted her eyes from slaughtered fowl and from meat on the salting board or in the soaking dish. If she found a fly in her groats, she would eat nothing for the rest of the day. She had no friends in Shidlovtse. She complained that the girls of the town were common and backward; as soon as they were married, they became careless and slovenly. Whenever she had to go among people, she fasted the day before, for fear that she might vomit. Although she was beautiful, clever, and learned, it always seemed to her that people were laughing and pointing at her.

Zise Feige wanted many times to talk to her husband about the troubles she was having with their daughter, but she was reluctant to divert him from his studies. Besides, he might not understand a woman's problems. He had a rule for everything. On the few occasions when Zise Feige had tried to tell him of her fears, his only reply was, "When, God willing, she gets married, she will forget all this foolishness."

After the calamity with Ozer, Liebe Yentl fell ill from grieving. She did not sleep nights. Her mother heard her sobbing in the dark. She was constantly going for a drink of water. She drank whole dippers full, and Zise Feige could not imagine how her stomach could hold so much water. As though, God forbid, a fire were raging inside her, consuming everything.

Sometimes, Liebe Yentl spoke to her mother like one who was altogether unsettled. Zise Feige thought to herself that it was fortunate the girl avoided people. But how long can anything remain a secret? It was already whispered in town that Liebe Yentl was not all there. She played with the cat. She took solitary walks down the Gentile street that led to the cemetery. When anyone addressed her, she turned pale and her answers were quite beside the point. Some people thought that she was deaf. Others hinted that Liebe Yentl might be dabbling in magic. She had been seen on a moonlit night walking in the pasture across the bridge and bending down every now and then to pick flowers or herbs. Women spat to ward off evil when they spoke to her. "Poor thing, unlucky and sick besides."

2

Liebe Yentl was about to become betrothed again, this time to a young man from Zawiercia. Reb Sheftel had sent an examiner to the prospective bridegroom, and he came back with the report that Shmelke Motl was a scholar. The betrothel contract was drawn up, ready to be signed.

The examiner's wife, Traine, who had visited Zawiercia with her husband (they had a daughter there), told Zise Feige that Shmelke Motl was small and dark. He did not look like much, but he had the head of a genius. Because he was an orphan, the householders provided his meals; he ate at a different home every day of the week. Liebe Yentl listened without a word.

When Traine had gone, Zise Feige brought in her daughter's supper—buckwheat and pot roast with gravy. But Liebe Yentl did not touch the food. She rocked over the plate as though it were a prayer book. Soon afterwards, she retired to her room. Zise Feige sighed and also went to bed. Reb Sheftel had gone to sleep early, for he had to rise for midnight prayers. The house was quiet. Only the cricket sang its night song behind the oven.

Suddenly Zise Feige was wide awake. From Liebe Yentl's room came a muffled gasping, as though someone were choking there. Zise Feige ran into her daughter's room. In the bright moonlight she saw the girl sitting on her bed, her hair disheveled, her face chalk-white, struggling to keep down her sobs. Zise Feige cried out, "My daughter, what is wrong? Woe is me!" She ran to the kitchen, lit a candle, and returned to Liebe Yentl, bringing a cup of water to splash at her if, God forbid, the girl should faint.

But at this moment a man's voice broke from Liebe Yentl's lips. "No need to revive me, Zise Feige," the voice called out. "I'm not in the habit of fainting. You'd better fetch me a drop of vodka."

Zise Feige stood petrified with horror. The water spilled over from the cup.

Reb Sheftel had also wakened. He washed his hands hastily, put on his bathrobe and slippers, and came into his daughter's room.

The man's voice greeted him. "A good awakening to you, Reb Sheftel. Let me have a schnapps—my throat's parched. Or Slivovitz—anything will do, so long as I wet my whistle."

Man and wife knew at once what had happened: a dybbuk had entered Liebe Yentl. Reb Sheftel asked with a shudder: "Who are you? What do you want?"

"Who I am you wouldn't know," the dybbuk answered. "You're a scholar in Shidlovtse, and I'm a fiddler from Pinchev. You squeeze the bench, and I squeezed the wenches. You're still around in the Imaginary World, and I'm past everything. I've kicked the bucket and have already had my taste of what comes after. I've had it cold and hot, and now I'm back on the sinful earth—there's no place for me either in heaven or in hell. Tonight I started out flying to Pinchev, but I lost my way and got to Shidlovtse instead—I'm a musician, not a coachman. One thing I do know, though—my throat's itchy."

Zise Feige was seized by a fit of trembling. The candle in her hand shook so badly it singed Reb Sheftel's beard. She wanted to scream, to call for help, but her voice stuck in her throat.

Her knees buckled, and she had to lean against the wall to keep from falling.

Reb Sheftel pulled at his sidelock as he addressed the dybbuk. "What is your name?"

"Getsl."

"Why did you choose to enter my daughter?" he asked in desperation.

"Why not? She's a good-looking girl. I hate the ugly ones—always have, always will." With that, the dybbuk began to shout ribaldries and obscenities, both in ordinary Yiddish and in musician's slang. "Don't make me wait, Feige dear," he called out finally. "Bring me a cup of cheer. I'm dry as a bone. I've got an itching in my gullet, a twitching in my gut."

"Good people, help!" Zise Feige wailed. She dropped the candle and Reb Sheftel picked it up, for it could easily have set the wooden house on fire.

Though it was late, the townsfolk came running. There are people everywhere with something bothering them; they cannot sleep nights. Tevye the night watchman thought a fire had broken out and ran through the street, knocking at the shutters with his stick. It was not long before Reb Sheftel's house was packed.

Liebe Yentl's eyes goggled, her mouth twisted like an epileptic's, and a voice boomed out of her that could not have come from a woman's throat. "Will you bring me a glass of liquor or won't you? What the devil are you waiting for?"

"And what if we don't?" asked Zeinvl the butcher, who was on his way home from the slaughterhouse.

"If you don't, I'll lay you all wide open, you pious hypocrites. And the secrets of your wives—may they burn up with hives."

"Get him liquor! Give him a drink!" voices cried on every side.

Reb Sheftel's son, Tsadock Meyer, a boy of eleven, had also been awakened by the commotion. He knew where his father kept the brandy that he drank on the Sabbath, after the fish. He opened the cupboard, poured out a glass, and brought it to his sister. Reb Sheftel leaned against the chest of drawers, for his legs were giving way. Zise Feige fell into a chair. Neighbors sprinkled her with vinegar against fainting.

Liebe Yentl stretched out her hand, took the glass, and tossed it down. Those who stood nearby could not believe their eyes. The girl didn't even twitch a muscle.

The dybbuk said, "You call that liquor? Water, that's what it is—hey, fellow, bring me the bottle!"

"Don't let her have it! Don't let her have it!" Zise Feige cried. "She'll poison herself, God help us!"

The dybbuk gave a laugh and a snort. "Don't worry, Zise Feige, nothing can kill me again. So far as I'm concerned, your brandy is weaker than candy."

"You won't get a drink until you tell us who you are and how you got in here," Zeinvl the butcher said. Since no one else dared to address the spirit, Zeinvl took it upon himself to be the spokesman.

"What does the meatman want here?" the dybbuk asked. "Go on back to your gizzards and guts!"

"Tell us who you are!"

"Do I have to repeat it? I am Getsl the fiddler from Pinchev. I was fond of things nobody else hates, and when I cashed in, the imps went to work on me. I couldn't get into paradise, and hell was too hot for my taste. The devils were the death of me. So at night, when the watchman dropped off, I made myself scarce. I meant to go to my wife, may she rot alive, but it was dark on the way and I got to Shidlovtse instead. I looked through the wall and saw this girl. My heart jumped in my chest and I crawled into her breast."

"How long do you intend to stay?"

"Forever and a day."

Reb Sheftel was almost speechless with terror, but he remembered God and recovered. He called out, "Evil spirit, I command you to leave the body of my innocent daughter and go where men do not walk and beasts do not tread. If you don't, you shall be driven out by Holy Names, by excommunication, by the blowing of the Ram's Horn."

"In another minute you'll have me scared!" the dybbuk taunted. "You think you're so strong because your beard's long?"

"Impudent wretch, betrayer of Israel!" Reb Sheftel cried in anger.

"Better an open rake than a sanctimonious fake," the dybbuk answered. "You may have the Shidlovtse schlemiels fooled, but Getsl the fiddler of Pinchev has been around. I'm telling you. Bring me the bottle or I'll make you crawl."

There was an uproar at the door. Someone had wakened the rabbi, and he came with Bendit the beadle. Bendit carried a stick, a Ram's Horn, and the Book of the Angel Raziel.

3

Once in the bedroom, the rabbi, Reb Yeruchim, ordered the Ram's Horn to be blown. He had the beadle pile hot coals into a brazier, then he poured incense on the coals. As the smoke of the herbs filled the room, he commanded the evil one with Holy Oaths from the Zohar, the Book of Creation, and other books of the Cabala to leave the body of the woman Liebe Yentl, daughter of Zise Feige. But the unholy spirit defied everyone. Instead of leaving, he played out a succession of dances, marches, hops—just with the lips. He boomed like a bass viol, he jingled like a cymbal, he whistled like a flute, and drummed like a drum.

The page is too short for a recital of all that the dybbuk did and said that night and the nights that followed—his brazen tricks, his blasphemies against the Lord, the insults he hurled at the townsfolk, the boasts of all the lecheries he had committed, the mockery, the outbursts of laughing and of crying, the stream of quotations from the Torah and wedding jester's jokes, and all of it in singsong and in rhyme.

The dybbuk made himself heard only after dark. During the day, Liebe Yentl lay exhausted in bed and evidently did not remember what went on at night. She thought that she was sick and occasionally begged her mother to call the doctor or to give her some medicine. Most of the time she dozed, with her eyes and her lips shut tight.

Since the incantations and the amulets of the Shidlovtse rabbi were of no avail, Reb Sheftel went to seek the advice of the Radzymin rabbi. On the very morning he left, the mild weather gave way to wind and snow. The roads were snowed in and it was difficult to reach Radzymin, even in a sleigh.

Weeks went by, and no news came from Reb Sheftel. Zise Feige was so hard hit by the calamity that she fell ill, and her assistant Zalkind had to take over the whole business.

Winter nights are long, and idlers look for ways to while away the time. Soon after twilight, they would gather at Zise Feige's house to hear the dybbuk's talk and to marvel at his antics. Zise Feige forbade them to annoy her daughter, but the curiosity of the townspeople was so great that they would break the door open and enter.

The dybbuk knew everyone and had words for each man according to his position and conduct. Most of the time he heaped mud and ashes upon the respected leaders of the community and their wives. He told each one exactly what he was: a miser or a swindler, a sycophant or a beggar, a slattern or a snob, an idler or a grabber. With the horse traders he talked about horses, and with the butchers about oxen. He reminded Chaim the miller that he had hung a weight under the scale on which he weighed the flour milled for the peasants. He questioned Yukele the thief about his latest theft. His jests and his jibes provoked both astonishment and laughter. Even the older folks could not keep from smiling. The dybbuk knew things that no stranger could have known, and it became clear to the visitors that they were dealing with a soul from which nothing could be hidden, for it saw through all their secrets. Although the evil spirit put everyone to shame, each man was willing to suffer his own humiliation for the sake of seeing others humbled.

When the dybbuk tired of exposing the sins of the townsfolk, he would turn to recitals of his own misdeeds. Not an evening passed without revelations of new vices. The dybbuk called everything by its name, denying nothing. When he was asked whether he regretted his abominations, he said with a laugh: "And if I did, could anything be changed? Everything is recorded up above. For eating a single wormy plum, you get six hundred and eight-nine lashes. For a single moment of lust, you're rolled for a week on a bed of nails." Between one jest and another, he would sing and bleat and play out tunes so skillfully that no one living could vie with him.

One evening the teacher's wife came running to the rabbi and reported that people were dancing to the dybbuk's music.

The rabbi put on his robe and his hat and hurried to the house. Yes, the men and women danced together in Zise Feige's kitchen. The rabbi berated them and warned that they were committing a sacrilege. He sternly forbade Zise Feige to allow the rabble into her house. But Zise Feige lay sick in bed, and her boy, Tsadock Meyer, was staying with relatives. As soon as the rabbi left, the idlers resumed their dancing—a Scissors Dance, a Quarrel Dance, a Cossack, a Water Dance. It went on till midnight, when the dybbuk gave out a snore, and Liebe Yentl fell asleep.

A few days later there was a new rumor in town: a second dybbuk had entered Liebe Yentl, this time a female one. Once more an avid crowd packed the house. And, indeed, a woman's voice now came from Liebe Yentl—not her own gentle voice but the hoarse croaking of a shrew. People asked the new dybbuk who she was, and she told them that her name was Beyle Tslove and that she came from the town of Plock, where she had been a barmaid in a tavern and had later become a whore.

Beyle Tslove spoke differently from Getsl the fiddler, with the flat accents of her region and a mixture of Germanized words unknown in Shidlovtse. Beyle Tslove's language made even the butchers and the combers of pigs' bristles blush. She sang ribald songs and soldiers' ditties. She said she had wandered for eighty years in waste places. She had been reincarnated as a cat, a turkey, a snake, and a locust. For a long time her soul resided in a turtle. When someone mentioned Getsl the fiddler and asked whether she knew him and whether she knew that he was also lodged in the same woman, she answered, "I neither know him nor want to know him."

"Why not? Have you turned virtuous all of a sudden?" Zeinvl the butcher asked her.

"Who wants a dead fiddler?"

The people began to call to Getsl the fiddler, urging him to speak up. They wanted to hear the two dybbuks talk to each other. But Getsl the fiddler was silent.

Beyle Tslove said, "I see no Getsl here."

"Maybe he's hiding?" someone said.

"Where? I can smell a man a mile away."

In the midst of this excitement, Reb Sheftel returned. He looked older and even smaller than before. His beard was streaked with gray. He had brought talismans and amulets from Radzymin, to hang in the corners of the room and around his daughter's neck.

People expected the dybbuk to resist and fight the amulets, as evil spirits do when touched by a sacred object. But Beyle Tslove was silent while the amulets were hung around Liebe Yentl's neck. Then she asked, "What's this? Sacred toilet paper?"

"These are Holy Names from the Radzymin rabbi!" Reb Sheftel cried out. "If you do not leave my daughter at once, not a spur shall be left of you!"

"Tell the Radzymin rabbi that I spit at his amulets," the woman said brazenly.

"Harlot! Fiend! Harridan!" Reb Sheftel screamed.

"What's he bellowing for, that Short Friday? Some man— nothing but bone and beard!"

Reb Sheftel had brought with him blessed six-groschen coins, a piece of charmed amber, and several other magical objects that the Evil Host is known to shun. But Beyle Tslove, it seemed, was afraid of nothing. She mocked Reb Sheftel and told him she would come at night and tie an elflock in his beard.

That night Reb Sheftel recited the Shema of the Holy Isaac Luria. He slept in his fringed garment with the Book of Creation and a knife under his pillow—like a woman in childbirth. But in the middle of the night he woke and felt invisible fingers on his face. An unseen hand was burrowing in his beard. Reb Sheftel wanted to scream, but the hand covered his mouth. In the morning Reb Sheftel got up with his whole beard full of tangled braids, gummy as if stuck together with glue.

Although it was a fearful matter, the Worka Hassidim, who were bitter opponents of the Radzymin rabbi, celebrated that day with honey cake and brandy in their study house. Now they had proof that the Radzymin rabbi did not know the Cabala. The followers of the Worka rabbi had advised Reb Sheftel to make a journey to Worka, but he ignored them, and now they had their revenge.

4

One evening, as Beyle Tslove was boasting of her former beauty and of all the men who had run after her, the fiddler of Pinchev suddenly raised his voice. "What were they so steamed up about?" he asked her mockingly. "Were you the only female in Plock?"

For a while all was quiet. It looked as though Beyle Tslove had lost her tongue. Then she gave a hoarse laugh. "So he's here—the scraper! Where were you hiding? In the gall?"

"If you're blind, I can be dumb. Go on, Grandma, keep jabbering. Your story had a gray beard when I was still in my diapers. In your place, I'd take such tall tales to the fools of Chelm. In Shidlovtse there are two or three clever men, too."

"A wise guy, eh?" Beyle Tslove said. "Let me tell you something. A live fiddle-scraper's no prize—and when it comes to a dead one! Go back, if you forgive me, to your resting place. They miss you in the Pinchev cemetery. The corpses who pray at night need another skeleton to make up their quorum."

The people who heard the two dybbuks quarrel were so stunned that they forgot to laugh. Now a man's voice came from Liebe Yentl, now a woman's. The Pinchev fiddler's "r"s were soft, the Plock harlot's hard.

Liebe Yentl herself rested against two pillows, her face pale, her hair down, her eyes closed. No one rightly saw her move her lips, though the room was full of people watching. Zise Feige was unable to keep them out, and there was no one to help her. Reb Sheftel no longer came home at night; he slept in the study house. Dunya the servant girl had left her job in the middle of the year. Zalkind, Zise Feige's assistant, went home in the evenings to his wife and children. People wandered in and out of the house as if it did not belong to anyone. Whenever one of the respectable members of the community came to upbraid the merry gang for ridiculing a stricken girl, the two dybbuks hurled curses and insults at him. The dybbuks gave the townspeople new nicknames: Reitse the busybody, Mindl glutton, Yekl tough, Dvoshe the strumpet. On several occasions, Gentiles and members of the local gentry came to see the wonder, and the dybbuks bantered with them in Polish. A landowner said in a tavern afterward that the best theater in Warsaw could not compete with the scenes played out by the two dead rascals in Shidlovtse.

After a while, Reb Sheftel, who had been unbending in his loyalty to the Radzymin rabbi, gave in and went to see the rabbi of Worka; perhaps he might help.

The two dybbuks were meanwhile carrying on their word duel. It is generally thought that women will get the better of men where the tongue is concerned, but the Pinchev fiddler was a match for the Plock whore. The fiddler cried repeatedly that it was beneath his dignity to wrangle with a harlot—a maid with a certificate of rape—but the hoodlums egged him on. "Answer her! Don't let her have the last word!" They whistled, hooted, clapped their hands, stamped their feet.

The battle of wits gradually turned into storytelling. Beyle Tslove related that her mother, a pious and virtuous woman, had borne her husband, a Hassid and a loafer, eight children, all of them girls. When Beyle Tslove made her appearance in the world, her father was so chagrined that he left home. By trickery, he collected the signatures of a hundred rabbis, permitting him to remarry, and her mother became an abandoned wife. To support the family, she went to market every morning to sell hot beans to the yeshiva students. A wicked tutor, with a goat's beard and sidelocks down to his shoulders, came to teach Beyle Tslove to pray, but he raped her. She was not yet eight years old. When Beyle Tslove went on to tell how she had become a barmaid, how the peasants had pinched and cursed her and pulled her hair, and how a bawd, pretending to be a pious woman, had lured her to a distant city and brought her into a brothel, the girls who were listening burst into tears. The young men, too, dabbed their eyes.

Getsl the fiddler questioned her. Who were the guests? How much did they pay? How much did she have to give the procurers and what was left for her to live on? Had she ever gone to bed with a Turk or a blackamoor?

Beyle Tslove answered all the questions. The young rakes had tormented her in their ways, and the old lechers had wearied her with their demands. The bawd took away her last groschen and locked the bread in the cupboard. The pimp whipped her with a wet strap and stuck needles into her buttocks. From fasting and homesickness she contracted consumption and ended by spitting out her lungs at the poorhouse. And because she had been buried behind the fence, without Kaddish, she was immediately seized by multitudes of demons, imps, mockers, and Babuks. The Angel Dumah asked her the verse that went with her name, and when she could not answer he split her grave with a fiery rod. She begged to be allowed into hell, for there the punishment lasts only twelve months, but the Unholy Ones dragged her off to waste places and deserts. She said that in the desert she had come upon a pit that was the door to Gehenna. Day and night, the screams of sinners who were being punished there came from the pit. She was carried to the Congealed Sea, where sailing ships, wrecked by storms, were held immobile, with dead crews and captains turned to stone. Beyle Tslove had also flown to a land inhabited by giants with two heads and single eyes in their foreheads. Few females were born there, and every woman had six husbands.

Getsl the fiddler also began to talk about the events of his life. He told of incidents at the weddings and balls of the gentry where he had played, and of what happened later, in the hereafter. He said that evildoers did not repent, even in the Nether Regions. Although they had already learned the truth of things, their souls still pursued their lusts. Gamblers played with invisible cards, thieves stole, swindlers swindled, and fornicators indulged in their abominations.

The townsfolk who heard the two were amazed, and Zeinvl the butcher asked, "How can anyone sin when he is rotting in the earth?"

Getsl explained that it was, anyway, the soul and not the body that enjoyed sin. This was why the soul was punished. Besides, there were bodies of all kinds—of smoke, of spiderwebs, of shadow—and they could be used for a while, until the Angels of Destruction tore them to pieces. There were castles, inns, and ruins in the deserts and abysses, which provided hiding places from Judgment, and also Avenging Angels who could be bribed with promises or even with the kind of money that has no substance but is used in the taverns and brothels of the Nether World.

When one of the idlers cried out that this was unbelievable, Getsl called on Beyle Tslove to attest to the truth of his words. "Tell us, Beyle Tslove, what did you really do all these years? Did you recite Psalms, or did you wander through swamps and wastes, consorting with demons, Zmoras, and Malachais?"

Instead of replying, Beyle Tslove giggled and coughed. "I can't speak—my mouth's dry."

"Yes, let's have a drop," Getsl chimed in, and when somebody brought over a tumbler of brandy, Liebe Yentl downed it like water. She did not open her eyes or even wince. It was clear to everybody that she was entirely in the sway of the dybbuks within her.

When Zeinvl the butcher realized that the two dybbuks and made peace, he asked, "Why don't you two become man and wife? You'd make a good pair."

"And what are we to do after the wedding?" Beyle Tslove answered. "Pray from the same prayer book?"

"You'll do what all married couples do."

"With what? We're past all doing. Anyway, there's no time—we won't be staying here much longer."

"Why not? Liebe Yentl is still young."

"The Worka rabbi is not the Radzymin schlemiel," Beyle Tslove said. "Asmodeus himself is afraid of his talismans."

"The Worka rabbi can kiss me you know where," Getsl boasted. "But I'm not about to become a bridegroom."

"The match isn't good enough for you?" Beyle Tslove cried. "If you knew who wanted to marry me, you'd croak a second time."

"If she's cursing me now, what can I expect later?" Getsl joked. "Besides, she's old enough to be my great-grandmother —seventy years older than I am, any way you figure it."

"Numbskull. I was twenty-seven years old when I kicked in, and I can't get any older. And how old are you, bottle-bum? Close to sixty, if you're a day."

"May you get as many carbuncles on your bloated flesh as the years I was short of fifty."

"Just give me the flesh, I won't argue over the carbuncles."

The two kept up their wrangling and the crowd kept up its urging until finally the dybbuks consented. Those who have not heard the dead bride and groom haggle about the dowry, the trousseau, the presents, will never know what unholy spirits are capable of.

Beyle Tslove said that she had long since paid for all her transgressions and was therefore as pure as a virgin. "Is there such a thing as a virgin, anyway?" she argued. "Every soul has lodged countless times both in men and in women. There are no more new souls in heaven. A soul is cleansed in a cauldron, like dishes before Passover. It is purified and sent back to earth. Yesterday's beggar is today's magnate. A rabbi's wife becomes a coachman. A horse thief returns as a Community Elder. A slaughterer comes back as an ox. So what's all the fuss about? Everything is kneaded of the same dough—cat and mouse, bear hunter and bear, old man and infant." Beyle Tslove herself had in previous incarnations been a grain merchant, a dairymaid, a rabbi's wife, a teacher of the Talmud.

"Do you remember any Talmud?" Getsl asked.

"If the Angel of Forgetfulness had not tweaked me on the nose, I would surely remember."

"What do you say to my bride?" Getsl bantered. "A whittled tongue. She could convince a stone. If my wife in Pinchev knew what I was exchanging her for, she'd drown herself in a bucket of slops."

"Your wife filled her bed before you were cold. . . ."

The strange news spread throughout the town: tomorrow there would be a wedding at Reb Sheftel's house; Getsl the fiddler and Beyle Tslove would become man and wife.

5

When the rabbi heard of the goings on, he issued a proscription forbidding anyone to attend the black wedding. He sent Bendit the beadle to stand guard at the door of Reb Sheftel's house and allow no one to enter. That night, however, there was a heavy snowfall, and by morning it turned bitterly cold. The wind had blown up great drifts and whistled in all the chimneys. Bendit was shrouded in white from head to foot and looked like a snowman made by children. His wife came after him and took him home, half frozen. As soon as dusk began to fall, the rabble gathered at Reb Sheftel's house. Some brought bottles of vodka or brandy; others, dried mutton and honey cake.

As usual, Liebe Yentl had slept all day and did not waken even when the ailing Zise Feige poured a few spoonfuls of broth into her mouth. But once darkness came, the girl sat up. There was such a crush in the house that people could not move.

Zeinvl the butcher took charge. "Bride, did you fast on your wedding day?"

"The way the dead eat, that's how they look," Beyle Tslove replied with a proverb.

"And you, bridegroom, are you ready?"

"Let her first deliver the dowry."

"You can take all I have—a pinch of dust, a moldy crust. . . ."

Getsl proved that evening that he was not only an expert musician but could also serve as rabbi, cantor, and wedding jester. First he played a sad tune and recited "God Is Full of Mercy" for the bride and groom. Then he played a merry tune, accompanying it with appropriate jests. He admonished the bride to be a faithful wife, to dress and adorn herself, and to take good care of her household. He warned the couple to be mindful of the day of death, and sang to them:

> "Weep, bride, weep and moan,
> Dead men fear to be alone.
> In the Sling, beneath the tide,
> A groom is waiting for his bride.
> Corpse and corpse, wraith and wraith,
> Every demon seeks a mate.
> Angel Dumah, devil, Shed,
> A coffin is a bridal bed."

Although it was a mock wedding, many a tear fell from the women's eyes. The men sighed. Everything proceeded according to custom. Getsl preached, sang, played. The guests could actually hear the weeping of a fiddle, the piping of a clarinet, the bleating of a trumpet, the wailing of a bagpipe. Getsl pretended to cover the bride with the veil and played a melody appropriate to the veiling ceremony. After the wedding march he recited the words of "Thou Art Sanctified," which accompany the giving of the ring. He delivered the bridegroom's oration, and announced the wedding presents: a shrouded mirror, a little sack of earth from the Holy Land, a burial cleansing spoon, a stopped clock. When the spirits of the guests seemed to droop, Getsl struck up a kozotsky. They tried to dance, but there was scarcely room to take a step. They swayed and gesticulated.

Beyle Tslove suddenly began to wail. "Oi, Getsl!"

"What, my dove!"

"Why couldn't this be real? We weren't born dead!"

"Pooh! Reality itself hangs by a thread."

"It's not a game to me, you fool."

"Whatever it is, let's drink and keep cool. May we rejoice and do well until all the fires are extinguished in hell."

A glass of wine was brought, and Liebe Yentl emptied it to the last drop. Then she dashed it against the wall, and Getsl began to recite in the singsong of the cheder boys:

> "Such is Noah's way,
> Wash your tears away.
> Take a drink instead,
> The living and the dead.
> Wine will make you strong,
> Eternity is long."

Zise Feige could not endure any more. She rose from her sickbed, wrapped herself in a shawl, and shuffled into her daughter's room in her slippers. She tried to push through the crowd. "Beasts," she cried. "You are torturing my child!"

Beyle Tslove screamed at her, "Don't you worry, old sourpuss! Better a rotten fiddler than a creep from Zawiercia!"

6

In the middle of the night there were sounds of steps and shouts outside the door. Reb Sheftel had come home from Worka, bringing a bagful of new amulets, charms, and talismans. The Hassidim of the Worka rabbi entered with him, ready to drive out the rabble. They swung their sashes, crying, "Get out, you scum!"

Several young fellows tried to fight off the Worka Hassidim, but the Shidlovtse crowd was tired from standing so long, and they soon began to file out the door. Getsl called after them, "Brothers, don't let the holy schlemiels get you! Give them a taste of your fists! Hey, you, big shot!"

"Cowards! Bastards! Mice!" Beyle Tslove screeched.

A few of the Worka Hassidim got a punch or two, but after a while the riffraff slunk off. The Hassidim burst into the room, panting and threatening the dybbuks with excommunication.

The warden of the Worka synagogue, Reb Avigdor Yavrover, ran up to Liebe Yentl's bed and tried to hang a charm around her neck, but the girl pulled off his hat and skullcap with her right hand, and with her left she seized him by the beard. The other Hassidim tried to pull him away, but Liebe Yentl thrashed out in all directions. She kicked, bit, and scratched. One man got a slap on the cheek, another had his sidelock pulled, a third got a mouthful of spittle on his face, a fourth a punch in the ribs. In order to frighten off the pious, she cried that she was in her unclean days. Then she tore off her shift and exhibited her shame. Those who did not avert their eyes remarked that her belly was distended like a drum. On the right and the left were two bumps as big as heads, and it was clear that the spirits were there. Getsl roared like a lion, howled like a wolf, hissed like a snake. He called the Worka rabbi a eunuch, a clown, a baboon, insulted all the holy sages, and blasphemed against God.

Reb Sheftel sank to the floor and sat there like a mourner. He covered his eyes with both hands and rocked himself as over a corpse. Zise Feige snatched a broom and tried to drive away the men who swarmed around her daughter, but she was dragged aside and fell to the ground. Two neighboring women helped her to get up. Her bonnet fell off, exposing her shaven head with its gray stubble. She raised two fists and screamed, sobbing, "Torturers, you're killing my child! Lord in heaven, send Pharaoh's curses upon them!"

Finally, several of the younger Hassidim caught Liebe Yentl's hands and feet and tied her to the bed with their sashes. Then they slipped the Worka rabbi's amulets around her neck.

Getsl, who had fallen silent during the struggle, spoke up. "Tell your miracle worker his charms are tripe."

"Wretch, you're in Hell, and you still deny?" Reb Avigdor Yavrover thundered.

"Hell's full of your kind."

"Dog, rascal, degenerate!"

"Why are you cursing, you louses?" Beyle Tslove yelled. "Is it our fault that your holy idiot hands out phony talismans? You'd better leave the girl alone. We aren't doing her any harm. Her good is our good. We're also Jews, remember—not Tartars. Our souls have stood on Mount Sinai, too. If we erred in life, we've paid our debt, with interest."

"Strumpet, hussy, slut, out with you!" one of the Hassidim cried.

"I'll go when I feel like it."

"Todres, blow the Ram's Horn—a long blast!"

The Ram's Horn filled the night with its eerie wail.

Beyle Tslove laughed and jeered. "Blow hot, blow cold, who cares!"

"A broken trill now!"

"Don't you have enough breaks under your rupture bands?" Getsl jeered.

"Satan, Amalekite, apostate!"

Hours went by, but the dybbuks remained obdurate. Some of the Worka Hassidim went home. Others leaned against the wall, ready to do battle until the end of their strength. The hoodlums who had run away returned with sticks and knives. The Hassidim of the Radzymin rabbi had heard the news that the Worka talismans had failed, and they came to gloat.

Reb Sheftel rose from the floor and in his anguish began to plead with the dybbuks. "If you are Jews, you should have Jewish hearts. Look what has become of my innocent daughter, lying bound like a sheep prepared for slaughter. My wife is sick. I myself am ready to drop. My business is falling apart. How long will you torture us? Even a murderer has a spark of pity."

"Nobody pities us."

"I'll see to it that you get forgiveness. It says in the Bible, 'His banished be not expelled from Him.' No Jewish soul is rejected forever."

"What will you do for us?" asked Getsl. "Help us moan?"

"I will recite Psalms and read the Mishnah for you. I will give alms. I will say Kaddish for you for a full twelve months."

"I'm not one of your peasants. You can't fool me."

"I have never fooled anyone."

"Swear that you will keep your word!" Getsl commanded.

"What's the matter, Getsl? You anxious to leave me already?" Beyle Tslove asked with a laugh.

Getsl yawned. "I'm sorry for the old folks."

"You want to leave me a deserted wife the very first night?"

"Come along if you can."

"Where to? Behind the Mountains of Darkness?"

"Wherever our eyes take us."

"You mean sockets, comedian!"

"Swear, Reb Sheftel, that you will keep all your promises," Getsl the fiddler repeated. "Make a holy vow. If you break your word, I'll be back with the whole Evil Host and scatter your bones to the four winds."

"Don't swear, Reb Sheftel, don't swear!" the Hassidim cried. "Such a vow is a desecration of the Name!"

"Swear, my husband, swear. If you don't, we shall all perish."

Reb Sheftel put his hand on his beard. "Dead souls, I swear that I will faithfully fulfill all that I take upon myself. I will study the Mishnah for you. I will say Kaddish for twelve months. Tell me when you died, and I will burn memorial candles for you. If there are no headstones on your graves, I will journey to the cemeteries and have them erected."

"Our graves have been leveled long since. Come, Beyle Tslove, let's go. Dawn is rising over Pinchev."

"Imp, you made a fool of a Jewish daughter all for nothing!" Beyle Tslove reproached him.

"Hey, men, move aside!" Getsl cried. "Or I shall enter one of you!"

There was such a crush that, though the door stood open, no one could get out. Hats and skullcaps fell off. Caftans caught on nails and ripped. A muffled cry rose from the crowd. Several Hassidim fell, and others trampled them. Liebe Yentl's mouth opened wide and there was a shot as from a pistol. Her eyes rolled and she fell back on the pillow, white as death. A stench swept across the room—a foul breath of the grave. Zise

Feige stumbled on weak legs toward her daughter and untied her. The girl's belly was now flat and shrunken like the belly of a woman after childbirth.

Reb Sheftel attested afterward that two balls of fire came out of Liebe Yentl's nostrils and flew to the window. A pane split open, and the two sinful souls returned through the crack to the World of Delusion.

7

For weeks after the dybbuks had left her, Liebe Yentl lay sick. The doctor applied cups and leeches; he bled her, but Liebe Yentl never opened her eyes. The woman from the Society of Tenders of the Sick who sat with the girl at night related that she heard sad melodies outside the window, and Getsl's voice begging her to remove the amulets from the girl's neck and let him in. The woman also heard Beyle Tslove's giggling.

Gradually Liebe Yentl began to recover, but she had almost stopped speaking. She sat in bed and stared at the window. Winter was over. Swallows returned from the warm countries and were building a nest under the eaves. From her bed Liebe Yentl could see the roof of the synagogue, where a pair of storks were repairing last year's nest.

Reb Sheftel and Zise Feige feared that Liebe Yentl would no longer be accepted in marriage, but Shmelke Motl wrote from Zawiercia that he would keep to his agreement if the dowry were raised by one third. Reb Sheftel and Zise Feige consented at once. After Pentecost, Shmelke Motl made his appearance at the Shidlovtse prayer house—no taller than a cheder boy but with a large head on a thin neck and tightly twisted side-locks that stood up like a pair of horns. He had thick eyebrows and dark eyes that looked down at the tip of his nose. As soon as he entered the study house, he took out a Gemara and sat down to study. He sat there, swaying and mumbling, until he was taken to the ceremony of betrothal.

Reb Sheftel invited only a selected few to the engagement meal, for during the time that his daughter had been possessed by the dybbuks he had made many enemies both among the Radzymin Hassidim and among those of Worka. According to custom, the men sat at one table, the women at another. The bridegroom delivered an impromptu sermon on the subject of the Stoned Ox. Such sermons usually last half an hour, but two hours went by and the groom still talked on in his high, grating voice, accompanying his words with wild gestures. He grimaced as though gripped with pain, pulled at a sidelock, scratched his chin, which was just beginning to sprout a beard, grasped the lobe of his ear. From time to time his lips stretched in a smile, revealing blackened teeth, pointed as nails.

Liebe Yentl never once took her eyes from him. The women tried to talk to her; they urged her to taste the cookies, the jam, the mead. But Liebe Yentl bit her lips and stared.

The guests began to cough and fidget, hinting in various ways that it was time to bring the oration to an end, and finally the bridegroom broke off his sermon. The betrothal contract was brought to him, but he did not sign it at once. First he read the page from beginning to end. He was evidently near-sighted, for he brought the paper right up to his nose. Then he began to bargain. "The prayer shawl should have silver braid."

"It will have any braid you wish," Reb Sheftel agreed.

"Write it in."

It was written in on the margin. The groom read on, and demanded, "I want a Talmud printed in Slovita."

"Very well, it will be from Slovita."

"Write it in."

After much haggling and writing in, the groom signed the contract: Shmelke Motl son of the late Catriel Godl. The letters of the signature were as tiny as flyspecks.

When Reb Sheftel brought the contract over to Liebe Yentl and handed her the pen, she said in a clear voice, "I will not sign."

"Daughter, you shame me!"

"I will not live with him."

Zise Feige began to pinch her wrinkled cheeks. "People, go home!" she called out. She snuffed the candles in the candlesticks. Some of the women wept with the disgraced mother; others berated the bride. But the girl answered no one. Before long, the house was dark and empty. The servant went out to close the shutters.

Reb Sheftel usually prayed at the synagogue with the first quorum, but that morning he did not show himself at the holy place. Zise Feige did not go out to do her shopping. The door of Reb Sheftel's house stood locked; the windows were shuttered. Shmelke Motl returned at once to Zawiercia.

After a time Reb Sheftel went back to praying at the synagogue, and Zise Feige went again to market with her basket. But Liebe Yentl no longer came out into the street. People thought that her parents had sent her away somewhere, but Liebe Yentl was at home. She kept to her room and refused to speak to anyone. When her mother brought her a plate of soup, she first knocked at the door as though they were gentry. Liebe Yentl scarcely touched the food, and Zise Feige sent it to the poorhouse.

For some months the matchmakers still came with offers, but since a dybbuk had spoken from her and she had shamed a bridegroom Liebe Yentl could no longer make a proper match. Reb Sheftel tried to obtain a pardon from the young man in Zawiercia, but he had gone away to some yeshiva in Lithuania. There was a rumor that he had hanged himself with his sash. Then it became clear that Liebe Yentl would remain an old maid. Her younger brother, Tsadock Meyer, had in the meantime grown up and got married to a girl from Bendin.

Reb Sheftel was the first to die. This happened on a Thursday night in winter. Reb Sheftel had risen for midnight prayers. He stood at the reading desk, with ash on his head, reciting a lament on the Destruction of the Temple. A beggar was spending that night at the prayer house. About three o'clock in the morning, the man awakened and put some potatoes into the stove to bake. Suddenly he heard a thud. He stood up and saw Reb Sheftel on the floor. He sprinkled him with water from the pitcher, but the soul had already departed.

The townspeople mourned Reb Sheftel. The body was not taken home but lay in the prayer house with candles at its head until the time of burial. The rabbi and some of the town's scholars delivered eulogies. On Friday, Liebe Yentl escorted the coffin with her mother. Liebe Yentl was wrapped in a black shawl from head to toe; only a part of her face showed, white as the snow in the cemetery. The two sons lived far from Shidlovtse, and the funeral could not be postponed till after the Sabbath; it is a dishonor for a corpse to wait too long for burial. Reb Sheftel was put to rest near the grave of the old rabbi. It is known that those who are buried on Friday after noon do not suffer the pressure of the grave, for the Angel Dumah puts away his fiery rod on the eve of the Sabbath.

Zise Feige lingered a few years more, but she was fading day by day. Her body bent like a candle. In her last year she no longer attended to the business, relying entirely on her assistant, Zalkind. She began to rise at dawn to pray at the women's synagogue, and she often went to the cemetery and prostrated herself on Reb Sheftel's grave. She died as suddenly as her husband. It happened during evening prayer on Yom Kippur. Zise Feige had stood all day, weeping, at the railing that divided the women's section from the men's in the prayer house. Her neighbors, seeing her waxen-yellow face, urged her to break her fast, for human life takes precedence over all laws, but Zise Feige refused. When the cantor intoned, "The gates of Heaven open," Zise Feige took from her bosom a vial of aromatic drops, which are a remedy against faintness. But the vial slipped from her hand and she fell forward onto the reading desk. There was an outcry and women ran for the doctor, but Zise Feige had already passed into the True World. Her last words were: "My daughter. . . ."

This time the funeral was delayed until the arrival of the two sons. They sat in mourning with their sister. But Liebe Yentl avoided all strangers. Those who came to pray with the mourners and to comfort them found only Jedidiah and Tsadock Meyer. Liebe Yentl would lock herself away in her room.

Nothing was left of Reb Sheftel's wealth. People muttered that the assistant had pocketed the money, but it could not be proved. Reb Sheftel and Zise Feige had kept no books. All the accounting had been done with a piece of chalk on the wall of a wardrobe. After the seven days of mourning, the sons called Zalkind to the rabbi's court, but he offered to swear before the Holy Scrolls and black candles that he had not touched a groschen of his employers' money. The rabbi forbade such an oath. He said that a man who could break the commandment "Thou Shalt Not Steal" could also violate the commandment "Thou Shalt Not Take the Name of Thy God the Lord in Vain."

After the judgment, the two sons went home. Liebe Yentl remained with the servant. Zalkind took over the business and merely sent Liebe Yentl two gulden a week for food. Soon he refused to give even that and sent only a few groschen. The servant woman left and went to work elsewhere.

Now that Liebe Yentl no longer had a servant, she was compelled to show herself in the street, but she never came out during the day. She would leave the house only after dark, waiting until the streets were empty and the stores without other customers. She would appear suddenly, as though from nowhere. The storekeepers were afraid of her. Dogs barked at her from Christian yards.

Summer and winter she was wrapped from head to toe in a long shawl. She would enter the store and forget what she wanted to buy. She often gave more money than was asked, as though she no longer remembered how to count. A few times she was seen entering the Gentile tavern to buy vodka. Tevye the night watchman had heard Liebe Yentl pacing the house at night, talking to herself.

Zise Feige's good friends tried repeatedly to see the girl, but the door was always bolted. Liebe Yentl never came to the synagogue on holidays to pray for the souls of the deceased. During the months of Nissan and Elul, she never went to visit the graves of her parents. She did not bake Sabbath bread on Fridays, did not set roasts overnight in the oven, and probably did not bless the candles. She did not come to the women's synagogue even on the High Holy Days.

People began to forget Liebe Yentl—as if she were dead—but she lived on. At times, smoke rose from her chimney. Late at night, she was sometimes seen going to the well for a pail of water. Those who caught sight of her swore that she did not look a day older. Her face was becoming even more pale, her hair redder and longer. It was said that Liebe Yentl played with cats. Some whispered that she had dealings with a demon. Others thought that the dybbuk had returned to her. Zalkind still delivered a measure of flour to the house every Thursday, leaving it in the larder in the entrance hall. He also provided Liebe Yentl with firewood.

There had formerly been several other Jewish households on the street, but gradually the owners had sold to Gentiles. A hog butcher had moved into one house and built a high fence around it. Another house was occupied by a deaf old widow who spent her days spinning flax, guarded by a blind dog at her feet.

Years went by. One early morning in Elul, when the rabbi was sitting in his study writing commentary and drinking tea from a samovar, Tevye the night watchman knocked at his door. He told the rabbi that he had seen Liebe Yentl on the road leading to Radom. The girl wore a long white dress; she had no kerchief on her head and walked barefoot. She was accompanied by a man with long hair, carrying a violin case. The full moon shone brightly. Tevye wanted to call out, but since the figures cast no shadow he was seized with fear. When he looked again, the pair had vanished.

The rabbi ordered Tevye to wait until the worshippers assembled for morning prayer in the synagogue. Then Tevye told the people of the apparition, and two men—a driver and a butcher—went to Reb Sheftel's house. They knocked, but no one answered. They broke open the door and found Liebe Yentl dead. She lay in the middle of the room among piles of garbage, in a long shift, barefoot, her red hair loose. It was obvious that she had not been among the living for many days—perhaps a week or even more. The women of the burial society hastily carried off the corpse to the hut for the cleansing of the dead. When the shroud-makers opened the wardrobe, a cloud of moths flew out, filling the house like a swarm of locusts. All the clothes were eaten, all the linens moldy and decayed.

Since Liebe Yentl had not taken her own life and since she had exhibited all the signs of madness, the rabbi permitted her to be buried next to her parents. Half the town followed the body to the cemetery. The brothers were notified and came later to sell the house and order a stone for their sister's grave.

It was clear to everyone that the man who had appeared with Liebe Yentl on the road to Radom was the dead fiddler of Pinchev. Dunya, Zise Feige's former servant, told the women that Liebe Yentl had not been able to forget her dead bridegroom Ozer and that Ozer had become a dybbuk in order to prevent the marriage to Shmelke Motl. But where would Ozer, a scholar and the son of a rich man, have learned to play music and to perform like a wedding jester? And why would he appear on the Radom road in the guise of a fiddler? And where was he going with the dead Liebe Yentl that night? And what had become of Beyle Tslove? Heaven and earth have sworn that the truth shall remain forever hidden.

More years went by, but the dead fiddler was not forgotten. He was heard playing at night in the cold synagogue. His fiddle sang faintly in the bathhouse, the poorhouse, the cemetery. It was said in town that he came to weddings. Sometimes, at the end of a wedding after the Shidlovtse band had stopped playing, people still heard a few lingering notes, and they knew that it was the dead fiddler.

In autumn, when leaves fell and winds blew from the Mountains of the Holy Cross, a low melody was often heard in the chimneys, thin as a hair and mournful as the world. Even children would hear it, and they would ask, "Mamma, who is playing?" And the mother would answer, "Sleep, child. It's the dead fiddler."

Translated by Mirra Ginsburg

The Lecture

I WAS on my way to Montreal to deliver a lecture. It was mid–winter and I had been warned that the temperature there was ten degrees lower than in New York. Newspapers reported that trains had been stalled by the snow and fishing villages cut off, so that food and medical supplies had to be dropped to them by plane.

I prepared for the journey as though it were an expedition to the North Pole. I put on a heavy coat over two sweaters and packed warm underwear and a bottle of cognac in case the train should be halted somewhere in the fields. In my breast pocket I had the manuscript that I intended to read—an optimistic report on the future of the Yiddish language.

In the beginning, everything went smoothly. As usual, I arrived at the station an hour before train departure and therefore could find no porter. The station teemed with travelers and I watched them, trying to guess who they were, where they were going, and why.

None of the men was dressed as heavily as I. Some even wore spring coats. The ladies looked bright and elegant in their minks and beavers, nylon stockings and stylish hats. They carried colorful bags and illustrated magazines, smoked cigarettes and chattered and laughed with a carefree air that has never ceased to amaze me. It was as though they knew nothing of the existence of world problems or eternal questions, as though they had never heard of death, sickness, war, poverty, betrayal, or even of such troubles as missing a train, losing a ticket, or being robbed. They flirted like young girls, exhibiting their blood-red nails. The station was chilly that morning, but no one except myself seemed to feel it. I wondered whether these people knew there had been a Hitler. Had they heard of Stalin's murder machine? They probably had, but what does one body care when another is tortured?

I was itchy from the woolen underwear. Now I began to feel hot. But from time to time a shiver ran through my body. The lecture, in which I predicted a brilliant future for Yiddish, troubled me. What had made me so optimistic all of a sudden? Wasn't Yiddish going under before my very eyes?

The prompt arrival of American trains and the ease in boarding them have always seemed like miracles to me. I remember journeys in Poland when Jewish passengers were not allowed into the cars and I had to hang on to the handrails. I remember railway strikes when trains were halted midway for many hours and it was impossible in the dense crowd to push through to the washroom.

But here I was, sitting on a soft seat, right by the window. The car was heated. There were no bundles, no high fur hats, no sheepskin coats, no boxes, and no gendarmes. Nobody was eating bread and lard. Nobody drank vodka from a bottle. Nobody was berating Jews for state treason. In fact, nobody discussed politics at all. As soon as the train started, a huge Negro in a white apron came in and announced lunch. The train was not rattling, it glided smoothly on its rails along the frozen Hudson. Outside, the landscape gleamed with snow and light. Birds that remained here for the winter flew busily over the icy river.

The farther we went, the wintrier the landscape. The weather seemed to change every few miles. Now we went through dense fog, and now the air cleared and the sun was shining again over silvery distances.

A heavy snowfall began. It suddenly turned dark. The day was flickering out. The express no longer ran but crept slowly and cautiously, as though feeling its way. The heating system in the train seemed to have broken down. It became chilly and I had to put on my coat. The other passengers pretended for a while that they did not notice anything, as though reluctant to admit too quickly that they were cold. But soon they began to tap their feet, grumble, grin sheepishly, and rummage in their valises for sweaters, scarves, boots, or whatever else they had brought along. Collars were turned up, hands stuffed into sleeves. The makeup on women's faces dried up and began to peel like plaster.

The American dream gradually dissolves and harsh Polish reality returns. Someone is drinking whiskey from a bottle. Someone is eating bread and sausage to warm his stomach.

There is also a rush to the toilets. It is difficult to understand how it happened, but the floor of the car becomes wet and muddy. The windowpanes become crusted with ice and bloom with frost patterns.

Suddenly the train stops. I look out and see a sparse wood. The trees are thin and bent, and though they are covered with snow, they look bare and charred, as after a fire. The sun has already set, but purple stains still glow in the west. The snow on the ground is no longer white, but violet. Crows walk on it, flap their wings, and I can hear their cawing. The snow falls in gray, heavy lumps, as though the guardians of the Treasury of Snow up above had been too lazy to flake it more finely. Passengers walk from car to car, leaving the doors open. Conductors and other train employees run past; when they are asked questions, they do not stop, but mumble something rudely.

We are not far from the Canadian border, and Uncle Sam's domain is virtually at an end. Some passengers begin to take down their luggage; they may have to show it soon to the customs officials. A naturalized American citizen gets out his citizenship papers and studies his own photograph, as if trying to convince himself that the document is not a false one.

One or two passengers venture to step out of the train, but they sink up to their knees into the snow. It is not long before they clamber back into the car. The twilight lingers for a while, then night falls.

I see people using the weather as a pretext for striking up acquaintance. Women begin to talk among themselves and there is sudden intimacy. The men have also formed a group. Everyone picks up bits of information. People offer each other advice. But nobody pays any attention to me. I sit alone, a victim of my own isolation, shyness, and alienation from the world. I begin to read a book, and this provokes hostility, for reading a book at such a time seems like a challenge and an insult to the other passengers. I exclude myself from society, and all the faces say to me silently: You don't need us and we don't need you. Never mind, you will still have to turn to us, but we won't have to turn to you. . . .

I open my large, heavy valise, take out the bottle of cognac, and take a stealthy sip now and then. After that, I lean my face against the cold windowpane and try to look out. But all

I see is the reflection of the interior of the car. The world outside seems to have disappeared. The solipsistic philosophy of Bishop Berkeley has won over all the other systems. Nothing remains but to wait patiently until God's idea of a train halted in its tracks by snowdrifts will give way to God's ideas of movement and arrival.

Alas for my lecture! If I arrive in the middle of the night, there will not even be anyone waiting for me. I shall have to look for a hotel. If only I had a return ticket. However, was Captain Scott, lost in the polar ice fields, in a better position after Amundsen had discovered the South Pole? How much would Captain Scott have given to be able to sit in a brightly lit railway car? No, one must not sin by complaining.

The cognac had made me warm. Drunken fumes rise from an empty stomach to the brain. I am awake and dozing at the same time. Whole minutes drift away, leaving only a blur. I hear talk, but I don't quite know what it means. I sink into blissful indifference. For my part, the train can stand here for three days and three nights. I have a box of crackers in my valise. I will not die of hunger. Various themes float through my mind. Something within me mutters dreamlike words and phrases.

The diesel engine must be straining forward. I am aware of dragging, knocking, growling sounds, as of a monstrous ox, a legendary steel bull. Most of the passengers have gone to the bar or the restaurant car, but I am too lazy to get up. I seem to have grown into the seat. A childish obstinacy takes possession of me: I'll show them all that I am not affected by any of this commotion; I am above the trivial happenings of the day.

Everyone who passes by—from the rear cars to the front, or the other way—glances at me; and it seems to me that each one forms some judgment of his own about the sort of person I am. But does anyone guess that I am a Yiddish writer late for his lecture? This, I am sure, occurs to no one. This is known only to the higher powers.

I take another sip, and another. I have never understood the passion for drinking, but now I see what power there is in alcohol. This liquid holds within itself the secrets of nirvana. I no longer look at my wristwatch. I no longer worry about a place to sleep. I mock in my mind the lecture I had prepared.

What if it is not delivered? People will hear fewer lies! If I could open the window, I would throw the manuscript out into the woods. Let the paper and ink return to the cosmos, where there can be no errors and no lies. Atoms and molecules are guiltless; they are a part of the divine truth. . . .

2

The train arrived exactly at half past two. No one was waiting for me. I left the station and was caught in a blast of icy night wind that no coat or sweaters could keep out. All taxis were immediately taken. I returned to the station, prepared to spend the night sitting on a bench.

Suddenly I noticed a lame woman and a young girl looking at me and pointing with their fingers. I stopped and looked back. The lame woman leaned on two thick, short canes. She was wrinkled, disheveled, like an old woman in Poland, but her black eyes suggested that she was more sick and broken than old. Her clothes also reminded me of Poland. She wore a sort of sleeveless fur jacket. Her shoes had toes and heels I had not seen in years. On her shoulders she wore a fringed woolen shawl, like one of my mother's. The young woman, on the other hand, was stylishly dressed, but also rather slovenly.

After a moment's hesitation, I approached them.

The girl said: "Are you Mr. N.?"

I answered, "Yes, I am."

The lame woman made a sudden movement, as though to drop her canes and clap her hands. She immediately broke into a wailing cry so familiar to me.

"Dear Father in heaven!" she sang out. "I was telling my daughter it's he, and she said no. I recognized you! Where were you going with the valise? It's a wonder you came back. I'd never have forgiven myself! Well, Binele, what do you say now? Your mother still has some sense. I am only a woman, but I am a rabbi's daughter, and a scholar has an eye for people. I took one look and I thought to myself—it's he! But nowadays the eggs are cleverer than the chickens. She says to me: 'No, it can't be.' And in the meantime you disappear. I was already beginning to think, myself: Who knows, one's no more than human, anybody can make a mistake. But when I saw you come back, I knew it was you. My dear man, we've been waiting here since half past seven in the evening. We weren't alone; there was a whole group of teachers, educators, a few writers too. But then it grew later and later and people went home. They have wives, children. Some have to get up in the morning to go to work. But I said to my daughter, 'I won't go. I won't allow my favorite writer, whose every word I treasure as a pearl, to come here and find no one waiting for him. If you want, my child,' I said to her, 'you can go home and go to bed.' What's a night's sleep? When I was young, I used to think that if you missed a night's sleep the world would go under. But Hitler taught us a lesson. He taught us a lesson I won't forget until I lie with shards over my eyes. You look at me and you see an old, sick woman, a cripple, but I did hard labor in Hitler's camps. I dug ditches and loaded railway cars. Was there anything I didn't do? It was there that I caught my rheumatism. At night we slept on plank shelves not fit for dogs, and we were so hungry that—"

"You'll have enough time to talk later, Momma. It's the middle of the night," her daughter interrupted.

It was only then that I took a closer look at the daughter. Her figure and general appearance were those of a young girl, but she was obviously in her late twenties, or even early thirties. She was small, narrow, with yellowish hair on her back and tied into a bun. Her face was of a sickly pallor, covered with freckles. She had yellow eyes, a round forehead, a crooked nose, thin lips, and a long chin. Around her neck she wore a mannish scarf. She reminded me of a Hassidic boy.

The few words she spoke were marked by a provincial Polish accent I had forgotten during my years in America. She made me think of rye bread, caraway seeds, cottage cheese, and the water brought by water carriers from the well in pails slung on a wooden yoke over their shoulders.

"Thank you, but I have patience to listen," I said.

"When my mother begins to talk about those years, she can talk for a week and a day—"

"Hush, hush, your mother isn't as crazy as you think. It's true, our nerves were shattered out there. It is a wonder we are not running around stark mad in the streets. But what about her? As you see her, she too was in Auschwitz waiting for the ovens. I did not even know she was alive. I was sure she was lost, and you can imagine a mother's feelings! I thought she had gone the way of her three brothers; but after the liberation we found each other. What did they want from us, the beasts? My husband was a holy man, a scribe. My sons worked hard to earn a piece of bread, because inscribing mezuzahs doesn't bring much of an income. My husband, himself, fasted more often than he ate. The glory of God rested on his face. My sons were killed by the murderers—"

"Momma, will you please stop?"

"I'll stop, I'll stop. How much longer will I last, anyway? But she is right. First of all, my dear man, we must take care of you. The president gave me the name of a hotel—they made all the reservations for you—but my daughter didn't hear what he said, and I forgot it. This forgetting is my misfortune. I put something down and I don't know where. I keep looking for things, and that's how my whole days go by. So maybe, my dear writer, you'll spend the night with us? We don't have such a fine apartment. It's cold, it's shabby. Still, it's better than no place at all. I'd telephone the president, but I'm afraid to wake him up at night. He has such a temper, may he forgive me; he keeps shouting that we aren't civilized. So I say to him: 'The Germans are civilized, go to them. . . .'"

"Come with us, the night is three quarters gone, anyway," the daughter said to me. "He should have written it down instead of just saying it; and if he said it, he should have said it to me, not to my mother. She forgets everything. She puts on her glasses and cries, 'Where are my glasses?' Sometimes I have to laugh. Let me have your valise."

"What are you saying? I can carry it myself, it isn't heavy."

"You are not used to carrying things, but I have learned out there to carry heavy loads. If you would see the rocks I used to lift, you wouldn't believe your eyes. I don't even believe it myself anymore. Sometimes it seems to me it was all an evil dream. . . ."

"Heaven forbid, you will not carry my valise. That's all I need. . . ."

"He is a gentleman, he is a fine and gentle man. I knew it at once as soon as I read him for the first time," the mother said. "You wouldn't believe me, but we read your stories even in the camps. After the war, they began to send us books, and I came across one of your stories. I don't remember what it was called, but I read it and a darkness lifted off my heart. 'Binele,' I said —she was already with me then—'I've found a treasure.' Those were my words. . . ."

"Thank you, thank you very much."

"Don't thank me, don't thank me. It's we who have to thank you. All the troubles came from people being deaf and blind. They don't see the next man and so they torture him. We are wandering among blind evildoers. . . . Binele, don't let this dear man carry the valise. . . ."

"Yes, please give it to me!"

I had to plead with Binele to let me carry it. She almost tried to pull it out of my hands.

We went outside and a taxi drove up. It was not easy to get the mother into it. I still cannot understand how she had managed to come to the station. I had to lift her up and put her in. In the process, she dropped one of her canes, and Binele and I had to look for it in the snow. The driver had already begun to grumble and scold in his Canadian French. Afterward, the car began to pitch and roll over dimly lit streets covered with snow and overgrown with mountains of ice. The tires had chains on them, but the taxi skidded backward several times.

We finally drove into a street that was reminiscent of a small town in Poland: murky, narrow, with wooden houses. The sick woman hastily opened her purse, but I paid before she had time to take out her money. Both women chided me, and the driver demanded that we get out as quickly as possible. I virtually had to carry the crippled woman out of the taxi. Again, we had to look for her cane in the deep snow. Afterward, her daughter and I half led, half dragged her up a flight of steps. They opened the door and I was suddenly enveloped in odors I had long forgotten: moldy potatoes, rotting onions, chicory, and something else I could not even name. In some mysterious way the mother and daughter had managed to bring with them the whole atmosphere of wretched poverty from their old home in Poland.

They lit a kerosene lamp and I saw an apartment with tattered wallpaper, a rough wooden floor, and spider webs in every corner. The kerosene stove was out and the rooms were drafty. On a bench stood cracked pots, chipped plates, cups without handles. I even caught sight of a besom on a pile of sweepings. No stage director, I thought, could have done a better job of reproducing such a scene of old-country misery.

Binele began to apologize. "What a mess, no? We were in such a hurry to get to the station, we didn't even have time to wash the dishes. And what's the good of washing or cleaning here, anyway? It's an old, run-down shanty. The landlady knows only one thing: to come for the rent every month. If you're late one day, she's ready to cut your throat. Still, after everything we went through over there, this is a palace. . . ."

And Binele laughed, exposing a mouthful of widely spaced teeth with gold fillings that must have been made when she was still across the ocean.

3

They made my bed on a folding cot in a tiny room with barred windows. Binele covered me with two blankets and spread my coat on top of them. But it was still as cold as outside. I lay under all the coverings and could not warm up.

Suddenly I remembered my manuscript. Where was the manuscript of my lecture? I had had it in the breast pocket of my coat. Afraid to sit up, lest the cot should collapse, I tried to find it. But the manuscript was not there. I looked in my jacket, which hung on a chair nearby, but it was not there either. I was certain that I had not put it into the valise, for I had opened the valise only to get the cognac. I had intended to open it for the customs officers, but they had only waved me on, to indicate it was not necessary.

It was clear to me that I had lost the manuscript. But how? The mother and daughter had told me that the lecture was postponed to the next day, but what would I read? There was only one hope: perhaps it had dropped on the floor when Binele was covering me with the coat. I felt the floor, trying not to make a sound, but the cot creaked at the slightest movement. It even seemed to me that it began to creak in advance, when I only thought of moving. Inanimate things are not really inanimate. . . .

The mother and daughter were evidently not asleep. I heard

a whispering, a mumbling from the next room. They were arguing about something quietly, but about what?

The loss of the manuscript, I thought, was a Freudian accident. I was not pleased with the essay from the very first. The tone I took in it was too grandiloquent. Still, what was I to talk about that evening? I might get confused from the very first sentences, like that speaker who had started his lecture with, "Peretz was a peculiar man," and could not utter another word.

If only I could sleep! I had not slept the previous night either. When I have to make a public appearance, I don't sleep for nights. The loss of the manuscript was a real catastrophe! I tried to close my eyes, but they kept opening by themselves. Something bit me; but as soon as I wanted to scratch, the cot shook and screamed like a sick man in pain.

I lay there, silent, stiff, wide-awake. A mouse scratched somewhere in a hole, and then I heard a sound, as of some beast with saw and fangs trying to saw through the floorboards. A mouse could not have raised such noise. It was some monster trying to cut down the foundations of the building. . . .

"Well, this adventure will be the end of me!" I said to myself. "I won't come out of here alive."

I lay benumbed, without stirring a limb. My nose was stuffed and I was breathing the icy air of the room through my mouth. My throat felt constricted. I had to cough, but I did not want to disturb the mother and daughter. A cough might also bring down the ramshackle cot. . . . Well, let me imagine that I had remained under Hitler in wartime. Let me get some taste of that, too. . . .

I imagined myself somewhere in Treblinka or Maidanek. I had done hard labor all day long. Now I was lying on a plank shelf. Tomorrow there would probably be a "selection," and since I was no longer well, I would be sent to the ovens. . . . I mentally began to say goodbye to the few people close to me. I must have dozed off, for I was awakened by loud cries. Binele was shouting: "Momma! Momma! Momma! . . ." The door flew open and Binele called me: "Help me! Mother is dead!"

I wanted to jump off the cot but it collapsed under me,

and instead of jumping, I had to raise myself. I cried: "What happened?"

Binele screamed: "She is cold! Where are the matches? Call a doctor! Call a doctor! Put on the light! Oh, Momma! . . . Momma! Momma!"

I never carry matches with me, since I do not smoke. I went in my pajamas to the bedroom. In the dark I collided with Binele. I asked her: "How can I call a doctor?"

She did not answer, but opened the door into the hallway and shouted, "Help, people, help! My mother is dead!" She cried with all her strength, as women cry in the Jewish small towns in Poland, but nobody responded. I tried to look for matches, knowing in advance that I would not find them in this strange house. Binele returned and we collided again in the dark. She clung to me with unexpected force and wailed: "Help! Help! I have nobody else in the world! She was all I had!"

And she broke into a wild lament, leaving me stunned and speechless.

"Find a match! Light the lamp!" I finally cried out, although I knew that my words were wasted.

"Call a doctor! Call a doctor!" she screamed, undoubtedly realizing herself the senselessness of her demand.

She half led, half pulled me to the bed where her mother lay. I put out my hand and touched her body. I began to look for her hand, found it, and tried to feel her pulse, but there was no pulse. The hand hung heavy and limp. It was cold as only a dead thing is cold. Binele seemed to understand what I was doing and kept silent for a while.

"Well, well? She's dead? . . . She's dead! . . . She had a sick heart! . . . Help me! Help me!"

"What can I do? I can't see anything!" I said to her, and my words seemed to have double meaning.

"Help me! . . . Help me! . . . Momma!"

"Are there no neighbors in the house?" I asked.

"There is a drunkard over us. . . ."

"Perhaps we can get matches from him?"

Binele did not answer. I suddenly became aware of how cold I felt. I had to put something on or I would catch pneumonia. I shivered and my teeth chattered. I started out for the room where I had slept but found myself in the kitchen. I returned and nearly threw Binele over. She was, herself, half naked. Unwittingly I touched her breast.

"Put something on!" I told her. "You'll catch a cold!"

"I do not want to live! I do not want to live! . . . She had no right to go to the station! . . . I begged her, but she is so stubborn. . . . She had nothing to eat. She would not even take a glass of tea. . . . What shall I do now? Where shall I go? Oh, Momma, Momma!"

Then, suddenly, it was quiet. Binele must have gone upstairs to knock on the drunkard's door. I remained alone with a corpse in the dark. A long-forgotten terror possessed me. I had the eerie feeling that the dead woman was trying to approach me, to seize me with her cold hands, to clutch at me and drag me off to where she was now. After all, I was responsible for her death. The strain of coming out to meet me had killed her. I started toward the outside door, as though ready to run out into the street. I stumbled on a chair and struck my knee. Bony fingers stretched after me. Strange beings screamed at me silently. There was a ringing in my ears and saliva filled my mouth as though I were about to faint.

Strangely, instead of coming to the outside door, I found myself back in my room. My feet stumbled on the flattened cot. I bent down to pick up my overcoat and put it on. It was only then that I realized how cold I was and how cold it was in that house. The coat was like an ice bag against my body. I trembled as with ague. My teeth clicked, my legs shook. I was ready to fight off the dead woman, to wrestle with her in mortal combat. I felt my heart hammering frighteningly loud and fast. No heart could long endure such violent knocking. I thought that Binele would find two corpses when she returned, instead of one.

I heard talk and steps and saw a light. Binele had brought down the upstairs neighbor. She had a man's coat over her shoulders. The neighbor carried a burning candle. He was a huge man, dark, with thick black hair and a long nose. He was barefoot and wore a bathrobe over his pajamas. What struck me most in my panic was the enormous size of his feet. He went to the bed with his candle and shadows danced after him and wavered across the dim ceiling.

One glance at the woman told me that she was dead. Her face had altered completely. Her mouth had become strangely thin and sunken; it was no longer a mouth, but a hole. The face was yellow, rigid, and claylike. Only the gray hair looked alive. The neighbor muttered something in French. He bent over the woman and felt her forehead. He uttered a single word and Binele began to scream and wail again. He tried to speak to her, to tell her something else, but she evidently did not understand his language. He shrugged his shoulders, gave me the candle, and started back. My hand trembled so uncontrollably that the small flame tossed in all directions and almost went out. I let some tallow drip on the wardrobe and set the candle in it.

Binele began to tear her hair and let out such a wild lament that I cried angrily at her: "Stop screaming!"

She gave me a sidelong glance, full of hate and astonishment, and answered quietly and sensibly: "She was all I had in the world. . . ."

"I know, I understand. . . . But screaming won't help."

My words appeared to have restored her to her senses. She stood silently by the bed, looking down at her mother. I stood on the opposite side. I clearly remembered that the woman had had a short nose; now it had grown long and hooked, as though death had made manifest a hereditary trait that had been hidden during her lifetime. Her forehead and eyebrows had acquired a new and masculine quality. Binele's sorrow seemed for a while to have given way to stupor. She stared, wide-eyed, as if she did not recognize her own mother.

I glanced at the window. How long could a night last, even a winter night? Would the sun never rise? Could this be the moment of that cosmic catastrophe that David Hume had envisaged as a theoretical possibility? But the panes were just beginning to turn gray.

I went to the window and wiped the misty pane. The night outside was already intermingled with blurs of daylight. The contours of the street were becoming faintly visible; piles of snow, small houses, roofs. A street lamp glimmered in the distance, but it cast no light. I raised my eyes to the sky. One half was still full of stars; the other was already flushed with morning. For a few seconds I seemed to have forgotten all that had happened and gave myself up entirely to the birth of the new day. I saw the stars go out one by one. Streaks of red and rose and yellow stretched across the sky, as in a child's painting.

"What shall I do now? What shall I do now?" Binele began to cry again. "Whom shall I call? Where shall I go? Call a doctor! Call a doctor!" And she broke into sobs.

I turned to her. "What can a doctor do now?"

"But someone should be called."

"You have no relatives?"

"None. I've no one in the world."

"What about the members of your lecture club?"

"They don't live in this neighborhood. . . ."

I went to my room and began to dress. My clothes were icy. My suit, which had been pressed before my journey, was crumpled. My shoes looked like misshapen clodhoppers. I caught sight of my face in a mirror, and it shocked me. It was hollow, dirty, paper-gray, covered with stubble. Outside, the snow began to fall again.

"What can I do for you?" I asked Binele. "I'm a stranger here. I don't know where to go."

"Woe is me! What am I doing to you? You are the victim of our misfortune. I shall go out and telephone the police, but I cannot leave my mother alone."

"I'll stay here."

"You will? She loved you. She never stopped talking about you. . . . All day yesterday. . . ."

I sat down on a chair and kept my eyes away from the dead woman. Binele dressed herself. Ordinarily I would be afraid to remain alone with a corpse. But I was half frozen, half asleep. I was exhausted after the miserable night. A deep despair came over me. It was a long, long time since I had seen such wretchedness and so much tragedy. My years in America seemed to have been swept away by that one night and I was taken back, as though by magic, to my worst days in Poland, to the bitterest crisis of my life. I heard the outside door close. Binele was gone. I could no longer remain sitting in the room with the dead woman. I ran out to the kitchen. I opened the door leading to the stairs. I stood by the open door as though ready to escape as soon as the corpse began to do those tricks that I had dreaded since childhood. . . . I said to myself that it was foolish to be afraid of this gentle woman, this cripple who had loved me while alive and who surely did not hate me now, if the dead felt anything. But all the boyhood fears were back upon me. My ribs felt chilled, as if some icy fingers moved over them. My heart thumped and fluttered like the spring in a broken clock. . . . Everything within me was strained. The slightest rustle and I would have dashed down the stairs in terror. The door to the street downstairs had glass panes, but they were half frosted over, half misty. A pale glow filtered through them as at dusk. An icy cold came from below. Suddenly I heard steps. The corpse? I wanted to run, but I realized that the steps came from the upper floor. I saw someone coming down. It was the upstairs neighbor on his way to work, a huge man in rubber boots and a coat with a kind of cowl, a metal lunch box in his hands. He glanced at me curiously and began to speak to me in Canadian French. It was good to be with another human being for a moment. I nodded, gestured with my hands, and answered him in English. He tried again and again to say something in his unfamiliar language, as though he believed that if I listened more carefully I would finally understand him. In the end he mumbled something and threw up his arms. He went out and slammed the door. Now I was all alone in the whole house.

What if Binele should not return? I began to toy with the fantasy that she might run away. Perhaps I'd be suspected of murder? Everything was possible in this world. I stood with my eyes fixed on the outside door. I wanted only one thing now—to return as quickly as possible to New York. My home, my job seemed totally remote and insubstantial, like memories of a previous incarnation. Who knows? Perhaps my whole life in New York had been no more than a hallucination? I began to search in my breast pocket. . . . Did I lose my citizenship papers, together with the text of my lecture? I felt a stiff paper. Thank God, the citizenship papers are here. I could have lost them, too. This document was now testimony that my years in America had not been an invention.

Here is my photograph. And my signature. Here is the government stamp. True, these were also inanimate, without life, but they symbolized order, a sense of belonging, law. I stood in the doorway and for the first time really read the paper that made me a citizen of the United States. I became so absorbed that I had almost forgotten the dead woman. Then the outside door opened and I saw Binele, covered with snow. She wore the same shawl that her mother had worn yesterday.

"I cannot find a telephone!"

She broke out crying. I went down to meet her, slipping the citizenship papers back into my pocket. Life had returned. The long nightmare was over. I put my arms around Binele and she did not try to break away. I became wet from the melting snow. We stood there midway up the stairs and rocked back and forth—a lost Yiddish writer, and a victim of Hitler and of my ill-starred lecture. I saw a number tattooed above her wrist and heard myself saying: "Binele, I won't abandon you. I swear by the soul of your mother. . . ."

Binele's body became limp in my arms. She raised her eyes and whispered: "Why did she do it? She just waited for your coming. . . ."

Cockadoodledoo

COCKADOODLEDOO! In your language this means good
morning, time to get up, day is breaking in Pinchev. What
a lot of words you people use! For us chickens, cockadoodledoo says everything. And how much it can mean! It all depends on the melody, the accent, the tone.

I am a great-grandson of the rooster who perched on King
Solomon's chair and I know languages. Therefore I tell you
that one cockadoodledoo is worth more than a hundred
words. It's not so much a matter of voice as it is of the flap of
the wings, the way the comb quivers, the eye tilts, the neck
feathers ruffle.

We even have what you call dialects. A Litvak rooster crows
cookerikoo, a Polish rooster crows cookerikee, and there are
some who can even manage cockerikko. Each has a style inherited from generations of roosters. Even the same chicken will
never crow the same way twice. But for such distinctions you
need a good ear.

On my mother's side I have blood of the Ancient Prophetic
Woodcock. If you put me in a dark cage, I can tell by the pitch
of the roosters' crowing and the hens' clucking whether it is
daybreak or twilight, clear or cloudy, whether it is mild or a
frost is coming, if it's raining, snowing, or hailing. My ear tells
me that the moon is full, half full, or new. I even can tell
an eclipse of the sun. I know a thousand things that don't
even occur to you. You talk too much, you drown in your own
words. All truth lies hidden in one word: cockadoodledoo.

I wasn't born yesterday. A world of hens and roosters has
passed before my eyes. I have seen a rooster castrated and
force–fed. I know the end all too well: death. Whether they'll
make a sacrifice of me for Yom Kippur, whether they'll put me
aside until Passover, Succoth or for the Sabbath of Moses'
Song of the Red Sea, the slaughterer waits, the knife is sharp,
everything is prepared: the tub for soaking, the salting board,
the gravy bowl, the stew pot, or maybe the roasting oven.

The garbage dump is crammed with our heads and entrails.
Every good-for-nothing housewife carries around one of our

wings for a whisk broom. Even if by some chance I should miss the slaughterer's knife, I still can't last indefinitely. I might get a nail in my gizzard. I might catch the pip. I might have—may it not happen to you—pox in my bowels. I might gulp down a wire, a pebble, a needle, a little snake. Every fowl ends up in the bowl.

So then what? Cockadoodledoo resolves all questions, solves all riddles. The rooster may die but not the cockadoodledoo. We were crowing long before Adam and, God willing, we'll go on crowing long after all slaughterers and chicken-gluttons have been laid low. What is rooster, then, and what is hen? Nothing more than a nesting place for the cockadoodledoo. No butcher in the world can destroy that.

There exists a heavenly rooster—his image is our own; and there is a heavenly Cockadoodledoo. The Rooster on High crows through our windpipes, he performs the midnight services through us, gets up with us for prayers when the morning stars sing together. You people pore over the Cabala and rack your brains. But for us the Cabala is in the marrow of our bones. What is cockadoodledoo? A magical name.

Maybe I'm betraying secrets. But to whom am I talking? To deaf ears. Your ancestors were never able to find out the secret of the cockadoodledoo; it is certain that you won't either. It is said that in distant countries there are machines where they hatch out hens by the millions and pull them out by the shelf-ful. The slaughterhouse is as big as our marketplace. One butcher boy ties, one cuts, one plucks. Tubs fill up with blood. Feathers fly. Every moment a thousand fowl give up their souls. And yet, can they really finish us this way?

Right now, while I'm talking, the under side of my wing begins to itch. I want to hold myself back, but I can't. My throat tickles, my tongue trembles, my beak itches, my comb burns. The quill of every feather tingles. It must come out! Cockadoodledoo!

2

Apropos of what you say about hens: you mustn't take them too lightly. When I was a young rooster, a hen was less than nothing to me. What is a hen? No comb, no spurs, no color in her tail, no strength in her claws. She cackles her few years away, lays eggs, hatches them, rubs her what-do-you-call-it in the dirt, puts on pious airs.

At an early age I began to see the hypocrisy of hens. They bow down to every big shot. Among themselves, in their own yard, whoever is stronger picks on the others. I have a hatred of gossip and a hen just can't hold her tongue. Cluck-cluck and cluck-cluck. My rule is: don't talk too much with a chicken. It is true that you can't get along without them. Everybody has a mother. But what of it? You can't stay stuck in the eggshell forever.

But that's the conceit of young roosters. With age I found that it must be this way. In all lands and in all the heavens there is male and female. Everything is paired, from the fly to the elephant, from the Rooster on High to the ordinary cock. It is true that cluck-cluck is just not the same as cockadoodledoo, but a hen, too, is not to be sneezed at.

Your so-called philosophers love to ask: which came first, the chicken or the egg? Garrulous chickens argue endlessly: which came first, the cockadoodledoo or the cluck-cluck? But all this is empty chatter. My opinion is that there was no first egg and there's not going to be any last egg. First is last and last is first. You don't understand? The answer is: cockadoodledoo.

I have five wives and each one is a tale in herself. Kara is a princess. Where she got her pedigree, I couldn't say. She is fat, easygoing, has golden eyes and a tranquil heart. She does not hobnob with the other hens. When the mistress scatters a handful of millet, the rabble run to grab it, but Kara has both patience and faith. The kernel destined for her will reach her. She keeps herself clean, doesn't look at other cocks, avoids bickering. She has the right to peck at all her competitors but considers it beneath her dignity to start up with every silly hen. She clucks less than the others and the eggs that she lays are big and white.

I have no great passion for her nor she for me, but I have more chicks by her than by any of the others. Every year she hatches two dozen eggs and without complaint she does everything that a hen should. When she's through with her laying, they'll put her away and she'll make a rich soup. I suspect that she doesn't even know that there's such a thing as death, because she likes to play around with the guts of her sisters. That's Kara.

Tsip is the exact opposite: red, thin, bony, a screecher, a glutton, and jealous—fire and flame. She picks on all the hens, but loves me terribly. Just let her see me coming and down she plops and spreads her wings. In your language you would say she is oversexed, but I forgive her everything. She twitches, every limb quivers. Her eggs are tiny, with bloody specks. In all the time I've known her she's never stopped screaming. She runs around the yard as though she were possessed. She complains and complains. This one pecked her, that one bit her, the third one pulled some down from her breast, the fourth grabbed a crumb from under her beak. Lays eggs and doesn't remember where. Tries to fly and almost breaks a leg. Suddenly she's in a tree and then on a roof. At night in the coop she doesn't close an eye. Fidgets, cackles, can't find any place for herself. A witch with an itch. They would have slaughtered her long ago if she were not so skinny, eating herself up alive—and for what? That's Tsip.

Chip is completely white, a hen without any meanness in her, as good as a sunny day, quiet as a dove. She runs from quarrels as from fire. At the least hubbub she stops laying. She loves me with a chaste love, considers me a hen-chaser, but keeps everything to herself. She clucks with a soft-tongued cluck and gets fatter every day.

If she feels like sitting on eggs and there are none to sit on, she might sit on a little white stone; she isn't very bright. The other day she hatched out three duck eggs. As long as the ducklings didn't crawl into the water, Chip thought they were chicks; but as soon as they began to swim in the pond, she almost dropped dead. Chip stood by the bank, her mother's heart close to bursting. I tried to explain to her what a bastard is, but try to talk to a frightened mother.

For some strange reason, Chip loves Tsip and does everything to please her. But Tsip is her blood enemy. Anyone else in Chip's place would have scratched her eyes out long ago; but Chip is good and asks for no reward. She's full of the mercy which comes from the Heavenly Chicken. That's Chip.

Pre-pre is the lowest hen I've ever met. Has all the vices a hen can have: black as coal, thin as a stick, a thief, a tattletale, a scrapper, and blind in one eye from a fight with her first husband, may the dunghill rest lightly on him. She carries on with strange roosters, slips into other people's yards, rummages in all kinds of garbage. She has the comb of a rooster and the voice of a rooster. When the moon is full, she starts to crow as though possessed by a dybbuk.

She lays an egg and devours it herself or cracks it open from sheer meanness. I hate her, that Black Daughter of a Black Mother. How many times I've sworn to have no dealings with the slut, but when she wants what's coming to her, she begins to fawn, flatter, gaze into my eyes like a beggar.

I'm no fighter by nature, but Pre-pre has a bad effect on me. I grab her by the head feathers and chase her all over the yard. My other wives avoid her like the plague. Many times our mistress wanted to catch her and send her to the slaughterer, but just when she's wanted she's not at home, that gadabout, that dog of a hen. That's Pre-pre.

Cluckele is my own little daughter, Kara is her mother, and a father doesn't gossip about his daughter even when she's his wife. I look at her and I don't believe my own eyes: when did she grow up? Only yesterday, it seems, this was a tiny little chick, just out of the eggshell, hardly covered with down. But she's already coquettish, already knows hennish wiles and lays eggs, although they're small. Very soon I'll be the father of my own grandchildren.

I love her, but I suspect that her little heart belongs to another rooster, that cross-eyed idiot on the other side of the fence. What she sees in that sloppy tramp, I have no idea. But how can a rooster know what a hen sees in another rooster? Her head could be turned by a feather in the tail, a tooth in the comb, a side spur, or even the way he shuffles his feet in the sand and stirs up the dust.

I'm good to her, but she doesn't appreciate it. I give her advice, but she doesn't listen. I guard her like the apple of my eye, but she's always looking for excitement. . . . The new generation is completely spoiled, but what can I do? One thing I want: as long as I live, may she live too. What happens afterward is not up to me.

3

Your experts in the Cabala know that cockadoodledoo is based on sheer faith. What else, logic? But faith itself has different degrees. A rooster's little faith may give out and he will become crestfallen. His wings droop, his comb turns white, his eyes glaze over and his crow sticks in his gullet. Why crow? For whom and for how long? Roosters have been crowing since ancient times and for what? When one begins to think about time, it's no good. Occasionally a rooster will even weep. Yes, roosters are capable of weeping. Listen sometime to the roosters crowing the night before Yom Kippur when you people are reciting the midnight prayers. If your human ears could hear our weeping, you would throw away all your slaughtering knives.

But let me tell you something that happened.

The night was dark. The chickens dozed or pretended to doze. It was during the Ten Days of Repentance before the Yom Kippur sacrifice of fowls. All day long it was oppressively hot. At night the sky clouded over, hiding a sliver of moon. The air was warm and humid like the mud in the duck pond. There was lightning, but no thunder, no rain. People closed their shutters and snored under their feather comforters. The grass stood motionless; the leaves on the apple trees were still; even the grasshoppers fell asleep. The frogs in the swamp were voiceless. The moles rested in their molehills.

Everything was silent, everything held its breath. It seemed as if the world had asked the ultimate question and was waiting for an answer: yes or no, one way or another. Things cannot go on like this. If a clear answer does not come, creation will return to primeval chaos. I did not move. My heart didn't beat, my blood didn't flow, nothing stirred. It was midnight, but I had no urge to crow. Had the end come?

Suddenly a flap of wings and from somewhere close at hand: cockadoodledoo! I trembled. I became all ears. It was the old cockadoodledoo, but with a new meaning. No, not the old one, but a brand-new one: a new style, another approach, a different melody. I didn't know what it was saying, but suddenly everything was light, I felt rejuvenated. Is it possible? I asked myself. Millions of generations of roosters had crowed, but no one before had ever crowed like that. It opened doors in my brain, it cheered my heart. It spilled over with hope and happiness. Could it really be? I asked. And I, fool that I was, had doubted! I felt both shame and joy. I, too, wanted to crow, but I was shy. What could I say after him? Tsip woke up and asked, "What's that?"

"A new voice, a new word," I said. "Chickens, let us join in a blessing. We have not lived in vain."

"Who is he, where is he?" asked Chip.

"What difference does it make who he is? The power lies in the crowing, not in the rooster."

"Still—"

I didn't answer her. I closed my eyes. The crowing had stopped, but its sound still echoed in the silence from trees, roofs, chimneys, birdhouses. It sang like a fiddle, rang like a bell, resounded like a ram's horn. It sang and didn't stop singing.

The dog in the kennel awoke and barked once. The pig in his sty uttered a grunt; the horse in the stable thumped the ground with his hoof. The clouds parted in the sky and a moon appeared, white as chalk. For a while I thought: who knows, perhaps I only imagined it. True, the hens heard it too, but perhaps it was a dream, perhaps it was only the wind. Perhaps it was a wolf howling, the sound of a trumpet, a hunter's call, a drunkard's shout.

Even though fowl wait all their lives for a miracle, still, when it happens, they can't believe it. I expected the other roosters to answer him as usual, but I didn't hear a sound. Had all the roosters been slaughtered, with only this one left? Perhaps I myself was already slaughtered and the voice I heard was only the dream of a chopped-off head? The stillness was not of this world. I stuck my beak in my feathers and pinched my own skin to see if it hurt. Suddenly: cockadoodledoo! It was the same rooster and the same crow. No, not the same, already different: a song which rent the soul and then revived it; a melody lifting a rooster's heart into heights where no eagle ever flew, above all towers, all clouds, into a brightness that made the stars seem dark.

Everything I know I learned that night. I can't reveal secrets

—my tongue is tied—but there is a cockadoodledoo which rights every wrong, forgives every sin, straightens all crookedness. Everything is cockadoodledoo: butcher and fowl; knife and throat; feathers and plucker; the blood in the veins and the blood in the ditch. Crow, rooster, and ask no questions! We must accept all: the crow of the rooster, the cluck of the hen, the egg which is hatched, the egg which is eaten, the egg which is stepped upon, the egg with the splotch of blood in it.

Sing, rooster, praise God, love your hens, don't fight with other roosters unless they attack you. Eat your grain, drink your water, stand on the rooftop and crow as if the whole world—all four corners of it—were waiting for your crowing. It is really waiting. Without your crowing, something would be missing. You don't understand? God willing, you will understand. You have eternity behind you and eternity before you. You will go through many lives. If you knew what awaits you, you would die of joy. But that wouldn't do. As long as you live, you must live. . . .

All night long that rooster crowed and not a single rooster dared answer him. He was a cantor without a choir. Just at daybreak, when it began to redden in the East, he let out his last crow—the loudest, the loveliest, the most divine.

The next day there was a furor among the neighboring roosters. Some swore by their comb and spurs that they had heard nothing. Others admitted they had heard something, but it wasn't a rooster. As for the hens, every one of them had forgotten. What will chickens not do to avoid the truth? They fear the truth more than the knife, and this is in itself a mystery.

But since that rooster crowed—exalted be his name—and I had the privilege to hear and to remember, I have wanted to spread the word, especially since tomorrow is the day before Yom Kippur. Happy is he who believes. A time will come when all will see and hear, and the cockadoodledoo of the Rooster on High will ring throughout heaven and earth.

Cockadoodledoo!

Translated by Ruth Whitman

The Plagiarist

THE RABBI of Machlev, Reb Kasriel Dan Kinsker, paced back and forth in his study. From time to time he would stop, grasp his white beard with his left hand, and let go, spreading all five fingers, a typical gesture when he was faced with a problem. He was talking to himself: "How could he ever do such a thing? He's actually copied word for word!"

The rabbi was alluding to one of his disciples, Shabsai Getsel. During the several years that Shabsai Getsel had studied with the rabbi, he had often made use of the latter's manuscripts. As a matter of fact, the rabbi had even asked him to copy out several of his responsa.

Reb Kasriel Dan had for the last forty years been writing homilies and commentaries on Talmudic texts, but he had never yet been able to bring himself to permit the publication of even one of his works. He had heeded the verse in Ecclesiastes: "And further, by these, my son, be admonished: of making many books there is no end."

Authors streamed to Machlev to sell prepublication subscriptions or to raise money to pay for getting their works printed. Some asked Reb Kasriel Dan for approbatory prefaces. There were those whose disquisitions totally missed the point of the Talmud text. Instead, they piled sophistry on sophistry and read into the words of the ancients meanings that had never been intended.

The rabbi hesitated before refusing to write such a preface lest his unwillingness be interpreted as an offense against the author. On the other hand, to praise work he could not approve was equally wrong. It also took a lot of time and good eyesight to read these manuscripts. Some of the handwriting was difficult to decipher, with afterthoughts frequently scribbled in the margins. Whenever the matter of why Reb Kasriel Dan did not bring out a book of his own came up, he would say: "There are quite enough books, thank the Lord, without mine. Let Jews abide by what has been written until now."

One of his grandfather's pithy Bible interpretations occurred to the rabbi. "It is written in Psalms that when the

Messiah comes, 'Then shall all the trees of the wood rejoice.' The question that arises is: Why should the trees rejoice? What concern is it of theirs? The answer is that by the time the Messiah arrives, authors will have written so many volumes that books will supply the necessary fuel for stoves. Thus there will no longer be any need to burn wood, and the trees will rejoice at having been spared."

That was all very well, but what Shabsai Getsel had done was so heinous that the rabbi for weeks on end was like a man obsessed. The young fellow had copied whole sections of the rabbi's manuscripts and had them printed under his own name. That was theft plain and simple. The rabbi could not believe that Shabsai Getsel was capable of such behavior, and he was still trying to think up some excuse on Getsel's behalf.

Yet the more the rabbi compared his own manuscripts with Shabsai Getsel's printed book, the more astounded he became. The rabbi realized the Shabsai Getsel knew himself to be safe against exposure. He could be sure that the rabbi would not stoop to shaming another man even though that man had sinned. Besides, Shabsai Getsel was also the son-in-law of Reb Tevia, the warden of the congregation, who had many relatives in Machlev. To bring the matter into the open would cause a scandal and profanation of the Holy Name.

But what had Shabsai Getsel been thinking as he sat copying out dozens of pages of Reb Kasriel Dan's manuscripts? Had he imagined some kind of heavenly dispensation for himself? Or was he, God forbid, a heretic who did not believe either in the Creator or in his judgment?

The more Reb Kasriel Dan pondered the matter, the more confounded he became. He grasped at his beard over and over again. It was not his habit to talk to himself, but the words forced themselves from his lips. He wrinkled his lofty forehead under his skullcap, knitted his brows, grimaced as if he were in physical pain. He paused in front of his bookcase, as though seeking an answer in the spines of the ancient volumes.

There was, of course, the fact that no man sinned unless a touch of madness entered his soul. On the other hand, that was true only of sins committed on impulse in a fit of rage, even if one went so far as to steal, or, God forbid, to commit adultery. But to sit day in, day out, week in, week out, plagiarizing another's works was sheer wantonness. Moreover, how did Shabsai Getsel still dare to look Reb Kasriel Dan in the face?

The whole thing was a riddle. Reb Kasriel Dan called out to himself and to the world at large: "The End of the Days is at hand!" Was not this event similar to those described in the Sotah tractate when it speaks of the omens preceding the coming of the Messiah: "In the Messiah's footsteps brazenness will grow, prices will soar, the vine will bear fruit, but wine will be dear. Idolatry will become heresy practiced with impunity . . . And the wisdom of the scribes will be dulled, while those who fear sin will be held in contempt; the truth will be absent. Boys will mock their elders, and the aged will rise before youth. . . .

"Have things really gone so far?" the rabbi asked himself.

The rabbi knew he ought not to be wasting so much time on this matter. His duty was to pray, study, and serve the Lord. This brooding over Shabsai Getsel led only to vexation. It robbed the rabbi of his sleep, so that he had difficulty in concentrating on his predawn studies. He had even vented his bitterness on his wife. He must keep the whole business hushed up. Certainly now he would have to give up any idea of publishing his own writings, for that would set tongues wagging and result in gossip and accusations.

"Who knows?" thought the rabbi. "Perhaps this is heaven's way of preventing the publication of my works. But was this reconcilable with the free will which is granted to all men?"

The door opened and in came Shabsai Getsel.

Outwardly there was nothing unusual in this. Shabsai Getsel had been coming to see the rabbi for years and still acted the part of pupil. Indeed, it was Reb Kasriel Dan who had ordained him the year before. But now the sight of Shabsai Getsel alarmed the rabbi.

"I'll not utter a cross word, heaven forbid, nor make any insinuations," Reb Kasriel resolved. He forced himself to say, "Welcome, Shabsai Getsel!"

Shabsai Getsel, short, swarthy, with pitch-black eyes, black eyebrows, and a little black beard, was wearing a fox coat, with foxtails dangling from the hem; a sable hat was perched on his head. He trod softly in his fur-lined top-boots. He applied two fingers to the mezuzah on the doorpost and kissed it. Carefully he removed his fur coat and woolen scarf, remaining in his caftan.

The rabbi indicated a chair at the table for Shabsai Getsel and seated himself in his armchair.

Reb Kasriel Dan was taller than Shabsai Getsel. From under his white bristly eyebrows, a pair of gray eyes peered forth. He was wearing a satin robe, breeches, half-shoes, and white knee-length stockings. The rabbi was barely sixty years old but looked closer to eighty. Only his gait was still firm and his gaze piercing. Whereas Shabsai Getsel did everything with deliberation, the rabbi moved with haste. He opened a book and promptly closed it again. He shifted pen and ink forward and drew them back.

"Well, Shabsai Getsel, what's the news?" he inquired.

"I've received several letters."

"Aha!"

"Would you like to see them?"

"Yes, let's have them."

Reb Kasriel Dan knew in advance what letters these were. Shabsai Getsel had sent copies of his book out to various rabbis, who had written back praising his work. He was already being addressed as "The Great Luminary," "The Living Library," "The Uprooter of Mountains."

The rabbis were eloquent in expressing their pleasure in his exegeses, describing them as "deep as the sea," "sweet as honey," "precious as pearls and jewels."

As the rabbi read the ornate scripts, he prayed to God to preserve him from evil thoughts. "Well, that's fine. 'A good name is better than precious ointment,'" he declared.

Suddenly the rabbi saw it all. He was being tempted. Heaven was testing him to see how much he could stand. One false move and he would fall into the trap laid for him by Satan. He would sink into hatred, sorrow, fury, and who knows what other transgressions. There was only one thing to do: keep his lips sealed and his brain pure. Most assuredly, Shabsai Getsel had erred; but he, Reb Kasriel Dan, was not the Lord of the Universe. It was not for him to pass judgment on a fellow man. Who could tell what went on in another's heart? Who could measure the forces which drove flesh and blood to vanity, covetousness, folly? Reb Kasriel Dan had long since come to understand that many people were made half mad by their passions.

The rabbi took out his pocket handkerchief and wiped his forehead. "What good errand brings you here?"

"I'd like to take a look at the responsum you wrote to the Rabbi of Sochatchov."

Reb Kasriel Dan was about to ask whether Shabsai Getsel was preparing another book. But he stopped himself and said: "It's in the drawer of the commode. Wait, I'll fetch it."

And the rabbi went into the next room, where he kept his manuscripts. He soon returned and handed Shabsai Getsel a copy of the responsum.

2

Shabsai Getsel remained with the rabbi for several hours. No sooner had he left than the rabbi's wife came in.

Reb Kasriel Dan saw at once that she was angry. She swept into the room, the hem of her dress swishing over the floor. The tassel on her bonnet shook. Her narrow, deeply wrinkled face was paler than usual. Even before she reached the table at which her husband sat, she began shrieking: "What does he want here, that worm? Why does he spend entire days here? He is your enemy, not a friend! Your worst enemy . . . !"

Reb Kasriel Dan pushed his book away. "Why are you screaming? I can't show people the door."

"He comes here to spy, the hypocrite! He wants to sit in your chair! May he never live that long, dear Father in heaven! He's inciting everybody against you. He's in league with all your enemies . . . !"

Reb Kasriel Dan pounded his fist on the table. "How do you know?"

The old woman's narrow chin, sprouting a few white hairs, began to tremble. Her bloodshot eyes, embedded in pouches, flashed angrily. "Everybody knows, except simpletons like you! Apart from that Talmud of yours, you're blind, you don't know your hands from your feet. He's determined to be rabbi here. He's produced a book and sent it out to everyone. You scribble a whole lifetime and nothing comes of it. But he, a

young man, is already famous. Wait until they throw you out
and appoint him in your place."

"Let them! I must get on with my studies."

"I'll not let you study! What comes of all your learning? You
get paid eighteen guldens a week. Other rabbis live in comfort,
while we starve. I have to knead the dough with my own crippled hands. Your daughter does the washing, because we cannot afford a washerwoman. Your robe is worn through. If I
didn't patch and mend every night, you'd go about in rags.
And what's to become of your son? They promised to make
him your assistant. It's two years since they promised, and not
a penny has he seen."

"Is it my fault if they don't keep their word?"

"A proper father would do something for his child. He
wouldn't allow the matter to drag on and on. You know the
communal busybodies, you know they can't be counted on.
Let me tell you something." The rabbi's wife changed her
tone. "They're going to appoint Shabsai Getsel as your assistant. And when your time comes—a hundred years from
now—it will be he who steps into your shoes. As for Pessachia,
he'll be left without bread."

She uttered the last words in a hoarse shriek and clenched
her hands into tiny fists. Everything about her was aquiver: her
bonnet, her earrings, her sunken mouth, in which not a single
tooth remained, her empty double chin.

Reb Kasriel Dan watched her with grief. He pitied his son,
who for these past twenty years had not been able to find himself a living and had to be supported by his father. Reb Kasriel
Dan was afraid that his wife was about to suffer an attack of
gallstones—inevitably they came when she got overly excited.
Indeed, the moans that presaged the first spasms had already
began.

Reb Kasriel Dan knew full well that the town worthies had
no use for Pessachia. Pessachia did not know how to flatter the
elders. He held himself aloof. His appointment as assistant
rabbi was constantly being deferred on all manner of pretexts.
But, after all, could a man be foisted on a community against
their will?

This was, however, the first time Reb Kasriel Dan had heard
any mention of appointing Shabsai Getsel to Pessachia's place.

"Still waters run deep," he thought. "Shabsai Getsel, my pupil, has become my deadly enemy. He wants to take everything from me."

Involuntarily something within Reb Kasriel Dan cried out, "He'll not live to see the day!" But he immediately remembered that it is forbidden to curse anyone, even in thought. Aloud he said to his wife, "Stop fuming! We don't know whether it's true or not. People concoct all kinds of lies."

"It's true. The whole town knows it. One hears about it wherever one goes. Beginning next Sabbath, Shabsai Getsel is to preach in the House of Study. He's to receive twenty guldens a week, two more than you do, just to show who's the real master here."

Reb Kasriel Dan felt a void around his heart. "Like Absalom rising against David," flitted through his mind. "May he share Absalom's fate."

Reb Kasriel Dan could no longer contain his ire. He lowered his head, his eyelids dropped. After a while he roused himself. "Heaven's will be done!"

"Ay, while you sit with folded hands doing nothing, others are busy. In heaven, too, you're of no importance."

"I have not deserved better."

"Old fool!"

Never had Reb Kasriel Dan heard such language from his wife. He was sure that she would soon be sorry for what she had said. Suddenly he heard her gulp and suppress a wail. She began to sway as though she were about to fall. Reb Kasriel Dan jumped up and caught her by the arms. She trembled and moaned. He half walked, half carried her to a bench. In his alarm he called for help.

The door opened, and in ran Teltsa Mindel, the rabbi's divorced daughter. Teltsa Mindel's husband had turned Hassid and gone to live at the court of the Wonder Rebbe of Belz, from where he had sent her a bill of divorcement. When Shabsai Getsel, as a yeshiva student and orphan, first came to board and study with Reb Kasriel Dan, the townsfolk assumed he would marry Teltsa Mindel, despite the fact that she was several years his elder. Reb Kasriel Dan himself had favored the match.

But Shabsai Getsel had instead become betrothed to the daughter of Reb Tevia, a rich man and leader in the community. Reb Kasriel Dan had borne his pupil no grudge. He had officiated at the wedding. When the rabbi's wife had railed against Shabsai Getsel, calling him a hypocrite and a wolf in sheep's clothing, the rabbi had scolded her and reminded her that matches were made in heaven.

The incident of the book and now Shabsai Getsel's attempt to take Pessachia's place as assistant rabbi could not be forgiven so easily. Reb Kasriel Dan shot a quick glance at his daughter and ordered: "Put your mother to bed. Heat up a warming pan. Call Feitel the leech."

"Don't drag me! I'm not dead yet!" cried his wife. "Woe is me! Alas and woe for all that has come upon me!"

Reb Kasriel Dan again looked toward his daughter. It seemed such a short time since she had been a little girl, since Reb Kasriel Dan played with her, seated her on his knees and rocked her up and down on an imaginary "coach ride." Now there stood before him a woman with a grubby kerchief on her head, misshapen slippers on her feet, and a soiled apron. She was short like her mother, had yellow eyebrows and freckles. There was a silent dejection in her pale blue eyes, the misery of an abandoned woman. She was getting fat. She looked older than her age.

Reb Kasriel Dan had had little joy in his children. Several had died in infancy. He had lost a grown son and a daughter. Pessachia had been a boy prodigy, but after his marriage he had grown taciturn. It was impossible to get a word out of him. He slept by day and stayed awake at night. Pessachia had immersed himself in the Cabala.

Was it any wonder that the community rejected him? Nowadays a rabbi needed to be businesslike, to know how to keep accounts and even speak a little Russian. Reports had reached Reb Kasriel Dan that rabbis in the big towns themselves dealt with the authorities and went to Lublin to see the governor. They enjoyed the hospitality of the wealthy. One rabbi had actually published an appeal to Jews calling on them to settle in colonies in the Land of Israel, where they would speak Hebrew every day, not just on the Sabbath. Conferences were being called, newspapers were being read. Machlev was a blind alley, cut off from the world.

Just the same, why should Shabsai Getsel, who had a rich father-in-law, take away a poor man's living?

Mother and daughter, taking tiny steps, made their way out of the room. Reb Kasriel Dan began to pace back and forth. "The wicked haven't taken over yet," he murmured to himself. "There is a Creator. There is Providence. The Torah is still the Torah. . . ."

Reb Kasriel Dan's thoughts reverted to Shabsai Getsel's book. As a result of his plagiarism, the only thing for the rabbi to do with his own works was put them out of reach once and for all. Otherwise they would be found after his death and Shabsai Getsel would be discovered and shamed, or it could even happen that Reb Kasriel Dan would be suspected of plagiarizing from the younger man. But where could he hide the manuscripts so that they would not be found? The only thing to do was to burn them.

Reb Kasriel Dan glanced at the stove. After all, what difference did it make who the author was? The main thing was that the commentaries were published and would be studied. In heaven the truth was known.

3

The rabbi lay in bed all night without closing an eye. He recited "Hear, O Israel" and then pronounced the blessing "Causing sleep to descend," after which one is not supposed to utter a word. But sleep would not come.

Reb Kasriel Dan knew what his duty was. The Biblical injunction stated, "Thou shalt rebuke thy neighbor and not suffer sin upon him." He should summon Shabsai Getsel and bring his grievances out into the open. What would be the use? Reb Kasriel Dan could already hear the other's slippery excuses. He would play the innocent, shrug his shoulders, insist he was being pressed by the congregation to accept the office. As for the manuscripts, the rabbi no longer possessed them. They had all gone up in smoke. Reb Kasriel Dan tossed from side to side. He either froze under the eiderdown or became flushed with heat. When he was not thirsty, he felt the need to urinate. He had put on fresh underwear, yet he itched. His pillow and mattress, although made of down, were as hard to his head and back as though someone had placed stones in the bedding.

Frenzied thoughts came to him of the sort that jeopardized his chances in the hereafter. Who knows? Perhaps the heretics were right, perhaps neither Judge nor Judgment existed . . . Maybe heaven, too, sided with the strong. Was it not written in the Talmud that "he who is stronger, to him shall victory go . . ." Maybe that was why the Jews suffered exile, because they were the feeblest among the nations. Maybe the slaughter of beasts was permitted simply because man was clever enough to wield a knife. It might even be that the strong sat in paradise while the weak fried in hell . . .

"I'm headed for perdition," Reb Kasriel warned himself. He placed his hand on his forehead. "Father in heaven, save me . . . I'm sinking, God forbid, into the infernal depths . . ." The rabbi sat up so abruptly that the boards under his mattress creaked. "Why do I lie here allowing the evil spirits to tear me to pieces? There's only one remedy—the Torah!"

The rabbi dressed hastily. He lit a lamp and entered his study. Shadows wavered on the wall, on the cross-beams. Though the stove was stoked up, Reb Kasriel Dan's teeth chattered with cold. Normally, on rising before dawn, he would light the samovar and brew tea; but now he did not have the energy to fill it with coals and pour water into it. He opened a book, but the letters danced giddily before his eyes. They darted about, played leap-frog with one another, changed color.

"Am I going blind, heaven forbid?" Reb Kasriel Dan asked himself. "Or perhaps the end has come. Well, so much the better. It seems that I have lost the power to control my will . . ."

Reb Kasriel Dan's head slowly dropped down on his book and he drowsed off. He apparently slept several hours, for when he awoke, the gray of daylight lined the cracks in the shutters. Snow was falling outside.

"What have I been dreaming?" the rabbi asked himself. "Shouting and yelling and the ringing of bells. A fire, a funeral, slaughter, all at one and the same time . . ." The cold ran along his spine. His legs had grown stiff. He wanted to wash his hands and say the morning prayers, but he was unable to rise to his feet.

The door opened slowly and Pessachia came in, a little fellow with a gray face, wide-set eyes almost devoid of eyebrows, a roundish little beard that was usually yellow but on this wintry morning looked like gray cotton wool. Pessachia did not walk but shuffled in his slippers. His caftan was unbuttoned, revealing the long, ritual fringes and shabby trousers tied with tape. His shirt was wide open at the neck, and his skullcap was covered with bits of feather down.

"What do you want?" the rabbi asked.

Pessachia did not reply immediately. His yellow eyes blinked and his lips twitched like those of a stutterer. "Father!"

"What's the matter?"

"Shabsai Getsel is ill . . . very ill . . . Collapsed . . . He needs mercy . . ."

Reb Kasriel Dan felt a pang all the way from his throat to his intestines. "What's wrong with him?"

"They called the doctor . . . They don't know . . . His wife has come to ask you to pray for him . . ."

"What value have my prayers? Well, leave me!"

"Father, his mother's name was Fruma Zlata . . ."

"Very well . . ."

Pessachia went out. The rabbi noticed that his son was limping. "What's happened to him," Reb Kasriel Dan wondered. "He doesn't look well, either."

Reb Kasriel Dan closed his eyes. The reason for Shabsai Getsel's sickness was clear enough. The rabbi's involuntary curse was to blame. A verse from the Book of Proverbs came to his mind: "Also to punish the just is not good." According to the commentaries the real meaning of it is: "Nor is it proper for the righteous to mete out punishment." Even calling himself righteous in his thoughts made the rabbi feel ashamed. "I, a righteous man? A man with evil power like Balaam the Wicked!"

The rabbi began praying for Shabsai Getsel: "Lord of the Universe, send him perfect healing . . . I have done much harm, but I do not wish to be a murderer . . . I forgive him everything, absolutely and forever."

The rabbi rose and took a Psalter from the bookcase. He located the Psalm of intercession for the sick: "Happy is he who comprehends the feeble . . ." It was time for the morning prayers but the rabbi continued his argument with Providence: "I have no strength left for all these upsets. If I cannot have peace in my old age, then better take me . . ."

For several days Shabsai Getsel contended with the Angel of Death. At times it looked as though he were improving but then he would have another relapse. A doctor came from Zamosc. The sick man was treated with cups and leeches. He was rubbed with alcohol and turpentine. His mother-in-law and his wife visited the graveyard to invoke the aid of dead ancestors. Candles were lit in the House of Study. The doors of the Holy Ark were flung wide open. Schoolchildren were made to recite the Psalms.

Reb Kasriel Dan went to visit his sick disciple. He passed through a corridor and a drawing room, entered a carpeted bedroom with curtained windows. On a chair stood bottles of medicine. The rabbi saw an orange, cookies, and sweets. Shabsai Getsel's face was livid. He murmured something, and his little beard moved up and down as though he were chewing. A pointed Adam's apple protruded from his throat. His brow was knotted as though he were considering a difficult problem.

Reb Kasriel Dan bowed his head low. That is what happens to flesh and blood. Aloud he said: "Shabsai Getsel, get well! You are needed here, you are needed . . ."

Shabsai Getsel opened one eye. "Rabbi!"

"Yes, Shabsai Getsel. I pray for you day and night."

It seemed as though Shabsai Getsel wished to say something, but nothing came out except a gurgling sound. After a while he closed his eyes again. The rabbi murmured: "Be healed! In the name of the Torah . . ." Yet all the time he knew, with a certainty that was beyond his understanding, that Shabsai Getsel would never rise from his sickbed.

He died that same night and the funeral was held in the morning. In the House of Study the rabbi spoke the eulogy. Reb Kasriel Dan had never wept when delivering a funeral oration, but this time he covered his face with his handkerchief. He choked over his words. Shabsai Getsel's father-in-law demanded that a copy of his son-in-law's book be placed on the bier; and thus they bore him away to the cemetery. Shabsai Getsel had left no children; the rabbi recited the first Kaddish for him.

A few days later the congregation appointed Pessachia assistant rabbi. They drank brandy, ate honey cake. Pessachia wore a new caftan, new shoes, a skullcap without feather down on it. He promised to fulfill all his rabbinical duties and to help his father lead the congregation. The elders wished him luck.

A few weeks went by. The rabbi remained secluded during the day, delegating the handling of all ritual questions and law cases to his son. He even stopped going to the House of Study to pray. As a rule, he ate one meal a day, gruel, bread, meat. Now he left his food almost untouched. On the Sabbath he sang no hymns. He no longer prepared the samovar at night. The household would hear the rabbi striding about in the dark, sighing and talking to himself. His face grew yellow and his beard shriveled.

All at once Reb Kasriel Dan announced that he was giving up his position as rabbi. He requested the community to appoint Reb Pessachia in his place. He stated that he had sinned and must go into exile to do penance.

The weeping of his wife was of no avail. Reb Kasriel Dan took off his satin robe and round rabbinical fur hat. He put on a shaggy long coat and peaked cap of cloth. He said farewell to his wife, Teltsa Mindel, to Reb Pessachia, to the townfolk. A wagoner gave him a lift to Lublin.

As the rabbi sat in the wagon, a young man noted for his insolence dared to ask him what sin he had committed. And the rabbi answered: "The Commandment 'Thou shalt not kill' includes all sins."

Translated by J. M. Lask and Elizabeth Shub

Zeitl and Rickel

I OFTEN hear people say, "This cannot happen, that cannot be, nobody has ever heard of such a thing, impossible." Nonsense! If something is destined to happen, it does. My grandmother used to say: "If the devil wants to, he can make two walls come together. If it is written that a rabbi will fall off a roof, he will become a chimney sweep." The Gentiles have a proverb: "He who must hang will not drown."

Take this thing that happened in our own town. If anybody told me about it, I'd say he was a liar. But I knew them both, may they intercede for us in heaven. They've surely served their punishment by now. The older one was called Zeitl; the younger one, Rickel.

Zeitl's father, Reb Yisroel Bendiner, was already an old man of eighty when I knew him. He had buried three wives, and Zeitl was the daughter of the third. I don't know whether he had any children with the others. He was in his late fifties when he came to live in our town. He married a young girl, who died, may God preserve us, in childbirth. Zeitl was taken out of her with pincers. Reb Yisroel's father-in-law had left his daughter a large brick building in the marketplace, with thirteen stores, and Reb Yisroel inherited it.

Strange stories were told in town about Reb Yisroel. There had once lived in Poland a false Messiah, Jacob Frank; he had converted many Jews. After he died, a sect remained. He had a daughter somewhere, and barrels full of gold were sent to her. These people pretended to live like other Jews, but at night they would gather in secret and read forbidden parchments.

Reb Yisroel dressed like a rabbi, in a velvet caftan, a round rabbinical hat, slippers, and white socks. He was forever writing something, standing before a high desk, and people said that Zeitl copied all his manuscripts. He had a wide beard, white as snow, and a high forehead. When he looked at anyone, it seemed as though he saw right through him. Zeitl taught the daughters of rich families to read and write. I was one of her pupils.

It was said of the members of the sect that they liked loose women and secretly practiced all sorts of abominations. But with whom could Reb Yisroel have sinned in our town?

Zeitl got married, but six months later she was divorced. Her husband had come from Galicia, and people whispered that he was one of "the clan"; that was how our townsmen called the sect. Nobody knew why the marriage had come to such a quick end. Everything in Reb Yisroel's house was veiled in secrecy. He had trunks hung with double locks. He had large cases full of books. He came to prayer only on the Sabbath, at the cold synagogue. He seldom exchanged a word with anyone. When the storekeepers came to pay their rent, he would put the money into his pocket without counting it.

In those years it was unheard of that groceries should be delivered to anyone at home. The richest women went to market with baskets to do their own shopping. But Zeitl had everything sent to her from the stores: bread, rolls, butter, eggs, cheese, meat. Once a month she received a bill, as though she were living in Warsaw. She had aristocratic ways.

I remember her as if it were yesterday: tall, dark, with a narrow face and black hair braided like a round Sabbath bread. Imagine, in those years—and she did not shave her hair. When she went out, she wore a kerchief. But when was she seen in the street? Reb Yisroel had a balcony upstairs, looking out upon the church garden, and Zeitl would sit there on summer evenings, getting fresh air.

She would give us girls dictation twice a week, not from a letter book but from her head: "My most esteemed betrothed! To start with, I wish to let you know that I am in good health, pray God that I may hear the same from you. Secondly. . . ." Zeitl also knew Polish and German. Her eyes were wild, huge as a calf's, and filled with melancholy. But suddenly she would burst into such loud laughter that all the rooms would echo with it. In the middle of the year she might take a fancy to bake matzo pancakes. She was fond of asking us riddles and of telling tales that made our hair stand on end.

And now about Rickel. Rickel's father was the town's ritual slaughterer, Reb Todie. All slaughterers are pious men, but Reb Todie had the reputation of a saint. Yet he had bad luck. His son had gone one day to the ritual bath and was found drowned. He must have gotten a cramp. One of his daughters died in an epidemic. A few years later strange noises began to be heard in his house. Something knocked, and no one knew what or where. Something would give a bang so that the walls would shake. The whole town came running, even the Gentiles. They searched the attic, the cellar, every corner.

A regiment of soldiers was stationed in our town. The colonel's name was Semiatitsky. He was supposed to have descended from converted Jews. He had a red beard and cracked jokes till your sides would split with laughter. When Semiatitsky heard that a demon was banging in Todie's house, he brought a platoon of soldiers and commanded them to look into every crack and every hole. He did not believe in devils; he called them nothing but old wives' tales. He ordered everybody out and Cossacks stood guard with whips, allowing nobody to come near. But suddenly there was a crash that nearly brought the roof down.

I was not there, but people said that Semiatitsky called to the unholy one to tell his name and what he wanted and that the spirit gave one knock for yes, and two knocks for no.

Every man has enemies, especially if he has a job with the community, and people began to say that Todie should be dismissed as a slaughterer. It was whispered that he had slaughtered an ox with a blemished knife. Reb Todie's wife took it so hard that she died.

Rickel was small, thin, with red hair and freckles. When her father slaughtered fowl, she would pluck the feathers and do other small chores. When the knocking began, suspicion fell on Rickel. Some people said that she was doing it. But how could she? And why? It was said that when she went away for the night the knocking stopped. There's no limit to what evil tongues can invent. One night there was such a loud bang that three windows were shattered. Before that, the devil had not touched the windows. This was the last time. From then on, it was quiet again.

But Reb Todie was already without his job, and he became a teacher of beginners. The family had gone through Rickel's dowry and she was now affianced to a yeshiva student from Krashnik, a lame young man. He was a Hassid, and soon after the wedding he went on a pilgrimage to his rabbi. At first he would come home for Passover and the High Holy Days. Afterwards he disappeared altogether. Rickel became an abandoned wife. Her father had died in the meantime and all she had left was the old house—little more than a ruin.

What could a husbandless wife do? She went around, teaching girls how to pray. She took in sewing and mending. On Purim she carried presents of holiday delicacies for wealthy families. On Passover she would become a sort of women's beadle and deliver gifts of herbs. When a woman was sick and someone was needed to watch at the bedside, Rickel was called. She learned how to cup and bleed the sick. She did not shave her head but wore a kerchief. She read many storybooks and loved to invent wild and improbable tales.

Old maids, you know, also end up half crazy. But when a woman who has had a man is left alone, it goes to her head. Rickel might have found her husband if she had had the money to send a messenger to look for him, but Todie left her without a groschen. Why did her husband forsake her? Who can tell? There are such men. They get married and then they tire of it. They wander away and nobody knows where their bones have come to rest.

2

I do not know exactly how Zeitl and Rickel got together. It seems that Reb Yisroel fell ill and Rickel came to rub him down with turpentine. People said he had cast an eye on her, but I don't believe it. He was already more dead than alive. He died soon afterwards, and both girls, Zeitl and Rickel, were left alone in the world. At first people thought that Rickel had stayed on with Zeitl as a servant. But if Zeitl had never had a servant before, why would she need one now?

While Reb Yisroel was alive, few matchmakers came to Zeitl with offers. They knew that Reb Yisroel wanted his daughter for himself. There are such fathers, even among Jews. She waited on him hand and foot. If his pipe went out, she would bring him an ember to relight it. I don't know why, but he never went to the bath, and it was whispered that Zeitl bathed him in a wooden bathtub. I've never seen it, but those false believers are capable of anything. To them, a sin is a virtue.

Anyway, Reb Yisroel gave the matchmakers such a reception that they forswore repeating their visits to the tenth generation. But as soon as Zeitl was alone, they were back at her doorstep. She sent them off with all sorts of excuses: later, tomorrow, it's not yet time. She had a habit, whenever she spoke to anyone, of looking over his head. Rickel had moved in with her, and now whenever anyone knocked, she would answer from behind the door chain: Zeitl is out, she is asleep, she is reading.

How long could the matchmakers keep coming? Nobody is dragged to the wedding canopy by force. But in a small town people have time, and they talk. No matter how you may try to keep away from strangers' eyes, you can't hide everything.

It was said that Zeitl and Rickel ate together, drank together, slept together. Rickel wore Zeitl's dresses, shortened and made smaller to fit her. Rickel became the cashier, and she paid the bills sent by the storekeepers. She also collected the rents. In the daytime the two girls seldom went out together, but on summer evenings they went strolling down Church Street, along the avenues leading to the woods. Zeitl's arm would be around Rickel's shoulders, and Rickel's around Zeitl's waist. They were absorbed in their talk. When people said good evening, they did not hear. Where did two women find so much to talk about? Some people tried to follow them and listen in, but they were whispering, as though they had secrets between them. They would walk all the way to the mill or the woods.

Rumors were brought to Reb Eisele, our rabbi, but he said: "There is no law to keep two women from walking to the mill."

Reb Eisele was a Misnagid, a Lithuanian, and they have a law for everything: either it is permitted or it's a sin.

But the talk would not die down. Naftali, the night watchman, had seen Zeitl and Rickel kissing each other on the mouth. They had stopped by the sawmill, near the log pile, and embraced like a loving couple. Zeitl called Rickel dove, and Rickel called her kitten. At first nobody believed Naftali; he was fond of a drop and could bring you tales of a fair up in heaven. Still, where there's smoke, there must be fire. My dear folks, the two girls seemed so much in love that all the tongues in town started wagging. The Tempter can make anybody crazy in his own way. Something flips in your head, and everything turns upside down. I heard talk of a lady in Krasnostaw who made love with a stallion. At the time of the Flood, even beasts paired themselves with other kinds. I read about it in the Women's Bible.

People went to Reb Eisele, but he insisted: "There is nothing in the Torah to forbid it. The ban applies only to men. Besides, since there are no witnesses, it is forbidden to spread rumors." Nevertheless, he sent the beadle for them. Rickel came alone and denied everything. She had a whittled tongue, that girl. Reb Eisele said to her: "Go home and don't worry about it. It is the slanderers who will be punished, not you. It is better to burn in a lime pit than to put another to shame."

I forgot to mention that Zeitl had stopped teaching the girls how to write.

I was still very young at that time, but something of all that talk had reached me too. You can't keep everything from a child's ears. Zeitl and Rickel, it was said, were studying Reb Yisroel's books together. Their lamp burned until late at night. Those who passed their bedroom window saw shadows moving this way and that behind the drapes, and coming together as in a dance. Who knows what went on there?

Now listen to a story.

One summer it turned terribly hot. I've lived through many a summer, but I don't remember such heat. Right in the morning the sun began to burn like fire. Not only men but even girls and older women would go down to the river to bathe. When the sun blazes, the water gets warm. My mother, may she plead for us, took me along.

This was the first time I bathed in the river. Men went into the water naked, but the girls wore their shifts. The roughnecks came running to peep at them, and it was impossible to drive them off. Each time there'd be a squealing and a panic. One woman started drowning. Another screamed that a frog had bitten her. I bathed and even tried to swim until I was so tired that I lay down among the bushes near the bank to rest. I thought I'd cool off in the shade and go home, but a strange sleep came over me. Not just sleep; may heaven preserve us, it was more like death. I put my head down and remained there like a rock. A darkness seemed to fall over me and I sank into it. I must have slept for many hours.

When I awakened, it was night. There was no moon. The sky was cloudy. I lay there and did not know where I was or who I was. I felt the grass around me, moist with dew, but I did not remember that I was on the outskirts of town. I touched myself; I had nothing on but my shift. I wanted to cry, to call for help, when suddenly I heard voices. I thought of demons and was terror-stricken, yet I tried to hear what they were saying. Two women were speaking, and their voices seemed familiar.

I heard one ask: "Must we go through hell?"

The other answered: "Yes, my soul, but even going through hell together with you will be a delight. God is merciful. The punishment never lasts more than twelve months. We shall be purified and enter paradise. Since we have no husbands, we shall be no one's footstools. We shall bathe in balsam and eat of the leviathan. We shall have wings and fly like birds. . . ."

I cannot recall all their talk. I gasped. I knew who they were now: the questioner was Rickel, and Zeitl gave the answers. I heard Zeitl say: "We shall met our fathers and mothers there, and our grandparents, and all the generations: Abraham and Isaac, Jacob and Rachel, Leah, Bilhah, Zilpah, Abigail, Bathsheba. . . ." She spoke as though she had just come from there, and every word was like a pearl. I forgot that I was half naked and alone out late at night.

Zeitl went on: "Father is waiting for us. He comes to me in dreams. He is together with your mother." Rickel said: "Did they get married there?" And Zeitl answered: "Yes. We shall get married up there too. In heaven there is no difference between men and women. . . ."

It must have been past midnight. There was a flash of lightning, and I saw my clothing, shoes, and stockings on the grass nearby. I caught a glimpse of them too. They sat by the river in nothing but their shifts, their hair down, pale as death. If I did not die of fright that night, I'll never die.

"And then?"

Wait a minute. I came home in the middle of the night, but my mother had left earlier in the evening for the fair; she was a storekeeper. My father was spending the night at the study house. I slipped into bed, and when I woke next morning, the whole thing seemed like a dream. I was ashamed to tell anyone about it. However, as the saying goes, heaven and earth conspired that there should be no secrets.

People began to say that Zeitl and Rickel were fasting. They would eat nothing all day and merely take a bite at night. We had pious women in town who would climb up the stairs into the women's section of the synagogue at dawn to pray. Every Monday and Thursday they went to visit graves in the cemetery. Suddenly we heard that Zeitl and Rickel had joined the pious company in lamentations and penitential prayers. They had shaved their heads and put on bonnets, as though they had just gotten married. They omitted no line or word, and wept as on the Day of the Destruction of the Temple. They also visited the cemetery, prostrating themselves on Reb Yisroel's grave and wailing.

People ran to Reb Eisele again, but the rabbi sent them off with a scolding. If Jewish daughters wanted to do penance, he said, was that wrong too? He was fond of poring over his books, but the affairs of the town meant little to him. He was later dismissed, but that's another story.

There are busybodies everywhere, and they took the matter to the colonel. But he said, "Leave me out of your Jewish squabbles. I have trouble enough with my soldiers." Cossacks are good soldiers, but sometimes they got letters from home that their wives were carrying on with other men and they went wild. More than one Cossack would go galloping off on his horse, slashing away with his sword right and left. After they had served their five-year terms, they would come into the stores to buy presents for their mothers and fathers, sisters and brothers, the whole family. The shopkeeper would ask, "And what will you get for your wife, Nikita?" "A horsewhip," he would say. They'd go back to their steppes on the Don and find bastards at home. They'd chop off the wife's head and be sent to Siberia for hard labor. . . .

Where was I? Oh, yes, penance. Zeitl and Rickel clung to each other and spoke only of the next world. They bought up all the books from every peddler passing through town. Whenever a preacher came, they questioned him: How long was the punishment inflicted on transgressors after death? How many hells were there? Who meted out the penalties? Who did the whipping? With what kind of rods? Iron? Copper? The wags had plenty to joke about.

We had many visiting preachers, but one, Reb Yuzel, was famous. Whenever he went up to the lectern, it was like the Day of Atonement all over again. When he painted a picture of hell, everybody shuddered. People said that it was dangerous for pregnant women to hear him; several had had miscarriages after his sermons. But that's how it is: when you must not do a thing, you're sure to do it. When Reb Yuzel preached, the synagogue was full. The railing closing off the women's section was almost bursting with the crush. He had a voice that reached into every corner. Every word cut like a knife.

The last time he came, I also ran to hear him. There was not one hell, he said, but seven, and the flames in each were sixty times hotter than in the last. There was a man in our town, Alterl Kozlover. He had a screw loose, and he figured out that the seventh hell was myriads of times hotter than the first. Men cried like babies. Women screamed and wailed.

Zeitl and Rickel were also there. They had entered among the men and stood on a bench, wrapped in their shawls. Ordinarily, women are admitted in the men's section only on the Festival of Rejoicing in the Law. But when the women's section was too crowded, some women were allowed into the antechamber, and from there they'd move inside.

Reb Yuzel handed out punishment to everybody, but the worst of his wrath was reserved for the women. He described how they were hung by the breasts and by the hair; how the imps laid them out on boards of nails and tore pieces from them. From fiery coals they were thrown into snow, and from the snow back onto heaps of coals. Before they were admitted to hell, they were first tortured in the Sling, by devils, imps and evil spirits. It made your hair stand on end to hear him. I was still a young girl, but I began to sob and choke. I glanced at Zeitl and Rickel: they did not cry, but their eyes were twice as big as usual, and their faces were like chalk. A madness seemed to stare out of them, and I had a feeling that they would come to a terrible end.

On the next day Reb Yuzel preached again, but I had had enough. Someone said later that Zeitl had come up to him after the sermon and invited him to be her guest. Many people asked him to their homes, but he went with Zeitl. Nobody knows what they spoke about. I don't remember whether he had stayed there for the night. Probably not; how could a man remain with two women? Although it's true the Lithuanians have an argument for everything. They interpret the Law as they like. That's why they are nicknamed "heathens." My grandfather, may he intercede for us, used to tell of a Lithuanian Jew from Belaya Tserkov who had married a Gentile woman and had gone on studying the Talmud.

After Reb Yuzel left, the town was quiet again. By then the summer was over.

One winter night, long after all the shutters had been closed, we heard a wild outcry. People ran out in panic. They thought the peasants had attacked. The moon was bright, and we saw a strange sight—Fivel the butcher carrying Rickel in his arms. She screamed and struggled and tried to scratch his eyes out. He was a giant of a man and he brought her straight into the rabbi's judgment chamber. Reb Eisele sat up late, studying and drinking tea from a samovar. Everybody shouted, and Rickel kept fighting to break away and run out. It took two men to hold her. The rabbi began to question her.

I was there myself. Ordinarily I went to bed early, but that night we had been chopping cabbage and all the girls had gathered at our house. This was the custom in our town. We chopped cabbage for pickling in barrels, and everybody ate bread with cracklings and told stories. One day the girls would gather in one house, the next in another. Sometimes they'd break into a dance in pairs. I had a sister-in-law who could play all the dances on a comb: a Scissor Dance, a Quarrel Dance, a Good Day.

When we heard the uproar, we all ran out.

At first Rickel would not say anything. She merely screamed to be allowed to go. But Fivel testified that she had wanted to throw herself into the well. He had caught her when she had already flung her leg over the edge.

"How did it come into your head to do such a thing?" the rabbi asked, and Rickel answered: "I am sick of this world. I want to know what goes on in the next." The rabbi argued: "Those who lay their hands upon themselves do not share the rewards of the next world." But Rickel said: "Hell is also for people, not for goats." She screamed: "I want to go to my mother and my father, my grandmother and grandfather. I don't want to keep wandering in this vale of tears." Those were her words. It was clear at once that she had learned all this from Zeitl, because the other knew the texts printed in small letters too. Somebody asked: "Where is Zeitl?" And Rickel answered: "She is all right, she is already up there. . . ." My dear folks, Zeitl had thrown herself into the well a moment earlier. She had gone first.

Half the town came running. Torches were lit, and we went to the well. Zeitl lay with her head in the water, her feet up. A ladder was lowered, and she was dragged up, dead.

Rickel had to be watched, and the men of the burial society took her to the poorhouse. She was turned over to the caretaker, who was told to keep an eye on her. Zeitl was later buried outside the fence. Rickel pretended that she had come to her senses and regretted her deed. But the next day at dawn, when everybody was asleep, she rose from the bundle of straw and went to the river. It was frozen, but she must have broken the ice with a stone. It was only in the afternoon that people realized she was gone. They found her footprints in the snow and ran down to the river. Rickel had followed Zeitl. She was buried near the other one, without a mound, without as much as a board to mark the place.

The burgomaster locked and sealed Zeitl's house, but later on, a letter she had written was discovered. She explained why she was leaving the world: she wanted to know what went on in the hereafter.

Who can tell what goes on in another's head? A person gets hold of some melancholy notion and it grows like a mushroom. Zeitl was the leader, and Rickel drank in every word she said. Forty years have gone by since their deaths, and they have probably suffered their allotted share.

As long as I was in the town, Reb Yisroel's house was boarded up and nobody moved into it. People saw lights flickering in the windows. A man said that he was passing by at night and heard Zeitl speak and Rickel answer. They kissed, laughed, cried. Lost souls remain on earth and do not even know they don't belong. . . .

I was told that an officer had later moved into the house. One morning he was found hanged.

A house is not simply a pile of logs and boards. Whoever lives there leaves something behind. A few years later the whole marketplace burned down. Thank God for fires. If it were not for them, the stench that would accumulate would reach high heaven. . . .

Translated by Mirra Ginsburg

The Warehouse

IN A WAREHOUSE in heaven, a number of naked souls stood around waiting for the issuance of their new bodies. Bagdial, the angel in charge of such goods, was a trifle late that morning. To be precise, Bagdial handed out a card entitling the spirit to receive a body but did not hand out the body itself. In heaven there is as much red tape as on earth, the dignitaries finding it necessary to make work to keep unemployed angels busy. But angels who have got used to an easy life resent having to do anything too strenuous.

It was now ten o'clock in the morning. The angelic choirs had long since finished chanting their lauds. The righteous in paradise had already had their second helping of leviathan. The wicked, lying on their fiery beds in hell, had just been turned onto their other side. But in the commissariat not a single card had been issued. Finally Bagdial, a corpulent angel whose wings were not sufficiently large to conceal either his massive legs or his navel, entered and, without even bothering to say good morning, shouted, "Cut out that shoving. There are enough bodies for all. The day's still young. When your number is called, step forward. In the meantime, shut up." Bagdial headed for his private office. "I'll be back in a minute."

"The morning's almost over, but he must see to his private business," an impatient soul muttered. "According to regulations, work is supposed to begin promptly with the cock's crow."

"Stop that grumbling. If you don't like what goes on here, report me to the Lord Malbushial. You keep your right of appeal until your departure."

"No, Bagdial, we're more than satisfied," a number of humble souls called out.

"I will return soon."

As Bagdial shut the door of his office, one of the souls remarked, "An absolutely worthless caterpillar. In the old days that sort of angel was kicked out of heaven and exiled to earth to consort with the daughters of Adam. Some were changed into devils and imps. Now, since they have organized, they do as they please. It almost seems that God Himself is afraid of them."

"How can God be afraid of one of His own creations?"

The soul of one who had once been a philosopher tugged at its spiritual beard. "That's one of the ancient problems. My opinion is that though God is very powerful, He is not omnipotent. He can destroy a world or two if He has a tantrum, but not the entire cosmos. Omnipotence would mean He could destroy Himself and leave the universe godless, an obvious contradiction. Although I've roasted in Gehenna for a full year, it's made me no wiser. I still concur with Aristotle that the world had no beginning. The notion that the world was created from nothing is repugnant to reason."

"I am no scholar, just an ordinary woman," another soul said, "but it's obvious to me that there's no order here. Thirty-one years ago I was exiled to earth from the Throne of Glory, where I used to polish one of the legs, and imprisoned in a beautiful body. Why they sent me to earth I did not understand until today. People say it's men who are the lecherous ones; my lust was more powerful than that of any ten men. My mother baked delicious pretzels with caraway seeds which the yeshiva boys loved, but they liked me even better. She warned me against men, but already when I was nine I could think of nothing else. I saw two dogs coupling once and after that. . . ."

"All right, we catch on. You became a whore."

"Not right away."

"How long did you fry in Gehenna?"

"An entire year."

"Well, you got off easy. There are lots of whores that they sling into the desert. When they get to Gehenna, they think it's paradise. What did they do to you?"

"The usual. I was hung by my breasts, hurled from fire into ice, and from ice into fire, and so on, except, of course, Sabbaths and holidays."

"You were lucky not to have to remain in the vale of tears longer," another soul remarked. "I lived there for eighty-nine years three months five days two hours and eight minutes."

"Were you also a whore?"

"No, a man."

"That's what I'd like to be. If I have to be dressed in blood and flesh, let it be male."

"What's so wonderful about being a man?"

"You are not a female."

"So I became a miser. A woman of pleasure has at least some pleasure. My sack of bones could do nothing but gather money. I got married but never gave my wife enough for the household and accused her of being a spendthrift. You don't need me to tell you that women hate a tightwad. All females are wasteful. My wife was always cooking twice the porridge we could eat. There was always a pot of spoiling food in our larder. We had so much schmaltz it turned rancid. Our flour became moldy. The Angel of Good pleaded with me: 'Let her have her will. She enjoys it. Why quarrel?' But my bag of money obsessed me."

"Was she any good in bed?"

"Even there I was stingy. Those who hoard money hoard everything. The upshot of it was that she ran off with a shoemaker."

"I would have done it, too."

"After that happened, I was afraid to take another wife. For all I knew, the woman I got would be crazy about marzipan. It got so bad I broke my teeth on stale bread because it cost a half cent a loaf less than the fresh. The moment I entered my house, I took off my gaberdine and, forgive my expression, even my underwear to keep them from wearing. I even saved snuff."

"How did you do that?"

"I would stretch out my hand when I saw someone taking a pinch and ask him for some. Instead of using it, I hid it in a bag."

"Did you save much?"

"Two sacks full."

"How long did it take you to do that?"

"More than forty years."

"If I become a man, I won't stint my wife. I'll give her anything she wants. If you ever become a woman, you'll find out what pleases women."

"If you become a man, you'll forget all this feminine nonsense."

"What do you want to be?" the whore asked.

"I don't want to be anyone," the miser answered.

"Perhaps they will make you a woman."

"For all I care, they can make me a flea."

"It could be that you'll be stillborn."

"The stiller the better."

"I don't care what you say, I would like the taste of being a man."

"You won't be consulted. You'll be handed a body whether it fits or not. I know. I've been here now for more than thirty years. For ten years I worked sorting bodies. The whole thing's just one enormous mess. A woman's torso is given a man's head. Just a short time ago, a man's body turned up with a pair of breasts of a wet nurse. They even get mixed up on who gets what genitals. You know about hermaphrodites, don't you? That Bagdial is both lazy and incompetent. If he weren't Malbushial's second cousin, he would have been scrapped long ago."

"What about God?"

"Does anyone believe in God here? Here in the lowest heaven we have only atheists. He is supposed to dwell in the seventh heaven, which is an infinity away. One thing we can be sure of, He's not here."

"Be quiet. Here comes Bagdial."

2

Bagdial scratched his left buttock with his right wing. "I'm not deaf, miser. If Malbushial knew of your barkings, he'd give you the body of a dog. No, we're not atheists here. But when you've hung around here some 689,000 years and been continually told about a boss who never shows up, you begin to have your doubts. Why does He sit there forever in His seventh heaven? Oughtn't He to come down here occasionally and see what's going on? Souls are shipped in this direction and that, wearing this or that body.

"You think that we warehouse people are negligent, but can we do anything if the manufacturers and the cutters send us poor products? We almost never receive a well-lathed nose. The noses we get are almost all either long as a ram's horn or short as a bean. Our suppliers have been in the nose business since the time of Methuselah, but they don't know their trade. The lips we're sent are either too thin or too thick. Almost none of the ears has decent proportions. The angel in charge of procreation is supposed to adjust the genitals of the sexes to fit correctly, and he's the worst bungler of all. He is capable of mating an elephant to a mouse.

"All of you clamor for beautiful bodies, but if you get one, what use do you make of it? It's destroyed, either by drinking or by lechery or by sloth. A short time ago we did a splendid job; soul and body fitted perfectly. Once a millennium we do such a good job. But that pampered little body started eating as if it had been given a bottomless stomach. It ate for forty years and returned round as a barrel, a mere heap of repulsive flesh. Miser, if you continue your blasphemies, I will. . . ."

"I didn't blaspheme. Honest, I didn't. What style body am I to get?"

"A eunuch."

"Why a eunuch? I was just saying that for all I cared I could be turned into a flea."

"I heard you. We have one eunuch-style body on hand which will fit you perfectly. You'll never be in a position to support a wife. And you certainly don't deserve to have someone else support you."

"What sort of temptations does a eunuch have?"

"Money."

"Will I be rich?"

"The wealthiest inmate in the poorhouse of Pinchev."

"What do I have to correct?"

"You'll return all the tobacco you stole to its rightful owners. The snuff was given to you to use, not to hoard."

"Where will I get so much snuff?"

"That's your problem. Hey there, whore."

"What style have I been given?"

"A woman."

"Again?"

"Exactly."

"Why not a man this time?"

"Don't bargain with me. I distribute the cards, not the bodies. We don't have our full quota of males in this batch.

Eighty male bodies were ruined in the factory yesterday. This year we've overproduced women. But we'll get rid of them all because Rabbi Gershom's edict against polygamy is about to be repealed. Every schlemiel dreams of having a harem. Even tailor's assistants want to become King Solomons. If you ask me, it's better to be a mortar than a pestle."

"I would like to be a man just once."

"We all have unfulfilled desires. I would have preferred to have been a seraph and sit in paradise between Bathsheba and Abigail. Instead, I have to come here six days a week and hand out cards for defective bodies. Everyone haggles with me as though I had the power of Metatron. I don't know what it's like in the other heavens; here in the warehouse it's chaos. At times I even envy the miserable creatures who are sent down to earth. At least there are temptations in the lower world. If you try hard you can achieve sainthood and receive your reward in paradise. What do I have? Nothing. No one tempts me and I'm fed with sour moon milk. I'm slandered disgracefully. I'm begrudged even a little stardust. Evil tongues make me feel that if I weren't Malbushial's second cousin I'd be nowhere."

"Maybe you could do me a small favor?"

"What sort of a favor, whore? Take your card and leave. You were a wanton for eighteen years; you'll be chaste now for exactly the same amount of time. If not, you'll return again, a double hunchback, one in the front and one in the rear."

"Have you already had a look at my body?"

"I caught a glimpse of it."

"What does it look like?"

"What's the use of telling you? Once you get to earth, you'll forget that the body is only a garment. Down there they think the body is everything. All around you, people will be saying that there isn't a soul."

"What will I look like?"

"Since you must correct the errors you made in your former existence, you will not be exactly a beauty. The body you receive will make your task easier."

"Ugly, eh?"

"Men will not care for you, nor will you care for them. You

have been given nine measures of shyness, which is exactly what is required to create a spinster."

"You dirty scoundrel."

Another soul flew over.

"Who are you?" Bagdial asked. "I don't recognize you."

"Leibke the thief."

"Well, no more stealing for you. You'll be robbed by others. Everything will be taken from you—your money, your wife, even the pillow you rest your head on. You'll hide your money in your boot tops, go to the steam bath, and leave your boots again and yet not be able to resist the urge to do so. Every body is made with its own particular obsession.

"Once we had a gambler here. Do you know what he'd done? He was playing draw poker and threw his wife into the pot. Can you imagine what he had? A pair of jacks. He was a big bluffer, only you can't bluff a man who has four aces. When his wife came back to him three months later, she was pregnant. He swallowed a ladle in an attempt to kill himself!"

"Did he get it down?"

"It stuck in his throat. Was there any sense to it? But you know how people are. The angels are no wiser. Who are you?"

"Hayim the coachman."

"Since you had a beautiful wife and in addition fornicated with a Gentile, what did you need the mare for?"

"I don't know."

"Hadn't you ever heard that horses kick?"

"It just slipped my mind."

"Those down below are always forgetting. Is it their fault? The most defective of all the organs is the portion of the brain containing the memory. They put on two pairs of underwear in the winter and only take off one when they go to the out-house. The only things they never forget are the injuries done them. Two sisters in Frampol quarreled over the tail of a herring for sixty years. When the older died, the younger urinated on her grave. You, Hayim, will be the horse this time. You'll pull freight from Izbitza to Kransnistaw."

"Has that road been fixed?"

"It's as muddy as it was, but a little bumpier."

"If that's so, there is no God."

"And suppose there isn't. Will that make pulling the wagon any easier? Anyway, you'll only last three years. Zelig the Red will whip you to death."

"Is that murderer still around?"

"He has a score to settle. He hasn't forgotten that you sold him a lame stallion."

"That happened thirty years ago. I was swindled myself. I got the horse from a gypsy."

"We know that. It's all on record here. The gypsy is now a stallion, and the stallion a gypsy. But the whip remains what it was and still has seven knots. Hey, who are you?"

"Shiffra the cook."

"You're not supposed to spit into your employer's porridge, even though he did spit in your face."

"What will I become?"

"Your employer's spittoon."

"Will I feel his spit?"

"Everything knows and feels. Your employer suffers from consumption and will spit out his last piece of lung into you. Both of you will be back in three quarters of a year."

"Together?"

"You will be married. You will be his footstool in the ante-chamber of paradise."

"I'd rather be a pisspot in Gehenna."

"Little fool, that amorous ass loved you. That's how men are. What they can't have, they spit at."

Bagdial scratched the nape of his neck with one of his lower wings and brooded in silence. "Is it much better in heaven?" he finally asked. "I stay here all day surrounded by rabble and listen to their needling. Other angels sing hymns three times a day and that's the end of it. Some can't even sing, only bellow. The higher your position, the less work you do. He created the world in six short winter days and has been resting ever since. There are those who are of the opinion that He didn't even work that hard."

"Do you mean by that that He wasn't the First Cause?" the philosopher demanded.

"Who else is the First Cause? He is a jealous God. He would never delegate such power. But being the cause and keeping order are different things altogether."

Henne Fire

Y ES, there are people who are demons. God preserve us! Mothers see things when they give birth, but they never tell what they see!

Henne Fire, as she was called, was not a human being but a fire from Gehenna. I know one should not speak evil of the dead and she suffered greatly for her sins. Was it her fault that there was always a blaze within her? One could see it in her eyes: two coals. It was frightening to look at them. She was black as a gypsy, with a narrow face, sunken cheeks, emaciated —skin and bone. Once I saw her bathing in the river. Her ribs protruded like hoops. How could someone like Henne put on fat? Whatever one said to her, no matter how innocently, she immediately took offense. She would begin to scream, shake her fists, and spin around like a crazy person. Her face would turn white with anger. If you tried to defend yourself, she was ready to swallow you alive and she'd start smashing dishes. Every few weeks her husband, Berl Chazkeles, had to buy a new set.

She suspected everybody. The whole town was out to get her. When she flew into a rage, she said things that would not even occur to an insane person. Swear words poured from her mouth like worm-eaten peas. She knew every curse in the holy book by heart. She was not beyond throwing rocks. Once, in the middle of winter, she broke a neighbor's windowpane and the neighbor never learned why.

Henne had children, four girls, but as soon as they grew up they ran away from home. One became a servant in Lublin; one left for America; the most beautiful, Malkeleh, died of scarlet fever; and the fourth married an old man. Anything was better than living with Henne.

Her husband, Berl, must have been a saint. Only a saint could have stood such a shrew for twenty years. He was a sieve-maker. In those days, in the wintertime, work started when it was still dark. The sieve-maker had to supply his own candle. He earned only a pittance. Of course, they were poor, but they were not the only ones. A wagonload of chalk would not suffice to write down the complaints she hurled at him. I lived next door to her and once, when he left for work at dawn, I heard her call after him: "Come back feet first!" I can't imagine what she blamed him for. He gave her his last penny, and he loved her too. How could one love such a fiend? Only God knows. In any case, who can understand what goes on in the heart of a man?

My dear people, even he finally ran away from her. One summer morning, a Friday, he left to go to the ritual bath and disappeared like a stone in the water. When Henne heard he was seen leaving the village, she fell down in an epileptic fit right in the gutter. She knocked her head on the stones, hissed like a snake, and foamed at the mouth. Someone pushed a key into her left hand, but it didn't help. Her kerchief fell off and revealed the fact that she did not shave her head. She was carried home. I've never seen such a face, as green as grass, her eyes rolled up. The moment she came to, she began to curse and I think from then on never stopped. It was said that she even swore in her sleep. At Yom Kippur she stood in the women's section of the synagogue and, as the rabbi's wife recited the prayers for those who could not read, Henne berated the rabbi, the cantor, the elders. On her husband she called forth a black judgment, wished him smallpox and gangrene. She also blasphemed against God.

After Berl forsook her, she went completely wild. As a rule, an abandoned woman made a living by kneading dough in other people's houses or by becoming a servant. But who would let a malicious creature like Henne into the house? She tried to sell fish on Thursdays, but when a woman asked the price, Henne would reply, "You are not going to buy anyhow, so why do you come here just to tease me? You'll poke around and buy elsewhere."

One housewife picked up a fish and lifted its gills to see if it was fresh. Henne tore it from her hands, screaming, "Why do you smell it? Is it beneath your dignity to eat rotten fish?" And she sang out a list of sins allegedly committed by the woman's parents, grandparents, and great-grandparents back to the tenth generation. The other fishmongers sold their wares and Henne remained with a tubful. Every few weeks Henne washed her clothes. Don't ask me how she carried on. She quarreled about everything: the washtubs, the clotheslines, the water pump. If she found a speck of dust on a shirt hanging up to dry, she blamed it on her neighbors. She herself tore down the lines of others. One heard her yelling over half the town. People were afraid of her and gave in, but that was no good either. If you answered her she raised a rumpus, and if you kept silent she would scream, "Is it a disgrace to talk to me?" There was no dealing with her without being insulted.

At first her daughters would come home from the big towns for the holidays. They were good girls, and they all took after their father. One moment mother and daughter would kiss and embrace and before you knew it there would be a cat fight in Butcher Alley, where we lived. Plates crashed, windows were broken. The girl would run out of the house as though poisoned and Henne would be after her with a stick, screaming, "Bitch, slut, whore, you should have dissolved in your mother's belly!" After Berl deserted her, Henne suspected that her daughters knew his whereabouts. Although they swore holy oaths that they didn't, Henne would rave, "Your mouths will grow out the back of your heads for swearing falsely!"

What could the poor girls do? They avoided her like the plague. And Henne went to the village teacher and made him write letters for her saying that she disowned them. She was no longer their mother and they were no longer her daughters.

Still, in a small town one is not allowed to starve. Good people took pity on Henne. They brought her soup, garlic borscht, a loaf of bread, potatoes, or whatever they had to offer, and left it on the threshold. Entering her house was like walking into a lion's den. Henne seldom tasted these gifts. She threw them into the garbage ditch. Such people thrive on fighting.

Since the grownups ignored her, Henne began to quarrel with the children. A boy passed by and Henne snatched his cap because she imagined he had stolen pears from her tree. The pears were as hard as wood and tasted the same; a pig wouldn't eat them. She just needed an excuse. She was always lying and she called everybody else a liar. She went to the chief of police and denounced half the town, accusing this one of being a forger and that one of smuggling contraband from Galicia. She reported that the Hassidim were disrespectful of the Tsar. In the fall, when the recruits were being drafted, Henne announced in the marketplace that the rich boys were being deferred and the poor ones taken. It was true, too. But if they had all been taken, would it have been better? Somebody had to serve. But Henne, good sort that she was, could not suffer injustice. The Russian officials were afraid that she would cause trouble and had her sent to the insane asylum.

I was there when a soldier and a policeman came to get her. She turned on them with a hatchet. She made such a commotion that the whole town came running. But how strong is a female? As she was bound and loaded into a cart, she cursed in Russian, Polish, and Yiddish. She sounded like a pig being slaughtered. She was taken to Lublin and put in a strait jacket.

I don't know how it happened, but she must have been on her good behavior, because in less than half a year she was back in town. A family had moved into her hut, but she drove the whole lot out in the middle of a cold night. The next day Henne announced that she had been robbed. She went to all the neighbors to look for her belongings and humiliated everybody. She was no longer allowed into the women's synagogue and was even refused when she wanted to buy a seat for the Days of Awe. Things came to such a pass that when she went to the well to get water everyone ran away. It was simply dangerous to come near her.

She did not even respect the dead. A hearse passed by and Henne spat at it, screaming that she hoped the dead man's soul would wander in the wastelands forever. The better type of people turned a deaf ear to her, but when the mourners were of the common kind she got beaten up. She liked to be beaten; that is the truth. She would run around showing off a bump given her by this one, a black eye by that one. She ran to the druggist for leeches and salves. She kept summoning everybody to the rabbi, but the beadle would no longer listen to her and the rabbi had issued an order forbidding her to enter his study. She also tried her luck with the Gentiles, but they only laughed at her. Nothing remained to her but God. And according to Henne she and the Almighty were on the best of terms.

Now listen to what happened. There was a coachman called Kopel Klotz who lived near Henne. Once in the middle of the night he was awakened by screams for help. He looked out the window and saw that the house of the shoemaker across the street was on fire. He grabbed a pail of water and went to help put it out. But the fire was not at the shoemaker's; it was at Henne's. It was only the reflection that he had seen in the shoemaker's window. Kopel ran to her house and found everything burning: the table, the bench, the cupboard. It wasn't a usual fire. Little flames flew around like birds. Henne's nightshirt was burning. Kopel tore it off her and she stood there as naked as the day she was born.

A fire in Butcher Alley is no small thing. The wood of the houses is dry even in winter. From one spark the whole alley could turn into ashes. People came to the rescue, but the flames danced and turned somersaults. Every moment something else became ignited. Henne covered her naked body with a shawl and the fringes began to burn like so many candles. The men fought the fire until dawn. Some of them were overcome by the smoke. These were not flames, but goblins from hell.

In the morning there was another outburst. Henne's bed linen began to burn of itself. That day I visited Henne's hut. Her sheet was full of holes; the quilt and feather bed, too. The dough in the trough had been baked into a flat loaf of bread. A fiery broom had swept the floor, igniting the garbage. Tongues of flame licked everything. God save us, these were tricks of the Evil Host. Henne sent everybody to the devil; and now the devil had turned on her.

Somehow the fire was put out. The people of Butcher Alley warned the rabbi that if Henne could not be induced to leave they would take matters into their own hands. Everyone was afraid for his kin and possessions. No one wanted to pay for the sins of another. Henne went to the rabbi's house and wailed, "Where am I to go? Murderers, robbers, beasts!"

She became as hoarse as a crow. As she ranted, her kerchief took fire. Those who weren't there will never know what the demons can do.

As Henne stood in the rabbi's study, pleading with him to let her stay, her house went up in flames. A flame burst from the roof and it had the shape of a man with long hair. It danced and whistled. The church bells rang an alarm. The firemen tried their best, but in a few minutes nothing was left but a chimney and a heap of burning embers.

Later, Henne spread the rumor that her neighbors had set her house on fire. But it was not so. Who would try a thing like that, especially with the wind blowing? There were scores of witnesses to the contrary. The fiery image had waved its arms and laughed madly. Then it had risen into the air and disappeared among the clouds.

It was then that people began to call her Henne Fire. Up to then she had been known as Black Henne.

2

When Henne found herself without a roof over her head, she tried to move into the poorhouse but the poor and sick would not let her in. Nobody wants to be burned alive. For the first time she became silent. A Gentile woodchopper took her into his house. The moment she crossed the threshold the handle of his ax caught fire and out she went. She would have frozen to death in the cold if the rabbi hadn't taken her in.

The rabbi had a booth not far from his house which was used during the Succoth holidays. It had a roof which could be opened and closed by a series of pulleys. The rabbi's son installed a tin stove so that Henne would not freeze. The rabbi's wife supplied a bed with a straw mattress and linen. What else could they do? Jews don't let a person perish. They hoped the demons would respect a Succoth booth and that it would not catch fire. True, it had no mezuzah, but the rabbi hung a talisman on the wall instead. Some of the townspeople offered to bring food to Henne, but the rabbi's wife said, "The little she eats I can provide."

The winter cold began immediately after the Succoth holiday and it lasted until Purim. Houses were snowed under. In the morning one had to dig oneself out with a shovel. Henne lay in bed all day. She was not the same Henne: she was docile as a sheep. Yet evil looked out of her eyes. The rabbi's son fed her stove every morning. He reported in the study house that Henne lay all day tucked into her feather bed and never uttered a word. The rabbi's wife suggested that she come into the kitchen and perhaps help a little with the housework. Henne refused. "I don't want anything to happen to the rabbi's books," she said. It was whispered in the town that perhaps the Evil One had left her.

Around Purim it suddenly became warm. The ice thawed and the river overflowed. Bridge Street was flooded. The poor are miserable anyway, but when there is a flood at night and the household goods begin to swim around, life becomes unbearable. A raft was used to cross Bridge Street. The bakery had begun preparing matzos for Passover, but water seeped into the sacks and made the flour unusable.

Suddenly a scream was heard from the rabbi's house. The Succoth booth had burst into flame like a paper lantern. It happened in the middle of the night. Later Henne related how a fiery hand had reached down from the roof and in a second everything was consumed. She had grabbed a blanket to cover herself and had run into the muddy courtyard without clothes on. Did the rabbi have a choice? He had to take her in. His wife stopped sleeping at night. Henne said to the rabbi, "I shouldn't be allowed to do this to you." Even before the booth had burned down, the rabbi's married daughter, Taube, had packed her trousseau into a sheet so she could save it at a moment's notice in case of fire.

Next day the community elders called a meeting. There was much talk and haggling, but they couldn't come to a decision. Someone proposed that Henne be sent to another town. Henne burst into the rabbi's study, her dress in tatters, a living scarecrow. "Rabbi, I've lived here all my life, and here I want to die. Let them dig me a grave and bury me. The cemetery will not catch fire." She had found her tongue again and everybody was surprised.

Present at the meeting was Reb Zelig, the plumber, a decent man, and he finally made a suggestion. "Rabbi, I will build her a little house of brick. Bricks don't burn."

He asked no pay for his work, just his costs. Then a roofer promised to make the roof. Henne owned the lot in Butcher Alley, and the chimney had remained standing.

To put up a house takes months, but this little building was erected between Purim and Passover, everyone lending a hand. Boys from the study house dumped the ashes. Schoolchildren carried bricks. Yeshiva students mixed mortar. Yudel, the glazier, contributed windowpanes. As the proverb goes: a community is never poor. A rich man, Reb Falik, donated tin for the roof. One day there was a ruin and the next day there was the house. Actually it was a shack without a floor, but how much does a single person need? Henne was provided with an iron bed, a pillow, a straw mattress, a feather bed. She didn't even watch the builders. She sat in the rabbi's kitchen on the lookout for fires.

The house was finished just a day before Passover. From the poor fund, Henne was stocked with matzos, potatoes, eggs, horseradish, all that was necessary. She was even presented with a new set of dishes. There was only one thing everybody refused to do, and that was to have her at the Seder. In the evening they looked in at her window: no holiday, no Seder, no candles. She was sitting on a bench, munching a carrot.

One never knows how things will turn out. In the beginning nothing was heard from Henne's daughter, Mindel, who had gone to America. How does the saying go? Across the sea is another world. They go to America and forget father, mother, Jewishness, God. Years passed and there was not a single word from her. But Mindel proved herself a devoted child after all. She got married and her husband became immensely rich.

Our local post office had a letter carrier who was just a simple peasant. One day a strange letter carrier appeared. He had a long mustache, his jacket had gilded buttons, and he wore insignia on his cap. He brought a letter for which the recipient had to sign. For whom do you think it was? For Henne. She could no more sign her name than I can dance a quadrille. She daubed three marks on the receipt and somebody was a witness. To make it short, it was a letter containing money. Lippe, the teacher, came to read it and half the town listened.

"My dear mother, your worries are over. My husband has become rich. New York is a large city where white bread is eaten in the middle of the week. Everybody speaks English, the Jews too. At night it is as bright as day. Trains travel on tracks high up near the roofs. Make peace with Father and I will send you both passage to America."

The townspeople didn't know whether to laugh or cry. Henne listened but didn't say a word. She neither cursed nor blessed.

A month later another letter arrived, and two months after that, another. An American dollar was worth two rubles. There was an agent in town, and when he heard that Henne was getting money from America, he proposed all kinds of deals to her. Would she like to buy a house, or become a partner in a store? There was a man in our town called Leizer the messenger, although nobody ever sent him anywhere. He came to Henne and offered to go in search of her husband. If he was alive, Leizer was sure he would find him and either bring him home or make him send her a bill of divorcement. Henne's reply was: "If you bring him back, bring him back dead, and you should walk on crutches!"

Henne remained Henne, but the neighbors began to make a fuss over her. That is how people are. When they smell a groschen, they get excited. Now they were quick to greet her, called her Hennely, and waited on her. Henne just glowered at them, muttering curses. She went straight to Zrule's tavern, bought a big bottle of vodka, and took it home. To make a long story short, Henne began to drink. That a woman should drink is rare, even among the Gentiles, but that a Jewish woman should drink was unheard of. Henne lay in bed and gulped down the liquor. She sang, cried, and made crazy faces. She strolled over to the marketplace in her undergarments, followed by cat-calling urchins. It is sacrilegious to behave as Henne did, but what could the townspeople do? Nobody went to prison for drinking. The officials themselves were often dead drunk. The neighbors said that Henne got up in the morning and drank a cup of vodka. This was her breakfast. Then she went to sleep and when she awoke she began to drink in earnest. Once in a while, when the whim seized her, she would open the window and throw out some coins. The little ones almost killed themselves trying to pick them up. As they groped on the ground for the money, she would empty the slops over them. The rabbi sent for her but he might just as well have saved his breath. Everyone was sure that she would drink herself to death. Something entirely different happened.

As a rule, Henne would come out of her house in the morning. Sometimes she would go to the well for a pail of water. There were stray dogs in Butcher Alley and occasionally she would throw them a bone. There were no outhouses and the villagers attended to their needs in the open. A few days passed and nobody saw Henne. The neighbors tried to peer into her window, but the curtains were drawn. They knocked on her door and no one opened it. Finally they broke it open and what they saw should never be seen again. Some time before, Henne had bought an upholstered chair from a widow. It was an old piece of furniture. She used to sit in it drinking and babbling to herself. When they got the door open, sitting in the chair was a skeleton as black as coal.

My dear people, Henne had been burned to a crisp. But how? The chair itself was almost intact, only the material at the back was singed. For a person to be so totally consumed, you'd need a fire bigger than the one in the bathhouse on Fridays. Even to roast a goose, a lot of wood is needed. But the chair was untouched. Nor had the linen on the bed caught fire. She had bought a chest of drawers, a table, a wardrobe, and everything was undamaged. Yet Henne was one piece of coal. There was no body to be laid out, to be cleansed, or dressed in a shroud. The officials hurried to Henne's house and they could not believe their own eyes. Nobody had seen a fire, nobody had smelled smoke. Where could such a hell fire have come from? No ashes were to be found in the stove or under the tripod. Henne seldom cooked. The town's doctor, Chapinski, arrived. His eyes popped out of his head and there he stood like a figure of clay.

"How is it possible?" the chief of police asked.

"It's impossible," the doctor replied. "If someone were to tell me such a thing, I would call him a filthy liar."

"But it has happened," the chief of police interrupted.

Chapinski shrugged his shoulders and murmured, "I just don't understand."

Someone suggested that it might have been lightning. But there had been no lightning and thunder for weeks.

The neighboring squires heard of the event and arrived on the scene. Butcher Alley filled with carriages, britskas, and phaetons. The crowd stood and gaped. Everyone tried to find an explanation. It was beyond reason. The upholstery of the chair was filled with flax, dry as pepper.

A rumor spread that the vodka had ignited in Henne's

stomach. But who ever heard of a fire in the guts? The doctor shook his head. "It's a riddle."

There was no point in preparing Henne for burial. They put her bones in a sack, carried it to the cemetery, and buried her. The gravedigger recited the Kaddish. Later her daughters came from Lublin, but what could they learn? Fires ran after Henne and a fire had finished her. In her curses she had often used the word "fire": fire in the head, fire in the belly. She would say, "You should burn like a candle." "You should burn in fever." "You should burn like kindling wood." Words have power. The proverb says: "A blow passes, but a word remains."

My dear people, Henne continued to cause trouble even after her death. Kopel the coachman bought her house from her daughters and turned it into a stable. But the horses sweated in the night and caught cold. When a horse catches cold that way, it's the end. Several times the straw caught fire. A neighbor who had quarreled with Henne about the washing swore that Henne's ghost tore the sheets from the line and threw them into the mud. The ghost also overturned a washtub. I wasn't there, but of a person such as Henne anything can be believed. I see her to this day, black, lean, with a flat chest like a man and the wild eyes of a hunted beast. Something was smouldering within her. She must have suffered. I remember my grandmother saying, "A good life never made anyone knock his head against the wall." However, no matter what misfortunes strike I say, "Burst, but keep a good face on things."

Thank God, not everyone can afford constantly to bewail his lot. A rabbi in our town once said: "If people did not have to work for their bread, everyone would spend his time mourning his own death and life would be one big funeral."

Translated by the author and Dorothea Straus

Getzel the Monkey

M Y DEAR FRIENDS, we all know what a mimic is. Once we had such a man living in our town, and he was given a fitting name. In that day they gave nicknames to everybody but the rich people. Still, Getzel was even richer than the one he tried to imitate, Todrus Broder. Todrus himself lived up to his fancy name. He was tall, broad-shouldered like a giant, with a black beard as straight as a squire's and a pair of dark eyes that burned through you when they looked at you. Now, I know what I'm talking about. I was still a girl then, and a good-looking one, too. When he stared at me with those fiery eyes, the marrow in my bones trembled. If an envious man were to have a look like that, he could, God preserve us, easily give you the evil eye. Todrus had no cause for envy, though. He was as healthy as an ox, and he had a beautiful wife and two graceful daughters, real princesses. He lived like a nobleman. He had a carriage with a coachman, and a hansom as well. He went driving to the villages and played around with the peasant women. When he threw coins to them, they cheered. Sometimes he would go horseback riding through the town, and he sat up in the saddle as straight as a Cossack.

His surname was Broder, but Todrus came from Great Poland, not from Brody. He was a great friend of all the nobles. Count Zamoysky used to come to his table on Friday nights to taste his gefilte fish. On Purim the count sent him a gift, and what do you imagine the gift turned out to be? Two peacocks, a male and a female!

Todrus spoke Polish like a Pole and Russian like a Russian. He knew German, too, and French as well. What didn't he know? He could even play the piano. He went hunting with Zamoysky and he shot a wolf. When the Tsar visited Zamosc and the finest people went to greet him, who do you think spoke to him? Todrus Broder. No sooner were the first three words out of his mouth than the Tsar burst out laughing. They say that later the two of them played a game of chess and Todrus won. I wasn't there, but it probably happened. Later Todrus received a gold medal from Petersburg.

His father-in-law, Falk Posner, was rich, and Falk's daughter Fogel was a real beauty. She had a dowry of twenty thousand rubles, and after her father's death she inherited his entire fortune. But don't think that Todrus married her for her money. It is said that she was traveling with her mother to the spas when suddenly Todrus entered the train. He was still a bachelor then, or perhaps a widower. He took one look at Fogel and then he told her mother that he wanted her daughter to be his wife. Imagine, this happened some fifty years ago. . . . Everyone said that it was love at first sight for Todrus, but later it turned out that love didn't mean a thing to him. I should have as many blessed years as the nights Fogel didn't sleep because of him! They joked, saying that if you were to dress a shovel in a woman's skirts, he would chase after it. In those days, Jewish daughters didn't know about love affairs, so he had to run after Gentile girls and women.

Not far from Zamosc, Todrus had an estate where the greatest nobles came to admire his horses. But he was a terrible spendthrift, and over the years his debts grew. He devoured his father-in-law's fortune, and that is the plain truth.

Now, Getzel the Monkey, whose name was really Getzel Bailes, decided to imitate everything about Todrus Broder. He was a rich man, and stingy to boot. His father had also been known as a miser. It was said that he had built up his fortune by starving himself. The son had a mill that poured out not flour but gold. Gretzel had an old miller who was as devoted as a dog to him. In the fall, when there was a lot of grain to mill, this miller stayed awake nights. He didn't even have a room for himself; he slept with the mice in the hayloft. Getzel grew rich because of him. In those times people were used to serving. If they didn't serve God, they served the boss.

Getzel was a moneylender, too. Half the town's houses were mortgaged to him. He had one precious little daughter, Dishke, and a wife, Risha Leah, who was as sick as she was ugly. Getzel could as soon become Todrus as I the rabbi of Turisk. But a rumor spread through the town that Getzel was trying to become another Todrus. At the beginning it was only the talk of the peddlers and the seamstresses, and who pays attention to such gossip? But then Getzel went to Selig the tailor and he ordered a coat just like Todrus's, with a broad fox collar and a row of tails. Later he had the shoemaker fit him with a pair of boots exactly the same as Todrus's, with low uppers and shiny toes. Zamosc isn't Warsaw. Sooner or later everyone knows what everyone else is doing. So why mimic anyone? Still, when the rumors reached Todrus's ears he merely said, "I don't care. It shows that he has a high opinion of my taste." Todrus never spoke a bad word about anyone. If he was going down Lublin Street and a girl of twelve walked by, he would lift his hat to her just as though she were a lady. Had a fool done this, they would have made fun of him. But a clever person can afford to be foolish sometimes. At weddings Todrus got drunk and cracked such jokes that they thought he, not Berish Venngrover, was the jester. When he danced a kozotsky, the floor trembled.

Well, Getzel Bailes was determined to become a second Todrus. He was small and thick as a barrel, and a stammerer to boot. To hear him try to get a word out was enough to make you faint. The town had something to mock. He bought himself a carriage, but it was a tiny carriage and the horses were two old nags. Getzel rode from the marketplace to the mill and from the mill to the marketplace. He wanted to be gallant, and he tried to take his hat off to the druggist's wife. Before he could raise his hand, she had already disappeared. People were barely able to keep from laughing in his face, and the town rascals immediately gave him his nickname.

Getzel's wife, Risha Leah, was a shrew, but she had sense enough to see what was happening. They began to quarrel. There was no lack in Zamosc of curious people who listened at the cracks in the shutters and looked through the keyhole. Risha Leah said to him, "You can as much become Todrus as I can become a man! You are making a fool of yourself. Todrus is Todrus; you stay Getzel."

But who knows what goes on in another person's head? It seemed to be an obsession. Getzel began to pronounce his words like a person from Great Poland and to use German expressions: *mädchen, schmädchen, grädchen*. He found out what Todrus ate, what he drank, and, forgive me for the expression, what drawers he wore. He began to chase women, too. And, my dear friends, just as Todrus had succeeded in everything, so Getzel failed. He would crack a joke and get a box on the ear in return. Once, in the middle of a wedding celebration, he tried to seduce a woman, and her husband poured chicken soup down the front of his gaberdine. Dishke cried and implored him, "Daddy, they are making fun of you!" But it is written somewhere that any fancy can become a madness.

Getzel met Todrus in the street and said, "I want to see your furniture."

"With the greatest pleasure," said Todrus and took him into his living room. What harm would it do Todrus, after all, if Getzel copied him?

So Getzel kept on mimicking. He tried to imitate Todrus's voice. He tried to make friends with the squires and their wives. He had studied everything in detail. Getzel had never smoked, but suddenly he came out with cigars and the cigars were bigger than he was. He also started a subscription to a newspaper in Petersburg. Todrus's daughters went to a Gentile boarding school, and Getzel wanted to send Dishke there, even though she was already too old for that. Risha Leah raised an uproar and she was barely able to prevent him from doing it. If he had been a pauper, Getzel would have been excommunicated. But he was loaded with money. For a long time Todrus didn't pay any attention to all of this, but at last in the marketplace he walked over to Getzel and asked: "Do you want to see how I make water?" He used plain language, and the town had something to laugh about.

2

Now, listen to this. One day Risha Leah died. Of what did she die? Really, I couldn't say. Nowadays people run to the doctor; in those times a person got sick and it was soon finished. Perhaps it was Getzel's carryings on that killed her. Anyway, she died and they buried her. Getzel didn't waste any tears over it. He sat on the stool during the seven days of mourning and cracked jokes like Todrus. His daughter Dishke was already engaged. After the thirty days of bereavement the matchmakers showered him with offers, but he wasn't in a hurry.

Two months hadn't passed when there was bedlam in the town. Todrus Broder had gone bankrupt. He had borrowed money from widows and orphans. Brides had invested their dowries with him, and he owed money to nobles. One of the squires came over and tried to shoot him. Todrus's wife wept and fainted, and the girls hid in the attic. It came out that Todrus owed Getzel a large sum of money. A mortgage, or God knows what. Getzel came to Todrus. He was carrying a cane with a silver tip and an amber handle, just like Todrus's, and he pounded on the floor with it. Todrus tried to laugh off the whole business, but you could tell that he didn't feel very good about it. They wanted to auction off all his possessions, tear him to pieces. The women called him a murderer, a robber, and a swindler. The brides howled: "What did you do with our dowries?" and wailed as if it were Yom Kippur. Todrus had a dog as big as a lion, and Getzel had gotten one the image of it. He brought the dog with him, and both animals tried to devour each other. Finally Getzel whispered something to Todrus; they locked themselves in a room and stayed there for three hours. During that time the creditors almost tore the house down. When Todrus came out, he was as pale as death; Getzel was perspiring. He called out to the men: "Don't make such a racket! I'll pay all the debts. I have taken over the business from Todrus." They didn't believe their own ears. Who puts a healthy head into a sickbed? But Getzel took out his purse, long and deep, just like Todrus's. However, Todrus's was empty, and this one was full of bank notes. Getzel began to pay on the spot. To some he paid off the whole debt and to others an advance, but they all knew that he was solvent. Todrus looked on silently. Fogel, his wife, came to herself and smiled. The girls came out of their hiding places. Even the dogs made peace; they began to sniff each other and wag their tails. Where had Getzel put together so much cash? As a rule, a merchant has all his money in his business. But Getzel kept on paying. He had stopped stammering and he spoke now as if he really were Todrus. Todrus had a bookkeeper whom they called the secretary, and he brought out the ledgers. Meanwhile, Todrus had become his old self again. He told jokes, drank brandy, and offered a drink to Getzel. They toasted *l'chayim*.

To make a long story short, Getzel took over everything. Todrus Broder left for Lublin with his wife and daughters, and it seemed that he had moved out altogether. Even the maids went with him. But then why hadn't he taken his feather beds with him? By law, no creditor is allowed to take these. For three months there was no word of them. Getzel had already become the boss. He went here, he went there, he rode in Todrus's carriage with Todrus's coachman. After three months Fogel came back with her daughters. It was hard to recognize her. They asked her about her husband and she answered simply, "I have no husband." "Some misfortune, God forbid?" they asked, and she answered no, that they had been divorced.

There is a saying that the truth will come out like oil on water. And so it happened here. In the three hours that Getzel and Todrus had been locked up in the office, Todrus had transferred everything to Getzel—his house, his estate, all his possessions, and on top of it all, his wife. Yes, Fogel married Getzel. Getzel gave her a marriage contract for ten thousand rubles and wrote up a house—it was actually Todrus's—as estate. For the daughters he put away large dowries.

The turmoil in the town was something awful. If you weren't in Zamosc then, you have no idea how excited a town can become. A book could be written about it. Not one book, ten books! Even the Gentiles don't do such things. But that was Todrus. As long as he could, he acted like a king. He gambled, he lost, and then it was all over; he disappeared. It seems he had been about to go to jail. The squires might have murdered him. And in such a situation, what won't a man do to save his life? Some people thought that Getzel had known everything in advance and that he had plotted it all. He had managed a big loan for Todrus and had lured him into his snare. No one would have thought that Getzel was so clever. But how does the saying go? If God wills, a broom will shoot.

Todrus's girls soon got married. Dishke went to live with her in-laws in Lemberg. Fogel almost never showed her face outside. Todrus's grounds had a garden with a pavilion, and she sat there all summer. In the winter she hid inside the house. Todrus Broder had vanished like a stone in the water. Some held that he was in Krakow; others, that he had gone to Warsaw. Still others said that he had converted and had married a rich squiress. Who can understand such a man? If a Jew is capable of selling his wife in such a way, he is no longer a Jew. Fogel had loved him with a great love, and it was clear that she had consented to everything just to save him. In the years that followed, nobody could say a word against Todrus to her. On Rosh Hashanah and Yom Kippur she stood in her pew in the women's section at the grating and she didn't utter a single word to anybody. She remained proud.

Getzel took over Todrus's language and his manners. He even became taller, or perhaps he put lifts in his boots. He became a bosom friend of the squires. It was rumored that he drank forbidden wine with them. After he had stopped stammering, he had begun to speak Polish like one of them.

Dishke never wrote a word to her father. About Todrus's daughters I heard that they didn't have a good end. One died in childbirth. Another was supposed to have hanged herself. But Getzel became Todrus and I saw it happen with my own eyes, from beginning to end. Yes, mimicking is forbidden. If you imitate a person, his fate is passed on to you. Even with a shadow one is not allowed to play tricks. In Zamosc there was a young man who used to play with his shadow. He would put his hands together so that the shadow on the wall would look like a buck with horns, eating and butting. One night the shadow jumped from the wall and gored the young man as if with real horns. He got such a butt that he had two holes in his forehead afterwards. And so it happened here.

Getzel did not need other people's money. He had enough. But suddenly he began to borrow from widows and orphans. Anywhere he could find credit he did, and he paid high interest. He didn't have to renovate his mill either. The flour was as white as snow. But he built a new mill and put in new millstones. His old and devoted miller had died, but Getzel hired a new miller who had long mustaches, a former bailiff. This one swindled him right and left. Getzel also bought an estate from a nobleman even though he already had an estate with a stable and horses. Before this he had kept to his Jewishness, but now he began to dress like a fop. He stopped coming to the synagogue except on High Holy Days. As if this wasn't enough, Getzel started a brewery and he sowed hops for beer. He didn't need any of this. Above all, it cost him a fortune. He imported machines, God knows from where, and they made such a noise at night that the neighbors couldn't sleep. Every few weeks he made a trip to Warsaw. Who can guess what really happened to him? Ten enemies don't do as much harm to a man as he does to himself. One day the news spread that Getzel was bankrupt. My dear friends, he didn't have to go bankrupt; it was all an imitation of Todrus. He had taken over the other's bad luck. People streamed from every street and broke up his windowpanes. Getzel had no imitator. No one wanted his wife; Fogel was older than Getzel by a good many years. He assured everyone that he wouldn't take anything away from them. But they beat him up. A squire came and put his pistol to Getzel's forehead in just the same way as the other had to Todrus.

To make a long story short, Getzel ran away in the middle of the night. When he left, the creditors took over and it turned out that there was more than enough for everybody. Getzel's fortune was worth God knows how much. So why had he run away? And where had he gone? Some said that the whole bankruptcy was nothing but a sham. There was supposed to have been a woman involved, but what does an old man want with a woman? It was all to be like Todrus. Had Todrus buried himself alive, Getzel would have dug his own grave. The whole thing was the work of demons. What are demons if not imitators? And what does a mirror do? This is why they cover a mirror when there is a corpse in the house. It is dangerous to see the reflection of the body.

Every piece of property Getzel had owned was taken away. The creditors didn't leave as much as a scrap of bread for Fogel. She went to live in the poorhouse. When this happened I was no longer in Zamosc. But may my enemies have such an old age as they say Fogel had. She lay down on a straw mattress and she never got up again. It was said that before her death she asked to be inscribed on the tombstone not as the wife of Getzel but as the wife of Todrus. Nobody even bothered to put up a stone. Over the years the grave became overgrown and was finally lost.

What happened to Getzel? And what happened to Todrus? No one knew. Somebody thought they might have met somewhere, but for what purpose? Todrus must have died. Dishke tried to get a part of her father's estate, but nothing was left. A man should stay what he is. The troubles of the world come from mimicking. Today they call it fashion. A charlatan in Paris invents a dress with a train in front and everybody wears it. They are all apes, the whole lot of them.

I could also tell you a story about twins, but I wouldn't dare to talk about it at night. They had no choice. They were two bodies with one soul. Both sisters died within a single day, one in Zamosc and the other in Kovle. Who knows? Perhaps one sister was real and the other was her shadow?

I am afraid of a shadow. A shadow is an enemy. When it has the chance, it takes revenge.

Translated by the author and Ellen Kantarov

Yanda

THE Peacock's Tail stood on a side street not far from the ruins of a Greek Orthodox church and cemetery. It was a two-story brick building with a weather vain on its crooked roof and a battered sign over its entrance depicting a peacock with a faded gold tail. The front of the inn housed a windowless tavern, dark as dusk on the sunniest mornings. No peasants were served there even on market days. The owner, Shalom Pintchever, had no patience with the peasant rabble, their dances and wild songs. Neither he nor Shaindel, his wife, had the strength to wait on these ruffians, or later when they got drunk, to throw them out into the gutter. The Peacock's Tail was a stopping place for squires, for military men who were on their way to the Russian-Austrian border, and for salesmen who came to town to sell farm implements and goods from Russia. There was never any lack of guests. Occasionally a group of strolling players stayed the night. Once in a while the inn was visited by a magician or a bear trainer. Sometimes a preacher stopped there, or one of those travelers of whom the Lord alone knows what brought them there. The town coachman understood what kind of customers to bring to The Peacock's Tail.

When Shalom Pintchever, a stranger, bought the hotel and with his wife came to live in the town, they brought with them a peasant woman called Yanda. Yanda would have been a beauty but for a face as pockmarked as a potato grater. She had black hair which she wore in a braid, white skin, a short nose, red cheeks, and eyes as black as cherries. Her bosom was high, her waist narrow, her hips rounded. She was a woman of great physical strength. She did all the work in the hotel: made the beds, washed the linen, cooked, dumped the chamber pots, and, in addition, visited the male guests when requested. The moment a visitor registered, Shalom Pintchever would ask slyly, winking an eye under his bushy brows: "With or without?" The traveler understood and almost always answered: "With." Shalom added the price to the bill.

663

There were guests who invited Yanda to drink with them or go for a walk, but she never accepted. Shalom Pintchever was not going to have them taking up her time or turning her into a drunkard. He had once and for all forbidden her to drink liquor, and she never touched a drop, not even a glass of beer on a hot summer day. Shalom had rescued her from a drunkard father and a stepmother. In return she served him without asking for pay. Every few months he would give her pocket money. Yanda would grab Shalom's hand, kiss it, and hide the money in her stocking without counting it. From time to time she would order a dress or a pair of high-buttoned shoes or buy herself a shawl, a kerchief, a comb. Sunday, when she went to church, she invariably threw a coin into the alms box. Sometimes she brought a present for the priest or a candle to be lit for her patron saint. The old women objected to her entering a holy place, but she stood inside the door anyway. There was gossip that the priest was carrying on with her, even though he had a pretty housekeeper.

The Jews accused Shalom Pintchever of keeping a bawdy house. When the women quarreled with Shaindel, they called her Yanda. But, without Yanda, Shalom would have been out of business. Three maids could not have done her work. Besides, most servants stole and had to be watched. Neither Shalom nor Shaindel could be bothered with that. Husband and wife were mourning an only daughter who had died in a fire in the town in which they had previously lived. Shaindel suffered from asthma; Shalom had sick kidneys. Yanda carried the burden of the hotel. Summertime she got up at daybreak; in the winter she left her bed two hours before sunrise. She scrubbed floors, patched quilts and sheets, carried water from the well, even chopped wood when a woodchopper was not available. Shaindel was convinced Yanda would collapse from overwork. Husband and wife also feared that she might contract a contagious disease. But some devil or other impure power watched over her. Years passed, and she did not get sick or even catch a cold. Her employers did not stint on her food, but she preferred to eat the leftovers: cold soups, scraps of meat, stale bread. Shalom and Shaindel both suffered from toothaches, but Yanda had a mouth full of strong white teeth like a dog. She could crack peach pits with them.

"She is not a human being," Shaindel would say. "She's a beast."

The women spat when Yanda passed by, cursing her vehemently. Boys called her names and threw stones and mud at her. Young girls giggled, dropped their eyes, and blushed when they met her on the street. More than once the police called her in for questioning. But years passed and Yanda remained in Shalom Pintchever's service. With time the clientele of the inn changed. As long as the town belonged to Russia, its guests were mainly Russians. Later, when the Austrians took over, they were Germans, Magyars, Czechs, and Bosnians. Then, when Poland gained independence, it served the Polish officials who arrived from Warsaw and Lublin. What didn't the town live through—epidemics of typhoid and dysentery; the Austrian soldiers brought cholera with them and six hundred townspeople perished. For a short time, under Bolshevik rule, the inn was taken over by the Communist County Committee, and some commissar or other was put in charge. Yanda remained through it all. Somebody had to work, to wash, scour, serve the guests beer, vodka, snacks. Whatever their titles, at night the men wanted Yanda in their beds. There were some who kissed her and some who beat her. There were those who cursed her and called her names and those who wept before her and confessed to her as if she were a priest. One officer placed a glass of cognac on her head and shot at it with his revolver. Another bit into her shoulder and like a leech sucked her blood. Still, in the morning she washed, combed her hair, and everything began anew. There was no end to the dirty dishes. The floors were full of holes and cracks, the walls were peeling. No matter how often Yanda poured scalding water over cockroaches and bedbugs, and used all kinds of poison, the vermin continued to multiply! Each day the hotel was in danger of falling apart. It was Yanda who kept it together.

The owners themselves began to resemble the hotel. Shaindel grew bent and her face became as white and brittle as plaster. Her speech was unintelligible. She no longer walked, but shuffled. She would find a discarded caftan in a trunk and would try to patch it. Shalom protested that he didn't need the rag, but half blind as she was, she would sit for days, with her glasses on the tip of her nose, trying to mend it.

Again and again she would ask Yanda to thread the needle, muttering, "It isn't thread, it's cobweb. These needles have no eyes."

Shalom Pintchever's face began to grow a kind of mold. His brows became even shaggier. Under his eyes there were bags and from them hung other bags. Between his wrinkles there was a black excrescence which no water could remove. His head shook from side to side. Nevertheless, when a guest arrived, Shalom would reach for his hotel register with a trembling hand and ask: "With or without?"

And the guest would almost invariably reply: "With."

2

It all happened quickly. First Shaindel lay down and breathed her last. It occurred on the first day of Rosh Hashanah. The following day, the oldest woman in the town gave up her own shroud, since it is forbidden to sew on the Holy Days. The women of the burial society treated themselves to cake and brandy at the cemetery. Shalom, confused by grief, forgot the text of the Kaddish and had to be prompted. Those who attended the funeral said that his legs were so shaky he almost fell into the grave. After Shaindel's death Shalom Pintchever became senile. He took money from the cashbox and didn't remember what he did with it. He became so deaf that even screaming into his ears did not help. The Feast of Tabernacles was followed by such a rain spell that even the oldest townspeople could not recall its like. The river overflowed. The wheel of the watermill had to be stopped. The roof on the inn sprang a leak. The guests who had rooms on the top floor came down in the middle of the night, complaining that water was pouring into their beds. Shalom lay helpless in his own bedroom. It was Yanda who apologized to the guests and made up beds for them downstairs. She even climbed a ladder up to the roof and tried to plug the leaks. But the shingles crumbled as soon as she touched them. In the morning the guests left without paying their bills. Early Saturday, as Shalom Pintchever picked up his prayer shawl and was about to leave for the synagogue, he began to sway and fell down. "Yanda, I am finished," he cried out. Yanda ran to get some brandy, but it was too late. Shalom lay stretched out on the floor, dead. There was an uproar in the town. Shalom had left no children. Irreverent people, for whom the sacredness of the Sabbath had little meaning, began to search for a will and tried to force his strongbox. Officials from the City Hall made a list of his belongings and sealed the drawer in which he kept his money. Yanda had begun to weep the moment Shalom had fallen down and did not stop until after the funeral. She had worked in the inn for over twenty years but was left with barely sixty zlotys. The authorities immediately ordered her to get out. Yanda packed her belongings in a sack, put on a pair of shoes, which she usually wore only to church, wrapped herself in a shawl, and walked the long way to the railroad station. There was nobody to say goodbye. At the station she approached the ticket window and said, "Kind sir, please give me a ticket to Skibica."

"There is no such station."

Yanda began to wail: "What am I to do, I am a forsaken orphan!"

The peasants at the station jeered at her. The women spat on her. A Jewish traveling salesman began to question her about Skibica. Is it a village or a town? In what county or district is it? At first Yanda remembered nothing. But the Jew in his torn coat and sheepskin hat persisted until Yanda finally remembered that the village was somewhere near Kielce, between Chęczyn and Sobkow. The salesman told Yanda to take out the bank notes that she kept wrapped in a handkerchief and helped her to count the money. He talked it over with the ticket seller. There was no direct train to that area. The best way to go was by horse and buggy to Rozwadow, and from there on to Sandomierz, then to Opola, where she could either get a ride in another cart or go on foot to Skibica.

Just hearing the names of these familiar places made Yanda weep. In Skibica she had once had a father, a mother, a sister, relatives. Her mother had died and her father, not long before he died, had married another woman. Yanda had been about to become engaged to Wojciech, a peasant boy, but the blacksmith's daughter, a girl called Zocha, had taken him away. During the years Yanda had worked for Shalom Pintchever she had seldom thought of the past. It all seemed so far away, at the end of the earth. But now that her employer was dead there was nothing left for her but to return home. Who knew, perhaps some of her close ones were still alive. Perhaps somebody there still remembered her name.

Thank God, good people helped. No sooner had Yanda left the town where she had lived in shame than people stopped laughing at her, making grimaces, spitting. The coachmen did not overcharge her. Jews with beards and sidelocks seemed to know the whole of Poland as well as they knew the palms of their hands. They mentioned names of places which Yanda had already forgotten, and looked for shortcuts. In one tavern someone took out a map to find the shortest way home for her. Yanda marveled at the cleverness of men; how much knowledge they carried in their heads and how eager they were to help a homeless woman. But, despite all the good advice, Yanda walked more than she rode. Rains soaked her; there was snow and hail. She waded through ditches of water as deep as streams. She had grown accustomed to sleeping on pillows with clean pillowcases, between white sheets, under a warm eiderdown, but now she was forced to stretch out on the floors of granaries and barns. Her clothes were wet through. Somehow she managed to keep her paper money dry. As Yanda walked, she thought about her life. Once in a while Shalom Pintchever had given her money, but it had dwindled away. The Russians had counted the rubles and kopeks. When the Austrians came, the ruble lost its value and everything was exchanged for kronen and heller. The Bolsheviks used chervontsi; the Poles, zlotys. How was someone like Yanda, uneducated as she was, to keep track of such changes? It was a miracle that she had anything left with which to get home.

God in heaven, men were still chasing her! Wherever she slept, peasants came to her and had their way with her. In a wagon, at night, somebody seized her silently. What do they see in me, Yanda asked herself. It's my bad luck. Yanda remembered that she had never been able to refuse anyone. Her father had beaten her for her submissiveness. Her stepmother had torn Yanda's hair. Even as a child, when she played with the other children, they had smeared her face with mud, given her a broom, and made her take the part of Baba Yaga. With the guests in Shalom's hotel she had had such savage and foolish experiences that she sometimes hadn't know whether to laugh or cry. But to say no was not in her nature. When she was young, while still in her father's village, she had twice given birth to babies, but they had both died. Several times heavy work had caused her to miscarry. She could never really forget Wojciech, the peasant boy to whom she had almost been engaged but who at the last moment had thrown her over. Yanda also had desired Shalom Pintchever, perhaps because he had always sent her to others and had never taken her himself. He would say, "Yanda, go to number three. Yanda, knock at the door of number seven." He himself had remained faithful to his old wife, Shaindel. Perhaps he had been disgusted by Yanda, but she had yearned for him. One kind word from him pleased her more than all the wild games of the others. Even when he scolded her, she waited for more. As for the guests, there were so many of them that Yanda had forgotten all but a few who stuck in her memory. One Russian had demanded that Yanda spit on him, tear at his beard, and call him names. Another, a schoolboy with red cheeks, had kissed her and called her mother. He had slept on her breast until dawn, although guests in other rooms had been waiting for her.

Now Yanda was old. But how old? She did not know herself —certainly in her forties, or perhaps fifty? Other women her age were grandmothers but she was returning to her village alone, abandoned by God and man. Yanda made a resolution: once home, she would allow no man to approach her. In a village there was always gossip and it usually ended in a quarrel. What did she need it for? The truth was that all this whoring had never given her any pleasure.

3

The Jews who showed Yanda the way had not fooled her. She reached Skibica in the morning, and even though it had changed considerably, she recognized her home. In a chapel at the outskirts of the village God's mother still stood with a halo around her head and the Christ child in her arms. The figure had become dingy with the years and a piece of the Holy Mother's shoulder was chipped off. A wreath of wilted flowers hung around her neck. Yanda's eyes filled with tears. She knelt in the snow and crossed herself. She walked into the village, and a smell she had long forgotten came to her nostrils: an odor of soggy potatoes, burned feathers, earth, and something else that had no name but that her nose recognized. The huts were half sunk into the ground, with tiny windows and low doors. The thatched roofs were mossy and rotting. Crows were cawing; smoke rose from the chimneys. Yanda looked for the hut where her parents had lived but it had disappeared and in its place was a smithy. She put down the sack she was carrying on her back. Dogs sniffed at her and barked. Women emerged from the dwellings. The younger ones did not know her but the old ones clapped their hands and pinched their cheeks, calling, "Oh, Father, Mother, Jesu Maria."

"Yes, it's Yanda, as I love God."

Men, too, came to look at her, some from behind the stoves where they had been sleeping, others from the tavern. One peasant woman invited Yanda into her hut. She gave her a piece of black bread and a cup of milk. On the dirt floor stood bins filled with potatoes, beets, black radishes, and cranberries. Chickens were cackling in a coop. The oven had a built-in kettle for hot water. At a spinning wheel sat an old woman with a balding head from which hung tufts of hair as white as flax. Someone screamed into her ear: "Grandma, this is Yanda. Pawel Kuchma's daughter."

The old woman crossed herself. "Jesu Maria."

The peasant women all spoke together. Pawel Kuchma's home had burned down. Yanda's brother, Bolek, had gone to war and never returned. Her sister, Stasia, had married a man from Biczew and died there in childbirth. They also told Yanda what had happened to Wojciech, her former bridegroom-to-be. He had married Zocha and she had borne him fourteen children. Nine of them were still alive, but their mother died of typhoid fever. As for Wojciech, he had been drinking all these years. Zocha had worked for others to support the family. After her death three years before, he had become a derelict. Everything went for drink and he was half crazy. His boys ran around wild. The girls washed clothes for the Jews of the town. His hut was practically in ruins. As the women spoke to Yanda, somebody opened the door and pushed a tall man inside. He was as lean as a stick, barefoot, with holes in his pants. He wore an open jacket without a shirt; his hair was long and disheveled—a living scarecrow. He did not walk, but staggered along as though on stilts. He had mad eyes, a dripping nose, and his crooked mouth showed one long tooth.

Somebody said, "Wojciech, do you recognize this woman?"

"Pockmarked Yanda."

There was laughter and clapping. For the first time in years Yanda blushed.

"See how you look."

"I heard you are a whore."

There was laughter again.

"Don't listen to him, Yanda. He's drunk."

"What am I drunk on? Nobody gives me a drop of vodka."

Yanda gaped at him. Could this be Wojciech? Some similarity remained. She wanted to cry. She remembered an expression of Shaindel's: "There are some in their graves who look better than he does." Yanda regretted that she had come back to Skibica.

A woman said, "Why don't you have a look at his children."

Yanda immediately lifted up her sack. She offered to pay for the bread and milk, but the peasant woman rebuked her, "This is not the city. Here you don't pay for a piece of bread."

Wojciech's hut was nearby. The roof almost touched the ground. Elflocks of straw hung from its edges. The windows had no panes. They were stuffed with rags or boarded up. One entered it as one would a cave. The floor had rotted away. The walls were as black as the inside of a chimney. In the semidarkness Yanda saw boys, girls. The place stank of dirty linen, rot, and something rancid. Yanda clutched her nose. Two girls stood at the tub. Half-naked children smeared with mud crawled on the floor. One child was pulling the tail of a kitten. A boy with a blind eye was mending a trap. Yanda blinked. She was not accustomed to such squalor. At the inn the sheets had been changed each week. Every third day the guests got fresh towels. The leftover food had been enough to feed a whole family.

Well, dirt has to be removed. It won't disappear by itself.

Yanda rolled up her sleeves. She still had a few zlotys and she sent one of the girls to buy food. A Jew had a store in the village where one could get bagels, herring, chicory. God in heaven, how the children devoured those stale bagels! Yanda began to sweep and scrub. She went to the well for water. At first the girls ignored her. Then they told her not to meddle in their affairs. But Yanda said, "I will take nothing from you. Your mother, peace be with her, was my friend."

Yanda worked until evening. She heated water and washed the children. She sent an older child to buy soap, a fine comb, and kerosene, which kills lice. Every few minutes she poured out the slops. Neighbors came to look and shook their heads. They all said the same thing: Yanda's work was in vain. The vermin could not be removed from that hut. In the evening there was no lamp to light and Yanda bought a small kerosene lamp. The whole family slept on one wooden platform and there were few blankets. Yanda covered the children with her own clothes. Late in the evening the door opened and Wojciech intruded a leg. The girls began to giggle. Stefan, the boy with the blind eye, had already made friends with Yanda. He said, "Here he comes—the stinker."

"You must not talk like that about your father."

Stefan replied with a village proverb: "When your father is a dog, you say 'git' to him."

Yanda had saved a bagel and a piece of herring for Wojciech, but he was too drunk to eat. He fell down like a log, muttering and drooling. The girls stepped over him. Stefan mentioned that there was a straw mat in the shed behind the hut that Yanda could use to sleep on. He offered to show her where it was. As soon as she opened the door of the shed, the boy pushed her and she fell. He threw himself on her. She tried to tell him that it was a sin, but he stopped her mouth with his hand. She struggled but he beat her with a heavy fist. As she lay in the dark on wood shavings, garbage, and rotting rope, the boy satisfied himself. Yanda closed her eyes. Well, I'm lost anyhow, she thought. Aloud she muttered, "Woe is me, I might have been your mother."

Translated by the author and Dorothea Straus

The Needle

"MY GOOD PEOPLE, nowadays all marriages are arranged by Mr. Love. Young folks fall in love and begin to date. They go out together until they start to quarrel and hate each other. In my time we relied on father and mother and the matchmaker. I myself, did not see my Todie until the wedding ceremony, when he lifted the veil from my face. There he stood with his red beard and disheveled sidelocks. It was after Pentecost, but he wore a fur coat as if it were winter. That I didn't faint dead away was a miracle from heaven. I had fasted through the long summer day. Still, I wish my best friends no worse life than I had with my husband, he should intercede for me in the next world. Perhaps I shouldn't say this, but I can't wait until our souls are together again.

"Yes, love-shmuv. What does a young boy or girl know about what is good for them? Mothers used to know the signs. In Krasnostaw there lived a woman called Reitze Leah, and when she was looking for brides for her sons she made sure to drop in on her prospective in-laws early in the morning. If she found that the bed linens were dirty and the girl in question came to the door with uncombed hair, wearing a sloppy dressing gown, that was it. Before long everybody in the neighboring villages was onto her, and when she was seen in the marketplace early in the morning, all the young girls made sure their doors were bolted. She had six able sons. None of the matches she made for them was any good, but that is another story. A girl may be clean and neat before the wedding, but afterwards she becomes a slattern. Everything depends on luck.

"But let me tell you a story. In Hrubyeshow there lived a rich man, Reb Lemel Wagmeister. In those days we didn't use surnames, but Reb Lemel was so rich that he was always called Wagmeister. His wife's name was Esther Rosa, and she came from the other side of the Vistula. I see her with my own eyes: a beautiful woman, with a big-city air. She always wore a black-lace mantilla over her wig. Her face was as white and smooth as a girl's. Her eyes were dark. She spoke Russian,

Polish, German, and maybe even French. She played the piano. Even when the streets were muddy, she wore high-heeled patent-leather shoes. One autumn I saw her hopping from stone to stone like a bird, lifting her skirt with both hands, a real lady. They had an only son, Ben Zion. He was as like his mother as two drops of water. We were distant relatives, not on her side but on her husband's. Ben Zion—Benze, he was called—had every virtue: he was handsome, clever, learned. He studied the Torah with the rabbi in the daytime and in the evening a teacher of secular subjects took over. Benze had black hair and a fair complexion, like his mother. When he took a walk in the summertime wearing his elegant gaberdine with a fashionable slit in the back, and his smart kid boots, all the girls mooned over him through the windows. Although it is the custom to give dowries only to daughters, Benze's father set aside for his son a sum of ten thousand rubles. What difference did it make to him? Benze was his only heir. They tried to match him with the richest girls in the province, but Esther Rosa was very choosy. She had nothing to do, what with three maids, a manservant, and a coachman in addition. So she spent her time looking for brides for Benze. She had already inspected the best-looking girls in half of Poland, but not one had she found without some defect. One wasn't beautiful enough; another, not sufficiently clever. But what she was looking for most was nobility of character. 'Because,' she said, 'if a woman is coarse, it is the husband who suffers. I don't want any woman to vent her spleen on my Benze.' I was already married at the time. I married when I was fifteen. Esther Rosa had no real friend in Hrubyeshow and I became a frequent visitor to her house. She taught me how to knit and embroider and do needlepoint. She had golden hands. When the fancy took her, she could make herself a dress or even a cape. She once made me a dress, just for the fun of it. She had a good head for business as well. Her husband hardly took a step without consulting her. Whenever she told him to buy or sell a property, Reb Lemel Wagmeister immediately sent for Lippe the agent and said: 'My wife wants to buy or sell such-and-such.' She never made a mistake.

"Well, Benze was already nineteen, and not even engaged. In those days nineteen was considered an old bachelor. Reb

Lemel Wagmeister complained that the boy was being dis-graced by his mother's choosiness. Benze developed pimples on his forehead—because he needed a woman, it was said. We called them passion pimples.

"One day I came to see Esther Rosa to borrow a ball of yarn. And she said to me: 'Zeldele, would you like to ride to Zamosc with me?'

"'What will I do in Zamosc?' I asked.

"'What difference does it make,' she replied. 'You'll be my guest.'

"Esther Rosa had her own carriage, but this time she went along with someone else who was going to Zamosc. I guessed that the journey had something to do with looking over a bride, but Esther Rosa's nature was such that one didn't ask questions. If she were willing to talk, well and good. If not, you just waited. To make it short, I went to tell my mother about the trip. No need to ask my husband. He sat in the study house all day long. When he came home in the evening, my mother served him his supper. In those days a young Talmud scholar barely knew he had a wife. I don't believe that he would have recognized me if he met me on the street. I packed a dress and a pair of bloomers—I beg your pardon—and I was ready for the trip. We were traveling in a nobleman's carriage and he did the driving himself. Two horses like lions. The road was dry and smooth as a table. When we arrived in Zamosc, he let us off not at the marketplace but on a side street where the Gentiles live. Esther Rosa thanked him and he tipped his hat and waved his whip at us good-naturedly. It all looked arranged.

"As a rule, when Esther Rosa traveled any place she dressed as elegantly as a countess. This time she wore a simple cotton dress, and a kerchief over her wig. It was summer and the days were long. We walked to the marketplace and she inquired for Berish Lubliner's dry-goods store. A large store was pointed out to us. Nowadays in a dry-goods store you can only buy yard goods, but in those days they sold everything: thread, wool for knitting, and odds and ends. What didn't they sell? It was a store as big as a forest, filled with merchandise to the ceiling. At a high desk stand a man sat writing in a ledger, as they do in the big cities. I don't know what he was, the cashier or a bookkeeper. Behind a counter stood a girl with black eyes that burned like fire. We happened to be the only customers in the store, and we approached her. 'What can I do for you?' she asked. 'You seem to be strangers.'

"'Yes, we are strangers,' said Esther Rosa.

"'What would you like to see?' the girl asked.

"'A needle,' said Esther Rosa.

"The moment she heard the word 'needle,' the girl's face changed. Her eyes became angry. 'Two women for one needle,' she said.

"Merchants believe that a needle is unlucky. Nobody ever dared to buy a needle at the beginning of the week, because they knew it meant the whole week would be unlucky. Even in the middle of the week the storekeepers did not like to sell needles. One usually bought a spool of thread, some buttons, and the needle was thrown in without even being mentioned. A needle costs only half a groshen and it was a nuisance to make such small change.

"'Yes,' said Esther Rosa. 'All I need is a needle.'

"The girl frowned but took out a box of needles. Esther Rosa searched through the box and said: 'Perhaps you have some other needles?'

"'What's wrong with these?' the girl asked impatiently.

"'Their eyes are too small,' Esther Rosa said. 'It will be difficult to thread them.'

"'These are all I have,' the girl said angrily. 'If you can't see well, why don't you buy yourself a pair of eyeglasses.'

"Esther Rosa insisted. 'Are you sure you have no others? I must have a needle with a larger eye.'

"The girl reluctantly pulled out another box and slammed it down on the counter. Esther Rosa examined several needles and said: 'These too have small eyes.'

"The girl snatched away the box and screamed: 'Why don't you go to Lublin and order yourself a special needle with a big eye.'

"The man at the stand began to laugh. 'Perhaps you need a sackcloth needle,' he suggested. 'Some nerve,' the girl chimed in, 'to bother people over a half-groshen sale.'

"Esther Rosa replied: 'I have no use for sackcloth or for girls who are as coarse as sackcloth.' Then she turned to me and said: 'Come, Zeldele, they are not our kind.'

"The girl turned red in the face and said loudly, 'What yokels! Good riddance!'

"We went out. The whole business had left a bad taste in my mouth. A woman passed by and Esther Rosa asked her the way to Reb Zelig Izbitzer's drygoods store. 'Right across the street,' she said, pointing. We crossed the marketplace and entered a store that was only a third of the size of the first one. Here too there was a young saleswoman. This one wasn't dark; she had red hair. She was not ugly but she had freckles. Her eyes were as green as gooseberries. Esther Rosa asked if she sold needles. And the girl replied, 'Why not? We sell everything.'

"'I'm looking for a needle with a large eye, because I have trouble threading needles,' Esther Rosa said.

"'I'll show you every size we have and you can pick the one that suits you best,' the girl replied.

"I had already guessed what was going on and my heart began to beat like a thief's. The girl brought out about ten boxes of needles. 'Why should you stand?' she said. 'Here is a stool. Please be seated.' She also brought a stool for me. It was perfectly clear to me that Esther Rosa was going to test her too.

"'Why are the needles all mixed together?' Esther Rosa complained. 'Each size should be in a different box.'

"'When they come from the factory, they are all sorted out,' the girl said apologetically. 'But they get mixed up.' I saw Esther Rosa was doing her best to make the girl lose her temper. 'I don't see too well,' Esther Rosa said. 'It's dark here.'

"'Just one moment and I'll move the stools to the door. There is more light there,' the girl replied.

"'Does it pay you to make all this effort just to sell a half-penny needle?' Esther Rosa asked. And the girl answered: 'First of all, a needle costs only a quarter of a penny, and then as the Talmud says, the same law applies to a penny as it does to a hundred guilders. Besides, today you buy a needle and tomorrow you may be buying satins for a trousseau.'

"'Is that so? Then how come the store is empty?' Esther Rosa wanted to know. 'Across the street, Berish Lubliner's

store is so full of customers you can't find room for a pin between them. I bought my materials there but I decided to
come here for the needle.'

"The girl became serious. I was afraid that Esther Rosa had
overdone it. Even an angel can lose patience. But the girl said,
'Everything according to God's will.' Esther Rosa made a
move to carry her stool to the door, but the girl stopped her.
'Please don't trouble yourself. I'll do it.' Esther Rosa interrupted. 'Just a moment. I want to tell you something.'

" 'What do you want to tell me?' the girl said, setting down
the stool.

" 'My daughter, Mazel Tov!' Esther Rosa called out.

"The girl turned as white a chalk. 'I don't understand,' she
said.

" 'You will be my daughter-in-law,' Esther Rosa announced.
'I am the wife of Reb Lemel Wagmeister of Hrubyeshow. I
have come here to look for a bride for my son. Not to buy a
needle. Reb Berish's daughter is like a straw mat and you are
like silk. You will be my Benze's wife, God willing.'

"That the girl didn't faint dead away was a miracle from
heaven. Everybody in Zamosc had heard of Reb Lemel Wagmeister. Zamosc is not Lublin. Customers came in and saw
what was happening. Esther Rosa took a string of amber beads
out of her basket. 'Here is your engagement gift. Bend your
head.' The girl lowered her head submissively and Esther Rosa
placed the beads around her neck. Her father and mother
came running into the store. There was kissing, embracing,
crying. Someone immediately rushed to tell the story to Reb
Berish's daughter. When she heard what had happened, she
burst into tears. Her name was Itte. She had a large dowry
and was known as a shrewd saleswoman. Zelig Izbitzer barely
made a living.

"My good people, it was a match. Esther Rosa wore the
pants in the family. Whatever she said went. And as I said, in
those days young people were never asked. An engagement
party was held and the wedding soon after. Zelig Izbitzer
could not afford a big wedding. He barely could give his
daughter a dowry, for he also had two other daughters and
two sons who were studying in the yeshiva. But, as you know,
Reb Lemel Wagmeister had little need for her dowry. I went to

the engagement party and I danced at the wedding. Esther Rosa dressed the girl like a princess. She became really beautiful. When good luck shines, it shows on the face. Whoever did not see that couple standing under the wedding canopy and later dancing the virtue dance will never know what it means to have joy in children. Afterwards they lived like doves. Exactly to the year, she bore a son.

"From the day Itte discovered that Esther Rosa had come to test her, she began to ail. She spoke about the visit constantly. She stopped attending customers. Day and night she cried. The matchmakers showered her with offers, but first she wouldn't have anyone else and second what had happened had given her a bad name. You know how people exaggerate. All kinds of lies were invented about her. She had insulted Esther Rosa in the worst way, had spat in her face, had even beaten her up. Itte's father was stuffed with money and in a small town everybody is envious of his neighbor's crust of bread. Now his enemies had their revenge. Itte had been the real merchant and without her the store went to pieces. After a while she married a man from Lublin. He wasn't even a bachelor. He was divorced. He came to Zamosc and took over his father-in-law's store. But he was as much a businessman as I am a musician.

"That is how things are. If luck is with you, it serves you well. And when it stops serving you, everything goes topsy-turvy. Itte's mother became so upset she developed gallstones, or maybe it was jaundice. Her face became as yellow as saffron. Itte no longer entered the store. She became a stay-at-home. It was hoped that when she became pregnant and had a child, she would forget. But twice she miscarried. She became half crazy, went on cursing Frieda Gittel—that is what Benze's wife was called—and insisted that the other had connived against her. Who knows what goes on in a madwoman's head? Itte also foretold that Frieda Gittel would die and that she, Itte, would take her place. When Itte became pregnant for the third time, her father took her to a miracle-worker. I've forgotten to mention that by this time her mother was already dead. The miracle-worker gave her potions and talismans, but she miscarried again. She began to run to doctors and to imagine all kinds of illnesses.

"Now listen to this. One evening Itte was sitting in her room sewing. She had finished her length of thread and wanted to rethread her needle. While getting the spool she placed the needle between her lips. Suddenly she felt a stab in her throat and the needle vanished. She searched all over for it, but—what is the saying,—'who can find a needle in a haystack?' My dear people, Itte began to imagine that she had swallowed the needle. She felt a pricking in her stomach, in her breast, her legs. There is a saying: 'A needle wanders.' She visited the leech, but what does a leech know? She went to doctors in Lublin and even in Warsaw. One doctor said one thing; another, something different. They poked her stomach but could find no needle. God preserve us. Itte lay in bed and screamed that the needle was pricking her. The town was in a turmoil. She said that she had swallowed the needle on purpose to commit suicide. Others, that it was a punishment from God. But why should she have been punished? She had already suffered enough for her rudeness. Finally she went to Vienna to a great doctor. And he found the way out. He put her to sleep and made a cut in her belly. When she woke up he showed her the needle that he was supposed to have removed from her insides. I wasn't there. Perhaps he really found a needle, but that's not what people said. When she returned from Vienna, she was her former self again. The store had gone to ruin. Her father was already in the other world. Itte, however, opened a new store. In the new store she succeeded again, but she never had any children.

"I've forgotten to mention that after what happened between Esther Rosa and the two girls, the salesgirls of Zamosc became the souls of politeness, not only to strangers, but even to their own townspeople. For how could one know whether a customer had come to buy or to test? The book peddler did a fine trade in books on etiquette, and when a woman came to buy a ball of yarn, she was offered a chair.

"I can't tell you what happened later, because I moved away from Zamosc. In the big cities one forgets about everything, even about God. Reb Lemel Wagmeister and Esther Rosa have long since passed away. I haven't heard from Benze or his wife for a long time. Yes, a needle. Because of a rooster and a chicken a whole town was destroyed in the Holy Land, and because of a needle a match was spoiled. The truth is that everything is fated from heaven. You can love someone until you burst, but if it's not destined, it will come to naught. A boy and a girl can be keeping company for seven years, and a stranger comes along and breaks everything up. I could tell you a story of a boy who married his girl's best friend out of spite, and she, to spite him kept to her bed for twenty years. Tell it? It's too late. If I were to tell you all the stories I know, we'd be sitting here for seven days and seven nights."

Translated by the author and Elizabeth Shub

Two Corpses Go Dancing

I‌T HAS always tickled my fancy to amuse myself not only with the living but with the dead as well. That I do not have the power of resurrection is a well-known fact. This is something only the Almighty can accomplish. Nevertheless, I, the Evil One, can for a short time infuse a corpse with the breath of life, with animal spirits as the philosophers choose to call it, and send it to roam among the living. Woe unto such a one! one who is neither alive nor dead, but who exists somewhere on the borderline. What a delight it is for me to look in on a corpse as, wholly unaware of its status, it eats, worries about making a living, marries, sins—deceiving itself and others. When the game becomes boring, I end it. "Back to your sepulcher, Mr. Corpse," I order, "enough of your tricks." And the corpse crumbles like dust, for while it has been carousing, it has kept on rotting all the same.

This time I chose a young man named Itche-Godl. He had been dead more than a year and his widow, Tryna-Rytza, had remarried. Since he had lived in such a large city as Warsaw, had left behind no parents, no children, and certainly no estate, he had been completely forgotten. The truth of the matter is that he had been a corpse even when alive. You know the old saying: "A poor man is like a dead man." Well, Itche-Godl had been a pauper of the first magnitude. His wife had been the breadwinner, selling in the marketplace, and the couple had made their home in a cellar that was dark even during daylight hours. Itche-Godl, in tatters, had moped about the study houses or dozed on a bench behind the oven. A puny man, stooped, sleepy-eyed, with a beard like the wattle of a chicken, he wore trousers that drooped constantly, a ragged gaberdine girdled with a rope, an old cap lining on his head, and on his feet cracked shoes. So he had existed until his thirty-sixth year, when he fell prey to some mysterious illness. For several weeks he lay under a covering of rags in the rotting straw of his bench bed, with his face turning always yellower and more haggard. Until finally one morning while Tryna-Rytza was preparing her wicker basket to take to the marketplace, she realized her

682

provider, her lord and master whose footstool she would one day become in paradise, was no longer alive. Taking a pillow feather, she held it to his nostrils and waited to see if it would flutter. But it did not. Somehow or other, she managed to scrape together a few gulden for the funeral, and Itche-Godl was dispatched to the True World. Since the burial took place on a Friday, the neighbors were too busy to walk behind the hearse, and the body was hurriedly disposed of. Not even a marker was placed over the grave.

Usually after a man dies the Angel Dumah confronts him, demands his name, and then proceeds to weigh up his good against his evil deeds. But Itche-Godl lay rotting for months without anyone coming to question him, forgotten not only by the angels but by the devils as well. It was only by accident that I learned of this forsaken cadaver, and then it occurred to me why not have some fun with it.

"Listen here, Itche-Godl," I shouted at him. "What's the use of rotting underground? Why not get up and go into the city? There are plenty of corpses roaming around Warsaw. There might as well be another."

Itche-Godl rose, and since it was very late and the sexton was fast asleep, I sent him to the mortuary, where he stole the night watchman's trousers, boots, hat, and gaberdine. Then he set off walking toward the city.

Although he was dressed like any other pauper, there was something about him that was frightening. Dogs howled. The night watch shuddered and clutched their sticks when they saw him silently approaching. A drunk, staggering across his path, sobered instantly and dropped back. Since Itche-Godl did not know that he was dead and that he had not been home in over a year, he was now on his way to his cellar. Coming into the narrow street where he lived, he felt his way sightlessly down the cellar steps, hanging on to the narrow wooden rail.

"How late it is! My, my! Why did I stay so long at the study house?" he mumbled. "Tryna-Rytza will surely make mince-meat out of me."

He pushed at the door but to his astonishment found it fastened by a lock and chain. She must be in a rage, he thought. He rapped once, then again. Suddenly he heard what sounded like a man's sigh from the other side. What's going on here, he asked himself. Is it possible Tryna-Rytza has fallen upon sinful ways? But that's foolish. I must have imagined it. . . . At that moment the door was flung open and in the darkness Itche-Godl made out the figure of a man. It occurred to him that perhaps he had made a mistake and knocked on the wrong door. "Does Tryna-Rytza live here?" he blurted out.

"Who are you?" rasped a coarse male voice. "What do you want?"

"But I am her husband," said Itche-Godl, confused.

"Her husband?" the other bellowed, backing away.

"Who is it?" Tryna-Rytza called, getting up from her bed. Presently she too was at the door. Itche-Godl recognized her familiar shape, her stride, the sweet-sour odor of her body.

"It's me, Itche-Godl," he said.

Instead of replying, Tryna-Rytza began to scream. The man slammed the door. Itche-Godl was shut outside. He trembled. Tryna-Rytza let out shriek after shriek. Then came a sudden silence, as if she had fallen into a swoon. A little later he heard whispers, murmurs, and then Tryna-Rytza and the man began to intone "Hear, O Israel."

"What goes on here?" Itche-Godl inquired of himself. Rooted there in the darkness, he pondered, scratched his beard, furrowed his brow, but the longer he thought about it, the more astounding the entire incident appeared.

"No doubt about it, the woman has committed adultery," he told himself.

Though it grieved him sorely to leave his woman and his pallet and to seek shelter for the night in the poorhouse, what choice had he? It was not his way to argue and he had never even learned how to raise his voice properly. He decided to withdraw.

"What can I do?" he thought. "It has been destined so."

And on shaky legs he climbed back up the stairs and out into the city.

2

At daybreak, as Itche-Godl lay huddled on the floor in a corner of the poorhouse, believing himself asleep, I appeared before him in black, with the feet of a goose. "Why dream,

Itche-Godl?" I said. "Man does not live forever. If you don't get your portion in this world, in the next it will be too late. If your wife is an adulteress, you must become a lecher!"

"But that is forbidden," Itche-Godl answered. "One is punished for that in hell."

"There is no such place as hell," I informed him. "A corpse knows nothing and feels nothing. There is no Judge and no Judgment."

"But how can I, ragged and scabby as I am, become a libertine?" asked Itche-Godl.

"The rich have plenty of money," I said. "Go to the market and steal some. I'll help you."

"And suppose they catch me and throw me into prison?"

"Don't worry. They won't be able to do a thing to you."

Early that same morning, Itche-Godl went to the marketplace and walked into a store as if to make a purchase. But although there were no other customers, the proprietress did not approach him, nor, when he ambled over to a sack of beans and dipped his hand in, did she berate him for handling her merchandise. Presently, when the woman went into the back room, leaving the store unattended, Itche-Godl sidled over to the counter, opened the cash drawer, took out a handful of money, and stuffed it into his pocket. Then he slipped out and lost himself in the crowd.

Barely a minute later he heard the hue and cry. The shopwoman wailed that she had been robbed, and a great commotion ensued. Everyone was suspicious of everyone else. A beggar was stopped, searched, and, although nothing was found on him, severely beaten. But no one suspected Itche-Godl.

"What do I do now?" he asked.

"Aren't you at all hungry?"

"Yes and no."

"Well, never mind. Go to a soup kitchen and order a plate of tripe with calves' feet, egg noodles, a bowl of carrots and fried potatoes, and a glass of brandy to wash it all down. As you leave, take a decent fur coat and a sable hat from a hook. After that, we'll see."

Since Itche-Godl was not listed in the Book of Life, the angels were unaware of his existence and it was easy for me to bend him to my will. He followed my instructions and an hour later emerged on the street again, a well-dressed man. His face, to be sure, was pale and sunken and his eyes looked congealed in bony sockets, but the fur collar concealed nearly his whole visage. Since he appeared prosperous, the beggars pestered him for alms, but he, like any man of property, pretended not to see them.

"What shall I do now?" Itche-Godl asked me again.

"Would you care for a little sport with that harlot, your wife?" I asked him.

"Yes, why not?"

"Come along then, and do as I tell you. I'll see to it that all goes well."

I steered Itche-Godl to the marketplace, where Tryna-Rytza was standing over a basket of half-rotten apples. In contrast to Itche-Godl, she was a healthy wench with red cheeks and broad hips. As Itche-Godl was convinced that it was only yesterday she had deserted him, he could not fathom the changes he saw in her. Her face appeared more youthful, her voice lustier as she conversed with the other marketwomen, at the same time eating with gusto some fried groats from an earthen pot.

"Apparently sin agrees with her," thought Itche-Godl. It was I, of course, who caused him to think this, his mind being completely under my domination.

He went nearer. "Excuse me, woman, how much are the apples?"

Tryna-Rytza looked up and, bewildered at seeing such a distinguished man in a fur coat and sable hat, blurted out: "A penny a pound. Three pounds for two."

"Too cheap!" said Itche-Godl. "In Danzig, where I come from, such produce would bring at least three pennies a pound."

"Huh . . . what? That is a price!" Tryna-Rytza exclaimed, staring in amazement at the stranger. "Here everything is dirt cheap."

"Why do you work in the market?" he asked. "Don't you have a husband to support you?"

"I have a husband, may he live to a hundred and twenty," she replied. "But I have to help out."

"What does he do?" Itche-Godl asked, laughing to himself. He was certain that she was speaking of him, Itche-Godl.

"You might say he's a jack of all trades—porter, secondhand clothes dealer, sometimes a barrelmaker, sometimes a cobbler. But you know the saying: 'Trades aplenty, pockets empty!'"

"Do you have children?" he asked. She said she did not. "And why not?" he asked slyly.

"I'm with my second husband," Tryna-Rytza explained. "My first, may he rest in peace, was, begging your pardon, a weakling and a simpleton. He died a year ago. My second, may God spare him, has only been with me a few weeks."

Itche-Godl strained to keep from laughter. How could the woman lie so shamelessly?

"Tell me the truth. Which one do you love best: the second or the first, blessed be his memory?"

"Why do you ask me such questions?" she demanded. "People from Danzig must be terribly curious."

"In Danzig, when one is asked a question it's the custom to answer it," he said, marveling at his daring. It seemed, he decided, that with money one acquired a goodly measure of impudence. Tryna-Rytza also seemed lost in thought as she swallowed the last spoonful of groats.

"Well, what's the use of lying to you?" she replied after some hesitation. "My God forgive me, but this one is a man. The other, may his rest be easy, was, alas, a schlemiel."

Suddenly she looked closely at the man in front of her. Her blood grew cold, her face paled, and the earthen pot fell from her hands and shattered into bits.

"Who are you? What do you want?" she screamed in a voice unlike her own. Before Itche-Godl could manage an answer, she had fainted. The tradeswomen cried out and scurried about. Itche-Godl edged away into the crowd.

3

At the marketplace of the Old City stood a large dry-goods store belonging to a widow named Finkle. Widely known for her wisdom and education, she spoke both Polish and German and her witticisms and bons mots were repeated and relished among the merchants. The widow Finkle was olive-skinned and slim, with sharp eyes and an aquiline nose. She wore a curled wig topped by a silver comb, wore shoes with high heels and, even on weekdays, silk dresses and jewelry. She had her clothes custom-made for her by a tailor who sewed for the nobility.

She had been a widow for over twenty years but had never remarried. The reason? That was her secret. No one dared to ask. Her late husband, Reb Joseph Rappaport, had been heir to a fortune, a Talmud scholar, and learned in worldly matters as well. Obviously she could not forget him. It was rumored, too, that she had come to her husband on his deathbed and of her own volition made a vow never to remarry.

This widow, Finkle Rappaport, fell ill one winter with an internal ailment, and the most prominent Warsaw doctors were unable to help her. In Vienna at that time lived a doctor said to have performed miracles, literally bringing the dead to life again. So the widow Finkle traveled to Vienna, leaving the store in the care of her three clerks, a young man and two girls, all relatives upon whose trustworthiness she could rely.

When months passed without word from her, rumors began to circulate that she was no longer alive. Before her departure she had drawn up a will, leaving part of her estate to her relatives, the remainder to charity. Her costly gowns and silk undergarments were, in case of her death, to be distributed among indigent brides. And a sum of money was set aside to engage ten pious men to say Kaddish and to study the Mishnah for a full year after her demise. She had also provided that an eternal light in her memory be maintained in the prayer house. In short, the woman had attended to it that she should not arrive empty-handed at the Celestial Council of Justice.

But in the meantime no one knew what had happened to her and the Warsaw rabbis forbade that her estate be touched until there was definite proof of her death. Nine months passed. That the widow Finkle was no longer alive was clear to everyone, since in all that time nothing had been heard from her. Her near relatives had already mourned for her, and when her name came up, the usual eulogies were intoned. Several women had dreamed that she appeared before them in shrouds, pleading that her remains be returned to Warsaw so that she might be buried next to her ancestors and complaining that her soul could find no place in the impious cemetery of Vienna.

Suddenly the news spread that Finkle had returned. One evening, as her employees were about to light the oil lamp, Finkle entered. She was swathed all in black and her form appeared taller and more angular than it had been. The clerks were so frightened they were unable to speak.

"Apparently you decided you were already rid of me," Finkle said.

"God forbid," replied the male clerk, recovering himself.

"Why didn't Aunt write?" asked the older of the girls, bursting into tears.

"If I didn't write, obviously I was unable to write!" Finkle snapped in her severe manner.

She related tersely that she had been confined in a Vienna hospital, had been extremely ill, but was now recovered. It was clear that she was not disposed to discuss her absence. She seemed a changed person, her face drawn and spotted, her nose more crooked, her eyes sharper yet somehow more distant. In the days that followed, she sat behind the counter gazing into a volume of *The Lamp of Light*, although, as the younger of the girls observed, she never turned the page and the book remained open always at the same place. Women kept coming in to see her, to question her, but she received them coldly and unresponsively. She answered everyone in the same way, saying only that she had been very sick. And when the young matrons interrogated her about Vienna, how the women dressed, what the latest fashions were, and whether the city was truly as magnificent as some descriptions would have it, she simply reiterated: "I hardly saw the city. My mind was on other things."

Finkle was sitting in the store one day starting into *The Lamp of Light*, the yardstick on one side of her, the shears on the other, when Itche-Godl came in to purchase material for an overcoat, as I had ordered him. Getting into a conversation with Finkle, he told her that he was a merchant from Danzig, a widower.

"Is it long since your wife passed away?" Finkle asked. And Itche-Godl told her how long it had been.

"What are you doing in Warsaw?" she asked. And he explained his plans to erect a building on the marketplace four stories high and with three courtyards.

"Why such a large building?" Finkle asked.

"One does not build for oneself alone but for posterity as well," he replied.

"You have children, then?" asked Finkle.

"My first wife, may she rest in peace, was barren," he answered. "But I am thinking of marrying again."

Finkle asked him how many yards of cloth he required.

"What's the difference?" he answered. "So long as it covers the body." And he looked at her with lackluster eyes, and she looked back, the depths of her eyes blank.

The next morning I bade Itche-Godl send a matchmaker to Finkle. "But how can I?" he protested. "I have a wife already." "Do as I tell you," I ordered. "You have nothing." So the marriage broker spoke to Finkle, and she consented. When the clerks and neighbors heard that Finkle was contemplating marriage, they were greatly surprised. They came to offer congratulations but were thanked curtly. When they inquired: "Who is the groom? Where is he from? What does he do?" she said sharply: "Who knows? He's erecting a building or something in the marketplace."

"But there isn't an empty lot there," they pointed out.

"For my part, he can build on the wind," Finkle answered. But although her mouth smiled, her eyes remained stark. Moreover, the women noticed when they were near her a weird odor that seemed to emanate from her person. Mostly they stayed at a distance, however, for Finkle always reapplied herself quickly to her volume with its yellowed pages. The women, leaving the store, whispered among themselves. "Somehow it's not the old Finkle," they said and departed with heavy hearts.

The clerks in the store assumed that Finkle's wedding trousseau would be a costly one, but she ordered no new garments sewn. At home, too, her maid observed that she was behaving strangely. She barely touched the food placed before her, never attended to personal needs or washed herself or changed her clothing. In the morning her bed appeared unslept in, never disarranged, as smooth and cold as the day before. When she walked through the house, her footsteps made no sound, and often when the maid spoke to her there was no reply. The wedding date was set, yet Finkle made no preparations. One time the maid asked her: "Where will the master sleep?"

"What master?" Finkle answered.

"I mean . . . after the wedding," stammered the maid.

Finkle shrugged. "He'll sleep in the same place as the first."

On the evening of the wedding Finkle appeared at the ritual bath and the women, who had not counted on her coming, were greatly astonished. She looked, in her black clothes, unusually fleshless and elongated, nor did her figure cast any shadow on the wall. The bath attendant came to help her undress, but Finkle pushed past her and sitting down on the edge of the bench began to remove her clothes herself. Her torn stockings and spotted undergarments surprised everyone. When she was naked, she descended the steps promptly and silently lowered herself into the water. Her body was wasted, one could count every rib. Though she remained underwater for a long time, not even one bubble rose to the surface. Finally she poked her skull out, a skull that was neither trimmed nor shaved as is customary among pious women, but was overgrown with clumps of disheveled hair.

The next night was the night of the wedding, and the bride, having dressed herself in a black silk dress with a train, stationed herself at a window to wait for the groom. Her girls had filled the candelabra and chandeliers with lighted wax candles. Itche-Godl hastened in, accompanied by an assistant rabbi and by some street loungers who were to make up the quorum. The ceremony went off in the usual way. The marriage contract was filled in by the assistant rabbi with a goose quill. Itche-Godl slipped the ring from his bosom pocket and placed it on Finkle's index finger. When the canopy had been dismantled and the poles stacked behind the oven, the maid served cakes and brandy to the guests while they tendered their congratulations to the bride and groom. When the assistant rabbi said to Finkle: "May we soon celebrate a circumcision!" she snickered, revealing a row of blackish teeth, while Itche-Godl, lowering his head, giggled.

"A good night! A lucky night!" chorused the guests as they left.

The servant girl, who had been given the night off, had gone to sleep at her mother's, and the clerks had retired to their quarters in the basement. Finkle and Itche-Godl were left to themselves.

"Shall I put out the lights?" asked Finkle.

"As you wish," said Itche-Godl.

"You're mournful. Why?" asked Finkle.

"You're imagining it," answered Itche-Godl.

"Would you prefer to eat or sleep?" whispered Finkle.

"Sleep," said Itche-Godl.

"I, too." Finkle sighed.

She began to walk toward the bedroom, and Itche-Godl trailed behind, his legs shaky. The corridor was dark.

"How's your house coming?" Finkle asked.

"The lot—it's already there," replied Itche-Godl in an undertone.

"The lots are always there," said Finkle sternly. Itche-Godl suddenly felt as if she were moving far away from him. "Where are you going?" he called. "Come on. Don't be afraid," she replied.

The bedroom was not only unaccountably wide and dark, but it didn't seem to have any walls and a wind seemed to be blowing as if they were outdoors. "Get undressed," Finkle ordered.

"I'm cold," complained Itche-Godl. He was stumbling around in the dark looking for a chair where he could sit down and take off his shoes.

"What are you doing? Where are you?" called Finkle.

"Are you in bed already?" asked Itche-Godl, and Finkle murmured, "I think so."

"I can't find a chair . . ." said Itche-Godl.

"Truly, you are helpless," sighed Finkle.

Having no other choice, Itche-Godl laid his coat and hat on the floor. With trembling knees, he started for the bed. Suddenly it seemed to him that he was looking down into a pit.

"What's the matter? Why don't you come?" Finkle grumbled.

"I think I see a pit," whispered Itche-Godl.

"What kind of pit?" Finkle cried out.

"A pit . . . it looks like a pit . . . what else could it be?" At these words he fell in and there was the sound of rattling bones.

"What's happened?" Finkle demanded.

"I've fallen in! Save me!" moaned Itche-Godl, whose tongue was becoming numb. Finkle tried to get up but was unable to move.

"I don't understand. Where could you have fallen? There aren't any pits here!" she screamed. For a long time both were silent. Then Finkle spoke: "Woe is me. . . . We have made fools of ourselves."

"What's the matter? Are you sick or something, God forbid?" asked Itche-Godl in a muffled voice.

And Finkle answered, her voice funereal: "I am worse than sick!"

"Good heavens! Hear, O Israel: the Lord our God, the Lord is One," gasped Itche-Godl, and those were his last words. The God-fearing widow Finkle answered: "Blessed be His Name, Whose glorious kingdom is forever and ever. . . ."

The following morning the news spread throughout Warsaw that Finkle and her bridegroom had vanished on their wedding night. At first it was thought that the couple must have fled to Danzig, but why they should flee or from whom no one could conceive. Sometime afterward a letter came from Vienna which stated that Finkle had died three months earlier and been buried in a local cemetery. Only then did the people realize that the Finkle who had returned had been nothing but a phantom and the entire series of events an illusion. They discovered, too, that over a year ago a pauper named Itche-Godl had died in Warsaw. This man had returned twice to haunt his wife, who had remarried. In every household in the neighborhood the mezuzahs were examined. Ten Jews went to Itche-Godl's grave to beg his forgiveness, to pledge him to remain in eternal rest and to torment the living no more. To appease the corpse, the community erected a tombstone over his grave. Thus Itche-Godl, who went unmourned from the world, became famous after death. And when Tryna-Rytza, his former wife, was, with luck, delivered a son, she named him after her first husband: Itche-Godl.

So much for two of the corpses I sent dancing. But Itche-Godl and Finkle are not the only ones. I play such tricks often. The world is full of dead ones in sable capes and fur coats who carouse among the living. Maybe your neighbor, maybe your wife, maybe you yourself. . . . Unbutton your shirt. It's possible that underneath your clothes your body is wrapped in a shroud.

Translated by Joseph Singer and Elizabeth Pollet

The Parrot

OUTSIDE, the moon was shining, but in the prison cell it was almost dark. Although the single window was barred and screened, enough light filtered in to disclose parts of faces. New snow had fallen and gave a violet glow to the speck of sky which came through the window as through a sieve. By midnight it had become as cold as in the street and the prisoners had covered themselves with all the rags they had: cotton vests, jackets, overcoats. They slept in their caps, with rags stuffed in their shoes. In summer the chamber pot had given off a stench, but now the winter wind came in and blew away the odor. It had begun to get dark at half past three in the afternoon, and by six Stach the watchman put out the kerosene lamp. The prisoners went on talking for a little while until they fell asleep. Their snoring kept up till about one o'clock, when they began to wake.

The first one to wake was Leibele the thief, a married man, a father of daughters. He yawned like a bell. Mottele Roiskes woke up with a belch; then Berele Zakelkover sat up and went to urinate. The three had been there for months and had told one another all their stories. But this morning there was a new prisoner, a giant of a man with a snub nose, a straight neck, thick mustaches the color of beer, dressed in a new jacket, tight high boots, and a cap lined with fur. He had brought a padded blanket and an additional pair of new boots which hung over his shoulders. He seemed like a big shot who had influence with the police. In the beginning they thought him a Gentile. They even spoke about him in thieves' jargon. But he proved to be a Jew, a silent man, a recluse. When they spoke to him, he scarcely answered. He stretched out on the bench and lay there for hours without a word. Stach brought him a bowl of kasha and a piece of black bread, but he was in no hurry to eat. Leibele asked him, "A word from you is like a gold coin, eh?"

To which he answered, "Two coins."

They couldn't get any more out of him.

"Well, he'll soften up, the snob," Mottele Roiskes said.

If this new inmate had been a weaker fellow, the others would have known what to do with him, but he had the shoulders and hands of a fighter. Such a man might have a hidden knife. As long as there was light, Leibele, Mottele Roiskes, and Berele Zakelkover played Sixty-six with a pack of marked cards. Then they went to sleep with heavy hearts. In prison it's not good when a man thinks too highly of himself. But sooner or later he has to break down.

Presently all three of them were silent and listened to the stranger. Since he didn't snore, it was hard to know if he was asleep or awake. The few words which he had spoken he pronounced with hard *r*'s, a sign that he was not from around Lublin. He must have come from Great Poland, on the other side of the Vistula. Then what was he doing in the prison at Yanev? They seldom sent anyone from so far away. Mottele Roiskes was the first to talk. "What time can it be?" Nobody answered. "What happened to the rooster?" he continued. "He stopped crowing."

"Maybe it's too cold for him to crow," Berele Zakelkover answered.

"Too cold? They get warm from crowing. There was a teacher in our town, Reb Itchele, who said that when a rooster crows he burns behind his wings. That's the reason he flaps his wings—to cool off."

"What nonsense," Leibele growled.

"It's probably written in a holy book."

"A holy book can also say silly things."

"It's probably from the Gemara."

"How does the Gemara know what's happening behind a rooster's wings? They sit in the study house and they invent things."

"They know some things. A preacher came to us and he said that all the philosophers wanted to know how long a snake is pregnant and nobody knew. But they asked a tanna and he said seven years."

"So long?"

They became quiet; conversation petered out. Berele Zakelkover began to scratch his foot. He suffered from eczema. He scratched and hissed softly at the same time. Suddenly the stranger said in a deep voice, "A snake is not pregnant seven years, perhaps not even seven months."

All became tense. All became cheerful.

"How do you know how long a snake is pregnant?" Leibele asked. "Do you breed snakes?"

"No creature is pregnant seven years. How long does a snake live?"

"There are all kinds of snakes."

"How can the Gemara know? To know you have to keep two snakes in the house, a he and a she, and let them mate."

"Perhaps God told him."

"Yes."

They became quiet again. The stranger was now sitting up. One could barely see his silhouette but his eyes reflected the gold of the moon. After a little while he said, "God says nothing. God is silent."

"He spoke to Moses."

"I wasn't there."

"An unbeliever, eh?"

"How can you know what God said to Moses?" the stranger argued. "It's written in the Pentateuch, but who wrote the Pentateuch? With a pen you can write anything. I come from Kalisch, where there are two rabbis. When one pronounced a thing kosher, the other said unkosher. Before Passover the miller asked one of them to make the mill kosher. So the other one got angry that he hadn't received ten rubles and he said the Passover flour was unkosher. Does all this come from God?"

Mottele Roiskes was about to answer, but Leibele interrupted. "If you are from Kalisch, what are you doing here?"

"That's a different matter."

"What do you mean?"

The stranger gave no reply. The stillness became heavy and tense.

"Do you have a smoke?" the stranger asked.

"We're all out."

"I can do without food, but I have to have a smoke. Can you get it from the watchman?"

"We have no money."

"I have some."

"With money you can buy anything. Even in the clink," Leibele answered. "But not now. Wait until morning."

"The winter nights are rough," Berele Zakelkover began to say. "You go to sleep with the chickens, and by twelve o'clock you're already slept out. You lie in the dark and all kinds of thoughts come into your mind. Here you've got to talk or you'll go crazy."

"What is there to talk about?" the stranger asked. "There's a proverb: man spouts, God flouts. I'm not an unbeliever, but God sits in the seventh heaven and snaps his fingers at everything."

"Why did they put you in this cage?" Leibele asked.

"For singing psalms."

"No, I'm serious."

The stranger was silent.

"A big pile, eh?"

"No pile at all. I'm not a thief and I don't like anyone to steal from me. If somebody tries it, I break him in pieces. That's the reason I'm here now."

"In what yeshiva did they keep you before?"

"First in Kielc and then in Lublin."

"Did you polish off someone?"

"Yes, that's exactly what I did."

2

The stranger stretched out on the bench again. Berele Zakelkover went to scratching his foot. Mottele Roiskes asked, "Are you going to stay here?"

"They'll probably send me to Siberia."

Leibele walked over to the window. "A blizzard."

"It's a sin to let out a dog in weather like this," Mottele Roiskes said.

"I'd like to be the dog," Berele joked.

The stranger sat up again. He leaned his back against the wall and supported his chin on his knees. Broken moon rays reflected on his shiny boot tops. He said, "So what if they let you out? In half a year you'd be sitting here again."

"A half a year isn't anything to sneeze at."

"This is the last time for me," Leibele said, both to himself and to the stranger. "I've eaten enough half-baked bread. I have a wife and children."

"That's the usual song they all sing," remarked the stranger. "Where do you all come from? From Piask?"

"You're a thief yourself."

"I'm not a thief, and till now I wasn't a murderer. I could always swap blows, but for many years I've never touched anyone, not even a fly."

"So what happened all of a sudden?" Leibele asked.

The stranger hesitated. "It was fated."

"Who did you finish off? A merchant?"

"A woman."

"Your own wife?"

"No. She wasn't my wife."

"Did you catch her red-handed?"

The stranger gave no answer. He seemed to doze off while sitting there. Suddenly he said, "It all happened because of a bird."

"A bird? No kidding."

"It's the truth."

"What kind of a bird?"

"A parrot."

"Tell us about it. If you hold it in, you'll lose your mind."

"That wouldn't be so bad, but you can't choose when to lose your mind. I'm a horse dealer, or, rather, that's what I was. They knew me in Kalisch as Simon the horse trader. My father also dealt in horses; my grandfather too. When the horse thieves in Kalisch tried to sell me bargains, I sent them packing. I didn't need stolen goods. Sometimes I used to buy a half-dead nag, but under my care it recovered. I love animals, all animals. We're a family of horse traders. My wife died two years after our marriage and for thirteen years I was alone. I loved her and I couldn't forget her. We had no child. I had a house, stables; I kept a Gentile maid—not a young shiksa, an older woman. And not for what you think either. I lived, as they say, respectably. The matchmakers proposed all kinds of women, but I didn't like any of them. I'm one of those men who must love, and if I don't love a woman I can't live with her. It's as simple as that."

"Aha."

"I like animals. For me a horse is not just a horse. When I sold a horse, I wanted to know to whom I was selling it. There was a coachman in our town who used to whip the horses, and I refused to sell to him. For sixteen years I traded in horses and I never lifted a whip to one. You can get anything out of an animal with good treatment. It's the same with a horse, a dog, or a cat. Animals understand what you say to them; they even guess your thoughts. Animals see in the dark and have a better memory than men. Many times I've lost my way and my horses have led me to the right spot. The snow might be knee-deep, but my horses would take me to the peasant's hut and stop in front of it. Sometimes my horse would even turn his head, as though to say, 'Here it is, boss.'

"If you're alone, you have time to observe these creatures. Besides horses, I had dogs, cats, rabbits, a cow, a goat. I lived in the suburbs because in the city you can't keep a big stable, and can't take a horse to pasture. Oats and hay are good in winter, but in summer a horse needs fresh grass, green grass with flowers, and all the rest. The peasants hobble their horses and leave them all night in the pasture, but a hobbled animal is like a hobbled human being. Is it good to be in prison? I made a fence around my pasture, and the peasants laughed at me. It doesn't pay to build a fence around six acres of land, they told me, but I didn't want to hobble my horses, or let them stray into strange fields and get beaten. That's how I used to be before I became a murderer."

"What about the bird?"

"Wait. I'm coming to that. I kept fowl, and birds too. In the beginning, they weren't in my house but under the roof and in the granary. Storks used to come after Passover from the warm countries and build nests on my roof. They didn't have to build new ones, they just mended last year's nests after the rain and snow. Under the eaves, starlings had built theirs. People believe that crows bring bad luck, but actually crows are clever birds. I also had pigeon cotes. Some people eat squabs but I never tasted one. How much meat is there in a squab?"

"You seem to be a regular saint."

"I'm not a saint, but when you live in the suburbs you see all sorts of things. A bird flies in with a broken wing. A dog comes in limping. I'm not softhearted, but when you see a bird tottering on the ground and not able to lift itself up, you want to help it. I once took such a bird into my house and kept it until its wing was healed. I bandaged it like a doctor. Of course, the Jews laughed at me, but what do Jews know about animals? Some Gentiles understood. In summer my windows are wide open. As long as a bird wants to, it can stay and get its seed. When it's healthy again, it flies away. Once a bird returned to me, not alone, but with a wife. I was sitting on a stool fixing a saddle and suddenly two birds flew in. I recognized the male immediately because he had a scar on his leg. They stood on a shelf and sang me a good morning. It was like a dream.

"Matchmakers used to come to me and propose all kinds of arrangements, but when I looked over the merchandise she never pleased me. One was ugly, the other fat, the third one talked too much—I can't stand chatterboxes. Animals are silent; that's why I love them."

"A parrot talks."

"Yes."

"Well, what else?"

"Nothing. The years go by. One day it's my wife's first anniversary, then the second, then the eighth. Other horse dealers became rich, but I just made a living. I didn't fool the customer. I decided how much profit I wanted and that was all. I got used to being alone."

"What did you do when you needed a female?"

"What do you do?"

"In a prison you have no choice."

"If you don't like anyone, it's like being in a prison. There were whores in Kalisch, but when I looked at them I felt like vomiting. You could get a peasant girl or even a woman, but they were all lousy. Mine was a clean one. Each night she combed her hair. In the summer we bathed in a pond. She died from a lump in her breast. They cut it out but it grew again. Such suffering I don't wish my worst enemy."

"Was she beautiful?"

"A princess."

3

"Well, what about the parrot?"

"Wait. Where can I begin? I'm not a grandmother and I don't tell grandmothers' tales. Gypsies used to come to me to sell horses, but I never bought them. First of all, they're thieves. Second, their horses are seldom healthy and, if you're not an expert, you find the defect later. But I see everything the first minute. The gypsies knew that they couldn't put anything over on me.

"Once I was sitting and eating breakfast, millet with milk. I used to eat the same thing every morning. I always had a sack full of it for myself and for the birds. As I sat there, I saw a gypsy woman, a fat black one with large earrings and many strings of beads around her neck. She came in and said, 'Master, show me your hand.' I had never been to a fortune-teller; I didn't believe in it. Besides, what is the good of knowing things in advance? What must happen will happen. But, for some reason, I gave her my hand and she looked at my right palm and clucked in dismay. Then she asked for my left hand. 'Why do you need my left hand?' I asked. She said, 'The right one shows your fortune and the left one the fortune of your wife.' 'But I have no wife,' I said. 'My wife died.' And she said, 'There will be a second one.' 'When will she come?' I asked. 'She will fly into your window like a bird.' 'Will she have wings?' I asked. She smiled and showed her white teeth. I gave her a few groschen and a slice of bread, and she left. I paid no attention to her talk. Who cares about the babble of gypsies? But somehow the words were stored in my head and I remembered them and thought about them. Sometimes an idea ticks in your mind and you can't get rid of it.

"Now listen to what happened. They had just called me into a village to buy horses and I stayed overnight. The next day I came riding home with four horses, one my own mare and three which I had bought from a peasant. I walked into my house and there was a parrot. I didn't believe my own eyes. Local birds flew in and out, but where did a parrot come from? Parrots are not of this country. He stood on my wardrobe and looked at me as though he had been expecting me. He was as green as an unripe lemon but on his wings he had dark spots and his neck was yellow. He was not a large parrot; in fact, he seemed a young one. I gave him some millet and he ate it. I held out a saucer of water and he drank. I stretched out a finger to him and he perched on it like an old friend. I forgot all my business. I loved him immediately like my own child. In the beginning I wanted to close the window, because he could fly out as easily as he flew in. But it was summer, and besides, I thought, if he's destined to stay here, he'll stay.

"He didn't fly away. I bought him a cage, put in a saucer of millet, a dish of water, vegetables, a little mirror, and whatever else a bird needs. I named him Metzotze and the name stuck. In the beginning he didn't talk; he just clucked and cawed. Then suddenly he began to speak in a strange language. It must have been gypsy talk because it wasn't Polish or Russian or Yiddish. He must have escaped from the gypsies.

"The moment he came I knew that what the gypsy foretold would come true. Somehow I felt that this would happen. The summer was over and winter was coming on. I closed the windows to keep the house warm. He began to talk Yiddish and call me Simon, and when the Gentiles spoke in Polish he imitated them. The moment I entered the room he would fly up to my shoulder. When I went to the stable he stayed sitting there. He put his beak to my ear and played with my earlobe, telling me secrets in bird language. In the beginning I didn't know if he was a he or a she, but a magician passed by and told me it was a he. I began to look for a wife for him and at the same time I knew I would find my intended."

"A strange story," Mottele Roiskes interrupted.

"Just wait. Once I had to go to an estate to deliver horses, but since I loved my Metzotze so much, it was hard for me to leave him. But—how do they say it?—making a living is like waging a war. I took my horses and went to the estate. I told my maid—Tekla was her name—that she should watch the parrot like the eyes in her head. I didn't have to tell her—she was attached to the bird herself, as was my stable man. In a word, he was not among strangers. I sold my horses for a good price and everything went as smoothly as on greased wheels. I wanted to go home, but new business came up. The bird had brought me luck. I had to spend the night at an inn and the moment I entered I saw a woman: small, dark, with black eyes, a short nose. She looked at me and smiled familiarly as though I were an old friend. Outside, there was a blizzard, much as today, and we were the only guests. The landlady heated a samovar for us, but I said, 'Perhaps you have some vodka?' I'm not a drunkard but in business you sometimes have to drink. When the deal is finished, the buyer and the seller strike their palms together and have a drink. The landlady brought us a bottle and a bowl of pretzels. I asked the woman, 'Perhaps you want to taste some?' and she answered, 'Why not? I'm still able to enjoy life.' I poured a full glass for her and she tossed it off as if it were nothing at all. She didn't even take a pretzel afterwards. I saw that she could pour it down. When the landlady went to see a peasant about a cow, we were left alone. I took a glass, she took a glass. I don't get drunk quickly—I can pour down a large bottle and still stay sober. I was afraid she would get fuddled but she sat there and smiled, and we just became more cheerful and familiar. We talked like old cronies. She told me her name was Esther and she came from somewhere in Volhynia. 'What is a young woman doing alone in an inn?' I asked her.

" 'I'm waiting for a smuggler.'

" 'What do you need a smuggler for?' I asked, and she told me she was going to America. 'What's wrong with this country?'

"She told me she had had an affair and the man left her. She learned that he had a wife. He was traveling salesman, one of those skirt chasers who think tricking a woman is something to boast about. 'Well,' she said, 'I played and lost. I couldn't show my face at home any more.' It came out that she had had a husband and had divorced him. Her father was a pious man and it was below his dignity. In short, she had to leave. Some smuggler was going to lead her to the German border.

" 'What will you do in faraway America?' I said. And she answered, 'Sew blouses. If you do something silly, you have to pay for it.' I poured her a fourth glass, a fifth glass. She said, 'Why didn't I meet you before? A man like you would make a good husband for me.' 'It's never too late,' I said. Why should I drag it out? By the time the landlady came back from the peasant, everything was settled between us. I was drawn to her as to a magnet and she felt the same way. We held hands, kissed, and her kissing drove you crazy. She wasn't a female, she was a piece of fire. I didn't want the landlady to know what was going on and I went to sleep in my room, but I lay there in a fever. She slept right next door and I heard through the thin wall how she tossed on her bed. At dawn I fell asleep and in the morning I had to leave. We had already decided that she was going with me. The whole business of America was out. She didn't need a smuggler any more.

"I came out of my room and found my woman already packed and ready. She smiled at me and her eyes shone. When the landlady heard that she was going with me, she understood what had happened, but what did I care? My heart was with Esther. I took her in my sleigh and she sat near me on the driver's seat. She was afraid of falling and she held on to me and excited me all over again. Riding along, we decided to get married. We didn't need any special ceremonies. I was a widower and she a divorcée. We would go to Getzel, the assistant rabbi, and he would lead us under a canopy. I told her about the bird and she said, 'I will be a mother to him.' We spoke about him as though he would be our child."

"Did you really marry her?" Leibele asked.

"No."

"Why not?"

"Because she was divorced and I was Cohen. I had forgotten the law."

"Who reminded you? The assistant rabbi?"

"Who else?"

"What a story!"

4

"When Rabbi Getzel told me that we couldn't marry, I wanted to tear him to pieces, but was it his fault? I never went to pray except at Rosh Hashanah and Yom Kippur. Suddenly I was a Cohen, descended from a priestly line! I took Esther and went home with her. 'Let's pretend that I'm a Catholic priest and you're my housekeeper.' I lived far from the city and nobody would look through the keyhole. At first she was disappointed. What should she write to her family? But we were both so much in love that we could barely wait till night. Metzotze immediately became pals with her. The moment she entered, he perched on her shoulder and she kissed him on the beak and he kissed back. I said to her, 'He's our matchmaker,' and I told her the story of the gypsy and the rest of it.

"In the beginning everything went well. We lived like two doves. They gossiped about us in the city, but who cared? So what if Simon the horse dealer isn't pious? So they won't call me up to the reading of the scroll. Well, but Esther wanted a baby and that was bad. It would mean that the baby would be a bastard. Some student from the study house told me that such a baby is not exactly a bastard but is called by some other name. But it's bad just the same. Esther had written to her parents that she got married and they wanted to visit us. Now the complications began. I was satisfied to be alone with her. Esther and Metzotze were enough for me. But she only wanted to go to town. She asked me if I had friends, wanted to invite guests to show off her cooking and baking. Her cooking was fit for a king. She could bake a cake which you couldn't match in the best bakeries. She dressed nicely too, but for whom? In the fields she wore a corset. She tried to persuade me to go with her to America. I wish I had listened to her, but I had no desire to travel thousands of miles. I had a house, stables, grounds. If you have to sell all this, you get almost nothing in return. What could I do in America? Press pants? Besides, I was so attached to the bird that I couldn't leave him. And it's not so easy to drag a parrot over borders and oceans. I was attached to my mare too. And where could I leave her? She wasn't young any more and if she fell into the hands of a coachman he would whip her to pieces. I said to Esther, 'We love each other, let's live quietly. Who cares what people babble about?' But she was only drawn to people. She went to the city, made acquaintances, entangled herself with low characters and the devil knows what. I let her persuade me to invite a few horse dealers to a party, but in the years when I was a widower I had kept away from everybody and no one wanted to come to the suburbs. Those who came did us a great favor. After they left, Esther burst into tears and cried until daybreak.

"Why drag it out? We began to quarrel. I mean, she quarreled. She scolded, she cursed, she cried and screamed that I had trapped her. Why didn't I tell her I was a Cohen? I didn't remember that I was a Cohen any more than you remember what you ate in your mother's belly. She lay beside me at night and kept talking as though possessed by a dybbuk. One moment she laughed; the next moment she cried. She was putting on an act, but for whom? She talked to herself and did such strange things that you wouldn't believe it was the same Esther. She called me names that you don't hear in my part of the country. Suddenly she began to be hostile to the bird. He screamed too much, he dirtied the house, he didn't let her sleep at night. She was jealous too, complaining that I loved him more than I did her.

"When this began I knew that it would have a bad ending. Was it Metzotze's fault? He was as good as an angel. At night he was quiet, but in the morning a bird doesn't lie under a quilt and snore. A bird begins to sing at daybreak. Esther, however, went to sleep at two o'clock in the morning, and at eleven at night she might begin to wash her hair or bake a cake. I saw I was in a mess, but what could I do? One minute she was sane, the next minute crazy. There's a teahouse in Kalisch where all the scum gather together. She kept on dragging me there. I sat and drank tea while she made friends with all the roughnecks. She met some strange nobody and told him all our secrets. I must have been stronger than iron not to bury myself from shame. She could be clever, but when she wanted she could act like the worst fool. It was all from spite, but what did I do to deserve it? Another man in my place would take her by the hair and throw her out, but I get used to a person. Also, I have pity.

"I can tell you, it became worse from day to day. I never knew what Gehenna was, but I had Gehenna in my own house. She picked quarrels with the maid, the Gentile, and made her leave. I had never touched her, but Esther suspected the worst. She was only looking for excuses to make trouble. She also began to pick fights with the stable boy. For years both had worked for me with devotion. Now they had to run away, and in my business you need help. You can't do everything by yourself. Horses have to be scrubbed and groomed. There are imps that come into the stables at night. Don't laugh at me. I didn't believe it either until I saw it with my own eyes. I would buy a horse and put him in the stable. I'd come in the morning and he was bathed in sweat as though he had been driven all night long over hills and ditches. He was foaming at the mouth. I would look at the mane and it would be in pigtails. Who would come at night to braid pigtails on a horse? It happened not once but ten times. These imps can torture a horse to death. I had to go down at night and keep watch. But when the groom left, I had to do his work too. In short, it was bad. When I talked she flared up; when I was silent she complained that I ignored her. She was only looking for something to pick on. I couldn't write, and she tried to teach me. She gave me one lesson and that was it. We played cards just to kill time, but she cheated. Why did she have to cheat? I gave her enough money."

"For such a piece of merchandise there is only one remedy," said Leibele. "A good swat in the kisser."

"Just what I wanted to say," Mottele Roiskes chimed in.

"I tried that too. But I have a heavy hand and when I give a blow I can cripple someone. If I touched her I had to pay the doctor. She also threatened to denounce me. But what was there to denounce? I didn't make counterfeit money. She was far from religious, but if she felt like it she could become pious. To make a fire on the Sabbath was all right, but to pour out the slops was forbidden. She changed the rules whenever it suited her. The women in the city knew of my misfortune and laughed in my face.

"It happened two years ago in the winter. I don't know how it was here, but around Kalisch there were terrible frosts. Old men couldn't remember such cold, and heating the stoves didn't help. The wind blew and broke the trees. On my place, the wind tore off a piece of the fence. Usually it's warm in the stable, but I was afraid for my horses, for when a horse catches cold it's the end. To this day I don't remember what we quarreled about that evening, but then, when didn't we quarrel? It was one long war. Sometimes at night we made peace for a few minutes, but later we didn't even do this. She slept in the bed and I on a bench. When I had to get up, she went to sleep. I'm a light sleeper—it's easy to disturb me. She crept around, boiled tea, moved chairs; she began to say the Shema and suddenly she burst out laughing like mad. She wasn't mad—

she did it to spite me. She knew that I loved the parrot and she had it in for him. A parrot comes from a warm climate and if he catches a draft he's finished. But she opened the doors and let the wind blow in. He could have flown away, because he was an animal, not a man with understanding. I told her clearly, 'If anything happens to Metzotze, it's all over with you.' And she screamed, 'Go and marry him. A Cohen is allowed to marry a parrot.' I know now that it was all predestined. It's written on a man's palm or on his forehead: he will live this long; he will do this and that. But what did she have against me? I didn't stop her from going to America. I was even ready to pay her expenses.

"Where am I? Oh. Yes, I warned her, 'You can do with me whatever you want, but don't take it out on Metzotze.' Nonetheless, she screamed at him and scolded him as though he were a man. 'He's scabby, lousy, a demon's in him,' and so on. You know, a bird needs to have darkness at night. When a lamp is lit, he thinks it's day. She kept on lighting the candles, and the bird couldn't stand light at night and tucked his head under his wing. What does a bird need? A few grains of seed and a little sleep. How can a man torture a bird? One night I heard noises in the stable. I took my lantern and went to look at the horses. As I stepped over the threshold I somehow knew there would be misfortune."

For a while all was silent. Then Leibele asked, "What did she do? Chase out the parrot?"

The stranger began to murmur and to clear his throat. "Yes, in the middle of the night, in a burning frost."

"He wasn't found, huh?"

"He flew away."

"And you finished her, huh?"

The stranger paused.

"As I came back from the stable and I saw that the parrot wasn't there, I went over to her and said, 'Esther, it's your end.' I grabbed her by the hair, took her outside, and threw her into the well."

"She didn't fight back?"

"No, she went quietly."

"Still, one has to be a murderer to do something like that," Mottele Roiskes remarked.

"I am a murderer."

"What else?"

"Nothing. I went to the police and said, 'This is what I did. Take me.'"

"In the middle of the night?"

"It was already beginning to get light."

"Did they let you go to the funeral?"

"No funeral."

"They say that a Cohen is an angry man," Berele Zakelkover threw in.

"It looks that way."

"How much did they give you?"

"Eight years."

"Well, you got off easy."

"I'll never get out," the stranger said.

For a long while all were quiet. Then the stranger said, "Metzotze is still around."

"What do you mean?"

"You'll think I'm crazy, but what do I care?"

"What do you mean, around?"

"He comes to me. He perches on my shoulder."

"Are you dreaming?"

"No, it's the truth."

"You imagine it."

"He speaks. I hear his voice."

"In that case you're a little touched."

"He sleeps on my forehead."

"Well, you're out of your mind."

"A parrot has a soul."

"Nonsense," Leibele said. "If a parrot has a soul, so has a chicken. If all the chickens, geese, and ducks had souls, the world would be full of souls."

"All I know is that Metzotze visits me."

"It's because you miss him so much."

"He comes, he kisses me on the mouth. He flutters his tail against my ear."

"Will he come here too?"

"Perhaps."

"And how will he know that they sent you to Yanev?"

"He knows everything."

"Nonsense. Tell it to the doctor. They'll send you to the nuthouse. It's easy to run away from there. What about Esther? Does she visit you too?"

"No, she doesn't."

"Fantasies. The dead are dead. Men as well as animals."

The stranger stretched out on the bench again. "I know the truth."

Translated by Ruth Whitman

The Brooch

WHEN Wolf Ber returned from the road, he always bought gifts for Celia and the girls. This time Wolf Ber had been in luck. He had broken into a safe and stolen 740 rubles. In addition, traveling on the railroad second-class, he had met a wealthy Russian and had won 150 rubles from him in a card game. Wolf Ber had long ago reached the conclusion that everything depended on fate: sometimes everything goes wrong; sometimes it doesn't. This particular trip had started right immediately. Just for fun he had tried to pick a pocket (a safecracker is not a pickpocket) and pulled out a purse full of bank notes. Then he had gone to a Turkish bath, and there he found a gold watch! After such "business" he always gave thanks to God and dropped a coin in the poor box. Wolf Ber did not belong to a gang and he conducted himself respectably. He knew that thieving was a sin. But were the merchants any better? Didn't they buy cheap and sell dear? Didn't they bleed the poor dry? Didn't they, every few years, go bankrupt and settle for a fraction? Wolf Ber had once worked as a tanner in Lublin. But he had been unable to stand the dust, the heat, the stench. The foreman had yelled at the tanners and was forever trying to get more work out of them. The earnings had amounted to no more than water for groats. It was better to rot in prison.

Wolf Ber had long since gotten used to earning his living as a thief. He had been caught a few times but had been let off easily. He knew how to speak to the *natchalniks*: Sir . . . I have a wife and children! He never talked back and did not try to play tough. In jail, far from fighting with the other prisoners, he shared his money and cigarettes with them and wrote letters for them. Wolf Ber came from a respectable home. His father, a pious man, had been a house painter. His mother had peddled tripe and calves' legs. He, Wolf Ber, was the only member of the family to become a thief. Already near forty, Wolf Ber was of medium height, with broad shoulders, brown eyes, and a beer-yellow mustache twisted in the Polish way. He wore riding pants, and boots with tight uppers that made him look like a Gentile; the Poles believed a Jew could not get his feet into such boots, because Jewish feet grew always wider and never longer. Wolf Ber's cap had a leather visor. Over his vest a watch chain dangled, with a little spoon to clean out ear wax attached to it. Other thieves carried guns or spring-knives, but Wolf Ber never had any weapons on his person. A gun will sooner or later shoot; a knife will sooner or later stab. And why shed blood? Why take upon oneself a severe punishment? Wolf Ber was a self-controlled and careful man; he was inclined to think about things and liked to read storybooks and even newspapers. Women were always trying to entice him with their charms. But Wolf Ber had one God and one wife. What could he find in others that Celia did not have? Loose females disgusted him. He never stepped over the threshold of a brothel and he detested liquor. He had a faithful wife and two well-brought-up children. He had a house and garden in Kozlow. His girls went to school. On Purim, Wolf Ber sent the rabbi a gift. Before Passover the community elders came to him to collect for the poor.

Coming home this time, Wolf Ber had bought a pair of gold earrings for Celia from a jeweler in Lublin, and for his daughters, Masha and Anka, two medallions. Until Reivitz, the last station, he had traveled by train; then he had taken a carriage wagon, sitting up front with the driver and helping him drive. Wolf Ber had no patience with the sort of jokes and puns that the businessmen riding inside exchanged with the women. They always tried to make Wolf Ber join in the conversation but he preferred to look in silence at the trees and sky and to listen to the twittering birds. The snow was melting in the fields; the winter grain was sprouting; the sun hung low, yellow and golden, as if painted on a canvas. Now and again he saw cows nibbling fresh grass in their pastures. Warm breezes drifted over from the woods as if a summer land were hidden in the thickets. Once in a while a hare or a deer peeked out at the edge of the forest; or a turtle moved slowly across the road like a living stone.

As a rule, Wolf Ber set out from home four times a year. When things went smoothly, he never stayed away longer than six weeks. He went to the same towns, the same fairs. In Kozlow they knew what Wolf Ber did for a living—but he never stole from anyone there; and in his absence Celia could always get credit at the stores. All such debts were entered in a book, and when Wolf Ber returned he paid them to the last grosz. Once Wolf Ber had been imprisoned for several months in the Yanow jail, but the Kozlow merchants did not let Celia down. They advanced her goods for hundred of rubles. Many times Celia complained to Wolf Ber that the shopkeepers had given her false weight or short measure or had padded the bill, but he refused to argue. That was how the world was.

As always, Wolf Ber came back to Kozlow longing for Celia and the girls, looking forward to Celia's dishes, which he could not get on the road, and to the soft bed, better than at any inn. Celia's pillowcases and sheets, luxuriously clean, were as smooth as silk and smelled of lavender. Celia always came to him in the bedroom freshly washed and combed, with her hair braided, her feet in slippers with pompoms, and dressed in a fancy nightgown. She kissed him like a bride and murmured sweet secrets into his ear. The girls were growing up: one was ten; the other, eleven. Yet, like small children, they fell all over him, covered him with kisses, showed him their schoolbooks, their compositions, their marks, their drawings. His children were dressed like those of the gentry, in starched and pleated dresses, with alpaca aprons, hair ribbons, and shiny shoes. They spoke not only Yiddish but Russian and Polish too. They talked about foreign countries and cities of which Wolf Ber had never heard; they were versed in the histories of kings and wars and could recite by heart poems and rhymes. Wolf Ber never stopped wondering how so much knowledge could enter into such small heads. Their father's occupation was never mentioned. He was supposed to be a traveling salesman. His house stood on Church Street near the toll bridge. The Gentile neighbors did not know what he did, or perhaps only professed not to. On Christmas and Easter he would send them gifts.

The carriage wagon bringing Wolf Ber home stopped in the marketplace. Although it was not long after Purim, the sun already had a touch of Passover warmth. Golden rivulets trickled in the mud. Birds picked grain from horse dung. Peasant women, wading barefoot through the puddles, were selling horseradish, parsley, beets, and onions. Wolf Ber paid the coachman and, in the big-city manner, added twenty groszy "for beer." Lifting up his leather valise with its copper locks and sidepockets, he began to walk toward Church Street. The storekeepers followed him with their eyes. Girls parted their window curtains, wiping the mist off the glass. From somewhere Chazkele the fool emerged and Wolf Ber handed him some coins. Even the dogs around the butcher shop wagged their tails.

Thank God! Wolf Ber was going to be home for Passover. Celia would prepare a Seder; he would drain the four goblets, eat matzo pancakes, matzo balls, and gefilte fish. Since he had brought home a large sum of money, he would dress up the whole family. With such a trade as his, it was best to spend the money at once. Wolf Ber was suddenly aware of a familiar smell. He was passing a matzo bakery and stopped to look in the window. Women with flushed faces, wearing white aprons and kerchiefs on their heads, were rolling out the matzos, stopping frequently to scrape their rolling pins with pieces of glass. One woman was pouring water; another was kneading the dough; a third perforated the matzos with a pointed stick. At the oven a man was shoveling out those already baked. Near him another man with sidelocks and a skullcap gesticulated and grimaced—the overseer. Wolf Ber suddenly remembered his parents. Where were they now? Most probably in paradise. True, their son had not chosen the righteous way, but he had put up a headstone over their graves. Every year he lit a memorial candle, recited the Kaddish, and hired a man to study the Mishnah in their memory. God was merciful to sinners. If not, He would have sent down a second deluge long ago.

2

When Wolf Ber entered Church Street, where he lived, a sudden fear came over him. A power that knows more than man seemed to be warning him against too much exuberance. Inside him, a voice seemed to say: It's not yet Passover; you are not yet at the Seder. Wolf Ber halted. Was Celia ill? Had something happened to the children? Was he, Wolf Ber, destined to end up in prison? But how? He never left any traces. Trying to dispel the premonition, he began to walk briskly between the two rows of houses, built low as for midgets and closed in with spiked fences. Through the half-melted snow pocked with holes like a sieve, the stems of last year's sunflowers stuck out. On Marchinsky's roof the storks had already returned and were mending last year's nest. Wolf Ber soon approached his own house, which had a roof shaped like a mushroom. White smoke was curling from the chimney. One pane in the front window reflected the midday sun. Well, everything is all right, Wolf Ber comforted himself. He opened the door and there was the whole family. Celia was standing at the kitchen stove in a short underskirt, her blond hair brushed up with a knot on top, her face white and girlish, her waist cinched in; she was wearing a pair of red slippers, and her legs, broad at the calf, were narrow at the ankle. She had never looked so fresh and charming to him. The girls were sitting on stools, playing some game with bonesticks.

There was an outcry as they all ran toward him. Celia almost tipped over the pot on the stove. The girls hung on him, covering him with kisses. In the next room the parrot, apparently recognizing his master's voice, began to shriek. The moment Wolf Ber touched Celia's lips, he was full of desire. He kissed her again and again. Masha and Anka fought over him. After a while he opened his valise to take out the gifts, and that set off another outcry. When Wolf Ber went to greet the parrot, the bird, which was perched on one foot on the top of its cage, flapped its wings and landed on his shoulder. Wolf Ber kissed the bird's beak and let it taste a pretzel which he had bought for it in Lublin. The parrot had lost its winter feathers and had sprouted brightly colored new ones.

The parrot spoke. "Papa, Papa, Papa."

"Do you love Papa?"

"Love, love, love."

Well, there was no reason for fear. Wolf Ber examined the house with an expert eye. Everything gleamed: the floor, the copper pans above the oven, the brass samovar. It was the custom to whitewash the walls every year before Passover, but he could see no blemishes. "There is no better wife anywhere in the world," Wolf Ber said aloud. Earlier in the day, sitting on the wagon, he had felt tired and barely able to keep his eyes open, but now he was wide awake and gay. Celia brought him a Sabbath cookie and a glass of Vishniak.

When they had been alone in the room for a while, Celia questioned him with a glint in her eye. "How was business?"

"As long as I have you, everything goes well," Wolf Ber answered, ashamed of his profession. As a rule, Celia asked nothing about what he had done while away and he seldom told her anything. But now it seemed she had made peace with his way of making a living. Presently Wolf Ber started to talk about new clothes for her and the girls. Celia doubted that any tailor would accept new orders so near Passover. Nevertheless, they decided that she would walk over to the dry-goods stores and select materials. Celia loved to shop. Wolf Ber handed her a wad of bills and she left, taking the children with her. While shopping, she would also pay up her accounts. Wolf Ber lay down on the sofa to get some sleep. He knew Celia would prepare a rich supper and he wanted to be rested. He dozed off immediately and dreamed that he was in Lublin. He stood in an alcove somewhere, half undressed, washing himself from a trough; his body gave off a bad smell. He was again a tanner. A door opened and a woman in a disheveled wig, with a dirty face, looked in and spoke angrily to him: "How long are you going to wash yourself? It's time for the Seder." Wolf Ber woke with a start. What kind of a dream was that? There was a bitter taste in his mouth. The dream had been unusually vivid. In his nostrils he could still feel the stench of rawhide. Wolf Ber reached into his breast pocket to take out the Havana cigar which had been presented to him by the Russian from whom he had won 150 rubles. Wolf Ber never smoked cigars; he rolled his own cigarettes. But he was curious now to taste a cigar that cost half a ruble. He remembered that he had once had an amber cigar holder trimmed with gold. If he was going to smoke a Havana, he might as well do it in style.

Wolf Ber got up to hunt for the cigar holder but couldn't find it. He hated to lose things. He opened all the drawers, rummaged in nooks and crannies, and searched through the oaken chest. In a drawer in the linen closet there was a tin box where Wolf Ber kept the birth certificates, the marriage contract, the mortgage papers, and other valuable documents which were seldom looked at. It was improbable that the cigar holder would be there, but Wolf Ber opened the tin box just the same. The cigar holder was not there, but on the marriage contract lay a brooch with big diamonds. Wolf Ber was stunned. What was this? He knew jewelry. These were real diamonds, not imitations. The brooch looked like an antique. The longer Wolf Ber examined it, the more his amazement grew. How did this brooch come to be here? It was neither his nor Celia's. Could Celia have saved up a nest egg and bought herself a brooch for hundreds of rubles? But such a piece could not be bought in Kozlow! Wolf Ber examined the brooch carefully and found on the reverse side two engraved letters: an aleph and a gimel. After a time he put the brooch in his inner pocket. He became depressed. He returned to the sofa and closed his eyes, trying to solve the riddle, but no matter how he racked his brain, he could find no answer. Finally he dozed off again and once more he was washing himself in that alcove in Lublin. Once more it smelled of rawhide and of chemicals used in tanneries. The disheveled woman with the wrinkled face warned him again that he would be late for the Seder. Wolf Ber woke up. What explanation could there be? Did Celia have a lover who had given her the brooch as a present? Wolf Ber felt a bitterness on his palate. He hiccuped and an unsavory taste came up from his stomach. He spat into his handkerchief. Well, there must be some answer. And what did the letters aleph and gimel mean? Was there a Jew in Kozlow who would have an affair with a married woman? And was Celia likely to do anything like that? The longer Wolf Ber pondered, the stranger the whole thing seemed to him. He paced the room. He spoke to the parrot: "You know the truth. Speak up!"

"Papa, Papa, Papa! Love, love love!"

Dusk fell. The windowpanes turned green. Purple reflections from the sunset trembled on the wall. The parrot entered its cage, ready for the night. Wolf Ber lit the Havana cigar and sat in the dark, inhaling deeply. The outlandish aroma made him drunk. Again and again he put his hand into his inner pocket and touched the brooch. Whenever he heard a noise outside, he listened intently. Where was his wife? Why was she taking so long? He decided not to get into any argument so long as the children were up. After a while he heard steps and voices. Celia was back. She and the girls, all three carrying packages, burst in gaily.

Celia spoke happily. "Wolf Ber, are you here? Why are you sitting in the dark? What's that you're smoking—a cigar?"

"A Russian gave it to me on the train."

"The smell makes me dizzy. We've bought out the store. Just a minute. I'll light the lamp."

"I had an amber cigar holder once. Where is it?"

"Where is it? I don't know."

The girls pranced about with the packages in their arms. Celia lit the table lamp first and then a hanging lamp that was suspended from the ceiling on bronze chains and had a gourd filled with lead pellets attached to keep it in balance. Celia had bought yards and yards of all kinds of materials, silks, woolens, velvet, and she had already had a talk with Leizer the tailor, who had promised to finish a few dresses before Passover. Now, with housewifely dispatch, she began to prepare supper. Usually the children went to bed early, but the day their father came home was a holiday. Celia had already promised them they would not have to go to school tomorrow.

3

Wolf Ber sat at the table, praised Celia's dishes, and joked with the children, but he was not as jolly as he had been earlier. He hurried through his dinner, didn't eat much, and from time to time looked sharply at Celia. Immediately after the tea and jam and honey-cake, he urged the girls to go to bed. They protested that they hadn't celebrated their father's home-coming enough. They wanted to show him their books, their maps, their drawings. But Wolf Ber insisted that all this could wait until tomorrow and that children should not sit up till all hours of the night.

After some haggling and delaying, the girls said good night. Celia had seemed to side with him, but at the same time she smiled knowingly. Apparently he was in a rush to be with her. You are eager, eh? her look seemed to ask. Wolf Ber went into the bedroom and undressed. His boots with the stiff uppers stood by the bed in soldierly fashion. He sat down on the freshly made bed. Celia was in the kitchen combing her hair and washing herself as she always did before coming to her husband. She donned a fresh nightgown, sprinkled herself with lotion, and brushed her teeth with paste the way they did in the big cities. Glancing at her image in the mirror, she thought: He will certainly not poison himself with me. . . . Celia expected Wolf Ber to extinguish the lamp immediately and make love to her, but he remained sitting up in his bed and looked at her sideways.

"Be so good as to close the door."

"Has something happened?"

"Close the door."

"It's closed."

Wolf Ber brought out the brooch from under his pillow. "Where did you get this?"

Celia lifted her eyes and her expression changed. She looked at the brooch, her face astonished, grave. "I've had it for a long time."

"How long?"

"A few years."

"Where did you get it?"

Celia did not answer immediately. Finally she raised her eyebrows. "I found it," she replied in the tone of one who does not expect to be believed.

"You found it? Where?"

"In the women's section of the synagogue."

"How often do you go to the synagogue?"

"It was Rosh Hashanah."

"And you didn't ask who'd lost it?"

"No."

"How is it you've never told me?" Wolf Ber asked after a pause.

Celia shook her head. "I don't have to tell you everything."

Man and wife spoke in low voices since the girls were not yet asleep. Wolf Ber thought it over. "Two letters are engraved on the back, an aleph and a gimel."

"Yes."

"Whose is it?"

Celia was silent. She turned to the door and made sure it was firmly shut. She moved as though she were trying to block the sounds of their conversation with her person, to keep them from reaching the children. For the first time Wolf Ber saw signs of insolence in her eyes.

"After all, you are not an investigating attorney!"

"Whose is it?" Wolf Ber raised his voice.

"Don't shout. Alte Gitel's."

In one second Wolf Ber knew everything. He remembered it all. "Alte Gitel lost her brooch at Hanukkah—not Rosh Hashanah. The whole town was in an uproar."

"Have it your way."

"How did you get it?"

"I found it."

"Where?"

"In the street."

"A minute ago you said you found it in the synagogue."

"What if I did?"

"Alte Gitel lost her brooch at Deborah Lea's wedding." Wolf Ber spoke half to Celia, half to himself. "You were there. . . . You even told me everyone was searched. . . . I remember your telling me. . . . Well, where did you hide it?"

Celia laughed shortly. "See how he interrogates me! One would think he was a saint!"

"You are a thief, aren't you?"

"If you are, why shouldn't I be?" Celia spoke rapidly and in whispers. "Why all the fuss? The whole town knows what you do. Our children are taunted. The teachers make fun of them. If a girl loses something at school, it's our Masha and Anka who are suspected. I haven't told you all this because I didn't want to hurt you, but I'm disgraced ten times a day. So now why do you suddenly play the honest man? If I were a holy woman I would never have become your wife. That's plain enough."

"You did steal it, didn't you?"

"Yes, I stole it."

And Celia's eyes turned to him with a mixture of laughter and fear.

"How did you do it?"

"I took it off her cape—when the jester was reciting. I don't know myself why I did it. It's lain around here for years. Why were you going through my drawers?"

"I was hunting for my cigar holder."

"Your cigar holder I didn't take."

It became quiet. Wolf Ber sat up straight in his bed, his face stern, stiff. It was not that he was angry, but a sadness had come over him, as if he had heard belated news of a near relative's death. All these years he had thought Celia an honest woman and had reproached himself for bringing shame to the daughter of a good house. Occasionally she had complained about the bitter way of making a living he had chosen, telling him how the townspeople ignored her, reminding him how important it was for their children to grow up decent and with a good education. Then, when he had been arrested a few years ago in Yanow and had been in danger of a severe sentence, it was Celia who had come to Yanow and gotten him released. She had told him how she had thrown herself at the district attorney's feet, crying and pleading until he finally stopped her: "Get up, my beauty, I can't bear to see your tears any longer." It had never occurred to Wolf Ber before that perhaps this story was not the whole truth. Many times in the big cities women of dubious character had tried to entangle him, but he had always answered that he had a faithful wife in Kozlow, a fine woman who was a devoted mother of their children. He had risked his freedom so that she should want for nothing. He had even denied himself the more expensive restaurants and theaters. Now it was all for nothing. Something within him laughed: You are a fool, Wolf Ber, a damned fool! He felt nauseous and as though in these last few minutes old age had overtaken him.

He heard Celia's voice. "Shall I put out the lamp?"

"If you want to."

Celia blew out the night lamp and went to her bed. For a long time there was silence. Wolf Ber listened to himself. An icy coldness enveloped him, like a cold poultice around his chest.

"Did you sleep with the district attorney?"

"I don't know what you're talking about."

"You know very well!"

"You must have lost your mind."

Wolf Ber stretched out, closed his eyes, and lay silently on the cool sheet. In the other room the girls still whispered and giggled. An early spring breeze was blowing outside and it shook the shutters. Beams of moonlight sifted in through the cracks. From time to time Celia's bed creaked. Wolf Ber had come home full of lust for Celia, but now all desire had left him. Everything is finished, he said to himself. The seven good years are over. Something in him mourned. Who could tell— perhaps the children were not his own? There was no more point to dragging himself about on trains, sleeping in cheap hostelries, endangering his life at fairs. If she is a thief, I must become an honest man, he murmured. There is no place in the family for two thieves!

Wolf Ber was himself baffled at this queer idea. Nevertheless, he knew there was no other way. For some time he lay quietly and listened in the dark. Then he put his feet down on the floor.

"Where are you going?"

"To Lublin."

"In the middle of the night?"

"In the middle of the night."

"What are you going to do in Lublin?" Celia asked.

And Wolf Ber answered: "Become a tanner."

Translated by Alma Singer and Elizabeth Pollet

The Letter Writer

HERMAN GOMBINER opened an eye. This was the way he woke up each morning—gradually, first with one eye, then the other. His glance met a cracked ceiling and part of the building across the street. He had gone to bed in the early hours, at about three. It had taken him a long time to fall asleep. Now it was close to ten o'clock. Lately, Herman Gombiner had been suffering from a kind of amnesia. When he got up during the night, he couldn't remember where he was, who he was, or even his name. It took a few seconds to realize that he was no longer in Kalomin, or in Warsaw, but in New York, uptown on one of the streets between Columbus Avenue and Central Park West.

It was winter. Steam hissed in the radiator. The Second World War was long since over. Herman (or Hayim David, as he was called in Kalomin) had lost his family to the Nazis. He was now an editor, proofreader, and translator in a Hebrew publishing house called Zion. It was situated on Canal Street. He was a bachelor, almost fifty years old, and a sick man.

"What time is it?" he mumbled. His tongue was coated, his lips cracked. His knees ached; his head pounded; there was a bitter taste in his mouth. With an effort he got up, setting his feet down on the worn carpet that covered the floor. "What's this? Snow?" he muttered. "Well, it's winter."

He stood at the window awhile and looked out. The broken-down cars parked on the street jutted from the snow like relics of a long-lost civilization. Usually the street was filled with rubbish, noise, and children—Negro and Puerto Rican. But now the cold kept everyone indoors. The stillness, the whiteness made him think of his old home, of Kalomin. Herman stumbled toward the bathroom.

The bedroom was an alcove, with space only for a bed. The living room was full of books. On one wall there were cabinets from floor to ceiling, and along the other stood two bookcases. Books, newspapers, and magazines lay everywhere, piled in stacks. According to the lease, the landlord was obliged to paint the apartment every three years, but Herman Gombiner had bribed the superintendent to leave him alone. Many of his old books would fall apart if they were moved. Why is new paint better than old? The dust had gathered in layers. A single mouse had found its way into the apartment, and every night Herman set out for her a piece of bread, a small slice of cheese, and a saucer of water to keep her from eating the books. Thank goodness she didn't give birth. Occasionally, she would venture out of her hole even when the light was on. Herman had even given her a Hebrew name: Huldah. Her little bubble eyes stared at him with curiosity. She stopped being afraid of him.

The building in which Herman lived had many faults, but it did not lack heat. The radiators sizzled from early morning till late at night. The owner, himself a Puerto Rican, would never allow his tenants' children to suffer from the cold.

There was no shower in the bathroom, and Herman bathed daily in the tub. A mirror that was cracked down the middle hung inside the door, and Herman caught a glimpse of himself—a short man, in oversize pajamas, emaciated to skin and bone, with a scrawny neck and a large head, on either side of which grew two tufts of gray hair. His forehead was wide and deep, his nose crooked, his cheekbones high. Only in his dark eyes, with long lashes like a girl's, had there remained any trace of youthfulness. At times, they even seemed to twinkle shrewdly. Many years of reading and poring over tiny letters hadn't blurred his vision or made him nearsighted. The remaining strength in Herman Gombiner's body—a body worn out by illnesses and undernourishment—seemed to be concentrated in his gaze.

He shaved slowly and carefully. His hand, with its long fingers, trembled, and he could easily have cut himself. Meanwhile, the tub filled with warm water. He undressed, and was amazed at his thinness—his chest was narrow, his arms and legs bony; there were deep hollows between his neck and shoulders. Getting into the bathtub was a strain, but then lying in the warm water was a relief. Herman always lost the soap. It would slip out of his hands playfully, like a live thing, and he would search for it in the water. "Where are you running?" he would say to it. "You rascal!" He believed there was life in everything, that the so-called inanimate objects had their own whims and caprices.

Herman Gombiner considered himself to be among the select few privileged to see beyond the façade of phenomena. He had seen a blotter raise itself from the desk, slowly and unsteadily float toward the door, and, once there, float gently down, as if suspended by an invisible string held by some unseen hand. The whole thing had been thoroughly senseless. No matter how much Herman thought about it, he was unable to figure out any reason for what had taken place. It had been one of those extraordinary happenings that cannot be explained by science, or religion, or folklore. Later, Herman had bent down and picked up the blotter, and placed it back on the desk, where it remained to this day, covered with papers, dusty, and dried out—an inanimate object that for one moment had somehow freed itself from physical laws. Herman Gombiner knew that it had been neither a hallucination nor a dream. It had taken place in a well-lit room at eight in the evening. He hadn't been ill or even upset that day. He never drank liquor, and he had been wide awake. He had been standing next to the chest, about to take a handkerchief out of a drawer. Suddenly his gaze had been attracted to the desk and he had seen the blotter rise and float. Nor was this the only such incident. Such things had been happening to him since childhood.

Everything took a long time—his bath, drying himself, putting on his clothes. Hurrying was not for him. His competence was the result of deliberateness. The proofreaders at Zion worked so quickly they missed errors. The translators hardly took the time to check meanings they were unsure of in the dictionary. The majority of American and even Israeli Hebraists knew little of vowel points and the subtleties of grammar. Herman Gombiner had found the time to study all these things. It was true that he worked very slowly, but the old man, Morris Korver, who owned Zion, and even his sons, the half Gentiles, had always appreciated the fact that it was Herman Gombiner who had earned the house its reputation. Morris Korver, however, had become old and senile, and Zion was in danger of closing. It was rumored that his sons could hardly wait for the old man to die so they could liquidate the business.

Even if Herman wanted to, it was impossible for him to do anything in a hurry. He took small steps when he walked. It took him half an hour to eat a bowl of soup. Searching for the right word in a dictionary or checking something in an ency-clopedia could involve hours of work. The few times that he had tried to hurry had ended in disaster; he had broken his foot, sprained his hand, fallen down the stairs, even been run over. Every trifle had become a trial to him—shaving, dressing, taking the wash to the Chinese laundry, eating a meal in a restaurant. Crossing the street, too, was a problem, because no sooner would the light turn green than it turned red again. Those behind the wheels of cars possessed the speed and morals of automatons. If a person couldn't run fast enough, they were capable of driving right over him. Recently, he had begun to suffer from tremors of the hands and feet. He had once had a meticulous handwriting, but he could no longer write. He used a typewriter, typing with his right index finger. Old Korver insisted that all Gombiner's troubles came from the fact that he was a vegetarian; without a piece of meat, one loses strength. Herman couldn't take a bite of meat if his life depended on it.

Herman put one sock on and rested. He put on the second sock, and rested again. His pulse rate was slow—fifty or so beats a minute. The least strain and he felt dizzy. His soul barely survived in his body. It had happened on occasion, as he lay in bed or sat on a chair, that his disembodied spirit had wandered around the house, or had even gone out the win-dow. He had seen his own body in a faint, apparently dead. Who could enumerate all the apparitions, telepathic incidents, clairvoyant visions, and prophetic dreams he experienced! And who would believe him? As it was, his co-workers derided him. The elder Korver needed only a glass of brandy and he would call Herman a superstitious greenhorn. They treated him like some outlandish character.

Herman Gombiner had long ago arrived at the conclusion that modern man was as fanatic in his non-belief as ancient man had been in his faith. The rationalism of the present generation was in itself an example of preconceived ideas.

Communism, psychoanalysis, Fascism, and radicalism were the shibboleths of the twentieth century. Oh, well! What could he, Herman Gombiner, do in the face of all this? He had no choice but to observe and be silent.

"Well, it's winter, winter!" Herman Gombiner said to himself in a voice half chanting, half groaning. "When will it be Hanukkah? Winter has started early this year." Herman was in the habit of talking to himself. He had always done so. The uncle who raised him had been deaf. His grandmother, rest her soul, would wake up in the middle of the night to recite penitential prayers and lamentations found only in outdated prayer books. His father had died before Herman—Hayim David—was born. His mother had remarried in a faraway city and had had children by her second husband. Hayim David had always kept to himself, even when he attended heder or studied at the yeshiva. Now, since Hitler had killed all of his family, he had no relatives to write letters to. He wrote letters to total strangers.

"What time is it?" Herman asked himself again. He dressed in a dark suit, a white shirt, and a black tie, and went out to the kitchenette. An icebox without ice and a stove that he never used stood there. Twice a week the milkman left a bottle of milk at the door. Herman had a few cans of vegetables, which he ate on days when he didn't leave the house. He had discovered that a human being requires very little. A half cup of milk and a pretzel could suffice for a whole day. One pair of shoes served Herman for five years. His suit, coat, and hat never wore out. Only his laundry showed some wear, and not from use but from the chemicals used by the Chinese laundryman. The furniture certainly never wore out. Where it not for his expenditures on cabs and gifts, he could have saved a good deal of money.

He drank a glass of milk and ate a biscuit. Then he carefully put on his black coat, a woolen scarf, rubbers, and a felt hat with a broad brim. He packed his briefcase with books and manuscripts. It became heavier from day to day, not because there was more in it but because his strength diminished. He slipped on a pair of dark glasses to protect his eyes from the glare of the snow. Before he left the apartment, he bade farewell to the bed, the desk piled high with papers (under which the blotter lay), the books, and the mouse in the hole. He had poured out yesterday's stale water, refilled the saucer, and set out a cracker and a small piece of cheese. "Well, Huldah, be well!"

Radios blared in the hallway. Dark-skinned women with uncombed hair and angry eyes spoke in an unusually thick Spanish. Children ran around half naked. The men were apparently all unemployed. They paced idly about in their overcrowded quarters, ate standing up, or strummed mandolins. The odors from the apartments made Herman feel faint. All kinds of meat and fish were fried there. The halls reeked of garlic, onion, smoke, and something pungent and nauseating. At night his neighbors danced and laughed wantonly. Sometimes there was fighting and women screamed for help. Once a woman had come pounding on Herman's door in the middle of the night, seeking protection from a man who was trying to stab her.

2

Herman stopped downstairs at the mailboxes. The other residents seldom received any mail, but Herman Gombiner's box was packed tight every morning. He took his key out, fingers trembling, inserted it in the keyhole, and pulled out the mail. He was able to recognize who had sent the letters by their envelopes. Alice Grayson, of Salt Lake City, used a rose-colored envelope. Mrs. Roberta Hoff, of Pasadena, California, sent all her mail in the business envelopes of the undertaking establishment for which she worked. Miss Bertha Gordon, of Fairbanks, Alaska, apparently had many leftover Christmas-card envelopes. Today Herman found a letter from a new correspondent, a Mrs. Rose Beechman, of Louisville, Kentucky. Her name and address were hand-printed, with flourishes, across the back of the envelope. Besides the letters, there were several magazines on occultism to which Herman Gombiner subscribed—from America, England, and even Australia. There wasn't room in his briefcase for all these letters and periodicals, so Herman stuffed them into his coat pocket. He went outside and waited for a taxi.

It was rare for a taxi, particularly an empty one, to drive down this street, but it was too much of an effort for him to walk the half block to Central Park West or Columbus Avenue. Herman Gombiner fought his weakness with prayer and auto-suggestion. Standing in the snow, he muttered a prayer for a taxi. He repeatedly put his hand into his pocket and fingered the letters in their envelopes. These letters and magazines had become the essence of his life. Through them he had established contact with souls. He had acquired the friendship and even the love of women. The accounts he received from them strengthened his belief in psychic powers and in the world beyond. He sent gifts to his unknown correspondents and received gifts from them. They called him by his first name, revealed their thoughts, dreams, hopes, and the messages they received through the Ouija board, automatic writing, table turning, and other supernatural sources.

Herman Gombiner had established correspondences with these women through the periodicals he subscribed to, where not only accounts of readers' experiences were published but their contributors' names and addresses as well. The articles were mainly written by women. Herman Gombiner always selected those who lived far away. He wished to avoid meetings. He could sense from the way an experience was related, from a name or an address, whether the woman would be capable of carrying on a correspondence. He was almost never wrong. A small note from him would call forth a long letter in reply. Sometimes he received entire manuscripts. His correspondence had grown so large that postage cost him several dollars a week. Many of his letters were sent out special delivery or registered.

Miracles were a daily occurrence. No sooner had he finished his prayer than a taxi appeared. The driver pulled up to the house as if he had received a telepathic command. Getting into the taxi exhausted Herman, and he sat a long while resting his head against the window with his eyes shut, praising whatever Power had heard his supplication. One had to be blind not to acknowledge the hand of Providence, or whatever you wanted to call it. Someone was concerned with man's most trivial requirements.

His disembodied spirit apparently roamed to the most distant places. All his correspondents had seen him. In one night he had been in Los Angeles and in Mexico City, in Oregon and in Scotland. It would come to him that one of his faraway friends was ill. Before long, he would receive a letter saying that she had indeed been ill and hospitalized. Over the years, several had died, and he had had a premonition each time.

For the past few weeks, Herman had had a strong feeling that Zion was going to close down. True, this had been predicted for years, but Herman had always known that it was only a rumor. And just recently the employees had become optimistic; business had improved. The old man talked of a deficit, but everybody knew he was lying in order to avoid raising salaries. The house had published a prayer book that was a best-seller. The new Hebrew-English dictionary that Herman Gombiner was completing had every chance of selling tens of thousands of copies. Nevertheless, Herman sensed a calamity just as surely as his rheumatic knees foretold a change in the weather.

The taxi drove down Columbus Avenue. Herman glanced out the window and closed his eyes again. What is there to see on a wintry day in New York? He remained wrapped up in his gloom. No matter how many sweaters he put on, he was always cold. Besides, one is less aware of the spirits, the psychic contacts, during the cold weather. Herman raised his collar higher and put his hands in his pockets. A violent kind of civilization developed in cold countries. He should never have settled in New York. If he were living in southern California, he wouldn't be enslaved by the weather in this way. Oh, well . . . And was there a Jewish publishing house to be found in southern California?

3

The taxi stopped on Canal Street. Herman paid his fare and added a fifty-cent tip. He was frugal with himself, but when it came to cabdrivers, waiters, and elevator men, he was generous. At Christmastime he even bought gifts for his Puerto Rican neighbors. Today Sam, the elevator man, was apparently having a cup of coffee in the cafeteria across the street, and Herman had to wait. Sam did as he pleased. He came from the same city as Morris Korver. He was the only elevator man, so that when he didn't feel like coming in the tenants had to climb the stairs. He was a Communist besides.

Herman waited ten minutes before Sam arrived—a short man, broad-backed, with a face that looked as if it had been put together out of assorted pieces: a short forehead, thick brows, bulging eyes with big bags beneath them, and a bulbous nose covered with cherry-red moles. His walk was unsteady. Herman greeted him, but he grumbled in answer. The Yiddish leftist paper stuck out of his back pocket. He didn't shut the elevator door at once. First he coughed several times, then lit a cigar. Suddenly he spat and called out, "You've heard the news?"

"What's happened?"

"They've sold the building."

"Aha, so that's it!" Herman said to himself. "Sold? How come?" he asked.

"How come? Because the old wise guy is senile and his sonny boys don't give a damn. A garage is what's going up here. They'll knock down the building and throw the books on the garbage dump. Nobody will get a red cent out of these Fascist bastards!"

"When did it happen?"

"It happened, that's all."

Well, I *am* clairvoyant, Herman thought. He remained silent. For years, the editorial staff had talked about joining a union and working out a pension plan, but talk was as far as they had got. The elder Korver had seen to that. Wages were low, but he would slip some of his cronies an occasional five- or ten-dollar bonus. He gave out money at Hanukkah, sent Purim gifts, and in general acted like an old-style European boss. Those who opposed him were fired. The bookkeepers and other workers could perhaps get jobs elsewhere, but the writers and editors would have nowhere to go. Judaica was becoming a vanishing specialty in America. When Jews died, their religious and Hebrew books were donated to libraries or were simply thrown out. Hitlerism and the war had caused a temporary upsurge, but not enough to make publishing religious works in Hebrew profitable.

"Well, the seven fat years are over," Herman muttered to himself. The elevator went up to the third floor. It opened directly into the editorial room—a large room with a low ceiling, furnished with old desks and outmoded typewriters. Even the telephones were old-fashioned. The room smelled of dust, wax, and something stuffy and stale.

Raphael Robbins, Korver's editor-in-chief, sat on a cushioned chair and read a manuscript, his eyeglasses pushed down to the tip of his nose. He suffered from hemorrhoids and had prostate trouble. A man of medium height, he was broad-shouldered, with a round head and a protruding belly. Loose folds of skin hung under his eyes. His face expressed a grandfatherly kindliness and an old woman's shrewdness. For years his chief task had consisted of eating lunch with old Korver. Robbins was known to be a boaster, a liar, and a flatterer. He owned a library of pornographic books—a holdover from his youth. Like Sam, he came from the same city as Morris Korver. Raphael Robbins's son, a physicist, had worked on the atomic bomb. His daughter had married a rich Wall Street broker. Raphael Robbins himself had accumulated some capital and was old enough to receive his Social Security pension. As Robbins read the manuscript, he scratched his bald pate and shook his head. He seldom returned a manuscript, and many of them were lying about gathering dust on the table, in his two bookcases, and on cabinets in the kitchenette where the workers brewed tea.

The man who had made Morris Korver rich and on whose shoulders the publishing house had rested for years was Professor Yohanan Abarbanel, a compiler of dictionaries. No one knew where his title came from. He had never received a degree or even attended a university. It was said that old Korver had made him a professor. In addition to compiling several dictionaries, Abarbanel had edited a collection of sermons with quotations for rabbis, written study books for bar-mitzvah boys, and put together other handbooks, which had run into many editions. A bachelor in his seventies, Yohanan Abarbanel had had a heart attack and had undergone surgery for a hernia. He worked for a pittance, lived in a cheap hotel, and each year worried that he might be laid off. He had several poor relatives whom he supported. He was a small man, with white hair, a white beard, and a small face, red as a frozen apple; his little eyes were hidden by white bushy eyebrows. He sat at a table and wheezed and coughed, and all the while wrote in a tiny handwriting with a steel pen. The last few years, he couldn't be trusted to complete any work by himself. Each word was read over by Herman Gombiner, and whole manuscripts had to be rewritten.

For some reason, no one in the office ever greeted anyone else with a "hello" or a "good morning" on arrival, or said anything at closing time. During the day, they did occasionally exchange a few friendly words. It might even happen that, not having addressed a word to one another for months, one of them might go over to a colleague and pour out his heart, or actually invite him to supper. But then the next morning they would again behave as if they had quarreled. Over the years they had become bored with one another. Complaints and grudges had accumulated and were never quite forgotten.

Miss Lipshitz, the secretary, who had started working at Zion when she was just out of college, was now entirely gray. She sat at her typewriter—small, plump, and pouting, with a short neck and an ample bosom. She had a pug nose and eyes that seemed never to look at the manuscript she was typing but stared far off, past the walls. Days would pass without her voice being heard. She muttered into the telephone. When she ate lunch in the restaurant across the street, she would sit alone at a table, eating, smoking, and reading a newspaper simultaneously. There was a time when everyone in the office —old Mr. Korver included—had either openly or secretly been in love with this clever girl who knew English, Yiddish, Hebrew, stenography, and much more. They used to ask her to the theater and the movies and quarreled over who should take her to lunch. For years now, Miss Lipshitz had isolated herself. Old man Korver said that she had shut herself up behind an invisible wall.

Herman nodded to her, but she didn't respond. He walked past Ben Melnick's office. Melnick was the business manager —tall, swarthy, with a young face, black bulging eyes, and a head of milky-white hair. He suffered from asthma and played the horses. All sorts of shifty characters came to see him—

bookies. He was separated from his wife and was carrying on a love affair with Miss Potter, the chief bookkeeper, another relative of Morris Korver's.

Herman Gombiner went into his own office. Walking through the editorial room, and not being greeted, was a strain for him. Korver employed a man to keep the place clean —Zeinvel Gitzis—but Zeinvel neglected his work; the walls were filthy, the windows unwashed. Packs of dusty manuscripts and newspapers had been lying around for years.

Herman carefully removed his coat and laid it on a stack of books. He sat down on a chair that had horsehair sticking through its upholstery. Work? What was the sense of working when the firm was closing down? He sat shaking his head— half out of weakness, half from regret. "Well, everything has to have an end," he muttered. "It is predestined that no human institution will last forever." He reached over and pulled the mail out of his coat pocket. He inspected the envelopes, without opening any of them. He came back to Rose Beechman's letter from Louisville, Kentucky. In a magazine called the *Message*, Mrs. Beechman had reported her contacts over the last fifteen years with her dead grandmother, Mrs. Eleanor Brush. The grandmother usually materialized during the night, though sometimes she would also appear in the daylight, dressed in her funeral clothes. She was full of advice for her granddaughter, and once she even gave her a recipe for fried chicken. Herman had written to Rose Beechman, but seven weeks had passed without a reply. He had almost given up hope, although he had continued sending her telepathic messages. She had been ill—Herman was certain of it.

Now her letter lay before him in a light-blue envelope. Opening it wasn't easy for him. He had to resort to using his teeth. He finally removed six folded sheets of light-blue stationery and read:

Dear Mr. Gombiner:

I am writing this letter to you a day after my return from the hospital where I spent almost two months. I was operated on for the removal of a spinal tumor. There was danger of paralysis or worse. But fate, it seems, still wants me here. . . . Apparently, my little story in the *Message* caused quite a furor. During my illness, I received dozens of letters from all parts of the country and from England.

It so happened that my daughter put your letter at the bottom of the pile, and had I read them in order, it might have taken several weeks more before I came to yours. But a premonition—what else can I call it?—make me open the very last letter first. It was then that I realized, from the postmark, yours had been among the first, if not the very first, to arrive. It seems I always do thing not as I intend to but according to a command from someone or something that I am unaware of. All I can say is: this "something" has been with me as long as I can remember, perhaps even since before I was capable of thinking.

Your letter is so logical, so noble and fascinating, that I may say it has brightened my homecoming. My daughter has a job in an office and has neither the time nor the patience to look after the house. When I returned, I found things in a sorry state. I am by nature a meticulous housekeeper who cannot abide disorder, and so you can imagine my feelings. But your profound and truly remarkable thoughts, as well as the friendliness and humanity implicit in them, helped me to forget my troubles. I read your letter three times and thanked God that people with your understanding and faith exist.

You ask for details. My dear Mr. Gombiner, if I were to relate all the facts, no letter would suffice. I could fill a whole book. Don't forget that these experiences have been going on for fifteen years. My saintly grandmother visited me every day in the hospital. She literally took over the work of the nurses, who are not, as you may know, overly devoted to their patients—nor do they have the time to be. Yes, to describe it all "exactly," as you request, would take weeks, months. I can only repeat that everything I wrote in the *Message* was the honest truth. Some of my correspondents call me "crackpot," "crazy," "charlatan." They accuse me of lying and publicity-seeking. Why should I tell lies and why do I need publicity? It was, therefore, especially pleasing to read your wonderful sentiments. I see from the letterhead that you are a Jew and connected with a Hebrew publishing house. I wish to assure you that I have always had the highest regard for Jews, God's chosen people. There are not very many Jews here in Louisville, and my personal contact had been only with Jews who had little interest in their religion. I have always wanted to become acquainted with a real Jew, who reveres the tradition of the Holy Fathers.

Now I come to the main point of my letter, and I beg you to forgive my rambling. The night before I left the hospital, my beloved grandmother, Mrs. Brush, visited with me till dawn. We chatted about various matters, and just before her departure she said to me, "This winter you will go to New York, where you will meet a man who will change the direction of your life." These were her parting words. I must add here that although for the past fifteen years I have been fully convinced that my grandmother never spoke idly and that whatever she said had meaning, at that moment for the first time I felt some doubt. What business did I, a widow living on a small pension, have in far-off New York? And what man in New York could possibly alter my existence?

It is true I am not yet old—just above forty—and considered an attractive woman. (I beg you not to think me vain. I simply wish to clarify the situation.) But when my husband died eight years ago, I decided that was that. I was left with a twelve-year-old daughter and wished to devote all my energies to her upbringing, and I did. She is today good-looking, has gone through business school and has an excellent position with a real-estate firm, and she is engaged to marry an extremely interesting and well-educated man (a government official). I feel she will be very happy.

I have since my husband's death received proposals from men, but I have always rejected them. My grandmother, it seems, must have agreed with me, because I never heard anything to the contrary from her. I mention this because my grandmother's talk of a trip to New York and the man I would meet there seemed so unlikely that I believed she had said it just to cheer me up after my illness. Later, her words actually slipped my mind.

Imagine my surprise when today, on my return from the hospital, I received a registered letter from a Mr. Ginsburg, a New York lawyer, notifying me of the death of my great-aunt Catherine Pennell and telling me that she had left me a sum of almost five thousand dollars. Aunt Catherine was a spinster and had severed her ties with our family over fifty years ago, before I was born. As far as we knew, she had lived on a farm in Pennsylvania. My father had sometimes talked about her and her eccentricities, but I had never met her nor did I know whether she was alive or dead. How she wound up in New York is a mystery to me, as is the reason for her choosing to leave me money. These are the facts, and I must come to New York concerning the bequest. Documents have to be signed and so forth.

When I read the lawyer's letter and then your highly interesting and dear one, I suddenly realized how foolish I had been to doubt my grandmother's words. She has never made a prediction that didn't later prove true, and I will never doubt her again.

This letter is already too long and my fingers are tired from holding the pen. I simply wish to inform you that I will be in New York for several days in January, or at the latest in early February, and I would consider it a privilege and an honor to meet you personally.

I cannot know what the Powers that be have in store for me, but I know that meeting you will be an important event in my life, as I hope meeting me will be for you. I have extraordinary things to tell you. In the meantime, accept my deepest gratitude and my fondest regards.

I am, very truly yours,
Rose Beechman

4

Everything happened quickly. One day they talked about closing down the publishing house, and the next day it was done. Morris Korver and his sons called a meeting of the staff. Korver himself spoke in Yiddish, pounded his fist on a book-stand, and shouted with the loud voice of a young man. He warned the workers that if they didn't accept the settlement he and his sons had worked out, none of them would get a penny. One son, Seymour, a lawyer, had a few words to say, in Eng-lish. In contrast with his father's shouting, Seymour spoke qui-etly. The older employees who were hard of hearing moved their chairs closer and turned up their hearing aids. Seymour displayed a list of figures. The publishing house, he said, had in the last few years lost several hundred thousand dollars. How much can a business lose? There it all was, written down in black and white.

After the bosses left, the writers and office workers voted whether or not to agree to the proposed terms. The majority voted to accept. It was argued that Korver had secretly bribed some employees to be on his side, but what was the difference? Each worker was to receive his final check the following day. The manuscripts were left lying on the tables. Sam had already brought up men from the demolition company.

Raphael Robbins carefully put into his satchel the little cush-ion on which he sat, a magnifying glass, and a drawerful of medicine. He took leave of everyone with the shrewd smile of a man who knew everything in advance and therefore was never surprised. Yohanan Abarbanel took a single dictionary home with him. Miss Lipshitz, the secretary, walked around with red, weepy eyes all morning. Ben Melnick brought a huge trunk and packed his private archives, consisting of horse-racing forms.

Herman Gombiner was too feeble to pack the letters and

books that had accumulated in his bookcase. He opened the drawer, looked at the dust-covered papers, and immediately started coughing. He said goodbye to Miss Lipshitz, handed Sam a last five-dollar tip, went to the bank to cash the check, and then waited for a taxi.

For many years, Herman Gombiner had lived in fear of the day when he would be without a job. But when he got into the taxi to go home at one o'clock in the afternoon, he felt the calm of resignation. He never turned his head to look back at the place in which he had wasted almost thirty years. A wet snow was falling. The sky was gray. Sitting in the taxi, leaning his head back against the seat, with eyes closed, Herman Gombiner compared himself to a corpse returning from its own funeral. This is probably the way the soul leaves the body and starts its spiritual existence, he thought.

He had figured everything out. With the almost two thousand dollars he had saved in the bank, the money he had received from Morris Korver, and unemployment insurance, he would be able to manage for two years—perhaps even a few months longer. Then he would have to go to relief. There was no sense in even trying to get another job. Herman had from childhood begged God not to make him dependent on charity, but it had evidently been decided differently. Unless, of course, death redeemed him first.

Thank God it was warm in the house. Herman looked at the mouse's hole. In what way was he, Herman, better than she? Huldah also had to depend on someone. He took out a notebook and pencil and started to calculate. He would no longer need to pay for two taxis daily, or have to eat lunch in a restaurant, or leave a tip for the waiter. There would be no more contributions for all kinds of collections—for Palestine, for employees' children or grandchildren who were getting married, for retirement gifts. He certainly wouldn't be paying any more taxes. Herman examined his clothes closet. He had enough shirts and shoes to last him another ten years. He needed money only for rent, bread, milk, magazines, and stamps. There had been a time when he considered getting a telephone in his apartment. Thank God he had not done it. With these six dollars he could manage for a week. Without realizing it would come to this, Herman had for years practiced the art of reducing his expenditures to a minimum, lowering the wick of life, so to speak.

Never before had Herman Gombiner enjoyed his apartment as he did on that winter day when he returned home after the closing of the publishing house. People had often complained to him about their loneliness, but as long as there were books and stationery and as long as he could sit on a chair next to the radiator and meditate, he was never alone. From the neighboring apartments he could hear the laughter of children, women talking, and the loud voices of men. Radios were turned on full blast. In the street, boys and girls were playing noisily.

The short day grew darker and darker, and the house filled with shadows. Outside, the snow took on an unusual blue coloring. Twilight descended. "So, a day has passed," Herman said to himself. This particular day, this very date would never return again, unless Nietzsche was right in his theory about the eternal return. Even if one did believe that time was imaginary, this day was finished, like the flipped page of a book. It had passed into the archives of eternity. But what had he, Herman Gombiner, accomplished? Whom had he helped? Not even the mouse. She had not come out of her hole, not a peep out of her all day. Was she sick? She was no longer young; old age crept up on everyone. . . .

As Herman sat in the wintry twilight, he seemed to be waiting for a sign from the Powers on high. Sometimes he received messages from them, but at other times they remained hidden and silent. He found himself thinking about his parents, grandparents, his sisters, brother, aunts, uncles, and cousins. Where were they all? Where were they resting, blessed souls, martyred by the Nazis. Did they ever think of him? Or had they risen into spheres where they were no longer concerned with the lower worlds? He started to pray to them, inviting them to visit him on this winter evening.

The steam in the radiator hissed, singing its one note. The steam seemed to speak in the pipes, consoling Herman: "You are not alone, you are an element of the universe, a child of God, an integral part of Creation. Your suffering is God's suffering, your yearning His yearning. Everything is right. Let the Truth be revealed to you, and you will be filled with joy."

Suddenly Herman heard a squeak. In the dimness, the

mouse had crawled out and looked cautiously around, as if afraid that a cat lurked nearby. Herman held his breath. Holy creature, have no fear. No harm will come to you. He watched her as she approached the saucer of water, took one sip, then a second and a third. Slowly she started gnawing the piece of cheese.

Can there be any greater wonder, Herman thought. Here stands a mouse, a daughter of a mouse, a granddaughter of mice, a product of millions, billions of mice who once lived, suffered, reproduced, and are now gone forever, but have left an heir, apparently the last of her line. Here she stands, nourishing herself with food. What does she think about all day in her hole? She must think about something. She does have a mind, a nervous system. She is just as much a part of God's creation as the planets, the stars, the distant galaxies.

The mouse suddenly raised her head and stared at Herman with a human look of love and gratitude. Herman imagined that she was saying thank you.

5

Since Herman Gombiner had stopped working, he realized what an effort it had been for him to wake up in the morning, to wait outside for a cab, to waste his time with dictionaries, writing, editing, and traveling home again each evening. He had apparently been working with the last of his strength. It seemed to him that the publishing house had closed on the very day that he had expended his last bit of remaining energy. This fact in itself was an excellent example of the presence of Godly compassion and the hand of Providence. But thank heaven he still had the will to read and write letters.

Snow had fallen. Herman couldn't recall another New York winter with as much snow as this. Huge drifts had piled up. It was impossible for cars to drive through his street. Herman would have had to plow his way to Columbus Avenue or Central Park West to get a taxi. He would surely have collapsed. Luckily, the delivery boy from the grocery store didn't forget him. Every other day he brought up rolls, sometimes eggs, cheese, and whatever else Herman had ordered. His neighbors would knock on his door and ask him whether he needed anything—coffee, tea, fruit. He thanked them profusely. Poor as he was, he always gave a mother a nickel to buy some chocolate for her child. The women never left at once; they lingered awhile and spoke to him in their broken English, looking at him as if they regretted having to go. Once, a woman stroked Herman's head gently. Women had always been attracted to him.

There had been times when women had fallen desperately in love with him, but marriage and a family were not for Herman. The thought of raising children seemed absurd to him. Why prolong the human tragedy? Besides, he had always sent every last cent to Kalomin.

His thoughts kept returning to the past. He was back in Kalomin. He was going to heder, studying at a yeshiva, secretly teaching himself modern Hebrew, Polish, German, taking lessons, instructing others. He experienced his first love affair, the meetings with girls, strolls in the woods, to the watermill, to the cemetery. He had been drawn to cemeteries even as a youngster, and would spend hours there, meditating among the tombstones and listening to their stony silence. The dead spoke to him from their graves. In the Kalomin cemetery there grew tall, white-barked birch trees. Their silvery leaves trembled in the slightest breeze, chattering their leafy dialect all day. The boughs leaned over each other, whispering secrets.

Later came the trip to America and wandering around New York without a job. Then he went to work for Zion and began studying English. He had been fairly healthy at that time and had had affairs with women. It was difficult to believe the many triumphs he had had. On lonely nights, details of old episodes and never-forgotten words came to him. Memory itself demonstrates that there is no oblivion. Words a woman had uttered to him thirty years before and that he hadn't really understood at the time would suddenly become clear. Thank God he had enough memories to last him a hundred years.

For the first time since he had come to America, his windows froze over. Frost trees like those in Kalomin formed on the windowpanes—upside-down palms, exotic shrubs, and strange flowers. The frost painted like an artist, but its patterns were eternal. Crystals? What were crystals? Who had taught the atoms and molecules to arrange themselves in this or that way? What was the connection between the molecules in New York and the molecules in Kalomin?

The greatest wonders began when Herman dozed off. As soon as he closed his eyes, his dreams came like locusts. He saw everything with clarity and precision. These were not dreams but visions. He flew over Oriental cities, hovered over cupolas, mosques, and castles, lingered in strange gardens, mysterious forests. He came upon undiscovered tribes, spoke foreign languages. Sometimes he was frightened by monsters.

Herman had often thought that one's true life was lived during sleep. Waking was no more than a marginal time assigned for doing things.

Now that he was free, his entire schedule was turned around. It seemed to happen of itself. He stayed awake at night and slept during the day. He ate lunch in the evening and skipped supper altogether. The alarm clock had stopped, but Herman hadn't rewound it. What difference did it make what time it was? Sometimes he was too lazy to turn the lights on in the evening. Instead of reading, he sat on a chair next to the radiator and dozed. He was overcome by a fatigue that never left him. Am I getting sick, he wondered. No matter how little the grocery boy delivered, Herman had too much.

His real sustenance was the letters he received. Herman still made his way down the few flights of stairs to his letter box in the lobby. He had provided himself with a supply of stamps and stationery. There was a mailbox a few feet from the entrance of the house. If he was unable to get through the snow, he would ask a neighbor to mail his letters. Recently, a woman who lived on his floor offered to get his mail every morning, and Herman gave her the key to his box. She was a stamp collector; the stamps were her payment. Herman now spared himself the trouble of climbing stairs. She mailed his letters and slipped the ones he received under the door, and so quietly that he never heard her footsteps.

He often sat all night writing, napping between letters. Occasionally he would take an old letter from the desk drawer and read it through a magnifying glass. Yes, the dead were still with us. They came to advise their relatives on business, debts, the healing of the sick; they comforted the discouraged, made suggestions concerning trips, jobs, love, marriage. Some left bouquets of flowers on bedspreads, and apported articles from distant places. Some revealed themselves only to intimate ones at the moment of death, others returned years after they had passed away. If this were all true, Herman thought, then his relatives, too, were surely living. He sat praying for them to appear to him. The spirit cannot be burned, gassed, hanged, shot. Six million souls must exist somewhere.

One night, having written letters till dawn, Herman inserted them in envelopes, addressed and put stamps on them, then went to bed. When he opened his eyes, it was full daylight. His head was heavy. It lay like a stone on the pillow. He felt hot, yet chills ran across his back. He had dreamed that his dead family came to him, but they had not behaved appropriately for ghosts; they had quarreled, shouted, even come to blows over a straw basket.

Herman looked toward the door and saw the morning mail pushed under it by his neighbor, but he couldn't move. Am I paralyzed, he wondered. He fell asleep again, and the ghosts returned. His mother and sisters were arguing over a metal comb. "Well, this is too ridiculous," he said to himself. "Spirits don't need metal combs." The dream continued. He discovered a cabinet in the wall of his room. He opened it and letters started pouring out—hundreds of letters. What was this cabinet? The letters bore old datemarks; he had never opened them. In his sleep he felt troubled that so many people had written to him and he hadn't answered them. He decided that a postman must have hidden the letters in order to save himself the trouble of delivering them. But if the postman had already bothered to come to his house, what was the sense of hiding the letters in the cabinet?

Herman awoke, and it was evening. "How did the day pass so quickly?" he asked himself. He tried to get up to go to the bathroom, but his head spun and everything turned black. He fell to the floor. Well, it's the end, he thought. What will become of Huldah?

He lay powerless for a long time. Then slowly he pulled himself up, and by moving along the wall he reached the bathroom. His urine was brown and oily, and he felt a burning sensation.

It took him a long time to return to his bed. He lay down again, and the bed seemed to rise and fall. How strange—he no longer needed to tear open the envelopes of his letters. Clairvoyant powers enabled him to read their contents. He had received a reply from a woman in a small town in Colorado. She wrote of a now dead neighbor with whom she had always quarreled, and of how after the neighbor's death her ghost had broken her sewing machine. Her former enemy had poured water on her floors, ripped open a pillow and spilled out all the feathers. The dead can be mischievous. They can also be full of vengeance. If this was so, he thought, then a war between the dead Jews and the dead Nazis was altogether possible.

That night, Herman dozed, twitched convulsively, and woke up again and again. Outside, the wind howled. It blew right through the house. Herman remembered Huldah; the mouse was without food or water. He wanted to get down to help her, but he couldn't move any part of his body. He prayed to God, "I don't need help any more, but don't let that poor creature die of hunger!" He pledged money to charity. Then he fell asleep.

Herman opened his eyes, and the day was just beginning— an overcast wintry day that he could barely make out through the frost-covered windowpanes. It was as cold indoors as out. Herman listened but could hear no tune from the radiator. He tried to cover himself, but his hands lacked the strength. From the hallway he heard sounds of shouting and running feet. Someone knocked on the door, but he couldn't answer. There was more knocking. A man spoke in Spanish, and Herman heard a woman's voice. Suddenly someone pushed the door open and a Puerto Rican man came in, followed by a small woman wearing a knitted coat and matching hat. She carried a huge muff such as Herman had never seen in America.

The woman came up to his bed and said, "Mr. Gombiner?" She pronounced his name so that he hardly recognized it— with the accent on the first syllable. The man left. In her hand the woman held the letters she had picked up from the floor. She had fair skin, dark eyes, a small nose. She said, "I knew that you were sick. I am Mrs. Beechman—Rose Beechman."

She held out a letter she had sent him that was among those she found at the door.

Herman understood, but was unable to speak. He heard her say, "My grandmother made me come to you. I was coming to New York two weeks from now. You are ill and the furnace in your house has exploded. Wait, I'll cover you. Where is your telephone?"

She pulled the blanket over him, but the bedding was like ice. She started to move about, stamping her boots and clapping her hands. "You don't have a telephone? How can I get a doctor?"

He wanted to tell her he didn't want a doctor, but he was too weak. Looking at her made him tired. He shut his eyes and immediately forgot that he had a visitor.

6

"How can anyone sleep so much?" Herman asked himself. This sleepiness had transformed him into a helpless creature. He opened his eyes, saw the strange woman, knew who she was, and immediately fell asleep again. She had brought a doctor—a tall man, a giant—and this man uncovered him, listened to his heart with a stethoscope, squeezed his stomach, looked down his throat. Herman heard the word "pneumonia"; they told him he would have to go to the hospital, but he amassed enough strength to shake his head. He would rather die. The doctor reprimanded him good-naturedly; the woman tried to persuade him. What's wrong with a hospital? They would make him well there. She would visit him every day, would take care of him.

But Herman was adamant. He broke through his sickness and spoke to the woman. "Every person has the right to determine his own fate." He showed her where he kept his money; he looked at her pleadingly, stretched out his hand to her, begging her to promise that he would not be moved.

One moment he spoke clearly as a healthy man, and the next he returned to his torpor. He dreamed again—whether asleep or awake he himself didn't know. The woman gave him medicine. A girl came and administered an injection. Thank God there was heat again. The radiator sang all day and half the night. Now the sun shone in—the bit of sunlight that reached his window in the morning; now the ceiling light burned. Neighbors came to ask how he was, mostly women. They brought him bowls of grits, warm milk, cups of tea. The strange woman changed her clothes; sometimes she wore a black dress or a yellow dress, sometimes a white blouse or a rose-colored blouse. At times she appeared middle-aged and serious to him, at others girlishly young and playful. She inserted a thermometer in his mouth and brought his bedpan. She undressed him and gave him alcohol rubs. He felt embarrassed because of his emaciated body, but she argued, "What is there to be ashamed of? We are all the way God made us." Sick as he was, he was still aware of the smoothness of her palms. Was she human? Or an angel? He was a child again, whose mother was worrying about him. He knew very well that he could die of this sleepiness, but he had ceased being afraid of death.

Herman was preoccupied with something—an event, a vision that repeated itself with countless variations but whose meaning he couldn't fathom. It seemed to him that his sleeping was like a long book which he read so eagerly he could not stop even for a minute. Drinking tea, taking medicine were merely annoying interruptions. His body, together with its agonies, had detached itself from him.

He awoke. The day was growing pale. The woman had placed an ice pack on his head. She removed it and commented that his pajama top had blood on it. The blood had come from his nose.

"Am I dying? Is this death?" he asked himself. He felt only curiosity.

The woman gave him medicine from a teaspoon, and the fluid had the strength and the smell of cognac. Herman shut his eyes, and when he opened them again he could see the snowy blue of the night. The woman was sitting at a table that had for years been cluttered with books, which she must have removed. She had placed her fingertips at the edge of the table. The table was moving, raising its front legs and then dropping them down with a bang.

For a while he was wide awake and as clearheaded as if he were well. Was the table really moving of its own accord? Or was the woman raising it? He stared in amazement. The woman was mumbling; she asked questions that he couldn't hear. Sometimes she grumbled; once she even laughed, showing a mouthful of small teeth. Suddenly she went over to the bed, leaned over him, and said, "You will live. You will recover."

He listened to her words with an indifference that surprised him.

He closed his eyes and found himself in Kalomin again. They were all living—his father, his mother, his grandfather, his grandmother, his sisters, his brother, all the uncles and aunts and cousins. How odd that Kalomin could be a part of New York. One had only to reach a street that led to Canal Street. The street was on the side of a mountain, and it was necessary to climb up to it. It seemed that he had to go through a cellar or a tunnel, a place he remembered from other dreams. It grew darker and darker, the ground became steeper and full of ditches, the walls lower and lower and the air more stuffy. He had to open a door to a small chamber that was full of the bones of corpses, slimy with decay. He had come upon a subterranean cemetery, and there he met a beadle, or perhaps a warden or a gravedigger who was attending to the bones.

"How can anyone live here?" Herman asked himself. "Who would want such a livelihood?" Herman couldn't see this man now, but he recalled previous dreams in which he had seen him—bearded and shabby. He broke off limbs like so many rotten roots. He laughed with secret glee. Herman tried to escape from this labyrinth, crawling on his belly and slithering like a snake, overexerting himself so that his breathing stopped.

He awakened in a cold sweat. The lamp was not lit, but a faint glow shone from somewhere. Where is this light coming from, Herman wondered, and where is the woman? How miraculous—he felt well.

He sat up slowly and saw the woman asleep on a cot, covered with an unfamiliar blanket. The faint illumination came from a tiny light bulb plugged into a socket near the floor. Herman sat still and let the perspiration dry, feeling cooler as it dried.

"Well, it wasn't destined, that I should die yet," he muttered. "But why am I needed here?" He could find no answer.

Herman leaned back on the pillow and lay still. He remembered everything: he had fallen ill, Rose Beechman had arrived, and had brought a doctor to see him. Herman had refused to go to the hospital.

He took stock of himself. He had apparently passed the crisis. He was weak, but no longer sick. All his pains were gone. He could breathe freely. His throat was no longer clogged with phlegm. This woman had saved his life.

Herman knew he should thank Providence, but something inside him felt sad and almost cheated. He had always hoped for a revelation. He had counted on his deep sleep to see things kept from the healthy eye. Even of death he had thought, Let's look at what is on the other side of the curtain. He had often read about people who were ill and whose astral bodies wandered over cities, oceans, and deserts. Others had come in contact with relatives, had had visions; heavenly lights had appeared to them. But in his long sleep Herman had experienced nothing but a lot of tangled dreams. He remembered the little table that had raised and lowered its front legs one night. Where was it? It stood not far from his bed, covered with a pile of letters and magazines, apparently received during his illness.

Herman observed Rose Beechman. Why had she come? When had she had the cot brought in? He saw her face distinctly now—the small nose, hollow cheeks, dark hair, the round forehead a bit too high for a woman. She slept calmly, the blanket over her breast. Her breathing couldn't be heard. It occurred to Herman that she might be dead. He stared at her intently; her nostrils moved slightly.

Herman dozed off again. Suddenly he heard a mumbling. He opened his eyes. The woman was talking in her sleep. He listened carefully but couldn't make out the words. He wasn't certain whether it was English or another language. What did it mean? All at once he knew: she was talking to her grandmother. He held his breath. His whole being became still. He made an effort to distinguish at least one word, but he couldn't catch a single syllable. The woman became silent and then started to whisper again. She didn't move her lips. Her voice seemed to be coming out of her nostrils. Who knows? Perhaps she wasn't speaking a known language, Herman Gombiner thought. He fancied that she was suggesting something to the unseen one and arguing with her. This intensive listening soon tired him. He closed his eyes and fell asleep.

He twitched and woke up. He didn't know how long he had been sleeping—a minute or an hour. Through the window he saw that it was still night. The woman on the cot was sleeping silently. Suddenly Herman remembered. What had become of Huldah? How awful that throughout his long illness he had entirely forgotten her. No one had fed her or given her anything to drink. "She is surely dead," he said to himself. "Dead of hunger and thirst!" He felt a great shame. He had recovered. The Powers that rule the world had sent a woman to him, a merciful sister, but this creature who was dependent on him for its necessities had perished. "I should not have forgotten her! I should not have! I've killed her!"

Despair took hold of Herman. He started to pray for the mouse's soul. "Well, you've had your life. You've served your time in this forsaken world, the worst of all worlds, this bottomless abyss, where Satan, Asmodeus, Hitler, and Stalin prevail. You are no longer confined to your hole—hungry, thirsty, and sick, but at one with the God-filled cosmos, with God Himself. . . . Who knows why you had to be a mouse?"

In his thoughts, Herman spoke a eulogy for the mouse who had shared a portion of her life with him and who, because of him, had left this earth. "What do they know—all those scholars, all those philosophers, all the leaders of the world—about such as you? They have convinced themselves that man, the worst transgressor of all the species, is the crown of creation. All other creatures were created merely to provide him with food, pelts, to be tormented, exterminated. In relation to them, all people are Nazis; for the animals it is an eternal Treblinka. And yet man demands compassion from heaven." Herman clapped his hand to his mouth. "I mustn't live, I mustn't! I can no longer be a part of it! God in heaven—take me away!"

For a while his mind was blank. Then he trembled. Perhaps Huldah was still alive? Perhaps she had found something to eat. Maybe she was lying unconscious in her hole and could be revived? He tried to get off the bed. He lifted the blanket and slowly put one foot down. The bed creaked.

The woman opened her eyes as if she hadn't been asleep at all but had been pretending. "Where are you going?"

"There is something I must find out."

"What? Wait one second." She straightened her nightgown underneath the blanket, got out of bed, and went over to him barefooted. Her feet were white, girlishly small, with slender toes. "How are you feeling?"

"I beg you, listen to me!" And in a quiet voice he told her about the mouse.

The woman listened. Her face, hidden in the shadows, expressed no surprise. She said, "Yes, I did hear the mice scratching several times during the night. They are probably eating your books."

"It's only one mouse. A wonderful creature."

"What shall I do?"

"The hole is right here. . . . I used to set out a dish of water for her and a piece of cheese."

"I don't have any cheese here."

"Perhaps you can pour some milk in a little dish. I'm not sure that she is alive, but maybe . . ."

"Yes, there is milk. First I'll take your temperature." She took a thermometer from somewhere, shook it down, and put it in his mouth with the authority of a nurse.

Herman watched her as she busied herself in the kitchenette. She poured milk from a bottle into a saucer. Several times she turned her head and gave him an inquiring look, as if she didn't quite believe what she had just heard.

How can this be, Herman wondered. She doesn't look like a woman with a grown daughter. She looks like a girl herself. Her loose hair reached her shoulders. He could make out her figure through her bathrobe: narrow in the waist, not too broad in the hips. Her face had a mildness, a softness that didn't match the earnest, almost severe letter she had written him. Oh, well, where is it written that everything must match? Every person is a new experiment in God's laboratory.

The woman took the dish and carefully set it down where he had indicated. On the way back to the cot, she put on her house slippers. She took the thermometer out of his mouth and went to the bathroom, where a light was burning. She soon returned. "You have no fever. Thank God."

"You have saved my life," Herman said.

"It was my grandmother who told me to come here. I hope you've read my letter."

"Yes, I read it."

"I see that you correspond with half the world."

"I'm interested in psychic research."

"This is your first day without fever."

For a while, both were silent. Then he asked, "How can I repay you?"

The woman frowned. "There's no need to repay me."

7

Herman fell asleep and found himself in Kalomin. It was a summer evening and he was strolling with a girl across a bridge on the way to the mill and to the Russian Orthodox Cemetery, where the gravestones bear the photographs of those interred. A huge luminous sphere shimmered in the sky, larger than the moon, larger than the sun, a new incomparable heavenly body. It cast a greenish glow over the water, making it transparent, so that fish could be seen as they swam. Not the usual carp and pike but whales and sharks, fish with golden fins, red horns, with skin similar to that on the wings of bats.

"What is all this?" Herman asked. "Has the cosmos changed? Has the earth torn itself away from the sun, from the whole Milky Way? Is it about to become a comet?" He tried to talk to the girl he was with, but she was one of the ladies buried in the graveyard. She replied in Russian, although it was also Hebrew. Herman asked, "Don't Kant's categories of pure reason any longer apply in Kalomin?"

He woke up with a start. On the other side of the window it was still night. The strange woman was asleep on the cot. Herman examined her more carefully now. She no longer mumbled, but her lips trembled occasionally. Her brow wrinkled as she smiled in her sleep. Her hair was spread out over the pillow. The quilt had slid down, and he could see the bunched-up folds of her nightgown and the top of her breast. Herman stared at her, mute with amazement. A woman had come to him from somewhere in the South—not a Jewess, but as Ruth had come to Boaz, sent by some Naomi who was no longer among the living.

Where had she found bedding, Herman wondered. She had already brought order to his apartment—she had hung a curtain over the window, cleaned the newspapers and manuscripts from the large table. How strange, she hadn't moved the blotter, as if she had known that it was the implement of a miracle.

Herman stared, nodding his head in wonder. The books in the bookcases did not look so old and tattered. She had brought some kind of order to them, too. The air he breathed no longer smelled moldy and dusty but had a moist, cool quality. Herman was reminded of a Passover night in Kalomin. Only the matzos hanging in a sheet from the ceiling were lacking. He tried to remember his latest dream, but he could only recall the unearthly light that fell across the lake. "Well, dreams are all lost," Herman said to himself. "Each day begins with amnesia."

He heard a slight noise that sounded like a child sucking. Herman sat up and saw Huldah. She appeared thinner, weak, and her fur looked grayer, as if she had aged.

"God in heaven! Huldah is alive! There she stands, drinking milk from the dish!" A joy such as he had seldom experienced gripped Herman. He had not as yet thanked God for bringing him back to life. He had even felt some resentment. But for letting the mouse live he had to praise the Higher Powers. Herman was filled with love both for the mouse and for the woman, Rose Beechman, who had understood his feelings and without question had obeyed his request and given the mouse some milk. "I am not worthy, I am not worthy," he muttered. "It is all pure Grace."

Herman was not a man who wept. His eyes had remained dry even when he received the news that his family had perished in the destruction of Kalomin. But now his face became wet and hot. It wasn't fated that he bear the guilt of a murderer. Providence—aware of every molecule, every mite, every speck of dust—had seen to it that the mouse received its nourishment during his long sleep. Or was it perhaps possible that a mouse could fast for that length of time?

Herman watched intently. Even now, after going hungry for

so long, the mouse didn't rush. She lapped the milk slowly, pausing occasionally, obviously confident that no one would take away what was rightfully hers. "Little mouse, hallowed creature, saint!" Herman cried to her in his thoughts. He blew her a kiss.

The mouse continued to drink. From time to time, she cocked her head and gave Herman a sidelong glance. He imagined he saw in her eyes an expression of surprise, as if she were silently asking, "Why did you let me go hungry so long? And who is this woman sleeping here?" Soon she went back to her hole.

Rose Beechman opened her eyes. "Oh! You are up? What time is it?"

"Huldah has had her milk," Herman said.

"What? Oh, yes."

"I beg you, don't laugh at me."

"I'm not laughing at anyone."

"You've saved not one life but two."

"Well, we are all God's creatures. I'll make you some tea."

Herman wanted to tell her that it wasn't necessary, but he was thirsty and his throat felt dry. He even felt a pang of hunger. He had come back to life, with all its needs.

The woman immediately busied herself in the kitchenette, and shortly she brought Herman a cup of tea and two biscuits. She had apparently bought new dishes for him. She sat down on the edge of a chair and said, "Well, drink your tea. I don't believe you realize how sick you were."

"I am grateful."

"If I had been just two days later, nothing would have helped."

"Perhaps it would have been better that way."

"No. People like you are needed."

"Today I heard you talking to your grandmother." Herman spoke, not sure if he should be saying this.

She listened and was thoughtfully silent awhile. "Yes, she was with me last night."

"What did she say?"

The woman looked at him oddly. He noticed for the first time that her eyes were light brown. "I hope you won't make fun of me."

"God in heaven, no!"

"She wants me to take care of you; you need me more than my daughter does—those were her words."

A chill ran down Herman's spine. "Yes, that may be true, but—"

"But what? I beg you, be honest with me."

"I have nothing. I am weak. I can only be a burden . . ."

"Burdens are made to be borne."

"Yes. Yes."

"If you want me to, I will stay with you. At least until you recover completely."

"Yes, I do."

"That is what I wanted to hear." She stood up quickly and turned away. She walked toward the bathroom, embarrassed as a young Kalomin bride. She remained standing in the doorway with her back toward him, her head bowed, revealing the small nape of her neck, her uncombed hair.

Through the window a gray light was beginning to appear. Snow was falling—a dawn snow. Patches of day and night blended together outside. Clouds appeared. Windows, roofs, and fire escapes emerged from the dark. Lights went out. The night had ended like a dream and was followed by an obscure reality, self-absorbed, sunk in the perpetual mystery of being. A pigeon was flying through the snowfall, intent on carrying out its mission. In the radiator, the steam was already whistling. From the neighboring apartments were heard the first cries of awaking children, radios playing, and harassed housewives yelling and cursing in Spanish. The globe called Earth had once again revolved on its axis. The windowpanes became rosy—a sign that in the east the sky was not entirely overcast. The books were momentarily bathed in a purplish light, illuminating the old bindings and the last remnants of gold-engraved and half-legible titles. It all had the quality of a revelation.

Translated by Alizah Shevrin and Elizabeth Shub

Chronology

1904   Yitskhok Zynger (Isaac Singer) is born in Leoncin, a Polish village northeast of Warsaw (then part of the Russian Empire), the third surviving child of Basheve Zylberman and Pinkhos Menakhem Zynger. (Although his Polish passport issued in the 1930s and other sources give his birthdate as July 14, 1904, Singer told his biographer Paul Kresh that he was "born in the third week of the month of Heshvan on the Jewish calendar—which is roughly equivalent to the month of November." Father is a Hasidic rabbi from a family of distinguished rabbis, though because of his refusal to take Russian language examinations he was not certified to perform rabbinical duties by the Russian government, which limited his opportunities. Mother was the daughter of the rabbi of Biłgoraj, a town in the province of Lublin; her family were *misnagdim*, opponents of Hasidism. The couple were married in Biłgoraj in 1889. Their first child, Hinde Esther, was born in 1891, and son Israel Joshua was born in 1893. Two other young daughters died on the same day during an outbreak of scarlet fever. After making a meager living as an itinerant preacher, Singer's father was invited to serve as a rabbi in Leoncin, and the family moved there in 1897.)

1906   Brother Moishe is born.

1907   Hard times in Leoncin and increasing tensions with the local community cause Singer's father to look for a position elsewhere. He becomes head of the yeshiva in Radzymin and moves the family there, where he also acts as unofficial secretary to the local rabbi. Singer begins to attend *cheder* (religious primary school).

1908–14   The family moves to Warsaw, where father presides over a rabbinical court in the family's home at 10 Krochmalna Street, an unheated three-room apartment on the second floor. ("Krochmalna Street in Warsaw was always full of people," Singer later wrote, "and they all seemed to be screaming.") Most of the residents are poor, and some are involved in petty crime or prostitution. Family's income consists mostly of donations from those settling their affairs through the court as well as fees from private Talmud lessons given by Singer's father. Singer attends a series of *cheders* but much of his religious instruction is provided by his parents at home. Serves as messenger and collector of donations for his father. Develops friendship with a girl his age named Shosha. Browses with fascination through the books of the Kabbalah in his father's library, although he is told not to read them. Reads tales of Edgar Allan Poe and Arthur Conan Doyle as well as novels by popular Yiddish writers, such as the pseudonymous "Shomer," and detective stories featuring a hero named Max Shpitzkopf; writes stories with Shpitzkopf as a character. Brother Israel Joshua, who is drawn to secular literature and ideas and rejecting his parents' desire that he become a rabbi, has heated arguments with the family and moves out of the house at the age of 18. Sister Hinde Esther's relationship with parents grows contentious, and she consents to an arranged marriage with diamond cutter Abraham Kreitman, moving to Antwerp with him following their wedding in Berlin in 1912; after their son Moishe (later known as Morris Kreitman and Maurice Carr) is born the next year, the family sends money from Warsaw because Abraham is unemployed. Early in 1914, family moves to a larger apartment in the building next door. After the outbreak of World War I, Israel Joshua adopts an assumed name to avoid conscription into the Russian army. Singer visits him several times in the studio of a sculptor named Ostrzego. The Kreitmans flee Belgium and settle in London.

1915–16   Singer goes to Bresler's lending library for the first of many visits, borrowing books on philosophy in Yiddish and Hebrew and reading them with enthusiasm. German troops occupy Warsaw in August 1915, causing prolonged hardship and deprivation. With the city under German control, Israel Joshua comes out of hiding and resumes living with the family. Brother Moishe falls ill with typhus and the apartment is disinfected; Singer and his mother are ordered to a hospital and confined to separate quarters for more than a week.

1917–20   In summer 1917, Singer moves with mother and Moishe to Biłgoraj, where, he would later write, "the kind of Jewish behavior and customs I witnessed were those preserved from a much earlier time." The village, which is occupied by Austrian troops, had recently lost many inhabitants in a cholera epidemic. Singer's father remains in Warsaw briefly before departing for Radzymin, where he again works for the town's rabbi. Singer is bar-mitzvahed. Meets eight-year-old cousin Esther, with whom he develops an intense bond. Contracts typhus and spends several months convalescing. Israel Joshua, now in Kiev, publishes stories and works as a proofreader for a Yiddish newspaper; he marries Genia Kupfershtock in 1918. Father comes to Biłgoraj in summer 1918 hoping to secure a rabbinical position there; his bid is unsuccessful, and the family must rely on charity. Independent Polish republic is declared in November 1918, and Polish troops advance into Ukrainian Galicia and take Lemberg (L'viv); there are widespread pogroms throughout Poland and Galicia. During his four-year stay in Biłgoraj Singer continues his Talmud studies while also reading widely in philosophy (particularly Spinoza), popular science, and modern literature, including Strindberg, Tolstoy, Turgenev, Flaubert, London, and Maupassant, complementing earlier reading of Sforim, Sholem Aleichem, Peretz, Asch, Bergelson, and Dostoevsky. He studies Polish, German, Esperanto, and modern Hebrew, in which he writes sketches and poems. One of his Hebrew poems is published in a local newspaper, prompting threats to revoke the family's charitable stipend. ("I had to promise to recant my apostasy," Singer wrote in 1963, "and return to 'real' learning—to Judaism, the Talmud.") Singer teaches Hebrew in private homes to young men and women. Father accepts rabbinical position in nearby Dzikow and moves there in 1920. Israel Joshua, Genia, and their infant son Yasha move to Moscow.

1921–22   Singer goes to Warsaw to attend a rabbinical seminary in 1921 but is unhappy, poor, and often hungry. Returns to Biłgoraj, giving Hebrew lessons there and in a nearby village. Continues intensive study of Spinoza's *Ethics* and reads Kant's *Prolegomena* and Hamsun's *Hunger*. Goes to live with parents and Moishe in Dzikow; now extremely pious, Moishe lends Singer the works of Rabbi Nachman of Bratslav. Israel Joshua returns to Warsaw with wife and son and publishes his first collection of short stories the following year; the couple's son Joseph is born in 1922.

1923–25   Accepting a job as proofreader arranged through his brother, Singer moves back to Warsaw, living free in the apartment of editor and poet Melekh Ravitch (the pen name of Zekhariah Bergner). Begins frequenting the Warsaw PEN Yiddish Writers' Club, attending lectures and often taking meals there. Reads about psychic research and spiritualism. Lives alone in an unheated room he rents during the winter of 1923–24. Meets writer Aaron Zeitlin, who will become a lifelong friend. Looking for a new place to live, he meets an older woman (called "Gina Halbstark" in his memoirs) who becomes his mistress; they live together for several months. After reporting for conscription, receives deferment from the army. Despite Gina's protests, he moves to rented room in the home of an elderly doctor and his wife while continuing to see her occasionally. Israel Joshua contributes regularly to New York Yiddish newspaper *Forverts* (*Jewish Daily Forward*) at the invitation of editor-in-chief Abraham Cahan. In December 1924, Singer publishes his first review, using for the only time the pseudonym "Yitskhok Tsvi," in *Literarishe bleter* (*Literary Pages*), magazine recently founded by Israel Joshua, Melekh Ravitch, and two other writers; he also works as proofreader for the magazine. Using the pseudonym "Tse," publishes his first short story, "Oyf der elter" ("In Old Age"), in *Literarishe bleter* in June 1925; the story wins first prize in a competition sponsored by the magazine. In Hebrew newspaper *Ha-yom* (*Today*), where he occasionally works as a proofreader, Singer publishes Hebrew story "Nerot" ("Candles") and signs it "Yitskhok Bashevis," pen name under which most of his short stories in Yiddish will be published. "Be-hatser shel nokhrim" ("In a Gentile Courtyard") appears in *Ha-yom* in October, the second and final story he publishes in Hebrew.

1926–27   Singer contributes stories "A dorfs-kabren" ("A Village Gravedigger") and "Eyniklekh" ("Grandchildren") to PEN Writers' Club publication. Is now involved with mistress Runia Shapira, a rabbi's daughter who has become a devoted Communist; according to Singer's memoirs, other mistresses during his adult years in Warsaw include women referred to by pseudonyms such as "Marila," a servant girl, and "Sabina," who works in a library. General Józef Piłsudski leads a coup against the Polish government in May 1926. In the summer, Hinde Esther and her son visit Warsaw for three months. Diagnosed as having weak lungs, Singer is rejected for military service in the Polish army. Continues to publish stories in *Literarishe bleter*. Around this time considers leaving Poland, and the Palestine Bureau in Warsaw issues him a certificate of immigration that contains a marriage requirement; meets woman known in his memoirs as "Stefa Janovsky," who seeks to marry Singer, then divorce him when reunited with a lover in Palestine. Their joint immigration is canceled when she discovers her lover is already married and, after proposing that Singer go through with the marriage, she becomes engaged to a prosperous Warsaw businessman instead. ("Stefa" will translate the only story of his to appear in Polish during his Warsaw years.)

1928   In April, Singer publishes story "Oyfn oylem-hatoye" ("In the World of Chaos"), about a wandering corpse. His translations of Norwegian novelist Knut Hamsun's *Pan* and *Landstrykere* (*Wayfarers*) are brought out by the publisher Boris Kletskin, the first of Singer's published translations to be signed; during his Warsaw years Singer also adapts popular German novels for the Yiddish newspaper *Radio*.

1929   Singer's father dies in Dzikow. Runia gives birth to Singer's son Israel. Three novels translated by Singer are published in Yiddish: Hamsun's *Viktoria*, D'Annunzio's *Il piacere* (*Pleasure*), and Danish writer Karin Michäelis's *Mette Trap og hendes Unger* (*Mette Trap and Her Children*); his translation of Stefan Zweig's 1921 biography of Romain Rolland appears as well. Hinde Esther returns to Poland alone with plans to stay permanently; after ten months, in which she translates Dickens (*A Christmas Carol*) and Shaw (*The Intelligent Woman's Guide to Socialism and Capitalism*) into Yiddish to help support herself, she returns to England.

1930   Boris Kletskin publishes Singer's Yiddish translations of Remarque's *All Quiet on the Western Front* and Mann's *The Magic Mountain*.

1931   Israel Joshua begins writing *Yoshe Kalb,* novel about a 19th-century Galician mystic based on a Hasidic folk tale; he reads sections of the manuscript to Singer, who also helps with research. Singer's translation of Remarque's *The Way Back* is published by Boris Kletskin.

1932   With Aaron Zetlin, Singer founds, edits, and helps finance magazine *Globus*, publishing stories "Der yid fun Bovl" ("The Jew from Babylon") and "A zokn: a khronik" ("An Old Man: A Chronicle") in its second and fourth numbers. His translations of Moshe Smilansky's Hebrew stories are published as *Araber: Folkstimlekhe geshikhtn* (*Arabs: Stories of the People*). Singer is arrested briefly during an investigation into Runia's activities. On the recommendation of his brother, Paris newspaper *Parizer haynt* (*Paris Today*) asks Singer to write about show trials of anti-Piłsudski opposition leaders; Singer attends proceedings but does not pursue assignment. Israel Joshua is invited to New York to supervise the stage adaptation of *Yoshe Kalb*, and travels there in the fall with wife and son Joseph (son Yasha dies suddenly of pneumonia just before the trip); the family remains permanently in New York, where he works for *Forverts*. Singer begins writing historical novel *Der sotn in Goray* (*Satan in Goray*), set in the 17th century against backdrop of pogroms and religious fervor caused by the false messiah Sabbatai Zevi.

1933–34   *Der sotn in Goray* is serialized in *Globus* from January through September 1933. Singer's articles appear in *Parizer haynt* and the Warsaw daily *Ekspres* (*Express*).

1935   Israel Joshua writes that *Forverts* has accepted Singer's 1925 story "Oyf der elter" ("In Old Age") for publication and encloses payment from the newspaper. As the first volume in a series issued by the Warsaw Yiddish PEN Club, *Der sotn in Goray* is published in book form with an introduction by Aaron Zeitlin. Assisted by his brother, Singer plans move to the United States. Separates from Runia, who soon immigrates to the Soviet Union with their son Israel. Travels by train from Warsaw through Germany en route to Paris, where he spends several days, staying in the Belleville section of the city. He is greeted by members of the city's Yiddish Writers' Club and attends a performance of *Yoshe Kalb*. Sails from Cherbourg on the *Champlain* and on May 1 arrives in New York, where he is met at the dock by Israel Joshua and the journalist and translator Zygmunt Salkin. In June his sketch "Reyzele: A kharakter-portrait fun varshever lebn"

("Reyzele: A Character-Portrait of Warsaw Life") is published in *Forverts*. In September, unfinished autobiographical novel *Varshe 1914–18* (*Warsaw 1914–18*) begins serialization in Warsaw daily *Dos naye vort* (*The New Word*). Lives near Israel Joshua in Sea Gate, gated community not far from Coney Island in Brooklyn; becomes romantically involved with the landlady (called "Nesha" in his memoirs) of a boarding house where he rents a room. Buys typewriter with Hebrew characters that he will use for decades. With the help of the *Forverts* staff who write to American immigration authorities on his behalf, obtains an extension of his visa. Takes long walks, a habit that will continue for the rest of his life. Writes Aaron Zeitlin and expresses regret that he has immigrated to America rather than Palestine. *Der zindiker meshiekh* (*The Sinning Messiah*), novel about 18th-century heretical mystic Jacob Frank who believed himself to be Sabbatai Zevi reincarnated, begins five-month run in *Forverts*; it is also serialized in newspapers in Paris and Warsaw.

1936   Singer moves briefly to a rooming house on East 19th Street in Manhattan, then lives for a time in Croton-on-Hudson, N.Y., and in Sheepshead Bay in Brooklyn. Contributes numerous reviews, sketches and stories as a freelance writer to *Forverts*; story "Oyf an alter shif" ("On an Old Ship") is published in anthology edited by noted Yiddish writers Joseph Opatoshu and H. Leyvick. Israel Joshua's epic novel *Di brider Ashkenazi* (*The Brothers Ashkenazi*) is published in Yiddish and in English translation to critical acclaim. Sister Hinde Esther's novel *Der sheydim-tants* (*The Devil's Dance*, translated into English as *Deborah*) is published in Warsaw.

1937   Singer contributes a few stories and sketches to *Forverts* early in the year, then stops writing fiction for several years. In the summer, meets Alma Haimann Wassermann, a recent immigrant from Germany, while both are vacationing on a farm in the Catskills; she is married, has two children, and does not speak Yiddish. Denounced as a Zionist, Runia is expelled from the Soviet Union and flees with son Israel to Istanbul.

1938   After eight months in Turkey, Runia and Israel immigrate to Palestine, settling in Tel Aviv. At the invitation of Zygmunt Salkin, Singer spends the summer at the Grine

Felder (Green Fields) arts colony in the Catskills, direct-ing rehearsals of an English-language production of I. L. Peretz's *At Night in the Old Marketplace*; the play is not produced. Singer's translation from German into Yiddish of Leon Glaser's *From Moscow to Jerusalem (The Moral Perishes): The Autobiography of a Revolutionary* is pub-lished. First work of Singer's in English translation, an ex-cerpt from *Satan in Goray* entitled "Hail the Messiah!," appears in the anthology *Jewish Short Stories of To-day*, edited by Hinde Esther's son Morris and published by Faber and Faber in London; the collection also includes stories by Israel Joshua and Hinde Esther, as well as Morris Kreitman himself (writing under pseudonym Martin Lea).

1939   Singer resumes contributing to *Forverts* after a two-year hiatus in April when he begins writing a long-running column under the pen name Yitskhok Varshavski (i.e., "from Warsaw"); these short articles range from human-interest stories ("What Studies Have Uncovered About Talented Children") to summaries of current and histori-cal events ("English Jews Fought as Heroes, Died as Mar-tyrs in York Pogrom") to general philosophical and social observations ("Can a Person Change?"; "Shyness—A Plague Affecting Large and Small, Rich and Poor"; "Why Men and Women Divorce—No Rules But the Cases Are Interesting"). Also begins to review books regularly for magazine *Di tsukunft* (*The Future*). Meets journalist Si-mon Weber. After the Germans invade Poland Singer loses contact with his mother and brother Moishe. Israel Joshua becomes an American citizen. Aaron Zeitlin im-migrates to the United States. Alma Wassermann and her husband divorce.

1940   Singer and Alma are married in a civil ceremony on Feb-ruary 14 at Brooklyn City Hall. The couple move into a small apartment on Ocean Avenue in Brooklyn. Alma be-gins working as a salesperson in the women's fashion de-partment of the Arnold Constable department store, the first of several department-store jobs. Runia and Israel move to Jerusalem; their contact with Singer is sporadic, as it has been since 1935.

1941   The Singers move to Manhattan, renting an apartment on West 103rd Street. Singer publishes more than 45 "Varshavski" articles in *Forverts*; during World War II his columns include war news and commentary.

1942–43   Singer becomes a salaried member of the *Forverts* staff. Moves with Alma to a small apartment on Central Park West. Returns to writing fiction and composes several stories narrated by the Devil or by a demon (later published in English as "The Destruction of Kreshev," "From the Diary of One Not Born," "Zeidlus the Pope," and "Two Corpses Go Dancing"). Along with revised version of 1932 story "Der yid fun Bovl," these stories are collected with *Der sotn in Goray* and published in book form by New York Yiddish publishing house Farlag Matones in 1943. The book sells about 1,000 copies and Singer collects $90 in royalties. Begins to sign some of his *Forverts* articles "D. Segal." Becomes an American citizen in 1943. Publishes overview of Yiddish literature in Poland as well as long essay about the problems of Yiddish literature in America. ("Words, like people, sometimes endure a severe disorientation when they emigrate, and often they remain forever helpless and not quite themselves. This is precisely what happened to Yiddish in America.") Israel Joshua's novel *Di mishpohe Karnovski* (*The Family Carnovsky*) and Hinde Esther's novel *Briliantn* (*Diamonds*) are published.

1944   Israel Joshua dies of a heart attack on February 10. Singer publishes story "Der Spinozist" ("The Spinozan," later translated as "The Spinoza of Market Street") in *Di tsukunft*. Begins researching, plotting, and taking notes for realist novel *Di familye Mushkat* (*The Family Moskat*).

1945   Publishes stories "Gimpl tam" ("Gimpel the Fool"), "Di kleyne shusterlekh" ("The Little Shoemakers"), and "Der Katlen" ("The Wife Killer") in Yiddish periodicals. Some time after the war's end, is told that his mother and brother Moishe were deported to Kazakhstan during the Soviet occupation of eastern Poland in 1939–41 and froze to death while building log huts. In the fall, has exchange of letters with Runia in which they discuss the legal status of their son: although they appear never to have been married, Runia requests a divorce so as to legitimize Israel; Singer refuses and proposes to legally adopt him, an offer rejected by Runia. In November, *Di familye Mushkat* begins more than two years of serialization in *Forverts*. The novel is also performed in Yiddish as a serial on New York radio station WEVD.

1946–47   Farlag Matones publishes *Fun a velt vos iz nishto mer* (*From a World That Is No More*), Israel Joshua's memoir of his childhood in Leoncin, in 1946. Many of Singer's "Varshavski" columns in *Forverts* discuss the works of philosophers such as Aristotle, Plotinus, and Spinoza. With Alma, Singer sails to Europe in late summer 1947. Visits England, where he sees his sister Hinde Esther for the last time. Travels to France and makes the first of many visits to Switzerland. Publishes travel sketches in *Forverts*.

1948   Serialization of *Di familye Mushkat* in *Forverts* ends in May; Singer will continue to submit radio scripts based on his stories and memoirs to be performed on WEVD. With Alma, travels to Miami Beach during the winter, the first of many Florida visits.

1949   When English translation by Abraham Gross and Nancy Gross of *The Family Moskat* is submitted to Alfred A. Knopf for publication, editor Herbert Weinstock suggests numerous cuts that Singer refuses to make, prompting a rift about the final shape of the book; Knopf writes to Singer, "I agree heartily with everyone that this book is likely to have a very poor chance indeed with the American bookseller if it is not substantially cut." Though continuing to resent the publisher's interference, Singer eventually cuts more than 100 pages and alters the novel's ending. In December, novel *Der feter fun Amerike* (*The Uncle from America*) begins 15-month serialization.

1950   In January, Singer travels to Miami. Reviews a recently issued thesaurus of Yiddish and the Kinsey report on male sexual behavior for *Forverts*. In October, Knopf publishes *The Family Moskat*, which is dedicated to Israel Joshua: "To me he was not only the older brother, but a spiritual father and master as well." For the first time, name appears as "Isaac Bashevis Singer," which is how he will sign his works in English. The Yiddish version is brought out in book form by Morris S. Sklarsky, and a Hebrew translation is published in Israel. Hinde Esther's collection of short stories *Yikhes* (*Lineage*, later translated as *Blitz and Other Stories*) is published in England.

1951–53   Singer travels to Florida and Cuba early in 1951 and re-
           turns to Florida the following winter. His many "Var-
           shavski" and "Segal" columns for *Forverts* include "The
           Tragedy of Knut Hamsun," "My Spanish Neighbors,"
           and "America Ignores Yiddish Culture." Works on long
           historical novel *Der hoyf* (later translated into English in
           two separate volumes, *The Manor* and *The Estate*), which
           is serialized in *Forverts*. Jacob Sloan works on translation
           of *Der sotn in Goray* into English. Eliezer Greenberg
           reads "Gimpl tam" ("Gimpel the Fool") to critic Irving
           Howe; at Howe's request, Saul Bellow does a translation
           that is published in *Partisan Review* in May 1953. After
           reading the story, Cecil Hemley, publisher who had co-
           founded the Noonday Press in 1951, meets with Jacob
           Sloan and then Singer himself and arranges to publish
           Satan in Goray; Singer is also introduced to Hemley's
           wife, Elaine Gottlieb, who will serve as one of his transla-
           tors. *Der sotn in Goray* is published in Hebrew in Tel Aviv
           in 1953.

1954   *A Treasury of Yiddish Stories*, edited by Irving Howe and
           Eliezer Greenberg, includes "Gimpel the Fool" and the
           first English publication of "The Little Shoemakers."
           Partisan Review publishes "From the Diary of One Not
           Born" and includes "Gimpel the Fool" in its anthology
           More Stories in the Modern Manner. Hinde Esther Kreit-
           man dies in England and her body is cremated.

1955   In February, son Israel (who has taken the name Israel
           Zamir) travels to New York on behalf of his kibbutz and
           sees Singer for the first time in 20 years. Memoir of
           Warsaw childhood *In mayn foter's bes-din shtub* (*In My
           Father's Court*) is serialized in *Forverts* from February to
           September (published in 1954 as *Mayn tatn's bes-din
           shtub*). Singer travels to Israel for the first of many visits.
           Publishes stories about his maternal grandfather's rabbini-
           cal court in Biłgoraj in *Forverts*. Story "The Wife Killer"
           published in English in first issue of the American Zionist
           quarterly *Midstream*. Noonday Press publishes *Satan in
           Goray* in the fall.

1956   Serialized memoir *Der shrayber-klub* (*The Writers' Club*)
           runs in *Forverts* from January to December.

1957   In February the story "Fire," first work of Singer's to be
           published in English in more than a year, appears in

Commentary, which also includes "The Gentleman from Cracow" in its September number. Novel *Shotns baym Hodson* (*Shadows on the Hudson*) is serialized in *Forverts*. Israel Zamir returns to Israel after two-year stay in New York. *Gimpel the Fool and Other Stories* is published by Noonday in November; reviewing the collection, Anzia Yezierska calls Singer "the last of the great Yiddish fiction writers." In December, eight episodes from *Mayn tatn's bes-din shtub*, including "To the Land of Israel" and "The Suicide," are dramatized by the Folksbiene (People's Theater) at the Radin Theatre on New York City's Lower East Side.

1958–60   *Satan in Goray* and *Gimpel the Fool and Other Stories* are published in England in 1958 by Peter Owen. Singer receives $1,500 grant from the National Institute of Arts and Letters in 1959. *Die kuntsmakher fun Lublin* (*The Magician of Lublin*) is serialized in *Forverts*; Elaine Gottlieb and Joseph Singer's English version is published by Noonday in June 1960. Singer and Alma move to an apartment on West 72nd Street. He reviews Tennessee Williams' *Period of Adjustment* and Sean O'Casey's *The Plough and the Stars* for *Forverts*. Novel *Der knecht* (*The Slave*) begins six-month run in *Forverts* in October 1960.

1961   The appearance of Singer's stories in mass-circulation American magazines such as *Mademoiselle*, *Esquire*, and *GQ* exposes his work to a wider audience in the United States. By now Singer has established a method of supervising his translations by working closely with collaborators (many of whom do not know Yiddish, Joseph Singer and Mirra Ginsburg being notable exceptions); his numerous collaborators and translators during his career include Ruth Schachner Finkel, Evelyn Torton Beck, Herbert Lottman, Rosanna Gerber, Elizabeth Shub, Aliza Shevrin, and many others. Reviews production of Ionesco's *Rhinoceros* starring Eli Wallach and Zero Mostel for *Forverts*, as well as Tagore's *King of the Dark Chamber*, Neil Simon's *Come Blow Your Horn*, Ester Kaufman's *A Worm in Horseradish*, the musical *Show Boat*, and Frederic Knott's *Write Me a Murder*. Farrar, Straus & Cudahy (which has acquired Noonday Press) publishes story collection *The Spinoza of Market Street* in October. Cecil Hemley and Singer work on English version of *The Slave*. Lila Karpf, director of the subsidiary rights department at Farrar, Straus & Cudahy, begins serving as Singer's unofficial literary agent.

1962   *The Spinoza of Market Street* earns Singer the first of several National Book Award nominations. On June 11, Farrar, Straus & Cudahy publishes English version of *The Slave*, which is praised by Ted Hughes and Susan Sontag, among others. Singer reads Bruno Schulz and admires his work. Reviews Tennessee Williams' *The Night of the Iguana* and other plays for *Forverts*. Roth-Kershner Productions buys film rights to *The Magician of Lublin*. "Yentl the Yeshiva Boy," English translation of story "Yentl der yehive-boher" (which will be published in Yiddish the following year), is published in *Commentary*. French translation of *Satan in Goray* is published in Paris; *The Spinoza of Market Street* is brought out in England by Secker and Warburg.

1963   Novel *A shif keyn Amerike* (*A Ship to America*) begins nine-month serialization in *Forverts* in January. Singer reviews for *Forverts* Tennessee Williams' *The Milk Train Doesn't Stop Here Anymore*, Eugene O'Neill's *Strange Interlude*, Edward Albee's adaptation of Carson McCullers' *The Ballad of the Sad Café*, and many other plays. Story collection *Gimpl tam un anderer dertseylungen* (*Gimpel the Fool and Other Stories*) is published. Spanish translation of *Satan in Goray* is published in Buenos Aires. Autobiographical narrative *Fun der alter un nayer heym* (*From the Old and the New Home*) begins two years of serialization in *Forverts*. Extensive interview with Joel Blocker and Richard Elman is featured in November issue of *Commentary*; as Singer's fame grows, he gives many more interviews for English-language magazines and newspapers, through which his views on Judaism, philosophy, spirituality, politics, and literature become widely known.

1964   A *Forverts* column, "Knape tsvey yor a vegetaryer" ("Almost Two Years a Vegetarian"), suggests that Singer became a vegetarian in 1962, an impression he will reinforce in later writings and statements in interviews (other evidence of his own and others records his vegetarian habits as far back as the 1920s). "A Sacrifice," chapter from *In My Father's Court*, is the first of several stories Singer publishes in *Harper's*; his fiction appears in *Vogue* and *The*

Saturday Evening Post as well as smaller publications (*American Judaism, Hadassah Magazine*) aimed primarily at a Jewish audience. National Institute of Arts and Letters elects Singer as a member. He writes an appreciation of Sholem Aleichem for *The New York Times* in September. Farrar, Straus & Giroux publishes *Short Friday and Other Stories*.

1965   The Singers move to the Belnord apartment house on the corner of Broadway and 86th Street. *The Family Moskat* is restored to print when it is published by Farrar, Straus & Giroux. Singer contributes an introduction to a new edition of Israel Joshua's *Yoshe Kalb*, published by Harper & Row, and reviews Martin Buber's *Daniel* for *Commentary*. Hebrew translation of *The Slave* published in Israel; German translation published in Hamburg. Singer is nominated for the International Publishers' Prize (also known as the Prix Formenter) and wins a prize for Best Foreign Book in France. In response to a request from *Harper's* to discuss the profession of writing, submits article discussing his royalties and financial situation, acknowledging that his "main source of income is still derived from my journalistic work for the *Jewish Daily Forward*."

1966   After a hiatus in writing about theater for *Forverts*, Singer reviews Sartre's *The Condemned of Altona*, Bellow's *Under the Weather*, and Yiddish musical *The Poor Millionaire*, starring Leo Fuchs. In February, Modern Library issues *Selected Short Stories of Isaac Bashevis Singer*, edited by Irving Howe. *Sonim, di geshikhte fun a liebe* (*Enemies, A Love Story*) appears in serial form from February to August in *Forverts*. Essay "Once on Second Avenue There Lived a Yiddish Theater" is printed in *The New York Times*. On May 2, Farrar, Straus & Giroux publishes *In My Father's Court*, abridged version of *Mayn tatn's besdin shtub*; later that month, *Forverts* publishes "Di geshikhte fun Mazel un Shlimazel" ("The Story of Mazel and Shlimazel"), the first of the many children's stories that become an increasingly important part of Singer's literary output in his later years. Collection of children's stories in English translation, *Zlateh the Goat and Other Stories*, is published in October by Harper & Row with illustrations by Maurice Sendak. Singer serves as writer-in-residence at Oberlin College, the first of several such academic appointments. Gives interview on NBC television program *The Eternal Light*, produced by the Jewish Theological Seminary. In an article about recent Nobel Prize recipient S. Y. Agnon published in *Commentary* in December, Edmund Wilson recommends Singer for a Nobel Prize. Ballet inspired by story "The Gentleman from Cracow" is performed by the Sophie Maslow Company at Madison Square Garden.

1967   Story "Hene fayer" ("Henne Fire") published in *Forverts* on January 6; the following week *Der sertifikat* (*The Certificate*), autobiographical novel based on Singer's attempt to immigrate to Palestine with "Stefa Janovsky," begins five-month serialization. *The Manor*, first part of *Der hoyf* in English translation by Elaine Gottlieb and Joseph Singer, is published by Farrar, Straus & Giroux. Children's books *The Fearsome Inn* and *Mazel and Shlimazel; or, The Milk of a Lioness* are published by Scribner's and Farrar, Straus & Giroux, respectively. In October, story "Powers" is published in *Harper's* in which Singer shares translation credits with Dorothea Straus; the wife of publisher Robert Straus, she has been acquainted with Singer for several years and will help translate many stories in the late 1960s and early 1970s. Singer contributes introduction to new edition of Hamsun's *Hunger*. Receives Italian literary award, the Bancarella Prize. Profile of Alma, "The Novelist's Working Wife," runs in *The New York Times*. When "The Slaughterer" is published in *The New Yorker* on November 25, the magazine breaks long policy of refusing to print translations, eventually reserving the option of first serial publication for the English versions of Singer's stories; Singer will have a close working relationship with Rachel MacKenzie, his editor at the magazine. For the first time, *Playboy* publishes Singer stories; the third of these, "The Lecture," in its December number, wins the magazine's annual fiction award.

1968   Story "Di kafeterye" ("The Cafeteria") is published in *Di tsukunft*'s March–April issue. *The Séance and Other Stories*, dedicated to the memory of Singer's sister Hinde Esther (with her name erroneously printed as "Minda Esther"), is published by Farrar, Straus & Giroux, which also brings out children's book *When Shlemiel Went to Warsaw and Other Stories*. Barbra Streisand acquires film rights for "Yentl the Yeshiva Boy." Collection of short stories in German translation, including "Gimpel the Fool," "Taibele and Her Demon," and "The Spinoza of Market Street," is published in Hamburg.

1969   Publication of *The Estate* (translation of latter half of *Der hoyf*) and memoir for children *A Day of Pleasure: Stories of a Boy Growing Up in Warsaw*, much of which is adapted from *In My Father's Court*. In the summer, Singer leaves New York for more than three months, visiting France and Israel. Meets novelist and short-story writer Laurie Colwin, who will soon become one of his translators. "Envy; or, Yiddish in America," Cynthia Ozick's long story inspired by Singer and the resentment other Yiddish writers feel about his success, is published in *Commentary* in November. Singer's essay "I See the Child as the Last Refuge" published in *The New York Times.*

1970   Profile of Singer in *The New York Times* reports that his annual income now "comfortably exceeds" $100,000. Although he signs some of his short stories with the "Varshavski" pseudonym, he effectively ceases to write the regular column for *Forverts* that had run continuously under pseudonyms since 1939. Israel Zamir publishes account of his reunion with Singer in 1955 in Tel Aviv newspaper *Al ha-Mishmar.* After a trial run in East Hampton, N.Y., Robert Brustein's Yale Repertory Theater stages *Two Saints* in the fall, pairing dramatic adaptations of "Gimpel the Fool" and Flaubert's "St. Julian the Hospitaler." *A Day of Pleasure* receives the National Book Award in the children's literature category. Singer receives Creative Arts Awards Medal from Brandeis University. Farrar, Straus & Giroux brings out *A Friend of Kafka and Other Stories* as well as the children's books *Elijah the Slave* and *Joseph and Koza; or, The Sacrifice to the Vistula.*

1971   From now on, Singer signs his writings in Yiddish as "Bashevis" or "Bashevis Singer." In August, novel *Der fartribener zun* (*The Exiled Son*) begins six-month serialization in *Forverts.* Farrar, Straus & Giroux's *An Isaac Bashevis Singer Reader* collects stories, *The Magician of Lublin*, and four additional translated chapters of *In My Father's Court.* Children's works *Alone in the Wild Forest* and *The Topsy-Turvy Emperor of China* are published. Singer publishes essay "Hasidism and Its Origins" in the book *Tully Filmus: Selected Drawings.* Folksbiene revives

David Licht's stage adaptation of *Mayn tatn's bes-din shtub* in November, and it runs for several months.

1972   Robert Lescher becomes Singer's agent. Farrar, Straus & Giroux publishes *Enemies, A Love Story* and children's book *The Wicked City*. Photographer and filmmaker Bruce Davidson, who lives in Singer's apartment building, completes half-hour film *Isaac Singer's Nightmare and Mrs. Pupko's Beard*, a free adaptation of story "The Beard"; it wins first prize for fiction at the American Film Festival and is shown on public television in December, paired with a film about Marc Chagall.

1973   Yale Repertory Theater produces dramatization of short story "The Mirror"; while in New Haven to attend a performance, Singer does a radio interview with Irving Howe. *New York* magazine profile "The Cafeteria" is illustrated with Bruce Davidson's photographs of Singer in the Garden Cafeteria on the Lower East Side. Visiting Miami Beach for the first time in several years, Singer buys a condominium apartment at 9511 Collins Avenue in the Surfside neighborhood. Farrar, Straus & Giroux publishes *A Crown of Feathers and Other Stories* and children's book *The Fools of Chelm and Their History*. Crown Publishers issues *The Hasidim*, book of photographs with introduction and essay by Singer.

1974   *A Crown of Feathers* shares National Book Award for fiction with Thomas Pynchon's *Gravity's Rainbow*. The novels *Neshome ekspeditsyes* (*Soul Expeditions*; later translated as *Shosha*) and *Der bal-tshuve* (*The Penitent*) are serialized in *Forverts*. In April, Yale Repertory produces *Shlemiel the First*, based on portions of *The Fools of Chelm*. Children's book *Why Noah Chose the Dove* is published. Chelsea Theater Center's production of *Yentl*, adaptation of "Yentl the Yeshiva Boy" by Leah Napolin and Singer, directed by Robert Kalfin, opens on December 21 at the Brooklyn Academy of Music.

1975   Brooklyn performances of *Yentl* end January 12. *Passions and Other Stories* is published by Farrar, Straus & Giroux. In July Singer receives an honorary degree from the Hebrew University in Jerusalem; while there, *The Jerusalem Post* publishes an unflattering article about him by nephew Maurice Carr, who calls him "an escape artist, the sex-Houdini" and claims Singer had seen a "cherished mistress" while visiting Israel in 1969. In September, he is awarded the S. Y. Agnon Gold Medal by the American Friends of the Hebrew University. Receives honorary doctorate from Texas Christian University (one of his eight honorary degrees). Serves as writer-in-residence at Bard College, where he meets Dvorah Menashe (later Telushkin), who begins to drive him to speaking engagements and act as personal secretary; she translates many of Singer's works and becomes a close friend and companion. After a week of previews, *Yentl*, starring Tovah Feldshuh and John Shea, opens on Broadway at the Eugene O'Neill Theater on October 23, running for more than five months and then touring nationally.

1976   Children's book *Naftali the Storyteller and His Horse, Sus* is published by Farrar, Straus & Giroux; memoir *A Little Boy in Search of God* is brought out by Doubleday. In September, Singer meets Richard Burgin, who will conduct approximately 50 interviews over the next two years, excerpts from which will be published in *The New York Times* in 1978 and in *Conversations with Isaac Bashevis Singer* (1986). Philip Roth visits Singer in November to discuss Bruno Schulz for an interview published in *The New York Times Book Review* the following year. *Yarme un Keyle* (*Yarme and Keyle*), novel about the Warsaw underworld set just before World War I, begins ten-month serialization in *Forverts* in December.

1977–78   During the winter Singer is hospitalized in Florida for treatment of a prostate condition. Stage adaptation of story *Teibele and Her Demon* by Eve Friedman and Singer is performed at the Guthrie Theater in Minneapolis, starring F. Murray Abraham and Laura Esterman. *Shosha* is published by Farrar, Straus & Giroux in July 1978. Singer reviews Bruno Schulz's *Sanatorium Under the Sign of the Hourglass* for *The New York Times*. Shooting begins in West Germany for film of *The Magician of Lublin*, adapted and directed by Israeli filmmaker Menahem Golan and starring Alan Arkin. Memoir *A Young Man in Search of Love* is published by Doubleday. Collection *he-Mafteah: sipurim* (*The Key: Stories*), translated by Israel Zamir, is published in Tel Aviv in 1978. On October 5, 1978, Singer is awarded the Nobel Prize in Literature. Rents a hotel room so he can work on his acceptance speech without distraction; the publicity and fame of the award cause him to remove his name from the phone book. Travels to Stockholm with Alma, Simon Weber (now editor of *Forverts*), Roger and Dorothea Straus, and Israel Zamir. His acceptance speech, delivered on December 8, is in English but includes a sentence in Yiddish. *Forverts* dedicates Chanukah issue to Singer, including a diary of the Stockholm trip written by Weber.

1979   First full-length biography, Paul Kresh's *Isaac Bashevis Singer: The Magician of West 86th Street*, is published. English and Yiddish versions of Singer's Nobel lecture are published by Farrar, Straus & Giroux, as well as the story collection *Old Love*. Israel Zamir's Hebrew translation of *Enemies, A Love Story* is published in Tel Aviv. Menahem Golan's *The Magician of Lublin* is shown at the Venice Film Festival but its scheduled screening at the Cairo Film Festival is canceled by Egyptian censors; the film opens in New York on November 9 and is met with unfavorable reviews. David Schiff's opera *Gimpel the Fool*, sung in Yiddish with English narration, premieres at the 92nd Street Y in New York and is revived the following year in a longer and slightly revised version. *Teibele and Her Demon* is performed in Washington, D.C., then makes its Broadway premiere at the Brooks Atkinson Theater in December.

1980   *Teibele and Her Demon* closes in January after 25 performances. Novel *Der kenig fun di felder* (*The King of the Fields*) is serialized for more than ten months beginning in February. Having long maintained he would never return to Poland, Singer declines offer from Polish literary group to attend a conference in Warsaw. Contributes a forward to Aaron Zeitlin's posthumous collection *Literarishe un filosofishe eseyen* (*Literary and Philosophical Essays*). Book of stories in Russian translation, including "Gimpel the Fool" and "Teibele and Her Demon," is published in Tel Aviv. Two children's books are published by Farrar, Straus & Giroux: *The Power of Light: Eight Stories for Hanukkah* and *The Reaches of Heaven: A Story of the Baal Shem Tov*.

1981   Autobiographical novel *Farloyrene neshomes* (*Lost Souls*, posthumously translated as *Meshugah*) is serialized in *Forverts* beginning in April. *Lost in America*, sequel to *A Young Man in Search of Love*, is published by Doubleday.

1982   "Di mishpohe: Materyal far an oytobiografye" ("The Family: Material for an Autobiography") runs in *Forverts* from February to August, then resumes in October for five months. *The Collected Stories of Isaac Bashevis Singer* is published by Farrar, Straus & Giroux, as well as children's book *The Golem*.

1983   Yehuga Moralis's musical version of "Gimpel the Fool" is performed in Israel. When novel *The Penitent* is published, it receives mixed reviews. Polish translations based on the English versions of *The Magician of Lublin* and *The Estate*, as well as a collection of short stories, are published in Warsaw. After being out of print for decades, Hinde Esther's *Deborah* is published in England by Virago Press; when asked about the revival of interest in his sister's work, Singer chooses not to comment. *Yentl*, musical film directed by Barbra Streisand and starring Streisand, Mandy Patinkin, and Amy Irving, opens November 18.

1984   *Yentl* is a commercial success but Singer is deeply unhappy about the adaptation of his story and publishes an essay (cast as an interview with himself) criticizing the film in *The New York Times* in January. Amrak Nowak's television film *The Cafeteria*, based on Singer's story, is shown on PBS as part of the "American Playhouse" series on February 21. In October, *A Play for the Devil*, based on story "The Unseen," is performed in Yiddish by the Folksbiene; *Shlemiel the First* opens at the Jewish Repertory Theater in New York. Autobiographical books *A Little Boy in Search of God*, *A Young Man in Search of Love*, and *Lost in America* are collected with introduction "The Beginning" as *Love and Exile*, published by Doubleday. *Stories for Children* is published by Farrar, Straus & Giroux.

1985   Farrar, Straus & Giroux brings out *The Image and Other Stories*. *Der ver aheim* (*The Way Home*), is serialized in *Forverts*. Singer teaches weekly creative writing class with Lester Goran at the University of Miami.

1986   *Conversations with Isaac Bashevis Singer*, edited by Richard Burgin, published by Farrar, Straus & Giroux. On June 23 Singer receives the Handel Medallion, cultural prize awarded by the City of New York. Story collection *Gifts* is published by the Jewish Publication Society.

Dvorah Menashe works with Singer to collect his early work in a series called "Early Steps in Literature" to be published in *Forverts*, but the project founders. Amrak Nowak's film *Isaac in America: A Journey with Isaac Bashevis Singer* is screened at the New York Film Festival in September. Paul Mazursky acquires film rights to *Enemies, A Love Story* and begins working on adaptation with screenwriter Roger L. Simon. In November, the Israeli ministry of education bans several of Singer's works from religious schools because "his values do not conform to the values of the religious public."

1987–90 *Isaac in America* is nominated for an Academy Award and wins the Sundance Film Festival's Grand Jury Prize for a documentary. *The Death of Methuselah and Other Stories* and novel *The King of the Fields* are published by Farrar, Straus & Giroux in 1988. Singer's health is now failing, and the Singers live full time in Surfside. Ronald Sanders, writer and former editor of *Midstream*, is named his official biographer (plans for other biographies, by Khone Shemruk, Leonard Wolf, and Janet Hadda, will be announced; only Hadda's is completed). The American Academy and Institute of Arts and Letters awards Singer its Gold Medal. Paul Mazursky travels to Florida to meet with Singer. *Enemies, A Love Story*, starring Ron Silver, Angelica Houston, and Lena Olin, opens in December 1989; Huston and Olin are both nominated for Academy Awards. Singer is elected to the American Academy of Arts in 1990, the first author to write in a language other than English to be so honored.

1991 Biographer Ronald Sanders dies in January. *My Love Affair with Miami Beach,* book of photographs by Richard Nagler with a short essay by Singer and an interview, is published. Farrar, Straus & Giroux publishes *Scum* in a translation by Rosaline Dukalsky Schwartz. Singer dies on July 24 in his apartment in Surfside, Florida. He is buried at the Beth-El cemetery in Paramus, New Jersey.

Note on the Texts

This volume contains the 54 short stories by Isaac Bashevis Singer published in English translations in the collections *Gimpel the Fool and Other Stories* (1957), *The Spinoza of Market Street* (1961), *Short Friday and Other Stories* (1964), and *The Séance and Other Stories* (1968). The texts of these stories are taken from their first book publications.

Singer wrote his stories in Yiddish, his native language, and published regularly in periodicals such as *Di tsukunft* (*The Future*), *Di goldene keyt* (*The Golden Chain*), and especially *Forverts* (*The Jewish Daily Forward*), the newspaper to which he contributed stories and journalism as a freelance writer from 1935 through the early 1940s and thereafter as a salaried member of its staff. In 1953, eighteen years after Singer's immigration to the United States, "Gimpel the Fool," his first story in English translation, was published in *Partisan Review*. (An excerpt from his novel *Satan in Goray* had been included in a British anthology in 1938, and the English translation of his novel *The Family Moskat* had been published by Knopf in 1950.) This story and several others published in the 1950s in magazines such as *Commentary*, *Midstream*, and *Partisan Review* were translated without Singer's direct involvement. However, soon after his stories began attracting interest in the United States outside Yiddish-speaking circles, Singer began working closely with his translators (many of whom did not speak Yiddish) to produce English versions, revising and adapting the works for a new audience. In the 1960s translations of his stories appeared regularly in mass-circulation American magazines such as *Mademoiselle*, *The Saturday Evening Post*, *Harper's*, *Playboy*, and *The New Yorker* before being collected in one of his short-story volumes. When preparing these volumes, Singer would continue to make or authorize changes while working with his editors at Noonday Press (for *Gimpel the Fool and Other Stories*) or Farrar, Straus & Cudahy (later Farrar, Straus & Giroux). Once collected in book form, Singer did not revise these stories, though many were published later in collections such as *An Isaac Bashevis Singer Reader* (1971) and *The Collected Stories of Isaac Bashevis Singer* (1982).

Singer called English his "second original language," and the English versions of his fiction served as the basis for translations into languages such as French, German, and Italian. Although he would almost always publish a story in Yiddish soon after its completion, sometimes the English version of a story was published years or even decades after it first written in Yiddish. For example, four stories in the present volume, "The Destruction of Kreshev," "From the Diary of One Not Born," "Zeidlus the Pope," and "Two Corpses Go Dancing," were written in the early 1940s after Singer had returned to writing fiction following a hiatus of several years. Narrated by the Devil ("the Evil One") or by a demon, these thematically linked stories were included with Singer's novel *Der sotn in Goray* (*Satan in Goray*) and the story "Der yid fun Bovl" ("The Jew from Babylon") in the 1943 collection *Der sotn in Goray: A mayse fun fartsaytns: un andere dertseylungen* (*Satan in Goray: A Story of Bygone Days: And Other Stories*). Singer chose not to publish these stories together in English, and the four stories are spread out among the separate books collected in the present volume. As Singer's popularity in the United States grew, however, lengthy chronological gaps between composition and publication in translation became less common; most of his stories from the 1960s were published in English within a few years of their original composition in Yiddish.

The list below provides information about the publication history of each story in Yiddish and in English. For Yiddish publication, the present volume has relied primarily on three bibliographies: David Neal Miller's *A Bibliography of Isaac Bashevis Singer, 1924–1949* (New York: Peter Lang, 1984) and *A Bibliography of Isaac Bashevis Singer, January 1950–June 1952* (New York: Max Weinreich Center for Advanced Jewish Studies, YIVO Institute for Jewish Research, 1979) as well as Roberta Saltzman's *Isaac Bashevis Singer: A Bibliography of His Works in Yiddish and English, 1960–1991* (Lanham, Md.: Scarecrow Press, 2002). These bibliographies are thorough but not complete (no bibliography exists for the period July 1952–December 1959); Singer published under at least six pseudonyms in Yiddish periodicals in New York, Warsaw, Paris, and perhaps elsewhere during his career, and it is unlikely that there will ever be a comprehensive list of all his contributions to Yiddish publications. The English versions of Singer's works have been listed by Jackson R. Bryer and Paul E. Rockwell in "Isaac Bashevis Singer in English: A Bibliography" in *Critical Views of Isaac Bashevis Singer*, edited by Irving Malin (New York: NYU Press, 1969) as well as in articles published in the *Bulletin of Bibliography* by Bonniejean McGuire Christensen (January–March 1969) and David S. Hornbeck (March 1982). The list below includes the Yiddish title of each story, which is translated only if significantly different from the title of the English version. If no Yiddish title is given, the story does not appear in Miller's or Saltzman's bibliographies. Book publications are abbreviated as follows:

SG   *Der sotn in Goray: a mayse fun fartsaytns: un andere dertsey-*
        lungen. New York: Farlag Matones, 1943. (*Satan in Goray:*
        A Story of Bygone Days: And Other Stories).
GT   *Gimpl tam un andere dertseylungen.* New York: CYCO,
        1963. (*Gimpel the Fool and Other Stories*).
MHO   *Mayses fun hintern oyvn.* Tel Aviv: Farlag Y. L. Perets, 1971.
        (*Stories from Behind the Stove*).
DS   *Der shpigl un andere dertseylungen.* Jerusalem: Hebrew Uni-
        versity of Jerusalem, 1975. (*The Mirror and Other Stories*).
GF   *Gimpel the Fool and Other Stories* (New York: Noonday
        Press, 1957).
SMS   *The Spinoza of Market Street* (New York: Farrar, Straus &
        Cudahy, 1961).
SF   *Short Friday and Other Stories* (New York: Farrar, Straus &
        Giroux, 1964).
TS   *The Séance and Other Stories* (New York: Farrar, Straus &
        Giroux, 1968).
SR   *An Isaac Bashevis Singer Reader* (New York: Farrar, Straus
        & Giroux, 1971).
CS   *The Collected Stories of Isaac Bashevis Singer* (New York: Far-
        rar, Straus & Giroux, 1982).

As stated above, the present volume prints the texts of Singer's
English-language collections, in which the English versions of his
stories were published for the first time in book form. The source of
each story printed in the present volume is indicated by bold type.

Gimpel the Fool. "Gimpl tam." *Yidisher kemfer,* March 30, 1945. GT. English
    version: *Partisan Review,* May–June 1953. Included in *A Treasury of Yid-
    dish Stories,* edited by Irving Howe and Eliezer Greenberg (New York:
    Viking, 1954) and *More Stories in the Modern Manner from Partisan Review*
    (New York: Avon Publications, 1954). **GF**, SR, CS.
The Gentleman from Cracow. "Der bal" (The Ball). *Forverts,* May 19, 1957.
    GT. English version: *Commentary,* September 1957. **GF**, CS.
The Wife Killer. "Der katlen." *Yidisher kemfer,* September 7, 1945. GT. En-
    glish version: *Midstream,* Autumn 1955. **GF.**
By the Light of Memorial Candles. "Kegn der shayn fun yortsayt-likht." GT.
    English version: **GF.**
The Mirror. "Der shpigl." DS. English version: *New World Writing* 12 (1955).
    GF, SR.
The Little Shoemakers. "Di kleyne shusterlekh." *Di tsukunft,* April 1945. GT.
    Included in *A Treasury of Yiddish Stories,* ed. Irving Howe and Eliezer
    Greenberg (New York: Viking, 1954). **GF,** CS.
Joy. "M'darf zayn be-simhe" (One Should Be Joyful). GT. English version:
    GF, CS.

From the Diary of One Not Born. "A togbukh fun a nisht-geboyrenem." SG. English version: *Partisan Review*, March 1954. **GF.**

The Old Man. "A zokn: A khronik." *Globus* (Warsaw), October 1932. English version: **GF.**

Fire. "Dos fayer." *Forverts*, March 25, 1956. GT, DS. English version: *Commentary*, February 1957. **GF.**

The Unseen. "Der roye veetne-nire: Fun der serye dertseylungen 'Dos gedenkbukh fun yeyster-hore'" (Seer but Not Seen: From the Series of Stories "The Devil's Diary"). *Svive*, July–August 1943. GT. English version: **GF,** SR, CS.

The Spinoza of Market Street. "Der Spinozist" (The Spinozan). *Di tsukunft*, July 1944. GT. English version: *Esquire*, October 1961. **SMS,** SR, CS.

The Black Wedding. "Di shvarts hasene." GT. English version: *Noonday* 3, edited by Cecil Hemley and Dwight W. Webb (NY: Noonday Press, 1960). **SMS,** SR.

A Tale of Two Liars. "A mayse mit trvey ligners." *Forverts*, April 15, 1949. GT. English version: *Noonday* 1, edited Cecil Hemley (NY: Noonday Press, 1958). **SMS.**

The Shadow of a Crib. "Der shotn fun a vig." GT. English version: *Mademoiselle*, March 1961. **SMS.**

Shiddah and Kuziba. "Shida un Kuziba." English version: *Commentary*, March 1961. **SMS.**

Caricature. "Dos nokhrimenish" (Mimicry). *Forverts*, November 13, 1960. GT. English version: *GQ*, November 1961. **SMS.**

The Beggar Said So. English version: *Esquire*, May 1961. **SMS.**

The Man Who Came Back. "Der tsurikgeshrigener." English version: as "One Who Came Back," *Commentary*, February 1960. **SMS,** SR.

A Piece of Advice. "Di eytse." *Di goldene keyt* 31 (1958). GT. English version: *Hadassah*, September 1960. **SMS.**

In the Poorhouse. English version: as "At the Poorhouse," *Midstream*, Winter 1960. **SMS.**

The Destruction of Kreshev. "Der hurbn fun Kreshev." SG. English version: **SMS,** CS.

Taibele and Her Demon. "Taybele un Hurmiza." English version: as "Taibele and Hurmizah," *Commentary*, February 1963. **SF,** CS.

Big and Little. "Kleyn un groys." GT. English version: *Midstream*, Summer 1961. **SF.**

Blood. "Tryf blut" (Unkosher Blood). *Forverts*, December 23, 24, 30, and 31, 1966. English version: *Harper's*, August 1964. **SF,** SR.

Alone. "Aleyn." *Svive* 1 (1960). GT. English version: *Mademoiselle*, October 1962. **SF,** CS.

Esther Kreindel the Second. "Ester-Krayndl di tsveyte." *Di goldene keyt* 48 (1964). English version: *Saturday Evening Post*, October 17, 1964. **SF.**

Jachid and Jechidah. "Yahid un Yehidah." *Di goldene keyt* 49 (1964). MHO. English version: **SF.**

Under the Knife. "Unter'n messer." *Forverts*, October 7 and 14, 1966. English version: **SF.**

The Fast. "Dos faster" (The Faster). *Di goldene keyt* 40 (1961). GT. English version: *The Second Coming*, June 1962. **SF, SR.**

The Last Demon. "Mayse Tishevits" (A Tale of Tishevitz). English version: *Prism* 1 (1962). **SF, CS.**

Yentl the Yeshiva Boy. "Yentl der yeshive-boher." *Di goldene keyt* 46 (1963). MHO. English version: *Commentary*, September 1962. **SF, SR, CS.**

Three Tales. "Dray mayses." *Di goldene keyt* 49 (1964). DS. English version: *Commentary*, October 1964. **SF.**

Zeidlus the Pope. "Zaydlus der Ershter: Fun a serye dertseylungen 'Dos gedenkbukh fun yeyster-hore'" (Zaydlus the First: From the Series of Stories "The Devil's Diary"). *Svive*, January–February 1943. SG. English version: **SF, CS.**

A Wedding in Brownsville. "A hasene in Bronzvil." *Di goldene keyt* 42 (1962). English version: *Commentary*, March 1964. **SF.**

I Place My Reliance on No Man. "Lo al enash rehitsna." GT. English version: **SF.**

Cunegunde. English version: *Esquire*, December 1964. **SF.**

Short Friday. "Der kurtser fraytik." *Di tsukunft*, January 1945. English version: **SF, SR.**

The Séance. "Der seans." *Forverts,* May 14, 1967. MHO. English version: *Encounter*, July 1965. **TS, SR, CS.**

The Slaughterer. "Der shoyhet." *Forverts*, September 24 and 25, 1965. MHO. English version: *The New Yorker*, November 25, 1967. **TS, SR, CS.**

The Dead Fiddler. "Der toyer klezmer" (The Dead Musician). *Forverts*, September 2, 3, 9, 10, 16, 17, and 23, 1960. MHO. English version: *The New Yorker*, May 25, 1968. **TS, CS.**

The Lecture. "Di forlezung." *Forverts*, December 10, 11, and 17, 1965. English version: *Playboy*, December 1967. **TS, SR.**

Cockadoodledoo. "Kukeriku." *Di goldene keyt* (1959). GT, DS. English version: *Hadassah*, November 1964. **TS.**

The Plagiarist. "Di kopye." *Forverts*, November 11, 12, and 18, 1966. English version: *Israel Magazine*, November 1967. **TS.**

Zeitl and Rickel. "Tsaytl un Rikl." *Forverts*, August 19 and 20, 1966. DS. English version: *Hudson Review*, Spring 1968. **TS.**

The Warehouse. "Di garderob." English version: *Cavalier*, January 1966. **TS.**

Henne Fire. "Hene fayer." *Forverts*, January 6 and 7, 1967. MHO. English version: *Playboy*, May 1968. **TS, CS.**

Getzel the Monkey. "Getsl malpe." *Di goldene keyt* 55 (1966). MHO. English version: *American Judaism*, Fall 1964. **TS, SR.**

Yanda. "Unter der pave's ek" (Under the Peacock's Tail). *Forverts*, September 29 and 30, 1967. English version: *Harper's*, May 1968. **TS.**

The Needle. "Di nodl." MHO. English version: *Cosmopolitan*, August 1966. **TS.**

This volume presents the texts of the original printings chosen for inclusion here, but it does not attempt to reproduce features of their typographic design. The texts printed here are presented without change, except for the correction of typographical errors. Spelling, punctuation, and capitalization are often expressive features and are not altered, even when inconsistent or irregular. Transliteration of Yiddish and Hebrew words appear as presented in the source texts, even if the same words are transliterated differently elsewhere in the volume. The translation credits are those given by Singer, and no attempt has been made to verify the accuracy of these credits or to identify translators for stories in which no credit line appears. The following is a list of typographical errors corrected, cited by page and line number: 8.24, Nor; 26.26, from them; 48.36, yes,'; 74.18, boys'; 96.22, thorat; 98.39, challah's; 100.38, his; 100.39, him; 102.8, thought,; 114.13, benath; 125.30, than than; 126.13, feel; 127.35, hand,; 128.26, grace; 130.20, that,; 148.38, Danzig,; 148.40, exhuded; 150.37, Why?"; 167.19, Tishvitz; 167.24, a a; 172.27, wasteful,; 173.28, bakers'; 175.10, Klopfstock; 192.33, voice."; 219.24, woman,; 223.37, forgotton; 228.4, granery; 238.35, our our; 256.34, asked.; 288.17, Hearts; 301.26, commandments; 303.30, Fridays; 305.36, were books; 307.29, *Schloimele*; 310.13, *Hagith*; 311.7, Mendel; 312.38, concubine; 313.18, of Adonijah; 313.22, pited; 326.21, therein."; 343.22, Tailbele; 411.34, was no; 465.40, your; 480.9, honered; 481.3, his; 492.21, awhile; 506.21, moats; 509.3, [no ¶]; 532.2, MINDA; 539.20, Masters,; 572.31, anyway; 577.9, Tatars; 582.19, dotor; 619.14, hell..."; 644.36, alledgedly; 717.21, women; 717.34, Wolfe; 733.9, hemorroids; 742.26, The.

Glossary and Notes

The glossary below provides basic definitions of terms that occur more than once in Singer's stories. The spellings follow the usage in Singer's texts (variant spellings used in the stories printed in this volume are listed in parenthesis).

Angel Raziel: Anonymous collection of kabbalistic texts published as a book in Amsterdam in 1701 but compiled centuries earlier.

Asmodeus: According to some Jewish legends, king of the demons and husband of Lilith.

Baba Yaga: Predatory witch in Russian folklore.

Book of Creation: Sefer Yezirah, one of the fundamental kabbalistic books.

Britska: Carriage long enough to recline in.

Cheder: Religious primary school.

Cholent: Stew made during the week for consumption on the Sabbath.

Dumah: Angel who demands the name of a person shortly after death and makes an accounting of that person's good and evil deeds.

Dybbuk: The spirit of a dead person who possesses the bodies of the living.

Feast of Omer: Harvest festival between Passover and Shavuoth.

Gemara: One of the two parts of the Talmud, primarily an elaboration of the first part, the Mishnah.

Guide of the Perplexed: Theological treatise (1190) by Maimonides.

Hashanah Raba: Seventh day of Sukkoth.

Ketev Mriri: Chief of the devils in Jewish folklore.

Kol Nidre prayer: Prayer repeated three times at the opening of the evening service on Yom Kippur.

Kuzari: Prose work in the form of a dialogue between the king of the Khazars and a Jew who explains the principles of his religion, originally written in Arabic by the Spanish-born philosopher and poet Judah ha-Levi (c. 1075–1141).

Landsman (pl. *landsleit*)*:* Fellow-countryman.

Lilith: In kabbalistic literature and Jewish legend, a demon who was Adam's wife before Eve. After abandoning Adam, she mated with Asmodeus and other demons. She and her many offspring, the *lilin,* were believed to prey on children.

Malamed: Teacher, learned man.

Metatron: In the Kabbalah, the highest archangel, seated beside God in heaven.

Midrash Talpioth: Book (1698) of commentaries and glosses by the Smyrna kabbalist Elijah ben Solomon Abraham ha-Kohen (d. 1720).

Mikveh: Ritual bath.

Mishnah: The first of the Talmud's two parts (the other is the Gemara).

Namah: Demon who rules one of the levels of hell with Lilith and the demons Machlath and Hurmizah.

Peios: Sidelocks.

Rashi: French Talmudist (1040–1105), known especially for his commentaries.

Responsa (sing. *Responsum*): A form of commentary in which a rabbi answers a specific question addressed to him.

Sambation: Mythical river whose turbulent waters are supposed to rest on the Sabbath.

Shabriri: Demon of blindness.

Shames: Synagogue-keeper.

Shema: Prayer recited twice daily as an affirmation of faith; the first of its three scriptural citations is "Hear, O Israel: the Lord our God is one Lord."

Simkhat Torah (*Simchas Torah, Simkhas Torah*): Holiday marking the end of the yearly cycle of weekly Torah readings.

Selichoth (*Selichot*) *prayers:* Prayers for forgiveness recited in the early morning on the days leading up to Yom Kippur, as well as on several other fast days throughout the year.

Shadai: One of the names of God.

Shokhet (*shochet*): Ritual slaughterer.

Shulchan Aruch: Codification of Jewish law by Spanish-born Talmudist Joseph ben Ephraim Karo (1488–1575).

Tishe b'Av: Holiday marked by fasting to commemorate the destruction of the temple in Jerusalem.

Tree of Life: 'Etz Hayyim (1346), by Aaron ben Elijah (c. 1328–69), Karaite theologian who lived in Constantinople.

Treif: Not kosher.

Wonder Rabbi: Hasidic rabbi believed to have healing powers.

Zohar: Kabbalistic book probably compiled in the 13th century; its authorship was attributed by tradition to 1st-century mystic Simon ben Yochi.

In the notes below, the reference numbers denote page and line of this volume (the line count includes headings). No note is made for material included in standard desk-reference books. For further biographical background than is contained in the Chronology, see Richard Burgin, *Conversations with Isaac Bashevis Singer* (New York: Noonday Press, 1986); Grace Farrell (ed.), *Isaac Bashevis Singer: Conversations* (Jackson: University Press of Mississippi, 1992); Janet Hadda, *Isaac Bashevis Singer: A Life* (New York: Oxford University Press, 1997); Paul Kresh, *Isaac Bashevis Singer: The Magician of West 86th Street* (New York: Dial, 1979); David Neal Miller, *A Bibliography of Isaac Bashevis Singer 1924–1949* (New York: Peter Lang, 1984), and *A Bibliography of Isaac Bashevis Singer, January 1950–June 1952* (New York: Max Weinreich Center for Advanced Jewish Studies, YIVO Institute for Jewish Research, 1979); Roberta Saltzman, *Isaac Bashevis Singer: A Bibliography of His Works in Yiddish and English, 1960–1991* (Lanham, Md.: Scarecrow Press, 2002); Clive Sinclair, *The Brothers Singer* (London: Allison & Busby, 1983); Seth L. Wolitz (ed.), *The Hidden Isaac Bashevis Singer* (Austin: University of Texas Press, 2001); Israel Zamir, *Journey to My Father, Isaac Bashevis Singer*, translated by Barbara Harshav (New York: Arcade, 1995).

GIMPEL THE FOOL AND OTHER STORIES

39.7   Seven Blessings] Recited during the wedding ceremony.

63.13   even the fish . . . tremble.] Proverbial expression describing the ten Days of Awe culminating in Yom Kippur.

69.7–8   Chmielnitzki's pogroms] At least 100,000 and perhaps more than 1,000,000 Jews were massacred in 1648 and 1649 at the instigation of Cossack leader Bohdan Chmielnitzski (c. 1595–1657).

80.24   during the Austrian occupation] I.e., during World War I, when a cholera epidemic ravaged the region. Singer recalled that when he moved from Warsaw to Biłgoraj (a village near Frampol) in the summer of 1917, a third of its residents had recently died of cholera.

82.39–83.1   the battle of Gog and Magog] In Jewish eschatological tradition, Israel's battle against barbarian enemies led by the tribes Gog and Magog was prophesied to be one of the major events preceding the reign of the Messiah.

87.21   Pithom and Rameses] Two "treasure cities" built by the Israelites during their enslavement in Egypt (see Exodus 1:11).

88.1–2   "Now . . . alive."] Jacob's words when reunited with his son Joseph (Genesis 46:30).

THE SPINOZA OF MARKET STREET

162.2 *Amor Dei Intellectualis*] Intellectual love of God.

181.36 the story of Joseph De La Rinah] The thwarted attempt of kabbalist Joseph della Reina to defeat the evil powers was the subject of a legend with several versions.

185.13 The earth . . . Korah] Korah and his followers who rebelled against Moses and Aaron perished when "the earth opened her mouth, and swallowed them up, and their houses, and all the men that appertained unto Korah, and all their goods" (Numbers 16:32).

187.34 Yehudah the Chassid] Judah ben Samuel, 13th-century German-Jewish mystic also known as "The Hasid of Regensburg."

198.17 Chmielnicki] See note 69.7–8.

239.33 Wundt . . . Bauch] German psychologist Wilhelm Wundt (1832–1920); German philosopher and literary critic Kuno Fischer (1824–1907); German neo-Kantian philosopher Bruno Bauch (1877–1942).

240.30 Berchtesgaden] Adolf Hitler's Bavarian mountain villa.

241.5 *Ost-Juden*] German: Eastern Jews.

244.17 dialect of Great Poland] Spoken in western Poland.

246.29 "Hear . . . One."] The first verse of the shema prayer.

257.27–28 King Sobieski's time] Old-fashioned, anachronistic. John III Sobieski (1629–1696) was king of Poland from 1674 to 1696.

265.2 Baal Shem] Shortened form of Baal Shem Tov (Master of the Good Name), name of Israel ben Eliezer (c. 1700–1760), founder of Hasidism.

293.28–29 Sabbatai Zevi, the false Messiah] Smyrna-born kabbalist (1626–1676) who declared himself the Messiah in 1648 and attracted a large following of believers throughout the Middle East, Europe, and North Africa. His movement weakened after he was forced to convert to Islam to save his life in Constantinople in 1666. He continued to assert messianic claims while observing the outward forms of Islam. A sect of his followers, the Donmeh, still exists.

294.3 treatise of Kilaim] A tractate of the Talmud.

307.7 Sabbatai Zevi] See note 293.28–29.

316.19–20 A sinner . . . Nebat!] God chastised Israel "because of the sins of Jeroboam, who did sin, and who made Israel to sin" (1 Kings 14:16).

SHORT FRIDAY AND OTHER STORIES

333.1 *Her Demon*] In the original Yiddish title of the story: *Hurmizah*. She is a demon who rules one of the levels of Hell with Lilith, Machlath, and Namah.

347.2–4   like that story . . . giants.]   Men sent by Moses to "spy out the land of Canaan" returned and told of an encounter with the giants of Anak: "we were in our own sight as grasshoppers, and so we were in their sight" (Numbers 11:33).

353.9   *ehrlichman*]   Honest man.

359.26   *starosta*]   Local official.

393.40   Pan]   Polish: Mister.

398.2   Sheol]   Underworld.

421.35   Sabbati Zevi]   See note 293.28–29.

422.11   *The Beginning of Wisdom*]   Book on morals compiled and written by the 16-century kabbalist Elijah ben Moses de Vidas.

425.28–29   *The Covenant of Rest*]   Treatise attributed to kabbalist Abraham ben Isaac of Grenada.

430.17–18   Abraham Zalman . . . Joseph]   "Messiah, son of Joseph" is the rabbinic name for the "suffering Messiah" who precedes the reign of "Messiah, son of David." Sabbatai Zevi (see note 293.28–29) claimed that Abraham Zalman, slain in 1648, was the suffering Messiah foretelling his coming as the redemptive Messiah.

432.33–34   excommunication . . . Gershom]   The French rabbi Gershom ben Judah (c. 960–c. 1040) presided over a synod that issued a formal prohibition of polygamy.

432.36   *Shaddai kra Satan*]   God, destroy Satan.

479.30   Reb Chaim Vital]   Safed-born kabbalist (1543–1620), disciple of Isaac Luria.

489.39   Hadassah]   Zionist Women's Organization.

495.14   *gleichgeschaltet!*]   In German, "coordinated"; the Nazis used the word to describe a policy that consolidated their power and eliminated their opponents.

504.16–17   the time of King Sobieski]   See note 257.27–28.

506.10–11   "when all the stars . . . together."]   Cf. God's answer to Job out of the whirlwind (Job 38): "Whereupon are the foundations thereof fastened? or who laid the corner stone thereof; When the morning stars sang together, and all the sons of God shouted for joy?"

509.19–20   'Ye shall not . . . man.']   Deuteronomy 1:17.

526.30   the Onkelos]   The Targum Onkelos, an Aramaic translation of the Hebrew Bible named after its translator, who lived in the 2nd century C.E.

530.3–4   *Lovely . . . divided.*]   2 Samuel 1:23, in which David laments the deaths of Saul and Jonathan.

THE SÉANCE AND OTHER STORIES

537.31   Horst Wessel song]   Nazi Party song that became the second national anthem of the Third Reich.

577.21   Amalekite]   I.e. enemy, derived from the name of a nomadic tribe descended from Esau that waged war against the Israelites and was eventually destroyed by David.

577.37   'His banished . . . Him.']   2 Samuel 14:14.

580.1–2   subject of the Stoned Ox]   See Exodus 21:28: "And if an ox gore a man or a woman, that they die, the ox shall be surely stoned, and its flesh shall not be eaten; but the owner of the ox shall be quit."

589.10–11   Captain Scott . . . Pole?]   The expedition of Norwegian explorer Roald Amundsen reached the South Pole on December 14, 1911, five weeks ahead of a competing expedition led by British explorer Robert Falcon Scott.

601.18   coming. . . . "]   When published in *An Isaac Bashevis Singer Reader* (1971) this story included the translator's credit, "Translated by Mirra Ginsburg."

705.24   divorced . . . Cohen.]   Moses' pronouncement at Leviticus 21:7 forbids a Cohen, a member of a priestly caste descended from Aaron, to marry a divorced woman.

712.27   *natchalniks*]   Russian rural prefects.

Library of Congress Cataloging-in-Publication Data

Singer, Isaac Bashevis, 1904–1991
  [Short stories. English. Selections]
  Collected stories : Gimpel the fool to the Letter writer /
  Isaac Bashevis Singer.
      p. cm. — (Library of America ; 149)
ISBN 1–931082–61–8 (alk. paper)
    1. Singer, Isaac Bashevis, 1904–1991—Translations into English. I. Stavans, Ilan. II. Title. III. Series.

PJ5129.S49A273   2004
839'.133—dc22   2003066055

This book is set in 10 point Linotron Galliard,
a face designed for photocomposition by Matthew Carter
and based on the sixteenth-century face Granjon. The paper
is acid-free Domtar Literary Opaque and meets the requirements
for permanence of the American National Standards Institute. The
binding material is Brillianta, a woven rayon cloth made by
Van Heek-Scholco Textielfabrieken, Holland. Composition
by Dedicated Business Services. Printing and binding
by R.R.Donnelley & Sons Company.
Designed by Bruce Campbell.